THE INVISIBLE LARIAT

NOEL HILL

NEWMAN SPRINGS PUBLISHING
320 Broad Street
Red Bank, NJ 07701

First originally published by Newman Springs Publishing 2024

ISBN 979-8-89061-951-8 (Paperback)
ISBN 979-8-89061-952-5 (Digital)

Printed in the United States of America

To Jake and the ghosts of Timbuctoo

THE OLD HOMEPLACE
1814

1

He watched her as if he had been a man caged for the past five years. Supper was finished. The two boys were playing with blocks on the floor at his feet. She had her back to him trying her level best to put her kitchen back in order. He filled his pipe with homegrown tobacco, never taking his eyes from her lovely hips. He smiled quizzically when he noticed she was moving her lips again. He always wondered who she was talking to and what she was talking about when she did that. He wondered why, if she had something to say, why she didn't say it out loud to him.

He shook his head slightly as he remembered the first time he had seen her and how this peculiar quirk had piqued his interest in her. His eyes were drawn again to her hips. The intimacy they had shared the night before had been so sweet and so heartfelt it left him wanting more. It was all he had thought of the entire day, so much so that he didn't even notice the pain in his hands, back, and legs. He pulled his hand away from the pipe in his mouth for a moment to examine the new blisters on top of old calluses and wondered if she would allow him to touch her breasts with such a couple of hideous things.

His eyes returned to her hips. He shook his head slightly again as he watched her use her tattered skirt to dry her hands. The woman did not possess one single garment that didn't look like a rag, even though he gave her money to purchase new fabric three times a year. For a brief moment, he wondered what she did with all of that money, but his heart leaped to his throat and his groin throbbed when she bent over to put the cast-iron in a low cupboard. She had no concept of what she was doing to him, and she wasn't even trying yet.

Douglas clobbered William in the ear with a block, and his amorous thoughts were shattered as the screaming commenced. Grace Weatherford quickly turned from her task. George stood from the table and simply held up his worn hand. Grace stood silently as she watched her husband ease their boys into their bedroom for the night. George's soothing voice resonated through their small house as he reprimanded Douglas and calmed William. In a short time, their home was quiet.

Grace began to move her lips again as she looked the kitchen over trying to remember what she had been doing when her baby had broken out in tears. A few moments passed when she finally remembered she had been drying the dishes. She had seen other women who made this kitchen business look so easy, but to her, it seemed to be mentally taxing. It was that she had to stay so focused just to accomplish the thing. It was wearing to her.

Grace felt him coming toward her. She smiled as he came closer and closer and finally slipped his hands between her arms and sides and cupped her breasts. Her pulse quickened as he nuzzled her neck and then kissed her ear. "These dishes will dry themselves by morning, you know." His deep voice was just a whisper.

The man, the love of her life, was threatening to make her weak. She pulled away from him slightly, pretending her business was more important than him, but his grasp was firm, and his kisses on her neck could melt steel. She gasped as he gently eased his thumbs against her nipples. She was instantly filled with want.

She faced him, put her arms around his neck, pressing her body firmly against his. His muscular arms wrapped her up, his hands caressing her back as they kissed. He pulled her hips close to his. She could feel him, his lust, his want, his love. As she melded her pelvis to his, she reached for his right hand. He gave it. She held it to examine his palm; she kissed it sensuously as if she could heal his blisters. He gently put his head against her cheek, closed his eyes, and rubbed her breast with his free hand. He knew there couldn't possibly be another woman on the whole face of the earth who could make him feel so loved, so fragile, so strong, and so defenseless just by kissing the palm of his hand.

She turned toward his hot breath, and their lips met again. She smiled at his clean-shaven face and realized he had planned this evening long before supper had reached the table. The thought excited her. Just knowing he had been thinking of her and what they would do together intensified her desires. She thrust herself into his hardness and gently rocked her body against his. She started to undo his pants. He let out a moaning sigh, picked her up in his arms, and carried her away from her tormenting task. She was grateful.

The couple lay entwined in their bed. George noticed that it had started to rain. The cool Kentucky night made him pull Grace even closer, and she obliged him by caressing his back. Her hands were healing. Just having them on his back made his pain go away. He was twenty years her senior, and after six years, he still couldn't believe she had picked him. She was young and pretty and full of mountains of love to give. George was a friend of Grace's family. Her father had said to George, "No man in his right mind would take on that crazy girl. George Weatherford, I swear, you've lost your mind! But don't listen to me. By God, take her! Take her, I say!"

George hadn't been sure what to make of it at the time, but Grace had heard her father's comments, and that evening, young Grace had followed George home. She, too, had made her choice, much to George's shock and delight. He kept her for his own, and her family was pleased with the union. After six years with Grace, George now knew what his old friend had meant, but the good far outweighed the bad.

Grace began to kiss his chest as they listened to the rain fall outside.

George thought of how miserable his trip to Frankford was going to be in the morning. Grace nuzzled the soft hair on her husband's chest and thought of the contrast between it and his hard body.

"It's going to be miserable and cold tomorrow. I think I'll put off my trip."

"You shouldn't put it off. You can't keep going the way you are. No man can work this much land by himself," she whispered.

"Dad and I have been doing it for years."

"Your dad is passed now, and you are working yourself into the ground."

George sighed sadly. "I don't like this idea of having slaves."

"I think you waited too long to have sons, George. You should have got an earlier start. They'd be grown now and helping you." Grace kissed him and smiled, waiting for his reply.

George rolled his wife playfully onto her back and kissed her breasts. "I had to wait for you. You are the silliest woman in all of Kentucky and well worth the wait."

Grace laughed. He kissed her mouth and then laid his head against her chest. "No woman could ever fill my heart with more joy than you have."

"Don't feel bad about this thing. All our neighbors are using slave labor now, and this conversion from tobacco to cotton is going to take a lot more work. You don't think any less of Graham Evans for having slaves, do you?"

"I'm not in the habit of telling a man his business."

Grace sighed and thought of a strong argument to put forth to her husband. She, too, needed help. Most women wouldn't in her situation, but she wasn't most women and they both knew it.

"George, you know I can't tend to my own household as it is, let alone another four or five mouths to feed. Will you please bring a woman home tomorrow to help me with the laundry and the cooking?"

"It will be too cold to travel tomorrow. I doubt I'll go."

Grace sighed and silently prayed for the storm to pass quickly.

The couple fell asleep still entwined in each other's arms.

Morning came sooner than it should have as Grace listened for a moment to Douglas' screaming. She eased out of bed hoping not to disturb George, looked out the window, and saw the rain had stopped. Her prayer was answered as she quickly looked at the sky and saw the stars. She headed for the bedroom door.

"What is it, my love?" George asked softly.

"I think Douglas wet the bed again," she whispered.

"Oh, Lord, do you want me to go?"

"Get your rest, dear, you have a big day ahead of you."

Grace had been right about Douglas' reason for screaming and waking the entire house. She never could figure out why he just couldn't come to wake her up quietly. "Don't cry, Douglas, don't cry, I'll fix it," she said calmly, and then, "You sure are hard on the feathers. You have to try to remember to wake up and go outside."

Douglas screamed louder at this slight.

William woke and said, "Mama."

She sensed angst in his voice. "It's all right, go back to sleep, baby." Grace remade the bed with clean sheets and blankets. Douglas allowed her to change his clothes for him, even though at the age of four years he wasn't much help. He just continued to cry. "Douglas, there is nothing to cry about." Grace was exasperated. "See there, Mama fixed it. You can go back to sleep now."

"No!"

"It's still nighttime, baby. The bed is clean. Hop in now," Grace said soothingly.

"No!" Douglas was defiant. "I'm hungry!" he shouted.

"Mama," William whispered.

Grace wanted to spank Douglas and make him get in bed, but it seemed that spanking Douglas was all she did sometimes, and it never did any good. She tried hard to get through to him in different ways, but that didn't seem to work either. It was as if he knew she wanted nothing more than to crawl back into bed with his father, and he was opposed to it for some reason. She knew one way or the other that she wasn't going back to sleep. If she could quiet Douglas, George could get his rest. Grace sweetly said, "Well, then, let's go look for something to eat."

William followed his mother and brother out of the room. Grace thought it was curious, but she reckoned he was afraid he would miss out on something. The boys followed her out into the starlit morning. She doubted the hens had laid any eggs yet, but it was worth a try. The lantern lit the way of the trail leading from the house to the coup. Douglas complained of being cold while William carefully followed along. Two eggs were all she could find, which would be enough until the usual breakfast time.

The trio stopped by the limestone blockhouse and sliced off a thick hunk of ham. The boys sat at the table, watching their mother fight with the complexities of the wood cookstove. Her lips moved as she tried to remember where she had put her cast-iron skillet. With the onerous task complete, Grace turned to setting the plates in front of her boys. William had dozed off, face and arms sprawled on the table and Douglas was gone. She discovered that Douglas had gone back to bed. Grace shook her head, and her silent lips became softly vocal as she picked up her baby and took him with her to her own bed.

George woke just before dawn. He listened carefully for sounds of rain and then got up to take a look. He dressed. He knew Grace would hound him all day if he didn't go to Frankford. She would have even if the weather had been bad. He headed out to hitch the team, grabbing the ham on the untouched plates as he passed through the kitchen. It was comical to think of what his wife had gone through with the boys, sometime in the middle of the night, that would actually cause her to gather and cook food.

When he was ready to go, he went in to say goodbye. The room was barely lit now, and the sight of his wife and son sleeping in his big bed filled his heart. He smiled as he hoped he could always remember this moment and leaned down to kiss her.

"You're up already?" Grace whispered.

"Yes, I'm going now. I'll be back home this afternoon, I expect."

"What about breakfast?"

"Don't worry yourself, I found the ham you cooked for me. You're a good wife to get up so early and tend that blasted skillet."

"That's very funny, George." She said lethargically.

"I thought so."

*****

When Grace looked out her kitchen window and saw her husband coming home, she stopped her menial, exhausting task of kneading the bread dough for the evening supper and exploded with squeals of delight. When Grace saw the wagon full of Africans, she naturally assumed at least some of them would be female. She would never have to knead dough or do laundry again. Grace eased out of the house to greet her husband. He sighed when he saw her coming and tried to imagine what her reaction would be. She smiled as she took his hand in hers and glanced in the direction of the wagons. "Good afternoon, Graham."

"Good afternoon, Gracie," he replied as he stepped off his wagon, weary from the long road.

"Your trip went well, I expect?" Grace said through gritted teeth as she continued to examine the contents of the two wagons. George's wagon contained four Negro men, their belongings, and some supplies. Graham's wagon was filled with building supplies and stacked in such a way that Grace knew no woman could be concealed among them. There was not a Negro woman in the whole lot.

George donned a ridiculous smile that only a man in trouble with a woman would attempt and spoke, "Yes, the trip to Frankford went well. The weather was cool but not wet. Graham and I had dinner at an inn outside of Frankford, and then we continued on about our business."

Grace was squeezing his hand as hard as she could, and she smiled and nodded sarcastically. She could see it pained him, and she began to seethe with anger.

Graham sensed it and removed himself from the couple. It was his intention to take the wagons to the barn, start unloading supplies, and help George get his men situated, but he lingered too long.

Grace threw George's hand away.

Grace said, "Mr. Weatherford, have you no regard for me at all? What is the meaning of this? Why didn't you bring back someone who could help me in the house?"

"I am expanding the farm, my dear, not the house," George explained.

"If you think that you can have slaves and I cannot, then you are sadly mistaken. I have had quite enough of all this cooking and cleaning and laundry. I am ashamed as it is to be seen in town. Every one of my neighbors talks about me behind my back because I am the only lady left in the country that doesn't have a house girl. Now either you fix this problem or I will, and if I fix it, you can bet that I will have more than one girl in my house, and if you don't want to be sleeping in the barn with them," she said, pointing to the Negroes, "then the house will have to expand with the farm!"

"By God, Grace, you should be ashamed to be seen in town. You refuse to wear anything except those rags, and your neighbors talk about you behind your back because everyone knows of your hot temper and your inability to sew. Now you get yourself in that house right this minute or I will bend you over my knee and whip your ass. How dare you start up with this childish behavior in front of our neighbor! How dare you stand in front of me and tell me that you have had enough of taking care of your family. I cannot even begin to understand what would possess you to say such a thing when you were put on this earth to do just that."

Now the young woman had been provoked, and George knew it. Never taking his eyes away from hers, he smiled and waited for the blow. Grace had a way of kicking a man in the shin bone that would nearly make him wet his pants, and George was waiting. Grace's blue eyes could cut steel with the invisible flame that was materializing, but George had seen it many times. Like he always did with a horse that kicked, he did with his wife. With one long step, he was toe to toe and nose to nose with this tempestuous brat of a woman, so if she did kick, it wouldn't hurt as bad. He grabbed her shoulders with both hands, and in a slow, soft voice that he only used during intimate moments with her, he said, "Woman, now you get your sweet self into that house and make us all a fine meal and you be sure to be quick about it because it won't take no time at all to make these fellas presentable, and I reckon by the looks of 'em, it's been some time since they've had much more than a biscuit in their bellies. In case you haven't noticed, they are a might narrow compared to the Negroes we usually see. They need fed, my dear."

"For one thing, I haven't noticed. I don't usually make a habit of gawking at Negroes, and for another thing, I certainly ain't going to make a habit of cooking for them."

"Well, my dear," George said, pulling her close to him and bending his head down toward hers as if he was going to kiss her in front of God and everybody, "you best not be gawking at them or you will never see the light of day."

Grace wrestled away from George struggling to get far enough away for one good kick or slap. The flames in her eyes revealed the blind madness that had overwhelmed her brain, and she was out for blood.

George picked her up, threw her over his shoulder, and packed her to the porch. Sitting down on the top step, George battled to position Grace over his knees for the discipline that she so richly deserved.

The battle was such that Graham wondered if he ought to help his friend. God forbid if Grace won the engagement, they would all have to eat George's cooking. Graham chuckled at the thought and wondered what the Negroes might be thinking as they looked on with concern. Graham nodded and winked to put them at ease, but it wasn't much help.

Everyone waited and watched with great anticipation, Graham ready to be called into battle, the Negroes angry and confused about why they were even there. They were tired, hungry, and wanting to find their own wives that they had been separated from; they waited for what would happen next.

After what seemed to George, like hours, with sweat dripping from the tip of his nose, one large drip at a time, the conflict was won, and the spanking commenced.

Once Grace knew that she was not as strong as her husband, she decided to play possum, hoping he would think he had killed her in the struggle. She refused to scream, cry, or even flinch at the blows to her bottom that she was receiving from his big hand. In this case, her trick of playing possum only helped her to achieve dignity since her game ended up being just a state of mind. George was wholly intended on dishing out his discipline before he checked her health. He had fallen for this game of hers before and had spent two weeks walking around with a black eye to prove it.

During the swatting, the Weatherford boys came running out from the back of the house to see what all the commotion was about. They had seen the wagons and the Negroes arrive, but little boys were not in the habit of concerning themselves with matters having to do with grownups or work. When they heard the excitement start up on the porch, they decided to have a look.

Douglas was very excited about what he was seeing his father doing to his mother and began to point and laugh. Douglas always thought that it was amusing to see someone or something in pain. This was a particularly delightful sight since it looked as if his father had just killed his mother.

William, on the other hand, was crying with his hands over his eyes. He had come to the same conclusion as his older brother had about his mama being hurt, and he didn't like it, and he hated Douglas for laughing about it.

George loved his boys a great deal and, during the spanking of his wife, could only see poor little William crying. George ceased with the punishment for William's sake, not being able to bear seeing him in tears just because his mother was an awful brat.

Grace lay limp across George's legs, still playing her game and waiting for her opportunity to strike. William kept up with his bawling, but Grace refused to give into the toddler's anguish. George waited a bit for her to get up, but she didn't. Then he poked her in the ribs with his finger, knowing that she was ticklish. There was still no movement. Now he was a little unnerved. Grace knew it. He prodded her once more, in the ribs, a little harder this time, and she rolled off his lap, landing face up.

Finally, Graham was starting to show some concern over the fact that he had just seen George Weatherford spank his wife to death and started toward the couple. He was also sickened by the fact that one of the sons was laughing uncontrollably now.

Graham went to Gracie's side to see if she was breathing, wondering at the same time why George wasn't showing the same distress that he was feeling himself.

"Watch out, Graham. She's a mighty tricky one!" George said as Grace laid there, holding her breath.

"Tricky? She's not breathing. You must have broken her neck or something during the struggle. I think you killed your wife, George," Graham said, suddenly having an image in his mind of attending his neighbor's hanging.

"I didn't break anything of hers. She ain't dead, believe me. If I was you, I'd stay clear of her. She's wily I tell ya," George said with certainty.

"You must be in denial, sir. This woman is surely dead," Graham said, thinking his friend must be in shock over what he had just done.

In the meantime, the Negroes who had witnessed this event from beginning to end were not shocked or surprised about what the man had done to his woman. It made perfect sense that such things should occur, considering that these were the same type of people that took them away from their homes and separated them from their own families. This incident only proved to them that all the people in this strange land were evil. They discovered, however, that these people are not born evil and that it must be taught to them by someone who has not yet reached the littlest member of the family but is certainly getting better at his trade by the looks of the older child. Still these four men waited for what would happen next.

"I assure you she is faking the whole thing! She is only trying to get out of the business of cooking! It seems to be a task that she finds undesirable, and the taste of her meals reflects her mood! Most undesirable, I tell you!" George shouted as he stood up to get a better look at his pretty pretending wife.

George knew he was going to get it one way or another. He knew Grace would never allow her spirit to be broken by him, and she was playing this part that she had created for herself so well that the only way he was going to get his way and his meal was to let her have her shot at him. He reckoned that she could go on this way for hours, and eventually, Graham would see fit to leave and bring back the authorities. He couldn't believe she would keep up this charade, knowing that it was upsetting the boys.

Shaking his head, George sighed and finally said, "Graham, you better get back a bit."

He looked at George incredulously in shock himself and numbly did as George suggested.

George stood over Grace, straddling her, making sure to put himself in a very vulnerable position. Nothing happened. *Maybe she is dead*, George thought. He reached down to pick her up, putting his hands under her arms, and that is when she delivered her blow.

Grace punched him once in the face and was able to wriggle backward in the dirt and kick George in one shin bone, right under the kneecap.

George hollered in pain from the blow to his leg. Graham jumped back, thunderstruck, as if he had seen a ghost. Grace took to her feet, dusted herself off, and smiled with her head still held high. Basking in the pride she had for her performance, patience, and, of course, the amazing wallop she had just given her husband. Standing in the dirt with her hands on her hips, watching her husband hopping around on one leg, and holding the other leg that she had so brutally damaged, Grace's mood began to change from satisfaction to fury. She started kicking dirt and rocks at her hopping husband and shouting, "How dare you spank me, you wicked, uncaring man! You deserve the pain you feel for not bringing someone home to help me with my work! I still owe you yet for this new humiliation you've just put me through. It wasn't painful, you know, just humiliating! I'll get you, George Weatherford!"

George stood up, refusing to be affected by the physical pain that he had endured for one more minute, reaching his arms to the sky and tilting his head back. He screamed, "Oh my Lord God, save me from this sneaking, evil, disagreeable, spiteful girl!" Then turning to Grace, he said, "My dear, for one second of your pretending, I thought that possibly I had done you in. And do you want to know something? It was the best second all danged day!"

Grace swished toward her husband, swinging her hips from side to side and jovially stated, "George, the only thing that can save you now is me, and you know it. If you ask me nice in front of our audience with the same enthusiasm you had when you tried to command me earlier, you might just find me to be the agreeable, dutiful wife that I promised to be. I am not a colt to be broken, Husband. I am the woman you have vowed to love forever."

"Forever, you say!" George exclaimed. "I always hoped you'd run off before that." George balked at his wife's request. The pangs of hunger that he felt in his stomach were already more than he wanted to bear. He found himself to be between a rock and a hard place. Giving in to this stubborn woman would surely be mortifying by the time his neighbor finished exaggerating his version of this experience. Out of the corner of his eye, he noticed a movement. The Negroes were becoming restless now that it seemed as though peace negotiations were beginning among the evil ones.

George said, "Grace, look over there at those fellas. Do you have any pity in your heart or soul for their plight? Won't you please give them comfort with a hot meal?"

"I will do the best I can, George, but you can't possibly expect me to care for them as well as my own all by myself," she said, starting to cry.

George hugged Grace remorsefully, knowing that her tears were genuine and her strong spirit was bending. George, being the soft-hearted soul that he was, found Grace's tears to be more painful than any physical pain she could inflict upon him. "I'm sorry, Grace, but tonight, you will have to find a way to make do. I am sure those men would like to eat before they bathe, but first thing is first, and I've got to help them and show them around," George explained. "You understand, don't you? Surely you can have something ready for them by the time they've had a chance to clean up, can't you?"

"I will give it my best effort, Husband," Grace said, squeezing him back with the strength and love of a young wife. She walked into the house and calmly began the task that she loathed the most.

George followed her with his eyes until she was in the house. He hung his head and shook it. Another disagreeable episode had worn him down, and he felt old. His hands hurt from the battle, but there wasn't anything to be done about it. He wondered if his wife's behavior would get better or worse with age and how he would endure it if it turned out to be the latter. George started for the wagons. Graham and Douglas went with him.

"You sure have yourself a spirited wife there," Graham commented to George.

Still glum, George was too tired and worn out to reply to the comment. He only nodded his head.

"Don't be so down in the mouth, George. You have a good wife. My wife doesn't talk to me at all. She makes those Negro women wait on her hand and foot all day, and then she goes directly to her bedroom right after supper. I picked a fight with her about a month ago as to why she was always feeling tired when she didn't do a damn thing all day, and she told me that constantly ordering those slave bitches around was exhausting. At least your wife has a heart and will compromise with you," Graham said, trying to ease George's mind.

George was surprised to hear this from his friend as he was crawling onto the wagon with the Negroes in a way that would make one think that he was eighty years old. Douglas crawled up on the other side to ride with his father. "You don't say," George finally replied. "She sounds consistent at least. I never know what Grace is going to do from one minute to the next. It is exhausting always having to be ready for the worst."

*****

As soon as Grace went through the door of her home, little William ran to her and clutched her legs. Grace was such a mischievous, spirited girl that she could not understand what had gotten into William. She grabbed him up from the floor and lifted him above her head. She looked deeply into his eyes and smiled. "William, what are you so worried about?" she asked and then hugged and kissed him. "You act like you are the one that has to cook for that army of men. You know what the problem is? I just don't know what I'm doing, do I? You know and I know that I barely get by as it is, and now Daddy has brought home a whole bunch of work for us to do and us not knowing what we are doing." Grace went on as she carried William on her hip, looking around the house for an answer to her problem.

"One thing is for sure, William. Your daddy is right about those men being hungry-looking. I bet you are hungry, too, aren't ya?"

Grace rambled as she set William on his feet. "Well, the first thing we have to do is get a fire going." She continued on as she went outside to the firepit, "It's just too big of a job to do in my little kitchen, and you can play by the big oak." As Grace took the process of making supper step by step, she explained everything that she was doing to William, and he followed her from the firepit to the root cellar, to the blockhouse where the meat hung, to the house, back to the firepit, listening to her and watching her every move. Grace didn't mind because she had someone to talk to, but she didn't realize that William was afraid to let her out of his sight.

*****

The four Negro men kept one eye on the devil child, Douglas, as they unloaded the wagons and helped George tend the horses and tack. They understood they would be sleeping in the barn and the building supplies were going to be used to start construction of their new cabins. The spring evening had grown cold. The men stayed in the barn to perform their ablutions. George knew he had to kill a lot of time to give Grace a chance to scare up supper. He wouldn't be surprised if they had to wait until midnight.

The men used the new lumber and rounds of firewood to construct a table inside the barn out of the weather. George got down to business with the men. He knew they were tired and hungry. He prayed for his wife as he hoped she would remedy the situation. In the meantime, there wasn't any reason why this time shouldn't be used to explain his plans.

George and Graham shared a limestone quarry. Buildings would primarily be constructed of stone. Then he explained how he wanted to start farming cotton instead of tobacco. He still had quite a bit of land to clear. He explained his plans for horse breeding. The conversation was a bit one-sided as the Negroes could not understand why this man was conversing with them as if they were old friends. He had just purchased them at a slave auction as one would do for any other species of livestock. George sensed their confusion. It was profound, although George could not imagine all the reasons these men had for feeling it.

Graham thought George to be too amiable and wondered why he and George didn't retire to the comfort of George's warm house. The conversation turned to the war with the British. Graham enjoyed speculating about how it would turn out and repeating tales he had heard of skirmishes and engagements. George was grateful for the topic as it went a long way toward giving Grace some time to work the supper.

The Black men listened to the slow monotone voices of the two White men. All but John thought of their own families. They had wives and children in the east and fretted over how they might be being treated and what cruelty it was to be parted from them. They thought of this man who had purchased them today. He seemed to be so pleasant, and yet it had seemed for a moment that he might have killed his young wife. He talked of hard work, and it was easy to see that he knew of hard work. He had an evil little son who for the time being was pissing on the straw pile the men were going to be using for bedding.

As George contemplated out loud about supper, the Black men thought of how little they cared about this man's supper, limestone, horses, or cotton. They needed to sleep. They hadn't slept on their backs for days, being forced to stand, bound in chains on a ferry that took them down the Ohio River. Their stomachs still tossed inside their bodies as the currents had tossed the ferry boat, rocking from side to side, and then back to front, and then side to side. The men could not understand why these two White men lingered in the barn with them when they should be sipping brandy and smoking cigars in the big house. They wished for George and Graham to leave them to cope with their misery in their own way and to take the evil one with them. This little child, who should be harmless, was not harmless. He raised the hair on all their necks.

"I think Grace has been at it long enough. I'll go check on her." With that, he left Graham sitting at the makeshift table alone with four Negroes. He was bewildered but tried not to show his discomfort. The Negroes were more anxious about Douglas being left behind, and soon, so was Graham when Douglas came to him for no reason and kicked him in the leg. Graham gave the boy a look of dissatisfaction, and Douglas ran screaming to catch up with his father. All five men watched the small boy leave the barn, and all five men suddenly felt a sense of peace.

By the time George came back, there was a big pot full of root vegetables and venison boiling over the fire outside. Grace had never finished kneading the bread that she had been working on earlier, and by the time she remembered it, it was already starting to rise. Grace reckoned this was no time to be wasteful, so she put it in a Dutch oven and hung it over the fire next to the stew.

Usually, the bread is the best part of the meal, but at the Weatherford Farm, there were no overeaters. George was grateful when he arrived to find that Grace had been busy doing as he had asked and prayed for. George helped Grace bring the food to the barn.

"Why in the devil are we eating in the barn, George?" Grace bellowed as she carried William on her hip.

"Stop cursing, woman!" George admonished. "I feel like eating in the barn, dang it! I can eat in my barn if I want to!"

"Why do we even have a dang house then, George? Why not do everything in the barn, for heaven's sake?"

Grace and George continued to bicker as they brought the food in and set it on the table. "What the devil will everyone eat on, George? The bare wood?"

"Go get plates, woman!" George demanded.

"The devil if I will! If we were eating in the house, we wouldn't have to drag our dishes around with us."

"Oh my Lord!" George exclaimed as he headed for the house.

Grace sat at the table and sighed. She shook her head as she scrutinized the men.

William climbed into her lap. "Graham, do you have any idea why we are eating in the barn?" Grace asked with a weary expression.

"It's a celebration, Gracie, like a homecoming for these men."

"In a barn?"

"Yes, that is how things are done now in the west," Graham lied, praying for George to hurry.

"My foot!"

"Yes, ma'am," Graham replied.

Grace turned to John. "Have you ever heard of such a thing?"

Graham's eyes widened, and he wanted to make it stop but had no concept of how to do it. George and Douglas came, and Graham was relieved. It seemed Grace could create more trouble in less time than it took even Douglas.

As the Negroes sat in awe of what was taking place in front of them, they became aware of their appetites. They didn't have the privilege of dinner at the inn or food of any kind for days. The Weatherfords had no way of knowing this. George would have never guessed people could be treated in such a way. The turmoil that had plagued the farm two hours earlier was gone now. Grace scooped stew in a pail that she could easily take around the table, slopping spoonfuls of the stuff on each plate. She filled the pail again. As Grace walked around the makeshift table delivering spoonfuls of food, she commented on how nice the Negro men looked in their new work clothes and then berated George for not bringing her a new dress or even new material for a new dress.

"The last time I bought material for you, you didn't like it. You took it back to the mercantile, got the money back, and hid it from me. It's somewhere in that house. If you need material, you can walk to town and get it! Put that pail on the table and sit down and eat yourself. Maybe if you are eating, you won't be nagging at me!"

Before Grace could sit down, she noticed that the Negroes had empty plates again. "George, give these men some bread, would ya?" she ordered as she ladled more stew onto their plates. George stood up from the table, picked up the bread, and walked out the big double doors to the chopping block and set the bread down on it. Grace stopped dead in her tracks, setting the pail on the temporary table, and rested her fists on her hips and looked on with curiosity as George reached for the double bitted axe. Everyone was watching George. They really wanted to observe Grace's reaction but were too afraid of her.

George split the round loaf equally as if he had done it with a knife, had it been possible, and passed a piece to each person with a plate. No man dared to laugh for fear that hot stew would end up in their laps. "That's very funny, George," Grace whispered as she sat down to join the men.

"I thought so," he replied, smiling.

2

About an hour before sunrise, George heard the sound of hooves coming up the road to his house. George eased out the door with his musket, wondering to himself why any sane person would be coming by for a visit at this hour and decided that there must be trouble of some kind.

The carriage slowed as it started to approach George's home, which relieved George a little. It indicated to him that maybe there was no emergency, but still he had to wonder what the devil was going on.

"George Weatherford! Don't shoot!" the jovial voice of Graham hollered in the pale light of morning.

"Why, Graham, what in the world are you doing out and about at this hour?" George shouted as the horse-drawn carriage came to a stop at George's steps. George stepped down from the porch to greet his neighbor and realized that he was not alone. There was hardly any light coming from the house, but George greeted Graham's companion, reckoning that he was with his wife or a relative.

Before Graham could explain his reason for the early visit, Grace came out to the porch with a lantern. "What is it George? Is there trouble?" she whispered.

"It's Graham, and I'm not sure yet."

"For heaven's sake, come in the house, Graham. I've started a pot of coffee. Come in now, all of you. It's too early to be standing outside," Grace complained.

"I've brought someone, Gracie. I think you will be very pleased," Graham said as he and his passenger stepped out of the carriage.

"Well, bring 'em in, Graham, and be quick," Grace said, turning toward the door and waving him in. "Come on, come in, and show me who you have."

George was amazed as he watched Graham and his passenger enter his home behind Grace. Now he understood why his friend had decided to visit so early in the morning. George followed them in and closed the door, and at that moment, Grace turned around to greet her guests. Grace paused. The look of shock was apparent in her expression, transforming quickly to confusion, and then to hopeful happiness. "Graham, are you and this young lady traveling together? Did you stop to ask for some of my delicious bread to take with you on your trip?" Grace joked.

Graham laughed at the implications and was just about to comment when he realized that Gracie had caught him in a trap almost before he knew it. If he commented on how he wouldn't get caught dead running around with this particular woman, she would hate him. And if he commented on how he felt about Gracie's bread-making abilities, she would hate him. Still chuckling, he looked at George and slightly shook his head. "She's quick but not quick enough," he said to George as the two men sat down at the table.

"You've just been awake a little longer," George jested. "What is this all about Graham?"

"Well, I told you yesterday about how things were at my place," Graham said, winking at George. "And I told Mrs. Evans about Gracie needing some help, and we decided to bring Miss Lucy over and make her a gift to young Gracie."

Grace brought both hands up to her face, gasping with delight and hugged Miss Lucy like she was a sister. Lucy nearly jumped out of her skin, and not knowing what to do, she just stood there. No White person had ever shown her affection before.

"Mrs. Evans and I thought this would be a nice home for Miss Lucy, and she is really a hard worker. Also, we have found that our girls know how to cook for our slaves in a way that they are accustomed to. What do you think, George?"

George was reluctant to agree with the idea, but when he looked into Grace's eyes and saw that she was silently pleading with him to accept the offer, he accepted with a smile and the nod of his head. George knew that without Miss Lucy's help, every meal would be a fight. Hopefully, she would teach Grace a few things about cooking, but these things would be discussed after Graham departed for home. George was also pleased with Grace at this moment for holding her tongue for once in her life instead of bringing shame on him like she had done the day before.

"Well, let's have some breakfast then. Lucy—I mean Miss Lucy—there are four men out in the barn, and they need to build up their strength. As soon as they are able, we are going to get their cabins started. I guess we will have to fix up a place for you first, though. We can't have you sleeping in the barn."

Grace, still overwhelmed at the number of people that she felt responsible for, awkwardly began to show Lucy where the supplies were kept. When the two of them formed a plan as to what to make for breakfast and when the task was being carried out, Grace was able to relax. Now she was able to tell Lucy about her sons and herself, how she hated cooking and laundry, and how George had brought home four men the day before, and if Mr. Evans hadn't brought Lucy to her, everybody would have starved to death because Grace probably would have just run away.

Silently, Lucy listened as Grace poured her heart out to her. Lucy had never met a woman like Grace. Mrs. Evans had berated her every time she spoke to her, so Lucy was having a hard time believing that Mrs. Weatherford was as sincere as she appeared. Also, she was wondering why Mrs. Weatherford was attempting to help her prepare breakfast. Lucy was seventeen years old. She had been in the Evans house for five years and had never seen Mrs. Evans help anybody. Not her husband, not her children, and certainly not ever her slaves. Lucy reckoned that when the men left to begin their daily tasks, then she would find out what Mrs. Weatherford was really like. In between now and then, Lucy decided that she wasn't going to fall for any tricks.

For Lucy to think that Mrs. Weatherford wasn't just a younger and thinner version of Mrs. Evans would only be a dream. As nice as Mrs. Weatherford appeared to be now, even if it was so, Lucy reckoned it was only a matter of time before Mrs. Weatherford started to treat her like the slave that she was. So Lucy thought it best to face the fact that the only thing that had changed in her life was her location.

The breakfast of ham, eggs, and biscuits was coming along much to Grace's amazement. Lucy made the whole production look so very easy. She never seemed to work up a sweat or get excited about anything. Grace was in awe of her abilities and felt grateful for her. Grace realized that she had been talking the whole time since they had been in the kitchen, which Grace always did whether anyone was in there or not, but Lucy had not had a chance to say anything. Grace wondered what it was going to be like having someone to talk to all the time for a change. Not only would Lucy help her with her household burdens, but she would also be taking away her feeling of loneliness for feminine companionship.

Realizing this made Grace even happier, and she threw her arms around Lucy. "Thank you. Thank you so much for coming to my home. I just wish there wasn't so much work to do. I want to know all about you. I want us to be friends. When the men go away, we will have coffee and talk. Oh! Wait until you meet the boys. Won't they be excited!"

Lucy stood there in shock, still not believing that she could ever be friends with a White woman, and wondering what in the world the two of them would talk about. The smell of the biscuits brought Lucy out of her shock as if someone had snapped their fingers in front of her face. Her reaction was swift. Pulling them from the wood cookstove and checking the bottoms of them, she couldn't help smiling at their perfection as she set them on the counter. "Breakfast is ready, ma'am," Lucy said, smiling.

"It is already?" Grace exclaimed.

Lucy started to look around for plates, utensils, butter, and napkins while Grace looked at the biscuits as though she had never seen one before. Noticing that Lucy was rushing around, she hurried to help her find what she needed, and together they went to the dining room to set the table.

"What is all this?" George asked, bewildered because Grace usually shouted from the kitchen when a meal was ready, and he had to serve himself.

"I don't know," Grace said, shrugging her shoulders. "I'm just doing what Lucy is doing. She has breakfast finished already. Can you believe it, George?"

Graham laughed heartily at Gracie's childlike reaction to Lucy's efficiency at preparing meals and making sure that all the proprieties of society were conducted as well. These were the things that Mrs. Evans had beat into Lucy when she first came to be a servant, and now she was in a home that had no knowledge of such foolishness.

"I'll go get the men," George said, getting up from the table.

Douglas and William had been awakened by the smell of ham frying and those biscuits that they had never smelled before. As they wandered out to the table, yawning and rubbing their eyes, they looked around, unconsciously aware that something was very different but not being able to put their little fingers on what it was. Douglas and William sat down in their chairs and realized one thing that was strange. The only grown-up who was there was Graham.

William began to cry and climbed down from his chair and waddled into the kitchen to find his mama. The only person he saw there was Lucy. This made him cry even louder, and he waddled back into the bedroom that he came out of and closed the door. William didn't see his mama in the kitchen because she had taken a couple of biscuits outside while Lucy was making another batch. When she heard William screaming, she ran in, and Lucy pointed her in his direction. Grace ran into the dining room, and Graham did the same and kept waving her on.

Douglas didn't cry nor seem to be concerned about anything being out of the ordinary as he started to pound his eating utensils on the table. Even though it was very early for Douglas to be awake, he was able to comprehend that he had an audience, and he took this opportunity to show off for Graham by throwing his utensils and plate on the floor and then sticking his tongue out. Of course, now Douglas was realizing that he didn't have anything to annoy the man with, so he reached for the place setting next to him and proceeded to do the exact same thing. Now that Douglas had figured out that he hadn't got into trouble yet, he decided to go around the table and throw all the place settings on the floor, each time sticking his tongue out at Graham.

Graham recalled Douglas's behavior the day before and wanted nothing more than to pick the boy up by the neck, hold him in the air, and whip him with a switch, but he knew that as soon as he did, one of his parents would come into the room, and he would find himself no longer welcomed at the Weatherford home. So Graham ignored the child to the best of his ability but couldn't help noting every time this contemptible little animal stuck his tongue out at him.

George opened the door and walked in; the Negro men followed. George was bewildered to see all the place settings on the floor. His first thought was that Grace had a fit of some sort, but he couldn't make his brain imagine why. Grace was happy and excited when he left for the barn. Douglas was standing on the chair across from Graham and was about to step up onto the table. George looked at Graham with a questioning expression on his face, and Graham, with his jaw clinched and rippling, nodded his head toward Douglas with the hope that the boy animal would get his beating now.

George just shook his head, went to his son, took him from the table, and made him sit down in the chair—not a swat, shake, spanking or a foul word. Graham was some disappointed in Ol' George and wondered what Douglas was going to be like when he was grown and pictured in his own mind having to shoot the boy someday.

As the Negroes were taking their places at the dining room table, George started to pick up the place settings. Grace came out of the boys' bedroom with William. "George, what in the world happened here?" she asked in a frantic tone.

"Douglas is what happened. Where were you?"

"William was crying because everything was out of sorts around here, and I was tending to him," she explained as she helped her husband reset the table.

Little William was still upset by all the changes that were happening to him, and without even knowing of his own actions, he found himself crawling up into a chair and sitting beside one of the Negro men as far away from Douglas as he could get.

"Douglas, did you do this?" Grace asked, already knowing what the answer was.

Douglas picked up his plate and threw it on the floor and stuck his tongue out at his mother.

Grace gasped at her child's misbehavior and grabbed him up from his chair, which was across the table from Graham, lifted his night shirt and proceeded to spank him until his bottom turned bright red. Graham was finding it very difficult to contain his delight while viewing this comforting scene. Douglas was screaming at the top of his lungs, trying desperately to wriggle away from his mother's grasp by kicking and swatting at her and flopping down on the floor. This aggravated Grace even more than she already was when she started. She seized her son's wrist and dragged him into his room. "Douglas, you will stay in this room until you learn to be a good boy! When the rest of us are finished with breakfast, I will come and let you out to have yours. If I hear one word out of you until then, I will whip your butt again, and you won't get breakfast either!"

The light seemed to come back into the eyes of the Negro men when Lucy came out to serve them. Upon observing this, George was feeling for the first time that he was turning with the universe instead of against it. He saw that a change was coming, and it was going to be for the better. George, like most people, dreaded change, and when he had decided that the time had come to expand the farm, it frightened the devil out of him. He knew that if things were not managed properly, he would lose everything. George had spent over a year debating about whether he should do it, how to do it, and wondered if it would be worth all the extra worrying. He was already worrying all the time about what he already had.

George's father had crossed the Cumberland Gap shortly after the Revolutionary War to settle this land. He had cleared it, planted it in tobacco, built a home, and raised his son on it, and now he was gone, leaving the place to George and Grace to do the same. Even though the certificate of settlement entitled the family to four hundred acres, George and his father had never gotten around to clearing all the land. Approximately eighty acres of it was still in timber. George often debated the question as to whether he should harvest the huge black walnut and bur oak trees. Graham had pestered him about it numerous times as Graham had a small lumber mill at his place and fancied himself a furniture maker, but his father's words always came back to him. "If all else fails, George, pigs will eat those big walnuts and acorns, and you and your family will survive." George chuckled to himself now as he recalled the ludicrous statement, and yet he was still reluctant to harvest those majestic, beautiful trees that ran along the creek. Nevertheless, there was still a good one hundred acres that George was determined to clear within the next two years, and for this, he needed help.

He hoped four men would be enough to reach his goal. Grace and Graham's persistence about acquiring slave labor over the last year had given George the idea that with that kind of help, he could finally get the rest of the land cleared, start growing cotton, and then move right on to his lifelong dream of being a premier horse breeder. That was what he wanted to leave to his sons. He hoped one would love horses and one would love farming.

Lucy could not believe her eyes when she came out of the kitchen and saw the Negro men at the same table as the White family and with Master Evans there as well. Lucy had been taught by her former mistress to never look at the faces of White people. Lucy was in such shock that she gave herself away when she paused and let out a little gasp.

Graham was waiting for this reaction and chuckled slightly to himself when it happened. Grace came to her aid and took the food from her, saying, "Lucy, I'll let you tend those biscuits. When they are ready, bring them out and join us at the table."

"They's ready, ma'am," Lucy said, not looking at her.

"They are already? Go get 'em then. Your place is there across from my little William so you can get to know him. I'll serve." Grace turned away happily and began her task.

Lucy so desperately wanted to look at her previous master. She wanted to see something in his eyes that would tell her that she was going to be all right with these people when he left, but she would not allow herself to do it. She turned and left to go get the biscuits that her new mistress admired so much. When Master Evans had gathered Lucy up this morning and told her what was happening, she really hadn't been fearful about being in a new home. She knew that she would be treated the same way that she was treated the day before, maybe worse, but she really couldn't imagine anybody being as disagreeable nor as lazy as Mistress Evans. Now Lucy was here, and she was becoming more and more frightened by the moment. She had butterflies in her stomach. Lucy had never sat at a table with White people before, but she did want to see the baby boy.

By the time Lucy came out with the biscuits, she was shaking like a leaf and suddenly became paralyzed with fear. Grace noticed and went to her, handing George the food for him to serve, and he did. This caused Lucy more distress. Her chest became tight, dizziness came about, and as Grace took the biscuits from her hand, Lucy started to go down.

Graham knew that there would be a strong reaction from Lucy to the attitude of her new family. Graham had never seen anyone faint before, but something had told him to get up and do something just in time. He caught her before she hit the floor.

"Oh my Lord!" Grace screamed. "George! George! What is happening?" Grace continued.

"Easy now, Gracie, she has just fainted is all. She must be overwhelmed by her new surroundings. Splash a little water on her face. She'll come around all right," Graham said coolly.

Grace glared at her generous neighbor and asked in a whisper, "Is this woman pregnant, you old scallywag?"

"Not to my knowledge!" Graham said defensively, wondering just what Gracie was trying to imply.

"Well, the poor thing, is she sick or something?" Grace questioned.

"George, do you mind if I help Gracie bring Lucy around in the kitchen?" Graham asked as he picked Lucy up.

George agreed pleasantly with the nod of his head. "Go right ahead." George thought that was a splendid idea. Now he could enjoy the first well-cooked meal he had ever had in his married life.

With Grace and Douglas out of the room, it turned out to be the quietest meal as well.

While Grace put a cold damp cloth on Lucy's face, Graham explained to Grace what he thought might be happening. He described how Lucy was usually treated by Mrs. Evans and how she was taught the dos and don'ts when associating with white people. "Mrs. Evans was very strict with Lucy. If she wasn't my wife, I'd tell you my opinion of her for mistreating people. Fact is she doesn't treat me much better either. Anyway, you and George would be the only White people that have ever treated Lucy like a human being, and she just didn't know how to take it. Believe it or not, this is the first time I've ever talked to the girl, and she's been in my house for five years. Now I don't know if you are going to change your ways or change hers, and it's none of my business what you do, but now you know."

Lucy was coming around now, and Grace's eyes were swollen with tears. "Well, pardon me for saying this, but I'm glad you got this poor girl away from your wife. I didn't know people could get away with such cruelty. I'm surprised though that Mrs. Evans would let Lucy go so easily."

"Well, she didn't. Fact is she doesn't know about it yet. I expect to be home when she finds out, though. Long about midday, she'll be hollerin' for Lucy to come feed her in bed, and all she will get is me. I have decided that she isn't going to get away with her nonsense anymore. The only woman that's going to tend to that house from now on is her. I've also decided to have my mother move in with us. Now she'll know what it's like to be told what to do all day. Either that or she will leave," Graham said with a defiant smile. "I'm going to go eat now."

Grace looked Lucy right in the eye. Their faces were so close because Grace was holding Lucy's head in her lap, and Lucy couldn't avoid Grace's eyes looking into hers. It was a long, silent moment while they read each other's thoughts. They both began to laugh and giggle at the thought of seeing the look on Mrs. Evans' face when her husband put the hammer down on her bad behavior.

"I wish I could be there, don't you?" Grace laughed. And they laughed together some more as Grace helped her up from the floor.

"Things are going to be different for you now, Lucy. I'm not lazy. I'm just terribly inept. When I have time to try my best to do something right, it still turns out wrong. It's depressing. The only thing that I'm any good at is playing with the boys, and it's the only thing that gives me any joy. I've been asking George for help ever since William was born, but he works very hard every day and hasn't been able to help me out much. He's been needing help, too, and I feel bad about not being able to produce one single decent meal for the man. Your being here will change my life for the better, and I hope your life will be better now too. Not everybody is like Mrs. Evans."

Lucy didn't know what to think about all of this. She had been mistreated for so long that she couldn't remember a time when she felt like a human or when she even felt liked, let alone loved.

Grace could see the wheels turning in Lucy's head and realized that it was going to take some time for her to earn Lucy's trust. Just saying she wasn't anything like Mrs. Evans wasn't good enough for Lucy. Grace took Lucy's hands in hers and spoke, "I don't expect you to trust us, but I hope you will give us a chance. We'll just take it one day at a time, all right?"

Lucy looked at the floor again and nodded her head. Grace put her index finger under Lucy's chin and gently forced Lucy to look at her. "That's the first rule that we are going to throw out the door. You don't duck your eyes for anybody anymore. You should hold your head up high. If anybody doesn't like it, I'll kick 'em in the leg. I'm counting on you to teach me and help me, and I never heard of a teacher duckin' her eyes when she's teachin', all right?"

Lucy nodded her head, this time looking Grace in the eye.

This pleased Grace, and it showed. "Teachers always speak up too. How can you teach me anything if you let me do all the talking?"

"Yes, ma'am."

"Grace," she corrected. "Not ever ma'am. I ain't old enough to be no danged ma'am."

Lucy snickered. "Yes, Grace. I'll teach you to be a good cook. Pretty soon, you be cookin' for your husband all by yourself, and he'll give you big kiss."

"Yeah, someday he'll quit trying to run me off and figure out that he can't live without me," Grace jested mischievously.

George poked his head into the kitchen. "Grace, how is everything?" he asked, referring to Lucy's health.

"Oh, we're all right now, but Lucy's still under the weather a little bit, so we're not going to do much today. I want her to get to know the boys and get rested before we start supper."

"Well, Miss Lucy, that sure was a fine breakfast. I sure do thank you. Grace, we must go to work now. Make sure you keep Douglas out of my hair today, I don't want to drop something on his head while we are building Lucy's cabin. You better come get William. He fell asleep on John's arm, and he doesn't want to be the one to wake him up."

Grace and Lucy came out from the kitchen, and Grace smiled when she saw her precious baby leaning against the tall Black man named John. Lucy could tell from the look on John's face that he had been mistreated by White people too. He probably never touched a White person before, and now one of their babies was using him for a pillow. Two weeks ago, he would have been hanged for even looking at the master's children. Lucy touched Grace's arm and eased by her to pick up William, smiling at this fellow, John, while she did it, hoping for two things to happen. One, he would be assured that he wasn't in trouble and, two, that he would notice her. William stirred a little but didn't wake up, and John hurried to get out of the chair and left to go to work, bewildered by all the morning's drama.

Grace was just so pleased with herself at that moment about producing such a handsome baby boy that she didn't even notice that there had been a problem and Lucy had just helped to fix it. Grace gently took William when Lucy handed him to her, and they both admired the boy. "They are such angels when they are asleep," Grace marveled.

"Yeah, when they are asleep! You got that right," George said, kissing Grace on the cheek and leaving the house.

"You're just jealous that they are so much more adorable than you!" Grace hollered out the door at him.

3

1819

Five years had passed since the day the Negroes had come to the Weatherford farm. Douglas was nine years old now. He couldn't stand to be in the house near his mother and Lucy; he couldn't stand the fact that William constantly played with Lucy's little boy, Johnny Boy. And now as he hid behind foliage of the large, black walnut tree, high up, lounging on a big branch and spying on his father, he detested the fact that his old man worked side by side with slaves.

It was embarrassing to him that his whole family had made friends with these Black demons. As he watched his father nail fence rails on the posts that had been set by him and the slaves the day before, he tried to reason why his family thought everything he said and did was wrong. He wanted to live in a place with people who acted properly. It could not possibly be proper to befriend slaves. He knew his mother talked about him to that Lucy and despised her for it. He didn't think that Black bitch needed to know his business. He knew his own brother, William, was so afraid of him that he wouldn't even speak to him if he could avoid it. Douglas smiled at this. He liked the fact that his little brother was afraid of him. It made him feel powerful.

George was in the process of decorating his property with a white rail fence. He had always wanted white rail fencing just as he had always wanted to breed horses. Douglas laughed out loud every time he heard George complain to Grace about the stretch of fence that was being built now. He had set his line too close to the trees on the creek, and setting the posts was very difficult on account of the tree roots. It tickled Douglas to see his father on his hands and knees, sawing roots out of the way when he should be making the slaves do it. He couldn't believe that he was of the same blood of such a stupid man.

Douglas had been hiding high in the tree branches for the last two weeks while this latest undertaking had been in the works. No one had looked for him. He had never heard anyone say, "I wonder where Douglas is." His mother never asked him, "How are you? What have you been doing today? Have you been helping your father?" No one asked him anything. No one cared about him or what he did.

George and his men had noticed, though. They noticed that the evil one was no longer underfoot. They noticed a new disagreeable feeling of being watched and they noticed at the beginning of each new day that all the posts that had been set the day before had to be straightened because someone had pushed and pulled them askew in every direction. No one complained. This was better than having to see or hear Douglas. Every morning, George wished that he could laugh about the fence posts, that he could say it was a silly little joke his son was playing on him to get his attention, but he knew it wasn't true. It was destructive and was done to show Douglas' lack of respect for his father, for his hard work, and for anything that George touched.

Douglas watched quietly now, hardly breathing as his father worked directly below him. He wondered if he could time out a drivel of spit that would land on George's hat while he was nailing up a board. He wished he had thought of it sooner so he could have practiced. It might take two or three seconds for the spit to travel the long distance. George was going to nail two boards on the post below. Douglas made a mental note of how long it took him to nail the first one, and when he got set to nail the second one, Douglas tested the theory of gravity. Spittle landed on George's arm. He looked at it, knowing it had not come from a bird, but he looked at it anyway. What was a man to do? George ignored it, not wanting to give his son the satisfaction of being acknowledged. George wanted to beat the boy. He wanted to climb the tree and throw his son out of it. But he was patient. The boy would come out of his hiding come suppertime, and that would give George time to think of what to do or say to him about his ill manners.

*****

Grace stood on her porch. Her arms were wrapped around her as if she was cold, but it was early summer, and the weather was perfect. She looked out at the expanse of cotton fields. She could barely make out George and his wagon down by the creek. George's men were pulling weeds out of the cotton. William was playing in the backyard with Johnny Boy. She knew Lucy was busy getting the noonday meal prepared. Everyone had a purpose. Everyone had something meaningful to do. Grace felt like her life had come to a halt. She was in between two places, life and death. She couldn't grasp either one. She had had three miscarriages in the last five years, the last one happening only a month ago. The last one was the one that put her over the edge. She felt nothing. She couldn't feel emotions such as love, hate, happiness, sorrow, and she couldn't even pretend to. She couldn't cry, she couldn't smile, and she couldn't stand herself. This was the first day she had been out of her house.

Lucy knew this could be the end of the woman she had known. Lucy was worried that her friend was soon to do something drastic, something that you couldn't take back or at the very least become a bitter woman she didn't want to know anymore. Lucy wondered if Grace would start to treat her poorly and how Grace would take the news about her and John expecting their second child.

Lucy took out a cup of coffee to her. "Grace," she said softly.

Grace turned. "Lucy, I didn't expect you to bring me coffee. I thought you to be busy."

"The stew is brewin', Grace. I wanted to see how you're feelin'."

Grace sighed. "I wish I could feel anything. I was just thinking how everyone here has a purpose, and I have come to the awareness that the only thing I'm good at is doing laundry. That is a sad state to be in."

"Oh, go on, everybody feels bad like that sometimes. Think of the good you have in your life. Your man loves you, and you have your boys."

"The boys are growing up. Douglas is a terror, and George still works just as hard as he always did. I feel lost. I had such hopes for this last baby. I had plans of all the things we would do together."

The women stood in silence, sipping coffee. Lucy searched her mind for something positive to say but couldn't. She couldn't imagine what Grace was feeling and didn't want to. Sometimes silence was good. Lucy admired her husband from afar as he pulled his weeds and thought of how she would rub his back for him after they retired for the day. He would appreciate her for it and wrap her up in his massive, loving arms.

Grace thought of how her husband hadn't been with her intimately since she had lost the baby. Hugs and kisses had been abundant, but there was no lovemaking. It seems as if neither one of them had the heart to do it anymore. That had been the only thing she felt like she was any good at, and now that was lost too. How long could they go on without lovemaking to bond them?

"You need work," Lucy said suddenly.

"Pardon me?"

"I says you need work, Grace. Not just laundry and tendin' to your family. You need somethin' that's just yours. You need a reason that makes you happy to get out of bed every day. Some people paint pretty pictures, some people paint barns. Some people take pride in pulling weeds and buildin' white rail fences. Find the thin' that you can have pride and happiness doin', and do it for two or three hours a day every day, and then every day, you will have a reason for gettin' out of bed, puttin' your clothes on and smilin' again. Your man works so hard. Maybe you could walk out and see what he's doin' sometime."

Grace listened silently. Lucy couldn't figure out if she was listening or thinking. Lucy waited a few moments for a response, but none came. Lucy shook her head and wanted to cry. Two months ago, Grace would have cursed, teased, and joked about a long list of possible occupations or hobbies she might like to try, and now there was nothing. Lucy turned to tend to her own business when a sudden raucous noise stopped her.

William and Johnny Boy were coming around to the front of the house. William, seven years old now, was running while Johnny was trying to catch him and then falling down, pretending to trip. Johnny jumped on top of William. William screamed and tried to crawl away, acting like he couldn't because Johnny was too big and strong. William then pretended that miraculously, he was transforming into the biggest, strongest boy in the world, overpowering Johnny—gently, of course—and getting out from under Johnny and growling like a bear. Johnny ran in the opposite direction, screaming and laughing at the same time, and the chase was on again.

Lucy stood beside Grace as they watched the boys play. Grace started to smile as the game continued. Lucy started to snicker. Lucy's little snicker had always been a funny sound to Grace's ears, and she reluctantly started to giggle. Little Johnny Boy found a small stick, quickly picked it up, turned on William, and wielded it like a colossal club. The look in his eyes was purely theatrical. His expression was kill or be killed. That was it for Grace.

Now Grace was laughing heartily. "Would you look at that, Lucy? Those two are having such a time, and I've been wasting my life away, worrying about things that I can't change. I want to be like that." Grace laughed while gesturing toward their boys.

Lucy saw the light in Grace's eyes return, not quite as bright as the day that they had first met but most certainly brighter than they had been for months. Lucy nodded in agreement.

"Everybody want to be like that, Grace."

As the two women continued to watch with wonder, it occurred to Lucy that her job as a mother might ease up a bit if William played with Johnny like that every day. With Lucy being in her third month of pregnancy, she was tired and worn down and always longing for a small bit of rest, knowing that it couldn't be possible. "What time you start your book learnin' with Williams durin' the day, Grace?" Lucy asked, always calling him Williams, which never failed to make Grace smile because it was one of Lucy's endearing qualities.

"Oh, Lordy, Lucy, why did you have to go and bring that up? That is the worst part of my day, for God's sake," Grace said, grabbing her head. "I work with William after lunch now for as long as we can stand it, but Douglas has now been turned over to George's instruction. That boy does not listen to me whatsoever about anything whatsoever. He has a total lack of respect for me and not much more for George, but it's that little bit more that keeps him alive. I swear, if it wasn't for George, I can't say out loud what I would do to that boy. William can only take so much, and then he gets impatient and fails to concentrate. That's when I make him do his penmanship before he can go, and go he does. He loves to be on the go. Douglas, on the other hand, is just so distressful for me to handle that George has become his sole guardian. It's embarrassing to say this to you, but that boy is frightening. If I tied him up in a cave, he would find a way to burn it down, I swear!"

"Oh, Grace, it ain't as bad as all that. He's just a growin' boy," she said, making sure she wasn't looking at Grace when she made what was supposed to be a comforting comment.

Grace turned to face Lucy with a look of sad disbelief. Seeing that Lucy still wasn't looking at her and acting as though the floor was more intriguing than engaging in a serious conversation with Grace about her terrifying son, Grace said, "Oh, please, don't spare the truth with me, Lucy. A growing boy indeed. What do you suppose the growing boy will grow into? Certainly not a good man and certainly not a hard worker. As a matter of fact, I believe George and the men probably have to work a couple of hours extra every day to fix things that Douglas has done to purposely complicate whatever project the men are trying to complete. Surely, John has mentioned this to you. I know George comments on it frequently."

"Well, Grace, all I know is it ain't my place to say anythin' about your boy that would hurts your feelins', and I wouldn't know what to say to makes it better anyhow," Lucy said in self-defense.

Grace sighed, thinking that this was a mighty poor topic to be discussing anyway since there didn't seem to be a God-fearing solution for the problem, and knowing that Lucy certainly didn't want to be put in the middle of it, Grace thought it best to drop the subject.

Friend or not, Lucy was right. Douglas was his parents' responsibility, and if they couldn't make him right, who could? This was a question Grace often asked herself and prayed that someday, somebody would come along who could give her the answer. Lucy probably had an answer but was too timid to offer it for fear it would cause a rift between them and quite possibly between everyone on the farm. For now, it was just best to watch William and Johnny Boy play.

"I was just thinkin' that Williams could help with Johnny Boy when he wasn't doin' his book learnin' and that might free you up some too," Lucy said after several moments had passed by.

"Yeah, I hear what you're saying, Lucy," Grace said thoughtfully. "I'll ask George if he can find me something to do that isn't housework related. In the meantime, I had better start catching up on the housework related chores around here. I've been holed up for too long, like an old wintery snake."

"Oh, go on." Lucy snickered at the comparison.

Grace laughed. "I have a mountain of clothes to wash. If I can bum dinner off you again, I reckon I'll get started on it this afternoon."

*****

George mounted his wagon. "Are you coming to dinner, boy?" he asked loudly, knowing that Douglas was hiding in the tree. He wanted to give Douglas a ride to the house and have a little talk with him about spying and spitting on folks along the way, but Douglas stayed in the tree, pretending to be invisible. *Suppertime then*, George thought. George left his fence project and headed for the cotton field. "Come on, men, hop on and we'll go have dinner."

The men did so, grateful for the break in the day. For the next hour, they would eat and try to straighten out their backs. "You men are doing a damn fine job on those weeds. After dinner, we'll set posts in the shade for the rest of the day."

It sickened Douglas to see his father treat his slaves with kindness. Douglas knew he would take this place over someday, and he knew hell would freeze before he ever got caught talking to one of those Black devils, let alone giving one a ride in his wagon. His father was a fool to trust those people as much as he did. Douglas would make William the overseer since he liked the savages so well, but he would be damned if he would tolerate kindness toward them. How he wished his parents weren't so odd and probably the laughingstock of the entire Bluegrass region. Douglas couldn't stand this scene anymore. He knew after dinner was finished, all the men were going to be in his vast space, working below his secluded tree branches, and he would have to listen to his affable father. He reckoned he had better things to do.

*****

George was pleased to see Grace. There was a profound change in her. She greeted him as the wagon pulled up in the yard. For the first time in a month, she was the one to initiate the hugs. She took his hand in hers and headed for their house while the rest of the men went to Lucy and John's house to have their meal. "I bummed dinner off of Lucy again, but from now on, I'll be tending my family on my own."

George only smiled. Lucy was a fine cook. George enjoyed her meals, but he admired his wife when she tended to her duties, and Lucy had taught her a lot about cooking and organization. Grace no longer feared the task as she once had.

"Guess what Graham showed me this morning."

Grace smiled a little at the excitement in George's voice. "I can't guess, my love, what did he show you?"

"An iron plow! Some guy invented an iron plow! Can you believe it?"

"Did Graham buy one?"

"He sure did!"

"How much?"

"More than I'm willing to spend right now. I'll have to wait until the cotton sells before I can even think about it, but by God, we will have one by next spring I bet. Can you believe some guy thought up an iron plow? By God, I wish I would have thought of that."

Grace walked out of the kitchen without saying a word as George continued to eat dinner. His eyes followed her until they couldn't anymore. He feared he had bored her or that his enthusiasm had saddened her. He wasn't sure what to say or how to act around her these days. He heard her footsteps returning to him and waited for her to enter the room. In her hands was a tobacco can he recognized as one of her possessions that she had when she followed him home, ten or eleven years it had been now. He couldn't remember exactly.

Grace sat with him at the table. "This is now 'The Iron Plow Account,'" she said, gently pushing the can toward him.

George put his spoon in his empty bowl and looked at his wife curiously. "What is this?"

"Open it." She hardly smiled, but her eyes were twinkling, and this George had not seen for far too long.

He opened the old tobacco can, and his eyes widened. "Where did you get all of this?"

"That's the money you always give me for clothes. Now aren't you glad you married a woman who doesn't give a care about clothes?"

"I see you've been wearing Lucy's hand-me-downs, for heaven's sake. Why don't you just go to town for once in your life and buy some clothes of your own if you can't sew?"

"The clothes I have suit me fine! Now Lucy says I need work. She said that since I don't find pleasure in housework that I should do something a couple of hours a day that I would find pleasure in. She told me to paint the barn or work with you. What do you think? Do you have any ideas? Would you hate to have me help you?"

George arched his brows. "What about William?"

"William has become Johnny Boy's caretaker. Lucy says I need a happy reason, all of my own, to get out of bed, put my clothes on, and go to work at."

Moments passed as George and Grace had a staring contest. George scratched his head as he reasoned out what Grace was trying to tell him. He imagined her life. He imagined how he would feel if his jobs in life were to cook, clean, wash clothes, and try to teach the boys how to read, write, and cipher. He imagined he wouldn't last five minutes. He looked out the window at his barn, and the looks of it suited him. He hadn't planned on having to buy paint for it for a couple of years. He had been thinking about putting a few head of sheep or cows out on the wooded eighty acres, but they wouldn't take that much tending to.

Grace was starting to wilt. George wasn't saying anything, and she was starting to get the feeling he thought he had seen enough of her as it was.

"I don't think the barn needs to be painted right now. I'd have to buy paint and I don't want to buy paint. I want that iron plow."

"Oh George!" Grace hastily got up from the table.

George quickly grabbed her hand. "I have an idea. Will you take a walk with me?"

Grace smiled broadly this time. "You have an idea, really? Are you teasing me, George Weatherford?"

"Walk with me and see."

"All right, will we be long? I promised Lucy I'd be out to wash clothes after dinner."

"It won't take long. Come on." George was smiling. He was so attractive to her at that moment she almost implored him to forget the walk and take her to bed instead, but she was also very curious about his idea.

George took her by the hand and eased her out the back door. They passed by John and Lucy's house. Everyone was in the shade, having a smoke before they went back to work. Their heads turned with wonder as they watched the couple walk out of sight. Lucy giggled, and each man silently contemplated what it could mean.

"Have you seen our limestone quarry lately?" George asked his wife.

"No, I haven't been back there for years."

"Did you know limestone is softer than most wood when it is freshly cut?"

"I never gave limestone much thought at all, except it looked like damn hard work when you built the cabins."

"A guy can carve it with woodworking tools to make sculptures. Since you never go anywhere with me, you probably haven't seen the fine sculptures in Frankford or Lexington. I have seen a couple of sculptures that are mounted in the middle of man-made fishponds. Some of them are of men, women, women with children, and some of them are of horses. That's what I want, sculptures of horses at the entry of the property by my white rail fence. You and I could work on them together. I've seen your sketches, and I think you'd be good at it."

"George, what are you trying to do, make this place fancy?"

"Why not?"

Grace giggled at her husband. "I think you go to town too often." Grace shook her head and added, "What do we need all that fancy stuff around here for?"

George stopped, faced his wife, and lovingly put his hands on her shoulders. "One day, people will come from all over Kentucky to buy horses from us. I want this place to shine. I want them to know we work hard to make it shine and we take pride in what we do. Do you want to help me with that?"

"Yes, I do." Grace smiled broadly with twinkling eyes.

He embraced her. For the first time in a month, there was passion between them.

George had the feeling everything was going to be all right now. The couple continued, hand in hand. Grace thought of how she loved this man's hands. She thought of how much pleasure they had given her over the years. She loved holding his hand, kissing his hands, having them touch her breasts in a way that only his hands could. She loved having his hands on her back, thighs, and shoulders. She suddenly shuddered at the thought of having his hands touch every part of her body, but now was not the time. She tried to shake off the feeling until the day was transformed into night as it always miraculously did. There would be no more wasted opportunities to be intimate with this man.

"George, is that poor tree dying?" Grace pointed to a tree off to the left of the quarry. It was early summer, and it was losing its leaves instead of growing new ones. Grace began to pity it.

"That is the strangest tree I've ever seen. It's like a ghost tree or something. It was my dad's favorite tree in the whole place." The couple walked toward it. George wanted to show Grace the enormous pea pods it produced. "This is a Kentucky Coffee tree. The damn thing sheds its leaves in the spring instead of the fall and sits there with bare branches for six months. It doesn't make any sense, but that's what she does. Look at these pea pods."

"I'll be darned."

"Don't curse, dear," George said softly. Grace smiled slightly, both knowing she would curse whenever she saw fit to do so. The couple marveled at the tree for a while and then headed for the quarry.

Grace tried to remember if they had ever walked like this before. Maybe once or twice before the boys came along, she thought. She found it to be just as intimate as lying in bed, rubbing George's back. That was his therapy. This walk was hers. That was until they entered the quarry and found Douglas there. Extra precut blocks leftover from the last building endeavor had been left stacked in the quarry for the next project, should George or Graham have to build something new. Douglas had found a sledgehammer and was working away at trying to disfigure them. George remembered it had taken considerable time and effort to measure and cut those blocks to the precise size for building. Douglas knew this. Douglas had been constantly underfoot when the cabins had been built. It sickened George to see the willful, devastating tendencies in his son.

The happiness and pride he had felt for his wife had now given away to utter and complete disappointment in the son. His stomach turned at the sight of it. Grace sensed the emotion her husband was feeling. She wanted to make it stop. She wanted him to be like he was moments before. She wanted to protect him from the pain Douglas caused him.

Grace reprimanded her son quickly. Grace jerked the sledgehammer out of his hands and threw it down. She grabbed a fistful of shirt collar and shook her son. "What is wrong with you? Why are you destroying these blocks?" She waited for an answer, but the shock of being caught rendered Douglas speechless, not to mention he had no good reason for doing it except to make his father mad. He hoped his father would see it sometime, blame it on a slave, and then maybe he would get to see his father whip one of the Black devils, but he certainly wasn't going to admit all that now.

Grace searched her son's eyes. She could see his mind turning. She sensed whatever he was thinking was something frightening that she didn't want to know about anyway. "Get your ass out of this quarry and stay out of it until your father tells you otherwise!" Grace jerked him in the direction of the entry before she let go of his shirt.

Douglas stumbled, righted himself, turned around, and glared vehemently at her. Her hands were planted on her hips. She silently raised one arm and pointed to the mouth of the quarry. As Douglas walked past George, he spat. George remained as much of a stone as the stone he was surrounded by. He never wanted to beat his son more than he did in that moment and knew if he started, he might not be able to stop.

Grace picked up the sledgehammer and joined her husband. "We better do something with this. He looked like he wouldn't mind using it on me."

"If he even tries, I'll kill him, Grace. God forgive me, I'll kill that boy," George whispered.

*****

"Lucy, let me take a turn at bringing the water. I can't remember what we did with the soap."

"Oh, Grace, you gone and lost your mind. That soap is in the same place it always is. You go get it now, haulin' water ain't no work for you."

"I am losing my mind, thank you for noticing. I can't remember, I tell you. Now let me have a turn with the water so I don't lose my strength and grow old before my time," Grace argued.

"Grace, it's bad enough you do your own washin' without somebody comin' along and seein' you haulin' the water for it," Lucy reasoned.

"Who's going to see us, Lucy? If you mean George, you don't have to worry about him. He appreciates me all the more when he catches me working hard," Grace said, smiling and winking at Lucy. "If you get my meaning."

"Oh, go on now! No White woman supposed to talk that way, and if my man caught you haulin' water with me standin' here, I be in a heap of trouble."

"Well, your man ain't here. You look peaked to me, and I'm going to take a turn at the water for my strength, and that's all there is to it!" Grace said, putting an end to the argument.

"Peaked! What you mean peaked? I don't looks peaked, Grace," Lucy said, sounding hurt at the insult.

"How do you know what you look like? Do you have a looking glass in your cabin? No! I'm the one looking at you, and you look like something. If you're not peaked, then you're something, and it means to me that you don't need to haul all the water!"

Lucy yielded the water bucket to Grace and watched in wonder at what this White woman was doing. *No other white woman in the world would have cared if I felt poorly or not. And her talkin' 'bout her man that way? I'll be,* Lucy thought to herself shaking her head.

"Tomorrow's church day. You better go this time so's you can get yourself untouched. I ain't goin' to be standin' here when my man come 'round that house and sees you haulin' water. Just do my chorin' at night where you ain't 'round here, shamin' me," Lucy said, turning away to find something else to do out of Grace's sight.

"Where are you going? John ain't nowhere around here! Don't get mad about this, Lucy," Grace implored.

Lucy stopped and looked at the ground with her back to Grace and leaned forward as if she was going to vomit. Grace quickly dumped the water, bucket, and all into the washtubs and ran to Lucy's side. "Come in the house now, Lucy. I'll have one of the men go for a doctor. My word, you are a stubborn woman!" Grace declared as she grabbed Lucy's arm and waist, supporting her weight as they both went into the house. William rushed over to support the other side of Lucy.

"What's wrong, Mama?" he asked with a frightened look on his face.

"Run quick, find one of the men, and tell them to fetch the doctor right away," Grace told William.

"I can get the doctor, Mama, I run faster than a horse."

"No, I want you here to keep playing with Johnny like you've been doing, all right? Do just like I said."

"Wait!" Lucy weakly tried to shout.

William stopped.

"I don't needs a doctor, Grace, please, I just got hot arguin' with you is all. You tried to give me a heart attack talkin' 'bout your man that way."

"Damn it Lucy, are you pregnant and too afraid to tell me or what? Go now, William. Do like I said!" Grace shouted, lifting her face away from Lucy's before she did. "My God, woman! Here you are, the only friend I got, and you haven't told me about your baby, and now you're in trouble. You come in now and lay flat on my bed."

"Oh, Grace, I couldn't," Lucy argued, trying to pull herself away from Grace's grasp. "That's your bed and your husband's."

"Damn it, I know whose bed it is, and you're going to it right now. The cabin is too far away if this is serious. And speaking of my bed, don't you be blaming me for your pains. You shouldn't have been arguing with me in your condition or hauling water either, and you know it too. I'm plenty guilt-ridden enough without you piling this on to my shoulders too."

"I'm sorry, Grace. I don't want no doctor lookin' at me. Only man ever looked at me is John."

"Quiet now, we left Johnny outside. You sit still," Grace ordered. Visions of the well and the washtubs exploded in Grace's mind as she thought of little Johnny Boy outside by himself. As she rushed through the kitchen door to the backyard, the boy was not in sight. Grace ran to the tubs and to the well and was relieved that he was in neither place. She ran to the side of the house to look toward the fields where William must have gone to get help, and there was William, carrying Johnny and running as fast as he could, back for the house. Johnny was bouncing in William's arms, both looking uncomfortable, Johnny looking as if his head was going to spring from his shoulders and William looking as if he had a limp.

Grace raced to the front of the house to meet them, and together, they went inside and put Lucy in bed. The boys stayed with her while Grace went for water to cool Lucy with, and everybody waited for the doctor. The squabbling was over now, and all that was left was a tiny family of friends quietly hoping that whatever was wrong with their friend and Mama was going to be all right when the doctor got there. William went to the kitchen to retrieve a chair for his mama to sit in while she tended to Lucy and then went for another so Johnny could sit in his lap and see his mama's face.

To William, waiting for the doctor was harder than waiting for Christmas morning. He had never been sick enough to need the doctor, but the doctor came to help his mama and now his good friend, Lucy, and it seemed like it was taking forever. William reckoned that if he got here before dark, then Lucy would get better. He always came after dark for Mama, and even though Mama always got better, he knew that in a different kind of way, Mama wasn't better because something bad had happened. Something had changed that William didn't understand, but he knew it was bad. It always happened in this room too, William thought, and then he said, "Mama, is it too late to put Lucy in my bed? Maybe it will bring her better luck if the doctor gets here before dark." William was looking out the window at the daylight and the road and then back to his mama with a wise, questioning look on his face that made Grace realize that her baby boy was growing up and didn't miss much.

4

George was the one who had gone for the doctor because that is who William sought first. George didn't waste a moment. He didn't even ask who needed the doctor or what was wrong. It usually meant something was wrong with his wife. The first time that Grace miscarried, the doctor was requested. George had no idea of miscarriages and couldn't figure out why Grace would be asking for the doctor so early in her pregnancy. His first thought was that his overly dramatic wife was trying to get out of something, some chore or cooking, so instead of going for the doctor, he went to the house to find out what was really troubling her. She lay in bed that day, carrying on about needing the doctor, but George didn't believe her, and when he grew weary of her performance, he went back to work. Lucy had seen her through that day and understood George's reasoning because Grace often pretended and complained that she was being worked to death and was being abused by her husband, and when George walked out of the house that day, disappointed by his wife's tantrum, both women knew why.

Grace wailed for the next two days, and Miss Lucy just held her and rocked her and prayed that her poor Grace wouldn't slip away into insanity.

When George realized what had really happened, he was sick. There wasn't any place on his own property where he couldn't hear Grace's grieving cries, so he left. He grieved too. He wanted to be held too. There wasn't a soul on earth that would allow him the privilege of mercy after what he had done. He would never forgive himself for the decision that he had made that day.

A week later, when George returned to his home, he was greeted with love. His wife had missed him and had worried about him. Then she proceeded to tell him that she would never ask him for the doctor unless it was important and that her days of pretending to be in dire stress were over. She had most definitely learned her lesson and that he must never leave her again.

George never really took his wife's words to heart. He knew that she would do something to get him back. He also knew that when someone hollered for the doctor, he wouldn't waste a second, so on this day, he grabbed the nearest horse and rode bareback in his pursuit.

Douglas was torturing a nest of baby field mice near the road when he saw his father race by. Douglas ran to the road, screaming for his father to take him along, but his father didn't hear him in his haste. George probably had heard his son but pretended not to. Douglas was so distraught at being left behind that he cried and threw rocks in the direction that his father had gone. After a while of that, he went to the stable and retrieved a mount for himself and followed his father.

The doctor's house was about three miles from George's farm and back from the road about one hundred feet. The place couldn't be seen from the road due to the trees and vines that the doctor's wife had been growing.

When Douglas left the farm, he was under the assumption that his father was going to town without him, which he hated because he couldn't bother his father to buy him something. It never mattered what, just anything. The boy would impertinently ask for anything in the mercantile from lanterns to kettles, driving George into a blackened state of depression on account of being saddled with such a disgusting child.

While Douglas was racing down the road, trying to catch up to his father, an opportunity to inflict pain upon someone presented itself. Douglas saw a lone Black woman walking down the road in the same direction that he was going. Douglas quickly looked around to see if there were any witnesses and, determining that he was safe, abruptly ran the woman down. The chest of the horse knocked the woman to the ground, and she was then hit twice by the horse's hind hooves. The horse tripped, trying to miss the poor woman, and Douglas was almost thrown, but his mount righted himself, and little Douglas, feeling lucky at that moment, was able to press on, hoping that his father hadn't left the mercantile yet.

George alerted the doctor and then raced out of the yard, heading back to his farm. The doctor would be coming, but now George was in a rush to find out why the doctor was needed this time. Grace hadn't mentioned being with child again, so it must be something else, a bad cut or burn maybe, he couldn't imagine. Ahead of George on a straight piece of road by an open corn field, he could see someone waving their arms above their head. "Good Lord! What is it now?" George said to himself as he prepared to stop. A Black boy about his oldest son's age was pleading for help and looked very concerned.

"What is it, boy?" George asked as he dismounted.

"Look!" was his only reply as he pointed at the woman lying on the side of the road.

"What happened here?" George asked, turning the woman over to have a look at her face. The woman moaned, and George could see that she had a bloody nose and a large bump on her forehead.

"I don't know," the boy said, shrugging. "I's out in the field, lookin' for som'tin' to eat and hears some noise, so's I look see."

"Well, this poor woman has been trampled by something." George looked around, thinking that somebody's oxen had gone on a rampage but saw nothing. He looked down where the boy was standing and saw hoof prints and knew that someone had deliberately run this woman down. "Did you see who did this?"

The boy shook his head and shrugged his shoulders. George was in a fix now. A doctor was needed back at his place. Someone could be bleeding to death for all he knew, but this woman needed help too. He couldn't just leave her on the side of the road until his own crisis was over. Doc's house was closest, and Doc had a buckboard in addition to his carriage, so he went back for it, telling the boy to stay with his mother and he would be back.

As George was trying to mount by centering his weight in the middle of his horse and then swinging his leg over and sitting up, he saw Doc coming. George waved Doc down and told him about the woman and how he was going for the Doc's buckboard. "Tell the missus to give you some blankets. Cover her up and have the boy hold her head. I'll see you at your place," Doc ordered as he hurried away.

The boy watched as each grown man dashed away in opposite directions and wondered who they were and why either one of them would give two hoots about an old Black woman anyhow. The boy felt bad for the old woman, but he couldn't do anything for her. Even if he could pick her up and take her out of there, he didn't have any place to take her. The boy's real mother had been sold by her master, and he was trying to find her. His master wouldn't be looking for him because since he was small for his age, he wasn't much of a worker and surely wasn't worth feeding. The boy reckoned that it was probably his master that had trampled the poor old woman and maybe he was going to come back, so he took the old woman's wrists and tried to drag her off the road so they could hide in the foot tall corn, but he was too little and too weak, so he just hid himself, letting the old woman lie there and moan by herself.

"Get in the wagon, boy!" George yelled at him, able to see the boy from the seat of the wagon. George jumped from the wagon and picked up the trampled Black woman. "Hurry up and get in the wagon. Doc says you've got to hold your mother's head and keep those blankets on her. Get goin', I gotta get back to my place."

The boy scrambled up on the wagon by climbing on the wheels to get in. "Sit down there, and keep her head in your lap, do you understand? Don't let her head bang around on the floor, all right?" The boy nodded as George lifted the woman over the side of the wagon and gently set her in. George noticed the boy put his hands on each side of her face so her head wouldn't move too much as he quickly covered her with the blankets. George hadn't given orders to do that, and he almost said something to the boy but decided not to. The poor little fella's mother probably wouldn't make it. At the very best, she wouldn't ever be right in the head again, and the boy didn't need anybody's opinion on how to hold his mother's head. George quickly got in his seat and slapped the reins against his horse that had been going back and forth on this road all afternoon and they all raced home.

Old Mr. Grant happened to notice a horse speeding around the corner four buildings up from his shop and wondered if there was a fire. Then he recognized the rider. The child, Doug Weatherford, was heading straight for his mercantile. Mr. Grant struggled through his merchandise to get to the front door in time to lock it. One of his lady customers was in the store and wanted to know. "What is the meaning of this?" She was thinking that Mr. Grant had sadistic ideas about her.

"It's the evil Weatherford boy. Hide!" he whispered with urgency.

The woman looked out the window, gasped, and immediately dropped to the floor, doing a belly crawl to find a better place to hide as Mr. Grant ran for the back door to lock it and take cover.

Douglas looked around the front of the mercantile for the horse that he had seen his father on and then tried to open the door. He shook it and banged his fists on it until finally he realized that he was locked out. Douglas was frustrated over the fact that he wasn't going to get his father to buy him something today, so he proceeded to kick the door repeatedly. Each time, both Mr. Grant and his customer cringed and closed their eyes, terrified that the animal would kick the door open. Finally, Douglas gave up. Just to make sure his father wasn't in there, he pressed his dirty face and hands to the windows in several different places.

Mr. Evans happened to have business at the mercantile that afternoon. He had been fortunate in not running into Douglas Weatherford in some time. George had started coming to town on Tuesdays because the town wasn't as busy on Tuesdays, and he wouldn't have to be so embarrassed by his son. As Mr. Evans dismounted to enter the store on this Saturday afternoon, the obnoxious boy hollered at him, "The mercantile ain't open, mister!"

Mr. Evans swung his head around and immediately recognized the face of his friend's son. "Your father is not in this town, boy. What are doing here alone?"

"I'm lookin' for him. I saw him come to town, and don't you be callin' me boy, mister!" the disrespectful brat screamed.

Mr. Evans walked quietly but forcefully toward the boy. "I told you, your father is not in this town. You better get your tail home this minute." In Evans' mind, he imagined finishing the order by saying, "Because the day you are old enough to come to town on your own, you better hope that I'm too old to get here because I swear, boy, I'll hang you from the tallest tree."

Douglas tried to kick him as Evans knew he would. Evans caught the boy's leg and quickly lifted him until the boy landed on his back. "The next time you kick me, boy, I'll break this leg in as many pieces as humanly possible. Now you get!" he commanded as he flung Douglas away, causing him to roll from the porch of the mercantile. The two people glared intensely at one another as Doug managed to get mounted. Mr. Evans gave a big slap on the rump of the Morgan that had carried the boy to town. Doug almost fell from the giant, trying to hit Mr. Evans with the back of his hand. His reach wasn't quite as long as he had hoped for, but he felt lucky that he had been able to keep his seat. Falling off in front of his new enemy just wouldn't do.

Doug checked every building in town, looking for his father, but after a while, he was convinced that he had thoroughly missed out today and headed for home, thinking of ways to get his father back for not taking him to town. Doug wasn't in a hurry to get home. He needed this time to think about what he could do to hurt his father. He also hoped the Black woman would still be on the road somewhere so he could run her down again. The Morgan eased home gently, grateful that the boy wasn't making him run anymore. He was a strong plow horse, but he had worked his heart out the day before and racing down the hard packed road had hurt him today. He didn't know why the wicked boy wasn't running him to death, but he was glad of it.

Doug was disappointed in not finding the Black woman and reckoned that he hadn't hurt her none, and when his stomach began to growl with hunger, he kicked his tired mount and sped home. When he arrived and saw the doc's carriage in front of the house, he realized his father really had not gone to town after all, but he still resented the fact that he had been left behind. He quickly put his horse back in the stable, bruised frogs and all, and ran to the house to spy happily at whosoever was hurt or ill.

*****

Grace met George at the door as he carried the trampled woman in. "Where should I put her?" he pitifully asked his wife.

"Oh, put her in the boys' room. Lucy is in our room. Where is John?" Grace asked.

"I'll get him," George said as he gently laid the woman down and ran out at full speed.

Grace looked the strange woman over and turned to get water to wash her wounds and ran into the little Black boy that had followed George in. He had become attached to the woman that he had held and decided to stay with her instead of wandering off upon arrival at a new place where the owner owned slaves. He thought that his real mother might be at this place.

"Oh, I'm sorry. I got to get some water to wash your mama's face. I'll be right back." Grace had been warming water all afternoon while she waited for the doctor and George to return. She knew the doctor would need hot water as he always did. Grace took the time to fill a plate with pie and some leftover biscuits and bacon for the boy. She knew boys were hungry all the time unless they were preoccupied with play or catastrophic doings, but this strange boy looked like he had been through some hard times, and she was right. When she walked back into the room and handed him the plate, his sunken eyes got so big Grace thought that they would fall out of his head.

"Go on now, it's for you, eat up! What's your name?"

"Sam," he replied.

"What's your mama's name?" Grace asked. Sam shrugged his shoulders.

Grace laughed. "I know, you just call her Mama, don't you?"

Sam thought it was best for now not to answer and just eat his food. This nice woman might not be nice if she found out that he didn't know the woman on the bed. When she did find out, he wouldn't get any more free food.

William was worried about his own mother and found her in his room with new people he had never seen before. "Mama," he said, leaning on her shoulder looking at the woman on Doug's bed. "Who is it? What happened to her?"

"I don't know except that she is Sam's mama," Grace said, tossing her head in Sam's direction.

William looked at the boy sitting on his bed and smiled. He kissed his mother's cheek and went to join the strange boy called Sam. "This is my bed," William said because he was proud to have a visitor. Sam got up. "You don't have to get up. My name is William," he said, smiling.

Sam nodded as he continued to eat, hoping that he wasn't expected to share his bounty.

The doctor came in. "Miss Lucy isn't having an easy time of it. The only way she won't lose that baby is if she has complete bed rest for at least a week and no hard physical labor after that. Now what can we do for this woman? George said that she was driven to the ground by a horse?"

"He did? Who in the world would do such a thing? The evil in this world bewilders me," Grace remarked.

"Help me with these clothes. I need to check for more bruising," Doc ordered.

The boys left the room. William stopped Sam in the kitchen and explained to him that they didn't want to run into his brother with all the grown-ups busy with sick people. Johnny was waking up from his afternoon nap, and William went to the bench and gathered him up, took him to the kitchen, and they all ate the rest of the pie that Sam had already sampled. Johnny stuffed the rest of the bacon into his pocket, and they went outside to find a safe place to play. William decided that it was best to stay close so he could scream for help when Doug came around to torment him.

Sam quietly watched as this White boy took care of and looked after the little Black baby just like he was William's own flesh and blood. Sam wondered what kind of strange people these were to care for others the way they did, especially Black people. "Where is his mama? Out in the field somewhere?" Sam asked.

"His mama is the one that's sick, the one Doc was tending to before you came."

This shocked Sam. Then he figured that the White people must live in a bigger house somewhere else, except William said that was his bed in there. As hard as Sam tried, he could not understand. His own mother had never shown him the love and kindness that William was giving to Johnny right now. The notion was so abstract to him that he didn't even recognize that it was love and kindness. He only realized that it was pleasing and peaceful to be here with a full stomach. In his life, he knew nothing good ever lasted very long. The knot in his stomach would never leave, and he would never have a reason to trust anybody, especially these strange acting people.

Doug was happy to see Lucy grimacing with pain and John sitting with a worried look on his face. He didn't know what troubled her, but he hoped that it was bad. He knew that Lucy didn't like him, and sometimes he would catch her looking at him in a way that he didn't like. It seemed to him that she was thinking bad thoughts about him or cursing him without saying the words, just like his own mother did, only she said the words. Doug's mother and Lucy were just like that Mr. Evans who had threatened to kill him someday. Doug thought how easy it would be to sneak out some night and burn that man's big house down to the ground and hide in his tobacco field and watch. "That man made a big mistake today," Doug said to himself as he smiled at the thought and spied on John and Lucy. Then he thought of how Lucy's illness would affect his mother and how she would have to do all the cooking and cleaning again if Lucy died, and he began to think of all the ways that he could make her life more difficult.

"Doug, quit spying. If you want to see Lucy, go inside and see her," his father chastised.

"I don't want to see her!" the boy bellowed.

"Well, get the devil away from her window then and leave people be."

"I'm hungry."

"When the doctor is finished, we'll get supper working."

"I'm hungry now!" the boy yelled.

"You watch your mouth or else I'll bust your ass!" George advised and went into the house to see what could be done about supper since there was, in fact, a whole crew of people to be concerned with.

Doug decided to make destructive use of his time by throwing rocks at the doctor's horse. This gave Doug great pleasure when the horse flinched and whinnied and tried to get away and couldn't because Doc had set the break. But the pleasurable moment came to an end when George grabbed his wrist in the middle of a throw, lifted the boy, until only one toe touched the ground and dragged him toward the stable, looking for something the whole time, appropriate enough to beat the boy with. Many different weapons crossed George's mind. He saw a shovel, a pitchfork, a board, but all these things were too harsh, and George was afraid that if he started, he wouldn't stop until it was too late. So he ended up merely spanking the boy with his arthritic hand as hard as he could, and then he let the boy go. "You get your ass in that house and don't move a muscle until I say so because if you do, you'll be hungry all night! Do you understand me?" George shouted and pointed his bent forefinger at his son.

Doug didn't nod nor say a word. He just ran for the house. He didn't care anymore if he ate. He didn't need any favors from the son of a bitch that had just spanked him. He would just lock himself up in his room so he wouldn't have to look at his father. That would make the old man feel sorry for what he had done, even though the spanking didn't even hurt. Doug laughed to himself about how soft his father was. Doug knew if that spanking was the worst thing that could happen to him, then he could do whatever he wanted to, and he would.

Doug slammed the front door as he ran toward his room and prepared to throw himself on his bed and wail and scream for the hours to come over the mistreatment he had just incurred by his father. The sight of the Black woman in his bed stopped him dead in his tracks. He didn't recognize that it was the woman who he had run down. He had even forgotten about the incident. The doctor and his mother were still in the room when Doug screamed, "What in the hell is that Black bitch doing in my bed?"

He couldn't believe that his plan to disrupt the entire house was unraveling right before his eyes. That thought was quickly replaced by how he couldn't believe that his mother had just hit him so hard across the face that he had to check and make sure that his eye was still in its socket.

Doug glared at his mother, trying to burn her with sparks of malice and hatred, and slowly backed out of the room until he was out of sight and walked through the kitchen and out the back door.

William heard Doug coming and picked up Johnny and motioned for Sam to follow him, and they hid under the steps coming from the house. Doug walked out and took a deep breath, looked around, and wondered which direction he would go when he ran away. Then he walked over to the well and looked around at the laundry that was never finished that day. He kicked at the ashes that were under the washtubs, hoping to find a live coal so he could burn the linens and clothes that were still sitting in their baskets. Then he felt himself being watched and saw his brother out the corner of his eye. Without looking at him, Doug whispered just loud enough for William to hear, "I see you staring at me, you little whelp. Tonight, when you are sleeping, I'm going to come back here, steal your little Black Johnny, and throw him in the well."

William sat tight, staring his brother down and watched him slowly walk away, out of sight and without purpose. William knew that his brother would backtrack and find a spot where he could watch every move made at the place. He knew it would delight Doug if he showed his fear and ran around screaming for his mother and telling on his big brother, so he did the opposite and went back to playing for a little while, and then they calmly went back into the house.

Grace had managed to build a big stew for supper. It was more overwhelming than usual, and her biscuits couldn't hold a candle to Lucy's, but everybody knew that, and they were just grateful to get something to eat. Bread pudding was the quickest dessert that she

could think of making, but there wasn't any bread, so for the first time in five years, the crew and family went without dessert.

William had relayed the whereabouts of his brother and the threat that he had made against Johnny and George and Grace were beside themselves over what to do about the boy. Each one of them secretly wished that the boy would just keep going and never come back.

The Black woman in Doug's bed passed away that night from internal bleeding, the doctor reckoned, and then left the dead woman in the care of the Weatherfords to bury.

*****

The next day, George and John wanted to carve a marker for the grave, so they questioned little Sam some more about her name, but he only shrugged his shoulders.

George looked at John, shrugged his shoulders too, and spoke, "I guess we can carve on it 'Sam's Beloved Mother.' How would that be, Sam?" George said, asking the boy's opinion.

Little Sam looked down at his bare feet then and confessed that he didn't know the woman and that his own mother had been sold away and he had been looking for her when he saw this woman on the side of the road. As much as Sam had enjoyed the free food, he had never become accustomed to lying, and if these people sent him away, it would be all right because he needed to find his mama anyway.

George wrote down a few words for John to carve on the marker and told Sam to follow him. They found Grace at the back of the house with William and Johnny helping her for all they were worth with the laundry, and Grace was grateful for their effort.

George told Grace Sam's story. It never failed to sicken George how slave owners treated their people. Grace whispered to George, "The son of a bitch probably got her pregnant and sent her away." She was referring to Sam's mama. Then she looked at the boy and smiled. "I say we feed him up, muscle him up so no son of a bitch will recognize him if they come looking because with Lucy down in bed, I could use the help with this blasted laundry, and you look like you could use some meat and potatoes on your bones. How would that be, Sam?"

Sam didn't make a gesture of agreement. He couldn't seem to take his mind from his bare feet. Grace looked at George and wondered what else she could offer the boy to enhance the negotiations. "Maybe you could stay until Lucy gets better. Then George can take you to town and pay you with some traveling clothes and shoes. You'll be better outfitted when you go looking for your mama. I could sure use the help, but I won't make you stay if you would rather roam around the countryside by yourself, barefooted, with nothing to eat, hoping to find your mama," Grace said while she continued with her work and pretended that it didn't matter to her what Sam decided to do.

William couldn't contain his opinion anymore. He wanted Sam to stay and help him protect Johnny from Douglas, and he blurted out his point of view. It shocked Sam to know that William would think that his mother and father would allow such a conspiracy. Sam didn't think that under any circumstances would these grown-ups let him even touch their son, let alone fight him.

"That reminds me, George, when are you going to start on the well house?" Grace asked.

"After we bury that poor woman, but I'll have to go to town for a lock," George answered.

"Make sure it is tight, no windows, no windows on the door, and a complete roof. I don't put anything past Douglas," Grace ordered.

"Yes," was George's only reply as he clenched his jaw and looked out in the distance, knowing that Douglas was out there, watching. George walked away then to help John with the grave preparations, leaving Sam with his wife. He reckoned the two of them could finish the negotiations amongst themselves.

The wash water had become too dirty now, and Grace left it to start wringing out the things that had been rinsing. Looking at the sun to make note of the time of day, she determined that she had time to start again with a fresh tub of wash water. She didn't really care if she ever caught up with the laundry, but what concerned her most was missing out on dessert again. No one enjoyed dessert as much as she did, so laundry be damned. One more load, and that was it.

Ignoring Sam all together, Grace said, "William, get workin' at emptyin' that old water while I rinse and hang these things."

William knew the routine and got working at it right away. Sam jumped right in to help William, and Grace smiled to herself. The boy drove a hard bargain, but the deal was closed, and she reckoned it favored her. She only wished that she could add two feet and thirty pounds of muscle to his body before Douglas came back.

5

1826

As the years passed, the work never diminished. Grace had forgotten about having another baby and found peace in watching Lucy's children grow up. Lucy and John had three children, and Lucy was content with her life. She had grown accustomed to Grace's friendship and had learned to fully trust her and accept her help when offered.

One day, Lucy noticed that despite the work that her friend was doing, she was becoming plump around the midsection. "Been hittin' 'em pies in the middle o' the night, Miss Grace?" Lucy asked, knowing that her question would be answered with an abundance of curses which Lucy found to be humorous, and it always helped to break up the monotony of their work.

"What the devil did you just accuse me of? Eatin' pies in the middle of the dang night? What the devil would make you say such a blasted thing? If anybody's stealin' pies in the middle of the bloody night, it sure the devil ain't me!"

Lucy giggled.

"What the devil are you snickering about? Every day, you go and get me riled up about some dang thing, and then you snicker at me. Why in the devil do you do that?"

Lucy continued to giggle, happy that her friend's spirit was as robust as ever. "How long you been makin' biscuits now, Miss Grace?" This was also a sore subject that was sure to stir Grace's blood.

Grace scowled at the only friend that she had in the world, except for her husband. "Now you want to start in on that. You just love it that your bloody biscuits are better than mine after all the times I've tried. Look at yourself. That does it!" Grace ran out of the kitchen and came back with her looking glass. "There, now look at yourself! You are just so full of yourself over your dagnabbit biscuits that you are starting to run out of your own son of a gunnin' ears, for heaven's sake. Put that stuff back in there before it gets on the floor!" Grace said franticly as she tried to poke Lucy's ears with her fingers. Lucy put her hands over her ears and ran around until Grace stopped trying to poke her and giggled. "Don't talk to me about them darned biscuits then!" Grace said with a smile, pointing assertively at her friend.

Suddenly, after all the excitement, Grace became pale and dizzy. "You wore me out with your nonsense," Grace told Lucy as she reached for a chair.

"Well, it ain't been pies you been hittin' in the middle of the night Miss Grace, you been gettin' that mano' yourn," Lucy suggested, bringing Grace some water.

"What in the devil are you talking about now?" Grace asked softly, now feeling like she might vomit.

"You with child again, Miss Grace," Lucy said smiling and hoping that her friend would be happy.

Grace sipped the water, and her face was expressionless. She wasn't in shock, but the two emotions that she felt were hope and dread, and in that moment, they were equal enough to cancel themselves out, causing her great confusion.

"This time, you rest in bed, and me and my girls will take care of you. You go on to bed right now. I'll fetch your man," Lucy ordered, and because Grace was in no position to argue on account of past failures, she silently obeyed her friend.

*****

Everyone was hopeful. Grace had confined herself to bed rest and had stayed healthy and full of life, and she was looking forward to having another child. She never figured out why God had made her wait so long for another try at it, and she spent many hours in her room, looking out the window, wondering about it. She finally concluded that it must have something to do with Douglas.

Douglas had remained to be the contemptuous dark cloud in her existence. The only good thing that she could say about him is that he had not spoken to her since the day she slapped him. He still skulked around, taking food as if it was owed to him, and if he did look at Grace, it was only to glower at her. He was sixteen now, but William had surpassed his brother in weight and mass and was always fully prepared to drive his brother to the ground if Douglas gave him any reason to.

Over the years, Douglas had been responsible for many cases of arson, but George couldn't hang his own son, no matter how badly he wanted to. So far, he was grateful that his son hadn't seen fit to torch his friend's and neighbor's properties. George also felt fortunate that given the iniquity that his son possessed, no one had been killed during Doug's fits of revenge. The losses were one stable, half the crop of dried tobacco before they got it extinguished, and an entire field of corn before George and his hands and every neighbor for miles around were able to get it out before it jumped the creek and got on to Mr. Evans' place. Douglas had picked a particularly windy day to start that blaze. Eighty acres of corn were destroyed. That was the day Doug almost breathed his last breath, but William attacked Douglas that day before George could get to him because the smile he had on his face, when William and George came in the yard from fighting the fire, was so morbid and deliberate it filled William with instant rage.

Mr. Evans had been there that night and watched William beat the devil out of Douglas. Evans' stomach was turning because the more William hit him, the more Douglas would just grin. William knocked out five of his teeth for all his sinister evil grinning, but it didn't keep him from continuing to do it. When William had figured out that he had broken enough of Douglas' bones to keep his brother from roaming around in the fields for a while, he quit and stood up. "Keep smilin', you piece of work! You think you're a real spook, don't you? But you ain't, you ain't nothin' but a worthless piece of work!" William wanted to stomp his brother's brains out of his skull then, but Evans pulled him away.

Evans bent down to look at Douglas lying on the ground. Ready for anything, he said, "Gettin' 'bout time for the two of us to meet in town again, ain't it, boy?" Evans hoped that he would try to kick him again so he could break some bones too, but Douglas' only reply was a sickening, bloody, toothless grin. Evans shook his head and walked away. He knew that William had hit the nail right on the head.

Over the years, William and Sam had fortunately gotten out of the laundry business and had become John's right-hand men, taking care of the horses and all the harnesses and the equipment that was used on the farm. Their days were spent together, and they were good friends. Sam's demeanor had changed a little over the years from being unconcerned about others, especially White people, to learning how to have faith in people. Little Johnny was growing and big enough to stick to Sam and William like glue, which they encouraged. Neither one of them would forget the threat that Doug had made that day about throwing Johnny in the well. It would be some time before one of them would forget that. It would be some time before Johnny would be able to defend himself in case Doug tried to make good on it.

Sam had become strangely particular about where he slept. When he first struck his deal with Grace to stay on, John and Lucy had asked him to stay with them and help them watch over Johnny, but as their cabin filled up with children, Sam had taken to staying out in the stables. That was about the same time Douglas had decided to torch them, but Sam was able to get out easily enough. Douglas hadn't thought about locking him in there before he started the fire. He just assumed that Sam was asleep and wouldn't make it out, but Sam had still been awake, reading a book that Grace had given to him. When Doug saw Sam get out and start hauling water to the fire, Doug ran for the house and accused Sam of starting it. Much to Doug's disappointment, he never heard anybody say anything to Sam about it. There wasn't anything said to anybody about it. Not only that, but when George rebuilt the stables, he included a nice big room in it for Sam to live in and even bought a bed for him to sleep on. This had been Grace's idea. George had cringed at the expense; after all, he had just spent a fortune on the stables.

"Now you listen to me, George Weatherford. Sam and I struck an agreement that he would stay on and help me around here, and I ain't gonna let him sleep in horse dung!" And that was that.

Doug despised her for that. She didn't give a damn whether he came home or not, and she turned around and saw to it that some Black little stray was getting to sleep on a real bed. That's when Doug decided that from now on, he would wreak havoc with his father's profits.

As Grace laid in her bed, remembering all the despicable things that Douglas had done and also thinking in contrast about how fortunate she was in having such a good son in William, she couldn't help but wonder what the child she was carrying now would be like. She prayed that the new little he or she would be half as good as William. That would ensure that the new addition would be two or three rungs on the ladder above her, and that would suit her just fine. She knew the time was close now, and within a few days, she would know.

William knocked on the door as he strolled in, looking a little spent from a good day of work. He leaned down and kissed his mother's cheek. Grace smiled broadly at her son as he pulled a chair close to her bedside.

"Don't sit so blamed close to me, for heaven's sake, you smell like an old plow horse!" Grace fussed, teasing her son.

"Well, what the devil do you expect me to smell like? I've been workin' all day. We can't all lie around all day, smellin' like roses, like you seem to be gettin' away with," Grace's son jovially replied to her obvious tease. "Are you feeling good today? Is there anything that I can get for you?" William asked.

"Yeah, you can go take a bath and come back later," Grace teased.

William smelled himself and said, "Yep, I sure could use one."

"Have you seen your brother around?"

"You mean your son? No, I ain't seen him, have you?" William asked instantly, concerned that maybe Doug had been around, tormenting her.

"No, I ain't seen him. Hey, why doesn't Sam ever come to visit me? I miss seeing him."

"Oh, he's too embarrassed to come into your room. I told him to, but he won't even come into the house anymore, let alone come in here. If you want to see him, you've got to hurry up and have this baby and quit lying around all day. Are you getting excited?" William inquired because he was beside himself with excitement. His hope was that Doug would finally leave and never come back and there would be a peaceful atmosphere surrounding the new arrival, and William would finally have a normal sibling to be proud of. William was fourteen years old now, and the thought of being a grown up himself soon or leaving his father's farm to build his own hadn't yet occurred to him. In his mind, there was plenty of time to be spent with a little brother or sister.

"Right now, I'm just praying that everything works out all right. I'll get excited after I'm finished having he or she," Grace said, gently tapping her enormous belly. "Do you want to feel it move?"

William shook his head. "No, I felt one move in that old mare earlier today," he joked.

"I ain't no son of a gunnin' horse, and this ain't no foal! What in the devil is the matter with you, son?" Grace laughed.

"It's all the same to me. One moving belly feels like any other moving belly, doesn't it?" William shrugged at the experience.

Grace made a face and shook her head, not knowing how to respond to her son's reasoning. "You're going to be quite a man when you grow up, William. Some poor girl is going to fall for you someday, and you'll make her cry all the time with comments like that. Most women don't have a sense of humor like I do."

"Girls? I ain't gonna have time for girls. I'll be workin' and savin' my money. You can't have money and girls too. That's what Pa told me anyway," William replied, smiling broadly, knowing that his pa would be scolded in the near future.

"He said that, did he?" Grace took William's hand and looked at him seriously. "William, remember this: whatever you do with your life, I know you will do it well."

"Thank you, Ma." He leaned in and kissed his mother's cheek again. "I'm glad you told me that 'cause Miss Lucy told me and Sam to go catch some fish for supper. Now I know we'll catch a mess of 'em." William smiled as he stood up and as he left the room.

Grace said, "You two watch your backs out there."

"Don't worry, Ma, Douglas knows better than to come around me. I love you."

"I love you too, son."

William went to the kitchen and started scrounging up some food for himself and Sam to eat while they were fishing. "Whach you doin', Williams?" Miss Lucy asked as William was putting his bounty into a pail.

"Gettin' ready to go fishin'."

"Who told you that you could go fishin'?"

"I told Pa that I wanted to see Ma, and I told Ma that you told me and Sam to go catch some fish for supper." William's broad smile was irresistible to Lucy. She shook her head and looked at the floor.

"Did you see your ma, Williams?"

"Of course I did!"

"Well, fish would be nice for a change."

"That's what I thought," William said as he made for the front door. He ran to the stable where John and Sam were and explained to John that Lucy was sending him and Sam fishing, and the afternoon was won.

Both boys were vigilant as they walked to the creek. William wasn't afraid of his brother, just afraid that Doug would try something stupid while he was gone. But it was still daylight, and Doug was a nocturnal species, so as long as they got back before suppertime, William reckoned there was a good chance that Doug wouldn't bother anyone. He thought how nice it would be to think that the bane of his existence had left the country, but he couldn't think that because he could still feel Doug's presence and could feel him watching.

The two boys stepped into the creek. William had a rock on the other side that sat up out of the water, where he could sit and bait his line, while Sam favored a shadier spot where a tree had blown over, making a bridge across the creek. Sam sat on the downed tree in the shade, took his shoes off, and let the current of the water soak his feet. This usually only lasted a few minutes before he got a chill and moved into the sun and down the creek from William where there was a calm, deep hole. William fished from above this hole, and Sam fished from the bank beside the hole. William always caught more because he had the best spot to fish from, but the issue of who caught more fish never came up because it really wasn't a sport. It was just time off from the stables.

William said, "Ma asked about you today. She says she misses seeing you. What do you make of that? And then she told me I needed a bath."

Sam smiled at William and nodded.

"I guess you still think about your ma a lot," William inquired, wondering how anybody could survive having their own mother sent off. William admired the strength that Sam must have.

"I think about her every day," Sam replied. "I would have left a long time ago to find her, but John told me that no good would come of it. He told me that I'd never find her, and while I was lookin', people would do me more harm than I could imagine, maybe even kill me! He said it was best to just stay with Miss Grace because she would never let anybody hurt me. So I stayed, but I sure do wish that I could see my mama again," Sam explained.

The boys had picked a good day to fish. The breeze was slight and from the west, and by suppertime, they had caught enough for everybody to have a taste. They started back for the house. They were late and Miss Lucy would have supper ready, but they were hopeful she would still cook up the catch for an after-supper snack. "Damn! I forgot the pail that I brought the food in," William said.

"Take the fish to Miss Lucy. I'll go get the pail," Sam said. "I left my hat on a branch down there anyway."

"All right," William said, continuing with the fish. He watched Sam trot back toward the creek, and then, out of habit, he glanced around at his surroundings, looking for Doug. There was nothing. He proceeded toward the house, now able to see the yard and the roof of his home. He thought now that he was especially stinky with the smell of fish, he would visit his ma again and tell her how well he and Sam had done this afternoon before he sat down to supper.

A noise from the creek made him stop in his tracks and listen. Then he heard it again. It was Sam hollering. William dropped everything and ran for the creek as fast as he could. When he got there, Doug was standing in the creek, struggling with Sam, trying to drown him. William wondered why Sam was letting Doug do it. Sam could overpower Doug easily but was afraid that he would get into trouble for doing it. William quickly picked up a rock and smashed Doug on the head with it. He dropped like a sack of spuds. William grabbed one of Doug's legs so he wouldn't drift down the creek and reached over to help Sam up onto his feet. "Are you all right?" William asked.

"Yeah, he just ruffled me a bit," Sam replied.

"I don't know why you let him get on top of you like that. Ma and Pa both told you to beat the devil out of him if you see him," William scolded as he dragged Doug to the bank of the creek and left him there with a bloody skull. He walked over to the hat and pail that had been forgotten, tossed the hat to Sam, and recommenced his trek to the house.

Sam looked at Doug, and then at William. "Hey, are you just gonna' to leave him there like that? Don't you think we better take him to the house?"

"No."

"Won't we get in trouble?" Sam asked.

"No, we got fish to clean. Besides, that's a good place for him. I don't have to worry about looking for him, and he won't be botherin' anybody for a while."

Sam didn't want any part of William's decision, but he wasn't going to stand around and wait for what would happen when the heinous boy woke up either, so he ran to catch up with William.

"I hope I can find where I dropped those fish," William said, smiling slyly when Sam caught up to him.

*****

Two days later, Grace hollered for Miss Lucy. The time had come for the new arrival. Lucy ran out to the stables to tell John to find Mr. George and tell him to go for the doctor. Grace had given birth to Douglas and William back in the old days by herself with only George's help, but everyone agreed that after all of her troubles, a real doctor would probably come in handy this time.

William hopped out of a stall where he had been grooming the tail of a horse. "I'll go, Miss Lucy."

"Williams, nobody talkin' ta you. You do what John says. Mr. George will be the one wants ta go!" Lucy told him.

William leaned his upper body and head back as though he had just been hit by a strong gust of wind and made a face at his bossy old friend.

"You keep 'em eyes in your head. You do that to your ma, but you best not be doin' that nonsense 'round me!"

William rolled his eyes and went back to the stall. John had already disappeared, and when Lucy finished eyeballing William with her hands on her hips, she scampered back to the house to help Grace. William watched her from the window opening in the stall and laughed at how Lucy reminded him of an old hen chasing somebody away from her baby chicks. Lucy quickly turned around to catch the boy laughing at her. William dropped like a rock to keep from getting caught. "I hear you gigglin'!" Lucy shouted as she stomped up the steps to the front of the house.

If Lucy had stood around much longer teasing her Williams, she would have been run down by George, who raced through the yard on horseback, just as the screen door closed behind her. Lucy had been watching her friend's baby boy for twelve years now and loved him as much as she loved her own children. What she loved most was the man that he had grown into and how he loved and protected everyone who was near to him. She had heard from John the story that Sam had told him the day before of how William handled his brother at the creek. She had rejoiced with her husband, hoping that maybe the blow to the head would have either killed Doug or at least it would have knocked some sense into him. Lucy and John didn't know if they should mention the incident to Grace and George. Then they thought that since the baby was just about due, it would be best not to say anything.

Lucy had sensed in Grace, over the last few weeks, that she was worried enough without having to worry about whether Douglas was lying dead at the creek or not. John knew that George was worried about the baby too. Even though George didn't talk to John about his problems or worries, John felt that George was more afraid that Douglas would hurt the new arrival than he was that something might go wrong with the delivery.

"Williams, you best go sit in the house till your pa gets back," John told him, noticing that William was desperately watching the house and yard, anticipating that Doug might show up and do something wretched when the women wouldn't be able to defend themselves. William hopped out of the stall again and left the stables without saying anything and nonchalantly headed toward the house. He knew that if Douglas was watching, he would know that it was Ma's time to have the baby by the way Pa had raced away, but if there was any chance that he missed seeing that, he himself wasn't going to be the one to give it away.

John watched William walk to the house and then scanned the landscape himself out of habit. When he realized that he was doing it again, for probably the twentieth time already that day, he sighed and thought how disruptive it was to a person's soul to always have an evil spirit casting a shadow on such a big place and on so many people. He shook his head slightly at the absurdity of it all and glanced over at Sam who was watching the fields, searching for a sign of doom. Suddenly, John got a spine-tingling chill up his back and wondered what it would take for it to be over.

William sat down at the kitchen table that John had made for his ma. From there, he could see the front and back doors. He heard his mother moan with pain, but he wasn't alarmed as he sipped a cup of Lucy's coffee and swallowed one of her biscuits. He reckoned that it wasn't an easy thing to have a baby. Even an old mare will moan a bit. Lucy hurried in with hot water from the fire outside, and William expected her to raise Cain with him for not helping. "What can I do to help?" he asked before she was able to start in on him.

"You doin' it. Go give your ma a kiss 'fore things get too bad. Then you come back and sit right here 'til your pa gets back."

William opened the door to his mother's room and smiled. "'Bout time! Open the window, would you, son?" Grace asked. "Sit here with me a while." Grace put her hand out, and William took it as he leaned down and kissed her on the cheek. "Oh, you're a good boy for coming to see me. I'm surprised that Lucy will let you in the house."

"I guess she figures that I have enough experience with the mares that I ought to be able to handle you," William joked.

"Oh, blast you!" Grace said, smiling slightly and sighing. "You're lucky you got such a handsome smile or else I know some old gal that would knock you on your ass for such a comment." Another contraction started, and William watched his mother clench her teeth and tighten with pain. The strength she possessed when she squeezed his hand in hers lifted him up out of his seat.

"Ouch, ouch, ouch! Oh! You're bustin' the bones in my hands for heaven's sake! What the heck!" William screamed.

As the contraction faded, so did the grip Grace had on her son. She smiled slightly. "Sorry, son, I didn't mean to hurt you, but what's wrong? I thought you had so much experience."

"Mares don't have hands like you!" William exclaimed. "You could choke the life out of a mule, for heaven's sake. I guess that's why Pa's fingers are twisted."

Grace gave her son his bruised hand back and spoke. "I won't hurt you again like that. I sure am glad that you're here for my baby." Grace looked deeply into her son's beautiful eyes and wondered how many young men there were in the world, if any, that would help their poor old mother through a labor pain and make her laugh at the same time. Grace wasn't laughing out loud because she was saving her strength, but she was laughing heartily on the inside. Happy tears welled up in her eyes as she watched him examining his hand, opening it and closing it, checking for broken bones. With his eyebrows furrowed, he caught her looking at him. The concern that he had for his hand and the look that he had on his face made her chuckle then. She couldn't help herself. It was energy well spent.

"What the devil are you laughing at?"

"All you're joking about me being no different from a bloody old horse," Grace lied, whispering.

Lucy came in after a little time had passed. She brought cool water and a cloth and started cooling Grace down and soothing her. "This ain't no place for boys now, Williams," she said.

"Oh, don't make him go, Lucy," Grace implored.

"Lucy's right, Ma, I have things to tend to anyway. I love you," William said as he kissed her.

William went back to his post and waited. As he ate another biscuit, he heard something outside. Stepping to the back door, he saw that it was Sam out there, stoking the fire. William knew that John had sent him to the house to watch after Lucy and the girls. William opened the back door. "You better have some biscuits, Sam, before somebody else gets 'em. It's goin' to be a long day."

Finally, George and the doctor arrived, and William thought it might be all right for Sam and the children to go with him to the stables. He didn't like hearing his mother in pain and decided that he'd rather like to wait for the good news someplace else. Maybe he'd go back after dark and wait with his pa, if it took that long, but for now, he reckoned playing with John's children would take his mind off his ma's distress.

Shortly after sundown, William heard a bloodcurdling scream. The hairs went up on the back of his neck, fearful that something was terribly wrong; he dashed to the house and found his father pacing back and forth across the dining room floor, wringing his crippled hands.

"What was that? Is Doug in here?" William persisted.

"That was your ma trying to have a baby. It could mean that she's getting close," George replied.

John was grateful that the boys had done such a good job of wearing out the children and decided that it was time to find them all something to eat and get rested up for the next day. The girls were very excited to see a brand-new little baby, and they thought they should stay up and wait, but before they were able to finish their supper, they went to sleep right at the table.

Sam didn't have any hankering to follow his friend William to the house. He never liked seeing people in pain nor being around them and knew there wasn't anything that he could do to help his friend. He loved William and Grace as much as he was capable of loving White folks, but he figured that when babies were coming, it was strictly a family matter. So he read the book that Grace had given him, only jumping out of his skin twice when Grace screamed, and then he went to sleep.

Lucy finally came out of Grace's bedroom. She was greatly disturbed when she told George that the baby was a breech, and the doctor was trying to turn it around. Then Lucy hurried back into the room.

"Will everything be all right Pa?" William asked.

George nodded his head. Unable to tell a lie, he didn't see any reason to frighten his son unless it was necessary. George knew that if the baby was turned around the wrong way that he would surely lose either his wife or his child. He turned away from William and wondered how he would go on if he lost his beloved Grace. After all these years, given their rocky start, Grace had turned into the best wife and partner that any man could ask for. He was envied and praised by all his friends and neighbors at what a good wife Grace had become. They commented some about her foul language, but everyone agreed that it was a small price to pay for such a hardworking, fast-learning woman to have on a man's side. Grace didn't know it, but she had become a woman that men told their wives they should aspire to be.

Doug watched from afar as his father resumed his pacing after Lucy went out of the room. Doug figured that the child had been born and George and William were waiting to see it. He wouldn't have much time to get his revenge on Sam for not letting him drown the other day. He had already started a small campfire just beyond the stables with a branding iron resting in it when he saw that John had gone home and Sam had turned in, slowly but surely getting it hot enough to use. Doug quietly opened the door to Sam's room and sneaked in with a horsehair rope that Sam himself had braided. Gently, Doug slipped the loops of rope around Sam's wrists, and with one motion, he pulled the rope tight with one hand and shoved an old dirty sock in Sam's mouth with the other hand. Quickly, he tied Sam's hands to his bed, tied an old shirt around Sam's mouth so that he couldn't spit out the sock, and then battled with Sam to get his feet tied to the bed. After winning the engagement, Douglas gave Sam his strange, twisted, toothless grin and ran outside.

Sam struggled to get loose. He tried to flip the bed over, but it was too solid and heavy. He wondered what that evil little creep hoped to gain from simply tying him to his bed, then he reckoned the place was about to catch on fire again, and he began to struggle for all he was worth.

Doug came into the room with a hot branding iron, and without even taking a moment to gloat, he hastily seared Sam's chest with the same brand as every animal that Sam had spent his days caring for. Douglas held the brand on Sam until his red crying eyes bulged from his head and he passed out from the pain.

Doug simply dropped the hot iron on the floor and left the room as though nothing out of the ordinary had happened. As he walked back to the house to watch his estranged family through the window, he noticed Doc's horse. He realized that it was the same horse that had caused him to receive a spanking some years ago. He took a makeshift knife from his boot that he had worked on while he watched the house from the trees on the ridge and plunged it straight into the animal's heart.

The poor animal let out a shrill whinny and dropped to the ground, just as Grace gasped her last breath in this world.

"What was that?" William asked as he jumped up at the spine-chilling noise.

"Doc's horse. Just skittish probably," George answered, numb with worry.

Douglas watched his father and brother for a moment and then skulked away into the darkness of the night.

George and William then heard the horrible sound of a woman wailing, and they both jumped to their feet again, each one unable to breathe. They met the doctor as he came out of the bedroom. He was soaked in Grace's blood. William was aghast by the sight and ran outside to vomit. George looked into the eyes of the man who had been with his Grace during her last moments, and he knew what the man was going to say. Over the desperate cries of Lucy, the doctor said, "I'm sorry, George, they didn't make it. I did everything that I could, but it wasn't enough. I have never felt more incompetent in my life than I do right now."

George used the nearest wall to hold himself up with, but his mind, body, and soul gave way to anguish, despair, and grief. The doctor watched George sink to the floor and cover his face with his hands. No sound came out of George as the doctor headed for the door. Doc knew that for a moment, George's body had forgotten to breathe, but there wasn't anything he could do about that. He walked past William who was crying and heaving at the same time and continued toward his carriage, not wanting to see pain in the faces of his friends who had earlier been so full of hope.

Doc saw his beloved gelding lying on the ground, still in his harness, and knew the gloom of this particular farm would be everlasting after that night. His old horse, who had been with him through all the good and the bad, who had waited hours upon hours for his keeper to finish his job at one home or another, had either died or been killed. He assumed that Douglas had something to do with it, but now was not the time to tell George. Just like he couldn't help George right now, George was purely incapable of helping him.

Doc began to take the harness off of his old friend, and his emotions compelled him to burst into tears with the force of a strong rainstorm. Combined with the loss of a special woman and her child and the breaking hearts of the people who loved her, his spirit was completely overwhelmed with sadness as he sunk to his knees and cried, wondering how he would ever get his harness free from his dear old horse.

William went into the house and saw that his father was inconsolable, and for an instant, he thought of going into the bedroom to help Lucy, but he couldn't fathom the thought of what it would be like in there, and he couldn't stand the thought of seeing his mother lifeless. Slowly he backed away until he was out of the house. He wanted to be away from this place. He wanted to forget this night. Ignoring the doctor's plight, he headed for the stable to get a horse and leave.

As he entered the building with just that single thought on his mind, he smelled something familiar that brought him out of his trance. He smelled smoke. William looked all around and followed the faint smell that led him to Sam's room. He lit a lantern and saw the branding iron smoldering on the wood floor. He wondered what it was doing there as he examined it and then raised the lantern above Sam, lying on his bed. The sight of seeing Sam tied to his own bed with his flesh burned with his father's brand took him from a state of shock to madness. William thought surely that Sam was dead but cut the ropes and the gag and went for the doctor.

After a few moments of shaking the doctor out of his own sad fury and giving him a moment to comprehend what William was trying to say, he picked up the bag and went with William to help Sam. William stayed with Sam and Doc until he knew Sam would live and then started packing a few things that he thought they would need when Sam was able to travel. He got two horses ready and picked out one for the doctor to have since he saw that Doug had killed his with a knife to the heart. He went to the men's quarters, woke up two of them, showed them Doc's dead horse and handed over the one that he had picked out and left them to tend to the problem.

William went to the house one more time to get the money that his mother always set aside for fabric but never used. There was more there than William imagined and only took part of it. He wanted to tell his father that he was leaving as soon as Sam was able, but he was still on the floor, wailing now as Lucy's crying had subsided. William thought how awful it must be for Lucy to be tending to his mother and her baby by herself, and the thought of it made him convulse with fits of crying, and he ran from the house. In Sam's room,

William tried to stop his tears. When he finally gained enough composure to speak, he asked, "What can you do for him, Doc?"

"All I can do, I'm sorry to say, is keep this salve on the burn and keep a clean bandage of gauze on it. Try not to get it dirty. I've also bandaged his wrists and ankles. Fortunately, he's very healthy and strong. It's the worst thing that I have ever seen one human being do to another, except for that woman that you had here that had been purposely run down by someone."

Sam opened his teary eyes. William turned to the doctor as the doctor turned to look at him. "Douglas!" William whispered. Sam closed his eyes, remembering the evil, toothless grin that bastard had on his face while he burned the brand onto his chest.

"Doc, give me all the salve and gauze you have. Sam and I are leavin' as soon as he's able," William told him.

"You can't leave your pa. He'll need you now more than ever," the doctor advised.

"It's Pa's place to take that menace out of this world. If I hear that he's done that, then I'll come back. Thank you for helping Sam. Some of the men are out tending to your horse. I'm sorry for that," William said, knowing that he should shake the man's hand but not doing it.

"I only wish I could have—"

William held his hand up, indicating that he wished for silence. "I don't want to talk about that. That's over now." He walked over to Sam, hoping that the doctor had gotten the point and would leave now without saying another word. And the doctor did, closing the door behind him.

"Why do you say we're leavin', William?" Sam whispered.

"Ma and the baby died tonight, and I'm gonna get you out of here before it happens to you. There ain't nothin' or no reason to stay here. As soon as you're able, it will be time to get from this place," William said with finality and determination.

"Help me get dressed, I'm ready."

"Are you sure?" William asked, surprised that Sam wasn't going to argue the point. Sam had already heard what William had told the doctor and knew that he was right.

"I'm ready to breathe air that's not filled with darkness."

"Good! Let's go," William agreed, unable to feel happiness about his decision to go and Sam's willingness to go with him. He wondered if being happy and knowing love would ever be his to hold again.

Under the Influence
San Francisco, January 1849

1

Bennager would never forget the day he saw Rose Mary Briar get off the ship at the San Francisco pier. This was the second White woman that he had seen in six months. The first one had been the wife of a Mormon. She hadn't looked anything like Rose Mary Briar. It was plain to see that when Rose had started her trip from the East Coast harbor, bound for the coast of California, she had been healthier than she was now because it looked as if her dress had outgrown her.

As Bennager watched her walk up the hill toward town, he found himself suddenly confused. A large Black man was walking beside her, each one carrying a large handbag. What Bennager was confused about was why they were leaving the pier without the rest of their gear. He imagined that this once healthy, fair-to-look-at, fancy lady must have brought more baggage than one large Black man and two large carpetbags.

Since gold was found twelve months ago, Bennager had seen some strange things, but for the most part, people who got off the ships in San Francisco were pretty much all the same and with the same intention. Number one, none of them were women. Number two, they all at least brought mining tools with quite a few of them having enough merchandise to open shop. And number three, none of them made Bennager's curiosity as active as this lady did.

At one time, the dress that the young woman was wearing had been the type that the fancy well-to-do ladies were wearing when he had passed through Springfield, Illinois. Her coat was practical enough, gray wool. The large Black man wore the same type of coat. Her hair was light brown or maybe blonde. It was hard to tell what color it was since it looked like she had not bathed in some time, but he could see three things for sure. Her eyes were green, she was about five-foot-four inches tall, and if she was soaking wet, dress and all, she might weigh about one hundred pounds. Because of the hard trip that she had just finished, it was hard to guess her age. Bennager was never good at those guesses anyway. He had guessed his aunt's age once when he was a youngster and got his butt paddled for his effort. Another thing that made Bennager curious about this sight was the way the woman was with the Black fellow. He walked beside her, not behind. He carried one large carpetbag, and so did she, and though the trip had been hard, Bennager could hear the woman chatting with the Black man about things as if they were related or best friends. *Maybe they are*, Bennager thought, chuckling to himself.

Bennager was the type of man who had always thought that it was best to keep his nose out of other people's business because there were some things he should not know and most things that he didn't want to know; but, by God, this was just too much.

"Miss, my name is Bennager Rasmussen. Could you folks use some assistance or maybe a guide?" Bennager asked, tipping his hat politely.

The woman looked at the Black fellow, and then they both looked at the stranger, and before he knew it, the Black fellow had Bennager's throat in his big hand.

"Sam, don't break his neck until we find out what he wants."

Slowly, Sam let go of the stranger's neck, and Bennager quickly figured out why each one of them kept one hand free. The woman had found a knife to hold on to. "Now, Sam, when you walk into a strange country, you can't be killin' people just because they start talkin' to you. You're going to have to learn to be neighborly. Mister, what is it that we can do for you?" The woman directed the question to the stranger.

Bennager backed up a step or two and spoke, "Miss, I saw that you were new in town, and I was just trying to be helpful, but I can see that you have all the help you need. Welcome to California." With that, he turned tail to get the devil out of there.

86

The filthy woman was instantly intrigued by the man's lack of fear. She could see that he merely wanted to leave because he had been irritated by Sam. "Hold on there, mister. It just so happens that Sam and I could use a little guidance, and I do apologize for reacting too quickly to trouble. It's just that we sure have had our share of it in the last seven or eight months," the worn-out woman said.

"Well, I can believe that since you are the first White woman to arrive in California by sea, and I really doubt that any White women have arrived by any other form of transportation. Although, I guess it's possible."

She looked at Sam in a way that suggested defeat, and then she looked back at Bennager and talked. "The first White woman? Mister, I asked you for guidance, not storytellin'. Now the first order of business in your guidance service is going to be to guide our asses to beefsteak. Or are you going to tell me that there ain't but one cow in California too?" the lady asked sarcastically.

Bennager's eyes widened, and then in disgust, he glared at the woman, taken aback by this female's foul language and foul manners. Bennager did not even bother to answer this woman's surly remark. *What kind of woman who has not bathed in what looks to be months would eat before she bathed?* Bennager thought to himself and then simply said, "Follow me, Miss."

It did not take them long to get to the first hotel where Bennager knew that he could find a beefsteak to jam into her foul-mouthed face. They walked past the livery and two store fronts, and they were there. Bennager was raised to be a gentleman in the presence of a lady. Although he doubted that he was in the presence of one, he kept to his upbringing and said, "There you be, Miss. This outfit rarely runs out of beefsteak. I'll be seein' you folks around."

The woman had sized the man up as they walked to the hotel. She could see that he was a hard worker and a handsome one at that. His dark hair was accentuated with sparkles of silver and matched his blue eyes perfectly. The woman reckoned that his maker had done a fine job of putting this man together, and she wasn't finished admiring him yet. "Well now, Bennager Rasmussen, I know that you'd be hard pressed to eat beefsteak side by side with the likes of a filthy female and a big black boxer, but if you could stand our company and a beefsteak to boot, I believe that it would be a good trade for your guiding services."

The fact was that since the big rush had started, the price of beefsteak had increased so much that it had been some time since Bennager felt like he could splurge for one, so reluctantly, he agreed, even though he knew that it would be more trouble than it was worth.

With three beefsteaks ordered, the female got down to business. "Mister Rasmussen, my name is Rose Mary Briar, and this gentleman is my business associate, Samuel Washington."

Rose Mary Briar, Bennager thought. *Nothing but thorns, this figures just about right.*

"Now I am quite aware of the fact that Sam and I have not bathed in some time, and you may be wondering why a bath was not our first order of business. Did you come around the Horn, Mr. Rasmussen?" Rose asked.

"No, Miss Briar, I came across country on horseback."

"Call me Rose, Mr. Rasmussen. I came around the Horn because I was afraid to take my chances with the Indians, but after coming around the Horn, there isn't one damned thing that I'm afraid of now. The meat spoiled after the first month, the water turned orange with rust by the third month, and the only nourishment we had until we stopped in Peru were the weevils that we had in our biscuits. We damned near starved to death on that godforsaken vessel, and only White woman or not, I'm here to stay." During Rose's story, she kept pulling up the bodice of her dress, fearing that her constant jabbering would cause her to fall out of it. "This damned contraption fit me when I got on that damned vessel. You see, Mr. Rasmussen, my father put me on a ship bound for Europe. On that ship, I had in cargo all the things that a proper young lady should have—dresses, undergarments, combs, soap. Well, you get the point. And before he left me to sail across the Atlantic, he handed me these two large carpetbags," Rose said with a nod of her head toward the floor where the bags were. "Oh, here comes the grub, Sam!"

While the three of them ate, not a word was said. Bennager had figured out two new bits of information about the female; there was at least one thing that would shut her up, and she didn't talk with her mouth full. On the other hand, it appeared as though she could wield a knife as well as any Indian that Bennager had ever seen because her plate was cleaned up well before his or Sam's. The cook came out to fill the coffee cups, and Rose said, "Sir, that was real good for a start. Bring us three more plates, and I wonder if you have a pie around here someplace?"

"Yes, Miss, I have a pie, an apple pie. Would you all like a piece?" the cook asked.

Rose said, "Three more beefsteaks and the whole pie."

"Yes, Miss."

"Call me Rose," she called out after him.

"Rose, I do not believe that I could eat another steak, but I thank you just the same," Bennager said. At that, Sam smiled and shook his head, and Rose looked as if she hadn't heard him. Bennager knew deep down that it was time to be on his way, but the two large carpetbags and Rose's story kept his interests up, not to mention how she got here from Europe, but he guessed that might be the end of the story because when his plate was finally cleaned up, she had started on her second, and so had Sam. As Bennager was about to take his leave, knowing that it was the smartest thing that he could do, Rose motioned for him to stay put. After she swallowed, she said, "Dig into that pie, Mr. Rasmussen. I'll be finished shortly, and then I'd be obliged if you'd guide us to our next order of business."

The cook came and filled their cups again, and Bennager waited while Sam and Rose divided the steak that he couldn't eat into two pieces, and he wondered if he had ever seen anybody eat that much at one time, let alone a female. Then he figured that she was trying to fill that dress of hers back in, but even Sam was slowing down now. It looked as if Sam might not finish half of Bennager's steak, and Rose was finished and washing it down with coffee. She did not even look like she was full or needed a break to let what she had eaten hit bottom. In order to remain a gentleman, Bennager decided not to comment on the amount that this female could eat at one sitting and pretended that he saw girls eat like that every day.

Rose said, "I bet you have never seen a woman eat that much at one time in all of your life, have you, Mr. Rasmussen?"

"If I can call you Rose, then you will have to call me Bennager," he said quickly, changing the subject.

"Bennager, does the cook here poison his pies?"

"Well, no, I do not believe so, at least I have never heard of anyone complaining about the pies being poisoned," Bennager answered with one brow raised.

"Then you must join us!" Rose said, making her point that Bennager had no excuse for not joining them in one piece of pie. He took a small piece, just so she would know that he wasn't afraid to eat the pie, and Sam took a small piece. Bennager thought that maybe the cook was right to give each person just one piece until he saw Rose start eating right out of the pie tin. Sam looked at Bennager, smiled, and shook his head. The cook came around with more coffee, and when he saw the woman eating directly out of the pie tin, he gave Bennager a look that made him feel like he should be embarrassed, even though the cook knew that he had just met this duo. Bennager had been a patron of this establishment many times. Now with the pie gone and the three of them sipping their coffee, Rose was ready to get back to business.

"So, Bennager, if there aren't any women in this town, then I guess there aren't any dresses or undergarments or combs or anything at all that would make a woman look like a lady," Rose surmised.

"I'm afraid not, Rose, nor are there any White women in this whole country that you could borrow off of," Bennager replied.

"I won't need to borrow anything, Bennager, and I can't wait to get shed of this damned contraption I have on. My God, back home, a woman spends half the day putting all that stupid garb on. And for what? It never brought any man that I ever run into down to his knees. My father thought that I needed more education to snare a beau, and that is why he put me on a ship bound for Europe. I guess he thought that if I couldn't charm the men, then maybe I could buy one. That's why at the last minute, he gave me these two bags. When my father left the ship, I looked in the bags, and that is when I had a change of plans. I just walked off of that ship and found one that was headed for the gold country, and I imagine my father is wondering why in the devil he hasn't received a letter from me."

As Rose was telling her tale, Bennager could see past her dingy face and into the eyes of a girl who thought that she had pulled a good trick on her father. She looked like the cat that had eaten the canary. Anyone could tell that she was more pleased to be just where she was than to be anywhere that her father wanted her to be.

"Well, if you two don't mind me asking, just out of curiosity, is Rose your woman then, Sam?" Bennager asked.

Sam blushed and then became visibly angry. Rose looked at him like he was stupid, and Bennager thought that Sam was going to grab his throat again. Rose said, "For heaven's sake, Bennager, Sam is twenty years older than I am. Besides that, the man is Black. Sam and I met on that godforsaken, starvation, rat-infested vessel that we just got off, and no, I ain't his woman. I told you Samuel Washington is my business associate. Let's go." Rose got up abruptly. Rose paid the cook and commented on a job well done, and Bennager found that he was even more intrigued by Rose Mary Briar now than he was when he first saw her.

Bennager realized that he had just spent the better part of an hour with her and her business associate, and he had not learned what business they were in. *How can these two be in business?* Bennager thought to himself. Rose was walking to the nearest merchant building, and Bennager was following along, deep in thought, when he realized that Rose Mary had not yet asked where the nearest bathhouse was. Rose had made Bennager understand that her stomach came before cleanliness, but what would she be shopping for now that couldn't wait?

Bennager soon found out that Rose was not one to waste time purchasing goods like so many other females he had noticed in the east. She picked up two shirts, one pair of overalls, one pair of boots, and a hat. Sam did the same, and after a short discussion, they decided on one jug of rum and one jug of brandy.

"Bennager, what will you have? Rum or brandy?"

"Well, Rose, I never acquired the taste for either one. I pretty much stick to coffee. Thank you just the same."

"There's something wrong with a man that don't drink," Rose said under her breath to Sam.

Bennager heard the remark and became angry but quickly let it go because it didn't matter what this female thought of him anyway.

"Throw in a pound of coffee then, sir, and five plugs of tobacco. Do you use tobacco, Bennager?" Rose asked generously.

"I do have a smoke from time to time, but I happen to have all of the tobacco that I need for the now. Thank you just the same."

Rose paid the merchant, and she and Sam each grabbed their purchases and headed for the door. Bennager reckoned that it had been some time since the storekeeper had seen a female. The man was speechless. Rose was the busiest businesswoman that Bennager had ever seen, although he didn't recall ever seeing any. He had seen busy females, females busy working, busybodies, and females busy causing and getting into trouble.

Once outside, with a sigh of relief, Rose said, "Bennager, I don't see how anybody could be more ready for a bath than I am right now. Could you?"

Trying to be polite, even if it was one of the hardest things that Bennager had ever had to do, he passed on making a comment on just how much he agreed with her, so again he was quick to change the subject. "We are going to a bathhouse ran by a Chinaman." Bennager chuckled a little. "I've heard of people who have turned tail and ran the other way when they first see a Chinaman because they look so different from any other person that they have seen before. I just wanted to let you know that this old boy we are going to see is a fine fellow, and I didn't want you to worry yourselves about his looks. If Sam grabs this fellow by the throat, I doubt you two will get your baths."

Rose stopped in her tracks, and so did Sam, and she gave him a hard look and said, "Keep your hands to yourself, Sam. I've got to have a bath!"

Sam nodded his head with a most serious look on his face, and the three of them continued on. The trio passed two saloons, another merchant tent, and Chang's Chinese food tent. Chang's father ran the bathhouse.

"Here we are. It's been a pleasure meeting the two of you. Good luck," Bennager said.

"Bennager, I was hoping that you would stick with us long enough to guide our asses out of this town. If you would give us long enough to get human again, we'll get some gear together and get started," Rose ordered.

"Get started out of this town?" Bennager repeated. "Where do you think you're headed for?" Bennager acted surprised.

"First off, far enough inland so I can't smell that damned salt air. And second off, to start a business wherever it is where those boys found the gold. They are still finding gold, ain't they?" Rose asked naively.

"I would say so, yes! There are thousands of those boys in those hills finding gold. That's why it's best for you to stay here in San Francisco to start a business. I just came here from those mining camps to pick up some freight, and I wasn't storytellin' when I told you that you are the only White female that I know of in this whole damned country," Bennager warned.

Since Sam was her business associate and seemed to be her bodyguard as well, Bennager looked to him to help him convince this crazy female that what he said was in her best interest and his as well, but he seemed to be unconcerned as hell about the information that was just passed to the two of them.

"So you're a freight hauler, huh? Knowing a good teamster is going to be an important part of my business probably. Where is that Chinaman?" Rose asked, taking no heed to Bennager's advice whatsoever.

Sam and Rose entered the tent, and Bennager started to walk away. He knew that the best thing he could do was put as much distance between him and those two people—who were probably going to get him killed—as possible. As he rolled a smoke, he kept thinking about what kind of a business a tiny female and a Black man were going to be involved in and how much money they had in their pockets to get the business started, and also, he wondered what was in those bags that would make a woman jump off of a ship bound for Europe and onto a ship bound for the gold country. Then he figured when a female was as crazy as this one was, there probably was not anything in particular worth noting in those bags at all.

As much as Bennager wanted to keep walking away, it seemed like this whole situation had just taken control over him. He just couldn't tear himself away from Rose and Sam. He decided that he would do the best that he could to convince them to stay in San Francisco, and if they would not, then he would help them find their way to the gold fields. As Bennager thought the situation over, he remembered that he had come to California for an adventure and to see things that he had never seen before and to scratch up a business if he could. He knew many people who had very bad luck and had already given up on mining, but he had always been pretty lucky so far and figured that it probably wouldn't kill him to help Sam and Rose along. That is, of course, if he could not convince them to stay put in San Francisco.

Bennager headed back to where he had left Rose and Sam. The thought occurred to him that Rose might not have privacy in such a place. He cringed at the notion she might do something unseemly. With more careful contemplation, he felt it was easier to accept the situation was indeed completely unseemly and likely would continue to be in the future of his relationship with Rose.

As the bathhouse was a family affair that also included laundry and food from the Orient, Rose was compelled to try out the cuisine. She felt this was the last chance to indulge or to ever experience it again. She was certain Bennager would want to join them for another meal.

When Rose summoned Bennager, he decided that he was a doomed man on a doomed mission to help two doomed people get through their misadventure without getting raped or murdered. There was a good chance that if he took on this mission that he would have to give up his team and work with Sam as Rose's associate because from Bennager's point of view, Sam was doing a piss poor job of keeping Rose Mary Briar out of trouble. As far as he could tell, it was just dumb luck that either one of them was still alive. Bennager couldn't believe that this woman thought he could eat again. It had been no more than an hour ago that they had left the hotel, but he went in any way to make sure that Chang's pa didn't have a bathtub set up in the restaurant. When Bennager sat down at the table and started to take in the sights, satisfied that there were no bathtubs, he turned to Rose to ask her a question, and her new appearance made him lose track of what he was going to say.

As it turned out, her hair was light brown with tints of red running through it. Her skin had quite a bit of color to it, even though she claimed that she almost starved to death on her sea voyage, and now that she was cleaned up, it would have been easier to guess her age. Bennager guessed that she had not seen her twentieth birthday yet, but not out loud since he was a poor guesser. The way she looked in her new miner's uniform sure was a sorry sight. He was sure that a young girl like Rose would have looked much better in a dress than in a flannel shirt and overalls, but then again, this garb might be better suited for this particular woman who was apt to find nothing but trouble in her future. If this woman had a dress that actually fit her properly, Sam and Bennager would eventually get killed over it, and of that he was certain.

"What's wrong, Bennager? Don't you like Chinaman food?" Rose asked.

Bennager's thoughts had started to drift when Rose interrupted him. As he started to answer, he noticed that Rose was actually eating this meal as though she was enjoying it instead of devouring it. Maybe she was just checking every bite to make sure that everything in it was dead.

"I really don't think that my stomach will hold any more grub. The steak that I had back at the hotel will stick with me for a day at least," Bennager said.

"Well, Sam and I have never eaten Chinaman food before, and we probably won't get to again once we leave this town. I really just came in to get more of that wine that these fellas make. I've never had wine like that before."

"It seems to me that for such a young lady, you are quite the connoisseur of spirits," Bennager remarked in a questioning tone.

Rose answered, "I'm just a person that likes to try new things. That's why I'm here."

"What made you decide to come to the gold country to try new things instead of trying them in Europe?" Bennager continued on with his questioning.

"I've been to Europe before, and I didn't lose anything when I was there and I didn't see any reason to go back," Rose said in her sarcastic way, not even looking up from her plate of food.

"You sure have taken a chance by making that decision, Rose Mary, but I guess that you are stuck with it now. There hasn't been one vessel that came into the harbor that has left again, so if you thought that you could come here and change your mind, I think that you are out of luck."

"Sam and I have no intention of changing our minds. Sam came here to mine for gold, and I came here to start a business, and that is how it is going to be. Ain't that right, Sam?" Rose asked, confident in what his answer would be.

"Those are the facts as I see 'em Rose," Sam said seriously, nodding his head.

"Sam, you won't have any trouble at in the mining camps, but wouldn't you agree that it would be better for Rose to start a business right here in San Francisco, maybe a ladies' bathhouse for starters?" Bennager pleaded very convincingly, he thought.

When those words hit Sam's ears, the bathhouse scene came back to his mind, and a chuckle soon turned into knee-slapping laughter again. It looked like he was trying not to laugh, but he just couldn't help himself.

"A ladies' bathhouse!" Rose shouted. "Are you trying to sink me before I've even gotten started? You are the one who has been trying to tell me that there ain't no danged ladies around here, and you want me to start a ladies' bathhouse? What in tarnation is so damned funny about that, Sam? Why the devil won't he stop laughing?" Rose directed her question to Bennager. "That wine must not agree with him, I guess," Rose said, shaking her head in disappointment and bewilderment. Then she said, "Bennager, I mentioned before that this salt air makes me high-tempered, and the sooner that I get out of this town, the better I'll like it, and I really don't think that ladies' bathhouses are the way for me to make my fortune here or anywhere else for that matter."

"I wasn't trying to break you. I suspect that ladies will start coming to town more regularly now that you're here. Word will get back to the east that you are here, and there are probably plenty more on the way that we don't know about yet. By the way, where is that dress that you had on when you arrived?" Bennager asked.

"I told that old Chinaman to burn it. I didn't figure on having any use for that blasted contraption where I was going. Why, did you want it? Do you have a sweetheart hereabouts?" Rose asked with a smirk on her lips.

"No, I just thought that maybe you would have a use for it someday is the reason why I asked," Bennager said politely.

"Well, I believe that dress has seen better days. Sam, I guess we better get moving along. Pay the man and see how much of that wine you can get him to sell you." Rose picked up the two carpetbags, and as she straightened up, she staggered back a step or two. Bennager thought that he would have to catch her, but then she headed for the door, saying something about how she was still walking on her sea legs. Bennager watched Sam pay Chang, and Chang charged the full amount for three meals and all the rice wine that Sam could carry out of the place, and that satisfied his curiosity about whether Chang had been in the bathhouse with Rose.

Once outside, Bennager and Sam looked up and down the street for the young lady dressed as a miner. Rose soon found them. They had chosen to head toward the hotel that they had first eaten at, but Rose was waiting for them in front of the bathhouse.

"Hey, you lollygaggers," she said while biting off a piece of her plug tobacco.

"Oh my Lord, I thought that tobacco was for you, Sam. Where are you people from?" Bennager cringed as he watched the girl.

"That stuff isn't for me Bennager. I don't use tobacco. I spent enough time in my life trying to get away from that stuff. I bet you think that all this wine is for me, too, don't ya'? I guess when it's all gone, she'll have to chew grass and drink water." Sam smiled.

"Rose Mary, where in the world did a lady, like you surely must have been raised to be, learn how to curse, wield a knife, drink spirits, and chew tobacco?" Bennager asked sweetly once they joined her.

"Well, nobody had to teach me that. I've always had a gift for picking up on valuable information just by listening and doing what I've seen being done before. There's nothing to it." She chuckled and swayed a little while she tried to find a pocket to secure her tobacco in.

Sam put the jugs of rice wine inside the big carpetbags and surveyed his surroundings.

There were quite a few people who had come into town by midafternoon. Some had gotten off the ship with him and Rose and had already purchased shovels, picks, grub, a few cooking pans, and seemed to be heading east. There were also quite a few people with dark skin, not as dark as his, wearing hats with very large brims. These people didn't seem to be heading for the east. They seemed to be in town gathering supplies and milling around. Sam looked toward the sky to try to determine what time of day it might be.

"Bennager," Sam said, "it looks to be about two or three o'clock. I better go get my mining equipment gathered up and head in the direction those other fellas are headed for."

"Sam's right. I need to get a wagon and a team together. Sam, will you drive the wagon?" Rose asked, slurring her words by this time.

"Yep," Sam answered.

"Good. I'll see if I can purchase a tall mare, and we'll get started." Rose picked up one of the bags, and Sam grabbed the one that remained. Rose started down the row of tents and saloons toward the livery and fell directly face down on the ground. Sam looked at Bennager, then at Rose, bent over, and picked up her bag and then looked at Bennager again as if to say, "My hands are full."

Bennager shook his head, and he wished that as long as he lived, he would never have to see a female pass out from drunkenness face down in the dirt. That just proved to him that he should have stuck to his policy of never putting his nose in the middle of other people's business. Bennager bent over and picked Rose up by her underarms, thinking that if he guided her, then maybe her legs would still work, but his notion was wrong. She was dead drunk.

Sam started to panic. "Was that Chinaman food poisoned, Bennager? You didn't eat any. Am I goin' to die too? What am I goin' to do with these bags of money? All these White men are goin' to hang me! They will think that I killed her for her money!"

"Calm down, Sam, calm down. Rose ain't dead. She's drunk! Just dead drunk is all, she'll be fine. The only thing that poisoned her was too much alcohol in the rice wine. Why do you let her drink like that? She is just a girl, Sam, and you are her pard'. Don't you have any say in how your business is represented?" Bennager inquired.

"I can't tell a White woman what to do."

"It seems to me that somebody should tell her what to do and often! Her father should have taken her out to the woodshed daily and tanned her hide. If he had, she might have made some poor gentleman a good wife instead of running around in California with the likes of us, and dead drunk to boot." Bennager picked up Rose and put her over his shoulder. "Were you going to camp or stay in a hotel, Sam?" Bennager asked.

"It is still wintertime. Rose had better sleep in a bed and rest for a day or two. I have to get started for the gold fields, though. When Rose wakes up, tell her that she can catch up with me later."

"Whoa! Hold on right there, Sam! You're not going to leave me alone with this female. I can imagine that you have had a belly full of this gal, but I'll be damned if I let you push her off on me!"

"I've been itchin' for nine months to get to those gold fields. I don't think that I can stand around here waiting for Rose to wake up."

"Sam, those fellas that you saw heading east with their supplies are breaking their backs for nothing, and they will be sleeping on the banks of the bay tonight. You might just as well get some grub and some pots and pans together, bunk with Rose tonight, and we will all catch the steamboat in the morning," Bennager explained.

"Steamboat? In the morning?" Sam repeated. "Even if Rose wakes up by morning, I don't think that you will ever be able to get her on to another boat."

"It's the fastest way to the gold fields and away from the salt air that Rose dislikes so much."

"What about the tools and wagon and team that Rose wants?" Sam asked.

"All of that will be available in Sacramento City. I have a freight wagon filled with supplies for miners, so there is no sense in you carrying an extra load on your back when I can do it for you. As for the wagon and the stock, Rose will be able to find that along the way too. Now promise me that you won't leave me alone with this female."

"Are you sure that she will be awake by morning?"

"I promise," Bennager assured.

"Well, I don't think that it's right for me to bunk with Rose," Sam said flatly.

"She can't bunk alone in this condition, Sam!" Bennager argued.

"You bunk with her, and I'll get another room then."

"Darn it, Sam! She is your pard', and you're trying to push her off on me again. What I said about the steamboat is true. It's not going to do you any good to sneak out on me because I will find you on the banks of the bay in the morning, waiting for the same steamboat that I will be waiting for. This is how it is going to be. We get Rose a room, we get your grub, then we both bunk with Rose," Bennager said persuasively.

"Bennager, Rose and I are good friends. We helped each other get to this here place, but I am a free man. Rose told me that they don't have slaves in California. Is that right?"

"Some folks are using the Indians, but California is not a slave state. It's not even a state yet."

"Then I'll tell you what. There ain't no man alive that's goin' to make me sleep in the same room with Miss Rose Mary Briar."

"Someone has to watch her Sam!"

"I'll trust you to do it, Bennager."

"What makes you think that I won't hurt her or rob her?"

"You said yourself those ships in the harbor ain't goin' nowhere and you'll be at the banks of the bay in the morning. Besides, I trust you, Bennager. You ain't the kind that hurts ladies. Come on, I'll help you get her to a room."

With Rose over Bennager's shoulder, they walked to the hotel. The cook came out to help them.

"What happened to that fella? Is he dead? I ain't no undertaker, you know," the cook said.

"He ain't dead, just dead drunk! I want to get a room and throw him in it, and we'll be back a little later to bunk with him."

"All right, that will be six bits for each of ya, and you can have room number three."

Bennager gave Sam a hard look so he wouldn't kick up a fuss about not sleeping with Rose. "Sam, could you give the man the money? My hands are full at the moment."

Sam dug in the pockets of his new overalls and found the money needed to pay the cook.

"Hey, what did you fellas do with that charming young lady that you had with you earlier?" the cook asked in a sarcastic tone.

Sam and Bennager looked at each other, each one of them waiting for the other to answer. "She left us after we finished eating. I think that she wanted to talk to a man about a job," Bennager said, giving Sam a look that suggested that he should go along with the fib.

"Yep, that's what she did all right," Sam said convincingly and nodding his head for show.

"I hope that she went to ask a man about a bath. I never seen a woman let herself go like that," the cook said, shaking his head.

As Bennager headed for room number three, he shook his head, too, and said, "I know just what you mean."

Sam opened the door of room number three for Bennager, and he laid Rose down on the bunk. Sam set the two carpetbags down and headed for the door.

"Say, where are you headed? I'll go with you. It's pretty early in the day yet. What do you want to do?" Bennager asked.

"I was going to find a room in another hotel. I thought you said that you'd watch Rose."

"Sam, Rose ain't going to die if we take in the sights until it gets dark." Bennager chuckled a little.

"We can't leave those carpetbags just sitting there with Rose the way she is. Those have to be watched too."

"Well, if someone were to come in here and steal Rose's rice wine, it wouldn't bother me a bit," Bennager said, heading for the door. Sam gave Bennager a hard look and put his hand on his chest to let him know that he wouldn't be leaving this room at all until Rose came to.

"What's this all about, Sam?"

"Take a seat, Bennager," Sam said.

Bennager looked around, and since there were not any seats, he just sat on the floor with his back leaned up against the wall. Sam stepped in, shut the door, and did the same thing. "I've already said that I trust you with Rose, so I might as well tell you the rest. There is more than garb and rice wine and plug tobacco in those carpetbags. They are plumb full of money. I guess Rose's daddy knew that she would have a hard time finding a husband in this big old world, so he gave her all that money so she wouldn't have to."

"Well, Sam, I guess that she killed two birds with one stone. She took her daddy's money and ended up with her choice of probably ten to twenty thousand single men and no competition." Bennager chuckled.

"That's where Rose is goin' to have troubles. She's not lookin' for a husband. She's lookin' for a new home. I don't know what she's goin' to do with all that money, but if anyone finds out that she has it, we'll have a fight on our hands all the time. And there is something else. When her daddy finds out that she didn't make it to Europe, all hell's goin' to break loose. I suspect he'll have the law or the army lookin' for her, and if I'm with her when she is found, they might try to hang me."

"If she runs into bad enough trouble, they might hang us both for not keeping her safe," Bennager added.

"Rose is my friend, and I would do anything that I could to protect her anyway, but she makes it pretty hard on just one man. I'm goin' to need your help, Bennager. It's a good idea for her to stay in San Francisco and wait for more ladies to arrive but she will never agree to it. She is goin' to go inland with or without us, and if we are all together, maybe no harm will come to her," Sam pleaded.

"If Rose just goes along like she is nobody special and she doesn't have anything special, then we might do all right. There are still plenty of Indians in those foothills, though. Anything could happen to any of us at any time, so I hope the two of you are ready for a wild ride. Do you have any weapons in those carpetbags?" Bennager was starting to get worried.

"Rose has a derringer with her at all times, and I picked up a revolver at sea," Sam answered.

"Well, I have a musket loader. We will have to hunt along the way. It will take about five days to get to Sacramento City, if we don't see any trouble. How did you come by the revolver?" Bennager inquired.

"Rose shot the man that it used to belong to," Sam answered casually.

"You mean to tell me that Rose killed a man, and nobody did anything to her for it!"

"Nobody else knows about it but me. I threw him overboard, and no one missed him. He was a bad man, Bennager. Don't go thinkin' ill of Rose. It was him or her," Sam assured him.

"How many people did you have to throw overboard during your trip?" Bennager was in awe. He had never had to kill a human being.

"I only have one revolver, don't I? The men on that ship learned in a hurry not to bother either one of us."

"When did you two become business associates?" Bennager asked.

"Bennager, I suppose that you have guessed that I am a runaway. I had to be real careful gettin' on that ship. I got on when it was dark and found a place to hide and just waited. The next morning, men from all kinds of different places started to board the ship, and I didn't know how I was goin' to make it all the way to California just hidin' in one place like that, but I knew that I would have to or die tryin' or they would throw me overboard or make a ships slave out of me. Sometime that mornin', Rose boarded with nothin' but those two carpetbags, and she caused quite a commotion. It didn't take her long to figure out that she was the only woman on board, and she started lookin' for a place to hide too. That's when she found me."

"'Are you a runaway?' she asked.

"I was real scared. I said, 'Yes, Miss.'

"'Huh! Me too!' she said, laughing.

"That's when we became business associates. She figured that we could help each other if I made out to be her slave. The other men on the ship would know that she wasn't alone, and I could protect her at the same time. And if I was already her slave, then they couldn't make me into one of their slaves or throw me overboard. Over the last nine months, not many people bothered either one of us, and we became good friends. True friends, I guess you could say. She got me brushed up on my readin', writin', and speakin' properly, and I told her about hard work, tools, mules, livestock, and crops. She also told me about money. Some of that money is pert near wore out from her teachin' me what things are worth and us pretendin' that we were in a store or a bank."

"Was the man that Rose killed trying to take the money?" Bennager asked, more concerned with Rose's ability to kill than to count.

"No, it wasn't the money that he was after. He snuck up on us when we were both asleep and put his hand over her mouth and got on top of her. I guess that he didn't expect that a fine lady like Rose would shoot him in the liver. The shot woke me up, and I threw him in the ocean as fast as I could, and Rose and I made out like nothin' happened, just in case someone else heard the shot, but nobody came lookin' for that man."

"Is that when Rose started going crazy?" Bennager asked feeling pity for the girl now.

"Rose ain't crazy!" Sam laughed.

"What about the cursing and the tobacco and the spirits?" Bennager argued.

"Well, now, she was doin' all that when I met her. I don't know where she picked up those habits. She just must not have spent much time with the women folks, I guess," Sam explained.

"So if you bunked with her for the last nine months, then why are you so hell-bent on bunking alone if the two of you are such good friends?" Bennager questioned Sam.

"Protectin' Rose has been a full-time job for the last nine months. I just haven't slept much at all. And for just this one night, I want to get away from people and get one night of peace and quiet. I want to be able to think and get a full night's rest. Can you understand that, Bennager?"

"I guess I sure can, Sam. Rose will be safe with me, and so will the carpetbags. Go on ahead and do what you have to do, and I'll see you here in the morning."

"Thanks, Bennager, you are doin' me a great favor. I hope that I can do you a favor in return someday. I'll see you here in the mornin'." Sam got up, and the two men shook hands, and out the door he went. Bennager rolled a smoke and started to think about all that Sam had told him. He got up from the floor and checked on Rose. She lay there peacefully, looking like somebody's little girl. She looked like someone who could never shoot a man or take a nine-month-long ocean voyage or especially not someone who would drink so much rice wine that she would pass out face down in the street. She just looked like a sweet little girl lying there, sleeping. Bennager knelt to push the strands of her wavy hair out of her face so that he could have a closer look at her childlike features, and he noticed that she had a little line of brown drivel flowing from the side of her mouth. When Rose's body had told her that she had consumed too much alcohol, it forgot to tell her to spit out her tobacco. Gently, he opened her mouth and scooped out the plug that she never had the chance to enjoy with his forefinger and wiped the side of her face with his sleeve. "There," he said to himself. "Now you look like a sweet little girl."

Bennager didn't have anything to do, and he didn't have any reading material, so he decided that it wouldn't do any harm to see if there was anything to read in the carpetbags. He rolled another smoke and sat down on the floor again, this time closer to Rose and with the carpetbags. He opened the one that had all the rice wine in it first. After pulling out three jugs, one of rice wine, one of brandy and one of rum, he remembered what Rose had said about being in Rome. He chose the brandy to sip on while he went through the bag of money, looking for a book or a newspaper to read. He didn't find anything. He put everything back in its proper order, except for the brandy, and started rummaging through the second bag. He took out Sam and Rose's spare shirts that they had purchased earlier and set them on the floor beside him.

He looked closer into the bag to see if there was anything right on top. He decided to take out all the money, figuring that Rose had hoarded her reading material because he couldn't imagine that she wouldn't have any. Finally, he found what he was looking for. It was *The Odyssey* by Homer, a story that he had read before and liked. He sat the book down beside him and arranged the bag's contents just as he had found them. Bennager situated himself in the most comfortable position that he could get into on the floor and prepared to get ready to read himself to sleep. He opened the book, and a piece of paper slipped out onto his chest. He opened it up, and it read:

My Dearest Rose Mary,

Yesterday was the most glorious day that I have ever had in my life. Spending the day with you at your family's home was an enjoyment that I have never encountered before. Your family is delightful, and I cannot wait to be a member. Yesterday, your father gave me your hand in marriage, and I hope that we can be married within one month. I have started to make the arrangements already, and I hope to see you tonight to discuss them further. The day that you become my wife will be the happiest day of my life. I love you very much.

Yours truly,

Richard

"So, Rose Mary Briar, the men don't fall to their knees for you, huh? Something about your story doesn't add up," Bennager said to the girl who could not hear him. Now he had something to think about. He wondered if Sam knew about Richard, and he also wondered if Richard was already on his way with the law or an army. Rose was going to be in a heap of trouble, and so were he and Sam if they didn't find Rose a new home and quick. The army was probably waiting for her in Sacramento City or Stockton right now. Bennager said to himself, "Never again will I stick my nose into somebody else's business." He put the letter back in the book where it had been before and laid it down, sipped more brandy for a few hours, and thought himself to sleep instead.

The next thing that he knew was that the room was shaking as if ten thousand buffalo were on a dead run right outside the hotel. Bennager jumped up not knowing what was happening, only to realize that it was just Rose snoring.

"Oh my Lord, no wonder why Sam needed peace and quiet in a whole other hotel no less. A stupid man he is not. And me, I am the biggest fool that these two have ever met!" Bennager exclaimed. Morning was six hours away.

2

The snoring finally subsided, and Bennager was able to catch a short nap before he heard Sam quietly tapping at the door. With some labor, he managed to make it up from the floor and opened the door to find Sam looking five years younger than when he had first seen him walking up the hill with Rose yesterday.

"Morning, Sam, I see that you went somewhere and found that peace and quiet that you were looking for."

Sam said, smiling, "Good mornin' to you, Mr. Rasmussen. How is our Rose this fine mornin'?"

"First of all, there is nothing good or fine about this morning, and second of all, if you want to know how Rose is, then you will have to wake her up and ask her! I'll be downstairs having coffee. The steamboat leaves at eight o'clock!" Bennager was short and grumpy with Sam as he slammed the door when he left in order to help Sam wake Rose up, and then he stomped down the stairs. The same man from the night before came out of the kitchen with a pot of coffee and a mug.

"What else can I get for you?" the cook asked.

"That's all for now. Thanks," Bennager replied. As he waited for the steaming coffee to cool a bit, he walked around the restaurant and tried to get the stiffness out of his body from having to sleep on the floor the night before. He took his coffee and stepped outside to get some fresh air and found that they were going to be in for a foggy, damp day. *Sam must have gotten one devil of a good night's sleep to be able to think that this is a fine day,* Bennager thought. He walked back inside and sat at a table. Bennager reckoned that Sam was having a hard time getting Rose to wake up. He hadn't heard any commotion yet, and he was sure that Rose made a commotion in the mornings.

While Bennager was deep in thought about the day ahead of them, Rose and Sam walked quietly down the steps and sat at the table. Rose Mary was quite a vision the morning after near alcohol poisoning. Her face was slightly swollen and pale, eyes red and hair uncombed.

"Good morning, Bennager," she nearly whispered.

"Good morning, Rose Mary," he returned. "Sam, that was a dirty trick you did to me by making me stay with Rose. You knew that her snoring would wake the dead."

Sam didn't want to rub in the fact that he had pulled a good trick on Bennager, but he couldn't help himself from smiling slyly.

The cook brought out two more cups of coffee and waited for them to order something to eat.

"Do you have ham, eggs, biscuits, and pie?" Rose asked the cook.

"Yep," the cook replied, not looking up from his task of coffee pouring.

"That's what I'll have, thank you," she said.

"Will that be a whole pie, Miss?" he asked.

"Yep."

Sam and Bennager ordered the same, minus the pie. "Mr. Rasmussen, why do you start the day out by slandering me? I do not snore. Sam, have you ever heard me snore?" she asked very quietly.

Sam looked at Bennager and then looked away from both as if he was reading something off the ceiling. He did it so convincingly that Bennager looked too.

"What in tarnation are you two looking at?" Bennager snapped his head back to reality, satisfied that there wasn't anything out of the ordinary to see on the ceiling of the restaurant. Sam was still pretending that there was.

Bennager said, "Rose Mary, I don't think that Sam is going to answer you, and I guess the subject hasn't been mentioned before, but I am here to tell you the facts, and the facts are that you do snore and very loudly, so loudly, in fact, that I am sure that is the reason why you are whispering this morning. Your snoring gave you a head-ache in your sleep, and your throat is too tired to talk normally, and that, my dear, is not slander!"

Rose put her elbows on the table and held her head with her hands and didn't speak or look at either one of them. She just stared at the table until their breakfast was set down in front of them. Suddenly, she pushed herself back from the table, put her hand over her mouth, and ran outside. Bennager shook his head and looked at Sam. Sam was still looking at the door with confusion written all over his face. Bennager could tell by looking at him that he had never had enough liquor in his body to experience a hangover. As big and strong as Sam was, Bennager didn't think that Chang and his pop could make rice wine fast enough to get Sam to feel the way Rose was feeling right now.

Sam and Bennager were almost finished with their meal when Rose came in and sat down at the table. She was sipping her coffee when the cook came out to give them a warmup. Bennager could see disbelieve in his eyes when he noticed that Rose hadn't touched anything on her plate.

"Is there anything wrong, Miss?" the cook asked.

"Wrong with the grub? I don't think so. These fellas seem to be cleaning it up quick enough. Wrong with me? Yes, but I'll be fine after I eat something."

Rose started to push her food around on her plate, and Bennager and Sam got started on the pie. Bennager started thinking about the letter that he had found in Rose's book and decided that this would be a good time to ask her if she knew exactly how many soldiers and lawmen were after her. "Rose, the three of us have to talk about something before we leave town. After you passed out in the street from intoxication, Sam and I put you and the bags in the room upstairs, and then Sam coerced me into keeping an eye on you, and I discovered something very interesting."

"You discovered the money," she said smartly.

"I discovered something even more interesting than the money. I discovered that you read Homer," Bennager said mischievously.

"Why in tarnation were you rummaging through my bags, Bennager?" Rose asked, not looking up from her meal.

"Because you are quite boring when you are dead drunk, Rose Mary, and Sam told me that the two of you had read on your voyage, so I figured that you probably had something more interesting to look at than the walls, and I was right. What I didn't figure on was the fact that you are not entirely honest in your storytelling."

"I guess that what you are trying to tell me, with that monotonous tone of yours that is drumming in my head like a ricocheting cannonball, is that you found the letter from Richard. So what business is it of yours?"

"As sure as the sky is blue, it will be my business if I happen to be with you when Richard and your father catch up with you. I'm not going to get myself shot or hanged because of you!" Bennager yelled.

Sam said, "What do you mean shot or hanged? What are you talkin' about? Who is Richard?" Panic was setting in again.

Rose had just about cleaned her plate by this time, and as she was finishing her meal, she was looking straight ahead with a maddened expression. Bennager got the feeling that Sam's questions were not going to be answered by Rose Mary. "This mule-headed female right here jilted her fiancé that she had back east and stole all that money that the two of you have been packing around for all these months and got on the first ship bound for California. Her pa never put her on a ship bound for Europe at all. She is a runaway, all right, but my guess is that those people have been looking for her a lot longer than she has led us to believe!" Bennager accused.

Sam looked at Rose as if he was waiting for an explanation. Rose cut a piece of pie and put it on her plate, instead of eating directly from the tin, and continued to look straight ahead with that mule-headed look on her face. "Rose, is it true? Is that money stolen?" Sam asked.

"Are you going to answer your business associate, Rose Mary? I'm sure he would like to know when he's going to be hanged," Bennager jabbed.

"The fact is, Sam and Mr. Rasmussen," she said quietly but sarcastically, "that marriage was arranged by my father and Richard, not me. You might also be interested to know that Richard is a slaveholder, Sam. There was no way in hell that I was going to marry that vile pig son of a bitch, and if I had to steal money and run away, then that is what I would have done. But the fact is that my mother told me to run for my life and gave me the money to start fresh in a place where my father and Richard would never come looking for me. Besides, I'm too young to get married anyway. Now I hope you gentlemen are satisfied that you are not in the company of a thief."

"Rose, you still ran away, and your father will still be looking for you," Bennager tried to remind her.

"My mother told me that she would take care of everything. She said that maybe Richard could marry my sister. My mother understands me and knows that I had no intention of wasting my time pretending to be a mindless, doting wife to a pretentious prig and slaveholder like Richard Hawthorne." Rose served herself another piece of pie, and the cook came out with more coffee. Bennager looked at Sam to see if he could tell what he was thinking about this new information that Rose had put before them. Sam was sipping his coffee and looking at Bennager as if he was trying to figure out the same thing.

"What do you think, Sam?" Bennager asked.

"I think if Rose was willin' to make such a long, hard trip to get away from bein' the wife of a slaveholdin' son of a bitch and a father that won't let her make her own decisions about marriage instead of bein' a wealthy wife and daughter that she is a person who has a lot of sand. And I also think that someone with that much determination is worth bein' in business with. Now I'm goin' to the gold fields to look for gold, and if anyone comes lookin' for Rose, they will have to go through me first. Let's go catch that steamboat." Sam got up from his chair and walked toward the kitchen to find the cook and pay him.

Rose looked at Sam as if he was her new enemy, then she looked at Bennager incredulously. "Did Sam just say something about a boat?"

Bennager put his hand on Rose's arm and said, "Rose Mary, I know that you don't want to get on another boat but it's the fastest and easiest way. I have a wagonload of supplies that I must get to Sacramento City. If you and Sam just purchase some bedrolls, then we can be on our way."

"What about the supplies that we need to start a business?" Rose asked.

"You can get everything that you need in Sacramento City— wagons, horses, mules, grub, mining equipment, or whatever you need. Steamboats don't usually travel in the dark, so we will be camped on the shore, and that is why you will need bedrolls. We should be in Sacramento City in five or six days."

"Do you have tents?" Rose asked.

"Yep."

"Well, Bennager, a new adventure starts today. I knew that it would be rough getting to the gold fields. I just didn't know that I would be on another damned boat, but that's all right. I am ready to start making a life for myself, and five or six days more on a boat isn't going to kill me."

"Even after you get to Sacramento City, you will have to ferry yourselves and your equipment across other rivers unless you plan on stopping at the first river you come to."

"Which river is that?" Rose asked.

"It's the busiest one called the American. It's the one that Marshall first discovered gold on."

Sam came back and Rose and Bennager got up from their seats. "We better get goin'," Sam said. Sam was just as excited to start his new life as Rose was. Bennager reckoned that he would have and could have run from San Francisco to Sacramento City to get started on his quest to find gold and also to try out his new life as a free man, even if he might have to pretend to be Rose's slave from time to time.

"Do you folks want to walk with me to get my wagon?" Bennager asked.

"I'll help you hitch the team, Bennager," Sam said as though he would do anything to work off his excess energy.

Rose asked, "How long did you say it would take to get to Sacramento City?"

"Five to six days," Bennager answered, "if we don't get into trouble."

"And what if we get into trouble?" Rose asked as though his previous answer had exhausted her.

"Well, Rose Mary, if we run into big enough trouble, time won't matter to us anymore. On the other hand, there is trouble that could delay our journey for God knows how long, but I would say that your run-of-the-mill average trouble would only delay our trip for two to three days at the most. How does that answer suit you, Rose Mary?" Bennager said loud enough to make her eyes squint and her jaw muscles ripple. Bennager was sure that sometime before the day was over that he was going to hear Rose Mary Briar declare that she would never drink again. He was determined to make sure that her headache stuck with her, even if her hangover didn't. He just didn't think that he could stand to see a woman face down in the street from drunkenness again as long as he lived.

Rose started to feel around in her pockets when Bennager had stopped talking, and for a blink or two, he was afraid that she was looking for her derringer. Then he saw a look of relief come over her when she found what she was looking for. She took three steps toward him, and he took one back so he could hit her if the derringer was, in fact, what she had been after. She took out her tobacco, locked her eyes with his, and bit off a piece that would gag a mule. Then she opened her bag and took out her jug of rice wine and proceeded to drink a generous slug of it. Bennager cringed.

"Mr. Rasmussen, would you be so kind as to meet me in front of my favorite mercantile when you and Sam are ready to head out? I fear that there might be a thing or two that I have forgotten to purchase in the event that something should delay our trip to Sacramento City," Rose said sweetly.

"I'd be happy to, Rose Mary. That is, if I'll be able to recognize your backside when you pass out face down in the street again. Let's go, Sam."

"No chance of that, Mr. Rasmussen. I think that if I drink rice wine in the morning instead of in the evening, I'll do much better," Rose said to their backs.

After Sam and Bennager got out of earshot from Rose, Bennager said, "Sam, I think that Rose is more trouble than she is worth. What kind of business do you expect to prosper at with a careless, drunk female like that? If she gets drunk and passes out today, then I'm afraid that I will be parting company with you folks in Sacramento City. I just can't stand to see a lady behave the way Rose does."

"Bennager, you said yourself that the only way that we are goin' to make it through a country full of nothin' but men is for Rose to behave just as she is doin'."

"Sam, she draws too much attention to herself, and if she continues to drink and shoot off her mouth, she's going to be found out, have her money taken, and be kidnapped by someone who will turn her into a prostitute. Chang's pa saw her last night, so I just imagine that the news of her arrival here in San Francisco has traveled halfway to Sacramento City by now among the Chinese population at least. All that I'm trying to say, Sam, is that her actions make our job of watching her a devil of a lot harder than it has to be."

"Maybe you should give her a little time. She wasn't surly at all when we were at sea, and she was the only one that ever treated me like a human instead of a mule. She is the first friend that I have had in almost all my life. There is a lot of good in Rose, and I think that she is celebratin' because she is on land and also because she has found someone to talk to, besides an old Black man. I know one thing, Bennager, when things get bad, she is a good person to have on your side."

"Did it ever occur to you that things wouldn't get bad if she wasn't around?" Bennager asked with his mind intent on the task of hitching the team and checking his supplies.

"I think that you are forgettin' who you are talkin' to, Bennager!" The hostility in his voice made Bennager stop at what he had mindlessly been doing, and he turned to face the man who may or may not be thinking of killing him for the things that he had just said about his friend. Sam was looking into his eyes, but what made the hair stand up on the back of Bennager's neck was how Sam wasn't seeing him. He felt like Sam could see his soul. "I was on a ship once before. When I was a small child in Africa, I was playin' a huntin' game with my brothers, and I fell into a trap. White men threw nets over me and my brothers and beat us until we were too weak to run away. They took the nets off and tied our hands and tied us together and dragged us to the sea where I saw the ship. I thought that it was the biggest animal on earth, and the White men were goin' to use us to feed it, and they did. They put us in the belly of that big animal, and inside the belly, I saw my whole family. The only people that they didn't take from my village were the old ones. They just killed them and left them dead in the dirt.

"By the time that my feet touched the earth again, everyone in my family, except my mother, had died and been thrown away into the ocean. For the next three years, I was beaten every day because I didn't understand the White man's language. For most of my life until a year ago, I was hungry, I was worked like an animal, and I was treated like an animal. Two years before I ran away, the White men decided to make me a boxer. That was worse than workin'. I fought other slaves. If I lost the fight, the White men would beat me worse than I had been beaten in the fight, and if I won, the White men got richer. Things have been bad for me almost every day since that day in Africa, but nothin' bad will happen to me because of Rose."

"Sam, I apologize for what I said about your friend. I'm sure that you are right about giving her some time. She is obviously a headstrong girl, and that is what it takes in this country to find gold and start businesses. The two of you will do fine, even if Rose is found out to be a female."

Sam chuckled. "What you don't understand about Rose is that she doesn't care who knows that she is a female. She isn't afraid of anyone or anythin', and she doesn't think that she needs us to watch after her and wouldn't care if we were around or not. She just does what she needs to do. She got on that ship by herself, and she will do whatever she needs to do by herself if she has to."

"Everybody needs help sometimes, Sam."

"That's the way I figure it, too, Bennager. Rose helped me, and someday she might be able to help you too."

Bennager continued with his task until he was finished. "Well, Sam, we are set and ready to travel. Shall we go find Rose and get the two of you started on your new futures?"

"Yep, let's go!"

The two men boarded the wagon and pulled out of the livery with a six-horse team and started up the street to pick up Rose. She was waiting in front of the mercantile with a crate of goods and her carpetbags beside her. She actually looked happy to see that the men hadn't left her to fend for herself, and Bennager was happy that she wasn't lying face down in the street.

"Hello, fellas, are we ready to go find a steamboat?" she said almost charmingly.

"We are. Climb aboard," Bennager said.

Sam got down to help Rose load the supplies and their belongings, then directed her to the wagon seat beside Bennager, and he climbed up and sat on the freight. Rose said, "Damn, Bennager, this team of horses you have here is magnificent. I am used to seeing one-horse carriages or two horses pulling a wagon. I have never seen so much beautiful power and strength working toward the same purpose all at the same time. It will be quite a load for a steamboat."

"The steamboat only takes passengers who can pay, so there is always room for me. Besides, I have become well-acquainted with the steamboat captain, so I never have a problem getting aboard," Bennager said, realizing that this was the first conversation that they had had since meeting yesterday. Bennager noticed as they were making their way to the bay that when Rose wasn't being outrageous, she had an attractive way about her. Her comment about his team had seemed sincere as though she was a child again, back before the time that she felt that she had to run away from home and risk her life on a ship full of men to come to a land full of men. It was like seeing a glimpse of the real Rose Mary Briar before she grew the hard outer shell to protect herself from predators and the elements of her newly acquired surroundings. This was the side of Rose that Sam had seen on that ship and the reason for him to be such a devoted friend, and

Bennager hoped that he would be able to get to know Rose as well as Sam did.

When Rose spoke, it made Bennager flinch because he had been so deep in thought. "I have never been too concerned about whether people like me. That is why I have always done my darndest to drive them away or make them dislike me upon first meeting them. I like people who stick. I didn't expect you to come back with Sam, but you did. Now I don't know if you like me, and I don't much care, but now I know that you are a man who will stick."

"I guess we have a lot to learn about each other, but we'll have nothing but time on our hands for the next week," Bennager said, sizing up the situation.

She was looking at Bennager the whole time that they had been talking, and he got the feeling that she was waiting for him to look at her, but he was afraid that if their eyes met that something other than friendship would start to evolve. Rose was fearless, and he figured that she would try anything at least once, but he was aware of his rational fears. In this country now, there were three things to fear: thieves, rattlesnakes, and Rose Mary Briar.

He felt her turn away when they started down the hill to the bay because she noticed the steamboat and the big crowd that wanted to get aboard. Again, Bennager gathered that she was in awe of the new sights that she was experiencing. "Damn! Will all those men be on that steamboat? Are you sure there will be room for me and Sam? There must be two hundred men there."

"You and Sam have money to buy yourselves passage to Sacramento City, at least more than most of these gents have. Charlie doesn't play favorites or make reservations. He is in the business to make as much money as he can. I learned to become good friends with Charlie. He makes me pay a regular fee, but I always have to bring something to boot. You and Charlie have something in common. I have a whole barrel of rice wine for him and oranges too. As for a lot of these men, they will discover that nothing comes cheap here in California, and they will walk back to town, sell their mining equipment, and find jobs until they have enough money saved up to get to Sacramento City.

"I'm glad that I'm not goin' to be in some of those fellas' shoes today. I think that I would explode if I had to go back to town and find a job," Sam exclaimed.

Rose chuckled at Sam's outburst. "Adversity makes men stronger. You told me that, Sam. Perseverance and determination is what keeps their dreams alive. Isn't that how you got this far, Sam?" Rose asked him to keep him from feeling bad for the men who were going to be left behind on this foggy morning.

"You are right, Rose. Those fellas will make it if they want it badly enough," Sam said, shaking his head.

"Bennager is thinking right now that it is easy for me to say such things when I had someone hand me two carpetbags full of money and told me to run like a rabbit," Rose said mostly to herself or anyone who was listening.

This time, Bennager faced her, and she locked her eyes with his, and he realized that she had laid a trap for him to get him to look at her. Bennager said, turning away, "Rose Mary, don't ever make an assumption on my thoughts where you are concerned. I don't waste time thinking the worst about someone until I know for sure, and then I don't think about them at all." He paused to consider his thoughts about the girl. "Believe me, Rose, if I had something to say to you, I would say it loud enough for you to hear, just like I did in the hotel earlier."

Rose was smiling as she and Sam were climbing from the wagon preparing to board the steamboat. Sam took the bags and the crate of supplies down. Rose took the crate and waited as Sam was gripping the bags that were now much heavier than they had been before rice wine and other spirits had been stuffed into them. Bennager got off his wagon of freight and inspected the harness and the knots that he had tied his freight with to make sure that they were still tight and secure. He had left Charlie's supply of rice wine on top of his other freight so he could take it off with ease, but he didn't want to unload it until they were aboard and on their way. Charlie wasn't the type of man who was entirely honest. It would not surprise Bennager if he was the kind of person to take the money and the rice wine and steam out into the ocean until the rice wine was gone and he had to come back, and Bennager wasn't in the waiting mood on this day, especially if he had to wait in the fog.

"Freight wagon boarding! Everyone step aside! Look out! This could be a disaster! These beasts are spooky enough without any help from the crowd! Step aside! Look out!" Charlie hollered and carried on.

"Good morning, Charlie. How was the river this time?" Bennager asked as he drove the team onto the boat. The team plodded onto the boat as if they were still asleep. Charlie's carrying on and the crowd had not concerned them in the least. They had come to learn that this was the easiest part of the trip so there wasn't really anything to stay awake for.

"The river is in good shape. It hasn't changed much this month. It has been staying cold enough in the mountains and dry in the valley. It's been pretty boring, really. It's hard to be a notable steamboat captain when the river never changes," Charlie complained and waved his hands about.

"I would say that you are a pretty notable fella, Charlie. You are the only one with a steamboat west of the Mississippi," Bennager said, trying to make him feel better about the importance of his occupation. "Hey, Charlie, I'd like you to meet a couple of fellas here. This here is Sam, and this young fella is, uh, Pete. They are in a hurry to get out of this fog just like I am, and they can pay for the passage." Bennager tried to make his introduction believable.

"Everyone wants to squabble with me about what I charge for passage, and I get so tired of turning men away who can't pay. I like men who can pay. It's one less man to squabble with. Passage will be fifty dollars," Charlie said with his hand held out. Sam paid his fifty dollars and headed for the deck of the steamboat, and Rose followed him with her crate of supplies.

"Hold on there, young fella. I didn't make myself clear. Passage will be fifty dollars per head." Charlie said with his hand still held out.

Rose shot Bennager a scowling look as if to ask if this was normal procedure or robbery.

Bennager shook his head and shrugged his shoulders as if to say that it was robbery, but how bad did she want to get away from all this delightful sea air that she loved so much? Rose looked back at Charlie and said with an English accent, "Pardon me, my good man, being a foreigner in a new land certainly has its disadvantages."

"Everyone is a foreigner in this country, fella," Charlie said with a frown, looking at the money that Rose was putting in his hand.

The trio settled in on the steamboat, waiting to see who would be able to pay for their passage and who would have to go back to town. There wasn't much to do on the boat. A person could sit, stand, or lean over the edge and look at the bay. Bennager reckoned that Sam and Rose had their fill of looking at water because they just seemed to congregate around the wagon, sort of waiting and watching but pretending that they weren't so they wouldn't embarrass the men who were turned back.

Four redheaded gents with Irish brogues so thick that they could barely be understood were able to pay their passage. It was hard to tell what they were saying, but it was apparent by their tone and body language and all the carrying on that they thought that they had just been robbed. They didn't really bother Charlie about it because they knew from the look on Charlie's face that it would not have done any good. But all the complaining that they were doing amongst themselves was quite comical. They seemed to know that the joke was on them, but there wasn't anything that they could do about it. The joke was that they were coming here to get rich, but they were getting fleeced every time they turned around.

Rose enjoyed the display of emotion that the Irishmen exhibited. She didn't laugh out loud, but she turned to Sam and giggled and then turned back to watch them some more. One of the Irishmen in the merry little group was a lot more outgoing than the others. The man never stopped talking and said a greeting to everyone who boarded, and his greeting had a lot do with robbery and the gold fields. "Dia duit" seemed to be a common thread of all the statements. Simply commencing salutations to someone would never occur to this man because he was not the simple type.

The next man of some interest was trying to board with his dog. Bennager could tell by the man's garb that he had been in California for quite some time. He was a White man, but he wore the clothes of the Mexican men that Bennager had seen in San Francisco. He was most definitely the only one on Charlie's boat that day who was wearing a sombrero. Bennager shook his head and chuckled as Charlie collected fifty dollars from the man and then wanted twenty-five dollars to let the dog on. The bold Irishman overheard this transaction, and the commotion started again. They couldn't believe that Charlie would charge that much for a dog. A dog was an asset to have along if all of them were going to be camping on the banks of the Sacramento River with Indians and vermin all around. Bennager guessed that is what the fellow who owned the dog thought, too, because he didn't bat an eye at paying the twenty-five dollars. His dog looked up at him, seeming to smile, and the two of them came aboard.

Rose was delighted to see the dog, and that is when a new part of her personality was revealed to Bennager. There couldn't be too much wrong with somebody who liked animals. The determining factor about those types of people who liked animals was if the animal liked them back. Animals always seemed to have a sense if a person was good or bad.

It took Charlie about an hour to sift through the men who could pay their passage to Sacramento City and the men who couldn't. One by one, the trio watched men walk back up the hill with their mining equipment and bedrolls. There had been a deep path cut in the earth by these men and the men before them who had come to California, ill-prepared for the realities that faced them.

Thinking about how many of those men had left their families, homes, farms, and their businesses behind to venture to the gold country of California was dreadful. How many of those men would die out here, trying to make their fortune? How many would see their homes again? How many wives and families would starve, waiting for their husbands and fathers to send money or even word about their achievements or failures or even their welfare?

Since Bennager had been hauling supplies from San Francisco to Sacramento City, he had learned not to look at the faces of the men who tried to do business with Charlie until their transactions were complete and the men were aboard the steamboat. He knew that if he got a good look at the men that Charlie had to turn away, then he would be waiting to see them on the next trip, and if he didn't see them, he would spend time wondering or worrying about them, and he knew that thinking about that many men would put him in an early grave.

The boat began to move in the water, and soon they were all heading east for the Sacramento River. Just like every time before, the passengers were exhilarated to finally be on the move again. It was a new journey, a new adventure to add to long list of adventures that had gotten them this far already. Everyone seemed to be happy and excited, except for the dog. This was something new and out of the ordinary for her, and she made it clear that she did not like this particular type of travel at all. She ran to the edge of the deck and looked at the water, and everyone watching thought that she was going to jump. Then she ran to the steering room and barked until her owner whistled for her to come, but she didn't go to him. Instead, she shot right under the wagon, laid down, and trembled. The wagon and the horses made her feel safer than standing out in the wide-open space of the deck with her owner. The dog's owner did not seem surprised at his dog's discomfort, but Rose was fit to be tied. She couldn't help herself.

Rose had been sitting in the wagon, looking at the view of the bay. She got down and sat underneath the wagon with the dog and tried to give her some reassurance that everything was going to be all right. At first, the dog just tolerated Rose's attempts to be her friend, but after her owner came to the wagon and started talking to Sam and Bennager and gave his dog a little pat, she crawled right on top of Rose's lap, and Rose was delighted to make a new friend.

The bold Irishman approached the wagon and spoke, "That collie of yours is as lonely for women as everyone else is. The poor thing hates this boat all right. When will she be havin' her pups?"

Rose screamed from under the wagon. "Is this dog going to have puppies? Oh, can I have one, please? I really need a puppy. When is she going to have them? What is her name?" Rose's childlike excitement over the prospects of puppies made all the men at the wagon have quite a laugh, especially Sam and Bennager because neither one of them would have guessed in a million years that Rose, of all people, could give a care in the world about puppies.

The owner of the dog got down on his haunches, and with his hat in his hands, he said, "How do, Miss. My dog's name is Girl, and mine is Zeb, and you can have a puppy. I expect them to come anytime now. It's a lucky thing that you are here. This is Girl's first litter, and she might need your help. She sure does seem to like you. You are the only person besides me that she has ever let touch her."

"My name is Rose," she said and held out her hand.

Zeb took her hand in friendship and got back up on his feet, put his hat back on, and shook his head in sorrow. "Women. They'll break a man's heart every chance they get." Even though this was a cruel fact of life, they all chuckled anyway as they introduced themselves. The bold Irishman's name was Angus, and the men that he had come with were his brothers. His brothers didn't seem to be as trusting toward people as Angus was because they kept to themselves and didn't even pay any attention to Rose and Girl who had become quite a spectacle.

"Me brothers over there are a borin' lot. They are hatchin' plans all the time to get rich and talkin' 'bout what they will do when they get rich, and we haven't made a cent yet. Our life's savin's are almost gone, and they are flocked together over there, still talkin' 'bout gettin' rich." Angus turned to Zeb and asked, "Can I have a puppy too?"

"It looks like the bunch of us will have to stick together for at least six weeks," Sam said, chuckling.

"Maybe we are all going to the same place. Do any of you have plans for where you are going after we get to Sacramento City?" Zeb asked, smiling.

Bennager watched as the future miners looked at each other for an answer, and then he heard Rose holler from under the wagon, "No!"

"It looks like Girl will be the leader of our expedition for a while, fellas. Did any of you ever think that a dog would someday determine your fate?" Zeb asked, scratching his head.

Rose said from her place under the wagon, "I'd rather have Girl determine my fate than my father." The men talked it over, and they all agreed that it would probably work out just as well with Girl as the leader than it would if she wasn't. The dog wasn't really a factor since they didn't know what they were doing anyway.

Once Charlie had the boat in the middle of the bay and pointed in the right direction, he came out to the wagon to make the transaction with Bennager final. "Do you have something in that there wagon for me?" he asked.

Bennager had seen him coming and was starting to untie his barrel of sake. "It's right here on top, Charlie, just like always. I'll bring it in for you."

"Good, that's real good. You know, I ran out of sake just this morning. Say, what is Pete doing with that dog? If he has a dog, then I'm going to have to charge the same price that I charged that other fella."

Zeb was confused by all of this Pete business, but he told Charlie that the dog was his, and she was the only dog on the boat, and Charlie let the matter drop. He seemed to be more concerned about his new supply of sake at the moment anyway. Bennager put Charlie's sake away for him, and as he was walking back to the wagon, he felt a little pang of jealousy come over him when he saw that Zeb and Angus had joined Rose underneath his wagon. Sam was petting the neck of one of the horses, so Bennager joined him. "What is going on under there, Sam?"

Sam said, chuckling, "Rose felt the puppies move inside that dog's belly, and she screeched like a little girl, and those two grown men dove under that wagon so they could feel the puppies move too. I never knew that White men acted that way. It's been a long time since I've seen a good White man. That is, until I met you and you stayed with Rose so I could finally get some sleep."

"I have no doubt that you have been surrounded by an evil bunch, but to be honest, I have never known grown men to be all that concerned with the arrival of a litter of pups before. I think that their behavior is on account of Rose Mary Briar."

Bennager walked to the back of the wagon and got a blanket for Rose and her new friend and crawled under it to join the gathering. Rose's eyes were dancing with joy and excitement but not because of the men who were seated beside her. Much to Bennager's surprise, it looked as though the men were genuinely excited about the dog as well, and they didn't seem to notice that Rose Mary was probably the most beautiful woman in the world. It seemed that for the time being, Girl was the only female for miles around.

"Bennager, did you bring that for Girl? Say thank you, Girl. Maybe this will make her stop shaking. Thank you, Bennager," Rose said in a way that appealed to him deeply.

"Make sure that you keep yourself warm too, Rose. If you are going to sit with the dog for very long, you will end up with the chills. Is there anything else that you need while you are down here?" Bennager asked.

"I have some hardtack and dried fruit in one of my bags, and some coffee would be really nice, and it would help us to stay warm too," Rose said, grateful that he would ask.

"Coming right up. Will you take anything in your coffee, Rose?" Bennager asked, hoping to keep the words between them pleasant.

"Not yet. I'll celebrate later. Thank you, Bennager."

Angus and Zeb hopped out from under the wagon to help Bennager gather up the stuff that would make Rose and Girl more comfortable. Zeb spread his bedroll out under the wagon and tried to encourage Girl to get on it, but the dog would not budge from Rose's lap. "Rose, I would be obliged if you would sit on this bedroll, so you don't get the chills while you are taking care of my dog. Please make yourself more comfortable. I don't want Girl to make a mess on your blanket when she has those pups."

"Thank you, Zeb."

Bennager asked Sam to get out the things that Rose had requested from the carpetbags.

Angus walked over to his brothers, and Bennager went into Charlie's steering room where he had left the sake and oranges and got a cup of coffee for Rose. As he walked out with the coffee, a fight had erupted between the four merry men from Ireland. Angus' brother knocked him right into Bennager and Rose's cup of coffee and burned both of them. The cup fell to the deck and was about to roll over the edge when Bennager bent over to pick it up. Angus let out the call of a jersey bull and bailed right into the middle of the three men. As Bennager started to stand up with his captured cup, he realized that he was about to go overboard if he didn't hit the deck because Angus was coming at him with one of his brothers held over his head. Angus threw that man right over the edge into the San Francisco Bay. Bennager started crawling as fast as he could until it was safe to get to his feet and watched the two remaining brothers try to get the best of Angus. Someone yelled, "Man overboard!"

Angus yelled back, "Let 'em drown!"

Angus' two brothers looked like they were about to get him down when Angus picked up one of the men and used him as a weapon against the other man, hitting one in the head with the other one's head, then he threw the weapon into the bay and picked up his last remaining brother and threw him overboard too.

"Man overboard!" someone yelled again.

Angus was leaning over the rail, watching to see if his brothers would swim or drown. "Good riddance to the lot of you fool-hearted bastards. I hope ya get rich shovelin' horse shit and washin' the streets, you ignorant sons of bitches!" Angus laughed as he turned to Bennager. "That last one I threw over was the leader of all us brothers, so I thought he should go help the first two of me brothers that went overboard. Gold! Gold! Gold! That's all I've heard 'bout for months. Those fools are nothin' but dreamers. They just got tired of workin' for a livin', so they thought they could come here and fall into a pit of gold. Maybe they will find some out there."

"How did all of this start, Angus?" Bennager asked as he walked back into Charlie's office for some more coffee and motioned Angus to follow.

"I told them about wantin' to travel with the dog until me pup was ready, and they didn't like the idea of travelin' with strangers and thought it best if the four of us went our own way, so we had a vote, and I won," Angus said, jabbing himself in his chest with his thumb and smiling widely.

Bennager was surprised. "Do you mean to tell me that you threw your brothers in the bay over a pup? Do you know that sharks come in here from time to time?"

"I would rather have me pup than the lot of 'em. As for sharks, they will be after something tastier than the arses of the three of 'em," Angus replied.

Bennager shook his head. "Angus, I guess you are a hard man. Now I'm going to try one more time to get this coffee over to Rose. I hope that you don't have any more disagreements until she gets it."

Angus chuckled sheepishly. "Well, if I had seen you comin' last time, she would have it by now."

When Angus and Bennager got to the wagon, Zeb and Sam were sitting on the freight, getting to know each other better and looking over at the shore through the fog for any sight that might be of interest to them. Angus' brothers being thrown overboard did not seem to concern them very much, and Angus had been reassuring the passengers who inquired that his foolish brothers would be just fine. Rose had made herself pretty comfortable under the wagon with Girl, and Bennager decided to sit with her and find out if the pleasant conversation that they had had this morning was a fluke due to a severe hangover or if there could be a remote chance that this female could turn out to be a lady after all.

"Well, Rose Mary, it looks like you have found yourself a job," Bennager said, sitting down beside Rose and the dog and handing her the coffee.

"Thank you. Sam told me a lot about this sort of thing when we were at sea, only the animals that he cared for were bigger. I have never seen puppies be born before. What was all the commotion about a man being overboard?"

"Oh, Angus had a disagreement with his brothers and made them swim back to shore," Bennager explained.

Rose furrowed her brow. "What was the argument about?" She had to wonder if in some strange way that it had something to do with her.

"Angus told them that he goes where the dog goes until he gets his pup."

Rose smiled wickedly. "So he would throw his brothers away for a puppy? He must be crazy or just one mean son of a bitch. Don't you think so?"

"Don't let him hear you say that or he might throw you in the bay too. I don't think he liked his brothers very well, and I'm not sure if he is crazy or mean, but I know that he is tough. He took all three of them on at one time," Bennager enlightened Rose. He could see that the wheels in Rose's mind were spinning as she thought about what kind of man Angus was.

"I hope he doesn't find a reason to cross us. I think that I'd rather have him as a friend. I guess time will tell." Rose wouldn't be intimidated.

"He sure is good at spotting women. I think Zeb knew right off too. It doesn't look like your costume is going to fool anyone. I guess that I should have known it wouldn't. Even in those clothes and that big hat and that big coat that you have on, anybody can see that you are not a man. It's a good thing that you met up with Sam."

Rose said, "Yes, it's a good thing that I met up with Sam for my sake and his too. It's also a good thing that we met up with you. You have helped me and Sam a great deal. What do you think about Girl being the leader of this venture? Do you think that we will be doomed right from the start?"

Bennager had already come to that conclusion before the dog had come into the scene, but he said, "I don't think a mere dog and a litter of pups will make or break you, Rose Mary."

"Don't tell anyone, but I don't think that I would want to be a nurse maid in this situation again. This is boring, but I felt so sorry for the poor thing. When she was running around and feeling afraid, it reminded me of the day that I got on that big boat. I was never more frightened in all my life, but I couldn't let it show, not even to Sam. Do you think that Zeb and Angus will cause problems for us?"

"Rose Mary, I think that from now on, the best thing that you could do is just be yourself. It doesn't seem to concern these men that you are the only woman for miles around, and they seem to regard you as an asset in this particular situation, and from what Sam tells me, it won't be long before you are forced to prove yourself to be more than just an animal lover."

"What do you mean, Bennager?" Rose asked.

"Until you get settled, there will probably be a lot of hardships for you in the near future. There will be men that you are afraid of because they will see you and want you or want to hurt you or rob you, and there will be Indians who will want to scare you away from their land. There will be animals that will want to eat you, rivers to cross, and bad weather. These are the difficulties that we all have here every day until we get settled and get used to the everyday adversities and just learn how to take care of them as they come. You are young and strong, and I think that you are just as capable as any man here."

Rose's eyes beamed with delight and reassurance. "Damn, Bennager, I didn't think that you thought very much of me after what you saw last night."

"I do admire your appetite, and Sam said that your drunkenness was only in celebration on account of having your feet on land again, and I think the tobacco was just to make me sick, and I guess a person can't help it if they snore loud enough to raise the roof," Bennager teased.

"I hope that what you said about me being capable is right because everything else that you just said dead is wrong. You were right this morning when you said that we have a lot to learn about each other. First of all, I don't snore, and second, I have been sneaking tobacco since I was five years old, and I am very pleased with the fact that now I'm on my own, I don't have to sneak it anymore. As for celebrating, I do it as often as I can, and if I ate like that all the time, you would be able to use me to pull your wagon. I reckon none of us are perfect, and I don't guess that I'll be changing anytime soon," Rose said flatly, letting Bennager know that she didn't have any regrets about who she was.

At that very moment, the strangest urge came over Bennager. They were looking at each other, and he was seeing the pretty features of her face, but unlike last night, when he was watching her sleep and seeing the little girl in her, this time he was seeing the beautiful young lady who knew who she was but wasn't particularly proud of the fact that she wasn't who he wanted her to be. Slowly and gently, he put his hand to her face, cupped her cheek, and he wanted to kiss her to let her know that he understood that no one was perfect, but he was afraid of what her reaction would be. Bennager was afraid that she would beat him with the dog and have Sam choke him and have Angus throw him overboard. Bennager said, looking deeply into her eyes with his thumb rubbing her cheek bone gently, "Rose Mary, you do snore."

The expression on her face was that of utter perplexity, and Bennager knew that a kiss was out of the question. He removed his hand from her face, smiled, and scrambled out from underneath his wagon as fast as he could. She did take a swing at him, of course, hitting him directly in the rump before he was able to execute his exit, but she didn't have Sam kill him.

3

Sam got out of the wagon while Bennager was talking with Rose and started pacing along the railing of the boat. Angus and Zeb were passing the time with a deck of cards, so Bennager went to visit with Sam.

"What's going on, Sam, are you waiting for a pup too?" Bennager jested.

"No!" Sam chuckled. "I'm not waitin' for a pup, but I'm havin' a fit of some kind. I never felt like this before. How is Rose doin' under there with that dog?" Sam asked nodding toward the wagon.

"Oh, she's fine, snug, and comfortable. Has anyone given you a hard time?"

"No. These fellas don't seem to care about my past or Rose's either. They just seem happy to be goin' somewhere. They are probably just wonderin' where they are goin' to end up just like I am. You say California is not a slave state and that I am free as long as I am with Rose, but are there many slaves in California Bennager?" Sam's fit was due to anxiety. Suddenly, it felt like the weight of the world was on his shoulders, and at the same time, he was highly excited about his new future and worried that someone was going to capture him from his success and turn him into a slave again.

"To be honest, yes, there are slaves in California. Rich slave-holders have been drifting into this country off and on for years, since the Lewis and Clark expedition. They brought their slaves with them, and when they needed more, they captured the local Indians. Some men just ended up out here after guiding immigrants to the west and came upon riches by using Indian labor in the fields. The soil along the Sacramento River is very fertile."

Sam did not like this information that Bennager had just given him, and the fearful look on his face proved it. He resumed pacing along the railing, not knowing if the decision that he had made to come to California had been the right one or not, and also, he probably wondered if he was ever going to truly be a free man or if he would forever have to be tied to Rose. Sam paced back to Bennager. "It has been a long time since I have had a life of my own. I feel like havin' my own life again is right at the edge of my fingertips. It's like those dreams that I have all the time when I am sleepin' that somethin's chasin' me and I'm tryin' to run, and I can't move. It's right there, Bennager. I can see it, but I can't have it or even touch it. Rose is the only friend I've got, but someday, she will want to make a life for herself, too, and I don't think her husband will be wantin' to see me around. He might not allow Rose to have me for a business associate."

Bennager laughed heartily. "You are painting a mighty grim picture for yourself. For one thing, there is no man alive that is going to allow or not allow Rose Mary Briar to do anything. You are probably the first true friend that Rose has ever had, and I'm here to tell you that Rose would die before she would let anybody take you, and so will I, although the best thing that we could do is get out of the Sacramento Valley as soon as possible and never leave Rose's side when we do get to Sacramento City. I'll tell you what I told Rose. There are a lot of things to worry about that could or could not happen the way that we want them to, and the best thing that a person can do is just be vigilant about the hardships that will happen and not worry about when they will happen."

Sam considered Bennager's advice. "You are right, Bennager. That is what I've had to do all my life. Maybe I'm just ready to explode because nothin' bad has happened to me in a long time, and I don't know how to live right. Is Rose worried about somethin' too?"

"Well, we were just talking about how Zeb and Angus weren't fooled by her miner's garb. They knew right off that she was a female, and I just told her that life is difficult here whether a person is a man or a woman. As long as you and I can keep her safe from really bad men, she will do just fine, I reckon," Bennager said, shrugging his shoulders as if the task was a simple one.

Sam smiled and said, "The last really bad man that tried to cross her ended up dead, and she didn't need anybody's help. I think I'll go see how she is gettin' along with the dog. Good talk, Bennager."

Sam shook Bennager's hand and headed for the wagon where Zeb and Angus had started sharing a jug, and Bennager fully expected Rose to abandon her responsibilities to the collie by turning them over to Sam so that she may join the men in a drink and a business conversation, but she did no such thing. Bennager took this opportunity to feed his team. He had a sack for each horse that fit over its mouth and attached to its neck just behind its ears. He filled the sacks with a little grain and gave it to them. Then, for something to do, he groomed their tails. This was a mindless job that enabled him to think about things or just daydream. He always liked to take an hour or two a day to let his mind drift. A body spends so much time having to think about things it has to think about or that it doesn't want to think about, so he figured that it's good to drift when you have time. He had spent many hours letting his mind drift on this boat for lack of nothing better to do. Soon they would have to stop and camp for the night, and he would have to get a couple of men and go hunting, and then he would have to think about the task at hand.

The horses were content. The grain and the tail grooming helped to keep them from getting restless. He found himself wondering how many more men had come to the gold fields by the overland route since he had left Sacramento City, and he wondered what it was like now in the foothills of the Sierras. Bennager hadn't been up there since last fall, and he wondered how crowded it was getting by now, if there would be enough room for Rose and Sam and the rest of the fellas that were on the boat, if the Indians were becoming more hostile with the arrival of every new wagon and boatload of gold-seeking White men, and if their wrath would fall on Rose somehow. It looked as if Zeb and Angus were going to be traveling with Rose and Sam, and if that was the case, then Rose would have plenty of protection, but if for some reason Zeb or Angus decided that they didn't want to travel with a Black man, what would happen then? What if for some reason one of those men decided to harm Rose in some way? Maybe they would get drunk and take it into their head to be with her in a sinful way. Rose was too young to have all of these "what-ifs" flung upon her.

"Bennager, the wee little ones are comin' now!" Angus hollered, hopping up and down like a schoolboy, startling Bennager in the process and making him feel like he had just jumped out of skin. Bennager shook his head, heart still pounding vigorously, and he thought to himself that Angus must not be a mean person.

Sam came out from under the wagon as Angus dove under it to watch the pups come out, almost hitting Sam on his way. Sam turned to look at the streak that almost hit him to find out what it was and what it was doing. When Sam saw that Angus had settled across from Rose and was watching the dog with fierce intensity, Sam shook his head and rolled his eyes toward the heavens as if he was shaking his head at his Maker for creating an Irishman that was so strange, then he made his way toward Bennager and decided that grooming the horses' tails was a good way to pass the time.

"Rose reckons that she can handle bringin' the pups into the world. She said she can't wait until it's over so she can celebrate," Sam said, smiling his all-knowing smile.

Now it was Bennager's turn to look to the heavens. "Well, Sam, we are about ready to call it a day and find a place to camp. I guess Angus won't let anything happen to Rose while we go out to find something to throw in the pot for dinner. You'll go with me, won't you, Sam?"

Zeb chimed in just at that moment and asked if he was welcome to join the hunting party, so it was agreed that the three of them would go together as soon as they hit the shore and got the horses staked out for the night.

Bennager thought that he had better let Angus know that he was supposed to look after Rose, so he got under the wagon again, thinking that this place had sort of become Rose Mary's office or place of business. Bennager thought of how bothersome it was becoming now to have to keep crawling underneath the damn wagon in order to have a face-to-face conversation with someone. He sat next to Rose so that he would be able to make eye contact with Angus. "Angus."

He looked at Bennager, and he took that as a good sign.

"Angus, since it seems that you are overanxious to see your pup get born, the fellas and I decided that it would be a good idea for you to stay with Rose Mary and keep her away from harm while the rest of us go out and hunt up something to put in the cook pot. We are just about to call it a day and camp for the night. I guess the dog shouldn't be moved, so the three of you are going to have to stay here." Bennager paused to observe the man for a moment. "Now, Angus, if you are too excited about the pups that you can't be alert to trouble, tell me now, and I'll have Sam stay with Rose."

"No need for that, laddie, no harm will come to Rose or the pups while I'm on guard, and tomorrow, I will take a turn at huntin' while one of you looks after this fine lady and the wee little babes. You have me promise, Bennager, and I will keep it."

"That's fine. Does this suit you, Rose Mary?"

Rose contemplated the idea. "Yes, that will do, but do you have any reason to believe that there will be trouble while you are away?"

Bennager touched her arm and said, "Oh no, Rose, but trouble could come to us from the shore, so you need to watch out all the time. I'm sure everything will be fine."

"I think that I would feel more comfortable if I had my bags to lean up against. Would you mind getting them for me?" Sam must have heard the conversation or else he was thinking the same way Rose was because about the same time she said that, he handed Rose the carpetbags. "Thank you, Sam, you have been with me so long that you are starting to read my mind. Will you fellas be gone long?"

"I'll stake out the horses, and we'll probably be gone for an hour or so," Bennager assured her.

"Come see me when you get back. With any luck, Girl will be finished with her task, and we can all celebrate. I dearly hope that I don't have to sleep on this damned boat all night. What I would give to warm up to a campfire. I've never camped before." Rose managed to keep her tone calm and soothing for Girl's sake but had made it clear with her words that she was becoming weary of her obligations.

"How far apart are her contractions now, Rose?" Sam asked.

"I've been talking to Bennager and not keeping track. I'm going to have to be more diligent, I reckon. I'm sorry, Sam," she mockingly apologized.

Sam chuckled, still not believing that Rose was the type to give a care about dogs but thought that was a good diversion from complaining about the fog, swilling liquor, and being outrageous. This situation made Sam realize that Rose could adapt to anything that came her way, and it gave him another reason to like and respect her as a person and as his friend.

A few minutes later, the boat started heading for the dock that Bennager and Charlie had built the summer before. The horses had broken the ramp that Charlie used to put in the water when they decided to stop for the night. The ramp was never long enough to begin with. One time, when Bennager had led the horses off the boat and the ramp had been set on a sandbar, the ramp collapsed, and he was in over his head with the two lead horses on top of him. It was then that Charlie and Bennager decided to figure out the best places to build docks for all the bays on the way to the Sacramento River. It took them all summer and part of the fall to build docks approximately four hours apart. They had figured eight hours of travel in the wintertime and twelve hours in the summertime. This schedule usually gave the passengers time to set up camp and gather food for the night, and in the summer, if unforeseen events occurred which delayed the boat, Charlie could call it quits and dock early.

Of course, this would cause the passengers to become very aggravated. Not only were they being detained and losing precious time in the gold fields, but even worse than that were the mosquitoes that afflicted them. In order to get away from the mosquitoes, they would have to camp at least a half mile away from the bay. Not many men did this because they were afraid of Indians and bandits.

Charlie set the ramp on the dock and the passengers, happy to be taking a break from the floating feeling that being on a boat gives people and walked around on shore until they could get over the slight dizziness that happens when people make the transition from water to land. Bennager went to check on Rose and Angus one more time before taking the horses to shore. "How is Girl doing now, Rose Mary?" he asked, this time just bending over and looking under the wagon instead of crawling under it.

"I have been timing the contractions, and they are one minute apart now. Do you think they will be coming soon?" She spat tobacco juice on the deck of the steamboat as if she was putting a question mark on the end of her question.

"Yes, they should be coming anytime as best as I can figure," Bennager answered.

Angus started squirming around on his buttocks, jovially pointing and clapping his hands like a four-year-old boy. "One is comin' out! One is comin'! One is comin'!"

"Angus, shhh, settle down now. Girl feels your excitement, and you will make her nervous," Rose said, giving Angus a hard look as a mother would do to her child.

Angus stopped squirming immediately, but as Bennager watched Rose and Angus, he knew that wouldn't be the last time Rose would have to scold him before this ordeal of birth was over. Bennager also got the feeling that Rose was going to have to be in charge of Angus on this expedition because if a man had told him to stop squirming, Angus would have thrown him overboard.

"Angus, are you sure that you will be able to keep Rose Mary from harm while we go to shore?" Bennager asked him one more time.

Angus did not hear him, but Rose answered with a look that implied that Angus wasn't really needed if harm was to come looking for her, and she said, "Bennager, you get that campfire started, and the three of us will be there directly with the new additions and spirits in hand. Go on now. We'll be there when our leader is finished."

Bennager looked once more at Angus and could tell that Rose was going to have to admonish him again very shortly. "Angus," Bennager said.

Angus heard him this time.

"Angus, you know that you shouldn't touch those pups for a couple of days because their mama might disown them, and if she does that, then they might die, right?"

"Oh, no, no, nobody will touch these wee little babes. I will not let them. I promise, Rasmussen. No, we can't have that. Now if me fool brothers were here, they'd be sayin' I was the fool. I know that's what they'd be sayin' aye."

"Angus, shhh, you must not get so excited and noisy," Rose told him.

As Bennager left with the team, he knew that nobody would bother Rose. They might try, but even most evil-hearted people thought it best to leave loco people alone. It was his misfortune that he had never met any unusual people before yesterday because if he had acknowledged this fact before speaking to Rose and Sam, he would be keeping his distance just as the rest of the men on the boat had been inclined to do, although Angus throwing his brothers overboard had a lot to do with that, Bennager imagined. He staked out the team under an oak tree and gathered a few sticks for a campfire, and Sam and Zeb came over directly. Zeb got the flames started while Sam and Bennager gathered enough wood and bark to keep the fire going for an hour or so.

"Zeb, your dog has had one pup so far. If you want to, you can tend the fire and wait for Rose and Angus while Sam and I get some camp meat. Rose figured on beating us to the fire."

"Thank you, Mr. Rasmussen. I'd be obliged to you. That poor dog of mine has had a rough day. If she was to come looking for me and couldn't find me, it's likely that she would head for home."

"Where's your home?" Bennager chuckled, imagining that the dog would have to travel a great distance to get there.

"Monterey," Zeb said without looking up from the fire.

"Well, I guess that isn't far to travel. It would certainly delay our trip if Rose Mary and Angus had to follow Girl back to Monterey to get their pups," Bennager said, still chuckling and turning to leave camp. He came face-to-face with Sam who wasn't laughing at all.

"It's just a joke, Sam. You know the dog won't leave her pups and go back home. Come on, let's get a move on. It'll be dark shortly."

Bennager slapped Sam on his muscular arm, trying to hide the fact that he still wasn't sure if Sam had a mind to take hold of his neck again or not. Getting to the gold fields was so important to him that he didn't even have a sense of humor.

Sam and Bennager had managed to kill a turkey not far from camp and were able to get back before dark. Upon seeing it, they decided that Sam should try to kill it with his revolver because there wouldn't have been much left of it if Bennager had used his musket loader. Sam successfully shot it in the neck, and then it was quite a race to catch it. They both ended up on their backs, but the turkey wasn't able to elude them. Their mouths were watering before they got back to camp, thinking about how good a fresh hot meal was going to be.

Girl had finished having her pups, and Zeb had gone back to the boat to praise her for her efforts and to let her show off her brood. Rose Mary was sitting alone by the fire sipping on her jug of brandy, using her carpetbags for pillows. The only care in the world that she had was to make sure to get her bones warmed up. Bennager's first instinct when he saw her sitting alone by the fire was to raise Cain with her for being alone. He was opening his mouth to do just that when Sam touched his arm and shook his head at him. Bennager saw many things in Sam's face and in his eyes that told him not to give Rose any guff. Bennager realized that if the other men on the trip noticed that this person needed protection, they would wonder why. Also, Rose may already be in a drunken stupor and cause more attention to herself, not to mention the fact that Rose was more than able to take care of herself, just as Sam had explained to him earlier, so if she wasn't worried about it, then why should he be?

Bennager turned away from Sam, and he touched his arm again, this time holding it so that he would have Bennager's full attention. He had a solemn look on his face that made Bennager take notice of the importance of what he was about to say, and then he whispered, "When we stopped in Peru, Rose got on that brandy." He looked around to see if anyone was listening. "And since you and Rose don't seem to understand each other yet, you know, the two of you don't really see thin's eye to eye"—he looked around again—"if I were you, I think that I'd give her a wide berth this evenin'."

Bennager looked down at the ground and shook his head and immediately started feeling a dark depression coming over him. He had been looking forward to a mouthwatering hot piece of turkey, and now he felt like vomiting would be the only remedy for what ailed him. He couldn't believe that he would witness another unfortunate exhibit of misbehavior shown by a lady two days in a row. Bennager handed Sam the turkey. "I believe I'll take your advice, Sam. You folks take the camp meat and enjoy. Would you mind keeping an eye on my team for a while? I just remembered that it has been sometime since I laid my eyes on newborn pups."

Bennager started to walk away, and a thought occurred to him. He stopped but did not look at Sam and asked, "When Rose shot that man, did it have anything to do with the brandy?"

"I already told you about that, Bennager."

Even though his reply didn't really answer Bennager's question sufficiently, he thought it best to make camp on the boat. Having spent so much time alone over the last year or so and after not getting very much sleep the night before, he figured that he would be better off spending the night alone anyway, and since he wasn't sure about the amount of poison that Rose may have consumed since the last time that he saw her, he decided not to bid her good evening.

Charlie was on his boat, eating oranges and drinking sake, not yet cold enough to join one of the campfires that so many of his passengers were enjoying.

"How's it going, Charlie? Is the coffee still hot?"

"How the hell should I know, Benny? I ain't had a cup since this morning. Ain't there any coffee at your camp?"

"I'm running a cold camp tonight, Charlie."

"Huh, them fellers that's been hangin' 'round your wagon today is a strange bunch. You thought I was watchin' what I was doin', but in the bay, I have time to watch what other folks are doin' too, and I ain't never seen a man tend a bitch in labor the way that feller Pete did today. Have you?"

"No, you don't see that every day, do ya?"

"I ain't seen many men carry on that way over an animal. Why, my own ma helps the neighbor ladies out back home, and when I was a boy, someone would tell me, 'Hey, boy, run and get your ma, my missus is havin' a baby.' By golly, I'd run for all I was worth, and Ma would leave, and when she came back, I'd say, 'Ma, what did missus so and so have?' And Ma would say, 'A baby.' And then she would walk 'round the house, fussin' 'round and botherin' me 'bout my chores. Ma never missed a step and never got excited 'bout much neither. That's probably why I'm an only child."

"Well," Charlie continued after his brief recollection of his ma and pa. "Pretty soon, when folks were yellin' at me to run and fetch my ma, I only ran 'til they were out of sight, and then I just went back to walkin' 'cause Ma made it seem like it weren't much worth runnin' 'bout. Some people are just excitable, I guess."

While Charlie had been reminiscing about his tender mother, Bennager had found luck in a warm coffee pot. "I suppose that it is mostly comforting to a female to have someone by their side when they are having a baby."

"I guess it would be to the one that was sufferin'. It must be awful painful."

"Well, Charlie, thanks for the coffee. I'm going to hit the sack. Town was noisy last night, and I didn't get much sleep. See ya in the morning."

"Oh, well, yeah, I'll see ya in the mornin', Benny."

As Bennager laid beside the wagon trying to warm up in his bedroll, he thought of how cold it was going to be tonight without the warmth of a campfire and hoped that Rose Mary Briar would get all her supply of spirits downed so that he could sleep by the camp-fire tomorrow night. He could smell the turkey that he and Sam had brought back to camp roasting over the campfire, and he could hear the tenants of camp laughing and the anxiety in their voices about the gold fields as he chomped away on his hardtack. He wondered when he was going to hear Rose Mary's voice. It was just a matter of time before she ended up doing something atrocious. By tomorrow morning, everyone would know that she was a woman or that her carpetbags were full of money. God only knew what Rose was going to do that would give her identity away.

He laid there, listening to Zeb talk to his dog, and he discovered that he would probably sleep better if he had asked Sam what he thought that Rose might do tonight. If Bennager could know in advance, then he would not have been so curious. Then he decided there was no reason why he shouldn't make a campfire of his own and warm up and observe Rose in another one of her finer moments.

Zeb was watching as Bennager rolled his bed up and said, "I suppose Girl and me are keeping you awake. Sorry about that, Rasmussen."

Bennager stopped. "Oh no, Zeb, if I didn't have so much on my mind, the soothing tone that you have with that dog would lull me right to sleep." And then Bennager sat for a moment to watch the dog with her pups.

"Then I suppose that it is the woman that is keeping you awake. You must love her."

"I do not think that I love her, but what keeps my mind so occupied is the trouble that I believe will come to me because of her."

"One little delicate flower like her could not bring any trouble. Trouble comes whether we like it or not," Zeb argued.

"I'm afraid that there are sides of Rose Mary Briar that you have not become acquainted with yet Zeb. As a matter of fact, I was warned by Sam to stay away from their camp tonight on account of if I didn't like seeing her drunk on sake, then I was really going to have trouble with her if she was drinking brandy, so now you see my curiosity is getting the better of me. It is like if you know that a wagonload of supplies is going to go over a cliff, you know it will be a disaster, but you still want to watch it happen."

"Drunk! Cliffs! Oh, Rasmussen, why do you hate this girl so much that you would try to damage her reputation? She is just a young girl, and you make her out to be a woman of ill repute."

"Hey, I don't want you to think that about her, and don't say any such thing again, but I'm not lying either. She drinks, and when she drinks, it worries me, and that's why I can't sleep, that's all."

Now Zeb was silent. Bennager could tell that he didn't believe him nor was he going to argue with him about it anymore. Zeb's silence made Bennager feel like he had just made an ass out of himself somehow. In Zeb's eyes, Bennager might as well have said nasty things about his own mother. The one good thing that Bennager got out of the conversation with Zeb is that Bennager knew that Zeb liked and respected Rose and he wasn't going to put up with people doing any ill-will toward her. "Well, Zeb, I can see that you don't believe me, so I'm off to make my campfire now. If you get cold, I hope you will join me."

Bennager made his way out and away from the other campers without disturbing anyone or bringing unwanted attention to himself and picked a place where he could see Sam and Rose's camp and went about the task of gathering firewood. Once the fire was going, he laid his bedroll out, and with his backside to the fire, he was able to observe Rose. He heard Rose ask Sam if Bennager was coming to supper, and Sam answered her by saying that he thought that Bennager was probably too tired to eat. This information did not seem to concern her, but she asked why he wasn't at their fire, and Sam told her that he imagined that Bennager was probably somewhere away from the noise of the other travelers, trying to get some rest.

She thought that it would be best to save Bennager some turkey in case he decided to show up. It did not look like Rose was drinking at all to Bennager, and he wondered why Sam had told him to give Rose a wide berth. Maybe Sam thought of Bennager as an intruder. After all, it was Rose who had asked for his help, not Sam. Maybe Sam didn't like the tension in the air when Rose and Bennager were together.

"Damn, Rasmussen, she is a real witch woman! That is a disgraceful sight. Just look at that cliff!" Bennager had heard Zeb coming up behind him to his fire, so he wasn't startled by his making fun of him about the things that he had said earlier about Rose. Bennager knew that if he had said anything more about it, then he would only make things worse. If he had told Zeb that Rose had taken a bath with an old Chinese man watching her or that she had eaten a whole pie or that she had passed out face down in the street or that her snoring would wake the dead, he would not believe him and he would dislike him for saying it. And if Bennager told Zeb that there was some reason why Sam did not want him in camp that night, he was sure that Zeb would shake his head and walk away thinking that Bennager was crazy.

"How's your dog doing, Zeb?"

"She looks like she is going to be just fine, and she appears to be a good mother. She's darn proud of herself, all right. This was her first litter," Zeb replied.

"They still have some supper left over there, Zeb. I suppose you are right about me saying those things about Rose. You should know that I do not hate that girl. As a matter of fact, she happens to be the most interesting person that I have ever met. She seems to fear nothing, and I guess that is why I worry so much."

"I do see you love her."

When Bennager turned to argue with that statement, Zeb was gone on his way to have his supper.

With Zeb's help, Bennager convinced himself that last night was probably a one-time incident and that Rose was not going to do anything outrageous this evening. It was possible that her body was rejecting any additional abuse from alcohol anyway, and this night was going to be as quiet and normal as any other winter night on the bank of the bay, so he felt that it was safe to rest his eyes.

The next thing that Bennager heard was angry voices. He opened his eyes and saw that in Rose's camp, someone was getting kicked around on the ground by three men. He could see that Zeb and Sam had stood up, and as Bennager was getting out of his bedroll, he couldn't figure out why Zeb and Sam weren't doing anything to stop this. *Oh, Lord, where is Rose?* Bennager thought. *There must be another man that I can't see holding a weapon on them. Oh, Lord, where is Rose?*

Enough time had passed since Bennager had fallen asleep that the fires had died down, so if he was quiet, movement around the trees and brush would be easy without being noticed in order to find the man that had the jump on Sam and Zeb. He crouched behind a bush, looking for the fourth man, when in the blink of an eye, the person being kicked took the leg of the man that was kicking and tossed him backward and into the fire, and in the next instant, the other two men tried to jump on the man on the ground, but they were too late. Bennager realized then that it was Angus that the men had been kicking. Angus was on his feet when the two men hit the ground at the same time. Bennager saw Sam take two steps and bend down.

Bennager couldn't tell if he was going for a weapon or hiding the carpetbags, but he realized that there must not be anybody holding Sam at gunpoint, and now Zeb was helping Sam with whatever it was that he was doing.

Bennager came out from behind the brush in time to see Angus jump and crush the two men with the full weight of his body. The one that was in the fire had gotten up, and Zeb was picking a body up from the ground, and Sam had the carpetbags. Bennager's first thought was that the culprits had stomped Rose before they had started in on Angus. *God, I will kill them*, he thought.

Angus took the man coming out of the fire and lifted him over his head and threw him right at Bennager's feet as he was trying to get to Rose. He stopped and immediately put his musket loader to the man's chest, and Angus screamed, "No! No!" At the same, Bennager recognized that this man was one of Angus' brothers.

The idea of getting shot took all the fight out of this man, but the other two still had plenty of energy, and while Angus was screaming at Bennager, one of them was able to pick up a stick and thwack Angus on the back of his head.

By this time, Bennager had made it to where Rose was and leaned down to see what was wrong with her, only to hear her snoring, and he saw that she had fallen asleep with tobacco in her mouth again. "Did they hurt her, Sam?" Bennager asked as Angus threw the man that hit him with the stick into the trunk of an oak tree, face-first.

"No, they didn't hurt her. She is just a sound sleeper. I guess she can't hear anything over her own noisy self."

"Sam, do you see how she has fallen asleep with this tobacco in her mouth?" Bennager showed him as he scooped it out. "You must remind her not to do that. That juice will get in her lungs at night and drown her, I'm sure of it. Not to mention the fact that she will be a terrible mess in the morning." Bennager cleaned the juice off her face and brushed her hair back. He loved looking at her when she slept. There was no guilt, no enemies; there was just a look of innocence.

Sam grimaced as he watched Bennager fuss with tobacco in the sleeping girl's mouth and could feel the turkey trying to come out of his stomach, and he turned away from the sight, determined that he would never love someone enough to scoop tobacco out of their mouth like that.

Zeb stepped close to Sam and whispered, "You see? I see. I see love."

Sam rolled his eyes and shook his head, still trying to keep that turkey where it belonged.

Angus watched while the last brother standing went to tend to the one that Angus had thrown headfirst into the tree, and the brother that Bennager was going to shoot walked up to Angus. "You should not have thrown us out of the boat, you hotheaded, crazy bastard."

"Go to the devil if you don't like the water! You kick like a little girl. The next time you fools start in on me, I will bash all your heads into a tree! In the meantime, I'll thank you to stay the devil out of me sight!" Angus told his brother. Angus picked up his belongings and went to the boat. His brother went and helped collect the hurt one and started to leave.

Zeb had seen all manner of disputes in his life and learned to never pick sides, just pick up the pieces, so he went over and asked of the man's condition and if he needed help, and the two that could see looked at him as if he was dirt, and they all headed out into the night. Zeb shook his head and went back to his bedroll. In all the commotion, it hadn't even been wrinkled. "That's an odd bunch. I have been around, and I find it improbable that those four men grew up in the same country, let alone the same house, and I have even a harder time believing that they traveled this far together without killing each other."

Sam chuckled. "Maybe they started out with eight or ten brothers and that's all that's left." Bennager and Zeb looked at each other, and then they looked at Sam, and all three found themselves wondering if Sam's joke might have some truth to it.

"That is an interesting point, Sam. Were those men on the ship with you and Rose?" Zeb asked.

"Maybe they were. I didn't see 'em, though."

Bennager picked Rose up and put her back by the fire, Sam got the bags, and Zeb stoked the fire. Daylight was still sometime in coming, and they thought about Angus and if he was going to be all right. Finally, Sam asked if they should go check on him. He had taken an awful blow to the head, and Zeb said that when someone has a concussion, they shouldn't go to sleep right away. Bennager reckoned that he had had enough close calls for one day where Angus was concerned, and he didn't want to have any part in looking for him, finding him, or waking him up. Sam and Zeb didn't think that the matter could wait until morning, so they decided that they would go if Bennager would stay with Rose. As terrible as Bennager thought that the night before had been, he realized that was before he had met Angus and his brothers. Rose's snoring couldn't bother him compared to that. Besides, her snoring was only half as loud as it had been the night before. He went and got his things and settled in by the recently kindled fire.

*****

"Bennager, Bennager, wake up," was the next thing that he heard. Rose was speaking so softly, and at first, he thought the sound was as sweet as the sound of doves on a bright breezy summer morning. "Bennager, wake up," Rose whispered. Then he thought that Rose could only be whispering because there was trouble. He opened his eyes and saw the alarm in Rose's face but kept as still as he could.

"What is it?" Bennager whispered back to her.

"'Bout time you woke up. Where in tarnation is everyone? I need coffee. I need to relieve myself, and I don't know where Sam went to. Watch my things. I'll be back in a minute."

"Do you need Sam's help to relieve yourself?"

"I heard that!" Rose cackled.

"Watch your backside, Rose. Angus' brothers are out there somewhere," Bennager warned, thinking how the dove had turned into a hen.

The new day had presented itself as cold and foggy just as the day before. Bennager reluctantly crawled out of his bedroll and put his coat on that had previously been on top of his bedroll. Even though the fire had been stoked just a few hours ago, its warmth did not keep the dew of the wet fog from saturating his coat. This problem occurred on account of his own stupidity, of course. Usually, he placed his bedroll over his coat to prevent being wet all day, but in all the excitement of a few hours ago, the fog had not been a concern. The first order of business for the day was to get the fire stoked up again, and the second was to get some coffee brewing. Like Rose, Bennager needed coffee as well.

"What was that you said about brothers? God, would you look at this damned fog. When will we see the sun or even clouds again, for heaven's sake? Look at this! Everything is soaked! Is this what you call rain in California?"

Bennager realized that Rose was much quieter on the mornings when she woke up with hangovers but proved to not be much of a morning person either way. He did not bother to answer her because he doubted that she would shut up long enough to hear it, and also, it seemed as though she was talking more to the elements than to him anyway. While he was thinking up ways to avoid talking to her, she had come up beside him at the fire. He could see out the corner of his eye that she was looking right at him as she bit off a piece of her tobacco.

"Well?"

The moment had come. Bennager could feel the tension boiling up in his blood. She was requiring him to speak to her. Bennager looked into her eyes hesitantly and spoke. "Well?"

"What in tarnation do you mean, 'Well?' Didn't you hear anything that I said?"

"I didn't know that you were talking to me," Bennager replied.

"Who else would I be talking to? Are you blind? You are the only other person here besides myself, and I haven't taken up talking to myself, which brings me back to my first question, which was, where in the hell is Sam? We will take this one question at a time since it seems as though you are rummy. Did you get into the brandy last night?"

"That's two questions, smarty, and now I have one for you. Can't you make coffee for yourself?" Bennager fanned Rose's flames.

"Sam always makes the coffee."

Bennager looked around and made a big show of it and then looked into her eyes, thinking that he would see in them a sure sign of surrender and said, "Sam ain't here, is he? And if you need coffee, you will lighten up your tone and be a little more agreeable."

The sign of surrender never came. He could now see in her eyes that he expected to become intimate with her derringer. She did lighten up her tone, however. The cackling was replaced by what resembled a hissing sound that one would imagine a very angry rattlesnake to make right before its fangs entered one's body, leaving one to die of its poisonous venom.

"Mister, for the third time now, and I'll not ask again, where in the hell is Sam?"

"Rose Mary, dear, I'm sorry, but I could not say for certain. I am sure that he is nearby, though, if you would like to go look for him."

"When I am finished chatting with you, I will. Next question, what brothers are you talking about?" she hissed.

"Angus' brothers."

Her eyes were burning a hole through Bennager because he would not elaborate on his answer. He found that he really was enjoying this conversation. She wanted him to answer questions, and he was able to answer them and keep her inflamed with frustration at the same time.

"All right, Bennager, I savvy this little game that you are playing with me now. Can you tell me about Angus and his brothers?" She spat into the fire. "Please."

"His brothers showed up last night and tried to kick the devil out of him for throwing them overboard yesterday. He got the better of them, though, and ran them off, but one managed to inflict a hard blow to the back of his head. I don't know why he left camp, but he did, and Sam and Zeb went to render aid to him. The fog may blow out, but if not, you will have to be in the foothills of the Sierras if you want to see the sky again, and this is not rain, it's damp fog." Bennager looked into her eyes passionately and said, "And I am definitely not blind."

She rolled her eyes into the back of her head in a way that only a female can do. This was a woman's way of letting a man know that she thought that he was an ass. No one had rolled their eyes at Bennager that way since before he left home. This gesture was made in order to aggravate a man, but since it reminded him of a memory from home, he found it to be pleasing, and he couldn't help laughing at her.

"What in tarnation are you laughing at?" she asked, now reverting to her cackling.

The coffee was boiling over now. Bennager removed the pot from the fire and added cold water to settle the grounds. "Your coffee awaits you, my dear." He poured each of them a cup, fearing that she would burn herself if allowed to do it herself. Certainly, he would have to listen to more of her wrath were that to happen, and also, it made him look like a gentleman.

"Thank you," Rose said, and all was quiet until the first cup was down.

Bennager scowled with curiosity as he watched her drink. "Don't get rankled, but there's something that I've got to know."

"What is it?"

"How do you drink coffee with tobacco in your mouth? I have never seen anybody who could do that before. You don't eat like that, do ya?"

Rose looked straight ahead, pretending to study the fire. "I don't eat like that, but as for the coffee, it is just better when you have one with the other, same way with whisky and brandy. It's not good with sake, though. That makes me sick. Maybe just the sake makes me sick. I don't know. Yesterday, when I was sitting with Girl, it occurred to me that maybe those men make that stuff out of used bathwater. I still feel rummy from drinking that stuff."

Bennager was peering at her. "Do you always fall asleep with that tobacco in your mouth?"

"Not usually. Not that I recall anyway. Why would you ask me that?"

"Because for the last two nights, I have had to fish that stuff out of there."

"No, you did not! That would be disgusting!"

"So is seeing tobacco juice driveling down the side of your face while you are sleeping."

"What are you doing looking at me when I am sleeping any-way?" she asked as though she had been violated.

"Don't get mad at me, Rose. I had call the last two nights to look at your face. The first night I watched over you to make sure that you didn't die from alcohol poisoning, and last night, Sam and I made sure that you were not hurt by the hotheaded Irish brothers. When I woke up, Angus was on the ground, being kicked. Sam and Zeb were not moving at all. My first thought was that they mistook you for Angus and kicked the devil out of you first. But as it was, you are just a sound sleeper. I don't suppose that you could train yourself to sleep with one eye open?"

"Having one eye open is not sleeping. I should thank you for your concern, and I do, Bennager, but I don't think that you have to scrutinize me that thoroughly when I am sleeping, let alone dig chaw out of my face. If I should fall asleep with chaw in my face, you just go ahead and leave it there. That way, I will teach myself a good lesson."

"You will choke, Rose Mary."

"I will wake up and take care of it, Bennager."

"Well, I'm afraid that you won't wake up."

"Enough! What time does this vessel get moving? I had better collect my things and go find Sam. It wouldn't surprise me if he lit out on foot. He is a very impatient man."

Bennager watched Rose bustle around camp as though she was angry, but she must not have been angry with him or else she would have said so, leaving no doubt in his mind about it whatsoever. He supposed that he had embarrassed her with his talk of looking over her while she slept. He rolled up his bed, took the coffee pot, and went to the boat.

Angus had decided that he preferred the company of the little puppies and probably thought that he was causing problems for the rest of the party and feared that they would dislike him on account of what was proving to be an ongoing feud between him and his brothers. The fact that Sam and Zeb had looked him up to inquire about his health seemed to make him feel at ease about the situation, and when Bennager delivered the pot of hot coffee to his freight wagon, where the three men were gathered, he was greeted by three cheerful faces, although one of those faces was quite battered.

Rose was looking in on her new friend who was also more at ease than she had been the day before. Girl was contented with her new life, and the look that she was giving Rose seemed to say, "Thank you for your help yesterday, lady, but you don't need to bother me now. I have everything under control." With two flaps of her tail, she laid her head down and closed her eyes while her babies were having their breakfast.

Angus offered to help Bennager bring the team on the boat. Bennager thought that he would be better off to take it easy for the day, but Angus wouldn't have it, and Bennager wasn't inclined to argue with him. Bennager reckoned that he wanted to show that he could pull his weight, and he was very apologetic about what had happened with his brothers and for waking everybody up. He commented on what a sound sleeper Rose was. He had also been afraid that something had happened to Rose during the brawl and was happy to see her in good health this morning.

"How many siblings do you have, Angus?"

"There are ten, countin' meself."

153

"Are you four the last survivors?"

"Ha!" He laughed heartily. "No, the other six are me sisters. That is why us four ran away. If you think we are bad, you should see them. But they don't just fight amongst themselves, oh no, they boss us all around to the point of insanity. Those six should be allowed to fight in wars, and I, for one, wish that they would go and do that very thing. Me brothers are tryin' to boss me 'bout just like me sisters did back home. If I wanted to put up with that nonsense, I wouldn't have left home to begin with." Angus contemplated his present situation. "What is wrong with just takin' life as it comes? Plans only turn out to be disappointments anyway. Thin's never work out the way ye plan them, so why do people insist on bein' devil bent on plannin'? They can all go to the devil if they don't like the way I live. I don't think they will bother me anymore, Bennager. They wanted to get back at me for throwin' them off the boat, and now we are even. I'm sure they will be goin' their own way now."

"It's really none of my business, they are your brothers after all, but what makes you think you are even? That boy that you smashed into the tree looked like he was hurt pretty bad."

"They know that I've had enough of 'em, and no good will come if they keep botherin' me. Besides, ye might shoot 'em next time," Angus said excitedly.

"Angus, I didn't know who they were. I thought they were bandits or Indians. I would never shoot one of your brothers on purpose. I did recognize him before you told me not to shoot, though. The way Sam and Zeb were just standing there and not knowing what had happened to Rose was very confusing to me. But things have worked out all right, and I agree with you about making plans, especially in this country. You just never know what is going to happen from one moment to the next."

Angus nodded his head in agreement as they brought the team aboard, and in no time at all, the anxious passengers had joined them. Everyone was filled with anticipation for what this new day would bring. They all looked as if they were going to spring into action at any moment, and after a short time, they started to wonder why they weren't going anywhere. Not one of them had thought to go find Charlie to tell him that they were ready, and everyone except for Bennager just assumed that he should know.

This task of finding Charlie always proved to be quite a chore, particularly the first two or three nights after leaving San Francisco. He drank his sake every night until it ran out for fear that somebody someday would want to join him in a drink, which he would have gladly shared, but at the same time, he wanted to make sure that he got more out of that barrel than anybody else. Charlie was quite an athlete when he was drunk. When he drank until he couldn't drink anymore, instead of passing out like most people do, he would take off walking or running and sometimes even climbing trees. Fortunately for the passenger that had to go find him, his athletic feats caused him to get hot, and he would peel one layer of clothes off and then another until he had no clothes on at all. The clothes trail that Charlie left behind was sometimes hard to pick up at first, but once it was found, Charlie would easily be located.

"I think we will have to go find Charlie. Sometimes he makes his camp far enough away that he doesn't hear his passengers moving about in the morning," Bennager said, trying to protect the captain's reputation by embellishing the truth somewhat.

Sam seemed to be busting out at the seams, wanting to get a move on, and Zeb looked like he could track based on the fact that he was older and looked like he was capable of anything, so Bennager asked the two of them to go with him. As they were walking off the boat, Bennager shook Charlie's barrel of sake and determined that they were going to have two more mornings like this on their trip. Charlie was slowing down in his old age. After Bennager told Sam and Zeb what the situation was with Charlie, Zeb started tracking him right from the shoreline. Sam was fuming.

"Bennager, doesn't that man care at all that everyone on his boat is in a hurry? If I was a White man, I would bust his barrel with his head."

"We will find him, Sam. Sometimes when we are on his trail, we find him backtracking and putting on his clothes on his way back."

"I'm not sure he wants me to find him. Someone should teach him a lesson for holdin' us up like this."

"It won't do to teach him a lesson, Sam. He is the only one who knows the river, and once we get to it, you will be glad that he is there. Tomorrow, I will go find him before anyone boards. I completely forgot this morning on account of Rose."

"What do you mean on account of Rose?" Sam asked defensively.

"Oh, it's nothing much, Sam. In between the time that I fell asleep after the brawl and when Rose woke me up, it only seemed like ten minutes. She cackled at me until she got her first cup of coffee in her. I haven't been cackled at since I left home. I can't think straight when she is cackling like that, and she is always mad at me too."

"Oh," Sam said, not knowing what to make of what Bennager had said and choosing not to comment on it.

"There is your steamboat captain!" Zeb exclaimed.

"What did I tell ya, Sam? There he is, dressed and everything." Bennager shouted so Charlie would know that he had told his new friends about his routine.

Sam didn't show any pleasure at finding Charlie at all. When Charlie was spotted, they all three stopped and waited for him to join them. Sam stood with his arms crossed in front of his chest, and the look on his face showed a complete lack of caring or respect for this steamboat captain.

"Howdy, fellas. What are you doin' way out here, lookin' for me?" Charlie asked with his eyes on Sam as he said it. "What's wrong with him?" he asked, still looking at Sam over his shoulder.

Sam wasn't the type of man to look down his nose at a person, but right then, with his arms folded like that and as big as he was, he seemed to be making a larger-than-life statement of displeasure.

"Sam is in a hurry to find gold, Charlie, and we need to get a move on anyway," Bennager said in a calm voice.

Charlie stepped up to Sam, toe to toe, and said, "So you are in a hurry, huh, big fella?"

Sam nodded his head yes, not changing his expression.

"Ya don't talk much, do ya?" Charlie asked.

Sam shook his head no.

"Well," Charlie said to them all. "What are we standing around for? This man is in a hurry."

4

A sense of relief came over the group, even Sam. As badly as Sam wanted to throttle Charlie at that moment, he knew that no good would come of it, not because of what Bennager had said but because he was a Black man in a strange part of the world.

Anticipation came back to the faces of Charlie's passengers when they saw the four men return. Everyone except for Rose and Angus continued as if there had been no delay at all.

Charlie walked out among the passengers and started counting heads to make sure that he wasn't missing anyone. He counted the people, the horses, and the dog. Knowing that the dog was under the wagon with her pups, he stuck his head under it and counted them, then he stood up and asked, "Whose dog is this?"

In the time that it took for Charlie to finish his counting, Sam's patience had worn to threads, very thin threads. He walked over, tapped Charlie on the shoulder, folded his arms, and said, "Mine."

"Well, there are three more heads here today than there were yesterday," Charlie informed.

Sam held his ground without saying anything and shook his head no, which was a sure indication to all the people watching that Charlie wasn't going to get a dime out of Sam for transporting pups, nor was Sam going to put up with anymore of his nonsense.

"Hey, you!" Angus said walking up to Charlie. "What are you, some kind of cheat? The head count is the same today as it was yesterday, you fool. Them pups is takin' me brothers' places. What do ya think of that?" he finished by tapping Charlie on his chest.

"Oh, yes, that's right. That is right," Charlie said as he started his count all over again, this time starting with the pups just to double check himself.

"I think everyone is here. I think everyone was here and ready to go when we went to find you," Sam said to put an end to any further delay.

Bennager had never known Charlie to be much of a fighter, but he had never known him to put up with someone telling him how to do his job before either. He raised Cain, looked into Sam's face and eyes for a moment, and everyone felt sure that he was going to with Sam and his opinions, but whatever he had seen in Sam's face had convinced him to just get the boat moving. Within minutes, they were on their way.

"Ha! That is good." Angus laughed and slapped his legs as he was dancing about in good humor. "That is rich. If I ever see me brothers again, I'll tell 'em that they swam for a good reason, the same reason that I threw 'em off to begin with. Did you hear, that lassie?" He hollered under the wagon. "Ye don't have to pay a travelin' fee for your new family." Angus continued to have a chuckle about that periodically throughout the day. All at once, he would laugh robustly for what seemed like no reason at all, but the party that was led by Girl knew.

Rose Mary seemed to be just as content as Bennager's team was, which surprised Bennager after what he had put up with this morning. He figured that she would find something to peck at throughout the whole entire trip. When Charlie returned and no fight had broken out over his being late, she sprinkled a touch of brandy into the bottom of her cup, added coffee, and was perfectly happy just to stare in the direction of the shore. Bennager reckoned that she was trying to see something through the fog.

It was a typical day for the men, one of those days when there is nothing to do, so they gathered around the wagon and talked. The conversation consisted mostly of nonsense, memories of home, dreams, and the like. Even though there were plenty of people around, it was as though Rose was having a day to herself. No one asked or needed anything of her nor did she of anyone else. It was not their intention to exclude her from their conversation nor was she interested in it. When she was tired of standing in one place, she would walk a bit, visit the horses, and return to watching the invisible shore and sipping brandy.

Bennager found that he was intrigued by her contentment and wondered what was going on in her mind. He had never met a person who could stand and think and watch that long without moving or needing something to do to keep them busy. Long after the rest of them had finished their coffee and found some small menial tasks to do, Rose was still thinking and watching. By midday, Bennager found himself having the desire to visit with her, but he refrained feeling sure that he would break her concentration and the serenity of the day.

The mood of the people coincided with the weather. There was not the slightest bit of breeze on the cold winter day. Someplace in the foothills of the Sierras or beyond, it was probably sixty degrees and sunny. A little later in the day, Zeb mentioned to Bennager that by the same time as the next day, it would be raining, and the fog would be gone.

"How do you figure that, Zeb?" Bennager inquired.

"There's no breeze at all now. It's the calm before the storm. Lots of wind tonight, rain tomorrow, much rain. You see Rose? She wished it."

"She wished for rain? I don't think so. I think she is pretty fed up with water of any kind," Bennager quibbled.

"She wishes for the fog to leave. Fog can only leave if wind and rain push it away. Only a woman can wish hard enough for fog to go away. I bet tomorrow she will wish for sun, and the next day, we will see sun."

"You know, Zeb, it could be that you are setting to much store in a woman that just stands around in one place and thinks. My horses are doing the very same thing. Maybe they wish the fog would go away, and Rose is just standing over there, drinking brandy. I'll tell you what. If Rose Mary Briar doesn't fall down from drunkenness today, then I will be more inclined to believe that she can wish the fog to go away, all right?" Bennager slapped Zeb on the back as a friendly gesture but also to let him know that he was finished listening to his nonsense.

Shortly thereafter, Bennager saw Zeb going to Angus and Sam and telling them what he had told him. Bennager watched their faces out the corner of his eye. Angus' expression was that of awe. From now on, Rose would be his weather goddess. Sam nodded his head in agreement, just as though he had known these things about Rose all along. For one brief moment, Bennager was convinced that Zeb knew more about women than he had previously thought, but he shook that feeling off, figuring that he knew Rose better than Zeb did since at last glance, she had filled her cup up with brandy again, minus the coffee. Finally, Zeb decided that he would break the silence between the men and Rose.

Bennager assumed he was telling her his theories about her abilities to wish weather. Whatever it was that he was telling her made her laugh with jubilation, and Bennager found himself wishing that she would laugh like that with him. *Oh, maybe I should go tell my horses, which are just standing there thinking and watching, to make this wish for me*, he thought sarcastically. He watched as Zeb shared in Rose's jug of spirits, and they continued to talk and laugh at heaven knows what. Perhaps her day alone had put her in better spirits or perhaps it was just the ones that she was drinking. Bennager knew the former feeling of serenity that he had enjoyed was fading fast. His blood began to boil, and he decided that it was best not to watch anymore. He did not understand what was giving him that heart-wrenching feeling that he was experiencing, but he knew that it had something to do with that woman. Every time her face lit up with laughter, he saw the same beautiful young woman that Zeb's dog had seen right off.

Zeb's dog didn't care if she drank or used tobacco and snored all night. But to Bennager, these things about Rose caused conflict between them. Zeb's dog didn't care if she ate like a horse or cursed like a sailor. The dog only saw the good in Rose. As a matter of fact, Sam, Angus, and Zeb seemed to see only the good qualities that Rose possessed as well. "What the devil is wrong with me?" he cursed himself. "Dang, she's pretty when she laughs."

Bennager reckoned that he might be able to figure out what the devil was wrong with him if he laid down and closed his eyes and thought about it for a while, and that is what he did. *Why can't I just accept Rose for who she is? Am I so judgmental of people? What business is it of mine how she chooses to live her life? Running away from home, traveling alone on a ship with a Black man all the way around the Horn, having to kill a man on her way here, and apparently losing quite a few pounds judging from that dress that she was wearing two days ago. What she must have looked like when that dress was new! Had Richard ever seen her smile and laugh the way I just did with Zeb? If he had, he would be looking for her now. Who cares if Zeb makes her laugh and I make her mad? I don't make everybody that I meet mad, just her. Just because one person doesn't like me doesn't mean that it is the end of the world.*

Rose will get to Sacramento City, and I will probably never see her again. Sam will dig for gold. Angus and his pup will walk around the earth, running into his brothers and getting into fights with them or anybody else that wants to. Zeb will probably follow Rose to the end of the earth, and she will let him because he makes her laugh. I reckon if that is how it will be, then there is nothing that I can do except to help them get to Sacramento City. And I will go on about my business of hauling freight. I don't know why I was so concerned about Rose being the only white woman in these parts. Soon there will be plenty of women around. Most miners talk about bringing their families out to California when they have saved enough money, and soon, Rose will be surrounded by women of class that she can associate with.

I shouldn't have to worry about protecting her so much either. For one thing, she doesn't even want my protection, and for another thing, she is now in the company of people who will do that with or without my help. So since I never should have gotten involved in Rose's life to begin with, from now on, I will just stay out of it, and I won't feel bad about making her angry with me because if I'm not conversing with her, there won't be anything for her to get mad about. What a relief, the problem is settled. I figured out what the devil was wrong with me. I care too much about things that do not concern me and that is not any of my business.

Rose will be an acquaintance, a lady that I met on my travels, just like everyone else that I meet. Occasionally, I see these people, often for-

getting their names, and sometimes I never see them again. For a while, I thought that these people were going to be my friends, but more than likely, we will dock in Sacramento City, and I will not see them again. That will be all right. I should not get attached to people that I meet when I am traveling. They have their dreams, and I have my work, and I was a fool for even walking up to Rose Mary Briar two days ago.

Bennager was getting cold just lying down like that. Cold damp days of traveling by boat in the fog have a way of lingering on longer than they should. His bones were telling him to get by a fire.

Tonight, I will eat jerky and dried fruit for supper and sit by the fire and dry out these clothes. I wish I had purchased some slickers on this trip. If Zeb is right, we will all be soaked tomorrow, he thought. *I reckon I will have to set up some canvas to keep us all dry. Tomorrow will be just as foggy as it is today because by the way Rose is starting to stagger about, it would appear as though she is unable to wish the weather as Zeb had told me.*

As Rose approached Sam, she put her hand out in front of her, and when it touched Sam's arm, she stopped. Sam held his arm in a position that enabled Rose to hold herself up with it, and Bennager heard her ask Sam if they had anything to eat. Sam took her brandy from her hand and guided her to a place where she could sit down and not hurt herself, and then he went to the wagon for the box of goods that she had purchased for the trip.

"Rose, it looks like we have jerky, dried fruit, canned beans, bread, and cheese. I've been waitin' for you to want somethin' to eat. I'm hungry too."

"Oh good, some bread and cheese would sure hit the spot right now. You know how I get the shakes when I haven't eaten for a while, Sam?"

"Yeah."

"Well, I think that I'd have them right now if it wasn't for the brandy. Zeb knows of a drink that I have never heard of. He calls it tequila. Have you ever heard of that one, Sam?"

"No."

"Well, Zeb is married to a Mexican lady, and they live in Monterey, and they have very big trees there, and they drink tequila, and he told me to come to his house and have tequila and meet his wife and his children. He was telling me about how women can wish the weather and that he was happy to see me on this trip. Zeb is a very nice man, Sam, and I am going to get to have one of his puppies. He told me that yesterday. Sam, what is he talking about, wishing weather? The weather just is what it is, isn't it, Sam?"

"Yep, I think so, Rose. He told me you wished that you could see land today, and because of that, tonight, the wind will blow this fog out, and tomorrow it will rain, and you will be able to see land," Sam explained.

"Oh." Rose laughed, finishing her bread and cheese and finding a piece of jerky in the box of groceries. "Zeb is quite a joker. I think that he is mostly full of shit, though, Sam," she whispered, not wanting Zeb to overhear and get his feelings hurt. "I haven't figured out what I should and shouldn't believe when that man talks. He doesn't aim to hurt anyone, though, Sam. He sure does like to tell stories."

When Bennager overheard this conversation, he knew that Rose was not a gullible woman, and he found himself happy and relieved to learn that Zeb was married.

"Oh, that food made me feel much better. I hope we can get another good meal when we get to Sacramento City. I sure do like to sit in a restaurant once in a while. Where is Bennager, do you know, Sam?"

"I think he's takin' a nap," Sam said, getting up to put the box of grub away in the wagon.

"When he wakes up, I want to tell the two of you something. When Zeb thought that I was wishing weather, I was really thinking about what kind of business that I wanted to be in."

"Well, what is it?" Sam asked excitedly.

"It's a surprise. I want to wait until Bennager is awake. I get the impression that he thinks that I am going to open up a brothel or a saloon," Rose squeaked with incredulity. "He doesn't think very much of me, Sam. He thinks that I am some kind of a heathen because I like tobacco and I like to drink when there is nothing better to do. I could not have thought up this idea if I hadn't met you, Sam. I told Bennager that you were my associate, and I really want you to be if you get tired of looking for gold. You better remember that, you hear?" she told him in a scolding tone of voice.

"I hear. If your business is goin' to be close to where gold is, then I will always be there to help you out anyway, Rose. I'm not just goin' to leave you out here to fend for yourself while I go minin'."

"You're not?"

"No, mostly, I just want to start a new life. I don't like boats and water and salt air any more than you do. You know how I came to be in this country to begin with. You have no idea what it took for me to get back on a boat. You and I are friends, ain't we, Rose?"

"Oh, yes, Sam. How could we not be? We know everything about each other."

"Well, then, I don't want you to leave me behind either."

"I would never do any such thing. I have ideas for us to make money whether there is any gold out there or not. Of course, if there is no gold, then no one will pay us," she thought out loud. "Oh well, when Bennager wakes up, we will go talk to him and see what he thinks of my idea."

As Bennager laid there, pretending to be asleep, he tried to imagine what Rose Mary might think a good business would be, and he also remembered that he just got finished telling himself to stay out of that woman's life. *As soon as I move one muscle in my body, she and Sam are going to approach me with whatever this idea is, thus requiring me to speak, thus making Rose Mary angry with me again. Lord, help me. What am I supposed to do? I can't lie here like this much longer just to avoid them. I should have been on my feet now as it is because if I don't get up and walk around, I'm going to catch a chill.* Bennager sighed. *It's now or never. I sure can't risk getting sick this time of year, especially for such a petty reason. Be civil. That is all I ask of others, so that is the least that I can be to others.*

With his pep talk concluded, his big nap for the day was over. He yawned and stretched to keep up the charade, took a drink from his canteen, and went about the task of sacking his team.

Evidently, Angus had been waiting for Bennager to wake up too. Angus walked right over and asked him if he could help him with the horses. Of course, Bennager thought that would be all right seeming how there wasn't much else to do. And also, maybe Rose didn't want to reveal her plans in front of Angus, which would postpone his having to talk to her.

"What will you do when you get to Sacramento City, Angus?"

"That would depend on what there is to do. What sort of place is this Sacramento City?" Angus asked.

"At the moment it is pretty much a tent city. They did finally start building shops and saloons, and I did hear that a surveyor was hired to lay out a town site. Are you much of a carpenter, Angus?"

"What I don't know I could learn. I am good with the bricks. Me brothers and I, we laid the bricks back east for two years."

"Well, if you don't want to work the streams, mining, I think being a mason would be a pretty profitable profession. California isn't likely to get any smaller. Imagine walking to a place, building a town, and then walking to another place and building another town. There is likely to be a town wherever two rivers come together or where a stream comes into a river. You might even end up going into business with your brothers when they get sick and tired of picking at rocks."

Angus' eyes had been lit with joy when he had been imagining building towns and going from place to place until Bennager mentioned his brothers. Obviously, that would be a sore subject for years to come, judging by the way his expression turned from delight to despair.

"I don't need me brothers to put the bricks up, that is for certain. I was happy to stay back east. I liked the work. I liked havin' a steady job. I can never get rich, but I can eat every day. Me brothers didn't like the hard work, and when they heard about Sutter's mill, they got the idea that they could come here and bend over, pickin' up rocks, and be rich in one day. I told 'em they were fools. I told 'em that the Indians would have picked 'em rocks up by now if they were worth anythin'. They don't like hardship of any kind. The trip out here was very hard on 'em. I fought 'em many times. Last night was not the first time they ganged up on me in me sleep, Bennager. Many times, I think that I am not of their blood. They are mean and stupid, even me sisters too. They told me back when we were first gettin' on the boat that these men are foolish for purchasing picks and shovels. You see? They think that they can still just walk around, picking up gold. They will not listen to anythin' they are told. They can go to the devil before they work with me again, doin' anythin'."

"Sounds like a hard luck bunch. I would guess that if you started doing masonry right now in Sacramento City, you will be able to build yourself a brick house within five years," Bennager encouraged.

"What's that?" Angus asked, not believing his ears.

"Five years. Your brothers are not the only fools here. Sure, a lot of men come here under the same impression, and when they find out that mining is hard work and you're wet all day long, they turn tail and find jobs. If they have any money left, they will open a shop of some kind. Half of the miners are here for adventure. They are young men with nothing better to do anyway. But the others are here, looking for an easy way to get out of working for a living."

"I don't know about a brick house, Bennager. I will work in Sacramento City if I find a job, and then I will buy a horse. We walked everywhere we went back east. Sometimes I would have to take a rest before I could start work because I was already tired. I never had a horse before."

"In five years, you will have a horse, a carriage, and a brick house. You will eat every day. If more women make it out this way, you will probably be married. If you want to help build towns, then it's my guess that you will earn more gold than one hundred miners would earn."

"What's that?" Angus laughed as if Bennager was telling him tall tales. "I will find a job and eat and I will buy a horse. I cannot imagine walkin' from place to place, but I can imagine ridin' me horse from place to place with me wee little puppy runnin' beside us. Aye." Angus smiled, and now all was quiet. He was imagining his future, so Bennager kept quiet, too, so he wouldn't interrupt his daydreaming.

With the horses all in fine condition and content, Bennager walked over to the railing and stood. Knowing where they were in proximity to land, he thought about what the shore would look like if it wasn't for the fog. Rolling hills, oak trees, and the site of a ranchero now and then is what they would be seeing. Where would all these miners go when they got tired of panning for gold? He wondered if they would go back home or stay and build towns, just as he had told Angus. There was no doubt that the young, adventurous people would stay. He wondered about the future of his business. As the towns grew, would his business grow? Or would he just have more competition? He reckoned that soon, everybody would have more competition. Out the corner of his eye, he saw Rose and Sam coming his way, and since there was no place to go, he prepared himself for the inevitable: the pain in his stomach that he was going to feel when he said the wrong thing, and the hurt look in Rose's face when she became angry with him.

"Bennager, could Sam and I have a talk with you before Charlie docks for the night?" Rose asked.

"Of course, Rose, what is it? Is there a problem?" Bennager asked, knowing that there wasn't but not wanting them to know that he had eavesdropped on their conversation earlier.

Rose smiled. "There is no problem, Bennager. I was just hoping that you could give me some information. What are these miners in the hills eating?"

"Oh, probably salt pork."

She nodded her head and looked as if she was making a mental note. "How do these men travel and how do they get their supplies from place to place? Do they walk or do they have a team like you do?"

Bennager marveled at the fact that Rose had really given her carpetbags full of money some serious thought. "You know, Rose, those are some very good questions. If a man comes to California by the overland route, then he is likely to have a horse or burro, but when they need supplies, they use the animal to pack and then they must walk. As for teams, there are not many like mine. There are quite a few two horse teams, though."

"Well, Bennager," she said taking a bite of her plug tobacco. "I gave it a lot of thought this morning. I thought about your team, things that Sam has taught me about animals, and how much I like steak, and I have formed a rough plan of what I want to do. When I get to Sacramento City, I will purchase some cattle, mares, studs, and jacks. I will take them to a place that is above this damned fog, and that is where I will live. Miners will come to me if they want steak, and people like you will come to me if they want good horses and mules."

Sam and Bennager looked at one another in utter amazement. Neither one of them thought that a pretty little woman like Rose could be ambitious enough to attempt such a feat. Sam had met her on a boat, both runaways, and Sam knew that he wanted a new life, and he was going to start it as a miner, not a boxer and not a slave, and he had been prepared to pretend to be a slave in order to save his hide, but he had never really given any thought to what Rose was going to be doing while he was mining. Bennager, on the other hand, wondered all the time what Rose was going to do with her carpetbags full of money and what business she would get herself into. He really thought that she would end up squandering her fortune away on bad investments or simply build herself a saloon and drink up all the profits.

"Well, one of you say something. You don't think that cattle and horses are a good business? You think that I would go broke? Damn! I'll have to think of something else, but I'm still going to take enough cattle for myself, and I'll be damned if I walk anywhere," Rose exclaimed with disappointment.

"Hold on there a minute, Rose." Bennager laughed with a feeling of admiration in his heart. "I think your idea is a fine one. As a matter of fact, I wish I had thought of it. Although, if I had, it wouldn't have done me any good on account of I don't have the financial resources that you do. You will raise cattle in the foothills of the Sierras and also horses and mules. A few men have started cattle ranches in the Sacramento Valley, but your desire to get out of the fog will put you closer to the miners that will be on the Yuba and Feather Rivers and every stream in between. I would imagine that just as I am hauling freight from San Francisco to the towns around Sacramento City, soon men will be hauling freight from Sacramento City to the foothills. This idea of yours is more insightful than being able to wish weather. Imagine if you owned a butcher shop and the restaurant where your cattle would end up. Imagine if you owned the livery where your horses and mules would end up."

Rose Mary's eyes were lit up with happiness at the enthusiasm that Bennager showed for the idea. "I already have imagined owning those businesses. Sam, what do you think? I would really like to have your help getting started. Everything that you told me about mules is what gave me part of this idea."

Sam had been thinking hard about all of this, and Bennager could tell that he was riding the fence about what to say. "It is a good idea. It will be a lot of work, though. People will try to steal your cattle. You will want a house, restaurant, and livery built. Pens and corrals for the stock. When will I have time to mine?"

Rose looked a little disappointed. Bennager guessed that she thought that Sam would give up being a gold miner to work with her full-time since he had pretty much been following her lead ever since they met.

Charlie stopped at the landing, and this rejuvenated Rose. She forgot about Sam's answer and the matter of their faltering partnership. Everyone was ready for a campfire, and to get dried out and to get started was usually the dreaded chore of setting up camp, hauling in water, wood, and finding fresh meat. These things were work that wasn't appreciated after having to spend a day at work already, but after spending a cold dreary day on a steamboat, everyone was anxious to do a chore. There was always plenty of water, wood, and fresh meat at these camps. Men didn't mind walking as far as they had to in order to obtain wood and meat.

Rose and Sam helped Bennager stake out his team, Angus got the fire going, and in no time at all, Zeb was back with a deer.

"Oh Zeb, remarkable, that will make an amazing meal!" Rose hollered excitedly. "Red meat."

"I know you are a woman who likes red meat. This you also wished today. When there is no woman around for a man to give happiness to, the man will starve. He doesn't care if he eats or not. It gives me happiness to have you eat this red meat that you wished for."

"Zeb, I think it is you who wished for red meat today, and you are full of prunes with all this woman business," Rose finally said to Zeb's face.

"I cannot help it if you bring us good luck on our journey," Zeb teased.

"I don't bring anything on this trip but myself, and that is it. I can't wish weather or wish red meat and make it so," Rose reasoned. "The weather wasn't even on my mind today."

Zeb laughed, knowing that he had rankled her, which had been his full intention from the start. Zeb obviously liked to tease people. That was probably why his wife had stayed home in Monterey.

"I thought ye said that Rose Mary Briar was goin' to change the weather," Angus whispered to Zeb. "She said she didn't even think 'bout it."

Zeb whispered back, "She doesn't want anyone to know about the special powers that women have. I know about women. I know their powers. She has never met a man that knew of women's powers before, so she is denying these powers so the rest of you men won't know her secret."

Angus nodded his head to let Zeb know that he understood. He watched Rose Mary with a look of admiration as she went about her chore of fetching water.

Zeb knew that Bennager had heard what he told Angus, and he gave him a sly wink.

Bennager shook his head at him. Zeb figured that since Rose was finished being teased for the day, then he would just spend the evening teasing Angus. Tomorrow, he would probably think of something else to tease someone about.

Zeb skillfully boned out the deer and threw the back strap in the hot skillet. He also produced the liver from a burlap sack and put it in another pan. The rest of the meat was hung from a tree with a rope to give it time to cool down. The back straps and liver would be enough for the five of them to have a warm snack. Accompanied by beans, coffee, and cocoa, they were sure to all be in a relaxed frame of mind.

Rose was in very good spirits. She passed her brandy, rum, and sake around to those who wanted to imbibe. Sam's uncertainty about her plans didn't seem to be putting a damper on her cheerful mood. Sam was acting a little shy around her not wanting to disappoint her further, but she had not one ounce of animosity toward him or anyone else. While they were waiting for the rest of the meat to cool, Rose asked Bennager if he would take a walk with her. He agreed, figuring that she needed to take a nature walk and she didn't want to go out into the dark by herself. He was half right. She also wanted to get him alone so they could talk more about her future.

"Without Sam's help, Bennager, I will have to hire some men. I hadn't counted on that. I suppose that it will be difficult to find men to work for me. They will all be like Sam. They came here to be miners," Rose said.

"Well, if you are handing out jobs, then you might ask Angus. He has no desire to be a gold miner. You may have to live out of tents until you find lumber and men to get your buildings put up. I'll tell you something else. Sam was right about people trying to steal your cattle. You will have to have some full-time men that you can trust to keep an eye on your animals. I don't reckon that you will be the one cutting or cooking those steaks either," Bennager said jokingly.

Rose laughed. "By golly, I hope not. Sam is right. It will be a lot of work, too much even for two people. Do you really think Angus would work with me?"

"Oh yes, Zeb has convinced him that you are a weather goddess. Angus would follow you anywhere." Bennager laughed.

Rose touched his arm, and he stopped walking. "What about you, Bennager?"

"I know that you are not a weather goddess."

"I mean, is there any way that I could enlist you to join this venture? You said that if you had the resources that it would be something that you would do yourself."

"You want me to give up my business to come to work for you?"

"Not for me, Bennager. You and I both know no man alive will work for a woman, and that is the biggest problem facing me. I'm sure you like your business. I'm not asking you to give it up, just to relocate it. You said yourself that there would be freight wagons running in those foothills of yours. I trust you, Bennager, and you do seem to be a sensible businessman. What if you had more than one team and wagon? What if you had a company of freight haulers? We could work this thing together and end up having a profitable relationship."

"What about your associate, Sam?"

"Sam will always have a home and a place in my part of the business if he wants it. I made him that promise, and I won't go back on it now. I really hope that he finds a lot of gold and then comes to work. I planned this, thinking that he would be with me."

"And when he wasn't, you thought of me?"

"No, Bennager, I planned this hoping that you would join us."

This statement made Bennager's heart leap into his throat. A wonderful opportunity had found him, and he was afraid to accept it. He was speechless. He wondered how many times they would squabble if he accepted this wonderful offer. Would their quarrels ruin their partnership? He gently put his hands on her shoulders as he faced her. "Rose Mary Briar, this is a really good offer, and I appreciate you asking me, but you and I don't seem to get along very well, and I would hate for either one of us to get hurt in this deal." The idea that she might shoot him never left his mind.

"What in tarnation do you mean we don't get along? You are always honest with me, and that's why I trust you." Rose said, smiling.

"Well, then, why do you always get angry with me?" Bennager asked, wanting to kiss that smile of hers at that moment.

"The truth hurts, of course, why else?" Rose whispered, putting her arms around his waist.

The only other place Bennager's heart could go now was out of his mouth and on to the ground. A slap in the face right now would not be felt. He moved his hands slowly from her shoulders to her neck and face and leaned in toward her, waiting for her to pull back. He felt no resistance and lightly kissed her on the cheek, and as he reached with his lips for her other cheek, she caught his mouth with hers, and he a felt passion rise between them that could never be equaled by any other experience. He pulled back and waited to be slapped, but there was no violence. The smile that she had donned all evening had grown bigger, and the sparkle in her eyes was enchanting. Seeing her like this struck him in the same way as the sight of her sleeping did, minus the tobacco drivel. When she wasn't cursing like a sailor, these moments reminded him that she was somebody's little girl at one time.

Still smiling, Rose suggested, "Bennager, perhaps you should take some time and think about this offer. I wouldn't want a kiss to sway your decision."

"Why exactly did you kiss me, Rose Mary?"

A breeze from the south had come up while they had been talking, and it was only now that Bennager had noticed it. "I thought that you wanted me to, for one reason," Rose answered.

"Well, what is the other reason?" Bennager asked.

Rose blushed. "I have never kissed a man before, and I wanted to know what it was like."

Bennager held his breath. It was foolish of him to ask, but as was usually the case with Rose Mary, he just couldn't help himself. "I cannot believe—I mean, it doesn't appear…well, that was such a nice kiss for a first-timer."

"Really?" She blushed some more but continued to smile. "You really thought it was nice? Are you teasing me?"

"Oh no, I don't tease, lie, or exaggerate. I have always told you what I think about things. What did you think of it?"

"Yeah, like you said, it was nice." Rose took her plug tobacco out, bit off a piece, and put it back in her coat pocket. "This feels like a warm breeze. Is it warming up or am I imagining things?"

"Well, I certainly think that it is warming up," Bennager said, but he wasn't really speaking of the weather. *This female has just made my heart and head race with excitement, and she said, 'Yeah, the kiss was nice!' Unbelievable*, Bennager thought. "I guess we had better get back to camp. This is Zeb's storm he was talking about."

They started walking back. "Will you think about relocation, Bennager?" Rose asked with determination.

"Will there be any more kissing involved?" Bennager asked in an intimidating tone of voice.

"Not if it's bad business practice. Not if you don't want there to be kissing, there doesn't have to be any of that. I'm sorry now that it has happened, Bennager. It was wrong."

"It wasn't wrong. Don't be sorry for it, Rose Mary. Dang! Why did you have to say that?" Bennager was exasperated.

"Well, I'm sorry. You can't be doing business and things like that at the same time. I promise I won't do that anymore. It is just that I saw the chance to try something new and took it because I don't figure that I will get the chance again. I haven't been around much, you know. I hope that you can forgive my bad behavior," Rose apologized.

"There isn't anything to forgive, Rose Mary. I guess we shouldn't make a habit of it anyway. Birthdays and holidays would be acceptable. And weddings, of course. You don't have to worry about never getting the chance, I'm sure you will be kissed again," Bennager assured her.

"Weddings. I thought you said there weren't any women in these parts," Rose argued.

"You are here. Surely you will kiss your husband when you wed," Bennager teased.

"Me wed! When pigs fly! I came here to be a businesswoman, not a wife. Who the devil would marry me anyway?" Rose exclaimed.

Bennager put his hand on the small of her back as they walked along in the dark to help guide her. "Rose Mary Briar, you are truly uncommon."

"When we get back to camp, I am going to put rum in my cocoa. I've been thinking about it, and I think that would be good. Will you try some with me?"

"You know that I don't drink much, Rose Mary. I should really get some canvas set up on the boat so we can stay out of the rain tomorrow. I believe that Zeb has lived in this country long enough to predict the weather. If it rains like he says it will, we will be in for a longer day than this day was."

"Maybe if Sam and I help you, then you will have time to try my drink," Rose reasoned.

"Brandy and cocoa sounds good. I reckon one wouldn't kill me," Bennager compromised. He figured if he helped her drink up her supply, she would be less likely to turn up in an unpleasant situation. No one else minded having a drink with her so he might just as well too, he reckoned.

"Let me explain something to you, Bennager," Rose said seriously. "I believe brandy is too strong of a flavor to be putting into cocoa whereas rum won't take the taste of cocoa out of the drink. But if you like the taste of brandy more than the taste of cocoa, then you will probably like it."

They were back at the camp now. Sam still wasn't making eye contact with Rose, but that didn't stop her from sitting right by him. Bennager saw her whisper something in Sam's ear. The look on his face was one of confusion, and his blank stare was aimed right into the depths of Bennager's soul. When he finally investigated Rose's face, that same smile of delight that Bennager had witnessed on their walk reappeared, and he realized that she had told Sam about their kiss. Bennager was so embarrassed and frightened of what Sam would say or do that he became paralyzed. Bennager didn't know if he should leave quietly with a sense of purpose, sit tight, and see what would happen next or engage in a conversation with Zeb or Angus.

Sam could see that Rose was pleased about what had happened on her excursion with Bennager, so he didn't do or say anything to Bennager that would ruin her happy moment, but when he looked at Bennager, the look of doubt was obvious.

"Hey, Sam, let's go help Bennager set up shelter for the rain that's coming," Rose suggested.

"I will help Bennager. You should rest here by the fire," Sam replied.

Bennager hoped that Rose's determination to show her independence would prevail. There was no telling what would happen to him if Sam were to get him alone.

"No, we made a deal. He's going to have a drink with me if I help him, and if you come, too, our supper won't be cold when we are finished. Besides, it's warming up, and I didn't do anything all day. Why would I need to stay by the fire and rest, Sam?" Rose reasoned in her childlike way.

This made Bennager smile. The child in her was going to run them all ragged because a child's dreams are always grander than an adult's is. Adults usually cling to and adapt to their limitations. The fact that she was a woman was why they were all going to allow themselves to be worked to the bone. The wind had really picked up, making the canvas difficult to work with, so they agreed to wait until it looked like it would rain, figuring that the wind would die down once the rain started. Charlie wasn't happy about the thought of listening to the flapping canvas all night, so he suggested that they wait. He wasn't going to notice anything in a couple of hours anyway, but Bennager didn't fancy losing his canvas in a windstorm, so his suggestion seemed sensible enough to agree to.

Sam didn't waste any time in letting Bennager know how he felt about the walk that he had taken with Rose. When they had all agreed to wait until tomorrow to build the shelters, he turned to Bennager. "We have somethin' that needs to be talked about. What do you think you're doin' out there in the dark with Rose? First, you were worried about her gettin' hurt out here, and now you have her alone, takin' advantage of the fact that she is just a girl. What kind of man are you, Bennager? Because I don't think you're really the kind of man you want people to think you are," Sam scolded.

Sam's wrath had cut Bennager deep, and even though he thought that he was falling in love with Rose, he knew that Sam was right.

"Sam, don't talk that way to Bennager. I kissed him. He didn't do anything to hurt me or take advantage of me. And I will have you know that I am not a girl! I am a woman, Sam, and I believe I will kiss whoever will let me! Bennager is a good man. I trust him, and I know you do too."

"Rose Mary, Sam is right. You are a young woman who is too young to know what love is, and no man, including myself, should take advantage of that. I'm sorry if I've let you down, Sam," Bennager apologized.

Sam's face softened at Bennager's apology. Rose spat out her wad of tobacco right on the deck. "What the devil are you sorry to him for if you supposedly wronged me? Let me tell the two of you something. I am old enough to be kissed, and since that is all that happened, then I don't see any reason for anybody to be rankled about it. My very own father was trying to marry me off last year. Now that is taking advantage of somebody, don't you think? Now I am a firm believer that men shouldn't meddle in my life, and that includes the two of you, so let's just drop this subject. I smell that venison, and my stomach is telling me to get back to camp." And off she went.

Sam just stood there, rubbing his eyes as though he had a pounding headache. Bennager knew that's what it was because he had one as well. "She is right," Sam finally said, shaking his head. "I ain't her daddy, and her daddy ain't here. Maybe the men around here should worry more about themselves than about protectin' her." Sam ended the statement with a long sigh.

"When her mind catches up with the rest of her, she is going to be something to behold, Sam. To be honest with you, I hope she will kiss me again when that day comes."

"I thought you didn't like Rose and her ways," Sam queried.

"That was my fault. When I first laid eyes on her, I liked her, but like you said, it was her ways that I didn't like. That was only because I wanted her to be something that she wasn't. Once I figured out to accept her for who she was, I found out that I liked her even more. She has asked me to relocate my freight route and join the two of you in your venture. What do you think?"

"I think it's goin' to take more than just us to get everything that she wants done. That's what I think," Sam said, shaking his head and knowing that he was too old for a young person's dreams.

"She has plans for that, but we should talk about it later," Bennager said.

When Sam and Bennager made it back to camp, Rose was already enjoying the meal that Zeb had prepared. "She has a real knack for knowing when supper is ready, doesn't she, Sam?" Bennager said, laughing. Sam laughed, too, and when they had settled around the fire, Rose got up and fixed Bennager his drink.

"Here is your cocoa and brandy," Rose said in a whisper as if she didn't want anybody to hear, even though they had all watched her make it.

"What's that, cocoa and brandy? I've never heard of that one," Angus cried.

Rose shot him a dirty look and spoke. "Don't make fun, Angus!"

Zeb moved in close to Angus and said, "There, you see, Angus? I bet that isn't cocoa and brandy at all but some concoction that will make Rasmussen dream about her tonight when he is sleeping. Tomorrow, he will be in love with her. Let this be a lesson: never let a woman fix you a meal or a drink. Women have powerful knowledge of concoctions that can make a man do anything that they want them to."

"Ye mean like a witch or somethin'?" Angus was intrigued.

"Oh no," Zeb whispered. "A witch is much worse. They can bring harm and turn men into creatures. Women, on the other hand, are just women. Rose is no different from any other woman. They cannot help being born with these powers."

"What in tarnation are you whispering about, Zeb?" Rose shouted at him. "You are telling Angus a whole mess of lies again, ain't you? Angus, whatever he is saying, especially if it is about me, you should ignore it because he is teasing you."

"I bet she gives you something while you are sleeping tonight that will make you forget everything that I have been trying to teach you," Zeb kept whispering.

"Hey, weatherman, what time do you think it will start raining tomorrow?" Bennager asked Zeb so that Angus could have a moment of peace.

"Whatever time Rose wishes it," Zeb said stubbornly.

"Darn it, Zeb, that is enough! How about if I wish for a beautiful spring day, all the flowers in bloom, and all the birds singing to the tune of a seventy-degree day? What kind of idiot would wish for rain when it is already wet?" Rose shouted.

"If you wish it, Rose, then it will happen," Zeb said, not knowing when to quit.

"Oh yeah? Well, if it happens tomorrow, then I will get drunk and take off all of my clothes," Rose replied in a doubtful tone.

This statement certainly got the full attention of all of them. Even Sam couldn't believe Rose would say something like that in front of all the men, and he blushed with embarrassment. Angus had part of his supper get caught in his throat, and Zeb had to beat him on his back to get him back in working order, and Rose pretended not to notice what the reaction to her statement had been. This was the most delightful suppertime banter that Bennager had ever witnessed, and he couldn't help laughing. It was apparent that Rose was going to call Zeb on all his storytelling from now on, and Bennager figured that this was going to cause Zeb to think up bigger and better ways to annoy her daily.

"With talk like that, Miss Rose, you will have us all dreaming of you tonight. Your tongue is as toxic as your concoctions," Zeb charmingly replied.

Sam cleaned up his plate and filled his cup with sake and took a walk. Bennager was under the impression that he didn't like how the conversation was panning out and had enough of Zeb's teasing. Zeb was going to find out one of these days that Sam wasn't one to be teased at all.

After a couple of cocoa drinks, Rose offered Angus a job. Of course, Angus had never realized that she and Sam had been toting more around in those carpetbags than liquor and laundry, so with the offer came the explanation going all the way back to when Rose left home and why. Angus was more than willing to accept the offer. She told him that she would buy his horse for him since she intended to buy one for herself and Sam and that they might just as well stick together at least until the pups were weaned and the deal was made.

It seemed as though Zeb was more inclined to be a miner but offered to help pick out stock and help drive them to the unknown destination. He also made it very clear that he expected his wife to be missing him, and he didn't expect to be on his journey for very long. As it turned out, Zeb had ended up in California on a surveying expedition some fifteen years earlier. In two days', time he had fallen in love with his wife and with California. He told his captain that he wanted to stay and that he intended to marry. His Mexican neighbors and future in-laws had welcomed him with open arms.

As the evening wore on, more stories of the people in the party were exchanged, except those of Sam since he hadn't come back. Zeb's teasing had subsided. Bennager suspected that his teasing was a front that he put up to keep folks from really getting to know him. He also figured that his mockery was due to missing his family, even though he had proven to be quite an adventurer during his days of surveying for the United States government. He told them of the Rocky Mountain Rendezvous when the fur trappers and the Indians came together every year to trade furs, supplies, liquor, women, and anything else that they could think of until they were all broke and had to go back into the wilderness and get back to trapping beavers for the hat makers of New York and Europe.

The warm breeze that had touched Rose and Bennager earlier had now evolved into a windstorm. The branches of the big oaks that they had camped by were starting to sing a song about how old they were and how hot the autumn had been and how long it had been since they had a really good drink of water. Bennager noticed then that Zeb had put his bedroll out in the open where the branches would not hit him if they fell. As the oaks continued their long ballad, they all began to shift their bedrolls around. Bennager's team also understood what the oaks were trying to convey, and the horses were thankful when he and Angus came around to move them out of harm's way. They settled in again by the fire, but the campfire conversation had subsided. None of them were willing to shout at each other over the roaring and whistling of the wind, so they talked to the person beside them, moving around the fire, continuously trying to stay warm and trying not to get smoke in their eyes. The only good thing about this wind was that their coats had finally dried out. The wind had been warm enough that they were able to take them off and hang them on branches for a while.

Sam finally returned to camp, and he wasn't alone. Bennager knew now why Sam had been somber when he left earlier with his cup of sake. It wasn't Rose's kiss that had been under his skin. It was the fact that Charlie had stood his passengers up this morning, and it had still been bothering him, so he had somehow convinced Charlie to join their camp. He was also carrying a big crate in his arms, and Girl was running beside him with her head up, looking at the crate as if she was trying to see inside it. He set the crate down in the vicinity of Zeb's bedroll, and Girl looked in the crate, sniffed, and jumped in a sniffed some more. This, of course, caused a plentiful amount of whimpering that was barely heard above the noise of the wind.

This caught Rose and Angus' attention, and they were quite tickled by the way Girl sniffed and nuzzled and cleaned each pup before she would lie down with them. Girl appeared to be displeased with this sudden relocation, and it was evident that she didn't need Rose and Angus tormenting her any further.

"Zeb, I hope you don't mind, but I didn't think it would be good for them to stay on the boat by themselves with the way the waves are startin' to pitch it," Sam told him.

"That was a good idea. Girl doesn't like that boat much anyway, and we can't have her milk going sour. I see you brought our captain with you. I guess you don't plan on being delayed tomorrow," Zeb said.

"Nope, I can watch him tonight and sleep tomorrow if I have to. I think if a man is goin' to drink, then he should be able to hold his liquor. We shouldn't have to go find him every mornin'."

"Everybody has their bad habits, I guess," Zeb replied.

As for Charlie, he didn't seem to care one way or the other where he did his drinking, and he was plenty content being away from the white capping bay and staying warm by the fire. Rose and Angus held his attention for quite a while. He was studying on how they were still fussing around with that dog. The more he looked, the more he scratched his head. Bennager walked over by Charlie and stood to make sure that he would feel welcome at their camp since Bennager was the only one that he really knew.

"Say, Benny, you see that little fella over there with that dog? There's something funny about that guy. I haven't been able to put my finger on what it is yet, but I know there is somethin' strange about him," Charlie declared.

Bennager asked, "You mean besides the way he carries on over the dog?"

"Yeah, the big one is strange, too, but not in the same way. I reckon I'll figure it out sometime."

Bennager chuckled and replied. "I bet you figure it out as soon as that barrel of rice wine is empty and you start seeing things more clearly."

"Yeah, but by that time, I'll be too busy watchin' the river to worry about that guy. This warm wind is goin' to make a devil of a mess out of the Sacramento. I'm not too drunk that I don't reckon that," Charlie grumbled.

"It's likely to bring rain, too, I expect."

"Oh hell's bells, we'll make it," Charlie said as he went to his bedroll. "We always do. We ain't on no picnic, last I checked anyway."

As Charlie was acting as though he was going to turn in, Bennager decided that he might as well do the same. He noticed that Sam wasn't quite confident in Charlie's actions because he continued to stand by the fire with his arms folded, watching Charlie, just as he had done this morning when they had found Charlie on his clothes trail. Bennager reckoned that Sam had a pretty good work ethic.

When Bennager laid down, his thoughts and his eyes were trained on Rose. He was pleased that so far this evening, the consumption of spirits hadn't affected her enough to make her unreasonable, and he figured that if he made quick work out of falling asleep, then he wouldn't have to see the event when it occurred. He also reckoned that if he was quick, then Rose's snoring wouldn't keep him awake. Even with the wind howling the way it was, he was sure that it could be a likely possibility. After lying there for what seemed like an hour, he realized that little Rose Mary Briar had more than one way to keep a man awake. Between her business plans and the kiss earlier that evening, his mind was racing.

From Sacramento City to the foothills, this would be the trip where he would find out more about the foothills. The last time he was in the Sacramento Valley, he had noticed that things were starting to grow. The people there had already been farming and ranching for a few years now. It could be that they had already taken up the business that he wanted for himself. He told himself that by this time next week, he would know where he stood and there wouldn't be any sense in losing sleep over it tonight.

Soon, the thought of kissing Rose earlier started to plague his senses. Thinking about what the kiss had meant to him and how it had meant no more to her than just something new to try really rankled him. But he told himself that she was more of girl still than she was a woman. A girl in spirit with a woman's appearance could get a girl in to trouble if she didn't keep her wits about her. He reasoned with himself that he didn't have to be the one in charge of worrying about her all the time and started to shut his mind down by listening to the oak trees.

5

The crashing of a branch at the break of dawn was the first thing that Bennager heard. It had been a surprisingly peaceful night, even though the wind had howled the whole night through. Bennager surveyed his surroundings and noticed that more than just one branch had fallen overnight. Sam had kept the fire built up with at least a couple of them, and there were still quite a few lying around. Bennager's team hadn't run off, and he was able to determine with a quick glance that Charlie hadn't either. He tipped his hat to Sam on his way to check the horses and he shook his head.

Thankfully, these horses didn't get excited about much. They didn't care for wind any more than the rest of them did, but they didn't get skittish about it either, like a lot of other horses did. Bennager talked to each one of them and went back to camp to see if Sam had any coffee. He hadn't noticed when he left. He did notice though that the fog had cleared out and some high, thin clouds had moved in. He could see the bay from camp, but steam was coming from the water, so today was probably going to be as gloomy as the other two had been but in a different way. Bennager hated when the bay rolled and rocked the boat.

Sam saw Bennager coming back and poured a cup of coffee for him. Bennager sat with him on a branch that he had brought over during the night and surveyed their slumbering companions. He hoped that Rose would be the next one to wake up so that no one else would know about her loud snoring.

"You managed to sleep pretty well last night, Bennager. You must have been pretty tired," Sam commented.

"Yeah, two rough nights and a little cocoa does wonders. I guess there wasn't any trouble last night after I fell asleep."

"Rose and Angus stayed up with me for a while. I think they were tryin' to stay up all night. They said it would be better to sleep during the day on the boat anyway since there wasn't anythin' to do. So when we get ready to go, I guess we will just have to wake them up."

"How did you get Charlie away from that barrel of sake?"

"We had a talk, I talked, and he listened. I knew I was takin' a chance by tellin' him his business, and I didn't want him puttin' the law on my trail when we get to this Sacramento City, so I asked him if we could make a deal somehow about all this runnin' around at night business, and do you know what?"

"What?" Bennager asked.

"He told me that he would like to be able to quit all that runnin' around. He told me that every time he wakes up out in a tree or in the wide open that he is embarrassed as the devil. He said that he has seen tracks before of Indians, probably, who have walked up to him where he was passed out with no clothes on. And do you know what else?"

"What?" Bennager asked again.

"Well, you know how you said that it's hard sometimes to pick up his trail of clothes when you take off to go find him?"

"Yeah."

"He has the same trouble from his side of the trail."

"Well, I'll be danged. I never thought of that. I've never had to go all the way to his end of the trail," Bennager said.

"So he asked me if I would be willin' to just watch over him on this trip because he said it would be nice for a change to just rest up and have a cup of coffee in the mornin' instead of wastin' the dawn away, tryin' to chase up his clothes. I said I would, and I also told him that his barrel would last longer this way, and I told him to come to camp with us, and he did." Sam shrugged his shoulders and shook his head at the end of his account.

"Well, I'll be! I've known Charlie for quite a while now, and he's never let on to me that he was embarrassed. He always came back chuckling and sort of shaking his head about it. I never needled him about it much. I was usually just so happy that the Indians and bandits hadn't gotten him that I didn't talk to him about changing his habits." Bennager shook his head about this new information regarding his friend and sighed, thinking to himself that he was part of the reason why they could have lost Charlie to Indians or bandits many times. "I ought to kick the devil out of him for telling me to bring him that stuff. It's on account of me that he gets that way."

Sam shook his head. "No, he made the deal. It's not your fault that he doesn't control himself. A barrel like that would last you or me a month or better. Besides, maybe it never bothered him before and that is why he never brought it up before."

"Well, if I relocate my business as Rose suggested, I won't be bringing Charlie anymore barrels anyway," Bennager said.

Charlie and Zeb were starting to stir around in their bedrolls now. Sam and Bennager started scratching up some fried biscuits and bacon. By the time Charlie and Zeb came back from their morning walk, the brighter sky that neither of them had witnessed for a while had warmed the faces of Rose and Angus enough to even get them to wake up. Bennager was sure, too, that the smell of the bacon helped. He knew that Rose wasn't going to miss a meal, no matter how late she had stayed up the night before.

"What in tarnation? Is that damned wind still blowing? For heaven's sake!" Rose grumbled as she got up and staggered around.

As she took her morning hike, Bennager commented to Sam, "She isn't much for greeting a new day with a smile, is she?"

Sam chuckled. "I never noticed that about her before when we were on the ship. I guess it's because we never had to get up and go somewhere. I don't know, she is probably still half asleep."

Angus' battered face had changed colors overnight, but none of the men mentioned it.

Rose came back and sat by Sam where Bennager had been earlier and quietly sipped her hot coffee. With each sip, Bennager noticed that she was becoming more alert and was starting to comprehend her surroundings.

Angus walked up with his empty cup in hand and a tin plate and knelt by the fire to fill both utensils. "Ah, this grub looks good this mornin'. Me and me gut are thankful to ye fellas on this bright mornin'."

Rose looked at him with a scowl on her face because he was cheerful and she wasn't, but when her eyes met with his face, her expression quickly changed to astonishment. "Good Lord! Angus you look downright awful this morning. I didn't realize those brothers of yours had done that much damage. Sam, isn't there anything we can do for him?" Rose had managed to make Angus feel self-conscious about his appearance, and they all saw it except for Rose. She would have never done anything on purpose to hurt his feelings, and she would never believe that she had, even if Angus had told her right out. But the men knew that she had, and they also knew that she would help him if she could.

They hadn't eaten all the venison the night before, so Sam cut a thick slab of it and handed it to Angus. "Here, lay that up on your bruises, and it will help. We should have done this last night, but the meat wasn't cool enough. This is what I heard other fighters did after a match. I don't know if it will help, but I don't think there is much else we can do."

"Thank ye much, Sam. At least it will cover me ugly face."

Sam gave Rose a scornful look for hurting Angus' feelings. She noticed the look, but she didn't know what it was for and she didn't ask.

"I got it!" Charlie exclaimed. "I got it. I finally figured out what it is about you that isn't right," he joyously yelled and pointed at Rose. "You ain't no fella, you're a damned girl!"

Rose gave him her mama badger look, half of her lip curled up with some of her tobacco-stained teeth showing, one eyebrow up at an arch, and the other one creased and flat with her nose wrinkled. She got up to face her accuser, tossing what was left in her cup into the fire with a sharp, assertive flick of the wrist. Bennager noticed that like him, Zeb and Sam were trying not to laugh.

"What in tarnation are you calling me?" Rose snarled. "Damn girl, is it? You got something against girls, do ya? If you hadn't been so concerned about collecting money and counting heads, you would have realized that I was a girl two days ago like everybody else did, you jackass. Now if you got something against girls being on your steamboat, say so, and we'll settle it right now."

"Hey, I ain't got nothin' again' girls, just ain't seen one in a while. Besides that, Benny told me that you was a gent by the name of Pete here the other day. What do ya say about that, girly?" Charlie said, trying to defend himself.

"I say I'll call myself what I like whenever I feel like it, but if you call me 'girly' one more time, I'll kick the tarnation out of you."

"Hey, no need to be so vicious, Pete. I didn't mean no offense. It's just that I noticed over these last couple of days that you seemed to be awful feminine in your ways, and believe me, I'm real happy to know that you're a real lady instead of some strange-acting man."

Rose chomped off a bite of her plug tobacco and put it back in her pocket. "So you're saying that it's just my feminine ways that you're contrary to, not me?" she asked, being argumentative.

This tobacco business now had thrown Charlie for a loop, not to mention the fact that this person had threatened to kick the devil out of him. He was confused and speechless at this point. He knew now that he was dealing with a woman, and he was remembering that he could never win an argument with a woman, especially when they were the only ones arguing to begin with, so he realized that the easiest way to get out of it was to give up. "I give up!" he shouted. "Be whoever you want to be. I'll not say another word to you or about you if you quit lookin' at me and go away!"

"So you don't like my looks now? A person can't help the way they look, you know!"

"No, I don't mean it that way. It's the way that you're lookin' at me. You're just bein' mean and contrary now, and I won't take any more of it! What the devil kind of gal are you anyway? Chewin' tobacco, drinkin', and threatenin' folks? You must be half Indian and half wolf or somethin'. I never ran across a gal as wild-eyed as you before in all my days. Someone ought to throw you down and whop your tail!"

When this mess had started, the spectators were laughing under their breath because they reckoned it would all end in good fun and because Charlie wasn't at all a prejudiced type of fellow, and really, he was fairly easy to get along with. Rose's eccentric behavior had provoked Charlie into saying far too many insults at one time to Rose, even if he had come within a frog's hair of hitting the nail right on the head. And even though he had pegged her for a wild-eyed girl, he was the last one to expect that she might be tempestuous enough to kill a man in cold blood. Sam and Bennager knew her a little better. When the phrase "half Indian, half wolf" slipped out of Charlie's face, Sam and Bennager started to make their move.

Rose had her derringer pointed at Charlie before Sam could grab her arm and before Bennager could step in between the woman and her accuser, which Bennager later confessed was the most ignorant move that he had ever made in his life so far. It was only by the grace of God that Sam got to Rose when he did because by now, she was so tempered up that Bennager believed that she would have shot him just to get to Charlie. Sam got a hold of her waist and, with his other hand free, was able to throw her shooting hand toward the sky, and he just hauled her away until they were out of range so that no one would get hurt.

Zeb was the only one who hadn't stopped laughing during the whole fiasco. Angus' expression was quizzical, and Girl hadn't even stood up. Girl was lying on her side but had turned her head to rest her chin on the side of the crate so she could watch what was happening. When the clamor was over, Zeb looked down at her. She looked up at him without lifting her head, and with a look of laughter in her eyes, she flapped her tail twice. If Zeb was happy, then there wasn't anything for her to worry about.

Charlie was simply stunned. "What the hell just happened here, Benny? I don't even know how it all started. Suddenly, that wild-eyed gal was pointin' a pistol at me!" he exclaimed, still confounded.

Zeb and Bennager said it at the same time, "That's what started it!"

"What?" Charlie asked.

"All that blasted name-callin' is what started it! First it was 'damn girl' then 'wild-eyed girl.' You wouldn't call your mother or sister names like that, would ya?" Bennager asked.

"Well, guess what, Benny? That girl ain't no relation to me, and I'll be thankin' the good Lord for the rest of my days for that!" With that, Charlie hastily gathered his trappings and headed for the boat.

Bennager gave a holler to Sam and Rose's benefit that it was time to go, and the rest of them started packing up. Each one of them, still by the fire, grabbed their things and a pair of horses. Sam and Rose returned. Sam took the crate of pups, which again vexed Girl, but she was good-natured enough to not let it show too much. Rose took the carpetbags.

Within ten or fifteen minutes, all the passengers were aboard. With any luck, they would come to the Sacramento River by tonight or tomorrow. The passengers would soon be in awe of the valleys and the snowcapped Sierras for the first time.

Bennager noticed as they finally got settled that Rose looked a little gloomy. He didn't know if it was for lack of sleep or if it was on account of not getting to shoot Charlie. He thought it might be best to leave her be for now, not knowing for sure, so he sacked his team and walked a bit trying to loosen his bones and muscles. Charlie was in a poor mood still when Bennager stopped to talk with him, and he tried to apologize for Rose a little, and he did apologize to him for telling him that Rose was a man. After all, it was that lie that had started the whole mess anyway. Bennager told him why he did it, and Charlie seemed to understand his way of thinking but informed Bennager that the scheme would never work and that Rose was too cantankerous to let it work anyway.

Angus came by just about then, and overhearing the conversation, he interjected, "Ye know, Rose is a gem compared to me sisters back home. If they would have had guns, there wouldn't be anyone left in Ireland. I think maybe the poor lady is just tired, and maybe she regrets leavin' her home. She has had quite a journey for such a young lassie. I believe she is good inside."

"Good people don't kill other good people in cold blood," Charlie said flatly.

"Well, she is still better than me sisters," Angus said, turning away and shrugging his shoulders.

As Bennager watched Angus walk away, he saw Rose and Sam heading toward them. "Brace up, Charlie. Here she comes," Bennager warned.

"Excuse me, Bennager, Charlie," Rose said, and then she looked at her feet, reminding Bennager of a shy little girl. "Charlie, I'm very sorry for my behavior earlier. Sam explained to me that you weren't making fun of me for being a girl. You see, I thought you were, and I also didn't want anyone thinking that they could call me names and get away with it, and I also didn't know that it was against the law to shoot an unarmed man, even if he is calling you names."

Charlie shot Bennager a look of perplexity, and Bennager figured they were both wondering if this was an apology or if she was just going to shoot him later, sometime when he was armed. Sam gave Rose a little nudge, and she pressed on. "Anyway, I do feel very bad for letting myself get so tempered up at you, Charlie." Then she looked up at him finally. "And I hope you can forgive me and I hope I can make it up to you sometime. I don't want to have any enemies here while I'm trying to start a new life, but I wouldn't blame you if you turned me into the law either. All I ask is that you don't involve my business associate."

Bennager watched Charlie's face and knew that as mad as Charlie had been earlier, he wouldn't be able to turn down Rose's apology. She had appeared so innocent and misunderstood that no good man would keep holding a grudge against her for very long. After all, she didn't know that shooting unarmed men was against the law. Bennager laughed to himself. Charlie sighed and looked at the bay.

"Well, I ain't much for turnin' folks into the law, and there ain't much law around these parts anyway. Benny told me that I said some things I ought not of, so I'm willin' to forget about it if you are, but I'll be keepin' my distance if that's all right with you."

Sam nudged Rose again. "Hey!" Rose yipped and looked up at Sam. "What?"

"Tell Charlie that we want to have his company at camp," Sam said, crossing his arms in front of his chest and giving Rose a scornful look.

Rose wrinkled her face up at Sam. "Well, he just heard you say it."

Sam looked at her still harder, and Bennager thought that he heard Sam growl.

Charlie said, "I know what you're gettin' at, Sam, but after this mornin', my old ways don't seem that bad."

Sam nodded his head sadly, realizing that you could only push a man so far and resolved to be the first one to set out each morning to track Charlie. Rose put her hand out to see if her apology had really been accepted, and Charlie shook it reluctantly so she would go away.

The wind was blowing harder now, and being on the bay was what Bennager imagined the ocean to be like. The paddles of the steamboat were only able to work three quarters of the time because the waves carried the boat higher than the water, and the paddles couldn't always make the reach. It was going to be a wicked day weather wise. The high, thin clouds of this morning were being followed by dark rain clouds, and they were starting to build up overhead. Charlie and Bennager hoped that it would stay cool in the Sierras so the snow wouldn't melt and come rolling at them down the Sacramento River along with mud and trees that generally accompanied snow when it melted too fast. It looked to them by the size of the clouds that the rain was going to cause enough trouble for the river without the snow melting away on them too.

Poor weather conditions usually coincided with poor attitudes amongst people and animals as well. With all of life's usual misfortunes and regrets that all people live with every day, bad weather always seems to be the last straw, and they can't help letting the world see their innermost badness on days like this one was becoming. Bennager wanted to know if Rose, the most spirited person among them, was going to be able to make it through the next couple of days, at least without going crazy and killing anyone. He was hoping that Zeb wasn't going on about how Rose had wished this weather because she wasn't going to like being blamed for it. Bennager found Rose and Girl bunked down together under his wagon, almost just like they were on the first day out. "Rose, are you awake?"

"Is that you, Bennager?"

"Yes, do you mind if I talk with you a while?"

"Come on ahead. Get out of the wind with me and Girl."

He took his bedroll with him and crawled under the wagon. "Are you trying to sleep?"

"I think I'm just hiding. Hiding from people and hiding from the wind. I was wishing that I was a little girl again with nothing in the world to worry about," Rose said.

"Being a little child, yes, I guess we all wish for that from time to time." Bennager smiled.

"What did Charlie say about me after I left?"

"Nothing. We talked about this weather and how it was going to give us a hard trip. That's what I wanted to talk to you about. You need to brace yourself for some bad times. It looks to me like we are going to have a lot of rain, maybe for a couple of days. Make sure you stay dry or else you will get sick, and you need to keep your temper under control because you ain't the only one around here with a weapon, and there ain't any of us that are going to be in good spirits by the time this storm hits."

"Oh, I guess I have a reputation now for not being able to handle bad situations. Have you ever been in the ocean when a storm hits? Believe me, it's no Sunday after church picnic, not that I would know anything about those. I can handle a storm and I can handle getting wet. I won't like it, but I won't kill anyone over it either." It angered Rose to think that people didn't trust her to control her emotions. She looked into Bennager's eyes and said, "I really am embarrassed about this morning, but I didn't like being compared to an Indian. I really wouldn't have shot Charlie anyway. I just wanted him to know that no man was going to take me down and whop my tail without a fight."

"Well, Sam and I didn't know if your trigger finger knew your true intentions or not." Bennager chuckled.

This quip made Rose smile. "Even though I wish that I was still a little girl, and sometimes I act like one, I think I can still pull my weight around here. You fellas aren't giving me anything to do, and I'm getting damned impatient to get to work, too, just like everyone else. I wonder all the time where I'll end up and if I'll be able to make a business and if I just made a big mistake by coming here."

"I'm sure your life would have been easier if you had stayed home. Even though you didn't care for Richard, at least he would have made sure that you were well taken care of."

"Taken care of by his poor slaves, you mean. I would have felt like a big bird in a small cage. I could never live with someone that I couldn't respect. I could never let a man like that touch me either. I knew that if I stayed, I would have to shoot my way out of that, too, only I didn't know who it would be—him, my father, or myself. So staying would have been just as risky as leaving."

Bennager laughed. "Well, you're stuck now, that's for sure. At least until we get to Sacramento City. You might like it right there and decide not to travel anymore."

"Does it get foggy there?" Rose asked.

"Oh yes, the fog lingers there at times too."

"I would just as soon not stay there then," Rose said firmly.

"I better let you rest. I don't expect any of us will get much sleep tonight. Later, if you want to help me set up some canvases to keep us dry, I'd be obliged."

"I won't know what to do. You'll have to tell me," Rose said. "I don't really know much about things related to living in the outdoors, but I want to learn, so you and the others will have to teach me."

Bennager was pleased with the eager bright-eyed girl. "That will be our new project. If you are going to live out here, then it will be necessary for you to know how to live off the land. Money is always a good thing to have, but it isn't always much use when there is nothing around to purchase."

"I am finding that to be quite correct. Speaking of money, when we get to Sacramento City, I want to do something for Charlie to make up for me being so contrary this morning."

"Do something? Like what?" Bennager looked at her questioningly.

"I don't know yet. You know him, you must know what he likes or maybe there is something that he needs. I thought you could help me figure it out," Rose said.

"Oh, I see, you want my help. We'll poke around and see if we can come up with something other than sake, although I figure that is what he would like the best. I better let you and Girl get some rest. I want you to use my bedroll for an extra cushion if you have a mind to. You'll be doing me a favor by keeping it warm and dry. And don't forget to spit that stuff out before you fall asleep. You'll choke if you don't."

Rose touched Bennager's arm as he started to crawl out from under the wagon. "Thanks for talking with me after I made such a jackass out of myself. It makes me feel good that you don't hold it against me."

"You apologized to Charlie. It goes a long way with me when someone is willing to admit that they were wrong. Not many men would have done that, and someone would have ended up dead eventually, all because they wouldn't admit that they were wrong. You did the right thing, and I respect you for it."

"Thank you, Bennager. I'll be able to sleep now," Rose said with a smile and a look of relief in her eyes.

Bennager was again finding himself drawn to her, wanting to kiss her and hold her in his arms. He reckoned that she would let him, but he knew that it wouldn't mean much to her. "Rose," Bennager said, pausing. "I want to ask you something, but I was told as a boy that it was an impolite thing to ask a lady, but I really want to know, and I don't want you to be angry with me. May I ask?"

"Well, what in tarnation do you want to know about me that would be impolite to ask? Go ahead, I'm curious, and I don't have any secrets anyway," Rose said smiling.

"I want to know your age."

"I used to get in trouble for asking that too. I never understood what was so terrible about that. I think just old ladies hate that because when I asked my grandpa on my mother's side, he didn't get mad at all. I had my seventeenth birthday last month. How old are you?"

Bennager answered as he went back to his bedroll. "I'm twenty-five."

"When I was fourteen, my father asked me who my beau was, but I didn't have one. That is when he started having parties and dinners so boys would have to associate with me. I ran them all off with my particular charm, and I did it just to make my father angry with me. Of course, no boy had the nerve to tell my father that I could spit tobacco juice just as far as any farmhand and drink brandy just as well as any of them, not to mention the foul language that I used with them when Father couldn't hear me. I always figured that if I could find a fella that would tell my father about all of that and then still wanted to be with me, then at least he would have enough backbone to withstand the consequences. But they were all spineless and slithered away like the little snakes that they were." She paused.

"That Richard was the worst one of all, but my father told me this was it. I was too old for him to take care of anymore, and it was time for me to have a husband, and if I was to run Richard off, then it was the convent for me. Can you imagine me in a convent?" she asked Bennager as she laughed. Then she continued, "I was laughing on the inside the other morning when you and Sam were going on about my father and Richard coming after me with an army, and that note you found was meant to be sarcastic. I tried every trick I knew to try to run Richard off, too, but my father had covered his bets with that one. He threatened me with the convent, and he must have threatened him with something too. I don't know what, but it must have been big. As far as armies go, I'm sure that they are both relieved that I'm gone. That despicable cretin isn't being blackmailed anymore, and father doesn't have to feed me anymore either. Mother is as contrary as I am, so I reckon she weathered the storm."

"So why do you continue the charade now?" Bennager asked.

"It has all become a terrible habit now. How people react to my bad behavior tells me a lot about them, I guess. I learn more about a person right away rather than beating around the bush. Sam informed me this morning, though, that he has just about had enough of my antics. I was pretty quiet on the ship, and he doesn't understand why I'm doing crazy things now. I didn't have time to explain it to him this morning, but I suppose you frightened me a little when you said that there weren't many women here, so without realizing it, I have started to run off everyone that I meet."

"If you slow Sam's progress to those gold fields, you are going to wish that you were in that convent, right?" Bennager inquired.

"I don't think it would be that bad but pretty close. He wasn't very pleased with me. He made that clear." Rose chuckled.

"Did he take your derringer away from you?"

"No! I might need that! Sam doesn't take and he doesn't threaten, he just tells it like it is."

Girl got up to shift her pups around in their new home, the crate, and a barrage of whimpering commenced. Girl was sweet enough to let them look at her brood. "Have you picked out which one you want yet?" Bennager asked Rose.

"I think I'll wait until they're a little older."

"They don't have much character yet, do they?" Bennager commented.

"I try to leave them be. I think Girl gets embarrassed when I try to look at her babies."

"Well, I just can't sit under this wagon anymore, Rose Mary. I feel like I'm turning to stone. I have to go stretch my legs. I'll see you gals later. Get some rest."

"I think I will. I want to be able to help you set up camp tonight. Don't forget, you promised to teach me."

"You bet I will." Bennager patted her shoulder as he got out from under that blasted wagon. As Bennager stood up and stretched trying to get the kinks out of his back, he turned and saw Zeb sitting on the seat of his wagon. He had managed to crawl up there without Bennager hearing him, and it was obvious by the look on his face that he had been eavesdropping. Why anyone would willingly sit on that wagon in this windstorm was beyond Bennager's realm of comprehension. Mostly, no human would except for Zeb. Bennager reckoned that he would go to any length to find something to tease someone about. "Little breezy up there, ain't it?" Bennager asked, figuring that he might as well get this teasing started so it would be over sooner.

"The breeze tells me things, Rasmussen, so when it comes, I make sure that I can hear everything that it has to say," Zeb said, trying to be mystical.

"All right then," Bennager said in an uninterested tone, and he turned to take a stroll, then he heard a thump, that being the sound of Zeb jumping from the wagon to follow Bennager around and be bothersome.

"How are the ladies doing today? Do you gals need anything?" Zeb asked Rose.

For a moment, Bennager thought that he had lucked out. Perhaps Zeb was going to visit with Rose and his dog for a while. But then he heard Zeb say his good days and the fast pace of his steps were approaching him. It was at that moment that Bennager realized that besides Charlie, who was busy, Zeb and he were the only two from their group who had slept the whole night through, and by now, Angus and Sam had surely dozed off, and that was probably why Zeb had come over to eavesdrop, and now Bennager was going to have to listen to his nonsense for the rest of the day.

"Stretching your legs, are ya, Rasmussen?" Zeb started.

"Yes."

"Yes, my legs need stretching too."

"Did you walk from Monterey?" Bennager inquired.

"Oh no, my family has many horses. My brother-in-law and I rode to San Francisco with a pack horse for each one of us. It was a very nice ride. My brother-in-law took the horses home."

"So your family is in the horse business? I'll be. Is the business doing poorly? Is that why you have come to mine for gold?" Bennager quizzed.

"I like to explore. My feet were starting to itch after being in one place too long and seeing all the same people day after day. I will pan for some gold maybe, but mostly, I will explore. Our business is very good. Maybe I will move it to this country that I have not explored yet. Someday these miners will be rich and will want the best-bred horses in California. To have them, they will have to find me." Zeb smiled as he put his thumb to his chest, then continued, "You understand how being in love with a woman will change many things about you. I was an explorer. I rode with a surveying party of forty men for several years. Every day, I saw a new place, and at least once a week, I met a new group of people. We came to California one day, and I met my wife. For a while, she took me to new places too. We did things together that I never dreamed I would do, falling in love, having a roof over my head, having hot meals and having a family. Her family turned me into a vaquero. The biggest exploration I've had since I've been married is when we gather and I'm looking for cattle in the brush. So I asked my wife to let me go, and since the 'in love' part has turned into unconditional love, she did."

"Are you sorry that you gave up the surveying party?" Bennager asked.

"There was no more surveying for me after the first time that I saw my wife. I asked my captain to marry us, but she said no. I had to meet the family first, ask her father for her hand, and have a big wedding in a Catholic church. She was the oldest daughter, so she had to set a good example for her sisters, not that it would have happened any other way. My captain wished us luck, and I have been happy every day since."

"So you knew that you loved your wife from the first time that you saw her? How did you know that you loved her just from seeing her?" Bennager was obviously curious, and Zeb liked it.

"The same way that you know it about Rose. You caught sight of her in town. You met her and you have been with her ever since. That is how you know you love her. That is how I know you love her," Zeb answered, using Bennager as an example instead of himself.

"Wait a minute, Zeb," Bennager argued. "The reason why I wanted to meet Rose Mary when I first caught sight of her was not because of her looks or her charm. I simply found the sight of her and Sam and that dress she was wearing to be mighty curious, not to mention that I had never seen a woman in all my days look that unkempt. Then, after meeting her and Sam, I realized that I had never met anyone like that in all my life, man, woman, or beast."

"She is very special then, isn't she? I had never met anyone like my wife before either. No other woman had made me feel curious or concerned. It was like she was the only girl that I had ever seen, like you feel about Rose. Whether you love her or not, and I'm sure that you do, you said yourself that you will never meet anyone like her again, and now that you know her, ask yourself if you wish that you didn't. And ask yourself how you would feel if you were never to see her again. Then we will talk of love some more because I have been looking around here, and I think that I am the only one who knows anything about the subject. I have many children, many cattle, and many horses, and obviously, Girl knows things too. While I am having this talk with you, I think Girl is having one like it with Rose," Zeb explained, turned, and walked away, leaving Bennager to argue with the wind instead of Zeb.

It wasn't exactly the teasing nonsense that Bennager had expected from Zeb. He seemed to be genuine and sincere about this matter.

6

As day gave way to the evening, so too did the wind to the rain, light at first, it seemed, since the wind was still struggling to maintain its force and misery that it pushed upon the party. In no time, though, the wind moved on and left them to answer to the rain and they were all drenched. Everyone was prepared and ready to organize the camp for the night. All they had to do was make it to one of those docks that Charlie and Bennager had built. Everyone had a canvas wrapped around them, keeping themselves and their trappings dry, and the plan was, once they got to the shore, to use the canvases to construct shelters. Now that the wind had died down, it was sure to be a simple task. Once they docked, everyone got to their jobs without hesitation. Even Rose was helpful without knowing what to do. As soon as her canvas had been taken for construction, she went about looking for dry wood and grass to get a fire started. While they were building lean-tos, Zeb was building a tepee. "Zeb, what in the devil are you trying to do? Get us mixed up in an Indian war?" someone asked.

"My campfire will keep me warm and dry tonight. There is much to be learned from the Indians who all of you farmers think are so savage," Zeb responded.

"How in the devil can you have a fire in that damned thing?" one of the passengers scoffed.

Zeb ignored the jeers and continued on with his work. Angus went to help him.

Bennager looked at Sam, and both shrugged their shoulders. "What else do you need?" Bennager asked.

"One more canvas will do, Rasmussen," Zeb answered.

"Go ahead," Bennager told Sam. "I'll give this one to somebody else and get the team."

When Bennager had gotten back, Sam had gone to help Rose. She must have come back once because a campfire had already been started right in the middle of the tepee, and the smoke was headed out the hole that had been left in the top of the structure. Bennager guessed that he must be a farmer because he never dreamed that he would be in a tepee. He really had never imagined what one even looked like, and he realized that he had never even given Indians much thought at all until now. This was a very efficient dwelling. When Zeb had trimmed the crooked oak branches to make the frame, he only trimmed one side and left the other side alone so they could use the smaller branches to hang their wet clothes on.

"Make yourself at home, Rasmussen. I don't think you'll have an arrow loosed on you," Zeb joked.

Angus came in with Girl and the pups. Girl seemed to be getting accustomed to having her brood moved around from time to time. On this rainy night, her first priority was to get undercover herself. The day that she had spent on the steamer in the windstorm had been a terrifying experience for Girl. If she had not been such a good and protective mother, she probably would have taken leave of the pitching vessel if Zeb had let her. Thankful now to be in the presence of a warm fire and undercover, Girl showed her appreciation to her new friends by giving her coat a vigorous shake, just as Rose was leaning over to set down an armload of wood. Girl was showering Rose's face so well that Rose had to close her eyes. "Good Lord, Girl, as if I weren't wet enough already. Where are your babies?" Rose asked her as she gave her new friend a pat on the shoulder. Girl knew just what Rose had asked and immediately looked up at the crate that Angus was holding.

"Oh, would ye look at that!" Angus declared.

"Well, I'll be," Rose said in awe. "She knows just what I said!"

Angus set the crate down a few feet from the fire and took a shirt out that he had laid over the pups to keep them dry. He had been fearful that they might catch pneumonia if they got wet. Girl must have thought the same thing. She looked in at her litter, nuzzled and moved them around with her nose, but didn't get in with them this time. Instead, she walked over to Zeb who was arranging his wet clothes on the branch snags and stared at him with her tail wagging until he turned around and gave her a pat on the head accompanied by a few words of encouragement about the weather conditions. Girl wagged her tail and settled in as close to the fire as she dared. Feeling reassured now by her friend, she gave a little sigh as she laid her head on her front legs and began to relax, enjoying the fact that she was on solid ground now.

"This is a pitiful fire, Zeb," Rose commented. "There are quite a few large branches out there that broke off the trees, but they are too heavy for me to lift or even drag. All I could get was this little stuff, but I'll go get some more."

"I have an axe and a saw in the wagon, I'll go get them," Bennager said on his way out the opening.

"Just get the saw, Rasmussen. We can take turns sawing up those big branches in here out of the storm," Zeb said.

"The wagon, damn, I forgot to bring in my things!" Rose said, looking around for them in the tepee and wondering if Sam had brought them. The sound of something being dragged on the ground made Rose scurry outside, knowing that Sam had arrived after having dragged one of those big branches back that she had mentioned. "Sam, did you happen to bring our things or are they still on the wagon?" Rose asked.

"Oh no, I didn't bring them, Rose. The tarps got me sidetracked. I'll go get them now," Sam replied.

"No, you get in and warm up some. I'll run over there. Bennager!" Rose hollered over the sound of saucer-sized raindrops hitting the canvas. "Where in the wagon is your saw? I'll bring it back too," Rose suggested.

"I'll run over there with you. There are some other things I need," Bennager said as he came out into the weather. They both jogged to the steamboat together with no time to argue, bicker, or tease. Rose found her bags right where she had left them and felt very lucky that one of the other passengers had not picked them up, even though they were well hidden behind the wheel of Bennager's wagon. Then, remembering where Sam had set the crate of goods in the wagon, she went to the back and started to lift it out, just as Bennager had located the saw buried in the bottom of the wagon and gave it a good hard pull to get it out of there.

"Ouch!" Rose yelled, grabbing her right arm with her left hand.

"Get out of the way before you get hurt!" Bennager hollered.

Rose ducked under the saw and got on the less dangerous side and helped Bennager pull it out of the wagon because it had hung up on something. "Get hurt? What in tarnation do you think 'Ouch' means, for heaven's sake?" Rose growled, not loud enough for Bennager to hear.

"Thanks," Bennager said, taking the saw and a crate and heading for shore.

"Thanks yourself," Rose muttered as she made her second attempt to lift her hardtack out of the wagon. She tried to take everything at once but found that her arm really hurt too much to take two bags, so she kicked one under the wagon, sadly knowing that she would have to make two trips.

When Rose made it back to the tepee, the men were in the doorway, working at cutting up the big branches for firewood. Angus and Bennager had taken a turn at gathering up some more while Sam sawed and Zeb held the branch steady, with the end that Sam was cutting sitting on a piece of branch so the saw's teeth wouldn't touch the ground.

Rose looked things over before she went for the second carpetbag that she had left behind. "I brought the food, Sam, no red meat tonight."

Sam nodded his head in acknowledgment, and Rose went out looking for Bennager and Angus as she made her way to the wagon. Rose was so soaked by now that she didn't realize that her arm was bleeding. The arm of her wool coat that was once gray was now red. Even in the rainstorm, she could be tracked by the amount of blood that was dripping off her sleeve.

Rose kept her eyes peeled for Charlie as she approached his domain. Hoping not to run into him after causing trouble with him this morning, Rose decided that if she did see him, she might have to hide. Being alone with Charlie in the rain might be trouble. He might have thought that he could get rid of her without anyone knowing.

Quietly, Rose went to the wagon, bent down to retrieve her bag, but it wasn't there. She got down on her hands and knees, feeling the pain in her severed arm, and looked under the wagon thoroughly. She bounced up, fearfully aware that the bag was gone, but rifled through the wagon and under the seat, everywhere that she could think of to make sure of the fact before she had to go into a complete panic.

The tepee looked like a giant lantern now that Zeb and Sam had put more wood on the fire and Angus and Bennager were better able to see their way as they brought in more branches. They were also able to see some smaller ones and older ones that were not as green as the branches that had just been blown down in the windstorm. As Angus bent down to pick up some smaller pieces, he noticed something, something that he had seen hundreds of times but shouldn't be seeing here. "Good Lord, me damned brothers are around here someplace."

Bennager stood up, suddenly alarmed by the statement he had just heard. He looked at Angus who was looking into the darkness in the direction that the boot print had gone to, and then Bennager looked around in every other direction. Bennager quickly made his way to Angus. "How do you know that? Can you smell them or what?" Bennager asked.

"That boot print right there, ye see?" Angus replied, pointing to the ground. "I know that boot print."

"He sure did come awful close to the tent. He must be looking for you."

"He's not alone," Angus said, walking to the tent door. "Ho, did ye gents see me brothers walk past here?" he asked Sam and Zeb. Blank stares were their only reply. "They're 'round, so watch yourselves."

"Hey, where is Rose Mary?" Bennager asked, alarmed. Sam stood up, looking mildly unnerved.

"Isn't she with you?"

"No, why would she be with us?"

"I thought she went to gather wood with you."

"Well, I didn't see her out there."

"It's me brothers, they've got her!" Angus frightfully exclaimed.

"Why would your brothers take Rose?" Bennager asked.

"I reckon they want me to come for her. They aren't exactly an upstanding lot. As a matter of fact, one of them has been known to be unlawful. As matter of fact, the reason why we are in California is 'cause that one had to run from the law, and he convinced the rest of us to follow."

"Hold on now," Zeb said, trying to quell the panic. "Rose was here just a few minutes ago, right, Sam? She said, 'No red meat tonight.' Your trappings are right over there, I watched her set them down."

Sam walked over to where Zeb was pointing and saw that one of the bags was missing, but the crate of dried goods was there. "She couldn't get everythin' in one trip. I reckon she had to go back to the boat."

Sam was starting for the door when Bennager bolted for the direction of the boat. Sam stopped in his tracks, turned, and looked at Zeb in amazement and shrugged his shoulders.

"Love is quick, huh, Sam?" Zeb teased, and they went back to sawing firewood.

Angus wanted to take a tour and see if he could locate his brothers but decided to shirk his wet coat and dry it out by the fire instead before it was his turn to cut wood. He sat by the little puppies and looked at them in awe, wondering if something so tiny would actually survive this trip.

"Hey, Charlie, have you seen Rose?" Bennager asked excitedly.

"That wildcat, I ain't been lookin' for her, and if I seen her before she seen me, I'd get out of sight damn quick like."

"So you haven't seen her I take it?"

"No, she might have been here, though. I've been hearin' all kinds of trompin' around all evenin'. Folks been scurryin' around back and forth, but I ain't about to stand in the rain watchin' who's comin' and who's goin'. I got to watch for trees in the river tomorrow. Reckon I'll save my eyes for that."

During Charlie's lecture, Bennager was anxiously looking around only half hearing what Charlie was saying. "What's all this here?" Bennager asked pointing to the floor of the boat. "Did you kill something for your supper, Charlie?"

"No, what do you see there?" Charlie stepped over to look at what Bennager was pointing at. "Where in the devil did all that come from?" Bennager quickly tracked the blood straight to his wagon where he found Rose lying on her side as if she were sleeping, absolutely soaked through and through.

Charlie came up behind Bennager. "Who is it, Benny? Is it the woman?"

"Yeah, it's Rose."

"What happened? Is she sleeping?"

"I don't know what the devil is going on here. Shine that lantern on her, would you?" They saw that her arm had been cut, but the bleeding had stopped. She still had color, but she was unconscious. Bennager quickly grabbed her up, not thinking about looking for clues about how this could have happened, only wanting to get her dried out.

Charlie, though, not caring one way or the other about the crazy girl's welfare, was curious about what had caused the girl to be unconscious. It didn't seem like the cut on her arm would cause that much trouble unless the sight of blood would cause her to faint, which he doubted since she was so eager to draw his this morning. Charlie concluded that she looked like she had been hit over the head and remembered hearing somebody running from the boat earlier. Charlie remembered thinking at the time, *That fella is in a devil of a hurry to get out of the rain. He must think he's gain' to melt.*

As Charlie was heading to shore, Angus and Sam were coming aboard. Charlie was afraid that they were coming for him and was trying to think of a way to convince them that he had nothing to do with what had happened to Rose.

"Did you see anything?" Angus asked.

"No, but I was just on my way to tell Benny that I heard a couple of fellas runnin' off this boat like someone was chasing them. I think someone hit her in the head," Charlie explained as the three men walked toward the wagon. Sam looked under the wagon for the carpetbag that Rose had come for and found a shovel instead. The wagon looked like it had been gone through. Sam reckoned Angus' brothers were looking for a tarp and warm clothes, and Rose caught them in the act.

"They must have taken the bag, thinking there was food in it. We'll have to find them, Angus," Sam said, turning his head to meet Angus' eyes with a look of vengeful purpose and seeing that Angus was feeling disappointment in his heart.

"I didn't know they were that bad, Sam, but they are dead men when I find them. Tell Bennager I'll owe him," Angus said as he took a canvas from the wagon, cut it down with his pocketknife, and cut a hole through it to make a poncho.

"I'll come with you, Angus," Sam said and began to do the same thing with the left over canvas.

"I'll be killin' them three meself, Sam. I know what's in that bag, and you can be trustin' me to bring it back. I don't want to be holdin' you up, gettin' to 'em gold fields, Sam."

"I reckon a friend is more important than gold, Angus. I'm going with you for Rose and for you too. You can bet that I will let you do all the killin' you want, but I want to make sure you make it back. Three against one isn't very good odds," Sam said, trying to make Angus understand that he was really concerned for Angus' health and not so much for the money that had been stolen.

"Have it your way, Sam. I don't have time to argue with ye 'bout it. I just thought ye would want to watch over Rose, that's all. I'm going to get one of Bennager's horses," Angus said hastily, and in a way, that made Sam know that there was no time to ask Bennager, no time to tell anyone what their intentions were, and no time for anything if Sam wanted to go with Angus. The once jovial, happy-go-lucky Irishman that everybody liked to be around had now become the man with the serious purpose of seeking justice. The man who had been giggling and cooing at newborn pups was now showing a businesslike approach to dealing out a death penalty.

Sam found the change in character to be frightening. He remembered when Angus threw his brothers overboard the first day.

Angus wasn't like this then. He laughed as each one of them splashed into the water. But this was different. Sam hoped that he wouldn't be hung for riding with Angus since at the end of the ride, three White men were going to be dead. But he also knew Rose would want him to go. If it was him that had gotten hit over the head with a shovel, she would go after the person who did it, and she would probably be the only one.

Charlie was still milling around listening to what Angus was planning to do. "Tell Bennager, would ya, Charlie? I don't want him to think we're horse thieves," Sam said, running after Angus who was merely walking but with purpose.

"You bet I'll tell him," Charlie replied, heading to the lighted tepee to tell him right away.

When Angus and Sam got to where the team was staked out, they only found four horses instead of six. "Where's the other two?" Angus asked Sam franticly.

"Maybe your brothers were in a big enough hurry to steal them," Sam answered. Angus quickly looked the ground over but couldn't make out what happened exactly.

The rain had blurred out any sign that might have given him or Sam an idea about who had taken the horses, but it was safe to assume that Sam was right. It was darker than dark because of the black clouds overhead, so they weren't even able to determine which way to go. They mounted Bennager's horses after Sam had made makeshift halters from pieces of rope, and they headed for the most likely direction that a thief would take as far away from passengers camping on the shore as one could get: south.

"I better tell Bennager about the two missin' horses. If somethin' happens to us, I don't want him thinkin' that we took four horses and him thinkin' that we're comin' back anytime. I'll catch up with you." Sam figured that he wouldn't have a hard time catching up with Angus. Sam had ridden many, many miles on the bare back of a horse, and he had gathered from overhearing conversations that Angus had not had the chance to ride much at all in his young life.

Sam didn't make it all the way to the tepee camp before he ran into Charlie. He asked Charlie to relay his message to Bennager, and

Charlie nodded and waved. "Hey, do you want to use my lantern?" he hollered after Sam. It hadn't occurred to Charlie until just then that they were going into the darkness without any light because he himself had light. His offer wasn't answered. Sam was on a mission and didn't have time to hear it.

"I don't know how they expect to see anythin' when it's like this," Charlie grumbled to himself. "If I didn't know how much store Sam put into gettin' to them gold fields, I'd swear he was abandonin' ship," he jested to himself.

"It's bad news, boys!" Charlie said as he walked into the illuminated tepee that could have been seen a mile away. "Damn, you boys sure got it hot in here," he remarked.

"We're trying to get everything dried out around here," Zeb replied. "This girl is plumb soaked to the bone, Bennager won't take her clothes off, and he won't let me do it either. I've been telling him that she'll get pneumonia, but the damn boy is too awful shy about the whole thing. It's criminal, damn it!"

"What the hell? That don't make no sense. You know better'n that," Charlie upbraided Bennager.

"This ain't no damn sideshow, Charlie. What's the bad news you were jabbering about when you walked in?" Bennager asked as he was carefully cutting the sleeve of Rose's shirt to see about the cut on her arm.

"Damn it, Benny, get the hell out of the way. You don't have a clue about what the devil you're doin' here. I'm the ship's captain, and that makes me in charge of the doctorin'," Charlie said, shoving Bennager out of the way and kneeling to tend to Rose. "Get them damned clothes off her right now and don't give me any sass about it. You, get a dry blanket from somewheres and put it on her as soon as Benny gets her wet clothes off," he ordered Zeb.

Charlie looked inside each one of Rose's ears as best as he could without proper light to find out if there was any sign of a concussion due to the blow that the girl had taken to the head. "This here girl went for her other bag or whatever and caught that big redheaded fella's brothers, he thinks, goin' through your wagon out there," Charlie told them while he was looking at the gash in between Rose's ear and neck. "By God, this is a mess. I'll have to clean this and stitch it up. Boil me up some water, find clean rags. You, go out to the boat, right beside that barrel of sake. You'll find a box with a red cross on it," he ordered Zeb again, who didn't like being ordered around like he was a child but knew he hadn't been doing a very good job tending to Rose since he hadn't seen the cut on her head, so he ran like the wind or as fast as bowed forty-two-year-old legs could carry him.

Charlie was silent until Zeb returned because he didn't want to tell the rest of the news twice. While Bennager took off the last shirt on Rose's person, Charlie saw the bad cut on Rose's arm. "Good Lord, it's cut clean to the bone! What a mess! How the hell did that happen, I wonder?" Charlie exclaimed.

Bennager remembered now just how it happened. The last time he had even seen Rose was when the saw was stuck under all the supplies, and he was yanking it out of there for all he was worth, and Rose screamed and helped him get it the rest of the way out. He told Charlie how it happened, and then Charlie looked over at the saw.

"Well, I'll be goin' to hell! She's damn lucky that old crosscut saw didn't slice her whole damned arm off. She'll have to see a real doctor when we get to Sacramento City. I hope they have one there by now," Charlie said, shaking his head.

Zeb came blasting in through the tent flaps.

"By golly, you're quick. The water ain't even boilin' yet," Charlie teased, observing that Zeb was breathing hard from his big jaunt.

"Well, anyway, one of them Irish fellas hit this gal in the head with a shovel. We found it lyin' there under the wagon. So that Irish fella and Sam ripped up one of your tarps and made ponchos out of it and took two of your horses to go find 'em. You don't need to be coverin' up that arm, Benny, I need to work on it. Get a dry blanket now and cover her up and watch for that water to boil. You, come over here across from me, watch that I don't jumble this up. My eyes ain't what they used to be for this fine work. I still darn my own socks, though."

"I'll tell you something, Mr. Captain, my name is Zeb, and I like taking orders just fine when I am called by my name."

"You don't say. Well, Zeb, I'm Charlie. I want you to watch her for the fever while you're there because what Benny did to her with that rusty old crosscut saw is just terrible, I tell you. He must be out to kill her. She'll get the tetanus now, sure as hell."

Zeb looked at Bennager and saw his anguish. Once a person got tetanus in these parts, they were a goner. Zeb knew it, and Bennager knew it too. Zeb whispered to Charlie now so Bennager wouldn't hear because this wasn't a teasing matter, and Zeb didn't want Bennager to think that he was making light of Rose's pain. "Rasmussen loves this girl. Don't speak of tetanus again."

"Well, I'll clean this good and stitch it up," Charlie said in his usual tone of voice. "We better collect some rainwater for this in the cleanest buckets you have. That river water will be too dirty now, and Mother always said cleanliness is next to godliness."

Bennager moved quickly to collect water that was running from the canvas into a clean pail that he had brought in for the purpose of collecting water to make coffee with.

"There's no rust in that bucket, is there, Benny?" Charlie hollered.

"No, it's brand-new and never been used," Bennager replied.

"Rinse it out good. We can't be havin' dirt and dust in it neither," Charlie ordered. When Bennager brought in the bucket of water, Charlie said. "Put that on the fire, I've got to wait for it to boil. Anyway, when them friends of yours went to get two of your horses, they found out that two had already been taken and that fella, Sam, told me to tell you they are goin' after whosoever done all this. Now if you want worse news than that, this girl needs a doctor, even after I do the best I can, and if this warm rain is hittin' the Sierras as hard as it's hittin' here, I'm goin' to be delayed on account of dodgin' trees and such in that river. She's wide, but I got to keep that boat in the middle of the channel or else the debris will wipe us out. I'm thinkin' about sittin' here a day to see what happens."

"She probably shouldn't be traveling in the rain anyway, should she, Charlie?" Bennager asked.

"No, that would make matters worse for sure, but this gal needs a doctor," Charlie said with a pessimistic tone and looked at Rose in a woeful way.

"Bennager, seems how everybody has been helping themselves to your horses, maybe we ought to get the other two a little closer to camp. Maybe they would enjoy the warmth coming through the wall of my house. Do you want me to bring them?" Zeb asked thoughtfully.

"Oh, thanks, Zeb. You're right, but I'll get them, I haven't sacked them yet tonight. Do you need anything, Charlie, before I go?"

"No, just waitin' for the water to boil now, Benny."

Bennager walked to the boat where his wagon was. It was so dark as he neared the water that he had to walk slowly to feel his way with his feet, hoping not to trip on some small limb that might be lying on the ground, waiting to surprise him. He wondered how the other passengers were making out trying to survive this rainstorm in their lean-tos and remembered that most of them had probably weathered much colder and harsher storms than this if any of them were from the northeast. Of course, he didn't know where any of them were from, and he thought to himself that nothing could be worse than being soaked and not being able to dry out. Then he thought of Rose and decided that having a big gash on the head and dying of tetanus was much worse.

When he approached his wagon and reached for the sacks of grain, he found out that none of the things were where he had put them. Here he was, in the middle of a rainstorm, and he couldn't even find a lantern to light to look for his grain. "Damn it to the devil!" he yelled at himself and at all the people who had disheveled his load. He did find one thing as he walked around his wagon, still looking for a lantern; it was the shovel that had been used on Rose. Sam had just left it lying there on the deck after he found it under the wagon. Bennager stepped on the handle with his left foot, and his right toe hooked under the handle. He barely had time to get his hands out before he crashed onto the deck. "Damn son of a bitch!" he screamed this time at the top of his lungs. If he was hurt, he was too angry to notice. He was so quick to get to his feet one would think that he had fallen while he was walking in a parade.

Bennager grabbed that shovel from the deck floor and threw it as hard as he could into the water. "There just went four damned dollars! You'd think a man would pick that damned thing up off the damn deck so it wouldn't nearly kill some dumb son of a bitch who was trying to find a damned lantern in this damned dark rain!" Bennager hollered. "To hell with it!"

Bennager went to shore and gathered up what was left of his beautiful team, mad now, thinking that the other four hadn't been sacked before they were taken and hoped the first two thieves had been bucked off and stomped to death by now and wishing that he was with Angus and Sam instead of being here, wondering when the moment would come for Rose when the tetanus would take hold of her. The way back to camp was still lit well, but Bennager knew that the fire was starting to dwindle down, and he thought he should get busy cutting more wood. As he staked out his two horses, hoping that there would be enough grass for them to nibble, one of his horses stepped on his right foot.

"Ouch, you son of a bitch!" Bennager yelled, shoving his shoulder into the animal as hard as he could, but it didn't budge, not at first, not until it was ready. The animal took all Bennager's abuse and cursing. Finally, Bennager hollered up to the sky, "What do you want from me?" The heavens never gave him an answer, but the horse lifted his foot.

7

Charlie and Zeb went to sleep when they knew they had done everything that they could do for Rose. Zeb knew Bennager would not be able to sleep as long as the woman that he was in love with was suffering, especially since her pain was due to his own incompetence.

Bennager would never forgive himself for hurting Rose with that crosscut saw, and he wouldn't allow himself to think that Rose might die. During the night, Girl left her pups and laid down against Rose's leg, resting her chin on Rose's knee. Girl was worried about her new friend and thought she could comfort Rose the way that Rose had reassured her just a few days before.

Bennager didn't disturb the dog. The dog was probably going to cause Rose to add flea-bitten to her list of injuries, but Bennager didn't think Rose would mind that. He couldn't shoo away something that loved Rose any more than if somebody tried to shoo him away from her.

The fever that Charlie had predicted had a hold on Rose now, but she wasn't tossing or convulsing, and Bennager hoped that the cool wet cloth that he kept draping over her head would keep that from happening. He didn't feel like he was doing anything important. He didn't feel like he was doing enough. There had to be something more tangible that he could do to make Rose get well. But Charlie had assured him it was all that could be done. The fever would break or it would not.

Rose was young and strong. Even though she had been deficient of proper nutrition during her voyage, she was never sick from it, which meant that her body probably had the strength to overcome it. Bennager still prayed for a miracle.

Zeb woke up a couple of hours before daylight. The tepee had been a brilliant idea last night in the storm, but sleeping on the ground in a tepee was still just sleeping on the ground. A prolonged period of sleeping was impossible. Girl watched as Zeb slowly and painfully tried to stand up, and she flapped her tail. When Zeb returned from his morning stroll, he took over Bennager's job without even asking him.

At first, Bennager thought that he should start something with Zeb, an argument, an accusation, or maybe he would hit Zeb on the side of the head with his fist. Zeb gave Bennager a hard, surly look as if to say, "Go ahead, if you think it would make you feel any better." Then Zeb smiled, knowing that Bennager wasn't one to act on insane thoughts. Bennager relaxed the look of outrage on his face and gave Zeb a thin smile, knowing that Zeb would have handled any deranged move that Bennager would have tried.

"It doesn't seem to me like the fever has gotten worse during the night," Zeb remarked, looking at Bennager with the back of his hand on Rose's cheek. "Did she toss or mumble?" Zeb asked, taking his hand away.

"No."

Zeb considered the answer and thought to himself that was a good sign. Rose was in a deep state of healing and was probably winning the battle with the infection. Zeb kept his thoughts to himself. He knew, maybe more than most, what it was like to truly love a woman and what it was like to see that woman in pain and not be able to do anything about it. The feeling of helplessness was nothing compared to the feeling of inadequacy, especially when you know that something you did is now the cause of her pain. Zeb felt this way when his wife was giving birth to their children and when his baby daughter died. Zeb gave a few moments of thought to the future Bennager and Rose could have and how it was likely that the two of them would have many of the same experiences that he had shared with his wife and smiled without knowing it.

"Why are you smiling? Do you know that Rose will be all right now?" Bennager asked quietly with great hope and excitement.

Bennager had shocked Zeb slightly. He even flinched. Girl flapped her tail at this but continued to stare into Rose's face. Zeb knew she was staring into Rose's soul but never told anybody about it. The memories of Zeb's past were so vivid that he had been transported back in time. He was, for a few short moments, in a different place, and Bennager's spoken words were what brought him back to reality. "I was thinking of my wife and thinking of when the two of you have your first child." It was Zeb's way of giving Bennager a piece of joy without giving him false hope.

Bennager didn't know what to think or say about that statement. Confusion came over him. Bennager was too practical to think that far ahead. First thing's first, Rose had to wake up, beat infection, keep her arm, and survive possible brain damage. If all these things were to actually happen and she got back to being her old self, she would probably shoot him for almost cutting her arm off.

Zeb laughed, knowing Bennager well enough by now to imagine what he was thinking. Zeb knew Bennager was old enough to know where babies came from, but the look on his face reminded Zeb of a child that couldn't comprehend such an abstract notion. Zeb chanced to tease, "I don't doubt for a moment that as soon as Rose is able, she will shoot you, but I'm sure she will shoot you in the leg or foot. She won't kill you, she'll just pay you back. A woman like Rose will want you to be partners in every way."

Zeb's jokes didn't rankle Bennager. He would shoot himself right now if it would make Rose into her old self, but it wouldn't. "Well, I'll let her, and I won't flinch," Bennager said. He was tired and disappointed, and he wished that Rose would just wake up. Bennager lay down for the first time all night. He lay on his side so he could watch her. He was jealous of Girl for being able to lay her head on Rose's leg and he couldn't. He wished that her pups would wake up and start making a fuss so he could have Rose to himself. He slid his hand under Rose's blanket, found hers, and held it. It was warm and it gave him comfort. He closed his eyes, thinking that he probably wouldn't be able to hold her hand if she was awake. He heard Girl flap her tail against the ground, and he drifted off to sleep.

Zeb threw a blanket over Bennager and continued his soothing task of keeping Rose's fever at bay, seeing the face of his own wife as he looked at the face of Rose.

*****

Bennager was awakened by a voice that he didn't recognize. It was light, but with the dark clouds still drifting overhead, he was unable to discern what time of day it was. Looking around him, he wondered why there wasn't anyone tending to Rose. He felt the damp cloth on her forehead. It was wet and cool, so she hadn't been left alone for very long.

A stranger was in camp. He must have just arrived, Bennager thought to himself as he listened to the man's voice, which seemed easy; not exactly soft spoken, not forceful or excitable, just quiet and easy, like the stranger knew that someone was hurt and needed their rest. Rose's face seemed warmer to Bennager now, but he wasn't sure. He wondered what time it was. He felt rested, but as he stood up to go outside, he stumbled feeling like he had drunk too many spirits the night before, but he hadn't had any.

Stepping out of the tepee, Bennager saw a man on a horse wearing buckskin pants and a coat to match. He wore a broad-brimmed hat that kept all forms of weather, good and bad, from being bothersome. The stranger wasn't one to waste time with a barber. His hair was unkempt as well as his beard, but he had taken the scissors to his mustache recently because one side was shorter than the other. The stranger also had a mule in tow. He was obviously a traveler, looked much like a mountain man but seemed to be out of his element. What was a mountain man doing on the Sacramento River?

"Bennager, I want you to meet an old friend of mine. I still can't believe he's here," Zeb said with a smile that stretched the whole width of his face. "This is Bill Ford."

Bennager stepped up to the man who was still on his horse with his hand out. "Bennager Rasmussen, how do you do?"

"Better now that it quit rainin'," Bill replied. He dismounted and went to the other side of his horse and retrieved something out of his saddlebag. "This old teaser was tellin' me about your woman. Is she still fevered up?"

"Yes," Bennager said, looking at Zeb. "It seems like she is getting worse."

"Mind if I have a look? I've picked up a thing or two about doctorin' in my travels. I might be able to help her out."

Bennager looked at Zeb. Zeb winked and gave a nod of his head. "We'd be obliged, thank you," Bennager said.

The three men walked into the tepee. Girl greeted them at the opening. She was very intrigued with the buckskin garment that Bill was wearing but not to the point of being a nuisance. Bill reached down and gave her a pat, and she smiled and wagged her tail. "Who is this?" Bill asked.

"That's my girl, Girl. She has become Rose's keeper and nurse," Zeb teased. "It looks like she is as glad to see you as I am."

Bill watched Girl jump into a crate and heard the ensuing commotion of her pups. He looked in, and Girl was still smiling. "Look at that!" Bill said and gave her another pat. "What do you have there, little Girl? It looks like you've been busy!"

Girl answered Bill by smiling and nuzzling her happy family.

"Look at her showing off to Bill, that crazy dog," Zeb said to Bennager, shaking his head in disbelief.

Bennager noticed, but he was weary with worry and lack of sleep and was barely able to produce a thin smile.

Bill went to Rose and pulled back the cover to see the wound on her right arm, not looking at her face that was partially covered with the wet cloth. "Someone has sewed this up. That's good," Bill commented quietly. The wound was hot and festered with infection. Bill had seen something like this when he was younger, but that wound had been caused by a burn and had not been an accident. He was remembering the incident that had caused him to leave home and never look back. "Well, I have a plant here that is good for soothing infections. I use it to make tea once in a while. Let's heat up a little water."

Bennager did as Bill asked without wasting time to silently confer with Zeb or ask stupid questions about the plant.

"I remember that plant," Zeb said happily. "I have never seen that plant in these parts. I look for it all the time. As a matter of fact, I haven't seen that plant west of the Rockies."

"We ought to plant some then, Zeb," Bill said, smiling as Bennager put clean rainwater on the coals to heat.

"When were you east of the Rockies last, Bill?" Zeb asked.

"Oh, two winters ago, I reckon."

"You've got plenty of that stuff to spare, don't ya?"

"Well, I haven't been around any crosscut saws in a long time," Bill quietly joked, but the joke wasn't received well by Bennager or even Zeb, for that matter. *This woman must be loved*, Bill thought. While the water was warming, Bill examined the woman's face. He gently removed the cloth from her forehead, and a lovely memory came to mind. It was the memory of his mother when he was a small boy. "What did you say this woman's name was?" Bill asked, still staring into Rose's face and soaking the cloth in cool water.

"Rose Mary Briar. Why? Do you know her, Bill?" Zeb queried.

Bill smiled, knowing that the name had to be assumed but kept his thoughts to himself. He wouldn't know anything until she opened her eyes anyway. But if he was right and he was looking into the face of his niece, then what had Douglas done to make his daughter run away from home and change her name? "She reminds me of someone," Bill said, replacing the cool cloth.

Bennager listened to Bill's remarks but didn't pay much attention to them. He busied himself by making fresh coffee hoping that Bill might appreciate it since he didn't have much else to offer as thanks. "Your water is heated, Bill." Bennager brought the small cooking pan to him.

"All right, here's what we do now. We just make us a small poultice," Bill said, talking to himself quietly and pouring out some water. Of course, Zeb and Bennager were watching every move that he made and listening hard because they assumed that he was talking to them. "Then we put some of this stuff here in the water and let the plant soak it up, like that," Bill said, looking into the pan, calmly watching the plant do what it was told. Bennager and Zeb tried to look too. Bill watched and waited for what seemed like forever to Bennager, but Bill was waiting for the poultice to cool before he put it on the woman's arm and watched it as if it was going to perform magic. "Of course, I'm goin' to need a clean piece of cloth to use for a bandage," Bill said to Bennager, and he produced one immediately so as to not miss any of Bill's performances. Bill smiled and touched the concoction.

"Now it's ready, so we just scoop it out of there like so and put it on the cut, and we moisten the bandage and wrap it around like that and tie it, but not too tight, just so the stuff doesn't fall off and we hope for the best. Now, about every four or five hours, we do it again, cleaning the wound spotless each time with water that has been boiled, and we pray because I, for one, would like to see what this girl looks like with her eyes open."

"Do you want to see the head wound, Bill?" Zeb asked.

"Head wound? How the devil did she get a head wound?" Bill asked, scowling.

"From bad men," Zeb replied. "She was hit in the head during a robbery. Two of her friends are after them and what they took right now."

"This gal had a bad night all around. I guess when it rains, it pours," Bill said, examining the back of Rose's head. "This wound looks clean. It probably rattled her brain a bit, I reckon. She might not be the same as she used to be when she wakes up. A rattled brain will probably cause her to be cranky and irritable, like a rattlesnake or a badger. Once we get that fever to break, we will find out," Bill said, turning to Bennager to ask about the coffee. Bennager's eyes were as big as saucers, and the blood had left his face. "What's wrong with you, Bennager? Do you hate snakes so bad that they can't be mentioned?" Bill teased.

"Is there any chance that an ill-tempered person could get their brain rattled and wake up in a more pleasant state of mind?" Bennager asked hopefully.

"No, I never heard of it working that way."

Zeb shook his head and smiled to himself as both men rose to help themselves to coffee. Bennager had wanted to offer it but decided to take a walk instead.

Bill looked at Zeb quizzically and saw that Zeb was smiling. Girl hopped out of the crate and sniffed Rose's arm. Approving of a job well done, she smiled and wagged her tail while looking at Bill, and then lay down beside Rose's legs with her chin resting on her knee, willing her to wake up.

"Are you sure that's your dog and not the girl's, Zeb?"

"I'm beginning to wonder, all right. The two of them have become great friends in the last few days. Girl hates to see Rose this way. She hardly takes the time to feed her pups."

"What's with this Bennager, besides feeling guilty?"

"I think he fell in love with Rose when he first set eyes on her, like I did with my wife, you remember."

"Yeah." Bill laughed. "I remember that's the day you quit us."

Zeb laughed. "Yeah, I did. Bennager's problem is that she doesn't look like the person that she is, and they have had a devil of a time figuring each other out. It's been the most comical thing that I have seen in years. I can't tell you anymore about her than that. You'll see for yourself when she wakes up. I will say this, though, guilt is eating on Bennager, but not as much as fear is."

Bill thought about that statement for a moment and then understood that his niece was probably as coldhearted as her father was and thought that it might be best if he didn't wait around to meet her. Then he thought of the fondness that Zeb's dog had for her. "What do you think of her, Zeb?" Bill asked, digging for the truth.

Zeb thought for a few seconds. "Well, she's just the kind of gal that would have fought side by side with the men at the Alamo."

This comment shocked Bill and made his blood stir. He knew that Zeb had only heard about what happened at the Alamo. Bill had heard about the Alamo and had been on his way to help defend it. He arrived three days too late. He remembered seeing the bodies of men he had known, men he had met and men he had never seen before. Sometimes still, he didn't know if he should feel guilty for not getting there on time or if he should feel lucky for not hearing about it on time. Even catching up with Sam Houston before the battle at San Jacinto and defeating Santa Anna's troops didn't make him feel any better about the fellas that gave up everything at the Alamo. When Bill realized that Sam Houston wasn't going to execute Santa Anna, he just mounted up and left Texas without saying a word. When he stopped, he was at the Milk River. He reckoned that was far enough away from Texas and Sam Houston as he needed to be. Bill wasn't a cruel man, but he did believe in justice. He figured Houston had his reasons for letting Santa Anna go, political probably, but Bill wasn't a politician and always believed in cutting the head off the snake.

Bill didn't know if Zeb's statement was meant to be a compliment or not. That could mean that she just liked to kill people or it could mean that she had a lot of heart. Bill knew that his old friend liked to tease and surprise and keep important information to himself, so he wasn't going to give Zeb the satisfaction of asking any more questions or showing any more interest in the woman for now. Zeb always gave his secrets away eventually because he couldn't hold them. Bill would wait Zeb out and drink his coffee.

Bennager stuck his head through the opening of the tepee. "Would you like me to unsaddle your stock, Bill?"

"Thank you, I'd be obliged to you," Bill replied.

"Young fellas are fidgety, but Bennager's a good hand and a good friend," Zeb commented.

"What of these other friends of hers that you mentioned?"

"Well, she caught somebody going through Bennager's wagon probably. Bennager is a teamster. They hit her in the head and took two of Bennager's horses. Her friends, Angus and Sam, took two of Bennager's horses and went after them right away. Angus thinks that it was his brothers that did this to her. They've been following him since he threw them off the steamboat three days ago. Angus damned near killed one of them two nights ago when the three of them ambushed him while we were sleeping. They were probably only hungry and looking for food when Rose caught them last night, but that won't matter when Angus finds them."

"Irish, is he?"

"Yep," Zeb smiled. "Bricklayer, Bennager says."

"Who's Sam?"

"Sam came around the Horn with Rose. I judge he's our age or older. He's a Black man. I don't know if he is free or a runaway, and I didn't ask. Bennager said he was a boxer, and as far as I'm concerned, he can be whatever he wants to be. He's anxious to find gold."

Bill shook his head. "He'll be disappointed. They ain't pickin' that gold up off the ground like they thought they would. I just came from the hills after seein' what all the fuss was about. They are gettin' gold, but it's hard work. The thing is there ain't much to eat up in them hills. I stopped at a cook tent, and the price of a rotten deer steak was $20. I had the beans, if you can believe that, traveled around some, lookin' for beef, and there wasn't any to be had. That's when I decided to see if you were still alive. I knew you would cook me up a good piece of meat."

Bennager had sacked the horses, including Bill's stock, and had come in during Bill's conversation with Zeb. He checked the temperature of Rose's face and thought to himself that the fever was fluctuating. "Rose thinks the best way to make money in the gold fields is to raise and sell beef."

Bill laughed. "Well, that's a hell of an idea, all right, if you are a cattle rustler or if you have a lot of money already. It appears that your girl is a dreamer."

"I ain't a damned thief, that's for sure. All you damned men are making too much noise. What did you do, get drunk?" Rose said with her eyes still closed and grimacing with pain from the headache she surely had.

"We're not drunk and we're not hollering," Bennager whispered to her after going to her side and feeling her head.

"Oh, don't touch my head." Rose cringed.

"I don't have to ask how you are feeling, I guess."

"I'm thirsty. Get me my brandy, would you?" Rose whispered.

"The thieves took it. You'll have to settle for water," Bennager said, smiling because he knew the head injury had not changed her way of thinking.

"Thieves? What thieves? What did I miss?" Rose asked.

"The thieves that hit you in the back of the head with a shovel. You haven't missed much except Sam and Angus went after them and they're not back yet."

"They probably got lost. They don't know this country. The damned fog swallowed them up, and they are lost forever. Why didn't you go with them? You know this country."

"They left before I knew they were gone. Besides, I was more worried about you at the time than I was about them. You are right, though, they probably are lost, but it's not foggy today," Bennager said, beginning to focus his worry on Angus and Sam.

"If it ain't foggy, then Sam will make it back," Rose said, assuring Bennager not to worry, and then she drifted back to sleep.

"Bill, we better go and kill something to eat. The next time that girl wakes up, she'll be hungry as a bear. I do believe she would eat us if we don't have something ready for her at feeding time," Zeb joked.

Bill didn't laugh. He didn't think that was a very smart way to talk about a lady. As a matter of fact, he shot a glance at Bennager, thinking maybe he might take offense to Zeb's remark and jump him.

Bennager only produced a thin smile. He would have normally chuckled at Zeb's teasing, but he was still too worried about Rose. "Take one of the horses if you want to, Zeb. You might have to travel far today."

"I will. I'll keep my eyes peeled for the posse while we are out there," Zeb replied.

Bill stood up from the fire and gave Bennager the pouch with the dried plants in it. "You'll need to change that poultice when the time comes. Wash the old stuff off completely before you put the new stuff on. Do you remember how?"

"Yes," Bennager said, nodding his head. Bennager was grateful to Bill and Zeb for all they were doing to help Rose and was happy to finally be alone with her, even if she was oblivious to what was happening around her. Bennager was able to take her hand in his without anybody around to tease him about it. He wasn't sure how Rose would have felt about it if she was awake, but it made him feel better. He thought of how it was just like her to criticize him for letting Angus and Sam go off into country unknown to them, but no matter what the outcome would be with Sam and Angus, he would never feel guilty for staying with Rose, even if he had nothing to do with patching her up or breaking the fever. He just couldn't risk not being there when she woke up, and he hoped that he would be the first person Rose would want to see, even if he was to blame for half of her injuries.

Time passed while Bennager was consoling himself by holding Rose's hand. Girl took the opportunity to break herself from being a nurse to being a mother and went to be with her pups. She knew Bennager would take her place to will Rose to stay alive. Bennager sat with Rose for an hour or better and decided to get busy changing the poultice as Bill had instructed. While he was cleaning the wound on Rose's arm, Charlie hooted at the opening of the tepee.

"Come on in, Charlie," Bennager told him.

"How's the patient today?" Charlie inquired.

"I think she's coming along. Slow but sure, I hope."

Charlie knelt to look at his handiwork on Rose's arm. "It looks puffy and red," Charlie commented.

"It's better now than what it was this morning," Bennager said as he was fixing the poultice. "A fella by the name of Bill Ford showed up this morning. It turns out that he was an old friend of Zeb's and was looking for him. I guess he's been a mountain man. He didn't say much about himself except that he knew a little bit about bad wounds. He said you did a fine job of stitching her up."

"He did, did he?" Charlie said, seeming proud. He really had no idea if he had done a good job or not. He only knew that he had done the best job that he could. "Bill Ford, you say? Don't know him."

"Well, he seems to just travel around a lot. I guess he's been to California before. He seemed to know where to find Zeb."

"What was he lookin' for Zeb for?" Charlie asked.

"He said he couldn't find anything to eat in the foothills, so he was going to have Zeb cook him a steak."

"Sounds like a travelin' son of a bitch to me, all right," Charlie agreed with Bennager's assessment.

"How's the river looking?"

"Oh, so far, so good. Hopefully that storm brought more snow to the Sierras instead of melting what was there. I'm still goin' to wait until tomorrow, though. I'm not goin' to risk runnin' into trees floatin' in the river."

"Are the other passengers getting inpatient with you?" Bennager asked.

"They are still workin' at dryin' themselves out," Charlie chuckled.

"Speaking of that, I better cut some more wood while I'm just sitting here. Zeb and Bill went hunting. Rose woke up once because she was thirsty, and Zeb said the next time she wakes up, she'll be hungry. I think Zeb thought it was time that Angus and Sam should be back too."

"That was goin' to be my next question," Charlie said. "You don't reckon those thieving bastards got away, do you?"

"Only time will tell. It's likely that Sam and Angus might have gotten lost. I don't know."

*****

In the daylight, it was easy for Sam to find his way. The tracks of four horses running in the mud had left a deep trail that even the hard rain of the night before was not able to wash away. Sam had winded the horses bad in his desire to be away from the place where two men had been killed. He finally slowed them down to a walk. He didn't want to, but he had no choice. Bennager would already be agitated about the stress that had been put on his team without Sam killing the animals. Sam recalled the scene of Angus killing his brothers in the dark.

Sam could not see the image in his mind, but, from the sounds, was able to picture it. The most prominent sound that came to mind was the one a melon makes when it is crushed. Sam closed his eyes and shook his head, trying to get loose from it. After the event, Angus was ashamed to come back to the traveling party. He wanted to wander the valley alone and never be seen by humans again, especially Rose

Mary Briar. Sam had to get him drunk and bring him back against his will as he knew Rose would not tolerate Angus being abandoned.

Unfortunately, Sam could hear Angus coming to life and hoped that he was still drunk. Sam desperately wanted to make it back to camp before he had to tend to Angus. He was still very frightened that the law would find him before he got back, even though he had not seen a single soul since he had started. Ignoring the groans of pain coming from Angus, Sam soon realized that he wasn't going to get his wish and started looking for a big oak to use for cover while they all rested.

Before Sam was able to stop, Angus started pleading with him. His voice was so low that Sam could have easily continued to pretend that he couldn't hear the poor man, but Sam couldn't ignore his words. Sam decided to settle for the next oak that he came to and stopped. He untied Angus and helped him to stand up. He thought a minute later that he should have let Angus fall off the horse himself because once Angus was on his feet, he clubbed Sam on the side of his face with his enormous fist and whispered, "What did ye tie me up like that for?" Then he fell, lying on his back under the horse that he had been on.

"Are you passed out again?" Sam asked, getting up from the ground.

"I'll never pass out 'round ye again, ye mean, ruthless, old son of a bitch!" Angus hissed.

Sam knew he deserved the harsh words that were being thrown at him but thought that his days of being hit in the face were over. Then Sam realized that he was lucky that Angus was in a weakened state because he might have given Sam a fatal blow instead of just the love tap that he suffered. "We have to get back, Angus. Bennager might have a bunch of men lookin' for his horses. He might not trust us to come back on our own. If you are strong enough to belly ache and hit me, then you are strong enough to ride."

"Bennager can go straight to the devil if he don't trust me. I never gave 'em no cause."

"Come on, I'll help you get mounted."

"Ye'll not touch me at all, Sam! It's ye that cannot be trusted. Your puttin' a man on a horse so as all the blood in his body fills up to his aching head is a cowardly thin' to do. When I am able to mount up, then I will be strong enough to ride, and if ye don't like 'em terms, then feel free to leave me here. I can walk back when I get ready."

"I can't leave you here by yourself."

"I wish you would so I can rest in peace," Angus argued.

"Good to see you boys made it back," Zeb hollered. Zeb and Bill had been watching the argument since Sam had stopped and nearly fell from their horses with laughter when Angus hit Sam and then sprawled out underneath his own horse. This is when Zeb thought that it would be fun to sneak up on the two of them while they were bickering. Sam nearly jumped out of his skin but was so happy to see Zeb that he quickly forgave him for the joke.

Stepping up to shake hands with Zeb, Sam asked, "It's good to see you, Zeb. How is Rose?"

"How is me Rose Mary?" Angus rattled from underneath his horse with his eyes closed.

Zeb shook his head at the sight of the big Irishman being in such a state and then told Sam, "She is bound to live now that Bill is here. She's likely to keep her arm too. Sam, this here is Bill Ford."

Sam turned to shake hands with the man and immediately realized that he already knew him. Even with his face covered with hair, Sam would never forget the eyes of the boy that he had known so many years ago. Of course, seeing William again brought back the disturbing memories of William's brother, Douglas, and the day Sam and William ran off together. "Bill, is it?" Sam said as he shook William's hand, thinking maybe William wouldn't want anyone to know about their past together.

"It's a small world, ain't it, Sam? My Lord, it's been a long time since we split the trail."

"Yep, I should have followed along with you instead of heading north. I was caught."

Bill shook his head, not knowing how to respond to the simple recollection and decided that it was best not to.

"Bill, you must know half the people in this world." Zeb chortled.

"I sure don't know that big fella, what happened to him?"

"Sam tried to kill me. Hang 'im!" Angus answered.

Sam quickly turned and glared at Angus, wanting to walk over and kick him, but answered Bill instead. Still glaring at Angus, he said sadly, "I don't think we are friends anymore, and what really happened to him is that he found his two stupid brothers."

"Hang me! Hang me, I'm done for, I avenged me pretty Rose Mary, and now I'm done for. Put me out of me misery." Bennager's horse turned and looked under its belly at Angus and whinnied, wanting the crazy man to go someplace else. This loud noise caused Angus to become paralyzed with pain.

Sam snickered a little.

"What is he? Crazy in the head or what?" Bill asked.

Zeb replied, "Oh, yes, Angus is crazy in the head, even for an Irishman, but it looks like those head wounds have made him more confused than ever."

Sam walked over to Angus, making sure to stay away from his feet. Bill and Zeb dismounted and followed Sam. Sam bent down and told Angus, "If you can still feel pain, then you're not done for. Now get up."

"Ye go to the devil."

"If you keep being mean, then this horse is gonna kick you, Angus. Yesterday, that might have been a fair fight, but you're look-ing a little peaked today," Zeb teased.

"Peaked? Is that all I am? I killed me mother's sons last night, and now I'm feelin' a little peaked. That's rich, Zeb. Zeb the big teaser, the funny man. I've seen some clowns back there in New York, but ye take the cake. Do ye really think I care if this horse kicks the devil out of me? I'm goin' to the devil, boys, no doubt about it. As far as I'm concerned, the sooner the better," Angus mumbled.

Sam shook his head and backed away from Angus. "He's been like this since he finished his brothers. That's why I got him drunk and packed him up like that. He wanted me to leave him, but I knew Rose wouldn't stand for it. He doesn't want her to see him because he thinks he's a murderer. If I leave him, I know that he won't come back on his own, and he'll never get past this and do something with his life." Sam looked at Bill. "You might not believe this, but Angus is usually good to be around."

Zeb agreed by nodding his head. Zeb smiled suddenly and snapped his fingers. "I've got it. I'll be back." Zeb mounted and headed back toward camp.

Bill and Sam watched him leave and then turned to each other, each man with a quizzical look on his face. They shrugged and turned their attention back to Angus. "Let's move the horse. If it kicks him, maybe he'll cheer up a little," Bill suggested.

Sam nodded and took the rope, speaking softly; he asked the horse that had packed Angus all morning to move carefully away from the crazy man. The animal was grateful and only too happy to ease ahead and was able to accomplish the maneuver without even touching his crazy former passenger.

"Well done, Sam. You always were a sweet talker with horses," Bill praised.

"Well, we always had things in common, I guess."

"Where did the shade go? Me eyelids are as red as the devil's fire in hell. Finally, I've died and gone to the devil," Angus murmured.

His horse turned to get a good look at the redheaded lump that had been causing him to be nervous and decided to smell it. The animal was certain that it was some form of man but wanted to make sure, so it did. First, he sniffed and snorted, slowly getting closer until his nose was right at Angus' ear, and then he took a taste of it. Angus thrashed around on the ground, waving his arms. The horse whinnied again and moved backward. Angus hissed with pain and grabbed his ear with one hand and his head with the other hand while Bill and Sam stood by, watching and laughing. Bill didn't really want to make an enemy out of this man that he didn't know yet, but Sam was tired of Angus feeling sorry for himself and thought that it was time to move on. "I suppose that was the devil's steed with the teeth from hell," Sam hollered, still laughing.

"Help me sit up, Sam," Angus whispered.

"You'll hit me again. You can do it yourself. I see that you can move when you want to," Sam told him.

"Damn ye, mean son of a bitch. I wouldn't hurt half as bad if it weren't for you," Angus said as he rolled over on to his belly. As he rested in that position, getting ready for his next move, Zeb walked up with the crate of pups, and Girl was following.

"Oh Lord, wait until you see this, William," Sam said as he sat down, resting his back on the trunk of an oak tree and shaking his head in disgust.

Bill was shocked at being called William. No one had called him that in many years. He quickly realized that Sam had been transported back in time to when they were boys and had forgotten the bad times that had happened after. Bill sat on the ground with Sam and asked, "What's he got? Food or whiskey or something?"

"Just watch, you'll see."

Zeb set the box of puppies beside Angus' head, and Girl looked in the box and nuzzled her babies around to make sure they had all survived the hike, and then she turned to Angus. She didn't like him as much as she liked her friend, Rose, but she knew him, and she knew that something was terribly wrong with him. She looked back at Zeb, then at her pups. Finally, she just lay down with her face resting on her front legs and stared at Angus. Girl really wanted to go back and watch Rose, but these men had taken her babies hostage, so she had to stay.

As Girl stared at Angus, she devised a plan to start packing her babies back to the tepee, one by one. It would take her a while, and some of them would be alone while she was gone, but she would have to risk it. Rose needed her, and she couldn't be fooling around with this man much longer.

Angus moved a little, getting ready to lift himself up to his knees. Girl lifted her head up and waited. The man didn't move anymore. Girl was anxious. Playfully, she put her paw on Angus' head, and he groaned. Girl jumped up, nuzzled his face, and licked him.

Angus tipped over onto his back and petted Girl and moaned to her about his problems and his pain as if they were the two only creatures in the world. Girl jumped back and stood by her brood and wagged her tail. Angus rolled onto his side to see where she went and saw the box with the babies in it. "Oh, ye brought me the wee little babes. What a good girl ye are." Angus happily praised her as he half crawled, half squirmed so he could look in the box. "Oh, look at those tiny little babes ye have here." Girl lay down again, watching every move the strange, distorted man made, wondering when she could go look after Rose.

Sam shook his head in disgust.

Zeb smiled at his own quick wit at knowing what would bring Angus back to life.

Bill looked on in wonderment, this being some of the strangest behavior that he had seen amongst men. "That beating he took has really played hell with his head. It has turned his brain into mush."

Zeb's smile turned into a frown, and Sam said, "No, Angus is getting back to his normal self now."

"Oh, me wee little angels, oh so tiny and pretty," Angus said, resting on his knees now.

8

"Bennager," Rose whispered.

Bennager squeezed her hand. "Rose, I'm here."

"What in tarnation happened? It was raining, everyone was working to set up camp, and I remember my arm was hurt so I couldn't carry both bags in one trip. So I went to get the other bag… What happened?"

"Angus' brothers were scrounging around my wagon, probably looking for food or dry clothes, nobody knows for sure. When you went for the second bag, they hit you over the head with a shovel and knocked you out. Ordinarily, I think you would have bounced right up after that, but that arm is the reason why you are having so much trouble. You lost a lot of blood while you were running around out in the rain, and then the cut got infected." Bennager looked away and shook his head. "It's all my fault, Rose. I pert near cut your arm off. If that mountain man hadn't come along, we would have had to cut it off because of infection."

"That old saw almost cut my arm off, and then those stupid brothers hit me in the head? Damn! What a day! What day is it now?"

"It's the next day, about suppertime."

"Where is everybody?"

"Sam and Angus went after the brothers. Zeb said they are back, just a little way from camp. Angus took quite a beating, so Zeb took the pups and Girl out to cheer him up. Zeb and the mountain man, Bill, are out looking for supper. Charlie is watching the river." Bennager put the back of his hand on Rose's cheek. This was becoming a habit for him. He would forever be Rose's fever checker from this time forward. Rose closed her eyes. Her first instinct was to pull away and raise Cain with him, but she knew it would be too painful and require too much effort.

"Do you have any idea what you are doing?" she asked mockingly.

Bennager looked into her green eyes that were open now. He wanted to kiss her and hold her and tell her that he loved her, but she would have thought that it was all nonsense. "No, but I know that your face is cooler now than it was before, and Charlie told me to keep checking."

"Charlie?"

"Yeah, Charlie is the one that sewed you up. You have a bald spot on the back of your head now."

"Well, what makes you think—I mean, is the infection in my arm gone now or what?"

"Look for yourself." Bennager pulled the cover off Rose's arm so she could see it, but the first thing that she noticed was that her top was off.

"Did all of you men see me without my shirt?" Rose shrieked.

Still concentrating on the progress of the wound, Bennager jerked back and looked at Rose. His heart sank. Here they were, alone together. He was pleased for the first time in two days, and the gal he loved was mad at him again. "No, just me," he said proudly. Seems how she was going to fuss over nothing anyway, he figured he might just as well rankle her.

"Oh, just you, huh?"

"Zeb and Charlie turned their backs while I got you out of your wet clothes so as you wouldn't catch pneumonia. Or would you like to add that to your list of ailments? I didn't want to take your clothes off," Bennager said, smiling broadly. "But Charlie said we had to do it. Zeb said that I should be the one to do it, seems how I'm going to be the one doing it anyway. In the future, of course."

Rose began to feel around on the ground.

"What are you doing?" Bennager asked.

"Where is my pistol? Sam wouldn't leave me lying here without my pistol by me."

"Sam was in a hurry. He trusted me to take care of you. What are you going to do with your pistol? Shoot me?"

"Yes."

"Well, I deserve it. It's my fault that you're in this fix." Bennager reached into Rose's bag and handed her weapon to her. "Here, use it."

"I should. You're trying to rankle me on purpose."

"We were all just trying to care for you. Here is a dry shirt for you to put on before the others get back."

"Thank you."

"You'll need help with that. May I without getting shot?"

Rose searched the depths of Bennager's blue eyes, burning a hole through his soul, looking for trust. She laid her pistol down.

Bennager explained, "I was going to do this last night, but everything was wet. I'm going to help you sit up, and then we'll do the bad arm first. We'll get the hard part over with."

Rose wanted to do it herself, but when she tried to use her arm, it was impossible. She had never had an injury like this before. Bennager started to button the shirt for her, and unexpectedly, his fingers began to tremble. Rose was watching his face as he fiercely concentrated on the task. She found it amusing that suddenly, this very capable man, who she had witnessed do all sorts of complicated tasks with his hands, was unable to button a shirt. He looked into her eyes pitifully. "Are you laughing?" he asked.

She felt his cheek with the back of her good hand. Something about this moment had sent a shooting sensation from the depths of her throughout her entire body. It was strange and something that she had never felt before.

She looked down at the two buttons on the bottom that he had managed to get. She couldn't understand what had him so nervous. Everything was covered up. She looked into his eyes. "Why did you stop? Are you sick too?"

Bennager smiled broadly again, remembering that this was the naivest girl that he had ever met, at least compared to the other two that he had met, and her young mind had no idea what it was like for him to have his hands that close to her and not be able to touch her. "No, I'm not sick, little girl."

"It tickles when you shake like that," Rose said innocently.

"Yes, I'm sure it does. It tickles me a little bit too. It's good to have you awake and feeling better, Rose. It was mighty dull without you giving me a hard time," Bennager said, continuing with the buttons and trying not to think about what was under the shirt and trying not to shake. He really couldn't believe that this woman didn't know how she affected him, but if she didn't, he couldn't take any bold chances, except just to rile her occasionally. When he got to the buttons at the bust, Rose was unable to conceal her own strange feelings. She showed her hand by letting out a little shiver. This pleased Bennager, but he pretended like he didn't notice. She was trying to drive him mad, but he wasn't going to let her do it.

"I'm all finished," he said, looking at Rose and still grinning. Rose wasn't grinning.

Whatever was going on in her mind had made her too speechless to even say, "Thank you."

"I suppose that you want your overalls on too," Bennager said as he took them from the tree branch where they had dried.

"No, no, thank you. I'll use the blanket for right now."

"I have to change that poultice on your arm every so often. I guess I should have cut the sleeve off before we put it on," Bennager said, treating her like a patient now. "Let me help you lie down."

Rose watched his eyes as he gently supported her until she was lying down again. When he finished, he just stayed by her side, holding her good hand in his and smiling. She smiled back at him. For the first time, she was being honest. There was no fake fussing or arguing. She probably just wasn't up to it because of her headache, but she realized that it was nice just to be quiet and smile and mean it.

Bennager put her hand to his lips and kissed it. His chin started to quiver. "Rose, I'm so sorry for cutting your arm. I was in a hurry to get out of the rain and mad that the saw was buried under all the supplies. I was so stupid for not being more careful."

"It's not your fault. It was just an accident. I was in a hurry, too, and I got in the way."

"I thought that I was going to lose you, and then I felt so helpless when you were sick with the fever. If Bill hadn't come along, you would really be in a bad way."

"Bennager, it's over now, and Bill or no Bill, I'm sure I would have survived, and I don't want you to worry about it anymore." She took her hand from his and put it on his face, caressing his cheek with her thumb. He closed his eyes and let the weight of his face rest in her hand. She brought her hand closer to her until he was lying down beside her. She gingerly turned to her side to face him. "You're tired."

"I slept beside you this morning," Bennager replied. "Just like this, except you weren't holding me."

"I am now. I'm going to be all right. You rest. You'll wake up when the others get back," Rose whispered.

Rose wanted to hold him with her other arm, but she couldn't. She lifted her blanket with her leg and curled her leg around his, holding him close and tight. The regret that he felt over a stupid accident had touched her heart more than his shaking hands on her buttons ever could. She knew that she didn't have a clue as to what to do with this man. Zeb seemed to think that she was doing something to him all the time. What did Zeb mean when he said that Bennager would be the one undressing her in the future? It felt good to Rose to hold Bennager close like this, even though they hadn't known each other for more than a few days. The thought of being close like this with a man had always been a nonsensical idea to Rose. She always figured that it was the man's idea to get close like this, and she never thought it was possible to really love a man with her heart, but the feeling that she was having for him right now, right or wrong, was a serious desire to show him that she wasn't a little girl. She wanted him to know that when he needed to be cared for, then she would be there to do it. A week ago, Sam would have been the one to stay with her if she was ill, but Bennager said that Sam trusted him to do it.

Rose watched Bennager doze, and she kissed him on the forehead. "I'm not a little girl," she whispered, thinking that he was asleep.

"I know. You are a beautiful woman. You just don't know it yet," he whispered back, not opening his eyes.

"One day, it will be my turn to take care of you."

"You're doing it right now," he replied.

Rose kissed his forehead again, and Bennager smiled as he slid his hand carefully between her waist and her injured arm. He raised his mouth to hers, hoping that he wouldn't frighten her away. Being inexperienced, Rose's kiss was light and gentle, and Bennager hoped for more. Rose liked this loving feeling that she had charging through her body, and every kiss was better than the one before. His kisses grew more passionate as if he was the teacher, and she continued to match his level of intensity. The way he caressed her back and pulled her waist toward his, each time he kissed her, sent quakes through her body that she wasn't sure of, but the kisses were so pleasing and plentiful that she didn't want to think about the quakes. She was giving her heart to Bennager right now. She wanted him to know that she loved him.

Of course, there was no way in devil that she would ever tell him that with words. She didn't want him to think that he owned her. She pulled back. One more minute of this, and she would melt, and he would be able to do whatever he wanted. Rose opened her eyes. Bennager's eyes were still closed. Slowly he opened them, and Rose saw tears coming from both of his blue eyes. "What's this?" she asked in a whisper.

"You really do forgive me for your arm?"

"It was an accident."

"I just realized that I have been waiting for you my whole life, and I didn't know that I was waiting for anyone until I saw you the other day walking up the hill from the pier."

Rose kissed him and used her leg to pull him closer.

Bennager said, "I thought that I loved you that day, but now I know that I love you."

"I love you too," Rose whispered, crying now herself and kissing him again.

*****

A couple of hours later, Bennager was shaken awake by Rose's snoring. Shaking his head, he looked around and noticed that Girl was back with her pups and happily content to sit in the box with them, taking her duties as a new mother more seriously now that her friend, Rose, was obviously much better.

Angus was on a makeshift bed on the other side of the tent sleeping. His wounds were still covered with mud as was his whole person. Bennager couldn't believe that no one had cleaned him up.

Bennager stepped outside the tent. It was dark now, but he could smell the venison that was roasting over the fire and was grateful to whoever had brought it in. He hadn't eaten since yesterday afternoon, and that hadn't been much. Looking at the others, he realized that no one had eaten since Rose had gotten hurt.

Every man was quiet. Sam looked up at Bennager, glaring, but had been around enough killing for one day. He reckoned he could eat tonight and kill Bennager in the morning.

"I guess Rose ain't Catholic like my wife is, huh, Bennager?" Zeb needled.

"What?"

"Catholic, I say. I had to marry my wife before I could have a honeymoon," Zeb continued.

"Honeymoon?" Bennager queried.

Bill stood up, seeming taller now than Bennager had remembered him being. "If it weren't no honeymoon, then maybe you just like taking advantage of girls when they are out of their heads with fever."

"Fever?" Bennager turned to check on Rose. He hadn't noticed the fever being back when he woke up. Bill grabbed Bennager's neck before he could get back into the tepee.

Charlie walked up with a couple of jugs of sake to instigate a celebration and noticed Benny was in trouble. "What goes here?" Charlie hollered.

"What goes here is that this no account ain't right in the head!" Bill hollered back.

"No account? Benny's as sound as any I have ever seen. Let him go. We're goin' to celebrate tonight. You are all back, the river's holdin', the girl is well now, and we leave tomorrow. What are you pickin' on Benny for?" Charlie jovially asked.

Bill held his ground, not letting his prey out of his talon. "I've heard that there ain't no law out west, but I've lived with Indians, and they have more respect for their gods and ceremonies than this yellow coward does."

Rose opened the tent flaps and quietly said, "Meat." With her eyes fixed on the campfire, she started toward it slowly, watching her step, not wanting to injure herself anymore amid all the excitement over her favorite food. Then she remembered to give her sweetheart a kiss. "Hello, sweetheart," she said, smiling.

"You're not getting out of this," Bill said, squeezing his claws even tighter around Bennager's neck.

"Howdy, Mrs. Rasmussen, are you feeling better this evening?" Charlie asked sincerely.

"Why, yes, I am, much better, never better, actually," Rose said, blushing and gingerly sitting down by the fire, thinking how funny it was to be called Missus.

"I've brought some spirits to celebrate your nuptials."

"Well, Charlie, I never imagined that you would part with your reserves," Rose joked.

"Well, Mrs. Rasmussen, it does my heart good to know that you will be married well and up there in those hills somewheres and that I will hopefully never see you again after this trip is over," Charlie said sincerely.

"What a lovely sentiment, sir. Unfortunately for me, whenever I think of the happiest day of my life, your face will be in my memory," Rose jabbed.

"You should have closed your eyes during the ceremony, Mrs. Rasmussen."

"Yes, and let that be the first toast on my wedding day," Rose cheerfully stated as she raised the jug.

Bill tossed Bennager to the side and took the jug away from Rose. "You shouldn't drink with a head injury. Drink this," Bill said, handing her a cup of hot tea. Bill wasn't a drinking man and always had his hot tea ready made with plants that he collected during his travels.

Zeb and Sam were looking at each other in astonishment. It was too much for either one of them to take in at once. First, Bennager was in deep trouble, there was no doubt about that, and then Charlie was calling Rose "Mrs. Rasmussen'" for some reason they couldn't get their heads around, and now someone had the audacity to rip hard liquor from the hands of Rose Mary Briar.

"Sweetheart, that reminds me, would you be so kind as to bring me my pistol? I forgot it," Rose sweetly asked her new husband.

"No, I won't bring you your pistol right now. Rose, this man brought you back to me. He is your official doctor right now, and you need to listen to him. Rose Mary Rasmussen, meet Bill Ford."

"You mean to tell me that you two are married!" Zeb said, pointing, having finally caught on. "But how?"

"I'll have you know that the captain of a vessel has the authority to marry two people. Did my best to try to talk him out of it, but I couldn't. Now he has become this wildcat's keeper," Charlie informed.

Sam was glaring at Charlie when Rose said, "Honey, my pistol!"

"Not right now, dear!" Bennager said.

"He's doing a damned fine job of too," Charlie laughed.

"Ma'am, I believe that we were in the middle of being properly introduced," Bill said, facing Rose.

Rose looked up and saw a tall, wide-shouldered man with a hairy face and a wide-brimmed hat, and his image was so familiar that she suddenly felt sick. The flood of emotions overwhelmed her. She wondered if she was seeing his twin or his ghost. Her head quickly burst with pain, and her insides were shaking. Rose glanced at herself to see if it was showing on the outside. She told herself, *Don't let him shake you.* Slowly, Rose stood up to look this man in the eye. She thought, what would she do if it was him? She would hold her ground is what she would do. *I am a married woman now, even if my husband doesn't know my real name. I've gone off and accomplished just what he wanted me to do. He'll want his money back, though, damn him.*

Rose and Bill were standing face-to-face now. "Ma'am, you look mighty familiar to me, especially now with your eyes open," Bill said, smiling.

Rose wasn't smiling. She had a look in her eye that Sam knew well. She wasn't pretending to be the crazy, outrageous, misbehaved girl that would start a fight over a jug. This man had done something that had Rose scared to the bone. Something about the sudden quiet around the fire made the hairs on the back of Bennager's neck stand up, and when he happened to see the look on Sam's face, he quickly stood up to get in between Rose and Bill.

"What is it, Rose?" Bennager fearfully asked.

"It's nothing. This man says he's Bill Ford, and then he says that he recognizes me. It's strange, is all. Besides that, he's given me some sort of piss water to drink on my wedding day," Rose said all too calmly, which frightened Bennager even more. Bennager took Rose by her good arm and waist and helped her to sit down by the fire again. He could feel her body trembling on the inside. He wanted to ask her what was wrong, but he was truly afraid of what the answer would be.

Girl came out of the tepee to bark at the coyotes who were also celebrating the better weather. She didn't like them. Her shrill barks hurt Rose's head, and she put her good hand over one ear.

"There is the nurse," Zeb said. "Come here, Girl. Stop that now, you're giving pain to your patient."

Girl saw Rose and wagged her tail. She trotted over, sat beside Rose, and put one paw on her friend's leg.

"Oh, sweet Girl, I missed you! How is your little family?" Rose asked the dog while hugging her with her good arm.

"Your buddy was so worried about you she barely took time out to feed her pups," Zeb answered for his dog. "It's a wonderment to me how she got so attached to you."

"Is that right, Girl? You helped me heal up too? We're the only girls on this trip, ain't we?" Rose looked up. "I guess I owe all of you a big thank you. My husband tells me that you all did things to help me, and he says that even Charlie was concerned about my health. So thank you, everyone. I hope I'll be around to return the favor." Rose looked down at her feet, humble and embarrassed, never much for being in the position to thank anybody for anything. "When do you think Angus will wake up?" Rose asked.

"Oh, Lord, whatever you do, don't wake him up! Don't talk about him or even say his name!" Sam implored.

Bennager was curious. "What's wrong?" he asked, chuckling.

Rose scolded, "He really needs to be cleaned up. His face has cuts filled with dirt, and it's all swelled up and bruised, and his clothes are turning to stone with all that mud on him. I'm sure that he's tired and he needs his rest, but you should have cleaned him up, Sam."

Sam was nodding his head up and down deliberately, knowing that he was being scolded without even having to make eye contact with Rose. "First of all, he's your husband, so he's the one you can nag at now," Sam said, pointing at Bennager. "And second, your big Irish savior is crazier than hell, which you might like to know is where he is goin', and I can't take gettin' whipped anymore. Have your new husband clean him up or let him rot!" Sam threw his empty plate down to the edge of the fire. Bill and Zeb snickered at Sam as he got to his feet and began to stomp off. Sam suddenly turned sharply and scowled at the gigglers and then continued on.

Bennager was shocked to hear Sam talk to Rose that way and wondered if Sam hated the idea of the two of them being married. Bennager searched Rose's face to see if he could tell what she was thinking and could tell that she was agitated. Instead of saying anything, he just got up to tend to Angus. He hated to leave Rose's side, but no one else seemed to want anything to do with Angus. He had agreed with everything that his wife had said on the subject, and he realized the moment that Sam had stomped off that her friendships hadn't changed since this afternoon when they decided to get married. At least he hoped they hadn't.

"Damn it, Sam. Don't stomp off like that," Rose hollered as she gingerly got up to follow him into the darkness, away from the others.

Zeb stopped her. "Go slow, Rose. It was a bit of a nightmare for both of them out there, I hear."

Rose looked into the eyes of the joker and saw that he was being sincere. She nodded and then hollered for Sam to wait for her. When she caught up to him, she said, "Damn, Sam, what in the devil has gotten into you?" Subtlety wasn't a trait that Rose possessed.

"I'm ready to get movin'!" Sam snapped.

"Well, we're movin' in the mornin'! What in tarnation are you yellin' at me for?" Rose snapped back.

"I'm just ready to get from this place."

"I ain't deaf, you said that already. What's got you so nervous? I ain't seen you like this since the first month on that damned ship. You got any tobacco on you? That damned Bill Ford, which he ain't no Bill Ford, will probably take that away from me too," Rose said, glowering back at the fire where Bill was.

The statement about Bill not being Bill got Sam's attention. "You reckon you know him?"

"I thought I did for a minute. Looks just like my father, except for the clothes. I thought I was caught," Rose said, turning back to Sam and smiling. "But he ain't, I guess, 'cause my father wouldn't wear clothes like that, let alone lift a finger to save me from pain."

Sam knew Bill's reasons for leaving home and losing himself and part of his name in whatever land he had been in, and he didn't think it was necessary to give away his childhood friend's true identity. "What's your father's first name?" he asked nonchalantly.

"Douglas."

"Douglas Briar?" Sam asked.

Rose gave Sam a sideways glance and smiled. "Not exactly."

"Not exactly, huh? Maybe you ought to let things be then, Miss Not Exactly."

"I get the feeling you're right. I got the chills when he said he recognized me. How could that be?" she wondered.

"Leave it be," Sam repeated.

"What happened out there with Angus?"

"We caught up with his brothers this mornin', two of them anyway, I didn't see the other one. Angus rode in ahead of me. It was still dark. They both jumped him at the same time. He killed them both with his bare hands. It took a while. He took a lot of blows to the head before he got the better of 'em." Sam looked into Rose's eyes then. "He killed his own brothers for what they did to you. He left here with the purpose to do it, and he did, and they had it comin'. He reckoned it was all his fault for what they did, and he reckoned it was up to him to make it right. Now he has to live with himself, and I don't know if he can, and if he clubs me one more time, I'll kill him for it. Rose, I swear I will. And I'm afraid of being caught again by whatever law they have here."

"I see why you're nervous. I don't believe you have to worry much about any law. Maybe in the towns, I don't know. We're partners, Sam. Nobody is taking you anywhere you don't want to go as long as I'm alive," Rose assured him.

"Partners? You're partnered up with your husband. That's the only partner you got now, Miss Not Exactly," Sam said sarcastically.

"That ain't true, Sam," Rose said as she spat. "I got a tender, loving feeling for Bennager, and he feels that way for me. He knows how it is with you and me. He's got no reason to interfere with that."

"I can't remember. How is it between you and me?" Sam asked, being mean-spirited.

"How it is, is come hell or high water, we watch each other's backsides. That's how it was on the ship. That's how it is now, and that's how it's gonna be. Sound familiar, you old grump?" Rose scolded.

"Your husband doesn't even know your real name, does he?" Sam teased, trying to lighten up his mood.

"Sure he does. It's Rasmussen."

"What about the Rose Mary part?" Sam asked.

Rose spat, "It's pretty close."

Sam shook his head in disbelief.

"You must be pretty tired, Sam. Maybe some sleep will make you feel better," Rose advised.

"I'm too old to sleep. Besides that, that crazy knothead captain is drinkin' again, and if I want to get out of this place in the morning, then I best go keep an eye on him."

"All right then. Watch that Bill, though, I don't trust him," Rose said, glaring at Bill's image by the fire.

"Now why do you say that for? You don't know him," Sam said harshly.

"I don't trust anybody that looks like my father," Rose whispered.

"He ain't him, and let me tell you one thing that you can remember, Miss whoever you are. You can trust him with your life and anything else you got, and you better believe that," Sam told her.

"How do you know that?"

"I just know. Let it be," he said over his shoulder as he left to go find Charlie.

"Let it be! Let it be! What is he talking about?" Rose said, talking to herself.

Rose had been feeling her arm aching while she was talking to Sam and decided that she had better turn in. Hopefully, that Bill would be gone off somewhere so she could get a nightcap, but as she approached the fire, she saw that he was still there. "Gentlemen, thank you for another fine meal and the conversation. I believe I'll retire now." She decided not to mention the sake with Bill still there. Even though her mouth was watering, she wouldn't give him the satisfaction of knowing it.

Inside the tent, she found her husband gently soaking Angus' wounds. "Charlie told me to call him if I needed help," Bennager said.

"At least somebody is willing," Rose whispered. "Did he wake up?"

"He's awake now."

"He is?" Rose was surprised. "Angus, I'm sorry about your brothers. I'm sorry that you had to be the one to go after them. I don't think that it was your fault they hit me. I don't know what else to say except thank you for being my friend," Rose said softly.

"They were bad, Rose Mary," Angus painfully murmured from his broken mouth.

"Yes, but you are not, Angus, and I'm damn proud to know you," Rose said with a tear streaming down the side of her face.

Angus didn't reply. Only a light squeeze of Rose's hand was all he could manage. The warm wet cloth on his face was enough to make him feel worthy of evading hell for a while, but Rose's words, the angel that he thought he could never face again, made him feel like maybe he deserved to live. He decided that he would give it a try after he slept.

"How's your arm, Rose?" Bennager asked.

"It hurts," she said as she moved across the room to lie down.

"I'll get Charlie to take over here. It will take two of us to change his clothes anyway, and I'll get that arm cleaned up. Let me help you," Bennager said as he rushed to ease Rose to her bed. Then he called for Charlie. "I can't wait to get to Sacramento City. I'm going to find the nicest room in town, bring you breakfast, lunch, and supper in a real bed, get a real doctor to look at this arm, and before we know it, you'll be as good as new." Bennager had cut the sleeve length wise so it could be repaired later and was working at flushing away the bits of poultice while Rose held the sleeve back.

"I hope your plans for me in that nice room don't end with food and a doctor. The way I see it, first thing's first. When I finally get you alone, food and doctorin' will be the farthest thing from my mind, husband," Rose whispered in his ear.

Bennager was pleased the two of them were thinking alike. Bennager smiled and then blushed at the image that he had formed in his head about what his new wife had planned for him in Sacramento City. "You keep talking like that, and we'll end up being in that room, locked away from the rest of the world forever, and you will forget about all of those plans of yours."

Still grinning from ear to ear, Bennager said, "I could live with that, especially the part about locking you up where only I know and only I have the key. When I open the door, the only thing you do is what you were just thinking about doing to me. And then when we are finished, I lock you up again and leave. You'd see me a lot because I'd open that door probably twelve or thirty times a day."

Bennager looked into Rose's eyes then while he was doctoring her arm to see how she was taking his teasing, and it wasn't good, of course. She was scowling at him, which he reckoned would be her response. He smiled.

"You just can't stand to see me happy and content, can you? You're not happy unless I'm spittin' fire all over you! I know your little game, husband. You're trying to scare me out of this marriage because you're afraid you made a mistake," Rose whispered but wanted to be screaming.

"That's not true! That's not true at all, dear. I was just explaining to you what I expect my wife to do. I got you now, and no matter what you do or say, I'll never let you go. You'll get used to how things are now." Bennager was doing everything in his power not to laugh or smile while he teased and worked on Rose's arm. He could feel her become tense and knew that she was giving him a look filled with daggers, but he wouldn't look at her. He reckoned that she would start hollering for Sam to come rescue her any second. The poor, little, inexperienced girl wouldn't know if her husband was serious or not.

"If anybody is going to get locked up around here, it's going to be you for having strange, evil thoughts. And I bet one of these days, you are going to choke on those words about never letting me go, but they are your words, so I'm going to make sure that you live by them. I only wish we weren't whispering because it would have been good to have a witness when you said that," Rose remarked, being indifferent to Bennager's frightening joke.

Bennager faced her then and smiled. He leaned toward her, hoping for a kiss that would confirm that she still trusted him and knew that he would never hurt her on purpose. At first, it seemed as though he might be refused. Rose glared as though she despised the man and was repulsed by his presence, then suddenly, she smiled also, playing along with his joke the whole time. His sadistic ideas of marriage that he had spoken of only excited the quick of her being.

Even though she knew that neither one of them had time to be locked up and used as love slaves for one another, the idea of it set her soul on fire with thoughts of passion that would have made her husband blush for a week straight. As her smiling at him turned into a long, intense kiss, Rose decided that she would keep her own evil, strange thoughts of desire to herself until the time came to show her husband that he was right about her being a beautiful woman. She couldn't wait to get to Sacramento City and find out for herself what she was made of.

Bennager's shock was apparent when he pulled back and looked at her. How the mind of this woman worked would probably always be a mystery to him, but then he remembered that everything she did was an overwhelming surprise to him. As he finished bandaging her up, he found that for the first time since he had met his Rose, he was actually looking forward to her next round of outrageous behavior.

Smiling as though he would never stop, Bennager said, "Well, I'm finished with this arm. You lie down and rest now. I doubt you've done much praying in your life, but it wouldn't hurt to pray for good weather tomorrow." He supported her as she laid down and lovingly kissed her cheek, mainly because one more kiss on the mouth would have spiraled into an embarrassing situation for both of them.

She knew it too. "Chicken," Rose whispered as he kissed her hand for an added show of affection and joined Charlie to help Angus.

9

After the coyotes had worn themselves out, rejoicing over good weather, the night became quiet. Everyone had managed to sleep the night through without interruption. Even Charlie had behaved himself. After only a few drinks, he was able to fall asleep. Watching the water and waiting for mud and trees to come boiling down the river had made him too tired to get drunk and run around, so Sam was able to sleep as well. Everyone decided to sleep outside by the fire so as not to bother Rose and Bennager. Of course, they didn't know it, but Rose and Bennager were dead to the world before the rest of them had finished the evening's conversation.

Angus was having a dream. He was back in Ireland, walking through the fields, and the next thing he knew, there was a big black bull with red horns, snorting at him from behind. Angus saw it and turned to run. The bull chased him down the hill. Angus tried to scream, but nothing would come out. He turned to see if he was outrunning the bull, and there were fifty of them, all exactly alike, chasing him. He tripped on a rock wall and fell. Just as the hooves were about to beat him to a pulp, Angus woke up, screaming, "It's the bulls from hell!"

Bennager woke up right away, wondering if he was in the middle of a stampede. He had probably been having a similar dream because his lovely wife sounded like a herd of snorting cattle. Bennager and Angus looked at each other, and then they looked at Rose who hadn't yet been alerted by the impending stampede. The noise that she was making was obviously the source of fear that both men had just felt in their dream worlds.

Angus' outburst impacted him both mentally and physically. He had become stiff overnight, and his mouth and head were filled with intolerable pain. Waking up to the fact that the devil's bulls were after him and seeing Bennager and Rose wrapped up together was more than his brain could bear, so he just started moaning. His whole body was so stiff and sore that he couldn't make himself get up, but most of the pain was located around his brain.

"Are you feeling better today, Angus?" Bennager asked quietly as he dressed.

A moan was his only answer. In between moans, Angus listened to the sounds that were coming out of his Rose Mary. The droning of it, going on and on, was to Angus' way of thinking what it would feel like if he had an iron wedge in his head and it was being hit with a sledgehammer. He tried to say, "Make it stop!" But to Bennager, it sounded like more moaning.

Bennager nudged Rose gently, hoping that she would wake up peacefully and stop making that awful racket. The only problem was that she was so damned mean in the mornings that Bennager might be ridiculed for letting the bear out of the cage. He had to risk it, though. He knew that his beautiful wife was the cause of Angus' grief and pain at that particular moment.

When Rose started to stir, Bennager scampered over to Angus so she wouldn't know that he had anything to do with her waking up. Angus was angry with Bennager and didn't want the man anywhere around him. Bennager noticed the look on Angus' face but thought that his grimace was caused by his physical pain.

Rose struggled to sit up. Bennager could feel her eyes on him. "Good morning, beautiful," he said. Rose's only reply was a hateful scowl which was better than the usual hateful words that she greeted each new day with.

Bennager left the tent to get some coffee going, knowing that it was better to leave his wife be until she had her first cup. What he really wanted to do was start the day out with a kiss, but he assumed that the idea wouldn't be received well by the missus. She might not even remember that she had a husband until she had her first cup of coffee.

It was early, still dark on this late January morning. Charlie and Sam were still asleep. Bill and Zeb were sitting up by the fire. With the fog gone for now, the sky had cleared, and there was a thin layer of frost on Charlie and Sam's blankets. "It's chilly this morning," Bennager observed. "Is there coffee in any of those pots?" he asked.

"I've got tea brewing here for the sick, injured, and weak-minded," Bill said jovially, joking about the weak-minded. Bennager pondered the idea of taking tea to his bride. That hadn't gone over very well the night before, and he knew damn well that it would only cause a conbobberation now. Bennager thought, as the sun was beginning to rise, that it was going to be too pretty of a day to start telling Rose to drink Bill's tea. Zeb was watching his friend Bennager. He could see the wheels turning in his head.

"This tea that Bill made is just the thing that is going to get Rose back on her feet. That's what you want for her, ain't it? You want what is best for her, don't you? Course, I have a little coffee right here for you, Bennager." Zeb was smiling his all-knowing smile. He knew just how Bennager would solve the problem, which made Bill's remark about the weak-minded true.

Bennager added a little cocoa and sugar to the coffee and a little sugar to the tea and rushed back into the tepee without saying a word, not even a word of thanks. Zeb didn't let on to Bill that Bennager was going to be the one to drink the tea in order to keep the peace with his wife because Bill looked so pleased with himself. Zeb just shook his head and smiled.

Moments later, Bennager came out and sat down by the fire. Now he was thinking on what to rustle up for breakfast.

"How is Rose this morning?" Zeb asked with sincerity.

"Well, you know, Zeb, it's too early to tell. She doesn't like to be fussed with first thing in the morning. I believe that she had a peaceful rest. I'm worried some about Angus, though. He is awake, but he isn't getting up. I tried talking to him, but he won't look at me and waves me to go away," Bennager confided.

"I better go have a look," Bill said, rising to his feet. He took his pouch of plants and his pot of tea, and Zeb joined him, knowing that on his worst day, Angus could still be a handful. "Oh, is Rose decent?" Bill turned to ask Bennager before entering the makeshift dwelling.

"Yes, but don't look at her or talk to her. The best thing is just to ignore her," Bennager said seriously as though their lives depended on it.

Bill turned to Zeb, who was smiling, of course. "Jealous type of character, ain't he?" Bill whispered. Zeb looked at Bennager who was working at preparing some breakfast and just continued to smile. He knew Bennager wasn't jealous, and his old friend, Bill, was about to know it too.

"Good morning, Mrs. Rasmussen! You wished for one beautiful day so you could see the hills and the trees, and the day is here. We all have you to thank for it. And how are you feeling on this fine day, Mrs. Rasmussen?" Zeb asked, purposely being cheerful so Bill would know what Bennager's warning had been about.

"Zeb, you're damn lucky that I've had my coffee or else I'd have to shoot you for being so damned happy. It's too damned cold to be a beautiful morning, and my arm hurts like hell, and if you say one more word to me about wishing weather, Zeb Jones, I swear, I'll kick the devil out of you in your sleep!" Rose scolded as she threw a rock. She missed Zeb, and the rock went out of the tent flap and hit Sam in the leg. Zeb hooted and laughed at the girl to show Bill how easy it was to rile her.

"You better let me have a look at your arm, Mrs. Rasmussen. We need to see if that poultice is doing its job," Bill said stoically, thinking that for some strange reason, Rose would listen to him.

"You'll not be looking at anything of mine whatsoever. I'm finished being doctorin' by the likes of you," Rose upbraided as she tore off a piece of plug tobacco with her teeth and gingerly managed to get to her feet. "I'm fit as a fiddle now, so stay the devil away from me," she stated as she spat.

Bill's eyes were as round as saucers as he watched Rose stomp out of the tent. Zeb was giggling at the sight of the girl reprimanding the older gentleman who had saved her life, and Rose punched Zeb in the arm on her way out. Bill looked at Zeb in astonishment as Zeb continued to laugh. "Good Lord! She is just like my mother!" Bill remarked.

Both men knelt beside Angus. Zeb asked, "Are you fit to travel today?"

Angus nodded his head.

Bill asked, "Can you get up?"

Angus shook his head.

"Do you want us to help you up?" Angus nodded his head.

A third man would have been helpful, but Bill and Zeb finally managed to get the job done. Angus had been dead weight in the beginning, but when he got his feet under him, the task wasn't as great. They helped him to take a stroll, and when they got back to the fire, Bill and Zeb propped him up against an oak, and Bill made him sip some tea.

Angus tried to talk to Bill and Zeb, but his words couldn't be understood by either one of them. Angus didn't know who Bill was. He had questions about Rose Mary and Bennager, and he was starving to death but didn't know what he could eat. As he observed the party with the eye that wasn't swollen shut, he noticed that Sam was glaring at him, and he remembered hitting Sam the day before.

Angus started to feel bad all over again. The sweet words that Rose Mary had told him last night were starting to give way to regret. Zeb was calling her Mrs. Rasmussen, so somehow, the girl that he had fallen for and killed his brothers for now belonged to another man. Angus hadn't realized that he had fallen in love with Rose Mary until he saw her that night on the deck of the boat, bleeding, unconscious, and drenched from the rain. It had been that image that had driven him through the rain, and that had filled him with enough anger to be able to defeat two men, two men that he would never see again, not even in hell.

Angus decided then that he didn't want to be seen by any of these people, so he eased himself to the other side of the tree and started to cry. The anguish that he felt accompanied by his pain made him too weak to stay on his feet. He slid down the trunk of the tree and rested, wondering how he could ever forgive himself for making such a hasty decision and then reckoning that he never would.

Angus felt something on his face and looked to see this fellow Bill. Bill was studying Angus' face as if it was a creation from another world, and Angus didn't like it. He wanted Bill to go away, but he was putting some sort of slimy medication on his wounds and decided not to offend him the way he had done with Sam yesterday. Bill put a piece of dried fruit on Angus' tongue and many more in his pocket and told Angus that it was all they had that he would be able to eat for right now. "Use this to keep your wounds soft, and you'll be able to chew beans by nightfall," the strange man said, handing him the tin of salve that he had produced.

Angus nodded once, not wanting to waste his energy on questions or pleasantries and reckoned Bill didn't expect him to because he left directly. The dried fruit was refreshing, and Angus found that he was thinking more about beans than of his regrets.

Angus could hear the bustling of camp being broken down, and he felt guilty for not helping. Then he thought that if he was very still, they might forget about him. He could rest up and go back to San Francisco, find a job, and forget that he had ever known Rose Mary Briar. Angus overheard Zeb and Sam exchanging goodbyes with the man in the buckskin clothing. He heard Bennager gratefully thanking the man for saving Rose's life, and then the man said, "See you fellas in Sacramento City." Then he heard the sound of horse's hooves trotting away. The next thing he knew, Zeb and Bennager were there to help him up. He realized he must have dozed off as the camp was completely packed, and he was the last one to board the boat.

"What the devil is he going to Sacramento City for?" Rose protested after a new day of traversing the river had commenced.

"It's a free country, dear. He can go to Sacramento City if he wants to," Bennager answered.

"That's where we're going!" she proclaimed.

"So?" Bennager really had no idea of what Bill's plans were in Sacramento City, and he didn't think that it was any of his business. Rose continued to complain about it, but Bennager didn't know what to tell her.

Sam and Zeb had been leaning on the railing of the boat, finally enjoying being able to see the scenery. Sam informed his partner, "I asked Bill to meet us in Sacramento City. I asked him to locate some horses and gear. We'll be outfitted by the time we get there. Then we reckon to head south, buy some cattle, and get this rancho of yours started."

"You didn't give that witch doctor son of a bitch any money, did you, Sam?" Rose said as she scampered toward Sam to look him in the eye.

"Well, sure I did. How can he get us outfitted if he ain't got no money?"

"We! How can we have him? Damn it, Sam! What in tarnation has you so convinced that you can trust that…that—how can you trust someone that won't have a drink with you, for heaven's sake? That tea drinker!"

"I told you last night that you could trust him," Sam replied, not worried in the least that Rose was madder than a wet hen.

"Yes, well, you haven't told me why."

"Because I know him."

"I know him too. I believe him to be as trustworthy as me," Zeb interjected.

"Oh, as trustworthy as you? Oh, well, excuse me. I don't know you're trustworthy, Zeb. All I know about you is that you think you're funny when you are really just full of shit all of the time," Rose said forcefully.

"My arm hurts where you hit me this morning," Zeb teased, trying to make her smile.

It worked. Rose smiled broadly and said, "Good!"

"You only dislike the man because he looks like your father. If he was anything like your father, would he be here or on a big plantation somewhere, whipping folks who look like me?" Sam asked.

"He's a strange man, and I don't want him nowheres around me, and that's it!"

"You only say he's strange because he doesn't drink. Maybe he knows men who drink, and they hurt people around them, and he didn't want to be a man like that. What is wrong with being good?" Sam said convincingly.

Sam was obviously describing Rose's father by stating all the differences between the two men. Rose tried to remember the conversations that she had with Sam. She had told him everything about the drinking, the plantation, and the slaves, but she never mentioned the sadistic things that her father had done when he was drunk. The things that he had done to her mother and to the Black women that worked in the house had never been spoken of by her and never would be. She wouldn't want anybody to know that she had that kind of bad blood in her body.

"Until just recently," she said, looking at the men on the boat, "I was under the impression that you hadn't had very good luck with any White men. As a matter of fact, in the months that we've traveled together, you never mentioned being friends with one. So how is it that you have such a sweet feeling for this one?"

"Watch your mouth, girl!" Sam said, wide-eyed.

"I ain't goin' to let up on you, Sam, until you tell me! You gave someone, who is a stranger to me, some of our money, and if we're partners, then you're goin' to tell me why I am supposed to think that's all right!"

Zeb could tell this discussion was getting too serious and heated, so he decided to check on Angus and the pups.

Sam went back to leaning over the rail and staring at the land they were passing, not really seeing it, and trying to figure out what to tell Rose. He wondered if Bill would care if Rose knew the truth about him. He hadn't flinched a bit when he saw Sam again after so many years. If Sam was right about the connection that Rose and Bill shared, he figured Bill would be happy to know the truth.

"Son of a bitch! Is that what I think it is?" Rose exclaimed, pointing to the north.

Sam looked in the direction that she was pointing in and saw fog slowly rising and rolling in their direction. A new cycle was starting, he reckoned.

"Mrs. Rasmussen, that's who you are for sure, I guess," Sam half joked. Then he lifted his shirt so only Rose could see the brand that was on his chest. It looked like a lightning strike hitting the center of the letter W. Rose gasped remorsefully. She knew the brand. It was the brand that her father used. Her green eyes, full of hate, fear, and confusion met Sam's that were full of knowledge. Rose began to cry and to feel sick. She started to heave, mostly hoping that she could purge away the fact that her father had once done such a thing to the man that was now her friend and partner.

"Stop it, girl!" Sam scolded. "It's over now. You will never see that again, and you had nothing to do with it. It happened before your time."

Rose's mind was reeling, wondering how it was possible that they could wind up meeting the way they did. How long had Sam known who she was? Would he want to rid the world of her father's offspring?

"The day this happened, that stranger that you don't trust took me out of that place. I had hatred back then for White men and thought that I could find my mother, so we parted company after a few days, and that was the biggest mistake of my life. If I had trusted my friend then as much as I do now, my slave days would have been over a lot sooner. I'm not going to make that mistake twice. Bill is a smart, good man. He's like you," Sam added, hoping that Rose would know the truth of the matter without him having to spell it out.

"Who is he that he would be able to take you out of there?"

"You don't know that you have an uncle?" Sam answered with a question.

"No."

"Well, that stranger's full name is William Weatherford. I don't know if he shortened it because he shares the same name as an Indian warrior or if he did it for the same reason that you changed your name. Reckon you can ask him when we get to Sacramento City. I can tell you one thing: he'll never give you a reason to hate him the way you do, so you get to thinkin' right about him," Sam advised.

"How long have you known who I am?" Rose asked.

"I've known you to be a kind, unruly girl and the loudest snoring girl that I've seen for a very long time. But I didn't know your real name until last night. Between what you and William were telling me, I figured it out."

"What the devil did he say about me? That I'm like him?" Rose snarled.

"No, that you are just like his mother."

"My grandmother?" Rose smiled wondrously. "I never knew her," Rose said sadly. "I thought you were in a big hurry to look for gold. What about that?"

"According to William, there're more people looking for gold than I imagined. I don't think I want to be around that many people. I told you, William is smart, like you. He and Zeb agree with you that starting a cattle rancho and feeding the miners would make more money, in the long run, than standing in a little piece of creek panning for gold. William said that he rode through a lot of pretty little meadows in the foothills, and the miners ain't interested too much in those places yet. He said you were dreaming when he heard your plan. He didn't know how or where you would be able to round up a herd of cattle, but when I told him you had capital, he said that you could purchase cattle in the south and drive them home."

"So Zeb is willing to go, and you, Bill, and me. Do you think Angus will want to go? How long will this take? Going south and coming back to this area?"

"I couldn't say. I'm sure Zeb would have an idea about that. I don't know," Sam replied.

"I better go tell Bennager our plans." Rose started to head for the wagon where Bennager was reorganizing after the mess that was made on the night of the storm. Rose stopped because she remembered her plans with Bennager for their first night in Sacramento City. She walked back to Sam. "I can't leave Sacramento City to go cattle buying on the first day we arrive. I have to wait until the second day, all right?"

"I think we should start right away," Sam argued. Sam could imagine why his young friend wanted to stay one night with her husband, so he thought that he would take this opportunity to tease her. "I know Zeb and Bill will be in a hurry to get started. Zeb already knows which ranchos to go to. I don't think we should waste a minute. Besides, think of those miners up there who are willing to buy beef for four times what it's worth."

Rose eyeballed Sam. He could see the wheels turning in her head and knew that she was leaning toward practicality instead of lust. Rose turned and watched her husband as he fussed with his wagon, and Sam knew she would ask him to postpone their honeymoon night that they had planned. Sam smiled then, not being able to hold it back any longer, and Rose caught him.

"What are you smiling about?" she asked, beginning to blush.

"It will take us a while to get completely outfitted. I reckon you'll have time to be alone with Bennager, but it's funny to me that you are so ruthless that you would give that night up to make money," Sam said sarcastically.

"I'm not ruthless! I just didn't know if it was right to hold up men who were willing to work with us to get this thing started. I came here to work, not to…not to… Well, you know," Rose explained, starting to blush.

"You mean not to fall in love and become a wife and mother like women are supposed to do? Course, if you do have that night you're hoping for, you'll get pregnant. That will make for a mighty interesting cattle drive," Sam teased. "Someone has explained to you where babies come from and how they are made, right?"

Rose was really blushing now. She thought that she had a pretty good idea about the things that Sam was asking, but the way he said it made her think that he had more information about the subject that she didn't know yet.

Zeb had been watching the negotiations between Sam and Rose and wanted to know what they decided because he was excited to make the trip and see some of his old friends. "Well, are we going on the drive, Mrs. Rasmussen?"

Rose faced him, still blushing, and said, "Yes, sir, that's the plan."

"That old phrase 'Blushing Bride' sure fits you well. Are you fevered up again?"

Sam said, winking at Zeb, "We were just talking about brides. Rose was about to tell me if anybody ever had the talk with her."

"The talk? Oh, the talk. You mean the one about what husbands do to their brides on their first night together when nobody is around to see them or protect or save the poor girl from the animal?

Or do you mean the talk about where babies come from?" Zeb asked, trying to be as serious as he could bear.

Bennager hopped down from his wagon and happened to see Rose looking at him, so he smiled and waved to her. At that moment, Rose began to see her husband for the animal that he was. There he was, smiling at her, pretending to be innocent. She glared at him. Sam had to turn his head away so Rose wouldn't see him laugh. Zeb remained serious but didn't let Bennager see his face.

"The only way you will stand a chance at surviving the first night with an animal like a new husband is to take that pistol with you. You better buy some fresh powder for it because the old stuff is probably wet," Zeb advised.

Zeb didn't know that Rose had already killed a man. Sam moved behind Rose and started shaking his head at Zeb, indicating to him that he was giving poor advice. "That's a given!" Rose said with purpose, still glaring at her husband.

"You just make sure that he knows how things are, and I'm sure that you won't have to shoot him. I'm sure the two of you will have a lovely evening." Zeb was looking at Sam in confusion. Sam was telling him to stop his teasing. Zeb could have gone on for hours on the subject, and now Sam was ruining his fun. "Now, as far as where babies come from, well—"

"I know where babies come from, you idiots, and if I didn't, I wouldn't ask either one of you two! As far as buying cattle goes, I think we're on to something good, and I appreciate you two working with me on this. I'll talk to you later."

*****

"Hello, dear. How was the meeting of the minds?" Bennager asked, smiling.

"Good, this really is a nice day," she commented on the weather as she raised her face to the sun, enjoying its warmth. A slight south breeze had started about midmorning and had managed to keep the fog at bay.

"Yep," Bennager said, still smiling. All his smiling was starting to bother Rose. She couldn't be sure why he was smiling exactly, and she wondered what he had up his sleeve that she didn't know about.

"So we're heading south to buy cattle," Rose said soberly.

"Yep."

"Well?"

"Well, what?" Bennager replied.

"Well, I have to go."

"I know you have to go. What are you trying to say? You don't want me to go with you or what?"

"I want you to go!" Rose was shocked that he would imply that she wouldn't.

"Well, I just figured that Zeb had you convinced that maybe you should shoot me when I get you alone in Sacramento City. I also reckon those two tried to tell you that maybe I wouldn't allow you to go looking for cattle to buy," Bennager explained.

"Oh, they teased me some, that's for sure. Zeb started to tell me to shoot you, but it all fell apart when Sam started hopping around behind me. Zeb didn't know that I killed that one bastard, and Sam was afraid that I might really do that to you if Zeb kept on. I could see the disappointment in his face when Sam convinced him to quit. Then they teased me about babies, for Christ's sake. Those two need a job!" Rose finished by shaking her head.

"So have you decided that you can be nice to Bill? He's going, right?"

Rose was looking inside her bags now. Finding a new plug of tobacco, she bit off a piece and continued doing inventory on her supplies. She lifted out an empty jug and pulled the cork. "Damn it, the brandy is gone," she whispered, knowing that Angus had drunk it, which was all right, but she was hoping that he had drunk up the rum. "Bill's okay, but I will still have a drink whether he likes it or not," Rose stated.

"Why is Bill okay now? What changed?" Bennager asked as he practiced tying knots because there was nothing else to do.

"Sam knows him from a long time ago. It turns out that he's my uncle." Rose gave a nervous chuckle. She now had her husband's full attention. Bennager looked at her with astonishment. "Yep, it turns out that his real name is William Weatherford, and of course, my real name is Weatherford. My dumb father never mentioned that he had a brother."

"Hold up here! Your last name isn't Briar?"

"No, my last name is Rasmussen," Rose said, smiling.

Bennager rolled his eyes and shook his head.

"So anyway," Rose continued, "knowing that he's my uncle sure didn't make me feel better about having him around, but Sam assured me that he hates my father as much as I do, so he must be all right."

"Your father must be quite a villain for everyone who is related to him to change their names!" Bennager said, suddenly irritated about just learning this new fact about his wife.

"He is, sweetheart. He is as bad as they come. Zeb vouched for Bill too. I guess they worked together. Anyway, as long as Bill don't bother me about drinking, then we'll do just fine. So what about you? You had plans before we met. Will you be able to go with me? Or do you have things to do?" Rose inquired.

"Where you go, I go. That's how it is now." Bennager leaned in, hoping for a kiss but figured Rose wouldn't give him one in front of the other men, but she did because she was pleased with him for what he said. He smiled. He was happy that they hadn't fought all day. Rose was happy that her husband didn't seem concerned that she had lied about her last name. "The supplies on my wagon will be gone before you find the hotel that we are going to stay in. We'll load it up again with nothing but sugar to keep you sweet," he said, kissing her again, passionately this time. "And then we'll hit the trail. We'll get you some black leather chaps, big, roweled spurs, and a sugar loaf sombrero. And I'll live to see seasoned vaqueros fall out of their saddles when they see you coming," Bennager jibed.

"I need guns too," Rose said, looking like a big-eyed little girl.

"Oh, yes, lots of guns, we mustn't forget that. What are you going to do with all the guns?"

"I'm going to shoot people who bother me," Rose replied seriously.

Bennager laughed at her then. "We'll be digging eight or twenty graves a mile if you shoot every person who bothers you. All of your vaqueros will be too worn out to push a cow. That's if you don't shoot them first."

Rose looked a little confused. She could see that her husband was trying to be funny, but if she saw fit to shoot eight or twenty people a mile, then she would. "We ain't stoppin' to dig graves for people who bother me, that I am sure of!"

"Oh, that was a silly thing to say, wasn't it?" Bennager said, making a silly face at her. "The biggest problem that you've got, my dear, is that there are not as many people in the world willing to bother you as you wish there were. I'm certain that even the bears, rattlesnakes, and badgers will leave the state when they hear of your arrival."

"Well, these must be some pretty smart critters that you're talking about."

"Oh, they are, they are, my sweet little Rose. Your name is Rose, isn't it?"

Angus had been leaned up on the wall of Charlie's steering room. Everyone had stacked their blankets and bedrolls up to try to make him comfortable. He was waking from a restful snooze which was much needed after being woken up so early this morning. He was hungry and thirsty, but he could feel himself slowly regaining his strength. He felt like he could get up, so he began to stir. Zeb saw him and eased over to assist him. Rose saw him and began to prepare some cheese, bread, and dried fruit. She hadn't liked Bill this morning, but she had watched his every move and remembered the dried fruit. Bennager moved to get some of that tea working as he had been instructed.

Zeb thought that maybe Angus should sit tight and continue to rest, but the redheaded titan had to relieve his bladder, and that was that. Sam could see that Zeb was struggling and decided that he would risk getting hit again to help Zeb. With his number one objective finished, Angus asked his friends to lean him up on the wagon. "I want to get me legs workin' again. I can't be lyin' 'round for the rest of me life." His speech was still garbled, but Zeb and Sam knew what he was talking about.

Rose had food laid out for all of them, but Angus wouldn't take anything until Rose told him to, and she wondered why he was being strange about it.

Sam could see that Angus could stand on his own and started to walk away from him. Angus stopped Sam. Angus still had the strongest grip that Sam had ever encountered, even in his weakened state, and Sam prepared himself for battle. He wasn't going to be hit in the head again.

"I'm sorry, Sam. I had no reason and no cause to treat ye that way, no matter 'bout the pain or the drink, no matter. I'm truly sorry, Sam."

Sam nodded and shook the man's hand. He figured that was enough for now. It was a good apology, but Sam didn't think that he would ever be friends with this man again. Sam didn't forgive and he didn't think that Angus would ever be right in the head again anyway. Sam figured that once the man was recovered, he intended to stay the devil away from him.

"We're heading south to buy cattle, Angus. Do you want to go with us?" Rose asked as Sam gritted his old broken teeth.

Angus still had mixed feelings about Rose and didn't want to see her and Bennager together for the rest of his life. He shook his head as Bennager handed him his tea. "I'll work with the bricks."

"Work with the bricks! That's hard work. I'll pay you for your time," Rose nagged.

"It's better that I work with the bricks."

"Where will you be when Girl weans her babies?" Rose persisted. Sam elbowed her in the ribs then.

"I'll find me little puppy when ye come back," he mumbled, not looking at Rose and feeling sad now about how he would miss the babies.

Zeb offered, "The best thing to do is leave Girl and the pups with Angus until we get back. It wouldn't be a good trip for her. She'd wear herself out and neglect the pups. Would you look after them while we are gone, Angus?" Zeb had a good plan. He noticed a gleam in the Irishman's eye.

Angus nodded. "I'll take good care of the wee little babies. We can find ye when ye get back." Angus' one good eye was filled with gratitude. He was a trusted man and knew that he had a friend in Zeb. Zeb smiled and nodded his head at him.

As Angus leaned on the wagon, sucking cheese and working his legs, he thought about Rose and Bennager. He had no cause to be mad at them. He never made his claim on Rose. He didn't even know about his feelings until that rainy night. Nobody ever told him to kill his brothers either. Rose and Bennager didn't get married to harm him. They probably wouldn't have done it if they knew how he felt. He knew they were the same good people they were a couple of days ago.

He decided to give his legs a try. He used the wagon for balance at first and then hobbled over to the horses and used the back of one to rest on. He petted them and talked softly to each one, feeling more at ease around them than with people. He knew that he must be a gruesome sight but was surprised that his fiery little Rose Mary had held her tongue about it this time. *It must be beyond comment*, he thought. Angus' thoughts roamed as he eased to the railing and rested again, sucking on dried fruit and enjoying the warmth of the afternoon.

Rose sneaked a cup of rum to visit Girl with. Bennager could hear her telling the dogs what the plan was and how Girl was supposed to look after the big man while they were gone. Girl would lift her ears and cock her head every time Rose said the words *cows* or *cattle*. It occurred to Bennager that the dog probably knew exactly what Rose was telling her and that she had probably forgotten more about cows than any of them would ever know, but he didn't think she was going to like being left behind. Then he heard Rose tell Girl that her and her babies would have the nicest room in town, and people would bring her some cooked steak. "I bet you like yours rare. I like mine medium, but we can't be too picky out here in these rural parts."

Bennager raised his eyebrows and shook his head as he turned to Sam who had his arms crossed and a sad look on his face. "Are you thinking what I'm thinking?" Bennager asked him, smiling.

"If you think she'll go broke tending to Angus and those dogs, then we're thinkin' the same thing, all right," Sam replied, shaking his head.

*****

Two more days on Charlie's boat landed the party in Sacramento City. The rest of the river voyage had been fairly uneventful. As the rolling hills that separated the ocean from the town gave way to the flattest, largest piece of land that Rose and Angus had ever seen, Sam, Bennager, and Zeb had to chuckle at the expressions on their faces.

The fog had managed to keep its distance for the last two days, and Rose was grateful to be able to see the new country that she intended to make her home in. She didn't really care for the flatness of the Sacramento Valley. It made her feel small and vulnerable. There was no place to hide. The closer that she got to Sacramento City, the easier it was to see the foothills beyond the valley. She liked the idea of being high in those foothills with the trees to hide behind, looking down on the towns below.

"That's where I'm headed," she said with certainty, pointing to the hills.

The only one that was close enough to hear her was Angus. Everyone else was busy cleaning up what messes had been made and picking up garbage. Charlie's vessel would have to be ready for passengers that would be leaving Sacramento City to go to San Francisco. Angus only nodded at Rose's comment. The vast valley astonished him. He never imagined a place so flat could exist nor could he see spending any more time there than it took to get out of it. He had spent the last two days resting, building up his strength, and looking forward to the soft bed that Rose had promised, but now his stomach was rolling with fear and anticipation. Angus wasn't sure what he was going to do, but he wasn't going to sit in the middle of this valley by himself, even if he did have Girl for company. "This place looks like trouble," Angus commented.

Rose nodded her head in agreement and looked around at her husband and her other friends. "I think most of us here could use a break from trouble." Rose wondered what Sam was thinking of. Was he having the same unsettling feeling that she and Angus were? As she studied him at his task of picking up garbage, she saw him lift his head once in a while and look at the valley that surrounded them. Seeming content with the fact that the landscape had not changed, he would go back to work. Five minutes later, he was finished and joined Rose and Angus who were leaning on the rail.

"Your turn, Mrs. Rasmussen," Sam said, holding a bucket of soapy water that Charlie had given him.

Rose took the things from Sam. "What do you think of this place, Sam?"

"It reminds me of home. I think I like it," Sam replied.

"Really? What home do you mean?"

"Africa, only it's greener here."

THE RIVERS AND THE VALLEYS

SACRAMENTO CITY

1

Rose sat next to her husband on his freight wagon as they disembarked from Charlie's vessel. Sam, Angus, and Zeb hitched a ride in the back of the wagon to town. Everyone on Bennager's wagon tried to wave goodbye to Charlie as they departed, but he acted as though he had never known them and didn't wave back. Sam and Zeb chuckled and shook their heads as they watched Charlie start to get hot under the collar as he negotiated with his new passengers about what their fare would be. "I guess if those folks catch him waving to us, they will think he's a nice fella," Zeb commented. "He can't take a man's gold and be a nice fella at the same time, I reckon." Sam nodded his head and smiled, figuring that Zeb was probably right.

All the members of the party were shocked to see how big the town of Sacramento City was. Even Zeb and Bennager were dumbfounded by the number of gambling halls, about twenty, with more buildings being constructed right before their eyes. The number of hotels and shops was also surprising to the party, but what really raised everybody's eyebrows were the women. All the fussing that Bennager had made over Rose being the only White woman in California had been for nothing, and Rose was now giving him the evil eye.

"I thought you said there weren't any women! Look at them! They are all dressed as women should be, and you got me in this costume! What the devil is wrong with you?" Rose said, wanting to punch Bennager in the arm but not being able to on account of her own arm still hurting.

"Well, there weren't any when I was here last," Bennager replied, surprised at the sight as well. "I'm sorry that I went on so much about it now. We'll get you outfitted with whatever kind of clothes that you want, dear. I would love to see you in a proper dress that actually fits you."

"These clothes that I've got on suit me, I reckon," Rose said stubbornly.

"What are you mad about then?" Bennager asked.

"Nothing! What are they all doing here, though?"

It was easy for the men to tell by the way the women were dressed what they were doing in the populated town. Some of them had obviously come to California with their husbands and families by the overland trail. Those women wore bonnets and skirts and were going in and out of the shops. Each of these ladies had a look of concentration and purpose on their faces as they shopped for whatever was needed. Some of these women were even accompanied by children and were quickly losing their ability to focus.

As Bennager stopped his team in front of the mercantile that he had always done business with, Rose saw a woman come out of the store, wearing a solid green woolen skirt and jacket with a white ruffled blouse and a green feathered hat to match. To Rose, this woman looked like she might own the whole town, but mostly, Rose thought this by the way the woman lifted her chin in the air, and Rose watched her intently as the woman walked away, waiting for her to trip and fall because surely the woman couldn't be able to see where she was going. Rose glared at the woman with wonder until she was out of sight, and the thought of brandy and a good meal claimed her full attention.

"Where do we eat?" Rose asked bluntly.

"That hotel yonder serves the best food that I know of," Bennager said, pointing across the street.

Rose nodded and smiled at her husband and walked into the store. Bennager didn't have to wonder what she was purchasing and wasn't surprised when she walked out with a crate full of brandy and tobacco and began passing out jugs to Sam, Zeb, and Angus. "Let's go get some supper, fellas," Rose said, not giving her husband time to finish his business. Bennager only smiled at the way his new wife was unconcerned about whether he was able to join them or not. The other men ignored Rose's nagging about supper and seemed content to linger in front of the mercantile, sipping their brandy until Bennager was finished selling his goods.

Bennager spotted Bill Ford walking toward them as he made a final count of each item being sold to the mercantile but didn't let on to the others that he was coming as Rose was already becoming loud and obnoxious due to the rapid consumption of her spirits.

Bill could see there was a celebration being held but was concerned about the lady becoming drunk and shook his head as he approached her from behind and tapped her on her good shoulder. Rose turned slowly, wondering who in the town of Sacramento City would be trying to get her attention and was relieved to see that it was just her Uncle Bill.

"It's good to see that you're ambidextrous," Bill joked in reference to Rose being able to hold her jug with her left hand. Rose choked and coughed as the large, offensive word caused her brandy to go down the wrong pipe.

"What did you just call me?" Rose yelled at her uncle.

Bill laughed and patted Rose on the head while she glared and jerked her head away from him and made ready for a fight. Bill walked over to the men, ignoring Rose altogether, and not giving her the satisfaction of explaining what ambidextrous meant. "Hello, fellas, how was the rest of your trip on the river?"

Zeb answered as each man took a turn at shaking Bill's hand. "It was as smooth as a baby's bottom. It was good weather, thanks to Rose there, of course, and no trouble." Rose rolled her eyes at Zeb, and Bill took a closer look at Angus.

"How are you feeling? It looks like your wounds are healing. Did you use that salve I gave you?"

Angus nodded his head. He didn't like the attention that his ugly face was getting. "You should see a doctor, but I haven't been able to find one in this town," Bill told Angus as he reached over to pet Zeb's dog.

"Me bones will heal soon enough," Angus mumbled.

Bill dropped the subject, knowing that Angus was sensitive about his appearance, which everyone else thought was silly. But no one spoke of his pain or the incident that caused it.

Suddenly, every man's attention was directed to four young ladies approaching the mercantile. Each painted-faced lady smiled broadly and made eye contact with the men who were leaning on Bennager's wagon. Each man tipped his hat at the ladies and watched them as they swayed their hips while they walked away toward one of the gambling halls. Each lady wore a wool coat because it was winter, but each man wondered why they would bother since they left their coats open to expose their scantily clad, ample breasts.

Angus got lightheaded when the ladies walked by, and Zeb chuckled when he looked like he might faint. "Don't weaken on us now, Angus. The fun is just starting," Zeb jibed.

"I never knew a woman's legs looked like that," Angus said, referring to the short dresses the women were wearing.

Sam couldn't believe that one of the ladies had smiled at him, and he had dreamy thoughts of knowing her name and making her his own. Bennager was shocked and appalled at such a display and could only wonder what breed of woman would traipse around in broad daylight, exposing themselves in such a way. As Bennager stood there with his mouth gaping, watching the ladies walk away, Rose decided to walk away too.

Every head in the restaurant's dining room turned toward Rose as she stood in the entrance with one arm in a sling and the other filled with one carpetbag and her jug of brandy. Everybody looked twice, trying to determine if she was a man or a woman and wondered what had happened to her arm. It was evident to all that she was a new arrival, and everyone figured that she was looking for a room or a job. A plump woman came in from the kitchen, carrying four plates at once, heaped with food, and said, "I'll be right with you, honey."

Rose followed the woman through the dining room and found an empty table. The woman came to her table after she delivered the plates. "My name is Maggie, honey, what can I get for you?"

"The same thing that you just carried out and a pie will do me just fine, Maggie," Rose said.

"A whole pie?"

"Yes, ma'am."

"You look a might gloomy, miss. It looks like you had a hard trip. Where're your men folk?"

"My husband is at the mercantile, ogling at half dressed women. I don't know how long it's going to take him to get his jaw unstuck from the mud, so I came in without him."

"Oh, ain't those girls something?" Maggie chuckled. "Some dirty little man pulled in last fall with two wagons full of those poor girls and their trappin's. He built a big house of ill-repute on one end of town and a gambling hall on the other end. He parades those girls up and down the street every day, advertising, you see. Word has it he's got a wife back in Kentucky. Can you believe that?"

"She should have shot him," Rose remarked as she took a pull from her jug.

"Word has it she gave it a gallant try. That's why he left."

"How do you know all of this?" Rose asked, confused about how someone in Sacramento City would know what happened in Kentucky.

"A lot of people who are in town were in the same wagon train with this fella. He tried to sell his goods on his way out west. When the married women heard what he was up to, they raised a fuss, and the men made this fella travel at the rear for the rest of the trip, eating dust. Word has it he even tried to recruit some of the young daughters of the folks in the wagon train. They wanted to hang him, but they didn't know what to do with those girls, so they threatened him, and he left their daughters alone after that."

"I'm sure the girls would have been better off without him. Of course, those women I just encountered do seem to enjoy their occupation," Rose said.

"Well, they sure minded eating dust last summer, I can tell you that," Maggie said with a chuckle.

Rose smiled and nodded, thinking of all the hardships she had endured on her journey.

"Can I get you a cup of coffee to go with that medicinal purpose you're sippin' from?" Maggie asked sarcastically.

"You bet, all you can spare," Rose replied greedily.

Maggie was right back, pouring the coffee. "What did you do to the arm?" Maggie inquired.

"It was just an accident," Rose answered vaguely.

Rose saw Sam walk through the front door, and she stood up and waved him over. Sam sat at the table with her. "I got to get away from these people! There're too many people here! I got a sick feelin'! It's a bad feelin', Rose! I won't make it through the night!" Sam whispered intensely, wide-eyed, anxious and sweating, even though it was about forty degrees outside.

Rose was astonished at Sam's behavior. She had never seen him like this. As she studied him, she realized that he was scared. She had never given much thought as to what could ever scare Sam Washington, but she was wondering about it now. She had always assumed that after everything that he had been through that nothing could frighten this man, except maybe the threat of slavery.

"I'm not going to let anything happen to you, Sam. I know there are a lot more people here than we expected, but we won't be here long, just one night is all. You'll probably feel better after you've had a good hearty meal and a piece of pie," Rose said, knowing that Sam's concern about his safety was real, and her words were meant to reassure her as well as him because seeing her friend and traveling companion of the last year look and act this way made the hair on the back of her neck stand up.

"Spirits and pie, that's all you think about! If I was you, I'd lay off the brandy tonight. I'm tellin' you, something's not right about this town!" Sam exploded from the table to leave.

"Whoa, where are you going? Won't you even stay to eat?" Rose asked, jumping up from her seat to try to stop him.

Sam whispered as everyone in the dining room turned to see the commotion, and all found the scene to be very strange. "Look it there, you've got everybody in this room lookin' at us as if things weren't bad enough already. This is no place for us to be. You're headin' south tomorrow, right? I'll meet up with you tomorrow, and you best keep your wits about you." He turned to leave.

"Wait!" Rose whispered. "What's got you so riled up? A few minutes ago, you seemed pleased that one of those Sacramento City sluts had smiled at you, and now here you are, scaring the devil out of me. What did you see?"

"I didn't see anything. It's a feelin' I got, like a feelin' I get when somethin' bad is about to happen." This time, when he turned to leave, he did, and he didn't look back.

Rose followed him to the door and watched her friend brush past Bennager and Zeb, turning Zeb sideways as he kept going past without a word as though he hadn't even seen them. She observed Bill and Angus talking to Sam for a moment, and they all picked up their trappings and headed north out of town, toward the river.

"What was that all about? Another spat between you two?" Bennager asked sarcastically.

"He's just shy, I reckon," Rose answered, knowing there was a lot more to it than that. She continued to watch the three men ride out of town on the horses that Bill had purchased and wondered how many things on this earth could make Sam so unsteady and frightened. *Not a whole hell of a lot*, she thought, almost saying it out loud. Suddenly, the bad feeling that Sam had was beginning to possess her. Her chest became tight with anxiety, and her head began to pound. The more she tried to figure out just what exactly was wrong with this place that made Sam so nervous, the worse she felt, and Sam's departure hadn't made her neck hair lie down either, and now she had chills going up and down her spine. Gritting her teeth and keeping her head down, she went back to her table followed by Bennager and Zeb.

Maggie came back to the table again and looking brazenly at Bennager's chin and declared, "Well, I don't see any mud on this handsome young man's face." And then, teasing the older man, "But I see some on yours!" she exclaimed, nearly pushing Zeb over sideways in his chair with only two fingers.

"No you don't either!" Zeb said rapidly, quickly coming to his own defense, even though he really had no idea what the woman was talking about. The comedy of it made Rose smirk as she sipped her coffee. Taking Sam's advice, she decided to save the brandy for the trail.

Zeb looked Maggie up and down as she asked him if he wanted beef or beans. He was keeping a close eye on this accusing witch woman to ensure that she wouldn't try to poke him or cast a spell on him when he wasn't looking. He determined, during his vigilance, that she wasn't bad to look at either, but she was definitely some sort of a crone. Bennager and Zeb said, "Beef" simultaneously, and as Maggie turned to go into the kitchen, she hit Zeb quick and hard on the back of the head. "I don't take kindly to men lookin' at me the way you been lookin'. I'm a married woman, and I'd thank you kindly to treat me accordingly," Maggie explained.

"I knew it," Zeb said mostly to himself, wide-eyed, holding his head and looking in Bennager's general direction.

Maggie quickly presented herself right in front of Zeb's wide eyes and braced him. "You knew what?" she said.

Zeb closed his eyes so he wouldn't be accused of looking at a married woman and refused to speak attempting to trick the sorceress. What he didn't see was Maggie winking at Rose who was trying not to laugh out loud, and Bennager looking at him with a confused scowl on his face. Zeb felt the floor move under his feet and heard the footsteps, but he knew for sure she was a witch because he could see through his closed eye lids that she had left.

"Are you going to eat with your eyes closed like that?" Bennager asked.

"I hope I don't have to," Zeb replied, just opening one eye. Closing both again, he whispered, "That woman is a witch. She is the reason why Sam was in a hurry to leave town. She could be a witch or a vampire. She is probably a vampire because I don't think a mere witch would bother Sam that much." While he was disclosing this very important information to his young friend Bennager, who was too ignorant to know a witch or a vampire on sight like he was able to, with his eyes still closed, Maggie approached the table with two cups and a boiling pot of coffee.

"You best not be talking about me, old man, or else I'll hit you again," Maggie said, glaring at Zeb, willing him to open his eyes. The twinkle that she noticed in Rose's eyes led her to believe that Zeb was either crazy or harmless, probably both, and his behavior was just some sort of game he was playing. She noted that the other young man had not changed his expression in the time that she had been gone. He was still looking at the older man as if he was something that had oozed up from under the ground. The older man was handsome, Maggie thought, but that was no excuse for not minding his manners around a lady. He could look at those prostitutes like that, but not her.

When Zeb felt that Maggie had left, he leaned across the table to Bennager and whispered again, "She's probably not a vampire, just a witch woman." He nodded with certainty and tightly closed eyes.

Bennager decided that if Zeb wasn't going to open his eyes at the table and continue with his silliness, then he wasn't going to look at him anymore, so he looked at his wife instead.

Rose was waiting for Zeb to open his eyes, not realizing yet that he was perfectly content to keep them closed. Rose felt Bennager's eyes on her. He was willing her to look at him the way Girl had willed her to wake up when she was sick with fever a few days ago. Rose smiled and blushed, against her will, of course, and turned to face him. "You're about to get smacked like Zeb was for looking at me like that," Rose whispered to her husband.

The supper arrived, and as Rose ate, she thought of the moments she and her husband had shared since they had been married. Even though they had not had the private intimate moments that most newlyweds practiced, they had some that she really couldn't imagine could be outdone by what her husband was imagining right now. When Bennager put his hands on her back to give her a hug, they were gentle and powerful at the same time, but not in a controlling or possessive way. She remembered the first time that he put his hands on her back and how she wouldn't want to be the man whoever made Bennager mad enough to grab his throat. She laughed to herself when she thought back to the day when she had first met Bennager, and Sam had grabbed his throat. She knew now that Bennager could have killed Sam very easily that day, but he hadn't done it because his gentleness was the biggest part of him, and protecting people who he thought needed it was the second biggest part of him. She wouldn't want those hands to get a hold of her in anger. And then, when he gently squeezed her with his loving arms, she just instinctively knew that she would never have to worry about her man hurting her physically. His arms were like pillars of strength and protective pillows at the same time.

When he held her, she never wanted him to let her go, and when he kissed her, she never wanted to let him go. His soft, gentle, powerful way he had about him melted Rose and made them into one. She could not imagine how anything could be better than that. As she read Bennager's thoughts through his mischievous, devilish blue eyes, she wondered, *What if something could be better than that? If it is better than that, could I survive it? What if I melt away into pure liquid and was never found again?*

Rose thought about the men she had known in her life. Her father, an obnoxious drunk, cruel, heartless, basically a no-account man. And then there were the boys who had come around to court her—nervous, without confidence, easily manipulated or they surely wouldn't have been there, and they were lazy like her father because they all had grown up not having to do any work. They would never have made the journey that she had just endured, and if it hadn't had been for Sam, she wouldn't have either, but the difference was she listened to Sam, and they wouldn't have because no matter what difficulties they found themselves in, they would still think they were better than Sam. Then there was Richard Hawthorne, who was a perfect combination of her father and the other boys. She was happily pleased now that she had never let that thing taint her person with his touch. It was customary to let a suitor kiss your hand, but Rose had seen the cruelty in Richard's eyes as she had seen in her father's and had refused him every time he reached for her hand before his departure.

As for the other men in her life, these men she was traveling with now, they were certainly a group cut from a different cloth. Sam was intelligent in a quiet way and eager to share his knowledge and superstitions, but Sam carried much sorrow in his heart. There was nothing in this world that could ease the sorrow and pain that had taken away his dreams of having a family of his own. The dreams of having his own property and being a completely free individual to do as he pleased could not even happen in California, really. California was a place filled with people who knew that a Black man was likely to be a slave, and people would probably treat the man like a slave whether Rose liked it or not. They would forever have to continue with the charade of him working for her, just to keep him safe from businessmen from the Southern states that would take him and mistreat him. Bill would keep him safe for tonight, she thought, as she sipped her coffee with Bennager.

Rose couldn't help thinking of Angus and the pain he must be in. Rose had promised him a soft bed and a hot meal, and before she knew it, he was gone, preferring to spend another cold night out in the brush, sitting by a campfire with Bill and Sam.

"Zeb," Rose said with a curious look on her face.

Zeb turned his face toward Rose with his eyes still closed. "Yes?" Zeb asked.

"Zeb, I want to talk to you. Now look at me while I do it, would you please?"

Zeb shook his head from side to side. "Nope, I won't. That witch woman will swoop over and get me, and I'll never make it back home to my wife."

Rose shook her head and rolled her eyes, and then she leaned across the table and whispered. "Zeb, you crazy bastard, open your eyes and look at me or I'll put knots on your shin bones!"

Zeb compromised with Rose by just opening one eye. Rose gritted her teeth because Zeb was getting on her last nerve. "Why didn't Angus come in and eat with us?"

Zeb closed his eyes again and answered, "He's embarrassed about his bruised-up face and didn't want people asking him questions about it."

"So he's embarrassed about fighting two men and getting my things back for me, but it doesn't bother you to sit at a table in a public restaurant with your eyes closed tight because you think that the woman running this place is a witch." Rose shook her head and looked at Bennager. "This is quite a bunch! Zeb, I suppose you're going to sleep in the brush with the rest of them?"

Zeb nodded. "Yep, Angus has my Girl. I'm going to bring her a piece of this steak, if that witch doesn't catch me. Witches don't like dogs because like me, dogs know a witch when they see one. Girl knew that you were a good witch, a weather and a birthing witch. A good witch that helps a dog have her pups is always good at wishing weather."

"Shut up! I've had it with your witch nonsense. You are driving me crazy!" Rose put money on the table and got up. Bennager stood up too. "You are going to see to it that Maggie is paid for the meal and also that she gets something extra for having to put up with you and also because that is the way I want it," Rose ordered. "Do you understand me, Zeb?"

Zeb nodded with his eyes closed.

"And then I want you to take that pie out to the men. Sam always likes pie when he can get some, and I doubt Bill and Angus have had a piece of pie since they were children. You better not trip on something and drop it either."

Zeb opened his eyes and quickly stood up, reaching for Bennager's hand and shaking it. "You are a lucky man. Oh, how I envy you," Zeb said sarcastically and quickly sat down, assuming his previous idiotic pose.

Rose glared at Zeb for a moment, wanting only to make good on her threat of kicking Zeb in the shins, but when Bennager put his hand on the small of her back and gently eased her in the direction of the door, her tempestuous spirit quickly calmed, and as she passed Maggie, she felt like a little revenge would be won when she said, "Maggie, that gentleman over there is all yours."

"I'll take good care of him," Maggie replied, winking.

As they walked through the lobby of the hotel and up the stairs, Rose remembered what Zeb had said about Bennager becoming an animal, and she remembered the look in Sam's eyes from moments before, and nervousness combined with the hairs on the back of her neck standing up again brought her to a gasping halt.

"What is it? Did you forget something at the restaurant?" Bennager asked, feeling his fantasies being quickly dashed away.

Rose looked into her husband's eyes, and the genuine concern that she saw in them and what she heard in his voice immediately convinced her that he was not an animal. His quaking had stopped, and his focus was on her needs in the present instead of the not-so-distant future.

"Are you in pain?" he asked.

His mischievous, devilish blue eyes had become protective again, which was, so far, what Rose loved and trusted most about her husband. "Sam has me worried. He said he had a bad feeling. Sam was scared, Bennager. I can't figure too many things that would scare the man," Rose said, facing her husband and looking deeply into his gorgeous eyes.

Bennager wrapped her up into his wonderful, all-knowing arms and kissed her ardently. He could feel her melt into him, and as he lifted his mouth away from hers, he realized that it was possible to make her forget about everything and everybody except him for at least this one night. "Sam is surrounded by friends who will look out for him tonight. I promise you he would rather have you here with me than out there with him. If there is something to be afraid of, we'll take care of it tomorrow." He kissed her again, hoping that his wife would not speak another man's name for the next twelve hours or so and also that there was no imminent danger of interruption because on this night, he wanted them to be the only two people in the world.

"I need a bath," Rose whispered into his mouth when their lips parted.

"Well, my dear, after your performance in San Francisco, I took the liberty of arranging for you to have a bath in our room because from now on, the only man who is going to stand a chance of seeing you in that way is me," Bennager said with a smile.

"You aren't jealous of an old Chinese man, are you? For heaven's sake," Rose said, quietly giggling, her nerves more at ease now.

"Like hell I'm not!?" Bennager said, squeezing her. And then he took her hand and led her to their room. He opened the door and scooped Rose up into his arms, causing her to scream and laugh heartily, and carried her into their room and kicked the door closed with his foot.

"What in tarnation are—" was all Rose was able to get out of her venomous mouth before her husband put his lips to hers and kissed her lustfully while he put her back on her feet. As she pressed herself against him, she thought again of Zeb's jokes and wondered if she should have brought her pistol just in case, but as his hands moved down the backside of her body and back up again, she realized that she was just as likely to become an animal on this night as Bennager was. As Bennager moved with her toward the tub, Rose tore her arm sling away and put her hands around his neck and then ran her fingers through his black, silver streaked hair and pulled herself closer to him, wanting them to be as close as possible. His shaking was no longer an issue, and her husband seemed to be in complete control of every move that he made. Suddenly, Bennager pulled back and gasped and gently pushed Rose slightly away from him and spun her around.

"Your bath awaits you, my dear," he said happily as he pulled a curtain back to show Rose the tub. The new nightgown was front and center among a variety of new clothes. There were two new dresses. The black chaps and roweled spurs were present as well as new undergarments. "I couldn't find a sombrero. Maybe tomorrow, I'll have more time to look," Bennager said, pleased that he had surprised his bride.

2

"I have to say that I'm starting to get tired of this traveling and camp-fire life. That witch back at that restaurant sure did remind me of how sweet my wife is. I'm beginning to miss my wife and my soft bed," Zeb remarked as he licked pie crumbs off his fingers.

"That sounds familiar. That was the same attitude you had back in '33, the last time I saw you. I swear, Zeb, you have got to be the softest mountain man that I have ever been around. I bet you were on the tit at the age of four, weren't you? For a man who is scared to death of every woman he sees, you sure do hanker after their company. Why don't you forget how sweet your wife is and how other women are witches? Women are all the same, you fool! And for the record, it's my opinion that your wife is the best one at witchin' men into her bed. You were perfectly happy being a government surveyor with the rest of us until you laid your eyes on that Mexican girl, and then suddenly, you tell us that you are tired of travelin' and sleepin' on the ground. What a lot of palaver," Bill complained in a joking way, winking at Angus and Sam as he was doing it.

"Forget about witches? You must be out of your mind, Bill Ford! You know just as well as I do about witches. I seem to recall you getting hung up with one or two in your day. I remember one at Pierre's Hole that got you so confused you didn't even know who you were. Hell, you thought I was a monster and my head was on fire, and I was coming to burn you up, for heaven's sake! Next thing I know, you got me in the Teton River, trying to drown me. Me, your friend Zeb! How do you explain that? Do I look a man who has ever had his head on fire? Hell no!" Zeb was worked up by now and was pacing from the fire to Bill and back again, trying to defend himself to the other men, but all that he was accomplishing was convincing them that he was just a paranoid kind of character as he stomped back and forth, splattering mud into the flames.

Bill thought back to the time that Zeb was referring to and remembered making love to an angelic Indian girl, and afterward, the little beauty put some tobacco in a pipe for him to smoke. Things did become confusing for the rest of the night. But the strangest thing that Bill remembered was when he woke up the next morning. The angel that he was sure that he had been with all night wasn't really the beauty that he thought she was. As it turned out, she wasn't very pretty at all. She was a lot heavier, and some of her teeth were missing. The smell of her hair and her body would gag a maggot, and she looked to be about ten years older than he was. Bill remembered jumping up from the bed of buffalo robes and getting his clothes and running out of that tepee. He was convinced that his sweetheart was in camp with someone else and had switched places with the old toothless crone that he had just woken up to. He recalled running around the rendezvous, asking his companions, "Where did that pretty little Indian girl go that I was with last night?"

And they all rolled around on the ground, laughing and pointing as the older Indian woman exited from the same tepee from where he had just come. She was the same poor old Indian widow that he had started out with, but Bill wouldn't believe it at the time because the more his friends laughed at him, the more convinced he became that they were the ones playing a joke on him, but because of the alcohol and tobacco, he would really never know for sure what exactly had gone awry that day along the Teton River. "You boys set me up with the poor old widow woman and you know it, and I'm quite certain that you, my friend, were the biggest instigator of the whole affair, but that doesn't mean that she was a witch, for heaven's sake, she was just missing some of her facial features," Bill said, laughing.

Zeb shook his head irately. "You are a crazy, dumb son of a bitch! You will never learn no matter how many times I tell you, not one of us boys had anything to do with your choice of lovers that night. You did that all by yourself with the tricks that only an

Indian sorceress would know." Zeb looked at Sam and Angus then. Angus was laughing a little by this time, but Sam was horrified at the thought of what Indian women might be capable of.

"You would think that Horny Bill would have learned something after the rendezvous, but oh no! Guess what he did the next year? We ran out of tobacco and alcohol, so Horny Bill tried to make friends with a Crow medicine man to help him get over the shakes and cure him from seeing snakes and monsters everywhere he went on account of the fact that old witch had put a spell on him. That damned medicine man sent Horny Bill to go see the witch doctor to make the evil spell go away. Well, let me tell you, boys, the last thing that you ever want to do is get tangled up with a witch doctor when you are trying to defend yourself against witches. I don't know what went on in that witch doctor hut, but before long, Horny Bill was trying to kill that spooky warlock. They came out of that tent, rolling and wrestling around in the dirt and dust. The Indian was bare ass naked and screaming like a little girl. It was the damnedest thing anyone of us had ever seen.

"The Indians were laughing their asses off and pointing at Horny Bill and his new girlfriend. What got the riot started though was the Crow Indian woman that was sweet on Bill. She had been eyeballin' Horny Bill for weeks, and she got jealous of the naked warlock, so she jumped in the middle of the fight. Bill accidentally elbowed her in the nose and knocked her out cold. The Crows weren't laughing then since the woman was the chief's wife's sister, and the fight was on. The whole damned thing became a free for all. It was every man for himself.

"I was trying to get to Bill to beat the devil out of him for startin' the whole thing, but them damned Indians kept coming at me. When it started, there was only about ten of them standing around there, but when the fight broke out, they came up from the grass just like they were growing with it, only faster. Pretty soon, I don't see Horny Bill anywhere around there. I caught up with him the next day, and sure enough, true to his name, he had picked that Crow woman up off the ground while she was still dead to the world and hauled her out of there and spent the night with her. That woman walked around the next day with a swelled-up nose and a grin that stretched from one ear to the other, but when we found Bill, he was squirming around in the grass, whacking imaginary snakes with a stick."

For the first time in days, Angus was laughing so hard that his face hurt, but not from his bruises. The more that Zeb ran around camp, acting out the events of the Willow Valley Rendezvous, with Girl chasing him around, barking and nipping at him for acting crazy, the more Angus laughed, feeling like his guts might burst.

Sam was in awe of the events that he was hearing about his old friend's life. Sam had spent most of his life wishing that he hadn't parted ways with William all those years ago, and he wondered what Grace would have thought about her William growing into someone that became known as Horny Bill. Suddenly, Sam exploded with laughter, too, and Zeb was pleased with himself for making the men laugh at his antics around the campfire. Bill couldn't help laughing at his crazy companion of the old days, even if the story wasn't quite the way he remembered it. Zeb was always a good showman.

Bill remembered the days that he saw snakes and monsters, but it wasn't because he had a witch put a spell on him. It was because he had an addiction to alcohol. After he lost his mother and he let Sam run off on a fool's errand and found himself in the company of government surveyors in the middle of nowhere, his broken heart got the better of him, and the only things that he could find to dull the pain was alcohol, all forms of smoke and women. Any woman was sufficient to ease his guilt, but the day that crazy witch doctor wanted to be his girlfriend was the day he knew it was time for him to change his ways. It was a long time after that before Bill quit trying to whip off imaginary snakes. It was only with the help of his employer that he was able to get past that and the snakes and the sweats by using certain plants to make tea with.

"So that's why yer down on Rose for drinkin', isn't it?" Angus said.

"Well, I just don't think anybody should get as bad as I was back then, especially a lady who happens to be my niece. That surely is no way to live," Bill replied, shaking his head as he remembered his blurry past.

"Drinkin'? What the devil does drinkin' have to do with anything? Horny Bill was witched by them Indians, I tell you, just like that woman was trying to do to me tonight. Horny Bill wouldn't care that she was a witch, though. He would have grabbed her up and took her out behind the building and poured it too her, and if he had, you would be seeing him runnin' around the fire, slapping the ground with blood coming out of his eyes," Zeb assured the men.

"I've known some men who have had the problems with snakes and monsters, and witches didn't have anythin' to do with it. I will yield to the fact that a woman probably started it, but it was the drink that caused them to act crazy. When the time came that they couldn't get the drink, that's when the problems with seein' things would start," Angus said, taking a stand against Zeb's witch theory.

"Angus, I swear, if you had been there, you would believe in my side of the story. That's why I stayed here in California. When I first laid eyes on my sweet Anna, I knew that she was the purest little lady that I had ever seen or ever would see in this world, and I was determined not to let her get away from me. Now here I am, and there she is, and I'm going to be sleeping alone on the ground with a pack of fools, and my Anna is missing me. I can hear her crying herself to sleep and whispering my name." Zeb pouted.

"If her lungs are as big as her tits, you probably would be able to hear her, but she probably got drunk on margaritas and is sleeping with a wandering vaquero," Bill kidded.

"No, she's not! No, she's not! How do you know how big my Anna's breasts are? You take that back!" Zeb was running around the camp again with Girl running and barking behind him.

"All I remember is, when we pulled into Monterey, your Anna and her sister greeting each one of us by, asking which one of us was Horny Bill, and we all pointed at you," Bill jibed, trying to keep a straight face.

"No, she didn't! No, she didn't! Maybe her sister did that, but not my Anna!" Zeb argued.

"Well, that's the way I recall it. I don't know." Bill ended the joke, knowing very well that Zeb would ponder his recollections and wonder all night about if his purest Anna had ever kept company with someone in his bed, and maybe that would keep him quiet about witches and Bill's past for a while.

As Sam watched William's wicked ways of teasing a person, he remembered back to the days when he would listen to him tease his mother and Miss Lucy. William was always able to make his mother's face light up with his crazy fibs and storytelling. Sam thought back to those strange days back in Kentucky on the Weatherford farm. The times, events, and emotions were constantly contradicting. One moment, William would be happily teasing and at ease with the world around him, and the next moment, he was as serious and vigilant as a hungry cat. As fun and carefree as the joking times were was exactly how gloomy and tense the rest of the time was. There wasn't a moment that went by that William wasn't on full alert for the next thing that Doug would do, except the night that Grace had died.

Sam realized that what he was feeling now was the same type of feeling he always felt back then. It was the feeling of impending doom. Sitting here now with these men around the campfire and laughing about William's misadventures reminded Sam of how extreme life was then, and he couldn't stop looking over his shoulder and wondering what was out there, making him feel afraid. He knew that he had been shocked to see so many people loafing around Sacramento City because the creeks were running too hard this time of year to pan for gold, and he knew that he had to be careful when there were a lot of people around him, but he had been in his share of crowded cities before and had never had that old feeling of ruin creep back into his bones like it was now.

Maybe Zeb was right about witches. When Sam was in New Orleans, he had encountered old, mean, scary Black women who practiced a witchcraft called voodoo, so he knew firsthand that there really were witches, but he wasn't going to tell Zeb about it because it was clear to Sam that Zeb was obsessed with the topic. It was hard to get him to talk about anything else, and Sam knew it would be bad for Zeb and everyone around him to encourage his craziness any further.

Bill was smiling at the others and pointing at Zeb behind his back as they all watched him miserably stabbing the ground with a stick. Girl was standing in front of him with all four of her legs spread out and studying the stick because she was waiting for him to throw it for her. Zeb was pretending to be depressed because he was missing his wife to make the others jealous of him for having a wife when they didn't and driving Girl crazy in the process. His charade was working on the dog but not on the men. They were just grateful that he was being quiet for a few moments.

Bill was heating water for his tea, and he dreaded the moment when he would ask Zeb if he wanted some because he was certain that Zeb would get riled up again, but he would do it anyway because he really wanted his tea and couldn't wait any longer. Besides, if Zeb could get the redheaded titan and the nervous Black man, who never had a sense of humor a day in his life, to laugh out loud, then Bill guessed he could take whatever Zeb could dish out about his fuzzy past.

Bill marveled at Angus as he watched his wee little babies crawling around on top of each other, staying in constant motion for warmth. Angus knew it was too early in their little lives to make friends with them, but the way he looked at them was like watching a child waiting with anticipation for Saint Nick to arrive on Christmas Eve. Bill had tried to imagine how a man could become enraged enough to actually live through a battle to the death, in hand-to-hand combat with his two brothers, and then be so concerned about the welfare of some black-and-white puppies. Bill thought about all the times that he should have killed his own brother but could never bring himself to do it. The night he and Sam left out of that place was the night he should have stayed and took care of it once and for all, but he had always believed that it was his father's place to hand out justice to Douglas. Now he wondered why it never happened. Why didn't anyone ever kill that useless piece of work? And what evilness would that animal be doing these days? Hopefully something that would get him killed. Maybe he would ask Rose Mary about it sometime.

Zeb tossed his stick on the ground, which disappointed Girl very much, as Bill was about to finish the tea. "I'm turning in, I reckon, so my Anna will come to me in my dreams." Girl walked over to Angus and received a pet and then hopped into the box with her brood and rested her chin on the edge of the box, watching Zeb and hoping he would change his mind about a game of fetch. Angus smiled when he heard the wee one's squeak with delight when their mother came to feed them and keep them warm, and Sam was certain that he heard the big, strange man giggle just a little bit and thought that if there was anybody on this earth that had been touched by a voodoo woman, it was Angus Donovan. Sam glared at the man in puzzlement for a moment and then shook his head in disgust.

"Zeb, I was about to offer you some tea," Bill said.

"Let me tell you something about your tea. Rose Mary and I agree on this. All tea drinkers can go straight to the devil! Take back what you said about my wife, you horny old medicine man! Take it back!" Zeb screamed at Bill, and Bill only laughed at him, not taking back anything that he had said about Anna. Zeb scowled at Bill, waiting for an apology, and when one didn't come, he quickly rolled over onto his side, facing away from the men, and pulled his blanket up over his head.

Sam and Angus thought the scene was humorous, but they didn't laugh at Zeb because it was likely that Bill had hurt his feelings. Even if they thought that Bill probably owed him that, neither one of them felt like it was their payback to be satisfied with.

Angus fell asleep shortly after finishing his tea. His damaged body was still healing, and sleep came easy to him these days.

Sam was relieved to have this time to catch up with William. "So what do you think it is that's got you on your ear, Sam?" Bill asked, concerned and wanting to help his old friend sort out his anxieties.

"Don't you feel it, too, William? It's that gloomy feeling I used to get back when we were kids," Sam replied, hoping that William would know at least what he was talking about when no one else would.

The look of hatred sparked in Bill's eyes as he turned his head and looked into the fire, remembering the feeling that was set deep in his bones like an affliction that would never leave. "I should have stayed and killed that bastard for what he did to you," Bill said in disgust with himself as much as with his brother.

"We wouldn't have Rose, and I probably wouldn't be kind of safe here in California if you had done that," Sam replied.

"Maybe you're having these funny feelings on account of seeing me again. I got those old memories worked up in you," Bill reasoned.

"That's not it. I'm happy to see you again, and I've been hoping to see you again for a long time. No, that's not it at all, William. Something bad is going to happen. I just wish I knew what it was," Sam said, looking into the mesmerizing flames and shaking his head.

Bill studied Sam's concerned and serious expressions. This man wasn't joking. He didn't have false beliefs in witches that Bill knew of, and he never lied or made mountains out of mole hills. He was sincerely worried or maybe haunted. One way or the other, Sam was genuine. "I guess we will just have to keep our eyes peeled. I have no doubt that you are right. Something bad is always happening somewhere."

"We can't let anything happen to Rose," Sam said ominously.

"So you think it has something to do with her? She was already on the brink of death once, and that didn't rattle you half as bad as you seem to be now," Bill stated.

"I know. Curious, ain't it?" Sam said, pondering the puzzle. Both men stared into the fire, speculating about what was waiting for them in their futures and wondering if they could ever lay their pasts to rest, wishing that they could just throw their bad memories into the fire and let it devour them away. But there was one thing that Bill had to find out about Sam.

Bill cleared his throat, knowing that he was about to touch on a hurtful subject. "Sam, I have to ask, did you ever find your mama?"

Sam looked down at the ground and shook his head. "No, I never did. I never really got much of a chance to look for her. I was only on my own for five days when some men stopped me on the road and questioned me about the horse, and even though I had your note, they said that I didn't deserve to have a horse or shoes or clothes, and they told me that they ought to hang me, but they didn't. They put me in the fields until that other fella came around and made me fight. I traveled some while I was doing that, and I always watched for her, but I never did see her. She is probably gone now, I reckon. She never thought much of me anyway, not the way Miss Grace thought of you. I reckon Miss Grace was more of a mother to me than my own would have been anyway. I should have never gone after her William. I will always hate myself for it."

Sam choked up with feelings of loss and regret. He was trying desperately not to cry, but he couldn't manage it, and Bill pretended not to notice, continuing to watch the fire until his old friend was able to collect himself. A few moments passed, and Sam had a long drink of brandy. "Now I have a question for you. What would Miss Grace think of you being somebody called Horny Bill?"

Both men laughed with bittersweet emotion, not knowing whether they should laugh or cry.

"Oh, believe me, I've done everything that I could think of to make my mama proud of me!" Bill said, crying now more than laughing and thinking of Miss Grace looking down at him from heaven.

"Was Angus right about you and the snakes?" Sam asked.

"Yes, he was. The alcohol had the better of me for a while. I was trying to kill myself with it, I think, but it had an unexpected effect on me. Over these last few years, since I was able to quit, I've been traveling from one tribe of Indians to another, all over the country, learning about plants and their different uses. I just spent this last fall with the Yanas who told me how to soothe your skin if you get poison oak."

"What's poison oak?" Sam inquired.

"It's like poison ivy, but it looks different. I'll show you some when I see it."

"I want to learn about plants. That sounds like useful information," Sam stated. "I couldn't believe how you healed Rose and got that fever to break."

"I've learned something valuable in my travels. I believe that God puts evil, poisonous things on this earth. I don't know why, but he also puts the antidotes for them here too," Bill said with confidence in his belief and with his brother in the shadows of his mind. "Sam, why don't you get some rest? I'll stay up awhile and watch over things."

"Yeah, do you really think that I could sleep tonight? I'm so on edge that it would just be a good waste of time trying," Sam said, shaking his head. "You go ahead."

"All right, but take it easy on that brandy. It's pure poison, you know," Bill advised.

Sam didn't argue. He only just smiled at his old friend in a way that suggested that he would do as he pleased.

*****

Sometime in the night, Sam had managed to fall asleep. He was rudely awakened by a curious commotion. He jumped up and tried to focus his eyes because he was seeing double and finally realized that it was Zeb kicking dirt all over William and cursing him. William had his bedroll pulled over his head, and Sam could hear him laughing.

"You rotten son of a bitch! Damn your hide! It's about time I tried to drown you in a river, you bastard!" Zeb was trying to pull Bill and his bedroll to the river. Sam grabbed Zeb from behind, pinning his arms down and dragged him away from Bill.

"What in the devil is wrong with you?" Sam was confused and angry.

"He's a warlock! He witched me and Anna! She came to me in my dreams, but she was making love to another man, and she smiled at me and let the other man play with her breasts!" Zeb was red-faced and pointing at Bill and looked as if he was about to cry.

"Was she howling like a coyote while the guy was kissing her big tits?" Bill asked from inside his bedroll, still laughing.

At this comment, Sam decided that William was big enough to take care of himself, and Zeb probably wouldn't kill him anyway, so Sam let him go.

Zeb ran over to where Bill was wadded up in a ball, jumped up, and landed on him, using his knees as weapons. Sam cringed and shook his head as he heard the air come out of Bill. Fortunately, Bill's bedroll was thick, and as Zeb continued to thrust his knees into any piece of his body he could find, Sam could still hear Bill laughing and making the sounds that he thought his purest Anna would make when she was in the middle of an intimate moment, and then Bill teased Zeb some more by pretending to be Anna. "Oh, wandering vaquero, I want you some more! Don't stop! Don't stop! Zeb? Zeb who? I love only you, wandering vaquero! I want to wander around with you!" Then Bill howled like a coyote.

"You crazy witch! You bastard!" Zeb screamed as he continued to beat up Bill.

Suddenly, Angus woke up. In his dreams, he thought that his brothers had come back to life and were hurting Rose again. Quickly, he picked Zeb up off Bill and flung him to the ground ten feet away. Angus looked like a wild animal as he walked toward Zeb with his hands reached out in front of him as if he was going to choke the life out of him. Sam grimaced at the thought of having to stop Angus. This matter was about to become a free for all, and Sam didn't want Angus to hit him in the head again. Sam ran up behind Angus before he got to Zeb, tripped him from behind, and pushed him to the ground. Now that Angus was face down, Sam just sat in the middle of his back. Of course, Bill didn't know what trouble he was causing, but he knew that Zeb wasn't trying to hit him anymore, so he started squirming around in his bedroll, still pretending to be Anna. "Oh, wandering vaquero, where did you go? I need you!"

Zeb looked at Sam, and Sam nodded to him. Zeb ran over to Bill and began the long process of trying to drag Bill to the river. The whole time Bill was being dragged to the river, he never stopped with his teasing, and when Zeb would get tired, he would stop and kick Bill and tell him to shut up. Angus realized, after Sam had been sitting in the middle of him for a few moments, that his brothers were still dead, and he assured Sam that he wouldn't hurt anybody if he would just let him up.

Sam got off him, and together they followed and watched Zeb trying to get Bill to the river so he could drown him, but midway through the project, Zeb grew weary and lost interest. He kicked Bill a few more times and went back to his bedroll by the dwindling fire and yelled, "You bastard witch doctor, go to the devil!" Zeb had worn himself out and was fast asleep again in no time.

Bill crawled out of his bedroll and shook it out, still laughing about the aggravation that he had caused his old fellow surveyor. "It was always so easy to get under Zeb's skin. I just had to find out if it still was in his old age or if he had matured any."

Sam shook his head at Bill. "Would you say that you've matured any?"

"Of course not," Bill confessed proudly.

Angus was still perplexed by the event. Dreaming that his brothers were in camp again bothered him and made him sad, but the sight of seeing Zeb struggling with Bill's dead weight as he tried to pull him to the river was comical enough to ease the guilt that he was sure he would always feel. "What caused Zeb to start in on Bill in the middle of the night? What did I miss?" Angus asked Sam.

"He dreamt his wife was sleeping with another man and accused Bill of being the cause of it," Sam replied.

"Aye." Angus nodded his head, knowing full well that Zeb would think that and understood now why it happened in the middle of the night.

While they were all awake anyway, the men gathered more wood for the fire. Sam checked on the horses, and Angus looked in on the pups. Girl hadn't moved during the disturbance because she was still mad about Zeb not playing fetch with her earlier, but she flapped her tail to thank Angus for paying attention to her when he petted her.

As Sam was curling up under his blanket, he could see that William was going to stay up and make more tea probably. He watched William put more wood on the fire, put his bedroll away, and put on his hat. The sky was just beginning to lighten with the first sign of dawn, and Sam dreaded what the next day would bring. For the most part, this night had been quiet. At least Rose wasn't there snoring, he thought as he drifted off to sleep.

3

Rose and Bennager lay side by side in their big soft bed, wet with sweat and sighing languidly with delight from their lovemaking exertions. Rose caught her breath and cuddled with her husband, and looking into his celestial blue eyes, she said, "Husband, I need coffee and I need more guns."

"You're still of a mind to go around shooting anybody who bothers you, I take it," Bennager replied, smiling at his fiery wife.

"No, now I'm concerned with people who might bother you. You're mine, and I don't intend to let anybody change that," Rose said as she bounced out of bed and prepared herself to greet the outside world. She longed for another bath as she looked at the tub that had changed her outlook of melting away into nothing. It was in that tub that she concluded that it was every animal for himself or herself, as was the case, and she was grateful for the epiphany. Right now, she wanted coffee more than she wanted a bath, and she knew that Sam would have some boiling. She wanted to find him and the others and get started on her next enterprise. As she chose one of the new dresses to wear, she decided that she could arrange for another bath for later in the morning while the others were preparing for the trip.

She peeked at Bennager who looked too sapped to move an inch and laughed at his lack of enthusiasm for her pursuit of coffee and breakfast.

She picked the velvet green dress with the black collar, gathered up her undergarments and proceeded to dress slowly, teasing Bennager so he would remember what she looked like without clothes on until she got him back in that bathtub with her again. Bennager watched her dress and thought of how smart he was to have attached himself to a woman who had no inhibitions about anything whatsoever. All the things about her that he had found to be distasteful and completely unladylike had turned out to be to his advantage, although he did hope that she wouldn't become the type of woman who would put on shows like this in the middle of camp. He was pleased and delighted by her childlike, feminine playfulness that she possessed when they were alone together. He had no doubt that this temptress would kill anybody that tried to come between them, so he would have to be careful, for the world's sake that nobody tried to. He knew how she felt because even though he had never had the bloodthirsty desire to go around killing people like Rose had, he found himself feeling the exact same way about her.

She's mine! he thought as he watched every move she made, every string that she seductively tied. Every time she put her hands to her breasts to adjust her bodice made Bennager swell with lascivious desire. He would have to protect her now with every fiber of his being, with everything that he had, in every way possible so that he could have her and keep her for his own forever.

"Come on, get up. Come with me to find the others and have coffee. I know how you love Uncle Bill's tea. Let's go," Rose jested joyfully. Of course, he would go whether he wanted to or not. This woman would play devil ever leaving his sight if he had it his way.

Bennager didn't bounce as easily as Rose did. He was tired from his honeymoon night and was astonished that he had lived through it. In all his visions that he had of his first time with a woman, he had never imagined something like that. He had listened to other men brag on their exploits with women of the night and had heard complaints and the good times as well from men who had been married but had never heard of anything coming close to what he had experienced with Rose Mary Rasmussen. Now she was even helping him to get dressed. She pulled his pants up for him and buttoned them, slyly grazing her hand against his wilted manliness, and then she buttoned his shirt, taking in the scent of his chest hairs as she did it.

"You must be Aphrodite in the here and now. I might not believe in witches, but you've made me believe that goddesses do exist," Bennager said, not being able to resist cupping her breasts in his hands. She looked so beautiful in her new dress. The green velvet made her green, erotic eyes brighter than ever, and the red in her hair stood out.

Rose smacked his hands. "Don't muss my dress, you heathen! Besides, you don't have enough energy left in you to finish what you're trying to start. How do I look?"

"You are and always will be the most beautiful thing that I have ever seen, and I will muss your dress anytime I see fit to," Bennager sincerely replied.

"Thank you, my love, for that and for the dresses. You have made every inch of me, inside and out, feel like a woman." She went to him and kissed him lovingly, and he received her with a warm, heartfelt hug and kiss. She wanted those arms to be wrapped around her every second of every day, but there was work to be done. Her first decision of her new life as a married woman had been made just this very second, and it was time to make it happen. "Let's go now. I have business to tend to." And just like that, it seemed that the honeymoon was over.

*****

"Townsfolk coming," Zeb said to Sam motioning with his head at the couple walking toward them.

"So your eyesight is another sense that you've completely lost, huh?" Bill jabbed Zeb, making sure to keep him riled.

Zeb shot a searing look at Bill but didn't give him the satisfaction of answering his cutting question, and then he turned his attention to the arrivals. Sam could tell by the way the two people walked that it was Rose and Bennager. Zeb just didn't recognize Rose in her dress, but he didn't see any reason to get involved in William's obvious attempt to keep Zeb in a particular poor state of depression, just because the man missed his wife and his soft bed. Girl took leave of her pups and trotted up the foot trail, through the oaks and low brush that belonged to the black tail deer and turkeys who craved the river water and sweet grass year round.

Rose stopped in her tracks to greet her friend and only female companion, and at this, her identity was apparent. Bill gave out a whoop and a holler to the newlyweds and was delighted to see his niece finally carrying herself as a lady. His delights came to an abrupt halt, of course, when he saw her spit tobacco out of her mouth and then wipe her face with the back of her hand. Bill shook his head and cringed at the sight of it.

"Sam, I hope you have coffee boiling," Rose stated.

Sam answered with a smile as he waited for his turn to shake hands with Bennager. There were no jokes or jibes made about the honeymoon night. It seemed to the party that everything must have worked out pretty well. Bennager didn't have any bullet holes in him, but he did look pretty worn out. Everyone just assumed in their own minds that it was because of Rose's snoring, especially since she seemed to be so chipper herself. Zeb wanted to tell Rose how well she looked and how the soft bed must have put her in better spirits since she didn't seem to be in her usual discontented mood, but he didn't say anything because he knew it would provoke Bill into razzing him some more about something, and if he had to hear that witch doctor jab him anymore about his Anna, he was sure that there would be a more serious fight than the one that they had the night before.

Everyone sat around the fire, sipping coffee and tea. The men were mostly in awe of Rose's new attire, and without Zeb rambling on in his usual way and Rose complaining in hers, the morning coffee didn't seem to have its usual flavor.

"It's a quiet camp this morning," Bennager offered. He was hoping to gather some of his energy back by listening to some titillating conversation with his tea that he graciously accepted from Bill. Rose was only enjoying Sam's coffee with relish and hadn't noticed until Bennager mentioned it, and then she looked at the other men and wondered why there wasn't any teasing or at least the usual morning palaver. Rose thought that they were either upset with her and Bennager or else the thing that Sam had feared the night before had happened.

Easing into the puzzle, Rose stated, "You fellas hurried out of town so fast yesterday without eating that you must be hungry. Let's go in and get some breakfast." She stood up, expecting them to agree and follow. The men only shifted their seats and grumbled a little, and then Bill got up and started to prepare a meal of biscuits and bacon. Rose looked at Bennager and sat back down, and together they observed their friends and wondered what had happened that was making them so sour.

Sam stood up to help Bill, and Angus was watching his wee little babes. Girl was standing in front of Zeb, still hopeful that he would stop jabbing his stick in the ground and just throw it for her to fetch. As Rose and Bennager watched Zeb and Girl, with her tongue hanging out of her mouth in anticipation, they realized that Zeb must be the reason for the quiet camp and lack of jokes and jests. Rose decided that this was a grand opportunity to get revenge on Zeb for his embarrassing performance in the restaurant the night before and kick him while he was down.

Rose spat tobacco into the fire. "Zeb, I hope you were a gentleman to Maggie after we left the restaurant last night. She is a fine lady who doesn't deserve to have to serve crazy people like you. She told me this morning, on our way out here, that she thought you were a very handsome older gentleman but a very odd man as well, and she wondered if you had been in an accident and got your head hurt." Instinctively, as if she was given this very special talent handed down from God and his angels, Rose knew exactly where to dig. Bennager had found out about her talents before the sun came up this morning, and now it was Zeb's turn to receive her in a different way.

"She said all of that about little ol' me, did she?" Zeb said sarcastically, still looking at the ground.

Rose noticed that Sam and Bill were trying not to laugh, and she knew she was on the path of retribution. "Yes, she said all that, and then she told me if you needed a place to stay while you got well from your accident that she had a spare room and would look after you until you were well enough to travel."

Zeb continued to pout, and now he was poking the stick in the fire, causing ash to get on Rose's new dress, and Girl was standing to the side of him, watching the end of the stick that was causing the disruption. Rose nonchalantly stood up and walked a little to save her dress and waited for Zeb's reply, but one didn't come.

Bill and Sam were laughing like two little boys who were drunk on stolen whisky.

Rose decided to drop the subject as she got the sense that Zeb was having an off day for some reason. She figured it was likely due to something that took place in the night, given the behavior of her uncle. She noticed that Angus was deep in thought and wanted to find clarity in how their plan might intersect. "Angus, have you given anymore thought to working with me to build a cattle rancho in the foothills?"

"Does he have a choice?" Bill interjected.

Kindly, Rose said, "Of course you have a choice, Angus, but if you don't want to go with us to buy cattle and you don't want to stay here, there is something that I need help with, and I would hate to have to hire someone I don't know to do it. I'm sure my friend Maggie could suggest someone reputable, though, if you have other plans." Then she glared at Bill for interfering with her conversation and sat down beside her husband.

Angus didn't really have any plans. For the past few days, he had just been concentrating on getting over his beating. He knew he wasn't a miner, and he knew that he was running out of money. Soon the party would leave him and Girl behind with the pups to look after, and he didn't want to be trapped in Sacramento City, eating scraps of food and washing dishes for a living. He had already been down that road before when he first arrived in America and couldn't find a job as a mason. Rose had promised him and Girl a soft bed when they got to Sacramento City, but now that he was here, he couldn't wait to leave. And he was ready to get back to work. He would work the stiffness out of his lazy body once he had something else to do and to think about.

Bill watched Rose ignore Angus and chat with Bennager about how she would have to hire someone and how she was sure Maggie would know an honest man and how everything would work out just fine, and then Bill looked out the corner of his eye to see what Angus was doing and could tell that he was deep in thought. Bill closed his eyes and chuckled, only loud enough for Sam to hear, and shook his head. Bill whispered to Sam, "You mean to tell me that you've been traveling with that girl for nearly a year, and you never noticed that she is the spitting image of my mother?"

Sam smiled. "It was all the spitting that confused me, I reckon. Circumstances were a lot different on that damned boat. Mostly, all we did was guard the money and ourselves and live like rats since we were both runaways. I can sure see Miss Grace in her now. She brings on a lot of memories, the good ones too." Bill and Sam both noticed Rose slyly peek at Angus while she calmly talked and sipped her coffee.

Bill handed out the breakfast biscuits and said, "Rose, I noticed that your arm must be feeling pretty good. You don't even seem to be favoring it much."

Rose blushed a little bit, remembering the moment that she had thrown off the sling and nodded. "Thank you, Uncle, yes, the sling wasn't stylish enough to match the dresses that my husband gave to me, and I think if I use my arm, it will heal faster."

Bill smiled and nodded. He was thinking about all the things that he had been called in his life and how being called Uncle had strangely just filled him with joy, even if his niece had just blown her mouthful of tobacco into the fire.

"Oh, these are the best biscuits that I have ever had, Uncle," Rose complimented and wondered if calling Bill Ford "Uncle" would annoy him the way she hoped it would.

"It's an old family recipe," Bill replied kindly. His comment reminded him of asking Rose if she knew of her grandfather, but he would ask her some other time.

"Pretty damn close, Williams," Sam said of the biscuits, knowing whose recipe he was trying to imitate and wishing that there was a wagon load of them to eat.

"What do you mean close?" Bill asked, offended by the comment.

"Pretty close, you know."

"You won't find any closer on God's green earth, and you know it!" Bill said, defending his ability to cook as the rest of the party ate and looked on in confusion about what the argument was over.

Zeb came back to camp, and when offered breakfast, he impolitely said, "Horny Bill, I tired of your biscuits years ago, you bastard!"

"Maybe you ought to go out in the brush and scare up a tortilla then, you ill-mannered son of a bitch. Maybe one will come to you in your dreams tonight," Bill shot back, resenting Zeb's hurtful comment about his cooking.

Angus and Sam stood up from the comfort of the big oak branch that they had been using for a dining room chair and took a few steps back. They both knew that this joke of Bill's had come to an end, and there was going to be a real fight this time. Bennager sensed the serious tension surrounding the camp and put his arm around Rose's waist, urging her to get up and get out of the way as the others had done, disrupting her state of shock as she looked at the two men who were about to fight; over what, she could not imagine. She thought that the two men had admiration for one another, and now they were about to have a fight over biscuits and tortillas. She was still trying to figure out what was going on when she noticed Girl cowering to her box to be with her babies and hide. Rose closed her eyes in confusion, and then shaking her head, she started toward the two men to stop the fight. Bennager stopped her with just a slight touch, and Sam gave her a look that told her to stay back.

Bill wasn't laughing at Zeb now. Talking guff about his biscuits was uncalled for, and although he would never admit it because he knew he had it coming, being kicked in the middle of the night hadn't set well with him either. Zeb's lack of feminine touch was his own doing, not Bill's, and now they were going to clear the air. The two of them eyeballed each other as they moved in a circle with their hands out in front of them as if they were in a bizarre trance, watching and waiting for the other man to make his move.

Rose watched her uncle and Zeb in disappointment and reckoned that she had never witnessed anything as ridiculous as this in her life. She looked at Bennager in disgust and asked, "What are they doing?"

"I'm not really sure what they are doing, but you probably shouldn't watch it. Besides, it looks like it could take a while, and we should start getting ready for the trip." And then Bennager said to Sam, "I think we're going to start preparing things for the trip, unless you want me to stay."

Sam smiled as he always did when White people were being absurd. "There's no need to stay. Take this lady away from this nonsense. I'll make sure they don't hurt themselves too bad. Angus and me have been doing it all night." Sam laughed as he watched his grown friends act like children.

Bennager and Rose started for town, periodically looking over their shoulders to see if the fight had started yet. Angus trotted up behind them after they had lost sight of the scene behind the brush.

"Mrs. Rasmussen, I thought about me plans, and I don't have any. If ye have a job for me, I'd be happy to have it," Angus said, hoping that he hadn't missed out on the offer.

Rose smiled, content that she had gotten her way. If she hadn't of been a married woman, she would have hugged her gentleman titan. She shook his hand warmly with both of hers and said, "I'm very glad, Mr. Donovan, because you are the one that I want to do this job." Rose would have liked to be sitting by the warmth of the fire to tell Angus about his job, but she settled for the nearest available oak branch in the damp, cold valley floor of California and took out a map that she had purchased in the mercantile that morning.

Bennager and Angus sat down on each side of her as she spread the map out across her lap. "I want you to go stake some ground out for us where there is good grass and water for the cattle and centrally located so we can supply beef to many miners, and let's not forget that it has to be a place where there is no fog. I don't like fog or the smell of salty air. This map shows that after you cross the American River, you can follow the Feather River north, cross the Bear River, and continue to Marysville. Then I want you to follow this Yuba River east and find a place south of it, up in those hills," she said as she pointed to the oak-laden foothills of the Sierras that were facing her. "Then while you and Girl are waiting for us and the cattle, we are going to have you use Bennager's freight wagon and start getting in supplies. I heard last night in the restaurant that there is a sawmill in Grass Valley, so you can start bringing in the building supplies for our homes and a stable for the horses. When we get back, we'll start building," Rose finished by handing the map to Angus. His eyes were wide with excitement as he looked at Rose and Bennager.

They trusted his judgment about choosing land, and Bennager trusted him with his beautiful team. Angus was afraid of how he would do on his own. This was a lot of responsibility and a lot of work to do by himself, but suddenly, he was feeling like a brand-new man. He had a newfound feeling of pride, and he was grateful to Rose and Bennager for giving him the job and making him feel like a trusted friend. Angus smiled and looked down at the map.

"You know, Angus, you could hire somebody to help you. If you should meet somebody that you want working for you, then go ahead. That's up for you to decide. I'd hate to see you get lonely," Rose added.

"I'll have Girl and me wee little babes. I'll do me best for ye, Mr. and Mrs. Rasmussen. Thank ye for the job. I'll be gettin' started straight away," Angus said, getting up and heading for town. "I'll go get the team ready."

"I'll go with you, Angus," Bennager said, walking briskly to catch up with him.

Rose sat on the oak branch and watched her husband and friend walk to town. She had been forgotten but felt a sense of relief and was glad to have a private moment to herself. She missed moments like this. She would often venture from her home as a child and sit and think about what her life would be like when she was grown-up and what was waiting for her to discover out in the world, and now she was thinking about the same thing: her future. She thought of her future with Bennager, finances, and friendships. She wondered what it would be like to buy cattle from the rancheros to the south, and she was still puzzled about what a vaquero was, but she reckoned that she would find out soon enough. She suddenly realized she ought not be sitting alone in the brush. She could hear the sounds of the silly men back in camp. Then she heard Bennager call for her. She hurried to catch up with her husband.

Angus was hitching the beautifully matched six-horse team to the freight wagon, and Bennager was dealing with the livery owner on a wagon, team, and a couple of more horses and tack. Angus would need a saddle horse when he got to where he was going, and he knew that Rose would never settle for riding in the supply wagon on the trail with him, so he told her to pick out a mount and a saddle that felt comfortable. There wasn't much to pick from on either count, but when she caught sight of the Roman-nosed dun in the middle of the corral with his ears pinned back, taking a nip out of the horse beside it, she asked, "How much for that one?"

"Which one?" the livery man and Bennager said in unison.

"That sandy colored one there," Rose said, pointing to the one in the middle of the corral.

"I guess you must be a good rider, ma'am. That is the most spirited horse that I have, couldn't let him go for less than $45," the man said.

Sam crossed his arms and glared at the man.

Bennager piped up before Rose was able to get out the words, "I'll take him."

"By spirited, you mean hardheaded, mean, and difficult to handle. Now isn't that a better way of putting it, Jim? That horse was in there last summer, and he still is because nobody wants him." And then to Rose, he said, "That little bay in the corner might be better suited for you, sweetheart. She looks spirited enough to make the trip."

Rose looked at Sam and then back at the bay and smiled. "She's too small, spindly legged, and she has two white feet. I'll be buying the dun, but not for $45," she said as she stepped off the bottom rail of the corral and approached Jim. "I'll take your spirited dun off of your hands so you won't have to waste feed on him and doctor the bites on the others, and that saddle and that ring bit bridle over there for $20, Jim." Rose turned and spat on the ground beside her and looked back at the man, waiting for his reaction.

Sam raised one of his crossed hands up to his mouth to hide his smile and admiration from Bennager and Jim. Rose happened to know more about horses than the two of them thought she did.

Apparently, her evil father had taken to buying horses, and because he didn't know anything about them, he had only picked them based on their looks, and like Sam and William when they were young, Rose had spent as much time as she could in the stables, listening to her father's slaves scrutinize each animal and watched them try to train the nags to perform certain tasks. Rose had helped when she could and learned and rode in every spare minute. Her father never paid any attention to her as a child. It had only been in the last couple of years that he had started harassing her about beaus and getting herself married up.

Rose's hands-on knowledge combined with what Sam had told her about burros, mules, and draft horses made her more than qualified to pick out a mount and know its value, monetarily speaking. She also knew that the hardheaded Roman-nosed dun might well be valued as priceless on the trail when times got tough.

"Thirty dollars!" Jim haggled.

"Fifteen then!" Rose bargained defiantly with her arms crossed in the same way that Sam did when he was displeased.

"Fifteen? You're going backward, ma'am. You're supposed to meet me somewhere between twenty and thirty. I don't believe you know how to haggle," Jim said kindly, trying to teach her what he thought she didn't know.

Rose stood her ground stoically and spat, working the tobacco in her mouth and completely baffling Jim because her outward appearance was so contrary to her personality. She said again, "Fifteen."

Jim scratched his neck unable to make out what was happening. "Twenty-five, and I won't go any lower!" he said.

"Fourteen!" Rose replied.

"Fourteen? Ma'am, that would just be robbery now. You are an awful pretty girl, but I just can't go around giving away my stock and tack. I'll tell you what. For $20, I'll give away the horse and saddle, but the bit and bridle will cost you two more dollars."

"I'll give you nineteen for the works," Rose countered.

Jim smiled. Now the woman was haggling correctly. "Twenty!" Jim hollered happily. Rose smiled and put her hand out, and Jim shook it, relieved that the business was over.

"I told you that I'd take him for twenty," Rose said, gloating.

Bennager looked at his wife in amazement and thought of how he had underestimated her again, then he looked at Sam and Angus in bewilderment and saw that Sam was finished trying to contain his smile and admiration, and the awe that was showing on Angus' face was obvious for the world to see. Rose went to her husband and rubbed his arm with her hand. "I can't wait to try him out," she said, referring to the horse. "I'm going to change my clothes and come back. I'm afraid my moment of looking like a lady is over for now. After you've finished negotiating with Jim and I've tried out the Roman, I was hoping that we could pack our things for the trip together back at the hotel."

Her whispered words were gentle and inviting to Bennager's ears. His eyes twinkled as he gathered their meaning by the way in which they were said. His heartbeat raced at the thought of this woman wanting more of him, and he imagined his heart exploding in his chest. Her plea had caught him off guard, and all that he could say was, "Yes."

She smiled and stood there, waiting for a kiss to seal the deal with her husband. She would not initiate it in front of the other men, given what she had learned earlier about privacy between partners in life. Bennager put her hand to his lips and kissed her fingertip in a way that sent a sensual chill through her core, and then he kissed her cheek. Now she knew how this type of business was conducted in public places. She smiled warmly at him and made for the hotel, peering back at the Roman as she walked. Bennager followed her with his gaze and knew that he would lose the $25 that Rose had just made during her negotiations. His mind was no longer able to concentrate on the important job of bartering over stock and tack; he was at a loss and looked to Sam and Angus for help. The premier haggler had left the premises as far as he was concerned, and he didn't like the idea of the others watching him fail at the task.

"Sam, you've been watching the finances of this outfit longer than I have, so you better take over. Something tells me that my wife learned some of her talents from you anyway. Angus, I'd be obliged if you would help him," Bennager said and then walked away.

"Where are ye going?" Angus asked.

Bennager's mind was on Rose's request, and he wanted nothing more than to go to their room and make good on it right now, but he knew that now wasn't the time. "I believe I'll need a drink before I have to watch that woman try out that dun," he said, pretending to be angry to cover up his real thoughts.

"I thought you said you didn't drink!" Sam chuckled after him.

Bennager didn't bother to dignify Sam's comment with an answer. He walked to the nearest saloon and washed away the throbbing pulse that had overtaken his entire body. By the third shot of bad whiskey, he was beginning to think with his brain and realized that the female he was in love with, the one that he had sworn an oath to the heavens to protect, the woman that could very likely be carrying his baby right now was about to try out the most iniquitous animal that he had ever looked at through corral rails.

Bennager shook his head and slammed his empty glass on the bar and hurried out of the saloon and down the muddy street to try to stop Rose before it was too late. He tried to see if the dun was still in the corral as he approached and leaped to the middle rail to look closer when he got there. Sam was examining four burros that he had purchased to pull a wagon, about half the size of Bennager's freight wagon, and Angus was working on the broken seat that came with it and thinking on how to make a cover for it to keep its contents dry when the cattle purchasing party was out on the trail.

"Where is that cursed dun?" Bennager shouted to them from across the corrals, his voice tinged with fear. Sam and Angus looked around for the man that belonged to the voice until they saw him above the heads of the remaining stock. Sam looked at Bennager with a confused expression on his face and pointed in the direction of where the men had camped last night. The thought of borrowing Sam's horse to try to catch up with his wife hadn't entered his mind until he had run full out over a half of a mile on foot and felt his lungs burning. Then he was mad at himself for letting this female, who he should have stayed away from in the first place, make him run around, looking like a damned fool. He might just as well have stayed at the saloon and drank more whisky.

After another quarter of a mile of jogging, Bennager gave up, weakened by the liquor and remembering why he hated drunkenness, and was reduced to walking. He hoped that Zeb and Bill might have seen his daring wife as he approached them and found them breathing hard and flopped over on an oak branch that had been lying on the ground for years. It was like they were using it to keep afloat in the water, but they were on land. "Have you seen Rose on a dun horse come by here?" Bennager blurted, out of breath.

Bill was breathing hard too. His face was covered with bloody scratches embedded with mud. He looked up at Bennager and asked, "Is this a riddle?"

"No, damn it! Did you two fools see her or not?" Bennager was exasperated by the woman, the run, and these preposterous men.

Both men rolled their eyes at him and rolled over to sit on the ground and use the big branch as a backrest, and Zeb said, "I believe a rider came through here. It looked like someone was trying to ride out a green mount, but I didn't see who it was. They were wearing black chaps. I did notice that right before this cuss smeared my face with mud."

"That was right after you smeared my face with mud," Bill countered.

Bennager laid his hand across his brow and took off his hat, threw it to the ground, and held his head in both hands, making his hair ruffle through the openings of his fingers. "Good Lord in heaven, I've lost her!" Bennager's heart was in his throat.

"How did you lose her already? Did she ride off on a dun with a wandering vaquero?" Bill grinned, showing Zeb his old, weathered teeth with specks of mud and blood on them, but Zeb just rolled his eyes and shook his head. Bill was insufferable, and Zeb had forgotten that quirk in his personality, but he remembered now that it was best to ignore him, and then he might leave him alone, if he was lucky, for a little while at least.

The crackling of leaves and twigs breaking and branches moving made the three men look up. It was Rose on the Roman, and they were both fit and calm as could be. Rose leaned over and rested her sore arm on the saddle. She could tell that her husband was in some distress, but she couldn't walk on eggshells every second of her life. She also noticed the grown older men had continued their scuffing endeavors and was perplexed by the way they chose to exert themselves.

"I don't see any vaqueros with her. Reckon you were worrying over nothing," Bill said as Bennager eased up to the side of the Roman and touched Rose's chapped thigh. He wanted to admonish her, but he was afraid that it would spook her horse. The Roman was pawing the ground and nodding his head, so Rose gave him his head, and he nibbled the grass.

"I thought I had lost you, sweetheart," Bennager said through gritted teeth.

Rose smiled as she knew that what she wanted to tell her husband wouldn't sit well with him, and this was going to be an issue that they would always butt heads over. She searched her heart and mind for a gentle way to tell him because this man was the only man in the world that she would do it for. "My love," she said softly, "I know that you think that I am a child in many ways, and you're probably right, but in many ways, I am not. In all the ways that count, you will have to trust me. I know that you think you are my protector, but you should know that I feel like I am yours, so you need not worry so much every time I take it into my pretty little head to do something. I made one devil of a trip to get here to find you, and I fully expect to make many more to keep you, and I'm not afraid to go to the end of the earth to live my life well. Are you?"

"You take ten years off my life every time you take it into your pretty little head to do something," Bennager reasoned.

Rose smiled. "You can blame the whiskey for that, that's what held you up, isn't it?"

Bennager noticed that now it was her face that had the hurt look on it. He stood back as she put a gentle heel to the dun's flanks and reined him in Bill's direction.

"Uncle, I would sure be obliged if you would look the maps over with us. I've given Angus an idea of where I want him to go, but I want your opinion of what the country is like or if you've seen it.

I'll go to the livery and ask Angus to wait for you," Rose said nicely as she eyeballed her uncle intently.

"I'll be along directly, Miss Rose Mary."

"Do you intend to look like that when you represent my cattle company, Mr. Jones?" Rose asked Zeb.

"You have to have cattle before you can have a cattle company, Mrs. Rasmussen."

"What do you think my chances are of accomplishing that goal, Mr. Jones?" Rose gritted her teeth when she asked the question.

"Fair to good if they haven't all been ate up already." Zeb looked at his clothes when he answered in an attempt to hide from her scowl.

Rose wheeled the Roman around and stopped in front of Bennager. She took her foot out of the stirrup and asked him if he wanted a ride. He shook his head and said that he would walk. Rose shrugged her shoulders and said, "Suit yourself." And then she headed for town on the seemingly docile back of the dun.

"The honeymoon is over, I reckon," Bill said, starting in on Bennager.

"You shut up, Bill! You don't know anything about love. These young people are doing just fine," Zeb said in a positive tone. "Bennager, the best part about being married is the adventure of the navigation. Once in a while, a strange sandbar crops up, but with a little work, you can come free from it. You'll do fine," Zeb told Bennager and slapped him on the back for moral support as he observed the newlywed holding his head in his hands. "Taking to the whiskey won't help anything, by the way," Zeb whispered so Bill might not hear.

"It was a moment of weakness," Bennager confessed.

"You will have to brace yourself for many of those," Zeb laughed. "That is a woman's special gift, making a man weak in many different ways. You don't have the luxury of a carefree life anymore as a husband. In my case, it was well worth giving it up." Zeb stole a peek at Bill then who seemed to be ignoring the conversation. Bill had never told anybody that he had been married once for a short time, and like his mother, his Indian wife had died during childbirth.

Bill was thinking of both beloved women in his life, and he wished that he couldn't hear his friend's conversation because it only brought him pain. When Zeb had said that he didn't know of love, it cut him deep, but he would never admit his failure to protect his wife to anybody, especially to the perfect husband that Zeb thought himself to be.

"She told me that I have to learn to trust her, and she thinks that it's her job to protect me. What kind of man does she think I am that I need to be protected by a female?" Bennager inquired.

"I think that she means that she can handle herself in whatever situation that should arise and that it's a good thing to have her on your side. Trust her to pull you up when you fall the way that you want her to trust you to do the same. She'll be there for you, I have no doubt about that," Zeb promised.

Bill decided that it required too much effort to pick the mud from the buckskins and out of his hair, so he went to the river. Zeb watched him go and considered jumping him down there but decided just to join him and get the cold swift bath over with. Zeb slapped Bennager on the back again and said, "It's time to go wash up."

Bennager remembered the bathtub in his own room and simply said, "Yep." He got up from the oak branch that he had been sitting on and headed to town.

4

Douglas Weatherford had become accustomed to sleeping in, well past the breakfast hour, and thoroughly enjoyed the nightlife of women, gambling, and spirits that he had purchased for himself. He had spent the last eighteen years saddled with a woman who expected him to rise every morning at dawn's first light and earn an honest living. She had every right to expect this from her husband since he had married her for her money. Doug had taken over the old homeplace but was broke within six months, so he went clear to west Tennessee to court a woman that he knew could afford him and because there certainly was not a single person in his own surrounding area of Kentucky that wanted anything to do with him.

Last June, Sarah Weatherford found out that her husband completely broke the bank, and she caused quite a fuss over it. She made the mistake of threatening to kill her husband. He bided his time because his daughter, Lily, was taking Rose's place at the altar with Richard Hawthorne, and both families were amid wedding preparations. That was how Sarah Weatherford had found out that her worthless, womanizing husband had wasted away her fortune. There was no money left in the bank to buy fabric for Lily's wedding dress, and grudgingly, Sarah had to convince her daughter that it was Tennessee tradition to wear the mother's wedding gown, and Sarah began the alterations while she listened to her spoiled, naive daughter wail for two days.

Meanwhile, Doug tried to plan Sarah's death. He knew that he had a ruthless alliance with Hawthorne and that once his daughter was married to the man, he would be able to keep her quiet if she was to question her mother's death. Knowing Lily, she would be too self-absorbed to notice anything. That was how Doug liked women: dumb and unconcerned with the world around them.

Doug was having a hard time coming up with a way that would free him from suspicion, given his history in his area; his wife's death would have to look like a very simple accident. A properly placed snake had been enough to give his father a heart attack eighteen years ago, and it had made George Weatherford's friends and neighbors sick to their stomachs to see his son, Douglas, take over the farm. Him being the last survivor, to their knowledge, there was not anything that they could do to prevent it. When they heard of a wife, and then later two daughters coming on the scene, they all decided that it would be just as easy to leave Douglas alone as to spend every waking moment trying to figure out a way to get rid of him.

Two days after Lily had been married off, Doug came across a rabid raccoon. He was about to kill it when he remembered the pleasure his wife found every morning when she tended to her hens and collected eggs. Doug managed to catch the raccoon using his shirts without getting bitten and took it home and hid it. Sarah was surprised to find her husband up and moving at such an early hour the next day, but since her husband had a glass of whiskey in his hand, it was safe to assume that he had been awake all night, in a drunken stupor, trying to force his wilted willy into one of her two house girls. The sight of him sickened her, but the fuss that her beloved hens were making now was more important than wasting her time with evil thoughts about her husband.

When Sarah opened the door to the coop, she immediately saw what the problem was. She searched the small, dark building for the wooden pitchfork that she kept on hand for just such occurrences, but it wasn't where it was supposed to be, and when she hollered for her husband's help, the rabid animal lunged at her, bit her on the arm, and ran away. Sarah knew that she was done for. She also knew, in the depth of her soul, that her husband was responsible somehow. She went to the house holding her bleeding arm and saw that the drunken miscreant had passed out. She called for her house girls, and one went for help while the other cleaned the wound. The old doctor did his best to keep Sarah Weatherford comfortable, and in two days, the woman was dead.

A cold chill on Doc's spine gave him a shiver when he saw Douglas weeping over his wife's body. Doc had known Douglas too long to believe the charade, and that was what gave him away. Doc let Doug see him inspect the chicken coop and search around for the wooden pitchfork, but the doctor also knew that he would never be able to prove Doug's involvement. The search was enough to put a bluff on Douglas Weatherford. He went to Richard Hawthorne and made a deal. He said that he couldn't stand to be in that house without his Sarah, and he was willing to trade the farm for Lily's dowry. Richard had always assumed that the Weatherford's were very wealthy. Why else would he have put himself through so many torturous hours, first with Rose Mary and Douglas, and then with Lily and Douglas. It had been excruciating and had cut into his carousing time at the local inn.

Lily's dowry had been kept in a safe place, far away from Doug's knowledge, since the day she was born and consisted of $7,500. When the deal between him and Richard was sealed with a hand-shake, Doug wept. Richard assumed that he missed his wife, but the truth was that he wept for joy, knowing that he would have the satisfaction of getting to waste every penny of his malcontent wife's fortune. Sarah should have loved him more than she loved those damned chickens.

It tickled Douglas to no end to know that he was leaving Virginia with Lily's dowry and leaving his son-in-law $15,000 in debt since he had only been making the smallest of payments that he could get away with for his seed and other expenses for the past several years.

From the Hawthorne porch, he mounted his saddle horse and rode hard to Independence, Missouri. On the day of his arrival, he heard something about gold being discovered in California. As he caroused and slapped women of the night around for ten days straight, he was able to pick up bits of information about this gold strike and decided that he could go out west with wagonloads of whores and do just as he pleased to whomever he pleased, and no one would know him nor suspect him anymore. He figured that there might be a call for whores in California, he wasn't sure, but if there wasn't, he would own them and be able to do whatever he wanted to them. He couldn't convince any of the soiled doves of Independence to go to California with him because he had just spent the last week and a half offending every one of them, so he traveled the river, looking for naive, unsuspecting young women and told them how much better it would be in California. They could start a fresh life working for him, catering to the needs of rich goldminers, and he was able to find six girls who believed him. The rest of the women that he talked to were old enough to know better.

Douglas yawned and stretched his arms. He smelled of cigar smoke and rotten alcohol that was oozing through the pores of his skin. He rolled out of bed, still rummy from the night before, and headed toward the washbasin by the window of his hotel room. He stumbled over something on the floor but was able to catch himself before he fell and turned back to see what it was. He remembered now before he had passed out that one of his girls hadn't been able to get his pecker working, and he had hit her. "So that's where she landed," he said to himself.

Dried blood was stuck to her nose, mouth, and on the floor where her head rested. Her hair was red, and her skin was pallid and covered with freckles. He rubbed his balding head and tried to remember the girl's name, but it wouldn't come to him. He put his foot on her rump and pushed her back and forth. "Hey you, wake up! Hey, get out of here, go get yourself cleaned up!"

The girl didn't move. Doug reached down to see if she was breathing, and she was, faintly, which was good enough for him, and he decided to let her sleep it off. He thought about giving her a kick for failing him the night before, but his head hurt, and if she woke up and started bellowing, it would only hurt more, so he left her be.

Doug wetted a cloth and scrubbed his face, neck, and hair and looked out the window onto the street of Sacramento City. He noticed a curious sight that seemed to captivate his attention for more than a half hour. He watched as a Negro and a barrel-chested Irishman worked on a little wagon. He couldn't imagine what they were going to use it for, but they had one side put on already that looked to be as high as a person's head from the floor, and he wondered if it was being built to haul prisoners. Just as he was about to turn away, a young woman wearing black chaps rode up to them on a sandy colored horse and got off and talked to the two men for quite some time. Doug's imagination was running wild, trying to figure out what the trio was up to and what a young woman would have to do with prisoners. He watched as the familiar, well-proportioned girl talked to the Irishman and pointed in one direction and then another, and he really became curious when the Irishman took out a map, and they looked at it together, standing shoulder to shoulder.

"Huh, those two must be married," he quietly said to himself. Shortly thereafter, he became confused when another man walked up to the woman, the Irishman went back to helping the Negro and the other man slyly sneaked a full mouth kiss from the Irishman's wife. "Whoa, what a girl. That wagon's not for prisoners, that girl is taking her show on the road and customers are lining up. I would have never thought that Black chaps would be such a draw." Doug was struggling to search his pickled mind as to why this girl was familiar to him when suddenly, the Negro looked up from his work and looked right into Doug's window. Instinctively, Doug hid himself behind the wall so he wouldn't be seen. He hated Negros with a passion. He always thought that they were like animals in the way that they could always sense his presents. He peeked around the window jamb to see if the Negro was still watching, and he was, and so was the woman. He ducked his head back again. He hated being caught and he hated that Negro. "I think I'll watch these people and kill that Black son of a bitch," Doug said to himself, as if it was his duty and privilege to do such a thing, and began to dress.

When he stomped out the door with purpose and slammed it shut, Trina opened her eyes and scanned the room without moving her head to make sure that Doug had really left, and slowly, she pulled herself up and went to the window. If there was somebody out there who was taking a show on the road, she was going to be with them. If she told what she knew about the Black man being in danger, maybe she wouldn't have to beg.

As Trina studied what kind of folks they might be and wondered about the woman in the chaps, she saw two more men approach to form a crowd. When she saw the man in buckskins, she figured that these were traveling folks. She had seen men like him many times before; he was a trapper, most likely. Men like him had been coming and going across the Missouri River for as long as she could remember. If she was lucky, she might even know this man. Trina didn't know how the woman figured into the troop, except that she was married to the younger man that was standing beside her, but she reckoned that for a good sign since women usually weren't welcome to join manly adventures.

Trina's room was above the saloon on the north end of town, and she thought of what she would want from it to leave town with. She needed warm clothes, the old quilt that she had left home with, and what little gold that she had hidden away from her boss.

Trina was excited to be able to run away this soon. She had been told by different customers that nobody would be leaving town until the end of March or the first part of April. Trina looked at the sky and noticed that it was going to be another clear, cold day which meant that more than likely, that abysmal fog would be rolling in before nightfall. She was going to have to be sneaky to get past Weatherford, but he seemed pretty intent on spying, and maybe he wouldn't notice her doing the same thing.

*****

Sam had an old feeling come back into his bones. It was one that he felt like he had been born with. The one that he had known for so many years, and then it had gone away one traumatic night—the night that he had been branded, his best friend's mother had died, and he had left the state of Kentucky. Sam had spent his life having many different feelings, not being wanted, doom, regret, tremendous loss and loneliness, but the sense of doom was always the one that had sent a chill up his spine. He might just as well sleep in a graveyard in Louisiana because that was how strong he felt about this particular kind of doom that watched a man's every move and followed him waiting for its time to strike.

Sam knew as well as he knew his name that he was being watched from the second-story window of the hotel across the street from the livery. Ordinarily, he might sense somebody looking at him, and he didn't like it. He always worried about when the time would come when he would be forced back into the fields, but lately, since Rose had reassured him so many times that he was safe, he had been able to shrug off uneasy feelings better than he used to. "I think somebody's up there lookin' at us," Sam said to Rose and pointed to the window. "Can you see 'em?"

Rose turned around and peered. The midmorning winter sun was shining on the south side of the building, and Rose could only see a glare. "How can you see through that window, Sam? The sun's shining right on it."

"That's why I asked you," he grumbled. "I got a bad feeling."

"Oh, Lord, here we go again," Rose said under her breath, not really wanting to hurt her friend's feelings.

Bennager smiled at his wife for moral support, but he studied Sam and could tell that he had a burr under his saddle, and the fact that it had come on all of a sudden was curious to him. Sam had been completely relaxed and content with his work of fixing the wagon up to haul food and supplies, and now he was working like the devil to try to finish and leave town as soon as he could. Sam had told Rose and Bennager that his seat didn't fit into saddles very well, he said he was too old and had been broken up too many times to go around, bouncing on the back of a horse, and he would prefer to drive the wagon. Bennager was happy to let him. Now if he had to chase Rose down when she got out of hand, which might be six or twenty-seven times a day, he might at least be able to keep her in sight.

"I don't want to wait around for you to stock the wagon. I'll wait for you south of town," Sam said matter-of-factly.

"What? Why would you do that? Just wait, and we'll go together. Besides, you might see something in the mercantile that you need," Rose suggested.

"I don't need nothin'. I got to get out of this town!"

"I don't like the idea of you going alone, Sam!" Rose argued. "Zeb will go with me!"

"How do you know? Maybe Zeb needs something at the mercantile. Just take it easy, and we'll all go at the same time, for heaven's sake. What has gotten into you all of a sudden? Are you trying to drive me crazy or what?"

Sam mumbled something that Rose couldn't hear, and she studied him with a frown on her face while four of the men attached a canvas that formed a roof and reinforced the sides of the little wagon. Then Sam looked at the window again, but he didn't feel as agitated as he had before.

"Whoa, look at what the cats dragged in!" Rose hollered sarcastically as she greeted Zeb and Bill. "You two look as fresh as daisies. What did you do? Try to drown each other in the river?" Both men were soaked clean through.

"No!" they said at the same time.

Sam finished what he was doing and went to Bill before Rose and Angus could dominate his time with the map and talk of Angus' route to the foothills. This rankled Rose, but she hoped that her uncle could calm Sam down and not let him ride out of town alone, so she waited.

Angus tried to drive the point home by climbing on the freight wagon and waiting. He had already purchased enough supplies to get him to Marysville when Bennager went off looking for Rose, so he was ready.

"I know as sure as I'm standing here that your brother is in this place," Sam told William after they had stepped away from the others.

"Did you see him, Sam?" William asked pensively.

"He was looking at us from that window up there," Sam said, pointing to the window of the hotel.

"You recognized him after all of these years?" William had no doubt that Doug could very well be in Sacramento City, but he couldn't believe that Sam could recognize him.

Sam looked at the ground and rubbed the back of his neck. "There was a glare on the window, but I didn't have to see him to know that he was watchin' us. It was just like when we were young and you just knew he was there. I don't want to hang around here, waitin' while they buy supplies, and I ain't goin' into the mercantile, looking for something that Rose thinks I might need. I'm riding out to that cluster of trees yonder and waitin'."

William looked at Sam and remembered how hard he always was to convince once he had his mind made up, but he felt like Sam's life depended on him changing his mind now. "You never listened to me when we were boys. You never would beat the devil out of him when you had the chance, and you didn't stay with me after we left out of there. But I'm telling you now, Sam, if you are right and he's here"—the hair spiked on the back of Bill's neck, and he visibly shivered at the frightful thought—"then the last thing you want to do is sit out at those trees alone, waiting for a woman to finish shopping. Would you please, just this one time, stay close? If we see him for sure, I'll kill him."

"You can't kill Rose's father pert near in front of her!" Sam argued. "If I get out of here, maybe there won't have to be a fight."

"If you're right and he was watching, what do you think that worthless bastard will do to his daughter? Give her a big hug and kiss? Or wonder why in the devil she is here instead of in Europe where he thinks she is? Also, if he is here, what do you think happened to Rose's mother and sister? Did you tell Rose that you saw him? Hell, we were just boys. If he's out here, he will recognize his daughter before he does us, so we better stay close to her, all of us. And you better believe that I'll kill that bastard if I see him, no matter who is there to see it. My father should have done it, but if he didn't, then the duty falls to me. I should have gone back and did it a long time ago. As bad as he was then, just imagine how bad he is now." Bill shook his head, trying to cover up that shiver that hadn't stopped since Sam told him of his suspicion.

Both men were quiet. William had said his peace, and Sam was considering what he would do. William waited and wondered about how to protect Rose and get Angus heading north and the rest of them heading south as soon as possible. "Let's tell Rose so she will have a chance to be on guard, send Bennager and Zeb to shop with her, and then you'll stay with me while I study the map with Angus, and we'll leave at the same time," William reasoned.

Sam rubbed the back of his neck, pondering the compromise, and nodded his head. "Yeah, they should all know. If he recognizes one of us, any one of us could be in danger at any time, but let's get away from this town a little, out in the open when you're talkin' to Angus so we can see him coming. He'll come for me just because I'm Black, I know it as sure as I'm standin' here." Sam hoped William would know and remember that about Douglas.

William nodded. "You're right! Mount up and have Angus follow you to a place you see fit out there, and I'll talk to the others and be along directly."

"I'll head east."

"I'll meet you out there," William replied.

Rose studied the two men and could tell that they were finished, finally. She let out a disgruntled sigh as the men came toward her. "That's a lot of serious palaver for the middle of a workday. What's the matter? Is Sam trying to tell you how to box?" she said, being devilishly clever.

Sam completely ignored her and walked to Angus and said, "Follow me out of town aways. William will meet us in a minute." Sam gingerly mounted and eased out of town so as to not draw any attention.

Rose was puzzled. "Where are they going?"

"Now would be a good time to keep quiet," William said in a growl. Rose started to have a verbal fit, but one look from her uncle made her think otherwise. She knew that there must be trouble and serious trouble at that. She hadn't known the man very long, but what she had observed about him was that he preferred to joke and didn't seem to take life serious, and now he was growling at her, and she knew that disliking her, whether he did or not, had nothing to do with it. Nevertheless, his tone had still offended her. She didn't appreciate being growled at by anybody, and she wouldn't tolerate it. She made a quick move to get away from her uncle, and just as quickly, he grabbed her wrist tightly and used just enough force so she would stop and pay attention.

William feared that he recognized a semblance of his brother coming out in his niece and waited a moment to gauge her reaction, then he tried to incite one. "I have something to tell you, but I won't do it until you stop having vile thoughts about me and focus on what I'm about to tell you. You can listen now and hatch evil plans about what you are going to do to me later."

Rose let out an exhausted sigh and rolled her eyes. "What is it then?"

"There's a good chance that your father beat you to California, and if I see him, I aim to kill him. He's got it coming for many reasons that I'm sure you have no knowledge of, and I truly am sorry if you don't believe me or agree with me, but that's how it is. In the meantime, while you are here doing your business, you had better be quick about it and watch your back. If there were hundreds of thousands of people in this town, he is the only one you should be worried about doing harm." Then to Bennager and Zeb, he said, "Did the two of you hear that?"

They nodded their heads in unison.

"Don't let this woman out of your sight and you better not do anything to get into trouble." William directed the last instruction to Rose and turned to go meet Sam and Angus.

This time, Rose grabbed her uncle's arm with force. "Just wait a minute, I don't like to be left hanging. What in the world gives you the idea that my father is here?" Rose asked politely but in a state of confusion.

William looked into his niece's face. "Sam said so, and I believe him."

Rose whispered, "That was a long time ago, Uncle. How can he be so sure?"

"If you were Sam, you'd be sure too," William simply explained.

Rose thought that was probably true, given that her father had branded the man, even if it was a long time ago.

"Where did Sam and Angus go?" Rose asked, beginning to feel sick to her stomach. The thought of her father being in the area was a bad beginning for her new life.

"They are waiting for me outside of town, away from prying eyes. It's the eyes that bother us about Douglas," William said in a strange way, looking off into the distance.

"How come of that?" Rose brought him back to the present time.

"I'll look that map over with Angus, and then Sam and I will meet you folks on the trail. Be quick, don't cause a fuss, and try to get out of here without being seen until I can figure out what I'm going to do about him." William mounted and eased out of town.

Rose watched as Bill left town and wondered if she should believe him. It could have been a plot just to hurry her up and ruin the plan that she had with her husband for another bath. Rose glanced at the window that had caused Sam such distress, and she knew Sam wasn't the kind of man who tried to trick people to get his way. She also knew that he wouldn't use that particular threat in order to hurry up her shopping either. Rose looked at her husband with disappointment in her eyes and shook her head. Her future was being held hostage by the uncertainty that she was feeling. Her happiness was being held back by an invisible force. Her control over her own life was gone, and her tenacity was being squelched by a feeling that she couldn't put her finger on. She felt like she was being held down by the weight of the air.

She sighed, trying to shake off what she was feeling. "I think it's best to do what Uncle says. If my father is here, then I agree with him and Sam that we should get out of here as soon as we can. Is there any other town where we can go to get our supplies?" Rose asked the men as she checked her derringer.

Bennager looked at the little burros and then at Zeb. "How far is Stockton with an outfit like this? Two and a half, three days maybe?"

"Yes, that sounds about right to me. Stockton will have everything that Sacramento City has to offer by way of supplies."

"Well, I hope that it doesn't have my father. Bennager, would it be all right if you went back to our room and collected our things and let Zeb and me go get the supplies? I want to be quick like Uncle suggested, but I'll be damned if I leave those dresses behind," Rose said, starting to become enraged by the fact that her father was here and that he might have the ability to ruin her plans.

"I'll go get our things and meet the two of you in front of the mercantile. You won't give Zeb any trouble, will you?"

"No, don't worry, just hurry, please," Rose pleaded.

*****

Rose and Zeb got onto the little wagon and went to the mercantile. They purchased enough things to get them to Stockton and hastily loaded the wagon without incident.

Bennager was there shortly, and he walked with Rose to the livery, and they all left to go meet up with Bill and Sam.

"Your wife is the fastest woman in a store that I have ever seen," Zeb commented to Bennager later.

"I noticed that about her in San Francisco. How much plug tobacco did she buy?" Bennager teased, trying to lighten Rose's spirits.

"The only thing I will say about that is that it is a good thing that I went with her or else we would all be having plug tobacco for supper tonight," Zeb chimed in.

*****

Angus drove the freight wagon back into Sacramento. He wanted to be sure that he had what he needed to take good care of his responsibilities. He stopped at the mercantile and purchased sugar and more hardtack. Sam had given him a considerable amount of money to get things started in the foothills, more than he reckoned would be needed, which made him nervous to oversee, so he bought a money belt and then went to the livery and purchased more grain. He was happy now to be on his way out of town, finally, with only Girl as his companion. He watched the team as they plodded through town, like they had done hundreds of times, and he watched the horizon to try to pick a landmark to strive for.

Near the north edge of town, he was shocked to see an older man shaking a woman like a rag doll in front of a saloon. Angus thought that it was one of the women that had paraded through town the day before. The horses pointed their ears toward the commotion, and when the older man hit the young redheaded woman with his fist, Angus saw red. Without realizing what he was doing, he leaped from the wagon onto the man, and he didn't stop inflicting his wrath upon him until he felt someone pulling on his arms and neck. Angus stopped and looked at what he had done. There was blood, some of the man's appendages were contorted, and he was lifeless.

Angus couldn't believe that he had done it again. He looked around, and there were quite a few men and women looking at him. He looked at the redheaded girl who was bleeding from her mouth. Her face was black and blue, but her eyes were bright. She was amazed by what she had just witnessed, but she could see that the big man who had caused her satisfaction was disturbed. He looked as though he was ashamed about bringing pain to the lowest man that she had ever been acquainted with.

"Is he dead?" Angus' question was whispered.

Trina knelt and felt for a pulse. "No, but believe me, he should be." She stood up and kicked the unconscious man in the kidney. "It serves you right, you ugly, bald, toothless piece of scum!"

Angus was shocked and wondered if the man was her husband or her father. Trina grabbed Angus by his elbow and pulled him up. "Come on, he'll wake up eventually, he always does."

Angus looked at Bennager's team of horses who had obediently stopped to wait. Girl was looking at him and wagging her tail, and when the Irishman finally got to his feet, the people who had witnessed the beating applauded him and his efforts. Angus was confused. He was sure that he would be taken to jail and the law would find out what he had done to his brothers and he would be hanged.

"Sir, you were leaving town, were you not?" Trina asked, retrieving her trappings from where they had landed when Weatherford punched her.

"Aye, I was," Angus remembered and hastily returned to the wagon.

"Wait, please take me with you. He will wake up, and when he does, I don't think that I'll survive it," Trina pleaded.

Angus stopped and looked into her eyes that were swollen with tears and red. Her face was battered and bruised. There were new bruises on top of old ones, cuts that had been reopened and blood pouring from her mouth. Angus couldn't believe that anyone could do all that damage to a woman, even if she was a prostitute. Angus saw that she was ready to travel, but he also knew that women of ill-repute were likely to be thieves as well, but Trina's battered face was no competition for Rose's money. He would have to be careful, but he wasn't going to leave the woman behind. "Aye, you better come with me at that. Let me help ye."

Angus sat beside Trina in the driver's seat and eased out of town. He wanted to look back to see what the townspeople were doing now, but he didn't. He was leaving Sacramento City, and he reckoned that he would never return, so it didn't matter what they were doing.

Angus was silent. He had a pretty good idea about why the woman was being beaten, and he also figured out what kind of man was giving the beating. He wasn't sure if it would be a good idea to befriend the woman that he had saved, but he liked her for being quiet. It must have been his reward for getting her out of town. He didn't feel the need to ask her absurd questions because she would probably only answer with lies, and she didn't feel the need to make any explanations to a man that would never understand them.

Suddenly, Trina was overwhelmed with exhaustion and climbed into the back of the freight wagon, moved some things around, wrapped herself in her old quilt, and then rolled into a ball and went to sleep. She never even noticed the puppies that were tumbling on top of each other in their box. Girl wasn't sure about this new development and took Trina's spot beside Angus in the driver's seat. Angus petted her but didn't say anything.

*****

A feeling of calmness swept over Sam all at once when he saw Rose and the two men coming toward him and William. It was more than just the sight of them that had put him at ease, though. He could feel that he wasn't being watched. His smile was visible when Rose rode up on the Roman.

"Oh, would you look at this? First a grumpy old bear and now you're laughing at me. You two sons of bitches were lying about my father just to mess up my honeymoonin'!"

"Shut up and quit that name-callin'. Your grandmother was a fine woman, and nobody lied to you about your father," Bill scolded.

"Why is he laughing then, Uncle?" Rose yelled and pointed at Sam.

Bill looked at Sam who was smiling now because Bill had to handle a rankled Rose Mary Rasmussen. "Well, how in the devil should I know why Sam is laughing? He is an old Black man who has had his head bashed in a hundred times. He could be laughing at something that happened last week, for all I know. It's a free country. I reckon a man can laugh without your permission anyway. Now never mind him. Did you have any trouble? Did you see your father? Were you followed?"

Rose glared at him with her nose wrinkled, chin out, and eyes slatted just like a mean half-grown child would do.

Bill rolled his eyes, pushed the Roman out of his way, and talked to Bennager and Zeb instead. "Well?" he said forcefully, wanting an immediate answer.

"I don't know if we were followed, but we didn't have any trouble in town, did we, Zeb?" Bennager smiled as he watched the love of his life wheel her horse around so he might try to bite her uncle.

"There wasn't a bit of trouble, Bill, and I doubt we were followed. I watched," Zeb said with a curious smile on his face too.

Bill scowled at the two men, and then he said, "Listen, you little battle-ax, if that ugly horse bites me, I'll shoot him right out from under you!"

Rose turned her horse and circled around so that she was beside her husband. Bill was discouraged by the trio facing him. None of them seemed to grasp the seriousness of the situation regarding Douglas. "I guess that's real funny seeing me with a horse bite on my leg."

"Simmer down, Uncle, what kind of tea have you been drinking today anyway? I wouldn't have let the Roman bite you. You're excited over nothing, if you ask me. If Father comes for me, I'll shoot him myself. I'll not let him interfere with any part of my life," Rose said.

Bill was surprised and pleased that she felt that way, but he didn't believe that she would do it. "That's all well and fine, but there are others around here that I have my doubts about."

Grimly, Rose leaned forward and rested her sore arm on the saddle. "I said any part of my life. That means everyone here. You don't know me very well, Uncle, but the first thing that you can chew on is this: when I say something, I mean it!" The words came out slowly and deliberately. "My father is no longer the monster that you make him out to be anyway. He is nothing now except a scheming drunk. He is bothersome, but he won't be any harder to kill, if he comes looking for trouble, than anyone else would be." Rose was finished with this idiotic conversation, and she rode over to wait with Sam. "What in the devil were you laughing about anyway?"

"The bad feelin' went away just before you got here."

Rose nodded and took a bite from her tobacco. "Good, maybe my father wasn't the cause of it after all."

"He was, I'm sure of that. But I know he's not watchin' us right now, and that's worth smiling about."

"You would have been proud of the lady, Horny Bill. She's not like those Indian women at the rendezvous that shop all day. If the storekeeper had been quicker with his cipherin', we would have been here sooner," Zeb praised.

"Do you mean that she actually listened to somebody for once?" Bill asked in amazement.

"No, that's just how she shops. When we get to Stockton, we'll have to start all over again supplying the wagon. The only thing that we have to eat is beans," Bennager complained.

"Frijoles!" Zeb cheered.

"Christ! You would be the one to praise beans, you foolhardy son of a bitch," Bill told Zeb.

"I've been missing my Anna's beans for a week now!" Zeb exclaimed and then immediately regretted even bringing her up, but

Bill dropped the subject, much to Zeb's surprise. Bill was concerned about the journey ahead now and how the party would do while they were crossing the valley. He doubted that Rose and Sam had ever been through such an experience. He didn't want to see his child-hood friend fall apart in front of the other men, but as far as Rose was concerned, he reckoned it would do her good to fear something for a change. She was too damned independent to suit him, and he felt sorry for her husband. Bill feared that Bennager would grow weary of such a woman, and soon the whole party would have to listen to their bickering, and chaos would ensue.

Zeb was happy that Bill was keeping his big, fat mouth shut about Anna. He figured that he had done some damage to Horny Bill during their fight, and he reckoned that Bill wasn't going to give him anymore trouble. Bill watched Rose and Sam as they headed out across the valley, and he wondered if they had any idea what they were up against as far as crossing rivers this time of year.

"It's a good thing that it's been staying cold in the mountains. I hope this weather holds out until we come back with your cattle, Little Rose. If we get rain and warm temperatures, we might not be able to cross all the rivers on the way back," Bill needled as he watched the girl's reaction, which still seemed to be cool.

Rose had already been thinking the same thing, but she wasn't that concerned about it. It didn't matter to her if she had to wait for the rivers to recede. She had funds to buy supplies, the men could turn their hand at looking for gold, and Angus would have more time to build her rancho. "No worries, Uncle." She smiled, revealing bits of tobacco that were in her teeth. She didn't know yet what to make of being called Little Rose, but since her spirits were high now, she figured that she would save that argument for later. Besides, he was retaliating for her calling him Uncle anyway, and she would rather be called Little Rose than Horny Bill, so the wide smile on her face remained as they continued on.

An older man approached them from the south. "How do, folks!" The older gentleman seemed pleasant. He wore a wide-brimmed hat like Bill's, but his head and face were covered with white hair. His beard and mustache were grown together, and his hair was grown down past his shoulders. Everything about his face was covered, except his nose and his twinkling blue eyes. "Where are ya off to?" he asked.

"We're heading south, how about yourself?" Rose said, still sporting a rare and cheerful smile.

"Pretty lady," the gentleman said, smiling back at her and tipping his hat, "I'm heading north, of course. You folks be careful travelin' this time of year. The Indians are on the move, and the rivers are still high. I've decided to winter in the big city."

Rose smiled at the Kris Kringle of the trail. His presence was so pleasing that she couldn't help it.

"My goodness gracious, what is a pretty little girl like you doin' travelin' with this bunch of characters for anyway?"

"We thought we would head south and buy some cattle," Rose said jovially. Sam thought the stranger was a curious man, but the sweetness he showed for Rose was humorous. He was impatient to be moving along but couldn't help wondering what the rest of the party was thinking of this.

The man took his hat off, exposing his bald topknot, and then he scratched it with a confused expression on his face. "Why in the world would a pretty young thing like you want to travel around buying cattle this time of year? You ought to winter in the big city with me and stay out of harm's way."

Rose giggled at the sweet talker. He seemed so sincere that if she hadn't been a married woman, she might have taken the darling up on his offer. "We are all together and they made me the treasurer," Rose cheerfully lied.

"An angel treasurer. They picked the right woman for the job. You must be the only one who can count." The man chuckled as they began to move ahead. Bennager and Bill thought the air was getting thick enough without having to listen to the lonely old miner try to take Rose away. "Where are you folks headed for, miss?"

"My name is Rose," she said with her hand out to introduce herself.

"What a befitting name for an angel. My name is Nick."

Rose cocked her head and squinted at the man merrily. "Your name sure fits you, too, but Zeb calls me a witch, not an angel."

"Zeb is a fool!" Nick said hastily, not caring one wit that he didn't even know the man.

Rose laughed as she peered at Zeb over her shoulder. Zeb was intrigued with the man as well until he said that, and then he shook his head and rode on to catch up with the others.

"We are going south to buy cattle from Zeb's friends. We want to build a cattle rancho up on the Yuba River."

"You want to drive cattle this time of year with all of those little baby calves? That will take forever, Angel," Nick warned.

"Will there be baby calves?" Rose was excited.

"Yes, and it's not going to be as fun as you think when you find out that baby calves can't travel through the sloughs in the San Joaquin Valley, and neither can that wagon, for that matter. It would be best to wait for June or May, depending on what kind of spring we have."

"Thank you for the advice, Nick. We will just have to spend our spare time looking for gold, I guess," Rose said jovially, not letting Nick's warnings deter her from her plan of being a ranchero on the Yuba River.

"By June, you'll have a new set of problems, gold miners and Indians. They will take your herd, probably one at a time, but they will take it," Nick said plainly as he watched the others head down the trail.

"I won't let them, Nick!" Rose said loudly and still smiling as if she was invincible.

"Hey, Bennager, can you make your wife smile like that or is she just trying to be neighborly?" Bill hollered over the sound of Sam's wagon.

Bennager wheeled his mount around and rode up to Bill, facing him. "I owe you a lot for saving Rose back on Sacramento, but you have one devil of a big mouth. You are just barely tolerable, and I will not put up with you accusing my wife of lewd behavior. I can take a joke as well as anybody, Bill, but not when it comes to her, and I would advise you not to push me on the subject." Bennager noticed that Zeb was smiling at the confrontation, and Bennager knew that everything was a joke to these two characters, but on this subject, he would not back down.

Bill tipped his hat to Bennager. "My apologies, young man. I am an intolerable teaser. It's just that I've been curious to know what a man has to do to rile you."

Bennager set his jaw. "Now you know," he replied and looked at the man, waiting to see if the conversation was over or not. Bill admired him for that. He never could stand a man that would ride away and leave things unsaid.

Bill nodded his head and said, "Yep, now I know."

Bennager detected a slight look of regret and embarrassment in Uncle Bill's eyes and reckoned that that was the end of it.

Nick looked back at Rose and noted her positivity and said, "I'll make a bet with you, Angel, because of the fact that I am a betting man is how I ended up in California knee-deep in a creek, trying to scrape up a living. If you make it back here with a herd before July, I'll throw you a party in the big city and buy all the booze, but if you don't, then you will have to throw me a party because my birthday is in July, and either way, I'll get to celebrate it with you."

Rose turned the Roman to face Nick and shake his hand. "That's a bet, Nick, although I feel bad about taking it. I feel like I'm cheating you. I didn't tell you I am a determined woman."

Rose made him wait for her to track down Sam and the wagon. Bennager went back with her, and she gave Nick two bottles of ale. Nick's hairy face beamed with delight when he saw the gift, and he said, "I don't know which one of you is Zeb, but this lady is an angel, I tell you!" Nick shouted after them.

*****

The party traveled for the rest of the afternoon and an hour past dark until they heard the waters of the Cosumnes River. Zeb wanted to go upriver and stay the night with a man that he had worked with in Monterey a few years ago and who had been granted a tract of land by the Mexican government for his work, but he couldn't be sure that the man was there, and he was too tired to make the trip, so he helped the others with the task of camping.

Bill and Zeb had led the way all afternoon, and Bill was eager to get away from the man for a while. "Bennager, watch for Indians and ruffians. I'm going to go see if I can catch some salmon to eat with our beans." He directed the last part of his explanation at Rose as she was helping her husband with their makeshift dwelling.

"I'll holler when I see you coming, Bill, you're the only ruffian I know," Bennager joked, curious to know if their rift was really over.

Bill turned to go to the river and said loud enough for the two of them to hear. "Mock me now, thank me later." The casual comment left Bennager still wondering.

Sam built up a fire to get the beans started, and by the time he was finished, Rose and Bennager were there to help him stake out the burros. The one that Rose was leading kept nibbling at her overalls and finally became so pitifully bothersome that Rose was forced to part with a piece of her tobacco. "You are worse than I am. Don't tell the others, Toby." Rose chuckled at the burro as he bobbed his head up and down. "You wanted it, but I can't tell if you really like it or not. We'll get you some hard candy in Stockton," she whispered to the addicted animal and scratched him under his chin. She went to the campfire and quietly observed Sam making coffee. She figured that someday she might have to make her own, which she could do, but it was never as good as Sam's, and she was trying to figure out what his trick was.

"I'd go upriver and see Jared tonight, but if he wasn't home, I might starve to death before I got back," Zeb complained.

"Who is Jared?" Rose asked with genuine curiosity. Zeb's spirits were dwindling with each passing day that he was away from Anna now, and Rose was happy that he was complaining about something else for a change.

"He's a fella that I met in Monterey in '42. He's a good man. It'll be good to see him again. He's just up the river a little piece," Zeb said.

"Maybe he'll hear us and come down," Sam said.

"I doubt it. This is a well-traveled road. He probably doesn't come out to see every person that stops here. We'll stop by tomorrow for a few minutes."

The night was clear and cold. The fog had been on its way in before the wintery sunset, but now a slight east breeze was keeping it at bay, but the east breeze was colder and went through a person's skin and right down to the bone, bringing with it the freezing temperatures of the Sierras. The stars in the sky were beautiful to look at, but only Bill ventured far enough away from the fire to observe them.

"I don't like this wind. I'm chilled clean through, Sam. This is a night for brandy. If the weather's not giving us that wet drizzling fog or a rainy windstorm, then it's giving us this damned freezing wind!" Rose carped as she rummaged through the wagon looking for the brandy and rum. "I'd try this ale, but I know that my brandy is a for sure warm-me-upper."

"My Lord, it's a cold night," Bennager commented as he arrived at the wagon to see what Rose was doing. "I suppose that you are looking for your spirits to keep you warm. That is supposed to be my job now, my love," he said, only loud enough for Rose to hear, but Bill thought that it would be fun to see how close he could get to Bennager by sneaking up on him, after having no success at catching a fish. He didn't care who he scared, but as he got closer to camp, he realized that Bennager would be the easiest target on account of Rose being a distraction.

Bill was able to get right beside Bennager in the dark of the night, and he said in a low voice, "Will you keep me warm too, honey?"

Bennager jumped back, not knowing who it was, and with his heart racing, he almost elbowed Bill in the mouth. "I'm ashamed of you, Rasmussen. I told you to watch for ruffians, but you have such a one-track mind that all you do is watch your wife's backside while she's bent over in the wagon." Bill laughed and joined the others at the fire.

"Bill sneaks up on everybody, Bennager, he is an old bastard!" Zeb yelled.

"Eureka!" Rose exclaimed. "I found my brandy!"

Bennager held out his hand and helped her from the wagon, and they walked together to the fire. Brandy and rum were offered to everyone, and it lifted the glum spirits of those who were depressed about having only beans to eat and nothing else. "I reckon that you won't join me in a drink, will you, Uncle?"

"No thank you. I'll have to stay warm without that stuff. The fact is that I do stupid things when I drink. Zeb was kind enough to remind me of some of my particular past errors last night. The truth is on nights like this one, I surely do miss it," Bill explained. He thought that it was time for his niece to know that he wasn't just an herbalist all his life, and he wanted her to know that the devil spirit in alcohol could have a negative effect on a person's life. Rose gave him a nod of understanding, and nobody teased nor commented as they had done the night before. Besides, no man in the party would have thought the conversation from the night before would have been appropriate in the presence of a lady.

"How many rivers are there to cross?" Sam asked, changing the subject before Zeb could get the chance to bring up all the fat Indian woman that Bill had slept with in his life.

"We won't run out of water, that's for sure," Zeb answered. "There will be at least five more counting this one here. That doesn't count creeks. We won't have any trouble as long as this weather holds, even if it is colder than a witch's tit." Zeb put his hand to his mouth, embarrassed that he had used the old phrase in front of Rose. "Pardon my language, Rose."

Bennager smiled, knowing that Rose was hard to beat in the foul language department, but appreciated Zeb's apology. Zeb had his superstitions, but he was always a gentleman.

It had been Zeb's intention to tease Rose about wishing the weather again, but considering making what he thought was a crude comment, he decided not to speak of witches for a while.

As the night wore on over the rolling hills that accompanied the Cosumnes River, other travelers began to trickle in a few at a time, and Bill had to wonder if any of them might be Douglas. He watched Sam as the strangers came to the river, but none of them seemed to make Sam anxious nor did they him. He quietly told the group, "We had better take turns on guard tonight. This is a pretty fancy outfit compared to what the others have. Of course, their vittles are probably better than ours are. You two can take first watch together since you got to sleep in a feather bed last night, but ease up on the fire water so you don't shoot an innocent."

Rose blushed as they both nodded at the order given to them and remembered that there wasn't much sleeping going on in that feather bed last night. Bennager was sitting beside her. He put his arm around her waist and squeezed her into him. She knew that he was remembering too.

"Hey, Sam, come look at this rock that I found," Bill said, luring him away from the others.

"Is it gold?" Sam asked excitedly.

"Shhh, don't say that word around crazy gold miners. Just come with me for a minute."

Sam followed Bill away from the camp, and Bill asked, "What do you think? Reckon he's out there somewhere?"

"I don't think so," Sam replied, looking around and waiting for the unwanted sixth sense to strike.

"He could have hired someone to follow us. What do you think?"

"If that's all he did, then we won't have any problems. Nobody could be as bad as he is. Let 'em follow us," Sam said, shrugging his shoulders.

Zeb was testing the beans when they got back to camp. Zeb was tired and sore from his excruciating battle with Bill the night before and that morning. He knew that he had wrenched his back for sure, and he wasn't looking forward to sleeping on the ground, but there was no way that he was going to complain about it. He wanted Horny Bill to know that he was still tough in his old age, even if the only people that he wrestled with these days were his children. He wanted to eat and sleep. "The beans are still a might crunchy," Zeb commented.

"I didn't have enough time to soak 'em," Sam replied.

"I like them that way," Zeb lied. Bill shot Zeb a look and then rolled his eyes. Bill knew that Zeb hadn't had an undercooked bean in years, and he wanted to tease him about his beloved Anna being a poor cook, but he was tired and worn out also, so he retrieved some hardtack from his saddlebags and settled down for the night instead.

"I can't believe that I don't have any biscuit makings. I should have gone shopping myself, but that woman over there was rushing me," Bill moaned.

"I think you spent too much time wrestling with Zeb," Rose corrected Bill. "It's your own fault for fooling around."

"Bill wouldn't leave me alone," Zeb said in his defense as he made ready to turn in for the night. He poured himself two fingers of rum into his tin coffee cup to help him sleep through his soreness, and instead of saying goodnight, his parting words were to Bill, "Crunchy beans are better than the rotten buffalo that I've known you to eat, Horny Bill."

"Shut up, you old buzzard! You could have picked up my biscuit makings, but you are too selfish. I'm riding into Stockton tomorrow to get my own grub," Bill threatened.

Rose wrapped herself in a wool blanket and checked her derringer, and Bennager checked the revolver that Sam had loaned him for the night watch. They spread out, away from the fire and away from each other, and watched and listened. The long ears of the burros were highly sensitive to things that might wander around in the dark, and Rose referred to them from time to time. She heard the distant sound of men's voices talking at another camp down the river apiece, but they were too far away to make out what they were talking about. One pitiful lone coyote was in the distance, bewailing to anything that would listen to him, about the cold east wind and how a bald eagle had swooped down and took his rabbit that he had been chasing this afternoon. That was what Rose imagined that he was probably complaining about.

Rose and Bennager had to keep their backs to the fire so they could see in the dark, which meant that their backs were to each other, and he couldn't stand it. He kept peering through the darkness, trying to make sure that she was still there, and the dark wool blanket made it hard for him to see her still figure. Rose set her brandy down beside her about the time the coyote gave up. He was so pitiful that even his own kind wouldn't talk to him. She reckoned that her blood was warm enough now. She remembered Bill's warning and didn't want to shoot an innocent. She took out her plug tobacco and bit off a piece.

The addicted burro—Toby, she had named him—let out a bray that woke Bill and Zeb out of a dead sleep. Rose could hear Bill tell Zeb to shut up and quit acting like an ass, and Rose chuckled at the commotion that one bite of tobacco could cause, but she didn't accommodate Toby this time because she didn't want anybody to know that she was the cause of the uproar. The coyote was glad to hear that there was another crying soul in the world, and he started in again with his dirge, but Toby ignored him.

Before they knew it, their time on the watch was up, and Sam relieved them. Bennager and Rose turned their weapons and the brandy over to him, and they went to the privacy of their tent. The warmth of each other was warmer than the campfire, and within moments, they were sound asleep, wrapped in each other's arms.

Sam found it difficult to sit or stand in one place. His arthritic body couldn't take it, so he spent his watch wandering around. He petted the burros and examined the Roman, now that his owner was tucked in for the night, and determined that he was about five or six years old. He would last Rose a good many years more.

He studied the wagon that he and Angus had hastily fixed up for the trip and thought of ways to reconstruct it so that it would be more suitable at mealtime. Once he started thinking about that, he could have been hit in the head or robbed at any time. A kitchen on wheels would become his new obsession until it was finished, but he would have to wait until they got to Stockton to get more building materials, and he thought of how he was so tired of waiting for the things that he wanted. As Sam made pictures in his head repeatedly of the cook wagon that he wanted, Bill slipped up on him but stayed far enough away so he wouldn't get hit. "It's my turn at watch, Sam," Bill said quietly.

"I didn't hear you come up, William," Sam replied.

"My moccasins are quiet," Bill said.

Sam handed him the pistol and revolver, but Bill had a revolver of his own and a sharp skinning knife. "Keep 'em in camp with you Sam. You might need 'em yet." Bill slapped his old friend on the shoulder. "Good night, Sam."

"Good night."

Bill scampered up into an oak tree like a squirrel. He was close to the horses and could see the camp and the campfires of some of the others down river, and he could pounce on anyone who tried to steal the stock. He crouched on a big branch partway up the tree and watched Sam build up the fire and eat some beans before he turned in. Bill had determined that it was about one or two o'clock in the morning. He could hear his niece snoring slightly, and he envied the youth that were able to sleep peacefully anywhere.

The cold morning passed slowly for Bill, and he finally surrendered the crouching position and sat down on the branch to let his feet dangle. He decided that he would stay up for the sunrise and let Zeb get his rest. He owed him that much. He knew that he had pushed Zeb too far the night before and that they were both too old to be clobbering each other in the valley mud. Deep down, he was glad that Zeb had found happiness with his Anna, and he knew he shouldn't belittle what they had together. He knew that just because he couldn't live with a full-time woman anymore, it didn't mean that others shouldn't. Besides, he knew that it would rile Zeb that he didn't do his part on guard duty, and Bill loved to cause the man to complain.

*****

About five o'clock in the morning, a young Miwok Indian boy about the age of fourteen wandered into camp and was headed straight for Bill's horse. Bill smiled as he recognized the boy that Bill called Stud Colt. The boy was a bit of a legend among his own people for the size of his pecker. Bill had teased the boy's father about how the boy's mother probably had an affair with a wild stallion, and the comment had caused a fight. That was another time that Bill shouldn't have said nasty things about a man's mate. Bill knew that the boy was harmless, so he observed the boy sneak around camp. He petted the horse that Bill rode and popped the Roman on the nose for trying to bite him, then he looked in the wagon. He opened the tent flaps, and Bill cringed, hoping that Bennager was still asleep and wouldn't kill the boy.

The boy walked around the campfire and examined Zeb and Sam. He looked at Sam three times because he had never seen a Black man before, and then he walked toward the horses, stopped, and put his fists on his hips. Bill knew that the boy was wondering where he was, and he hoped that the boy would get closer to his tree. Bill had resumed his crouching position while the boy was studying Sam. Suddenly, the boy looked up at him and pointed and smiled.

"You were going to jump on me, but I found you," Stud Colt said in his native tongue.

Bill had an ear for dialect like nobody else. He could stay with a group for eight or ten days and be able to converse with them almost as if he was a native himself. California wasn't as easy as other places, though. Within ten miles, there would be a different group, and their dialect would vary entirely. Bill climbed down from the tree and gave Stud an Indian handshake, holding each other's forearms instead of hands, and then slapped him on the shoulder.

"Why are you here, Stud Colt?" Bill asked.

"I saw your track last night. You are traveling. I want to travel too. My home is boring. There is nothing to do this time of year, and my big brother is jealous of me," Stud explained.

"That is a familiar story, Stud Colt, much like my own. How are your mother and father?" Bill asked.

"They are well. My mother is about to have another baby, and I think babies stink. I will stay away until it is not a baby anymore," Stud said, making a face and holding his nose. "I go with you. Where are you going?"

Bill laughed at the boy, and he wondered if Rose would let him come along, although he doubted that she would have a choice. The boy seemed adamant about staying away from babies, and Bill didn't blame him. In such a rural environment, babies did stink in a way that only a mother could ignore. Bill walked to the fire with Stud as dawn approached and said, "We are headed south to buy cattle. We will have to get you a horse or else the cattle might walk on top of you. Do you have anything to trade?"

Stud Colt smiled. "I know what the White man likes." He took the pouch from around his neck and poured gold nuggets into Bill's hands until both were almost full.

"You can trade for whatever you want with this, Stud Colt. Reckon you can go if you want to, but you better not show this to anyone, especially while you are trading. The White man will over-charge you because they think that Indians don't know the value of gold." Bill picked out two pieces and put them in Stud's hand, which amounted to about thirty dollars' worth, and said, "This much for one horse and bridle." Stud Colt smiled at Bill, and they put the gold back in the pouch.

Bill stoked the fire and began to brew some tea. Finally, he had a companion that would truly enjoy it. Stud pointed at Sam and said, "That man was burned."

Bill shook his head and chuckled. "That man is from a different land. His skin is just a different color like mine is from yours," Bill explained by pulling up his buckskinned sleeve and comparing his arm to Stud's. Stud nodded his head. "He is Sam. He is a good man and friend."

Rose's snoring increased its decibel level, and Stud Colt giggled. "White man is noisy when he sleeps."

"White man is noisy when he is awake too." Bill laughed. He wanted the fact that Rose was a woman to be a surprise. While they were sipping their tea, Rose's snoring stopped. Bill assumed that it had woken Bennager, and now the two of them were saying good morning to each other silently the way married folks will do. Bill didn't want Rose to run Stud Colt off, and he was hoping that Bennager was putting her in a good mood right now. Stud Colt knew that they were awake, too, and Bill could see that he was getting anxious about having to meet strangers, but after an hour had gone by, he became curious about what the White men were doing with each other in that tent.

In the meantime, Zeb had risen, introductions were made, and he quietly sat by the fire, sipping tea. Zeb felt bad that he hadn't stood his turn at watch, and he planned on upbraiding Bill for it, but he would wait until later since everyone else needed their rest.

"Stud Colt sure is curious to meet Rose, ain't he?" Zeb noticed.

"Not really. It's just that he thinks that there are two men in there," Bill said, snickering.

"You are a devil. You better tell him. He's apt to run off when he sees that fiery woman barrel out of that tent, hollering about coffee."

"It will make for a good show. Stud Colt doesn't fear women. He will probably try to woo her away from Bennager." Bill snickered some more. Zeb chuckled and shook his head, trying to imagine what was about to happen.

5

Angus woke up next to the stream that was called Bear River. The morning was crisp and clear, and he was pleased to see that crossing the river wouldn't be anything to worry about. The American River had given him quite a fright, and he hoped he would never have to cross it again or any others like it. He stoked the campfire, checked on Girl and her brood, who seemed to be sleeping contently, and then he prepared breakfast. His traveling companion had never left the absurd comfort of her quilt and the freight wagon.

Angus decided to leave her where she was the night before, thinking that if she was sleeping, she wouldn't be bothering him or stealing Rose's money. As he peered at the wondrous mountains directly to the north of him, he hoped that he would be able to leave the woman in the next town that he came to. The valley trail that he was traveling on was paralleled by yellow rolling hills where the grass had dried from the heat of last autumn, and the oak groves were sparse, but near the stream, he was blessed by shelter in the way of wild roses and other brush that the valley deer seemed to enjoy. Angus was happily content to be camping out virtually on his own. For the first time in his life, he didn't have any relatives around to tell him what to do or the rest of the party that he had been traveling with. He was amazed and proud of himself for being at ease with the fact that he was in charge of his own doings and that Rose, Bennager, and Sam knew that he would be a capable man before he knew it himself.

Angus wondered why the smell of breakfast hadn't brought the girl in the wagon to life, so he got up and checked on her. He could see that she wasn't dead because she was breathing soundly, and as he examined the bruises and cuts on her freckled face, he remembered that he still had some salve that Bill had given to him for his own battered face. The coffee was boiling and spitting out the spout now, and he went to the fire to tend to it and flip the bacon over. It occurred to him then that if he didn't wake the girl now and feed her, she would surely want him to stop along the trail so she could eat and tend to nature when she did wake, and he didn't feel that his business should be delayed just because she had made some poor choices in her day. Even Girl had enough sense to know when it was time to get up and go to the river and take care of business.

Angus was delighted when Girl came back, quickly looked at her pups, and then sat patiently beside Angus with a thin single line of drool hanging from the side of her mouth while they both waited for the bacon to finish cooking. Angus added more to the pan for the girl in the wagon and fried biscuits in the grease while he and Girl enjoyed a couple of pieces, and he sipped his coffee. He thought of how he missed Bill's morning brew of tea but figured that he would have to make do until he saw him again. He made Girl go with him to wake up the redhead in the wagon so she wouldn't disturb the frying pan in an attempt to get more bacon. He put his giant hand on the girl's frail shoulder and shook her roughly. "It's time to wake up and eat, ye've slept long enough now, miss."

Trina was slow to react to the command, but she did eventually because Angus was persistent, and his constant grinding of her against the bed of the wagon was becoming painful. "I'm awake, sir. I'll get up right now, just stop, you're hurting me!" Trina moaned.

Angus stopped immediately. It wasn't his intention to hurt the girl, but he remembered how sore he was after his last battle and figured that it didn't take much to cause the girl pain after what she had probably been through. "Ye better come eat now. We won't have time to stop later, and I'll be leavin' as soon as breakfast is finished."

Trina gingerly eased out of the wagon and watched the uncompassionate man walk back to the fire with his dog. Trina walked to the river and splashed cold water on her face. She longed for a hot bath that would wash away the savage touch of her former employer.

She tore a piece of cloth from her dress and tried to wash the intimate parts of her body, and then she took off her shoes and stood in the river that was born by the snow of the Sierra Mountains.

Her feet became numb after several moments, and she wondered what it would be like if her whole body was numb. Could this water freeze away the filth that Douglas Weatherford had smeared on her? Or would she just freeze to death and never have to think of him again? Trina took her coat off and threw it on the rocks that lay on the shore. She hiked her dress up and held it tight at her waist, and with her bottom exposed, she waded out. The deepest part of the river was only knee-high, and she was furious. Hastily, she pulled her dress from her body and threw it toward the shore, but her dress landed in the water and drifted slowly away as she submerged herself into the freezing stream. The cold water surrounding her entire body was exhilarating, and she never felt anything as sensational. Every nerve ending felt like it was being pierced. She let the cold water have its way with her as she thought of the honorable Irishman who had come to her defense and his black-and-white collie.

Soon she wouldn't be able to feel anything. The water wouldn't feel cold anymore because she wouldn't be able to feel it. The cuts and bruises and filth would no longer hurt, and if the cold water would take her life, it would also take away the last surviving pain that still lingered in her heart. She rolled over onto her front side so that she could freeze her battered face and contemplate whether she would let the river take her. After a few minutes had passed, her brain started screaming with excruciating pain, and Trina realized that freezing to death in the Bear River in the middle of winter wasn't as easy as she thought it would be. She took a deep breath of water into her lungs to speed up the process of death that had originally started out as a simple splash of water to her face before breakfast. Her airway and lungs were in pain, and suddenly, so was her scalp. Before she knew what was happening, Trina was upright and gasping air instead of water, and as she coughed and sputtered, she opened her eyes to see that the Irishman was holding her up by her long hair as though she was a fish and looking at her as though she was absurd.

"What in God's name are ye doin', woman? You ought not to be bathin' in a river this time of year. Look at ye, ye're blue!" Angus said to the creature that must be tougher than him. "Ye got me friend over there worried 'bout ye. Even she knows better than to bathe in freezin' water!" Angus reprimanded as he picked the naked girl up and carried her to the shore and set her down by her coat that she had left on the rocks. Girl was sitting on the edge of the water, whining for her friend to hurry up before he froze too. When Angus set Trina down, Girl trotted up to them and barked at Trina, letting her know of her displeasure with the idiotic girl and upbraided her until Angus told her to stop.

Trina was blue and trembling. She thought that if she tried to reach for her coat that she would break in half. The temperature was just above freezing on this day of February first.

"What did ye do with your dress?" Angus asked, and the only reply was Trina's chattering teeth. She couldn't point, nod, nor talk, and she hated the man for pulling her out of the water when she was so close to being finished with her task. And now that he had hauled her out, he didn't even have enough sense to hurry up and put her coat on for her.

Angus was deliberately taking his time getting her coat. He knew what she was trying to do to herself in that river because he had thought of doing the same thing after the ordeal with his brothers. Now the stupid, selfish girl was probably going to get sick and die anyway, and he would have to be the one to tend to her. He was going to have to take the time to either get her well or he would have to dig a hole in the hard ground and bury her. So it didn't bother him to let her wait for her coat because if he was able to keep her from dying, maybe she wouldn't try to kill herself again.

Finally, he put the coat on for her, pretending that he didn't know that she couldn't do it herself, and he grabbed her up with ease and carried her through the brush back to the fire. He set her down by the crate of pups and went for her quilt. Girl was still mad at Trina, but her pups were cold, and she had to warm them up.

Trina was still shivering and froze stiff, so Angus resolved to start rubbing her body to get her blood flowing again, and he wished that he had just let the girl sleep. He could have given her cold biscuits and bacon later, but now he would have to spend the whole day putting this suicidal girl back in working order.

He went to the river and gathered more branches to put on the fire, and when he returned, the girl was despondent. She wasn't shivering, but her jaw was clenched, and her eyes were closed. She wasn't as blue as she had been when she was sitting on the shore, and Angus hoped that she would come around when he started to rub her feet and legs. After several minutes, the girl finally opened her eyes. Angus switched from her feet and legs to her hands and arms so she would be able to hold a cup of coffee. Finally, Angus had had enough, and he could see color coming back into her skin, so he handed her the cup of coffee to hold and figured that it was time for her to help herself.

"Can ye talk yet?" Angus asked as he broke off pieces of fried biscuits and gave them to Girl, one piece at a time, for breakfast and wondered what Rose Mary Rasmussen would do with a woman like this. Would she leave her, shoot her, or help her? Angus was just as willing to go along with the first two suggestions as well as the last.

Trina nodded as she felt her senses returning to her, and she hated herself for doing what she did, not finishing the job, and having to survive through the consequences. "Yeah, I can talk. You should have let me die. I asked you to give me a ride out of town. I didn't ask for your help or interference beyond that!"

The rudeness of the redheaded woman reminded Angus of one of his sisters, only she wasn't as thin as this one that sat before him. Her chin was trembling with rage and anguish. When tears came to her eyes, she dropped her head and her defiant look so Angus wouldn't see her face.

"What be your name?" Angus inquired.

"My name is Trina, my occupation is—"

"I know what your occupation is besides giving me a devil of a time! Me name is Angus Donovan, Miss Trina, and I won't put up with ye shoutin' at me. I'm not the cause of your troubles and I won't put up with ye causin' me anymore trouble. I'm a busy man and have more work than I can handle without havin' to tend to ye. Ye can quit feelin' sorry for yeself over your choice of occupations while I'm 'round because I don't have time for your selfish nonsense. Ye can be that way after I drop ye off in the next town," Angus said forcefully, hoping that this redhead wasn't as stubborn as his sisters were because if she was, then he had just wasted his breath. Girl flapped her tail in agreement.

Trina was startled at Angus' outburst. He was loud, and she jumped when he talked for fear that she would be hit, and she was relieved when he hadn't hit her for being a whore. She looked into the bottom of her coffee cup and began to sob. Gentle Angus had never done anything to her except save her life, and she shouldn't shout at him for anything. She had already worn out her welcome and she had only spent two waking hours with the man.

"Stop that cryin'. I didn't give ye reason to cry like that." Angus walked over to her and knelt in front of her with the salve in his hand. He gently put his hand under her chin. "Look at me now. I have somethin' for those cuts. See me face? I got into a fight like ye did just a few days 'go," he said, gently dabbing the salve into the cuts on Trina's face. She had stopped crying now and was waiting for the predator that she knew all men to be to take advantage of her, and she prepared herself to go along with it so he wouldn't leave her behind. She waited like a frightened rabbit and watched his eyes as he focused on his task. When he finished, he gently brushed her beautiful hair away from her face to examine a bruise that was on her forehead, and then he looked into her eyes and saw the distrust and fear that was in them. It hurt him to know what she was thinking, but he backed away easily, trying not to let her see what he was feeling, and then he gathered more wood for the fire.

Angus let a little time pass before he talked to Trina again. He sacked the team and peered through the brush at the strange mountain formation that was sitting in the middle of the Sacramento Valley. It bothered him because it was obvious that it didn't belong there, and he decided that he was going to go see it before he went up the Yuba River for Rose. He thought that he might not get the chance once she got back.

The sun was getting high, and an east wind was starting to blow cold air off of the Sierra's snowcapped mountains. Trina hadn't eaten anything yet, so he rummaged around in his supplies and got out some cheese and dried fruit and went back to the fire. He handed some food to Trina, and she took it.

"Thank you, Angus," Trina said. Angus put some more coffee in her empty cup, and she smiled.

"Ye ought to cut a hole in the middle of that blanket and drape it over ye so ye'll be fit to travel tomorrow, seems how ye lost your dress."

"I should, you're right, but I can't. My mother made this quilt for me, and I've damaged it enough as it is. It's the only thing that I have from home," Trina said sadly.

"Why are those mountains sittin' out there like that? They don't belong there!" Angus queried.

Trina wasn't one to think about Mother Nature's wonders, and why she might have put a mountain someplace didn't concern her unless she had to walk up it. The seriousness of Angus' expression made her laugh because to her, it was ridiculous to ask her such a thing as if she would really know the answer. She shook her head and said, "I don't know, Angus."

Angus hadn't expected her to laugh at his question, but he was glad she did. "Ye are feelin' better, aren't ye, Miss Trina? If ye behave yourself, we'll leave in the mornin' and maybe buy ye some clothes in this place they call Marysville. It's probably better that ye lost that old dress. Now ye can pick out some clothes that suit ye. I was told by me employer to hire someone if I needed to, and I've been thinkin' that ye must be pretty tough. Ye put up with beatin's and allow yourself to freeze in the river, and I don't know many men who could do that. If ye live through this, ye ought to work for me, buildin' me boss' rancho. I'll teach ye and pay ye."

Angus couldn't believe that the offer to hire the woman had just come out of his mouth. Rose would have a fit. He looked at Girl, and she flapped her tail twice and jumped out of the crate, licked Trina on the hand, and sat back patiently as if she was waiting for an answer to Angus' offer.

"I thought you were going to leave me in the next town," Trina stated suspiciously.

"Is that what ye want, for me to leave ye in Marysville to start a new life and have that fella in Sacramento City find ye and stand in line behind others who want to abuse ye? Ye are tough if that's what ye want," Angus said, then looked at the ground, imagining what it was like to live that way and how he was probably wasting his time on a lost cause again. He had met a similar woman in New York and told her to work with him, but she thought it would be easier to make her living on her back. Rose had been a lost cause, too, but at least he lost her to the true love of one man instead of the pitiful excuse that there is only one way for a woman to earn money.

Trina looked at the kind man, and Girl put one paw on Trina's knee. Trina smiled and gave Girl a piece of cheese and a pat on the head, which is exactly what she had wanted all along. Girl went back and sniffed her babies and lay down on her side, away from the fire, to enjoy the sunshine. "I never said that's what I wanted Angus. It's the last thing that I want. I don't want that man to find me. He's a disgusting monster, and he'll kill me over the good beating that you gave him," Trina said sadly, feeling like Angus might be giving her charity but also feeling an uncontrollable suspicion that her newly twisted life had taught her to feel. "I will take your offer until I've earned enough money to go home," Trina said.

"That's fine. That will be better than livin' in town. We've a mountain of work to do then. There had better not be any more nonsense out of ye, though. Ye wouldn't be the first one to think of such a thin', but it's time that ye started to make peace with it and be movin' on," Angus said still studying the puzzling buttes to the north.

"I'll be sure to work on that for ya," Trina said sarcastically.

By midday, Trina had warmed up, and her companion was putting her in a hateful, surly mood. She was so tired of men and having to need a man to get the pitiful, meager things that she needed. This new man in her life seemed harmless, in respect to her, but she knew that eventually he would want the only thing that she had to give, and she would give it reluctantly so she wouldn't be beaten or left behind. It was not the adventure that she thought it would be when Douglas convinced her to leave home and go to California, and she was homesick and downhearted. If this man wouldn't let her die, then she would just sleep. She couldn't dwell on her sorrows when she was asleep. Warily, she crawled back into the wagon and fell asleep, contemplating how many days it would take until Angus would want her and refuse to take no for an answer.

Angus watched the woman and wondered why she wasn't more excited about getting out of the whoring business and learning how to be a builder, but he thought that it was good that she was getting her rest because she was going to need it. The pups were over a week old now, and Angus couldn't stand it for one more minute. He looked at Girl where she was sprawled out on the grass, and he picked up one of the pups for the first time. He held the little thing in the palm of his big hand and gently rubbed his thumb up between its eyes to its forehead, and then he checked for gender. He spent some time with each one like this and determined that there were two little girls and one boy. Angus let the fire go down and was becoming bored. There was so much to do, and it was too late in the day now to travel on.

Girl got up and sniffed her pups and then sat by Angus. She was bored, too, and missed Zeb and Rose. Suddenly, she jumped up and ran to the river and brought back a stick in hopes that Angus would play with her, and he did. They played fetch on and off all afternoon while Trina slept in the wagon.

Angus prepared his supper, which was just like breakfast, while it was still light. He had enjoyed the cocoa that Rose had insisted on having at suppertime so much that he made sure to buy some for himself. He threw out what was left in the coffee pot and went to the river for water, thinking that the first thing that he would purchase for the new rancho would be a milk cow. Mixing water with cocoa seemed like a good waste of cocoa, but it was better than nothing, and Rose never noticed the difference anyway because she always doctored it with hard liquor.

The river was shallow, and there was a sandbar just a few feet out, so he jumped to it, hoping that the water would be deeper on the other side. He looked into the cold water as he filled his pot, and the wintery sun that was going down in the west reflected off the water in a way that made Angus think of what a miracle it was to be alive. He remembered thinking earlier what a shame it was that the redheaded girl didn't think that she had anything to live for, just moments before he yanked her out of the water by her hair. The light dancing on the water had mesmerized him as he thought of what would have happened if Girl hadn't alerted him to trouble.

A hard gust of cold east wind brought him back to his senses and reality. He dipped the pot into the water and accidentally collected some tiny rocks along with it. He threw the water out so he could start over, and when he checked the bottom of the pot to make sure that it was clean, four gold flakes, half the size of a pinky nail, remained in the bottom. "I'll be danged, me brothers were right! And this is what I could have been doin' all day!" He wrapped the flakes neatly in his handkerchief and got his water while Girl started barking at him in her frustrated tone.

Angus could see that Trina was having a bad dream as he approached camp, and that was what Girl was riled about. Girl thought that an invisible predator of some sort was tormenting Trina, and Girl didn't like it one bit. The woman suddenly stood up in the wagon, wide-eyed, looked into the depths of Angus' soul, and screamed, "Don't touch me! No, don't touch me!" Trina had her hands up in front of herself, and then she collapsed to the bed of the wagon. She had frightened Angus into stone, and if Girl hadn't jumped on him, he might not have survived the harrowing event. He investigated the wagon to see if the girl was still alive. Girl let out one shrill bark because she wanted to know too.

The woman was breathing soundly as if the episode had never happened, and Angus remembered all the things that Zeb had said about women and witches, and he thought that there might be some truth to back up his suspicions. He petted Girl and told her that everything was all right, and then he built up the fire for the night.

*****

Stud got up and walked behind a tree to relieve his bladder. A rock on the ground caught his eye, and he examined it for a while. It was just a round river rock that had washed up during some flood, but he thought that he could use it for something sometime, so he kept it. He walked closer to the river to see if he could find something that might interest him and found some quartz to show the Black man when he woke up. To Stud, quartz crystal was the prettiest rock. He always brought them to his mother, and she kept them.

While he was wandering around, Sam began to stir. The sun would be up very soon, and Sam couldn't believe that he had slept that long. As he was getting the coffee ready, he explained to Bill and Zeb about the idea that he had to fix up the wagon, and Bill was all for it. It would be nice to have a flat surface to work on instead of having to rely on an old dirty rock, or worse yet, the ground. Sam explained that he had thought about it for a while before he was able to go to sleep.

Stud walked up behind him after walking up from the river and tapped Sam on the shoulder to show him the quartz. Sam turned around and was startled to see a smiling Indian boy with a pretty rock in his hand, but Sam could tell by the look in the boy's eyes that he was friendly and meant no harm.

"Sam, meet my friend, Stud Colt," Bill said, standing up to make the introduction.

"I'll be. Is this an Indian?" Sam asked with delight.

"Yes, this is a fearsome Indian brave. He's scary, ain't he?" Bill joked.

Stud Colt gave Sam the rock in friendship, and Sam liked it very much. He hadn't taken the time to look at any rocks himself, and then Stud started talking to him. Sam was amazed by his language and his friendliness and just stood there, smiling, even though he didn't understand anything that the boy was saying, except that it had something to do with the river, and Stud wanted Sam to go with him, so he did. "Will you watch the coffee for me, Zeb?"

"Sure enough," Zeb answered. Then he became nervous about overseeing something that was so important to Rose. This kind of responsibility was overwhelming, and he began to fiddle with the coffee pot, and he never took his eyes off it. Then, much to his displeasure, Rose and Bennager came out of their nest. Rose was trying hard not to smile in front of the other men, but the twinkle in her eye was a dead giveaway. Bennager went right to work putting the bedrolls and tent away so that he would be ready when it was time to move.

Rose smiled at Bill and Zeb and cheerfully said, "Good morning." The two men looked at each other and giggled like two little children.

"Good morning, Mrs. Rasmussen," they said in unison as if they were greeting a schoolteacher, which neither one of them had ever had, Rose reckoned.

Rose knew that they were trying to get her riled, but it was too exhausting to be riled all the time. "I see that you two are behaving like gentlemen today. You must be taking a break to lick your wounds," Rose said with a broad mischievous smile that made the two men stop their giggling and begin to puff up like fighting roosters. "Is the coffee ready?" she asked pleasantly.

"Sam put it together, and then he left and told me to watch it!" Zeb bemoaned loudly, and then he threw his stick that he was messing with on the ground. "And it's not ready yet!" he finished and then continued to stare at the coffee pot.

"That's all right, Zeb, I can wait for it to finish. What in tarnation are you putting in this man's tea, Uncle? He's getting the peedoodles!" Rose joked.

"No, I'm not! I'm not getting any peedoodles!" Zeb argued rapidly.

"Oh, Lordy, take it easy. I'll watch the coffee, and you can go back to playing with your stick. I sure do miss Girl. I bet you do too. That must be the cause of your angst," Rose commented.

"No, it's not! I'm not a coffee watcher, that's all!" Zeb said nervously.

Rose widened her eyes in a way that meant that it was time for her to surrender the task of trying to converse with Zeb and she let out a sigh. Then she stirred the beans around and put some on a plate to have for breakfast.

Bill cringed at the sight but thought that it was better to see her doing with what she had rather than to complain about what she didn't. The coffee began to boil, and she watched it for about a minute and then took it from the fire, and after another minute, she added cold water to it. "That's for settling the grounds," she explained to Zeb.

"I know it! You don't have to tell me about settling grounds!" Zeb said in an agitated tone.

Rose's head went back as though she had been hit right in the middle of the forehead, and then she quietly laughed. Zeb was being so ridiculous this morning that she couldn't help it. Once she was able to stop laughing, she asked, "Didn't you sleep well last night?"

Zeb threw his stick down and stomped off. Rose shook her head, and then she glared at Bill. "You're putting something it that man's tea, sure as I'm sittin' here, ain't ya?"

Bill snickered like a rotten child, but he never answered the question.

"Well, you had better knock it off, Uncle. I'm depending on Zeb to lead me to people who will sell me cattle, and he can't do business when he's like this, for heaven's sake! He's completely unreasonable!"

"He's like that because he's jealous that you were kept warm by your mate last night, and he wasn't. And I don't like being blamed for his behavior, by the way," Bill argued.

Rose eyeballed her uncle, searching his eyes for truth, but didn't find much. "He might miss his wife, but you are giving him something, and I would appreciate it if you would quit. I was with Zeb on the river long enough to know that he wouldn't act like that no matter how much he missed his wife."

Bill didn't nod or answer. If he did, he would be admitting that Rose was right in her accusation, and he wouldn't concede. Bennager came to the fire, and Rose poured him a cup of coffee. Bill was grateful for the third party because Rose would probably leave him alone now.

"How about some beans, dear?" she offered, being mildly sarcastic.

Bennager shook his head. "I guess beans will have to do. For a lady who can eat half a beef and a whole berry pie in one sitting, you sure do run a poor camp," Bennager teased.

"You forget, my dear, I'm also a lady who learned how to live on practically nothing. These beans are a lot better than the weevil-filled biscuits. You wait until I get to Stockton. You'll have to drag me out of the next mercantile I patron."

Bennager and Rose had their backs to the river as the coldest part of the morning was upon them, just before the sun peeked over the eastern horizon. Sam and Stud walked up behind them, and Sam said his good mornings. Stud saw Rose's long flowing hair hanging down her back, but he was still confused because of her hat. Quickly he stepped in front of her where she was sitting on the ground and sat on his haunches and lifted her hat from her head.

Rose jerked back so forcefully at the sight of the Indian boy that she spilled hot coffee everywhere. Even the cup went out of sight. She jumped up and quickly pulled her overalls away from the skin of her legs to stop the burning and then looked at the boy with fierce anger in her eyes.

Stud felt bad. He stepped back a couple of paces and looked at the ground and then looked back at Rose with curiosity. Rose hadn't screamed during the incident, so he still wondered if she was a man. Rose could see that he felt bad, but she was speechless as she peered at the boy and tried to figure out what he wanted. In one quick motion, the boy stepped up and put both of his hands on her breasts, and Rose gasped. With the instinct given to her from her maker, she grabbed the boy's hand, twisted his arm behind his back, and tripped and pushed him at the same time until he hit the ground and then she sat in the middle of his back. The boy lay on the ground, wide-eyed, and looked at Bill.

Zeb had seen Sam and Stud coming and was watching from behind the nearest tree. Both men were laughing so hard that Rose was sure that they were urinating on themselves, and then she felt bad. Somehow, those two maniacs had coerced the poor boy into playing a trick on her, and she had fallen for it. She got up off the boy and helped him up. The boy smiled when he faced her and patted her hard on the shoulder and started talking hastily and pointed at her hair, hat, breasts, and privates, but he didn't offer to touch her again. Then he pointed to where her tent had been and at Bennager, the tree where he had relieved himself earlier, then to Sam and the river. Then he handed her a pretty quartz rock that had a line of gold running through it, and he stopped talking and just smiled at her.

Somehow, Rose seemed to get the gist of the story, and she took the rock and looked into his kind eyes, then she promptly kicked her uncle in the shin. She took the boy's hand in hers graciously and said loudly, "Uncle, quit that damned laughing! Do you know this poor boy? Or did you just pay him to scare me like that?"

Stud laughed and pointed at Bill. "Bill, you are bad. You could have told me that was a woman in that tent with that man. Now the joke is on you. Does your leg hurt?" Stud asked him, sporting a smile.

Bill nodded his head as he rubbed his leg, and when his tearful laughter dwindled down to just aftershocks, he said to the boy, "Just a little, but it was worth it. Snoring girl is loud when she is awake."

Stud was shocked and pointed to Rose with his free hand. "This is loud one?" he asked.

Bill nodded his head. Rose was infuriated that they were talking about her in another language and dropped his hand. She went to saddle the Roman. The big joke was over, and she felt that it was time to go anyway. She would be damned if she was to stand around, waiting for childish explanations from grown men. She bit off a piece of tobacco, and before Toby had a chance to beg, she gave it to him and then bit off a piece for herself. She was glad that the other burros didn't seem to have the same hankering or else she would be apt to run out.

Bennager was looking at Sam's rock that he found, the same kind that Stud had given to Rose, and smiled as he told Sam that the yellow streak was gold.

"I know, Stud told me!" Sam was delighted. He really never thought that he would actually find gold.

Stud walked up to Bennager and patted him hard on the shoulder. He pointed to Bennager, and then to Rose, and then to Bill as he talked. Then he pointed to the south, himself, and then to Bennager. Bill translated.

"He is apologizing for touching your woman, and it's my fault for letting him think that there were two men in the tent, fooling around with each other. He wants to go south with us to buy cattle, and he promises not to touch your woman again. His name is Stud Colt."

"That's quite a name," Bennager queried.

"It's what I call him, and he liked it when he was younger, but now that he is a man, he wants me to call him Stud Dick, but I told him that he would have to prove himself to be a man, and getting thrown to the ground by a girl won't cut it," Bill said loud enough for Rose to hear.

Zeb was getting eager to saddle his own horse because he wanted to go see Jared, but he didn't dare until somebody else went with him that would protect him from Rose. He didn't want to get kicked. Bennager started to help Sam hitch up the burros, but Bill said that he wanted to, in order to stay away from Rose, and Zeb's silent prayer was answered as he walked with Bennager to the horses. Zeb kept Bennager between himself and Rose until he was saddled and mounted, but he could feel Rose scowling at him. Her mean looks made his bones hurt and his skin flinch. That was how he knew that she was looking at him.

"I'm going to see if Jared is home. I'll come back for you if he is. Maybe he will sell us some food."

Zeb headed upriver hastily and never looked back. He had escaped being kicked by Rose or bitten by her wicked horse, and now that she couldn't see him, he could relax.

*****

Jared Sheldon was home, had food to spare, and was eager to meet Zeb's friends, especially Bill Ford. He had heard things about Bill and was excited to talk to him. Stud Colt walked beside the party, even though Sam had offered to give him a ride on the wagon seat. Jared shook hands with almost everyone as the introductions were made, and Rose was in awe of Jared's home. All that she had seen since she left the ship were hotels, shops, and tents. Seeing Jared's place made her remember that her dreams were capable of being realized and that what she was doing now, even if she did have to eat beans for breakfast, would be worth it someday.

"Hey, I know this young fella," Jared said when he was introduced to Stud Colt. "I never knew his name, though."

"That's what I call him, and he likes it, but I doubt that's his real name," Bill explained.

"It suits him from what I hear." Jared chuckled as Stud patted him hard on the shoulder. "This boy comes here from time to time and looks around until he finds out where the work is happening. Then he watches the men for about ten minutes until he can figure out what he can do to help, and then he just jumps right in, and he works with them all day. He has helped with the buildings, corrals, ditch-digging, and planting. I always try to feed him or pay him, but he never accepts anything from me. Some days, he shows up, and some days, he doesn't. At least now I know his name. He is probably the most pleasant person that I have ever met." Jared told the group while Stud stood next to him smiling.

Bill asked Stud about the puzzlement that Jared was speaking of, and Stud answered, "I am learning. I should not get paid for learning. When I am not learning, I am at home doing. But there is nothing to do there now, so I will go with you to the south." Bill only translated the first part of the explanation because he was afraid that if the White man knew that Stud was working his land, the White man would take it. Bill didn't know the man yet and had no way of knowing what kind of man he was. Bill decided that he would stake a claim on Stud Colt's land when they got to Stockton so that the boy could keep his work and his home safe. Generally, Indians were known to wander, but Bill figured if Stud was learning about land development and finding gold to boot, then he was probably planning on staying put. Nobody had told Stud that Indians didn't have any rights to land, and he wouldn't believe them if they did. Bill intended to, but he would wait until later.

"Stud decided that he is going to go with us for a while, but I'm sure you will see him again," Bill explained nonchalantly.

"Oh, where are you folks headed for?" Jared asked.

"Zeb is taking us to some ranchos to the south to buy cattle. I would—I mean, we would like to start a cattle rancho up on the Yuba River. I hear that the fog rarely reaches out that far," Rose told Jared.

"I suppose that a miner would eat anything, but those Mexican cattle don't have much meat on them," Jared said, and then he looked at Stud. "Is Stud going along with you afoot? He might be trampled!"

"He can keep up until we get to Stockton, then we will do some trading for a mount," Bill said in a way that made Jared think that they didn't have any money or gold, and they might have to trade weapons or keepsakes.

"Those ruffians in Stockton will rob you!" Jared proclaimed, laughing. Jared waved one of his employees over to the group and asked him to get a horse saddled for Stud to have. Then he told Bill. "That boy has done a good year's work in the last three years that he had been coming around, and a horse is the least that I could pay him, but it's a good start. Will you tell him to please accept my gift as thanks for the work that he's done for me?"

Bill searched the man's face for honesty and found some, so he told the smiling boy what Jared wanted to do, and the boy started to reach for his pouch of gold just as Bill knew that he would. Bill touched the boy's arm, and in a very friendly voice, he told Stud in his native tongue. "Don't show this man that gold, Stud. He'll probably kill your family, burn you out, and take your land if he knows that there are gold nuggets like that on it. Accept his gift of the horse, and if you don't want to keep it, then you can drop it off when you get back."

"Bill, this man is good. Why don't you trust him?" Stud asked.

"White men start out good and then change into bad men when they get greedy. White men always want more and more. Do you understand?" Bill explained, still smiling so no one would see the distrust that he felt for Jared regarding what could happen to Stud and his family. Bill reckoned that the man might always have some square dealings with most folks, but he also reckoned that he thought that Indians were easy to take advantage of, and Bill wanted to protect his friends.

Rose knew that her uncle wasn't acting naturally, and suddenly, she felt a dire need to go. Thankfully, some men were bringing out the supplies that Zeb had asked for, and Rose asked Bennager to pay them. She didn't want any more to do with this place and she didn't want to stay any longer palavering. She mounted up as Sam and Bennager were storing the food, and when the other man brought out Stud's horse, Bill and Stud promptly mounted up as well, and that is when she knew that her uncle had a bad feeling about the man.

She rode over to Zeb and said, "Bennager said the trail to Stockton is well marked. Go ahead and visit with your friend if you like, but I believe we had better get these burros going. I doubt that you will have any trouble catching up with us." Then she kindly eased the Roman out of the yard as Bill and Stud were doing and waved.

"Thank you for your hospitality, Mr. Sheldon." Bennager and Sam quickly said their goodbyes and thank-yous and hurried to catch up with the others.

Sam was happy to be going and not waiting around for Zeb to visit with his friend all day. When the introductions had been made, Jared Sheldon shook everyone's hand except for Sam's and Stud's. Sam was used to White men being that way, but he didn't like it. He reckoned that the others noticed, and they didn't like it either, and that made Sam feel good. As they crossed the Cosumnes River and widened the gap between themselves and the Sheldon rancho, everyone relaxed and began to act like themselves again.

As noon approached, so too did the Mokelumne River. Rose exercised her arm by helping the ferryman. When the crossing was finished, the party stopped to eat some of the bread and cheese and dried fruit that Mr. Sheldon had been able to sell them. Sam was eager to throw out the crunchy beans and decided that he would make a new batch sometime on the other side of Stockton when he would have time to soak them properly. Bill and Stud dined on hardtack, and they decided that they would replenish their supply by killing a deer as soon as they saw one.

Sam was rummaging around in the supplies and found some apples. He couldn't believe it. He hadn't seen a piece of fresh fruit in nine months. He took one out for Rose and said, "Catch," tossing it to her.

Rose caught it one-handed, examined it, and looked at Sam with a wondrous smile on her face. "Where did you get this?" she asked, reaching in her pocket for her knife to slice it with.

"That man sold it to you," Sam answered. "Where do you think that I would get an apple this time of year?"

"I'll be danged! I haven't seen a piece of fresh fruit for nine months!" Rose exclaimed, and Sam chuckled. She went to the wagon. "How many apples do you have in there?"

"I don't make pies, Rose. Do you?" Sam said, knowing from past experience that she liked her fruit surrounded by pie crust.

"No," Rose said with a disappointed look.

"Then you will have to enjoy them the way they are," Sam advised with a smile.

After a ten-minute stop, Bill was mounted again, and he rode up to Rose. "Ride beside me, Little Rose. I want to talk to you." Bill couldn't stand not knowing what had happened after he left the old homeplace, and he knew that he would never get his newly wedded niece alone on accident. Rose nodded and gave Bennager a queried look. Bennager smiled and nodded to her to go without him, and, reluctantly, she did.

They rode a little while in silence while Rose finished her apple. Bill kept looking over his shoulder for Zeb, but he knew not to worry about him. He had always been long-winded. "I was wondering if my father was still alive," Bill finally asked timidly, afraid of what the answer would be.

"Was his name George?" Rose asked.

"Yes."

"My father never mentioned George, but there was an older man who worked in the stables who told me that George had a heart attack before I was born," Rose said.

"What was that man's name that you talked to in the stables?" Bill asked.

"His name was John Foreman," Rose answered.

Bill had a sad trembling feeling as he remembered John and Lucy, and he had a hard time continuing with his inquiry. A few minutes passed, and then he said, "I knew John and his family. Did you know Lucy?"

Rose pondered the question as if it was hard for her to remember something that should be easy. Bill thought that if John had been part of her life, then certainly she should remember Lucy. But then Rose said, "The two girls who worked in the house told me that their mother's name was Lucy."

Bill's heart sank. "Did Lucy die?"

"I don't think so. They said that she had been sent away," Rose said in a remembering state.

Bill was silent. He was trying to puzzle out why Doug would keep Lucy's family but not Lucy. It was hard for him to think like Doug after all these years, but after a few minutes, he remembered that Doug was simply the most hurtful person in the world. He had never liked Lucy, and he knew that Lucy hated him, so he sent her away. Bill let out an angry sigh, and his jaw muscles rippled. "Lucy was my mother's best friend," Bill said sadly.

"That would be my grandmother. What was her name?" Rose asked inquisitively. Bill shot an appalled look at his niece, and the look in his eyes made her want to gasp.

She didn't think that she had said anything wrong, but apparently, she had. Bill stopped his horse, and Rose could feel a tension so thick that it was like a brick wall. He looked like he was going to hit her. His chin began to tremble, but he covered it up by moving his lips around and biting them, then he said, "No one ever told you anything about Grace Weatherford?"

"No, I thought maybe you would, but I won't ask if it's a sore subject." Rose wheeled the Roman around to go join her husband. Rose didn't understand why Bill was acting the way he was. Rose had never loved anyone in her family, and she didn't think that she would like her uncle any better. He looked enough like her father as it was without acting strange to boot. He gave her a peculiar feeling, but she couldn't pinpoint what it was. She just wanted to be away from him.

Bennager could tell that his wife was annoyed. "Did something happen?" he asked.

"No, there is a lot that I don't know about my family. I wish I wasn't part of that family. That's why I left, and I don't want to talk about it!" Rose stepped from her horse to the wagon and sat beside Sam. As she tied her horse to the seat, she said, "Sam, I have a chill. Do you have the brandy up here?"

Sam handed her the jug without saying anything, and Bennager knew that whatever had been said between her and her uncle had scared her. It was the first time that he had seen her that way, and even though he felt for her, he was glad to know that his wife was afraid of something. She had no fear or inhibitions about being a wife, crossing rivers, seeing Indians, or boarding an ocean vessel full of men, but now she was nervous and frightened of her own uncle, the man who had saved her life.

Bennager didn't think that it was necessary to go to Bill and fight this family battle for his wife. It was obvious to him that there was some strange force in the family that caused major disruption, and from what he gathered, the force was Rose's father. Bennager didn't think that it was worth getting in a row about, so he decided to stay out of the family affairs, for now anyway.

The cold day passed by slowly, and Rose was becoming vocally depressed about the fact that the fog had swallowed them up. Bill rode ahead until he was out of their sight and circled around so he could sneak up on his drunken niece. "I see that you are on your way to being worthless to the rest of us. What if we were all like you and we didn't give a damn about what could happen to us?" he said to Rose and was completely ignored by her. "I'm going to ride ahead and look at the next river. We'll have to camp on this side tonight and float the wagon across in the morning. Stud will show you where to camp," Bill said to Sam who was actually listening to him. Then he slapped Rose on the leg with his reins. "We're not finished talking yet, so lay off that liquor, you're too young to drink anyway." Bill put the heels to his horse and lopped away.

Rose was mad enough to kill. She quickly untied her horse and leaped on him from the wagon and raced to catch up with Bill. "Who in the devil do you think you are to be hitting me with your reins and telling me what to do?"

"You're drunk! Go back to the wagon like a good little girl and talk to me when you're sober," Bill said, not looking at her.

Rose saw red, and she wasn't as drunk as he thought. In a move that was cat quick, she was crouched on all fours in her saddle. She leaped on him, knocking him to the ground with the same faultless ability that any Sioux warrior would possess. Bill laughed until he realized that she was trying to choke him with her arm, and then he quickly flipped her over onto her back and sat on her, holding her wrists tightly against the ground so she couldn't procure any of her weapons. "You said you wanted to talk, you crazy son of a bitch, then start talking and quit threatening me with it. I ain't drunk either, you self-righteous old bastard!" Rose screamed as she scowled at Bill.

Bennager rode up and surveyed the situation from his saddle. "Are you all right?" he asked.

"I'll be better when this bastard gets off of me!" Rose hollered, pretending she couldn't breathe.

"I was talking to Bill," Bennager said and then rode off to join the wagon. "Nice move, my dear!" he hollered as he rode away from the family quarrel.

Bill knew that he had made Rose mad enough to gain her full attention, but he didn't put it past her to kill him if he let her up. "I guess we can talk here. You say that your father is nothing more than a bothersome drunk. Why do you think he is here? Why do you think that he sent Lucy away? Why do you think that my father died of a heart attack? Why don't you admit to what kind of man that you know your father to be? How many innocent people did he kill while he was raising you? You know as well as anyone what he is capable of, and you have the nerve to tell me and Sam that he is just a bothersome drunk? You want your husband and friends to think that there is nothing to fear from that man! And if you ever call me a son of a bitch again, I swear, I will cripple your ass for life!"

Rose closed her eyes, not wanting to hear nor admit what Bill was yelling at her. She thought that she had put the darkness behind her when she left to start her new life, and everything was going according to plan until this unwelcomed mountain man, know-it-all uncle appeared in her life and brought everything that she had hidden back to the light again. "I left out of there and changed my name, same as you. I won't allow you to blame me for my father's doings," Rose said forcefully.

"I'm not blaming you for anything, but you know how bad he is. Why won't you admit it?" Bill asked with compassion.

Rose paused; she didn't want to answer. She really didn't want to acknowledge her father's existence. "His blood is in me. If I was to speak out loud of everything that I know about him, then I would have to admit that I am like him," Rose cried. Bill let her weep until he couldn't stand to see her in pain anymore, then he pulled her to him and hugged her as she wept and shook, which was something that she had needed to do for a very long time. Bill knew what it felt like to be related by blood to someone that was so despicable and not having any way to get away from it. It angered him so much that it was he who had left and changed his name when he should have stayed and protected the farm and the people that lived there. He began to weep too, for all his losses, for his mother and father, and the little baby that was lost; for all the people that he would still have in his life if he would have stayed and found a way to stop Douglas. The two of them held each other for several moments.

Both wanted desperately to pull themselves together and stop crying in the presence of the other. Finally, Rose gently pushed him away, and several more minutes passed as they sat in the mud, not looking at each other.

"You are nothing like him. You are exactly like my mother, except she loved me," Bill said quietly.

Rose laughed a little through her tears, but she didn't look up.

"If you were anything like him, you would have stayed with him, but you are just like Grace Weatherford, and I bet he noticed that about you too. He hated all of us, but he especially hated my mother, and he hated our Lucy too. I suspect that he sent her away because it would torment John, and he probably made her daughters' lives miserable, didn't he?"

Rose looked at Bill then, with anguish in her eyes. Her uncle had just hit on another topic that she swore she would never reveal to anyone, but she never expected to meet anyone that knew her father either.

"He raped them. Anytime that he felt like it, he raped them." She sobbed into her hands, not wanting her uncle to see her grotesquely contorted face.

"What about your mother?" Bill asked almost in a whisper.

Rose shook her head. "He never hurt my mother or us in that way. Mother was the one with the money. Mother saw to it that he was fed, but she never cared about what he did to those people. There were so many unspeakable things. I don't want to say them."

Bill nodded his head knowingly and gave Rose time to gather her emotions. "I can imagine. When he was ten years old, he trampled a Black woman to death, but she didn't die right away. She ended up dying in his bed. He burned the stables, the crops, and on the night that we left, he branded Sam and killed the doctor's horse. We had a neighbor that always threatened to kill him. I wonder why he never did," Bill pondered.

Rose looked up at Bill with disbelief showing through the tears in her eyes. "Was his name Evans?"

Bill stared wide-eyed into her soul. "How did you know that?"

Rose shook her head and started to realize how bizarre and surreal this conversation was becoming. It was too overwhelming to even cry about, and she was becoming angry. "He was found dead in the creek that borders our two properties. Everyone assumed that it was an accident, but I heard that they had words with each other in town a couple of days before, and I always wondered. John was always afraid about me spending time with him in the stables. He was afraid that my father would kill him in some sneaky way. He always said that. But Mother would let me go, so I would only go when Father was gone."

"Didn't John ever tell you anything about us when we were growing up or about my mother?" Bill quizzed, remembering all the time he, Sam, and John had spent wondering what Douglas was doing or planning.

Rose shook her head. "No, John hated for me to be out there with him, but he did tell me about animals, and he taught me to ride. When his girls were outside doing their chores, he would stop what he was doing and wave at them, but they never looked at him. They were ashamed, but he didn't know that, and he would get quiet and hateful toward me, and I would go back to the house until the next time." Rose looked at the ground. "He only put up with me because he had to, but I couldn't stand to be in that house. When I got older, John would set out the saddle and put my horse in the corral every morning so he wouldn't have to see me, and when Mother would let me go from my studies, I would leave."

"What about Johnny Boy? Did you know him?" Bill asked.

Rose shook her head sadly. Bill shook his head, too sickened at the thought of what might have happened to Lucy's baby boy who he and Sam had spent so much time with. "Your mother didn't care for her people like she should have, but at least she got you out of there."

Rose nodded her head, remembering the look on her mother's face when Rose left as though it was a life-or-death situation. Rose always knew that her mother had wanted to leave, too, but she couldn't because her fortune was invested in the farm, and by the time she figured out that she wasn't making any money, she didn't have enough of her own left to get out. Rose wondered how her father was able to get to California and what her mother was doing right now.

Bill got up and held his hand out to Rose, and she took it and pulled herself up. Bill hugged her and repeated, "I knew who you were when I met you because you are just like my mother in every way, and I loved her, so I would know. You're nothing like him. The blood that flows through you is Grace Weatherford's, and somehow, that woman has brought us together from where she is perched in heaven." He held her tight until he got those words out so that she would hear them, and then he grabbed her shoulders, pushed her to the full length of his arms roughly, and looked her in the eye until he knew that she could stand on her own, and then he let her go.

"What in God's name are the two of you doing here in the fog by yourselves? Were you attacked?" Zeb startled them with his panicked hollering, and they stepped away from each other.

"Yeah, where in the devil have you been? We were charged by a herd of white buffalo and got split from the others. I fell off the horse, Rose is crying for her husband, and you're off reminiscing. Go see if you can track Sam and the wagon," Bill yelled, pretending to limp with a broken leg.

Zeb's eyes widened as he put his heels to his mount and rode hard and fast to go find Sam. It wasn't until about a mile up the trail when he found the rest of the party plodding along just as they should be that he realized that the likelihood of seeing a herd of white buffalos in California or any place else was pretty slim.

Rose laughed when she mounted. "You're bad, Uncle."

"That's the blood of Grace coming out in me. She was an awful teaser. I'm surprised that my father outlived her and her torments." Bill chuckled as he mounted his horse with ease. Rose bit off a piece of tobacco as she watched her uncle and thought of how different his life must have been from Sam's after they split from one another. She thought what a shame it was that Sam hadn't stayed with Bill and wondered how many years had been taken off of his life on account of all of the fighting he was forced to do.

"You're in pretty good shape for an old man. You must have lived a good life," Rose said in a way that she hoped would needle Bill slightly. Even though Bill and her father looked alike, their bodies were dissimilar. As she compared the two men, she realized that her disgusting father played his role right down to the last detail, being in a slovenly state at all times and unhealthy to boot. Rose knew that her wicked father drank a lot and smoked, and his bad deeds were probably weighing on his health, and Bill was probably right to reprimand her for her alcohol consumption.

"Who are you calling old? There are plenty of folks who know that I'm not too old to get the job done," Bill said, puffing his chest like a peacock.

Rose smirked. "So I hear, Horny Bill."

"Those aren't ladylike thoughts you're having, Little Rose. A young girl ought not be thinking that way about menfolk," Bill scolded.

Bennager had made Rose know that she was a woman, not a young girl, whether her uncle knew it or not, and Rose wouldn't know what a ladylike thought was anyway. Her uncle was right because most of the thoughts that she had running around in her head these days were of her husband and how she wanted him. Rose chuckled and shook her head as she slapped the Roman on the hind end with her reins. "I don't think you menfolk can ever get your stories straight on what women should and shouldn't think about," she said loudly as she rode away. Bennager had been out of her sight long enough, and she was longing for it to be time to camp for the night.

6

Douglas came back to life sometime after dark. He had lain there all afternoon with broken bones and blood pouring out of him, and no one had done anything to help him. The only one that had even checked for his pulse had been Trina. He wondered what had happened. All the buildings were upright, and there were no boulders in the vicinity, but he knew that some great force of nature had squashed him like he would step on a bug. He tried to get up and realized that it was worse than he thought. His arm and leg on the right side of his body were broken and probably some of his ribs were as well. He felt his face to see if it was still there because it felt like it had been ripped from the bone.

Douglas moaned in a low voice, "Ah, help me somebody! Help me out of the cold! Help me, bring me a doctor!" Time passed, but nobody came to help him, even though he was lying in front of his own establishment. "Rotten, worthless, low down, good-for-nothing bastards and bitches," he grumbled. "Somebody help me, damn it, right now! I can't walk!"

Time passed, and finally he heard the sound of slow, sauntering footsteps coming toward him. "It's about time," Douglas said. "Hey, you, help me to my room and go find me a doctor."

"You're pretty bossy for an old-timer that's a fall down drunk," Dan Dunaway said, standing over Douglas with his arms folded. "I'm a busy man. I doubt I have time to be fooling around with a fall down drunk, unless there's something in it for me."

"I'll have you know, you surly little cretin, that I own every whore in town, and I'll give you the run of them for a week if you do what I tell you," Douglas proposed.

"Have you been havin' at 'em?" Dan asked.

"Of course, take my word, they are all very pleasurable ladies," Doug answered.

"I can see why you're so popular. The townsfolk must love you. I think you'll have to come up with a different offer. I don't think that I would want a woman that would hump you," Dan said, lighting a smoke and waiting.

"I own this gambling establishment. I'll give you all the credit you need to enjoy yourself for a week." Doug gritted his teeth in pain while trying to negotiate a bargain when the man should just go get help and stop standing there, tormenting him.

"I don't gamble. I'm not a fool," Dan replied.

"Would you go in there and find a redheaded girl named Trina? She will help me, and it shouldn't be much trouble for you," Doug asked as nicely as he could but vowed to himself to kill this man as soon as he was able.

Dan went into the gambling hall to find Trina, but only out of curiosity. He wanted to meet the woman that would help a man who claimed to own whores.

An hour went by before Dan came out of the building again, and during that time, four men had stepped over Douglas, and two men had tripped over him. Douglas moaned for help to each one of them, but they kept going. Dan stood over him again with the same pose that he had held before. "It seems that your Trina has left town with a big Irishman driving a six-horse team. Do you remember the big Irishman?" Dan asked, pretending to be caring.

"No, I don't," Doug said, wondering how he was going to get out of this situation.

Dan smiled, showing his young, bright, straight teeth. "'Twas the Irishman that laid you out. I guess he was sweet on your Trina and didn't like seein' you whip up on her. Now who's gonna help ya?"

Since this little whelp was the only one in town that would even give him the time of day, Douglas thought it best to start dealing. "Is there anything I have that you want?"

"Yeah, come to think of it, I'll take the building you call the whorehouse. Yeah, I'll take that," Dan answered.

"I'll give you free room and board for a month." Doug countered.

"I want claim to the building and everything in it, except the women that you claim to own, or else you can lie here and wait for somebody else to come along to haggle with."

Douglas knew that he was between a rock and a hard place, so he agreed. He planned on killing the smiling, blue-eyed son of a bitch with raven black hair when he was better anyway, and then the agreement would be like it never happened. "Fine, I'll give you the hotel. Now get me on my feet and to my bed."

"Where's your bed?" Dan asked, smiling.

"It's in the whore house!" Doug ground out the words trying to control his anger.

"Then I'll have to take you someplace else. I'm afraid a man like you isn't welcome in my establishment," Dan said, laughing at Douglas.

"Very well, I have a bed in this building right here. Take me to it and get me a doctor," Doug said in such a calm way that Dan knew the man was plotting now.

The gambling house was as crowded as ever, and everyone there turned to see who was coming through the front doors and promptly turned their backs or looked away when they realized that it was Douglas Weatherford.

Douglas seethed with hatred for every person in the building as he directed Dan to take him to a small room in the back. "The doctor, if there is one in this town, will be coming as soon as I can find him. I'm going right now," Dan said, pretending to be concerned with the man's welfare.

"Thank you ever so much," Doug said sarcastically through gritted teeth. He watched as Dan rifled through the safe that was left ajar the night before. Doug's lustful intentions with Trina had overcome him in his drunkenness the night before and he had not made certain to lock it. Soon, Dan was able to produce the deed to the building he would soon convert to a hotel.

"It's my pleasure, sir," Dan said, taking the deed to the building out of the safe and waving it at Douglas. "You had better sign this over to me before I go, though. You might pass out again, and our business won't get finished." Dan held the ink bottle for Doug as he signed the piece of paper, and Dan flashed his perfect teeth and left the room without another word.

The out-of-work miners saw the young man with black hair and cigar in his mouth come out of Doug's office and whisper something in the ear of one of the working ladies. Doug's female employees followed Dan out of the building much to the surprise of the miners. They watched the women leave, then looked at each other and wondered what they were supposed to do. They finished their drinks, collected their winnings, and wandered aimlessly out of the building. Douglas heard them all leave as his consciousness swam away into the darkness.

Dan and the women split up in pursuit of a doctor, but the best that they could find was a veterinarian. He had a very nice medical bag, and Dan convinced him to put on a clean shirt and not tell his patient that he wasn't a people doctor.

"Who is the patient?" the vet asked.

"Douglas Weatherford," Dan replied.

"It would be my pleasure to work on that man. It must be my lucky day. I doubt a people doctor would come to his aid anyway, if they knew him as well as I do," the vet remarked as he tipped his hat to the ladies that were standing behind Dan. The six of them watched the man walk toward the empty gambling hall and close the doors behind him.

"Let's go home, ladies. You can rest tonight, but first thing in the morning, you will be living by my rules," Dan said, leading the way to his newly acquired business.

*****

Rose had risen to greet the new day with a scowl. She was slowly returning to her old self since the happiness of being a newlywed was starting to wear off and bleak reality was starting to manifest itself through the cold, damp fog. Nobody had taken the time to make coffee because the men were getting the wagon ready to cross the Calaveras River. There was no ferry at this river, which was a great disappointment to Rose when she had found out the night before. The water was just swift enough to wreak havoc with the wagon and the burros, so the men were sawing down a couple of trees and limbing them to use the logs as flotation devices for each side of the wagon. Rose didn't know how she would make it through the day without coffee, but she knew that she would only get in the way if she attempted to make some herself.

She went back inside the tent and washed the "coffeeless" morning down with brandy, bit off a piece of plug tobacco, and began dismantling camp. She thought of how the night before had been uneventful, and she was proud of herself for making through her turn at watch. Of course, the only thing that had kept her awake was the mischievous thoughts she had been having about what she was going to do to her husband when they got back to their nest. Now she was paying the price for staying up half the night, and she wanted nothing more than to go back to sleep.

Rose looked at Bennager to see how he was weathering the morning. He saw her glance, smiled broadly, and tipped his hat in a way that said to his wife, "Good morning, and thanks for last night."

Rose continued to scowl and thought, *The least that he could do is pretend to be as bedraggled as I am.*

Bennager was confused by the scowl, and when the wagon was ready for the crossing, he went to Rose and said, "Good morning, dear. How are you feeling this morning?"

"I'm so tired. I feel like I've been dragged through a knothole backward," she whispered as she gave her husband a heartfelt hug.

"So that's the reason for the dirty look. I thought you were mad at me on account of there being no coffee." Bennager smiled, knowing that his wife had every reason in the world to be tired after the night before. He gently pushed Rose away and put his forehead to hers. "You play too hard. You need to start getting some rest or else you will wear yourself plumb out." He gently kissed her on the lips. "Are you ready to cross the river?"

"When I mount up, I will be."

Sam was sitting on the wagon, waiting for the horsemen to cross. He knew there was no point in getting in a hurry because the burros wouldn't cross the river unless they were following the horses. Bill and Zeb were out in front with ropes ready in case the wagon tried to float away and the burros panicked. Wearily, Rose mounted the Roman and let out a long, luxurious yawn in preparation for the ride ahead. The Roman took this unguarded opportunity to remind his rider what real power and authority was. The Roman crow hopped straight up into the air three times, loosening Rose from the saddle. Her feet were out of the stirrups, and with every descent, she landed in a different spot on the Roman's back.

First, she was rammed into the fork, then on top of the cantle, and then back to the seat again. The Roman knew that he had woken her up because she was making an effort to turn his head, but he was a quick thinker. Now he began a series of full-on bucks, jumping high and landing hard with each kick until Rose was thrown over the Roman's head and to the ground, landing flat on her back but still in possession of one rein.

The Roman stood over her kindly, nodding his head with satisfaction. Rose looked up into his eyes, unable to speak or even breathe. All the wind had been knocked out of her, and she thought that she was dying since she had never experienced such a thing before. She realized that her Roman had bested her just like she had bested him on their first day, and in the Roman's mind, they were even now.

Bennager jumped off his horse and came to his wife's aid. "Rose, are you all right?"

"She's got the wind knocked out of her," Sam said. "Breathe in some air, Rose," Sam said, leaning over her with his hands on his knees.

Rose gasped and coughed, then Bennager asked. "Can you sit up? Did you break anything?"

Rose sat up and waited to feel debilitating pain exude from some part of her body. There wasn't any unordinary pain, and she waved the men away as she sat on the ground, looking at her horse's kind eyes. She pulled him to her with the rein, scratched him under his chin, and said, "You put me here, you hardheaded comic, now you can help me up." Rose stiffened her body like a board and with both reins in her hands, the Roman backed up until she was on her feet. "Thanks for the lesson, Roman, you bastard," Rose whispered in his ear as she eased by his head and gingerly made a second attempt to get the day started.

Bennager and Sam looked at each other and then looked at Rose. "Are you sure you're all right, dear?" Bennager asked.

"I'll make it, I reckon, except that I swallowed my tobacco," Rose replied and rode into the river.

Bennager and Sam looked at each other again wondrously and shook their heads.

Stud Colt watched Rose ride slowly into the water and start crossing, seemingly undisturbed by the swift current or the cold temperature of it as it slowly crept up her legs. He wasn't familiar with horses or their wicked ways and personalities. Being a native Californian Miwok Indian, he had never had any use for a horse before this trip, and he hoped that his horse would be kinder to him than the ugly one that Rose was riding was to her. Stud Colt felt bad that Rose was hurt, and when Rose approached him on the other side of the river, he reached out and patted her, gently this time, and looking at her questioningly. He asked in his native tongue if she was well, and then he glared at the man-eating ugly horse.

Bill and Zeb were waiting in the middle of the river to help Sam and the burros if they needed it while Bennager rode beside the burros with a willow switch and gently touched them on the rumps with it for added encouragement. Bill noticed his young Indian friend lending comfort to his niece and smiled broadly at Zeb, nodding his head toward the shore. "What did I tell you about Stud Colt Zeb? He's got a way with women!" Bill laughed.

Zeb saw the scene that Bill was referring to and laughed as well.

"Bennager's apt to lose his bride before we get Sam's contraption to shore," Zeb replied to Bill. "Hey, Bennager, did anybody ever tell you that Indians ain't too good about keeping their promises?" Zeb hollered, pointing to Rose and Stud on the shore.

Bennager shook his head at the teasing men and waved them off, continuing with the task at hand. The burros eased across the Calaveras carefully as if they had done it a hundred times, and Sam was thankful that he had picked the best burros in all of California. Rose was amazed that the team had done so well and vowed never to sell these little gems at any price. Carefully, she dismounted and gave all the burros a little pet. Toby brayed for a prize that he felt was owed to him, and when no one was looking, Rose slipped him a piece of tobacco. The men quickly built a fire so everyone could dry off, and Rose finally got her cup of coffee.

"We'll be in Stockton by midafternoon, don't you reckon, Zeb?" Bill asked.

Zeb nodded his head, smiling. He had already made up his mind that before the cattle buying part of the trip was over, he was going to rush home and see Anna and the children for a few days. Since the day he had made his decision, he had been in a better mood, and since Rose had told her uncle to stop putting harmful things in his tea, he had gone back to being his old, reasonable self. Bill simply ran out of the funny little plant that he had found along a creek in the foothills, but Rose had thanked him for stopping his nonsense, and Bill had tipped his hat in a silent reply.

"Well, when we get to town, us men are going to do the grub shopping this time. You wouldn't know the first thing about outfitting a party of hungry men, Little Rose. Why, our captain would have gut shot you if you had been our cook," Bill teased, trying to get a reaction out of his niece.

Rose looked at Bill as if he was insane. "What in tarnation would I be doing cooking for a government surveying party of forty men, Uncle?"

"Yeah, Bill, she wouldn't be the cook, she'd be the horse breaker and Indian charmer." Zeb chimed in.

"Well, I guess the captain might not have shot up her guts then," Bill confessed and gave his niece a sly wink. "We men will be doing the grub shopping, though," he boasted.

"That's a good job for you, Uncle," Rose said as she gingerly shifted her weight. "I've got my own shopping to do anyway."

"Spirits, I reckon?" Bill assumed.

"You bet." Rose smiled mischievously.

Sam and Stud didn't linger long by the fire. They thought their clothes would dry just as promptly as they looked for rocks by the edge of the water. Sam had a touch of gold fever now, and he didn't care if his pants were wet or not. Stud had a knack of knowing where to look for gold and a keen eye to see it, so while the rest of the men stood around the fire, giving each other heck for one thing or another, Sam and Stud kept busy during every minute of light that they could spare. Sam couldn't wait for the drive to be over so he could spend more time looking for gold. He could tell that the smiling boy was talking to him about Rose and her ugly horse, and he was replaying the accidental event that had happened earlier. He put his hands on his back ribs and rubbed them, pointed to Rose, and then made a motion with his hands that indicated a break and pointed to Rose again.

Sam nodded his head to let the boy know that he understood and laughed to himself over the fact that the boy wanted to make sure that Rose wasn't to hurt to ride. Stud cared more about Rose's well-being than she did. Sam would know if her ribs were broken or bruised if he examined her, but he didn't think that she would let him. He conveyed this to Stud, and he nodded. They heard Bill holler for them, and they hastily returned to the party. Everybody was mounted and ready to go when Sam and Stud got there, but they didn't offer to get going. Stud walked directly to Rose as she sat on her ugly horse, put his hand on her thigh, and looked pleadingly into her eyes. Bill translated, "He says he's worried that you might have broken ribs on your back and he wants you to let Sam have a look."

Rose smiled and waved the boy off, shaking her head no. Stud looked disappointedly to the ground and then went to Bennager and put his hand on his thigh. Bennager arched one brow since the only person who had ever touched his thigh in his life had been Rose. Bill translated, "He says you should make her if you love her."

"I do love you, dear, and Stud seems determined," Bennager said, almost laughing. He knew that he couldn't make Rose do anything, but when he saw Sam waiting for her to dismount with his arms folded, he knew that he might be able to talk her into not delaying the trip any further. "The sooner that you let Sam check you out, the sooner you can go shopping for guns."

Rose was embarrassed to be holding things up and embarrassed that she let the Roman throw her after she had been warned about him. Now she would agree to be humiliated further by letting Sam look at her rib cage, just so she could get to town before dark. She did as Stud asked, and Sam determined that she was bruised but not broken. Bill relayed the message to Stud Colt, and he gently patted Rose again and quietly mounted, keeping his distance from the teeth of the ugly man-eating horse that Rose still seemed to be proud of.

Bill, Zeb, and Stud always rode together to give Rose and Bennager their privacy. "I think that horse is a witch that just looks like a horse. It doesn't want anyone to be friends with Rose. It wants her to himself so he can abuse her. That's why he bites everybody. Tell Stud that's what I think," Zeb told Bill.

"If it's male, wouldn't it be a warlock?" Bill asked seriously.

"Yeah, a warlock, tell Stud what I think."

Bill talked to Stud for a couple of minutes, but he never mentioned Zeb's theory about warlock horses because he knew that Stud wouldn't understand such impractical, abstract thinking. Bill was telling Stud what to expect when they got to Stockton. When Bill was finished, Stud nodded his head, but he only wanted to talk about the Roman. He said that it had the same evil spirit of a rattlesnake and the sneaky way of a coyote, and he had a hard time sleeping at night because he was afraid the awful horse would try to eat him. Bill nodded.

"What did he say?" Zeb asked.

"He agrees with you, Zeb," Bill replied, and then he shook his head slightly. Bill was surrounded by two of the most superstitious men in the world. Even Sam could make the hairs on a man's neck tingle when he wanted to. Bill looked back at Rose and realized that out of all of them, she was probably the only one who just saw things for what they were.

Zeb was pleased that Stud Colt understood his theories about witches, and on the way to town, he asked Bill to translate for him about his thoughts on women, the moon, different animals, the ocean, and the tall redwoods near his home. Bill thought it was too much senseless palaver, but he did it anyway because there wasn't any reason not to. Stud didn't agree with Zeb about there being evil women. Stud loved all women, and the Creator put women on earth for that very purpose. The discussion became very heated, and when Stud stopped smiling, Zeb backed off and changed the subject, asking about the ocean. Stud didn't have an opinion about the ocean because he had never seen it, but he wanted to.

Their conversation quieted down the closer they got to town. The trail was starting to get crowded with miners who were coming to town for supplies and to beg for credit to get them with. When the water had become too cold to work in, the men had started building shelters on their claims. The tougher miners would rather weather out the winter in the hills than in town, especially those who were in debt, but once they got hungry, they would have to come in and do some bartering.

Sam observed their condition as they passed each man and thought that having a full-time job with Rose was better than being a full-time gold miner.

Rose and Bennager rode up beside the wagon, but they didn't comment on the health of the miners. Rose hoped she would do better as a cattle ranchero than these men were doing as gold miners, but she never said anything out loud. She had been practicing holding her tongue so as not to hurt people's feelings, and as long as she wasn't drunk, she did pretty well.

Bill, Zeb, and Stud Colt slowed their pace and waited for Sam to catch up. They were all afraid that there could be trouble before they got to town, so they encircled the wagon and continued. The hearty miners didn't pose any threat to the outfit. Even though they were hungry and poor, they knew that they would be rich someday, and they didn't want to jinx it with bad deeds. The older men of the party remembered similar scenes of disheveled men after the War of 1812 when they were small boys, except these miners weren't wearing bloody bandages.

Bill reckoned that one or two of these miners had been in the War of 1812 and wondered why in the devil an old man would take up gold mining. Then he wondered why a man his age was attempting to drive a cattle herd through the San Joaquin Valley, and he shook his head and chuckled.

The party arrived in Stockton well before dusk and split up in search of what they needed to make their trip easier. Sam and Stud were afraid that they wouldn't be treated fairly by the merchants, so Zeb and Bill split up to go with them. Sam wanted lumber to modify the wagon, and Bill wanted to outfit Stud with clothes better suited for driving cattle. Rose and Bennager went directly to the gunsmiths. Bennager hoped that if he went with his bride, he could keep her from buying out the whole town.

Rose was just about ready to dismount when a bald, middle-aged man approached her but stopped five paces from her. He said, "How do there, miss? That used to be my horse."

Rose was on the ground, having a hard time making her body get ready to walk. "Is that right?" she boldly questioned, wondering if she was being accused of horse theft.

"Yes, miss, that is right. I won him in a bet back on the Green River, and if I ever see that man that I won him from, I'm going to pay him back with flying lead. I would just as soon walk the breadth of the earth seven times as to straddle that horrible beast for one more second." The Roman recognized the man and pinned his ears back, snorted, then turned away, ignoring the man that he knew was saying bad things about him. The man continued, "How in the world did you end up with this animal, miss? Don't you have any friends in the world to advise you about horses?" The man started showing the scars on his arms and legs where the Roman had bitten him. "That beast barreled out of the Sierras last summer on a dead run. I couldn't control him whatsoever. You wouldn't believe the sheer rock cliffs that he tried to destroy us on when he ran off them. We slid down hill one time on shell rock for probably a mile before we landed in a creek, but he paid the price for that endeavor. He rubbed all of the hide off his hind end." The man pointed to the rear of the Roman and showed Rose the difference in color.

"He ran me right through a den of rattlesnakes, hoping that I would fall off and be consumed by them, and he tried to brush me off on every oak tree between the foothills and Sacramento City. When the trees became sparse, he would run out of his way to try to brush me off. From Donner Summit to Sacramento City, he went nonstop for forty-six hours. It wouldn't have taken him that long if he hadn't gone out of his way looking for cliffs, beehives, rattlesnake dens, badger holes, and oak trees. I tell you, miss, I was one sorry mess when I got to the Sacramento River and too sorry to be in public, if you understand my meaning. I rode this bastard—oh pardon me—I rode this animal right into the river, and we bathed together. I figured he would die of shock and float away, but when he was finished twitching, he dragged me out and we went straight to the livery, and I've been walking ever since."

The man stood there, waiting for Rose to be shocked and disturbed about the mistake that she had made in purchasing the dun.

"Maybe he didn't like Donner Summit," Rose ventured a guess in the Roman's defense.

The Roman gently put his chin on Rose's shoulder and snorted at his previous victim.

The man tipped his hat to Rose, passed by her, rolled his eyes at Bennager, and went to the nearest saloon.

Bennager chuckled at the story and the new admiration that was showing on Rose's face.

"Did you really do all that, Roman? I better get you some hard candy." She patted the beast on the neck, took Bennager's hand, and went shopping.

Rose was disappointed in the selection of weapons available for purchase. She settled for a flintlock Spanish pistol that wasn't any more efficient than Sam's, but the range was farther than her derringer. Bennager was excited when he saw a new .50-caliber Sharps Carbine, and he traded in his musket loader and cash to get it. Rose kicked a barrel of gunpowder over on the floor out of frustration when she noticed that Bennager was happier with his purchase than she was with hers. The man behind the counter was distracted by her anger.

"If you want to kick my gunpowder, then buy it and kick your own gunpowder, miss."

"Don't mind her," Bennager nonchalantly suggested.

"Well, sir, I do mind her walking around in here kicking my gunpowder on purpose, for heaven's sake!" the gunsmith said.

Rose smiled happily. "I'll buy four barrels and kick them all I want then!"

Bennager shook his head. "Dear, you don't need that much gunpowder."

"I think I might need it," Rose replied, indubitably.

Bennager walked up to Rose, hoping that he could come up with a good reason why she didn't need that much gunpowder in the time that it took him to cross the room. "There really isn't any reason for you to have that much gunpowder. It will just get wet and go to waste. Also, you will have to have another animal to haul it."

"There is a nice mule down at the livery. I saw her on the way in," Rose argued.

"Well, get the mule but leave the gunpowder here," Bennager pleaded.

"No, I need it," she said as she left the building to go purchase the mule.

The gunsmith looked at Bennager for a moment with a confused look on his face, and then he smiled. "Good Lord, mister, you must be a saint."

Bennager nodded his aching head. "That explains it then."

The man that owned the mercantile where Bill and Stud had gone for clothes and grub had started in on Bill about Indians not being allowed in his store, but one dirty mean look from Bill was all that it took to quiet the man down. He quickly determined that the mountain man had no regard for his opinion of Indians or his rules. The smiling boy seemed harmless anyway, so he didn't delay the mountain man with his arguments.

Sam and Zeb didn't have any trouble at the hardware store, except that it took Sam forever to pick out his hardware. He studied hinges for twenty minutes and nails for even longer. Zeb wanted to help but he couldn't see the picture that Sam had in his mind, so he looked around at everything else that was in the store until he was bored stiff. Finally, they went out to the back of the store to get the lumber, and Zeb was pleased when Sam picked out four ten-by-twelves, paid the man, and left. They moved the wagon down the street and parked in front of the general mercantile.

Zeb went in to help gather supplies while Sam started to work on his kitchen unit. Zeb walked right past Stud, not recognizing him in his new garb, and directly to Bill and complained about how long it took for Sam to pick out a hinge.

"What did you do with Stud Colt?" Zeb asked. The storekeeper looked up from his ciphering at this comment.

"He's right there, you walked right by him, you idiot. I knew you were blind," Bill said gruffly. The storekeeper looked at the Indian, knowing now who they were referring to.

"There you are, Stud Colt. I didn't recognize you. Are you going to get your hair cut while you're in town?" Zeb asked as he messed with Stud's hair.

The boy smiled but shook his head no, and then he complained to Bill about his shoes.

Bill told him in his language that he might need a bigger pair, and they went to the boot section and started to make the switch. The storekeeper had a fit.

"You'll have to buy the pair that the Indian already put his dirty feet in!"

Bill walked up to the man and waved at Zeb to continue helping Stud. "If I do buy an extra pair of boots that I don't need, they will be used for shoving up your ass."

"I won't have that kind of talk in my place. I'll kick you all out and you there," he said to Zeb. "Get that Negro of yours out from in front of my store!" the man hollered just as Rose walked through the door.

Rose hurried to the arguing men. "What did you just say about the man outside?"

"He's stinking up the front of my store!" the man growled.

"What should we do with this…this person, Uncle?" Rose asked as she looked the man up and down, wondering if she should kill him or just kick the tar out of him.

Zeb jumped into the fray, "Rose, you have a lot of money to spend. I say we just spend it someplace else."

Rose and Bill hadn't taken their flaming eyes off the storekeeper, and Zeb didn't think they were considering his suggestion either, so he tried to reason with the other guy. "You could apologize for saying mean things about our friends and live to see another day." Bennager had ridden up to the store front leading the mule and its cargo. He dismounted and asked Sam if he could help.

"There's my gunpowder, Uncle," Rose said, never taking her eyes from the bigot in front of her.

"We might be able to use that sooner than you thought," Bill said to intimidate the man but wondered what in the devil Rose wanted with gunpowder. It would just get wet.

The man went behind his counter. "Get what you need and be quick about it."

Bill ushered out his people. Zeb had fitted Stud with a bigger pair of boots and left the other pair on the floor. Bill stayed behind to pay for his friend's clothes and then purposely tipped over a barrel of sugar on his way out. "On a different day, that would have been your brains lying there on the floor," Bill said as he strolled out the door. "Mount up before I torch this place!" Bill hollered at the top of his lungs.

Everyone was shocked except for Rose. She was proud of her uncle for being as angry as she was. She smiled as everyone quickly got moving. Bennager could see that Bill was enraged, but he didn't know why, and he hoped that the man had good reason and wasn't just going crazy. He was still hoping that Rose would outgrow her strange behavior, but his hope was wearing thin when he saw Bill's outburst.

Bill leaped on his horse and raced to the end of town, turned, and raced to the other end, screaming an Arikara war cry the whole way before Sam had gotten his tools put up. This act of insanity went on for fifteen minutes as Rose waited for Sam to crawl on his wagon, and she calmly led the party southward. Zeb seemed to be Bill's target in his pretend counting coup outrage. Every time Bill screamed wildly up or down the street, he would pop Zeb on the elbow or in the ribs. No matter what Zeb did to get away from him, Zeb would still get hit. "Give me that new carbine. I'm going to blow that silly windbag out of his saddle!" Zeb said seriously and wide-eyed. "If that goofy son of a bitch hits me again, I'm going to tear him apart!" Zeb screamed as Bill made another pass.

Some of the townspeople had lined up against the buildings to watch the maniac who would surely kill his horse. Bennager and Sam didn't have any knowledge of why Horny Bill was going crazy in front of a passel of out-of-work, hungry miners in the middle of Stockton, California, but they knew that Rose had the answer. Bennager was afraid to ride to the front of the procession to ask her about it for fear that Horny Bill would run him down. "How long do you figure that he'll keep this up, Sam?" Bennager asked.

"Probably until Zeb kills him, I guess," Sam said, watching Bill go by as he made another pass. Sam looked at Bennager, shrugged his shoulders and shook his head, and then he laughed. "That's some kind of family you married into!" And he laughed even more heartily at his comment and the look on Bennager's face.

"That's what I was just thinking!" Bennager said loudly as Bill screamed again.

A storekeeper on the south end of town waved the party over. This wasn't the first time that his prejudiced competitor had caused turmoil for the town. "I'm in the business of selling if you folks are in the business of buying. I reckon you've all been acquainted with my competitor in the north end of town. It's a wonder how the man stays in business."

"He hasn't sold his first lot of goods yet. They still have last year's dust on them!" Zeb commented as he dismounted and shook the man's hand. "I'm Zeb Jones, this here is Stud Colt, and over there is Bennager Rasmussen and his wife, Mrs. Rose Mary Rasmussen, and our teamster, Sam Washington. That crazy wild-eyed bastard is Horny Bill Ford. He'll be finished directly, and you can meet him when he comes in to give me heck for buying too many beans. I don't outfit a company good enough to suit him, but I'm going to get started anyway because he is embarrassing the devil out of us."

"I need hard candy," Rose blurted out of the blue. Everybody in the group looked at her with confusion except Stud Colt. He was smiling, as usual, but he was particularly impressed with Bill's display of wild horsemanship. Stud didn't understand about counting coup. The natives of California never got around to warring with each other, let alone from the back of a horse, but Bill had told him about it, and now he was seeing how the game was played.

Sam and Bennager got the tools out and started working on the kitchen unit again. Sam looked over his shoulder at Bill who had given up running up and down the street and was just sitting on his horse in front of the bigot's store, chanting a war cry now. Occasionally, he would spin his horse in a circle. "I think he's running out of steam, Bennager," Sam said laughing. It was a long war song, but when it was over, he ran his horse faster down the street than he had before and slid his horse to a stop alongside Sam and Bennager and hopped off onto the ground. Stud Colt threw his arms straight into the air toward the sky. He liked the show very much. Bennager watched Bill go to Stud and talk to him.

"Stud is encouraging Bill," Bennager remarked.

"William knew we wouldn't encourage him, and that's why he's ignoring us. I would just as soon not be caught talking to him anyway," Sam replied with his head down, watching what he was doing.

Bill walked through the door of the general mercantile, and the owner immediately introduced himself with his hand out. "Well, hello, I'm Peter Harlan." Bill took his buckskin glove off and kindly shook the man's hand. "I'd apologize for my competitor up the street, but I won't because he's rotten to the core," Peter said, scowling.

"So's his merchandise, Pete." Bill laughed and slapped the man on the shoulder. "I have to make sure we get some biscuit makings for this outfit. These people are content to live on beans."

"Right this way, Mr. Ford," Peter directed Bill through his store.

Rose didn't bother looking through the store. She knew what she needed and she knew she wouldn't be asked by the men her opinion of what they needed. The selection of hard candy was lacking, in her opinion; she had a choice of licorice, peppermint, and lemon drops. She was in a hurry to leave the store, and reluctantly, she interrupted the men. "Pardon me, Mr. Harlan, I need some hard candy, plug tobacco, and two jugs of brandy, please."

"Right away Mrs. Rasmussen, I'm always eager to satisfy a lady's sweet tooth."

Rose arched one brow at Peter's comment, wondering if that was his way of being nice or if his mind was running rampant with wild thoughts.

Peter noticed Rose scrutinizing him, and he smiled innocently at her. "You must be a brave young lady to come all the way to California to look for gold. Most women would be too afraid of the wild Indians to make the trip," Peter kindly said, trying to make polite conversation.

Rose smiled. "I have my doubts about there being wild Indians. Mr. Colt is a very pleasant young man. Mr. Ford, on the other hand, is the wildest man I have ever met. I didn't have to worry about wild Indians anyway. I had the opportunity to come around the Horn, so I took it."

"Opportunity, you say. I would rather move in with the wild Indians than make that trip. I don't want anything to do with the ocean. Was it awful?"

Rose nodded her head and smiled. "Yes, sir, it was."

"You are a very brave woman, braver than me!" Peter laughed and shook his head. "You must be from the east. What state are you from?"

Rose cringed. She didn't want her past to encroach on her present, but this would probably be a question that people would always ask, and she wasn't going to start her new life by lying. "I lived in the state of Kentucky."

"Is that right? Well, I'll be. I was in a wagon train with a man from Kentucky last summer and fall. He seemed to be a notorious character. Somehow, he managed to collect a handful of unsuspecting young ladies from the Missouri River, and halfway through the trip, he informed the poor things that they were going to be his employees in a house of ill-repute. We were in the Great Basin about that time, and there wasn't any place for them to go. Then he had the nerve to advertise. We put him in the back of the train and made him eat dust the rest of the way."

"I heard that story in Sacramento City. That's where they are now," Rose said, shaking her head in disgust.

"Yep, that's right, that's where they are now. I guess I'll never forget that devil. Douglas Weatherford was his name," Peter replied.

Rose was speechless and wide-eyed. Bill looked up from what he was doing.

"You wouldn't know a man like that, though. You should feel lucky that you're not here with the Missouri River girls that he conned," Peter said, and then he looked up from his ciphering.

Rose was white as a sheet.

Bill quickly crossed the room. "Rose? Go give a piece of that candy to your horse. I'll finish up here directly."

Rose picked up the things that she had purchased and went outside. Rose put her things on the wagon seat and went to the back. "Sam, you were right about my father being in Sacramento City. He's the one that runs the house of ill-repute!" Rose was over her shock, and now she wondered what to do next. "How did you know that he was there, Sam?"

"Who told you this, Rose?" Bennager asked.

"Pete did, the man that owns the mercantile." She pointed behind her with her thumb.

"I'll be right back." Bennager wanted to know if Rose's fiancé was in the neighborhood as well.

"How could you have been so sure, Sam?" Rose continued to question.

"I just know when that man is lookin' at me, and so does William. That's why he was the one that believed me," Sam answered.

"I'll be darned. And he turned a bunch of poor girls into soiled doves. What am I going to do now? If he was looking at you, then he probably saw me, and he's probably following us, that bastard!" Rose exclaimed.

"He's not followin' us. I don't know why he's not, except I think somethin' happened to him and he couldn't. You would see him by now if he was. We haven't been travelin' very fast," Sam said, not looking up from his work. Bennager came back and continued to help Sam.

"Are those two maniacs finished yet or have they gotten into another brawl?" Rose asked her husband.

"They are behaving very well at the moment, for a change. How was your hard candy?" Bennager teased. "I never took you for a hard candy lover, little girl." Bennager had been reassured by Peter that Douglas Weatherford was not accompanied by another man and figured Rose was correct in her assumption that Richard probably married her sister, and as for Rose's father, he had not a care about him and knew with all his heart that the man couldn't come between him and Rose.

"I don't love hard candy!" Rose fumed. "I got that for the Roman."

Stud Colt patted Rose on the shoulder. He could tell that she was agitated about something. She smiled to let him know that he didn't have to worry about her, then she offered the boy some candy. He didn't like the licorice or the lemon flavors and made it known by sticking his tongue out and letting it fall to the ground. He looked at Rose as if she was trying to hurt him. She smiled and gave him a peppermint candy. Stud could barely stand it, but she seemed dead set about him having it, so he kept it in his mouth and went to find Bill. The Roman liked the lemon candy the best, the burros liked all the flavors, except Toby just wanted his tobacco, which Rose had plenty of now. And the new mule that hadn't been named yet didn't like candy and she didn't like Rose.

The mule moved away from Rose and looked to Bennager for help. She sensed that the woman was dangerous and reckless and Bennager wasn't. Rose thought nothing of the mule not liking candy, and after she put her things safely away in the wagon, she went back and talked to Sam and her husband again. The mule protested with a deafening bray that Rose was even standing next to Bennager, and when Rose reached out to pet her, she shied away. This happened three more times.

"That mule doesn't like you, Rose," Sam suggested.

"What? Why wouldn't she like me?" Rose asked incredulity.

"She just don't, mules are like that. She likes Bennager and she doesn't want you around him," Sam explained.

Bennager blushed. "What are talking about, Sam?"

"Just because you love Rose doesn't mean the mule does. The mule loves you, and she doesn't like Rose bein' around you. Mules are like that," Sam explained, not looking up from his work.

"Well, that's silly, Sam, I hardly know her," Bennager teased.

Rose got mad and went back into the mercantile to find out what was taking so long. When Rose left, Sam explained to Bennager that the mule knew that Rose was crazy and did crazy things, and mules don't do crazy things. When Rose entered the building, she found Bill and Zeb arguing over their purchases.

Bill thought that Zeb had too many beans, and it was a waste of space in the wagon, and Zeb felt the same way about the biscuit makings. Peter Harlan had a good sense of humor and found the whole ridiculous scene to be quite amusing. He had given up on ciphering the purchases until the argument was finished.

"Lord Almighty, do you two old ladies ever quit? Just get the stuff and let's go." Rose acted as if she was exhausted.

"He has enough biscuit makings for an army, and nobody likes his damned biscuits anyway," Zeb complained. "There's not enough room in the wagon for all that stuff."

"I like the biscuits," Rose said.

"Biscuits won't keep you alive like beans will." Zeb was sure of his statement.

"Uncle, how many biscuits can you make with all that stuff?"

"About a hundred millions!" Zeb cried.

Rose smiled at Zeb's distress. "Is that about right, Uncle?"

"It will make a fair amount all right," Bill confessed.

Rose surveyed the counter. The men had done well in getting together plenty of dried fruit, salt pork, coffee, salt, sugar, cocoa and even some fresh eggs for a treat. "What's this?" Rose asked, holding up a long, old, dried-out vegetable.

"That's a chili pepper, for the beans," Zeb explained.

"If it was summertime, this wannabe Mexican would have us eating grasshoppers!" Bill remarked loudly.

Rose made a face and decided to let the men come to a compromise by themselves for a change. "Well, you two need to hurry up and figure this out, we need to get going," Rose said as nicely as she could. Bill knew that the confirmation of her father being as close as Sacramento City was weighing on her, and she wanted to get as far away as possible from the area.

Bill put his hand on her shoulder to let her know that he understood, but he said, "Make Zeb put some of the beans back. I hate beans!"

Rose shook her head and looked at Zeb who was looking away defiantly. "He's the only one who likes beans," Bill whined.

"Maybe he could leave one of those fifty-pound sacks here if you asked nicely," Rose suggested. "Maybe he will do it if you put one of those barrels of flour back."

Both men did as Rose kindly suggested at the same time, glowering at each other like schoolboys while they crossed the room. Rose raised one eyebrow and shook her head. She directed Stud Colt to come over and help her haul the food to the wagon. He smiled, but he wouldn't come near her. "What's wrong with him now?" Rose asked.

Bill looked up to see what was going on. "Oh, I forgot to tell you, Stud hates whatever you were feeding him outside. What did you give him, tobacco? He came in here with his tongue hanging out and complaining about it."

Rose laughed. "It wasn't tobacco, it was candy. Tell him I'm sorry and I won't bother him about it anymore."

Bill translated, and Stud Colt crossed the room and patted Rose hard on the shoulder and helped her. When she got outside, she was pleasantly surprised by the smell of fresh apple pie. She investigated with her nose until she found the little restaurant where the pies were just coming out of the oven.

"Hello," Rose said to the couple in the kitchen. "I need some pie," she said absolutely.

The man and woman smiled pleasantly at Rose, and the friendly man teased, "You seem pretty sure about that, miss, but its better when it cools down for an hour or two. It gives the apples time to soak up their juice and soften up. You don't want to cut into an apple pie too early, you'll ruin it, and it takes a lot of work to make a good apple pie."

Rose was drooling. "How many pies can you sell me right now?"

"I can sell you two, but I won't sell them to you for at least an hour. I can see that you are the kind of girl that would cut into an apple pie and ruin it," the nice little man explained. He handed Rose a piece of cloth and silently directed her to wipe her chin.

Rose turned four shades of red and started counting the seconds away in her head since she couldn't find a clock. The man's wife could see that the young lady was having a difficult time waiting for the hour to pass and offered her a cup of coffee and a menu. It never occurred to Rose that she was in a regular restaurant because she was so fixated on the pies. "I'll be back," Rose told the sweet lady and left. Rose went back into the mercantile, where Bill and Zeb were settling the bill, and purchased a pocket watch, and then she asked everybody to come to the restaurant and have supper. She even convinced Peter Harlan to close the store and join them. He did because he wasn't in the mood to give miners anymore credit for the day, and he wondered what Mr. Ford and Mr. Jones would find to argue about next.

When Rose walked back into the restaurant, she showed the nice man her new pocket watch, and the man laughed heartily. The woman was pleased to see that many people come in at one time. She thought they were a merry group. "Well, hello there, Mr. Harlan. Have you closed early this evening?" the kind lady asked.

"Yes, I did, Mrs. Howell, these folks encouraged it." The smell of the apple pie aroused everybody's appetite, and Mrs. Howell's coffee was the best that they had ever had. Zeb didn't say one word about witches since the Howells were as kind as angels, as kind as Anna even.

Bill ordered fried chicken for himself and Stud, knowing that Stud was going to eat whatever was served to him with his hands. Everyone else ordered steak because they knew they would be able to eat all the fowl they wanted to once they were back on the trail. Mr. Howell continued to work on making more apple pies, and he laughed at Rose who was trying to see how he was doing it while trying to have good table manners at the same time. Mr. Howell finally waved her into the kitchen to give her a lesson while his wife cooked for the party.

He already had the apples cut up, so he showed her how to add flour, sugar, a dash of vinegar, and cinnamon. "Stir it all together, and let it set while you make the pie crust," he instructed her. Then he mixed flour, lard, salt, and cold water. Rose watched as he rolled the crust out into a perfect circle, put it in a round dish, scooped in the apples, added butter to the mound, laid the second crust over the mound, and pinched the two crusts together on the edge. "This keeps the juices in the pie, and never forget to slash the top to let out the steam. It has to cook for at least an hour, and it has to cool for at least an hour," Mr. Howell reminded her.

Rose was grateful for the lesson, but she didn't think that she would ever have time to perform such a task and she didn't have an oven either.

"I'll try to remember this lesson after I get settled if that ever happens," Rose said, laughing.

"Are you with a traveling circus?" Mr. Howell asked sarcastically.

Rose looked out into the dining room. "Let's see, there's me, an old Black fighter, an Indian boy, the two arguing mountain mean, and one normal man. I guess we could be part of a circus, we only lack an elephant." They laughed together. Mr. Howell was afraid that he might have hurt her feelings for a moment and was glad that he hadn't.

"Are you prospectors then?" he asked.

"We are aiming to start a cattle rancho northeast of here."

"Well, that might be a prosperous endeavor. I wish you lots of luck, Mrs. Rasmussen."

"Thank you, Mr. Howell," Rose replied.

Rose helped Mrs. Howell bring the plates of food to the table and then sat down next to her husband who was looking at her admiringly. Stud enjoyed his fried chicken but was curious about how the rest of the people were using their utensils. Bill convinced him to try the fork to eat his potatoes. He told Bill that such nonsense was a waste of time, but when Bill explained that it would please the ladies, he was eager to comply. He found that Bill was right when he saw Rose smiling at him for his efforts.

Finally, it was time for the pie. It was cut seven ways, and each person was in rapture. Stud Colt had never tasted such a thing; he had never had sugar in his diet whatsoever, except for the berries that grew near his home and the apples that Mr. Sheldon had given him. Stud finished his pie quickly and wanted more. Everyone else was full to the brim and couldn't eat another bite, even Rose. Stud was smiling broadly while he told Bill that he wanted more pie, but Bill shook his head and shrugged, and Stud stopped smiling. It was a sure sign of displeasure that everyone noticed.

"What's wrong with him?" Rose and Zeb asked in unison.

"He wants more pie," Bill translated. "I told him that the plate is empty, and he said that there is another one and he wants it." Stud was talking at the same time as Bill was, and Bill suddenly scowled at Stud and then laughed. "He says he's fixing to make war like I did if he doesn't get some more pie."

Everyone wanted to laugh, but to Stud, this was a serious situation, and they didn't want to offend his native right to make war over apple pie. Zeb quickly jumped to his feet making a big show of protecting the White people from the young Indian warrior and set the second pie down in front of Stud. The war was over. Stud was smiling again.

Rose was hoping to have the second pie for breakfast the next morning but figured coffee and biscuits would have to do in order to keep the peace.

"Supper was delicious, Mrs. Howell. That was elk, wasn't it?" Zeb asked.

"Yes, it was. There are a couple of men that we pay to bring us meat. I hope your cattle rancho is prosperous. It would be wonderful to put beefsteak on the menu, Mrs. Rasmussen," Mrs. Howell remarked.

"Yes, but that elk steak was the best meat that I've ever had. We ought to look into raising a herd of elk. I hear that the Mexican cattle don't have much meat on their bones," Rose commented.

"It's best to live on buffalo whenever you can" Bill said.

"I like elk better!" Zeb said loudly.

Bill closed his eyes tightly, bracing for the ensuing argument. "You can use every part of a buffalo, and the meat tastes better. Elk is too lean."

"I would rather rot in hell than eat another buffalo or one of your damned salty biscuits. Elk is better," Zeb whispered out of respect for the Howells.

The new argument delighted Peter Harlan and Stud Colt. This was why Peter closed early and joined the merry group for supper. Stud wanted to know what was being said. He was afraid that Zeb was saying bad things about women, but when he found out what they were talking about, he told Bill that elk was better than buffalo. Bill rolled his eyes at the boy on account of the fact that Stud had never even seen a buffalo let alone ate one.

Rose looked on in awe at how easily the two men could get into a squabble with one another and was surprised that they had managed to behave all the way through supper. Sam and Bennager knew how quickly a scene like this could escalate into a fistfight, and they decided that it was time to go.

Everyone said their thank-yous and good evenings to the Howells and Peter, and Zeb and Bill continued the loud discussion on the way out the door. Stud said thank you in his special way with the hard shoulder pat for each person that had shown him kindness. He praised the apple pie in his native tongue, and the Howells smiled, thinking that they were pretty sure of what Stud was talking about.

The party filled up their water barrels at the town well and camped for the night so they could get an early start. Sam was glad that they had eaten in town because now he could finish his carpentry on the wagon. Zeb and Bill had forgotten about their arguing for the time being while the discussion about Douglas was growing. Zeb and Stud Colt didn't care about Douglas Weatherford, so they stood around the campfire and tried to learn each other's language. The rest of the party stood around the wagon, consulting with Sam.

"I guess Doug came here for the gold rush like everybody else did, but he's so lazy that he's using those girls to make his fortune, Bill suggested.

"It's the same way that he used those poor girls back home," Rose said in disgust. "I can't believe that I'm related to that man."

"What do you reckon happened to your mother and sister if he came here on his own with a wagonload of women?" Bill asked.

"I'm sure that Mother must have kicked him out, but what I can't figure is how he got the money to build a hotel and a gambling house. Mother was the one with the money in the family. She's the one that sent me on my way. All that I can think of is she got so fed up with him that she paid him to leave. As for my sister, I'm sure that my father—" Rose paused, choking on her words. "I'm sure he married Lily off to that Hawthorne family."

"So your mother had enough money that she could pay Doug to go away, huh?" Bill questioned.

"I don't know," Rose answered, shaking her head and looking at the ground.

Sam was thinking that Doug probably stole the woman's money and left her destitute or he just killed her in some sneaky way, but he kept his thoughts to himself. Bennager was happy that Rose's father was more interested in running a whorehouse than looking for his daughter and wished that Rose could forget about the bastard. He didn't seem worth a damn to Bennager, let alone the time wasted on speculation and the apparent worry that was on the faces of the others, but Rose was his wife, and he wanted her to know that her worries were his, too, even if the conversation was grating on his nerves. Bennager rolled a smoke and tried to stay engaged in the conversation. It was a wonder to him why Bill seemed to be so concerned with the matter.

Bill was contemplating the topic while he helped Sam, and finally, he said, "If Doug had spotted you in Sacramento City, then he would be following us out of curiosity at least. He's not following us, so I say we go on about our business, and if he gets in the way, we'll deal with him then. I don't like him being this close and I do worry about what he will do if he spots you, but we all know what to do if he tries to make any trouble."

Rose was becoming sick to her stomach with fret, and her head was pounding at the thought of what might have become of her mother and sister. It wasn't much of a stretch for her to think that her mother had come to a terrible end, but she thought that if she made such a horrible claim out loud then it might be true. She wondered if she would ever know the truth and she knew there was only one way to find out. All she could do at this point was to hope for the best.

Rose turned to her husband. She needed to feel his strong gentle arms protecting her, and Bennager was competent in performing the task. Rose came to realize that as long as this man was by her side, her father couldn't be a threat that she couldn't handle. She took in a deep breath and let out a long sigh as if she was cleansing her spirit of fear and uncertainty. "I guess you are right, Uncle. When we get back to Sacramento City, I'll try to send word to Mother and Lily. Maybe I'll hear from them someday soon."

"I think Stud had too much pie!" Zeb hollered.

The group at the wagon looked over at the campfire and saw that Stud Colt was jumping back and forth over the fire, and then he would run around and tap Zeb on the head every time he passed by. "Look at what you taught him to do now, you old buzzard! You taught him how to bother me when there's nothing better to do!" Zeb complained to Bill.

Stud knew that Zeb was getting mad at him, so he started climbing trees instead. When he got to the tree that was sheltering the animals, he jumped onto the back of his horse, landing on his feet. He was proud of himself for accomplishing such a daring feat, and he smiled broadly and threw his arms straight into the air. Stud jumped up from his horse's back and into the tree again so he could attempt the daring feat twice. "Somebody better capture him. That ugly Roman-nosed son of a bitch will kill him if he gets the chance!" Zeb yelled, fearing for the boy's life.

Everyone made a mad dash for the stock. Sam didn't want his little burros to get hurt. The new mule was very happy to see Bennager come to her rescue, and in all the chaos, she was able to kick Rose in the leg and get away with it while Rose collected the Roman and Bill's horse. Bill waited at the bottom of the tree for Stud Colt after reprimanding him for his craziness.

"He ate too much pie! My children behave wildly when they eat too much food with sugar in it!" Zeb informed, trying to be helpful. "He's probably never had sugar in his life! I should have thought about that before I set that pie in front of him."

"He'll be all right, Zeb," Bill said kindly. "I should have known better, too, but when the rascal threatened to make war, I forgot about his health. I'll stand watch with him tonight. I doubt he'll be able to sleep for a while, and I'll keep an eye on him. Watch yourself tonight, Little Rose!" Bill hollered. "This boy reminds me of myself when I used to run out of whiskey. There's no tellin' what kind of trouble he'll get himself into tonight," Bill teased as they all watched Stud climb around on the branches of the big oaks that they had camped by.

7

Dan Dunaway woke up to the rancid smell that Douglas Weatherford had left behind in his hotel. It was the smell of filth, alcohol, and sin. Weatherford hadn't recognized Dan the night before, but Dan had been in the same wagon train with the ugly man last summer. Dan had spent the last four months witnessing the treatment of the girls and what Weatherford had forced them to become. Dan had always wanted to do something for the girls, but he didn't know how to help since he didn't have any financial resources. He was from a family of one brother and four sisters and had faced the loss of one sister after she made a poor choice in finding a husband. By the time that Dan and his brother had learned that their older sister was in trouble, in her first year of marriage, her husband had already beaten her to death the day before they arrived to collect her.

Dan had watched the six soiled doves parade up and down the street of Sacramento City, and as each day passed, their giddy gaits became an oppressed, black-and-blue, limping from time to time, trudging, and he knew that their way of life was weighing on their bodies and spirits. Dan had witnessed the big Irishman the day before. He knew that the Irishman didn't even know the redheaded Trina, but he knew it would bother Weatherford if he thought that she was in love with the man who had beaten the devil out of him. Dan thought that if the girl wasn't in love with the big man, then she was a fool. He was glad to see her safe, and he cringed at the thought of the ugly Weatherford touching any woman. It made him sick whenever he tried to put himself in their shoes.

Dan had waited all day to see what the townspeople were going to do for a man who lay crushed in front of his own gambling house, and he found it to be a very curious thing that not one person in Sacramento City had one ounce of sympathy for a man that could be dead or dying. Dan had sipped coffee and watched and waited all day, and then he came up with a plan to help the girls and himself at the same time. He had laughed to himself when he thought of it, thinking that it would be a pretty good coup if it worked out, but he had his doubts. He figured that eventually, some miner that owed him money would drag the wicked, revolting man out of the cold night air, but they didn't, and when Dan saw Weatherford squirm out of the blackness that the Irishman had put him in, he hurried to put his laughable plan into action.

"Wake up, ladies! Wake up, it's time for you to know what the new rules of the house are, wake up!" Dan hollered through the hall while he slammed two tin saucepans together.

Dan was waiting in the kitchen when the scantily clad ladies finally presented themselves. Each one of them glared at the man who boldly claimed to have new rules for them to live by, and Dan couldn't help but laugh when he saw the look of hatred and distrust in their faces and wondered if they would ever have regular lives after what they had been through.

"Well, your former employer didn't spare any expenses when he built this place. We have a brand-new wood cookstove that's never been used, a beautiful dining room collecting dust, and wagonloads of dirty sheets. Weatherford signed this building over to me last night, and I plan on running it as a hotel and nothing else. You ladies are free to do as you like since the man who claims to own you can't stop you now. He can't beat you and he can't foul you with his dirty stench anymore. If any of you are interested in having a real job, I'm hiring cooks and maids. If any of you have become accustomed to your present lifestyle, then I will have to ask you to leave." The girls looked at each other with doubtful expressions.

"What do you pay, smart man?" one of the girls jibed.

"I don't have any money, but I have this place, a roof over my head, and I think once the stench is gone, I'll have customers. I'll split the profits equally with anyone who wants to work here." He cringed when he said it, but he planned on going to the diggings in the summer to make his fortune anyway.

"If we work here, then we live here, right?" another girl asked.

"Yes, but instead of having separate rooms, I'll be asking you to bunk together so we will have more rooms for paying customers," Dan answered.

"Are you going to bunk with us?" a different girl asked, and all the girls giggled.

Dan was prepared for that question and calmly told them no without blushing. The girls were starting to circle him, mentally, like vultures. They figured that they had an innocent by the tail, and a couple of the girls began to use their hatred for men and their feminine wiles to wrap Dan around their little fingers. Dan had sisters and knew that girls were apt to try anything to get their way, and he was prepared for that as well.

"Oh, where will you stay, smart man? What's wrong? Are you afraid to sleep with us?" the first girl asked sarcastically.

Dan didn't want to hurt their feelings, but he expected them to get nasty with him. "I'm sorry to have to say this to you, ladies, but you would have to soak you privates in the American River for two years straight before I would even consider bunking with you. If you're lucky and you work hard and conduct yourselves as ladies, you might each one of ya' find a good man who would be willing to stick his pecker in you after you've been had at by Weatherford. You might even find a good man that doesn't know you were had at by Weatherford. I'm willing to give you gals a chance at that, but you'll never have to worry about where my pecker is, and if you don't want a legitimate job, I left Weatherford up the street. You are all welcome to join him, I'm sure he would appreciate it." Dan stood his ground and looked each one of them in the eye, waiting for them to decide.

A quiet, thoughtful blonde girl, who Dan had seen with black eyes a time or two, said, "Mister, I don't know who you think you are, but you should know that bastard isn't going to let you get away with this. There ain't no law here abouts, in case you haven't noticed, and when he gets healed up, he'll kill you, and you wouldn't be the first one he's killed either. What do you think will happen to us then?"

These girls were weak-minded. Dan figured they would be since they never made an effort to defend themselves. He reckoned most women didn't have the fighting spirit that men had, and they didn't have the sense to know a bad man when they saw one. Dan knew that the job offer would have to come with a commitment from him to keep these women safe and that meant that he probably wouldn't get to go to the diggings right away. "I'll guess you'll have to count on me not to let Weatherford kill me, and if you want to change your lives for the better, then you'll have to learn to disassociate yourselves from that kind of filth. That man can only hurt you if you let him. Think about that while you think about whom you want to work for. In the meantime, you gals need to wear decent clothes while you are under this roof. Do you have any?"

The girls looked at each other for a few moments, and then they all shook their heads silently.

"Can any of you sew?" Dan asked. Two of them nodded their heads. "How many of you want to stay and work this place?"

The girls looked at each other again, and silently, they all raised their hands as if they were in school. Dan stood up and put his hands on his hips and looked each one of them in the eye. "Then let's go to work!"

*****

Stud Colt had a hard time moving the next morning. He was sore and scraped up from wrestling with oak trees, had small burns on his hands and feet from falling in the fire, and he complained of an aching head. Shortly after the party got moving, everybody noticed that Stud had to keep hiding behind trees or riding ahead a good distance to hide behind a rolling hill. By the time the group arrived at the ferry that crossed the San Joaquin River, the only thing that Stud was talking about was his backside and how he thought that he must have rubbed the skin off it. Everybody could tell by the look on Bill's face and Stud's hand gestures exactly what Stud was complaining about, and they were grateful they didn't savvy his lingo.

"That's what you get for being greedy and threatening to make war on folks. Rose bought that extra pie so we could all have another treat tonight, but I reckon you think pies grow on trees or something, you damned big peckered Indian. I reckon if your brain was as big as your pecker, you would almost be as smart as me. You should apologize for threatening to make war on folks who buy you supper and teach you table manners and show you how to keep on good terms with the women folks," Bill told Stud. He could see that Stud felt bad about taking the pie and not just because he had it running out of his backside now.

Bill also noted that he hadn't bothered Zeb yet today, and that was why Zeb looked bored and ready to fall asleep in his saddle, so he continued with Stud. "I reckon if your brain was as big as your pecker, then you would be a little smarter than Zeb, but that's not saying very much." Stud produced a thin smile, but Bill couldn't make the boy's famous smile return with such a vulgar comment.

"What did you say about me, you damned old coyote?" Zeb asked loudly.

"Nothin'!" Bill replied.

"You said something! I heard you say my name!" Zeb argued.

"I was talking about another guy," Bill assured.

"What other guy?"

"Zeb, you damned idiot!" Bill yelled.

"Zeb who?" Zeb asked.

"I don't know his last name," Bill replied with a scowl on his face.

"What did you say about him?" Zeb asked calmly.

"That's none of your damned business! I was talking to Stud, not you, you nosy bastard!"

"Why can't you tell me what you said about him?" Zeb continued.

"Because I don't want to, and he wouldn't like it if I did."

"Who wouldn't like it?" Zeb asked.

"Zeb!" Bill yelled.

"Zeb who?"

Bennager, Rose, and Sam were following the others and were close enough to hear the ridiculous banter that the two men refused to break from. It was as if they were twins, and each one had the same amount of sass to keep the stupid argument going. Rose looked at Bennager and Sam and then shook her head in disbelief, and they all started to snicker on account of the fact that it seemed as though Zeb believed that Bill was talking about another guy named Zeb.

Rose struck up a casual conversation with the ferryman as they boarded. He told her that he was worried about his family and business was slow. He pointed out the little farm that he and his family had started back in '41, and he explained that he needed all the capital that he could get because his wife kept having babies. He claimed that she had one a year, whether he liked it or not, and he was afraid that after a couple of more years, he wouldn't be able to feed them all.

Rose widened her eyes in awe and wondered if this man was as brainless as he seemed or if he was just pulling her leg. She promptly dropped the conversation and patiently waited for the west shore to reach her and take her away from the ferryman so she wouldn't catch whatever ailment he must be suffering from.

Zeb quietly conceived a plan to torment the ferryman as how he looked to be an easy target. He had Bill ask Stud to show the ferryman his pecker on cue. Bill giggled like a schoolboy at Zeb's plan, and Stud agreed to do as Zeb asked. He liked that the old men were asking him to be a participant in one of their clever jokes.

Zeb and Stud walked up to the man while he labored at his rope. "I couldn't help but overhear your conversation with the lady and your complaints about your wife having children all the time. My wife does the same thing to me, but I finally figured out what causes it."

"What?" the ferryman asked, seeming to be excited to finally solve the mystery that had been causing so much work for his pea brain.

Zeb nudged Stud Colt, and the boy hauled his pecker out of his deerskins. The man looked at it, looked at the smiling boy, and furrowed his brows as if he was in deep thought, looked at his farmhouse, and came to the conclusion that Stud Colt was the father of all those screaming little toe-headed brats that were eating up all of his profits. Instinctively, Stud knew that the man was angry with him, and he quickly put himself together and ran for Bill at the same time. The ferryman stopped pulling his rope and tried to grab Stud, but the boy was too fast. "You little Indian son of a bitch! You've been banging my wife! When I get my hands on you, I'm gonna kill you!"

Stud was frightened and didn't know what to do except run. He weaved around the animals, which they didn't mind since they were used to Stud after the night before, but when the idiotic ferryman tried it, they all became very upset. They began to shift around to get away from the man, and in the blink of an eye, the ferry began to sway. Rose and Bennager were at the opposite end of where the clamor had started, and all they had heard was the ferryman's outburst. Rose looked back at the other end of the ferry and saw Zeb and her uncle bent over with laughter and slapping their knees. They had not a care in the world that the ferry was in danger of tipping over.

Bennager caught the ferryman by the throat as he and Stud passed by him. Rose had never seen Bennager when he was truly angry, but he was just as she suspected that he would be. Bennager held the man's life in his hand. He had no intention of killing him unless the ferry turned over and then Bennager planned on breaking his neck when they hit the water.

Bennager continued to hold the man by the throat while Stud Colt hid behind Rose. "You better hope these animals settle down, mister," Bennager said calmly and quietly. The mule began to bray a ballad of discontent and was sorry now that she had blindly followed the stupid horses onto the floating contraption. She was also very aware that her Bennager was upset, but she knew that he would save her as he had the night before. Stud put his hands over his ears, and Rose glared at the mountain men, who she figured were peeing on themselves by now, bit off a piece of her plug tobacco, and then mounted up on the Roman and watched the west shore in disgust.

When the animals calmed down, Bennager said, "I'm finished with your nonsense. We paid to cross, so get this thing across this damned river."

"That damned Indian's been bangin' my wife!" the ferryman cried over the mule's continuous braying.

Bennager backhanded the rude, simple-minded man across the face. "That's for being crass in front of my wife! That boy has never even seen your wife, you moron. I have a good idea of what's got you riled, but I don't give a damn about your problems. If I have to operate this ferry, then I assure you that you won't be on it, so are you going to pull that rope or are you going to swim?"

The ferryman skulked back to the spot where he had been, before Zeb went to pestering him, and finished his job. Everybody off-loaded, except for Bennager. Sam and the burros still had to cross, and Bennager was sure that the dimwitted man was incapable of performing the task without his presence. He was also certain that he needed to cool down before he faced the other maniacs that he had unwittingly become associated with. Bill and Zeb knew that they might have pushed Bennager too far with their last antic, but as soon as Bennager was out of earshot, they started laughing all over again, especially when Bill informed Stud Colt why the ferryman was chasing him.

"Zeb, you are bad. You didn't tell me that the man would be angry with me. Now I will have to swim this river to see my mother again," Stud told him.

Bill translated, and the mountain men started laughing all over again. Stud was sad, and he rode his horse to catch up with Rose to apologize for making Bennager angry and for eating all her pie and threatening war on folks.

Rose had reached her limit with the old surveyors, and like Bennager, she felt that she needed time to cool off, but she felt sorry for the Indian boy. Those men had used him again to play a joke, and she knew that it always made the pleasant boy feel bad when they did that to him. She listened to Stud's words compassionately and figured that she understood some of what he was trying to convey. Finally, she patted him hard on his shoulder, and he smiled slightly, but she could tell that he was still sad. Rose and Stud rode up the river a piece and watched Bennager and Sam make the crossing. Rose hoped that her husband would help her come up with a plan to get the mountain men back for their bad deeds.

"I thought you folks were going to roll this ferry over. What happened?" Sam asked Bennager while they crossed the river. Bennager was glaring at the ferryman, even though he knew that Zeb and Bill were behind the near catastrophe.

"You know something, Sam? Those two damned idiots don't care how much trouble they cause. I thought for sure we were going over, and those two never stopped laughing. They wouldn't have cared if we had gone over. They probably would have thought that to be even more hilarious. I don't know what they did to get this damned idiot riled, but they did something. That I do know," Bennager explained.

"I reckon they would be just as happy to swim this river as to cross it on this ferry. It probably doesn't matter to them one way or the other," Sam suggested.

"That one feller told me that damned Indian was pokin' my wife!" the ferryman hollered. He figured he was safe from Bennager's wrath now that he was talking mean about the two old men.

"Shut up! I already told you about that!" Bennager yelled.

"You'll have to pay me for these extra trips you're takin'!" the ferryman yelled back at him.

Bennager pointed his finger at the man. "I'll throw you over and pull this son of a bitch myself if you don't shut up!" Bennager retorted loudly.

The yelling was getting on Toby's nerves, and when he saw Rose on the other side of the river, he brayed in a pleading way for a piece of tobacco. The new mule brayed back, but she wasn't conversing with Toby. She wanted Bennager to hurry up and come back to her. Sam had to laugh since he was the only one who knew what the animals wanted.

"What's so funny, Sam?" Bennager asked.

Sam shook his head and thought for a moment about what a bizarre adventure they were all having. "I wish I had grandchildren to tell this story to. You're mad now, but you'll laugh about it someday. What gets me is I was watchin' this thing gettin' ready to tip over, and that crazy wife of yours decided to get on her horse. Why do you reckon she did that? You would think that crazy horse would be the first one to spook, and you would think that Rose would be gettin' ready to swim, but she just mounted up and waited for the shore while you had hold of this fella. Why do you reckon she did that?" Sam asked laughing in a confused way.

"I was so scared that we were going over I didn't notice that she had done that Sam," Bennager answered with wonder on his face.

Sam shook his head, still laughing. "That Rose is really somethin', what I'm not sure, but she's somethin' all right." Sam thought about the situation a little more. "I guess she trusted you to make the ferry stop swaying, either that or she was gettin' ready to swim for it."

The skulking ferryman finally completed his job. Bennager was admiring Rose as she and Stud rode up to meet him. The strange little ferryman with eight toe-headed children never said a word about Bennager having to pay for the two additional trips that he made, but Bennager paid the man's fee, and then he explained to him that the mountain men were bothersome jokers and they liked to tease people and that he shouldn't believe anything they say. "Do any of your children look like Indians? Now think about it real hard before you answer," Bennager advised.

The man did think about it until it looked like he might hurt himself. "Well, do they?" Bennager was becoming impatient.

"No," the man confessed.

"All right then. Do you understand those men were teasing you?"

"Yeah, I reckon," the ferryman said slowly.

"All right then, thank you for your time and goodbye," Bennager abruptly finished the conversation.

The man nodded his head sharply and sat down on a wooden box that he used for a chair and stared at the deck, waiting for his next customer.

The group decided to push on and stop for lunch later when they were out of sight of the ferry to avoid any further trouble with the dimwit. Bennager had cooled down a little, but he still wasn't in the mood to listen to the jokers, and he doubted that he would ever laugh about their antics of this day, no matter what Sam said.

"We have a storm coming," Zeb said about an hour after lunch.

Stud was the only one interested in his comment, and when it was translated, he nodded his head in agreement.

Rose looked at Bennager, who was still steamed at Zeb and Bill, and he returned her glance with a slight smile. No one bothered to argue with Zeb about the weather, not after the last storm that he predicted, but Bennager and Rose didn't want to talk to him about it either.

Sam finally broke the silence. "Will it be a bad one?"

"It will be a long one," Zeb answered downheartedly. They were a day and a half away from the rancho that he was leading them to, but he was four days away from Anna and he was going to have to travel through a torrential downpour to get to his wife.

"How long will it be?" Sam asked after five minutes when he realized that nobody else was going to ask.

"It will probably last for about a month," Zeb answered.

Sam pondered the answer and looked at Rose and Bennager who returned his look with the shaking of their heads. "What's Stud think?" Sam asked Zeb.

Zeb furrowed his brow and gave Sam a dirty look. Nobody challenged his weather predictions, but he didn't say anything. Because of Horny Bill's bad influence on him, he was going to lose his credibility. It would do him good to go visit his family and get away from that crazy buzzard for a while. Bill told Stud what Zeb said about the length of the storm, and Stud agreed.

Sam looked at Rose and Bennager again. "That's a lot of rain," he said quietly.

"If it blows this fog away, I bet we'll be able to see farther," Rose mumbled.

The party stopped for the night about an hour before dark. Bill started the biscuits, Zeb started the beans, Sam started the coffee, Rose set up the tents, and Bennager and Stud went out for more firewood and to find some camp meat. Bennager was eager to try out his new carbine, and if he didn't get away from Bill and Zeb, he thought he might try it out on them. He unloaded the gunpowder kegs off the mule and told Rose to get it undercover and away from the campfire or it would either blow up or get wet. "If it rains for a month, it's bound to get wet anyway. I don't know why you needed all of that gunpowder," Bennager said to her gruffly.

Rose rubbed her brow with the back of her hand, put her hands on her hips, and looked at her husband for a long moment, trying to think of a use for the stuff before it went to waste. Finally, she asked, "Zeb, when is this rainstorm going to hit us?"

Zeb was happy that the woman was taking him seriously, and even though he wanted to tease her like he had before on the Sacramento River, he didn't because he knew he needed to make up for being an ass on the ferry. "It will probably start tonight or first thing in the morning. If it wasn't for this fog, we would have been able to see the clouds building up. As for this fog, it probably won't go away for a while, I'm sorry to say."

Rose took Bennager aside. "Wouldn't the gunpowder be useful for starting fires in the rain?"

"Yes, dear, but only if you keep it dry," Bennager reminded her again.

"Well, maybe we could figure out a way to bother Bill and Zeb with it," Rose said with a smirk on her face.

For the first time since the ferry incident, Bennager smiled sweetly at his wife and kissed her. "Yes, let's think on that. I'll be back after a while, and I'll take my mule so she won't cry for me while I'm gone."

"That damned mule kicked me last night!" Rose exclaimed. "Sam was right, she hates me." Rose laughed.

Trees were scarce in the San Joaquin Valley, but Stud and Bennager traveled from tree to tree, picking up branches and sticks to keep the fire going for the night. Stud found tracks of two little children who had been doing the same thing two days earlier, and he tried to show Bennager, but Bennager heard turkeys roosting for the night, and he gestured to Stud to come with him. He couldn't shoot one with his new carbine, but Rose's new pistol was sufficient for the job. Stud went back to the tracks and made Bennager look at them, just before dark, and showed him that there were little children nearby. Stud held his nose, showing Bennager that he thought little children stank, and then they went back to camp.

Stud told Bill that there was a family of Yokuts nearby, and he wondered if Bill knew the language. Bill didn't because he hadn't spent much time in this valley. Stud said, "The family is close because I can smell those stinky children."

"Maybe they will stop stinking after it has rained for a couple of days," Bill said, smiling.

Stud shook his head and held his nose. "I don't think rain can wash away the smell of children."

"You will have children one day, and you won't think they stink," Bill said, thinking of his own child that had died and who he missed very much.

"I will run away until they grow big," Stud argued.

Bill patted him on the shoulder. "No, you won't," Bill said with deep sorrow in his eyes.

Stud dropped the subject. He had never seen this sorrow in Bill before, but he knew what it meant. Stud picked up some biscuits and bit into one.

"Good," Stud said to Bill in English, and the sorrow went away.

Later, when supper was finished, the party gathered by the fire. The mule started braying again because Rose was sitting next to Bennager. Bennager took his wife's hand. "Go get your candy, and let's get you two acquainted. It's time for that silly animal to know that you're my number one girl."

The mule was certainly not going to accept a piece of candy from Rose. She closed her eyes tightly when she saw the two of them walking together. It was as if she was having terrible pain. Bennager started scratching her throat while Rose just continued to stand by her husband. Finally, the mule opened her eyes to see if Rose was gone, and when she saw that she wasn't, the mule blinked profusely and threw her head up and to the side, shying away as if someone was standing in front of her, waving a coat around and trying to spook her away. She held her ground, but she was very aggravated and began to bray.

Sam was watching the scene, and he chuckled and shook his head. Bennager wasn't sure what to do next, but Rose knew that she was dealing with a jealous female. Rose eased her body into Bennager's, and he got the hint and welcomed her by wrapping her up with his loving arms, and he kissed his wife sweetly. The mule cried a song of deep pain, sorrow, and heartbreak until everyone else in the party felt sorry for her and started to harbor ill feelings toward Rose and Bennager. Bill gave Sam a hard look, waiting for Sam to make the couple stop, but Sam only shook his head.

Bill couldn't take it anymore. "Hey, quit tormenting that poor animal. You're breaking her heart and ours too!" he hollered.

"Oh, does it bother you, Uncle?" Rose said, smiling.

"Yes, by God, it does!" he hollered.

"Good!" Rose hollered back at him. Rose and Bennager gave up on trying to show the mule how things were, and they returned to the campfire.

Stud Colt went to the mule to console her. The old girl put up with Stud. Bennager was her favorite, but Stud was a pleasant, caring boy. He explained to the old girl that he didn't like Rose's candy either. He spoke to her in a way that soothed her, and she finally quieted down.

She knew that she would get the chance to kick the reckless woman again. That would teach her for fouling her Bennager with her craziness.

It was all that Zeb could do to bite his tongue. He desperately wanted to tease Rose about how the mule thought she was a witch and that the mule was just trying to warn an innocent man, but he didn't. He knew that the joke that he had played earlier had rubbed Rose and Bennager the wrong way, and his luck would run out with Bennager if he started flapping his jaw about Rose being a witch.

Sam cleaned and organized his kitchen, got a cup of coffee, and sat down by Rose as the night air grew damper and colder than any night so far since they had been off the Sacramento River. Sam could feel a definite change in his bones, his hands and knees especially, and he wished that Rose had purchased more brandy. He didn't know how he was going to survive his arthritic pain for a month straight of rainy weather.

"You didn't buy enough brandy to get my bones through a month of rain," Sam said chuckling, even though he wasn't joking.

"Reckon you'll have to learn to drink tequila," Rose suggested. "But I'll lay off the brandy, Sam."

"The folks that we're going to see don't drink. They won't have any tequila," Zeb said.

It was a lie, but he was bored and wanted to get a reaction out of Rose about folks who don't drink. It didn't work. Rose was bound to ignore the man.

Sam sighed. "I guess I'll have to live with it."

Zeb leaned over and tested the pot of beans. "I can bring some tequila or whatever you prefer back from Monterey."

"Monterey? What the devil? What are you doing, going home?" Bill complained.

"Yes, I'm going home to see my Anna and the children. They'll be missing me by now," Zeb said.

"You just want to see if she's still there," Bill jibed.

"I have no doubt about my Anna," Zeb said defiantly. "I'll get you folks acquainted with Pablo and his family, but then I'm going home. I'll be back in a couple of weeks."

That statement was music to Bennager's ears. He thought the break from Bill and Zeb's arguing and mischief would do him good. He wrapped his arms around Rose's waist and held her tight. She welcomed him by leaning her body into his warm chest. She could hear and feel his strong heartbeat, and she felt as warm and protected as if she was sitting with him in front of a fireplace surrounded by four walls. She was happy for Zeb that soon he would be feeling what she was feeling now. Rose dreamed of the day when she would have her four walls, but for now, she couldn't feel anymore content with what she had. The depth of her soul and body quaked when Bennager put his lips to her ear and whispered, "I think we should give the boys a reprieve. My head just stopped aching."

Stud Colt was complaining to Bill. "I want the rain to hurry. The smell of those children is getting bad. I should be smelling the turkey, but I only smell them," he said, holding his nose.

Rose gave the boy a quizzical look. "What's the matter, Uncle?"

"Oh, there's a family of Yokut Indians around here, and Stud is complaining about the smell of the children. He is gifted with an acute sense of smell when it comes to Indian children. As a matter of fact, he is wondering what is wrong with the rest of us because we aren't complaining about what he thinks is such a foul stench. He's like a hound dog," Bill explained.

"Are these Indians dangerous?" Rose asked.

"I don't know, I never met them," Bill replied smartly.

"Well, maybe we should stand watch after all," Rose suggested.

"I don't think there is anything to worry about. Pablo has never complained about trouble with Indians before," Zeb assured.

Stud was still holding his nose, and it was apparent that the smell was very annoying to him. He said to Bill, "They are so close that I can taste them in my mouth. I have to go now." Rose watched the boy take his bedroll and head south on foot. "Where is he going?"

"The Yokut family is coming in for a visit and they probably need some hot food, and Stud isn't staying around to smell them," Bill said as he rolled the turkey on the spit over the fire. "They probably smelled my biscuits and came a runnin'."

"Here are our guests now," Bill whispered.

*****

Angus awoke to the smell of bacon frying and coffee brewing over a fire. The night had been cold, and he was finding it harder to fall asleep with each day that passed when he wasn't working. It had been days of nonstop rest to recuperate from his fight with his brothers, but now that his body was on the mend, he needed to work hard before he could sleep well. Trina had gotten cold sleeping in the wagon and had built the fire up to warm herself. She had also gotten her appetite back and was starving for something to eat.

"Will ye be able to travel today then?" Angus asked quietly.

"Yes, it will be nice to get some clothes. I got so cold this morning," Trina replied.

Angus got up and shook out his bedroll, put it away, and returned to the fire to wait for breakfast to finish.

"I'm hungry," Trina said.

"Aye, ye should be. Ye haven't eaten much. Ye should keep your strength up." Angus was proud of the woman for going over to the river to get water for the coffee, and he thought of saying so, but he didn't. He looked in on his wee little babes instead. He held each one of them and whispered things to them that Trina couldn't hear, but it made her consider what kind of man Angus might really be.

"I like the way this one is colored. Look at its four wee little white feet and two wee little white tips on her ears," Angus said, showing Trina and smiling with glee. "This one will be mine," he said with certainty.

Trina turned over the strips of bacon. "Aren't they all yours?" she asked, looking into the box that was carpeted with black-and-white puppies.

"Nay, the mother belongs to Zeb, and one pup belongs to Mrs. Rasmussen," Angus answered.

"Who is Mrs. Rasmussen?" Trina inquired.

"She is the woman we work for," Angus answered putting his puppy back with its mother.

"What is she, an old, rich widow lady?" Trina asked, becoming increasingly curious about her employer.

"Nay, she is a very beautiful and very young lady. She married Bennager Rasmussen while we were traveling on the Sacramento River," Angus replied as he put the pups in the wagon.

Trina remembered seeing the young woman in the black chaps. "So she is a beautiful young lady. It sounds like you love her," Trina jibed.

Angus didn't give the woman the satisfaction of an answer or of continuing the conversation any further. His feelings for Rose Mary were nobody's business but his. He sat down by the fire, sipped his coffee, and finished his breakfast of bacon and cheese, and Trina wondered if he had heard her surly comment. She reckoned he had since she knew that he wasn't deaf, so she didn't repeat herself.

"Who is Zeb?" Trina asked while they were putting away their cooking utensils.

"He lives in Monterey. He is helping the Rasmussens buy cattle and drive them home."

"Would it be all right if I joined you in the wagon seat?" Trina asked. She thought that Angus might be offended by having to sit beside a whore.

"Of course!" He was surprised that she would ask such a thing, but when he thought about it for a few moments, he realized her reason but didn't comment on it.

They crossed the Bear River and passed through the patches of wild berries, wild roses, and leaf barren willows, cottonwood and oak trees, and emerged into the wide-open valley that was paralleled by the rolling foothills to the east, the Feather River on the west, and the mysterious buttes to the north. Trina said a silent goodbye to the river that she had wanted to take her life the morning before and a silent good riddance to the life and people that she had been forced to live with in Sacramento City and hoped she would never have to cross the Bear River again. Trina glanced over at Angus and could see that he was still fixated on his buttes, and the fact that she had just had a life-changing moment would never have crossed his mind.

"Are you thinking of building the rancho over there on those mountains?" Trina asked with sincere interest.

Angus looked at Trina searchingly, wondering if she was making fun of his intrigue or if she truly wanted to know. Angus was wondering how such a creation could be formed in the middle of a seemingly, perfectly flat valley. He had never been sure about Zeb's stories of witches and warlocks, although he had been very convincing, but Angus thought that if such creatures did exist, they would probably live in those mountains, and since Zeb had lived in California for fifteen years, then it was likely that he had seen those mountains and the people who lived there, and that was why Zeb was so certain that witches really did exist. "Nay, we won't have the rancho near those wicked mountains, and I'm thinkin' that I don't want to get any closer to them than I already am. I was told to go to Marysville to buy supplies, but I don't want to travel this trail anymore. I'm thinkin' of headin' east right now," Angus said as he started angling the team northeast toward the foothills. "I don't like this strange valley of flatness. It doesn't strike me as bein' natural. It's givin' me a strange feelin' in me stomach and heart. Don't ye feel it too?"

"No, this valley is wondrously beautiful and fertile compared to the Great Basin," Trina replied.

If Angus hadn't been so spooked, he would have been impressed with Trina's assessment. "Aye, I think it's too flat," Angus argued.

"You must not have seen the Great Plains on your way out here," Trina observed.

"Nay, I came here by boat," Angus said nervously. His spine was beginning to tingle, and he felt the desperate need to hurry to the cover of the foothills. He slapped the reins against the backs of the horses to encourage them into a gallop, and when the ground began to roll, Angus started to relax.

Trina could feel the tension emanating from Angus, and she didn't understand it and didn't like it. It caused her to become anxious and upset in the same way that she felt when she was summoned by Weatherford, but this was different. The danger was invisible, unidentifiable, and weird. She wrapped her quilt around her, tighter than it had been before, closed her eyes, and thought of her mother. She wished that she was home and safely protected from this life that she led now where every turn was frightful and unknown.

As time passed, Trina could feel the tension dissipating. Angus slowed the team down to a walking pace that they could better withstand in the rolling foothills. Clouds were starting to build against the snow-covered tops of the vast Sierras. It seemed to be a slow process, given that the breeze was slight and out of the southwest.

Angus noticed that Trina was clinging to the only cover that she had left in her wardrobe, her coat and her quilt. "Are ye cold?" he asked.

"Yes, my legs are cold," she answered softly with a shiver.

"We could stop and build a fire, have lunch and warm ye up," Angus suggested.

Trina surveyed the terrain that surrounded them and noted that they seemed to be in the middle of nowhere. They weren't even on a trail anymore. She wondered how Angus was planning on warming up her legs and replied, "I'm not hungry, I'd rather we just push on through until we reach a town."

"The next town is likely to be Grass Valley. It will probably be another day out," Angus said, taking out the map that Rose had given him and handing it to Trina.

Trina examined it and quietly resolved to withstand having cold legs.

"I have to find the Yuba River before I can go to Grass Valley." Angus looked at the clouds building in the east, peered at the open landscape, hoping to see a person or a dwelling, and then he looked at Trina. "I wish someone would come along and tell me if I was gettin' close."

Trina smiled and fidgeted with her quilt. Angus said, "I have extra shirts and trousers. They will be big on ye, but ye're welcome to use them until I find that town. We missed Marysville. I didn't like bein' that close to those mountains back there. I'm sorry, but I think this was best."

Trina climbed to the back of the wagon to find the clothes that Angus spoke of. "Whoa, miss," Angus said. "Let me give these horses a rest. There's no need in ye gettin' dressed out here in the open." Angus stopped the team, and Girl hopped out to stretch her legs. Her growing brood made a fuss at the sudden disappearance of her warmth, and Trina remembered a simpler time when she was a child and was able to spend endless hours with the litters of pups that her family dog would have every year. Then Trina contemplated Angus' comment for a moment.

"What difference does it make where I get dressed? There ain't nobody out here except us." Trina told her giant companion.

Angus was standing beside the wagon with his hand out. "Here, get down from there, and I'll hold the quilt up as a wall."

"A wall? A wall for what? There ain't nobody out here except you, and you already saw me," Trina argued.

"I didn't see ye, but an Indian could see ye, and I'm told that Indians are bothersome to women. Get down from there," Angus said.

Trina looked at the man questioningly. "What do you mean you didn't see me? You hauled my naked body out of the river yesterday."

"Ladies don't change their clothes in public and I wasn't lookin' at your naked body when ye were tryin' to drown yourself," Angus said with his hand out waiting for her to comply with his suggestion. They looked at each other for a long moment, each one thinking that the other was ridiculous, and then Angus looked at his feet and said, "I was so busy lookin' at your beautiful hair and wondering if ye were goin' to live that I didn't look at your body, and I'm not ready to see ye now, no matter how badly ye want me to."

Trina realized at that moment she didn't have as much experience as she thought she did with men. She had never been told by a man that her hair was beautiful. But she became enraged and screamed, "I don't want you to see my body!"

"Then get down from there and let me shield ye with your quilt!" Angus said, smiling a crooked smile that no other human had ever seen before.

Trina came to the edge of the wagon bed and waited. Angus held up both hands, and she leaned over, letting the herculean man lift her out and set her on the ground. The gentleman did as he promised and then handed the quilt back to Trina. "Well done, me lady." Then his eyes widened, and he smiled. "That's what I'll name me pup, Me Lady!" He turned away from Trina and looked in Girl's box at the brood and started to make cooing sounds at the pups. Trina raised her brows in wonder and then decided to take this opportunity to stretch her legs too. Girl brought her a stick, and naturally, Trina looked at it as a gift instead of throwing it for the dog.

"Come and eat, woman!" Angus said loudly to Trina as he rifled through the food. Hardtack, bread, cheese, and dried fruit were what he decided on for lunch since Trina was in a hurry. She walked over to the wagon, and Angus handed her half of the food that he was dividing. She put the hardtack and fruit in her coat pocket and started to walk away to get into the wagon, but Angus stopped her as he gave a couple of pieces of hardtack to Girl.

"What?" Trina was surly. She despised being handled.

"Easy now, I just want to put some salve on your cuts and bruises. It helps a great deal, doesn't it?" Angus said cheerfully, knowing from experience that it did, but Trina pulled away.

"I don't need you puttin' anymore of that bear grease on me. I'm not a child!" Trina said defiantly.

"Go ahead and do it yourself then," Angus said, handing her the container.

"I don't want to!" Trina went around and hoisted herself up and into the wagon seat. "Let's get going."

Angus shook his head and looked at Girl, who was already finished with her jerky and was hoping for another piece. He put the salve away with the food and stood at the back of the wagon, enjoying the bread and cheese. He hoped that the woman would try to order him around a few more times before the day was finished. He thought it was comical in an ironic way, but he wasn't going to let her get away with it. He liked it when they were able to compromise. He admired this woman for being tough and having a surly attitude and wondered how such a woman could wind up in the hands of a man that would mistreat her. Angus climbed up onto the wagon, looking into Trina's eyes questioningly as he did it. She turned away from him. She didn't want the man's eyes piercing into her soul and finding out something that she didn't want him to know. Angus shook his head at her again.

"Can ye drive a team?" Angus asked, looking at the backs of the horses instead of her.

"I don't know," Trina replied, looking at the horses also.

"Let's find out," Angus said, handing her the reins.

Trina took the reins studiously, leaned forward, and did what she had seen Angus do, and they were off. Bennager's team was fine, an excellent group of matched horses that always knew what they were doing, so Angus didn't have to give Trina hardly any direction, which was good because it would have only rankled her. Throughout the cold afternoon, they traveled toward the northeast. Angus had keen eyesight and was always looking far ahead for a human, a dwelling, or anything that might indicate the existence of a river such as willow trees or cottonwoods. Every time they topped a rise in the terrain, he could feel his spine tingle. The mysterious buttes in the middle of the valley were to the west of them, and river or no river, he knew that the site that he would pick out for the rancho dwellings would not include those ominous mountains in its view.

"My arms are tired," Trina complained.

"Ye did well, woman. Let me take over. It won't be long until we have to stop for the night," Angus said. Trina gladly handed the reins over and stretched. "Do ye want to stop and stretch your legs?" Angus asked.

"No, let's push on," Trina said, looking away from him again. She didn't want to be nice to this man and she didn't want him to be kind to her. She had thought of nothing else all afternoon but the comment that he had made about her hair and the way that he had said it.

When she tried to forget about it, then she remembered the way he had smiled at her and the gentle way that he had lifted her out of the wagon. She had never experienced a man who possessed kindness and didn't recognize it for what it was. She hated herself for thinking about him because she knew he was only being kind to her for one reason, and she dreaded the day when he would hit her or beat her for not giving him what he wanted.

"Do ye have good eyesight, woman?" Angus asked.

"Me name is Trina, ye giant Irishman!" Trina yelled, mocking Angus' accent.

"Well, do ye?" he asked, smiling but not looking at her.

"Yes, I do," Trina replied.

"Do ye see the river yet?"

"Are ye lost, laddie?" Trina jibed, not giving a damn about Mrs. Rose Rasmussen's river and hoping that the giant would just keep heading east until they reach the Missouri River. One raindrop hit Angus' face as the winter night closed in on them, and then another and another.

Angus stopped the team but never made a move to get down and set up camp. It wasn't so dark that they couldn't keep going, but he had come to a tiny creek, and firewood was abundant. His companion was a fiery, redheaded joker with a scar on her heart that ran deep, but she wasn't weak or full of sorrow like he had figured her to be when he found her drowning herself in the Bear River.

"What are we doing now?" Trina asked.

"I'm just sittin' here, what are ye doin'?"

"Why are you just sitting here?" Trina questioned.

"I'm lost, I'm gettin' wet, I'm stuck with a woman with a smart mouth, and I'm just tired. I'm restin'."

"Resting?" Trina yelled. "Christ Almighty, we don't have time to rest!" Trina jumped out of the wagon and started to unload it and set up camp. It was a task that she had done many times before when she had been on her way to California. "Get off that damned wagon and make yourself useful!"

Angus hopped off the wagon, looking as refreshed as a man who hadn't done anything all day, and he made himself useful. They quickly put up the canvas to shield them from the rain. Angus gathered the dogs and put them under it right away while Trina gathered firewood.

"Quit fooling around with those dogs and get a fire started," Trina ordered. She saw Angus glare at her, and she wished that she hadn't said anything, not because she was afraid that he would hit her but because she knew she had hurt his feelings. She knew that he had tender feelings for the puppies and yelling at him about them was as mean as yelling at a child. She looked at Angus when she brought in another armload of wood and was happy to see that he had ignored her harshness. He was still fussing with the dogs. He looked up at her, and she knew he was waiting to be yelled at again. His look was so pitiful that Trina couldn't help but smile. He was a giant, but his eyes were windows that she could see his heart through, and she saw the spirit of a man.

8

"Damn, Uncle, isn't there anything you can do about that smell? God, Stud was right! I bet I won't ever get that smell out of my nose or my mouth," Rose complained as she bit off a large piece of tobacco and rolled it around in her mouth. "You would think this rain would help, but I think it's getting worse, my Lord!" Rose looked behind her to check on Stud. He was still there, following the party at a distance of about a hundred yards. He was holding the reins with one hand and covering his nose with his free arm.

Bill had the two Yokut children riding with him. The girl was sitting side saddle on his lap, and the boy was riding behind him. The change in the weather had kept the fog from rolling into the valley so far for the day, and if it wasn't for the nasty stench, the day would be pleasant compared to the cold, icy, foggy days that they had been having. The rainstorm had brought warmer temperatures with it, and even though the party was soaked, they all agreed that it was better than traveling in the fog because they could see the country for a change.

"Quit picking on these poor children. They can't help how they smell," Bill reprimanded.

"They need a bath!" Rose hollered.

"Quit hollering around the children, they know you're talking about them. You're hurting their feelings," Bill scolded.

"I think we should stop, get rid of whatever they are using for cover, and wash them up," Rose said calmly so as to not scare the Indian children any more than she already had. Rose looked at the poor little girl who was curled up against Bill's chest. She was covering her face with her hands. The little boy was curious. He peered around the front of Bill from time to time, but mostly, he studied the people around him, especially Sam, who would smile when the boy looked his way. Sam thought back to the days when William was the great protector of Lucy's children when they were worried about Douglas doing harm to them, and then he laughed out loud about what Grace would say to Horny Bill and his filthy children, and then he laughed again about what William would probably say back to her.

"What do you think is so funny?" Rose asked Sam, which led the boy to jerk his head around to observe Sam's answer.

"William was in charge of the children when we were boys," Sam whispered. "He protected them and his mother and me and anythin' else that he was afraid that Douglas would want to hurt. It's funny to me that the only thin' that's changed about him is that people call him Horny Bill," Sam explained.

Bennager chuckled; his question had just been answered. He had spent the rainy morning wondering why a man they call Horny Bill would so graciously concern himself with two orphaned twins that stunk to the high heavens. Bennager could see that the children needed reinforcements, and no one in the party would have left the poor little things to fend for themselves, but Bennager found it odd that Bill took them in solely instead of putting them in the wagon with Sam or asking somebody to take one of the children so that his ride would be more comfortable. Zeb was an old hand at fatherhood and had offered to take one of the children with him, but Bill wouldn't let him. Zeb was grateful he hadn't, especially after their little deer hide clothes that hadn't been properly tanned and scraped became completely soaked. Zeb cringed when he saw the little boy scratching his belly and his back almost constantly. He also knew that the only one in the party that smelled half good was Mrs. Rasmussen, but at least the rest of them weren't wearing garments that probably contained maggots.

"Bill, I think those children must be miserable," Zeb said quietly. "They smell like that for a reason. Their clothes are fly blown or they are, and by the way, Little Bill is itching. I think we had better stop and find out," Zeb said in a reasonable manner.

"They could get pneumonia and die," Bill said in a way that made Zeb query at the comment.

"Bill, they could be dying of something right now. We really need to get those old deer hides off them and check for sores. Little Bill there still has the strength to itch, but the little lady looks like she's losing her will," Zeb said thoughtfully, wondering why Bill was being so stubborn about the children.

"She is just shy, she is hiding from Rose." Bill was making excuses.

Zeb stopped his horse, and the rest of the party followed suit. This was becoming a protest. "Bill, I know mountain men don't take baths until it's summertime in the Rockies, but you are wrongheaded about it this time," Zeb said.

"I agree with Zeb Uncle. The boy is scratching constantly, and the girl looks pretty peaked," Rose said convincingly.

Bill looked to Sam for advice, and Sam simply nodded his head. Bill balked. "They will catch pneumonia if they don't have anything to wear."

Rose looked at Bennager with sadness. Bennager knew what his wife was thinking. She was the only one in the party who had extra clothes, and they were the ones that he had bought for her as wedding gifts. Bennager nudged his horse toward the Roman and leaned in toward his wife, watching to make sure that he wasn't in danger of being bitten. He reached around her waist, squeezing her warmly, tenderly kissed her cheek, and whispered, "Make sure to cut up the green one because I've been dreaming about seeing you in the red one for a week."

Tears welled up in Rose's eyes, but she couldn't understand why, except that she just boiled over with love for her husband. She tried to shake off the loving feeling that she was having for him so she could talk to Bill, but she couldn't do it, so she dismounted and went to work.

Bennager watched his beautiful, loving wife and wished for a moment that they were the only two people on earth for just one day, and he sighed. He looked at Bill who was cradling the girl in his arms with a weird look of melancholy on his face. Bennager dismounted and walked over to where Bill was still sitting on his horse. "Rose has some garment material to keep these children warm, and I'll make them some little canvas ponchos to keep them dry."

Bennager waited for a few minutes for Bill to reply, but all he got was a stern look from the man. "We won't let them die from anything, Bill," Bennager assured in a light tone of voice. Bennager waited again, and then he looked at Zeb who obviously didn't know what to make of his old friend. Bennager looked at the ground and slapped his reins against his leg, showing minor frustration. Since Sacramento City, Bill and Zeb had been a pain in his ass in one way or another. Bennager had wanted to kill them both the day before, and now here they were today. Bill was acting senile, Zeb was acting perfectly reasonable, and Bennager was trying to figure out how to help the crazy bastard who had fallen in love with two stinky children and was being daft about checking them for bugs.

Bennager looked around and saw that Rose and Sam almost had the tent ready. He saw that Stud Colt was collecting firewood, and then he looked at Zeb again. Zeb dismounted and went to help Sam and Rose. Zeb knew that Bennager was about to get serious if it was required, and the old surveyor didn't want anything to do with the strapping young man when he was at his wits end. Bennager waited until the tent was up, and then he took his stand.

"Whatever we find wrong with these little kids will be fixed, Bill. Let's get them in undercover and give them some proper care," Bennager said, never taking his eyes off Bill's.

"They won't like this. They will run away and die out there," Bill said, waving his arm at the vast valley. "They won't trust me ever again."

"I won't let them run away, and they will love you even more for taking proper care of them. You might think that they are used to the way they smell or they like it, but I think they would like it better if they smelled good," Bennager said forcefully. "Have you made any progress in their language yet?" Bennager asked, hoping to bring the old mountain man around.

"Just enough to know their parents are dead or gone," Bill replied. "Will you take the boy down for me?" Bill asked as he prepared to dismount.

Bennager did it quickly before Bill had the chance to change his mind and slowly started walking toward the tent waiting for Bill to catch up with him.

Stud Colt was reluctantly back in camp trying to be helpful to Rose. She was the one who had let him come along, but if he had known then what he knew now, he would have taken his chances with the new baby back at home. He shook his head at his friend Bill who seemed to have an affinity for stinky children, and he asked Bill if they were finished traveling for the day.

Bill told Stud what they were doing and that he wasn't sure what they were doing after that. Stud continued riding from tree to tree gathering wood for the fire and was thankful to have a job that would take him away from camp.

Bennager and Bill stepped into the tent with the children. Rose was cutting the green dress apart to fashion something from it that would keep them warm and dry. She had her back to the men and Bennager knew that she was probably upset about losing the dress or maybe losing time. Zeb had said earlier that they would come to his friend's place if they pushed on through the evening, but they didn't think that they should push the children that hard.

Bennager set the boy down who went right over to Sam. Bennager leaned down, put his loving hands on his wife's shoulders, and kissed her cheek again. It was wet as he had assumed. "What's the matter, dear?" Bennager asked while he sat down on his haunches.

"It's these poor children. Have you ever seen anything so pitiful?" Rose asked.

Bennager smiled. The only thing that he had ever seen that came close was when he had first seen the beautiful woman that he was looking at now. He hadn't taken his wife for being a compassionate woman, but he was pleased now to learn that she was. He looked at the children who were glad to be out of the rain. Bill was still holding the girl, and the boy had decided to cling to Bill's leg after his inspection of Sam. "No, my dear, I guess I haven't seen such desperation, but we'll fix them up."

"What could have happened to their parents?" Rose asked shaking her head in sorrow.

"I don't know. Bill is still trying to figure it out. They might not even know, but they're safe now," Bennager assured.

"Bill doesn't know what to do with children. He's been living a bachelor's life since the day he was born. He had to be convinced to give them a bath, for heaven's sake. He'll probably only bathe them once a year," Rose complained.

Bennager looked at Bill again who was sitting on the ground with the children while they waited for the water to heat up. "I think Bill knows what he's doing, dear. You won't get those little kids away from him anyway. They already love him. What do you think should be done with them?" Bennager was afraid that Rose wanted to take the children and raise them herself.

"I think they should have their own parents." Rose was just emotional about the loss that wasn't hers to bear.

"Don't fret so much, they have a family now. They have a bunch of crazy people and me and Sam." Rose darted a pouty look his way, but his wide smile made her laugh. "They are pretty little. In time, they might not even remember their own parents," he said, gently hugging her. "I hope we don't run into anymore orphans. I won't make it if I don't get to see you in that red dress pretty soon. I'm going to set up our tent and make those ponchos that I promised Bill. Hurry up with the children and come see me when you're finished."

Rose returned his request with a kiss and a smile.

"I don't know what these babes will think of this," Bill complained quietly.

"It must be done, Uncle, for their sake as well as ours. We can't back out now after I've torn up this beautiful dress that my husband gave to me," Rose replied forcefully but calmly.

"A bath makes a man feel new all over again," Sam said smiling at the boy.

"When we get to Pablo's place, I bet one of his girls can make these little ones some proper clothes. It's good that you agreed with us, old friend. Pablo might have been leery about letting us on his place," Zeb said, trying to be jovial about the event.

"I thought you said you had been there before," Bill said with a confused look on his face.

"I have," Zeb replied.

"Well, if those people would let an old skunk like you come around, then they wouldn't shun Bud and Blossom," Bill said gruffly.

Zeb stood up and looked at his old friend in a way that suggested that he might be of a mind to start a fight, and then he smiled and slapped Bill on the back and laughed. "You old buzzard!" Zeb said and headed for the door. "I think I'll finish setting up camp. I don't think these poor little folks would want everybody gawking at them."

Sam stood up. "I'll go with you."

Bill and Rose looked at each other as the men left the tent, and then they both stood up at the same time to leave as well. "Where are you going?" Rose asked.

"I'm going to make some biscuits. Where are you going?" Bill asked.

"You are going to tend to the children and I'm going to help my husband," Rose said, putting her hands on her hips.

Bill crossed his arms in front of him. "Tending children is woman's work, and this was your idea."

Rose looked at the children who were clinging to Bill. She knew they would fuss terribly if Bill left them, and the bath business wouldn't be completed. She glared at Bill. "Is it your intention to make this as difficult as possible?"

"No, but I'm afraid to embarrass Blossom." Bill's fear was sincere.

Rose nodded her head. "Yes, and I have the same fear about Bud, although I doubt they are capable of such an emotion." Rose waited for Bill to agree to the obvious compromise.

"We will have to team up on them," Bill said.

"Right!" Rose reached her hand out to Blossom. The girl was so shy she wouldn't take her hands away from her face. It was her way of hiding herself from the world. Rose was sympathetic. She knew that she would feel the same way if she was in Blossom's position. Rose wished that they had a real bathtub to set the children in. It would have been much easier to wash their hair. The amount of scrubbing that was going to be required was going to be a long and tedious experience for the children, and they were going to need a lot more water to do a proper job. Rose hoped that the task could be completed without causing the children pain because if it was painful, they would never desire to do it again.

"This tepee invention sure is a good one for such an occasion. It wouldn't be good to have a sponge bath without a fire to stand by on a day like this. I wish we had a tub to put them in," Rose said quietly as she leaned down and gently nudged Blossom to one side of the pan of water. "Do you have your tea leaves and salves ready?" Rose asked Bill.

"They are in my saddlebags. I'll go get them," Bill said, gently easing Bud off his leg and communicating to him to stay with Rose.

"Ask Sam to bring one of the barrels of water. I think this is going to take a while," Rose said. Bud wasn't as shy as Blossom. He went right over to Rose to garner some of her attention and to inspect her. Rose realized that everything the boy was seeing was completely new to him, and his curiosity about everything made her laugh. She wished that Blossom would come around but resolved to the fact that she would probably always be in a state of camouflage.

Biscuits, bacon, and coffee were the first order of business on the wet morning. The night before had been quiet. Bill and the children worked on communication, and Bill had found out that Bud and Blossom had been told by their parents sometime back to sit still and hide.

The parents left. Bill figured they were using themselves as decoys, but for what? He didn't know because the children didn't know, and they never came back. The children had hidden for days and then finally started wandering around, looking for their folks, but the smell of food cooking two nights ago made their search come to an abrupt halt.

Stud Colt had forgiven the poor little beggars for being children and had worked with Bill to try to learn their language. He thought that it was a poor language and that Bill should just retrain them to speak Stud's language, but when Bill suggested that they should all be taught the English language, Stud wandered off and watched Zeb teach Sam a card game.

"I don't gamble," Sam told Zeb. No one had ever tried to teach Sam a card game before because he had never had anything that anybody wanted, but he had been won and lost by men who gambled with his life, and he knew that in some cases, card games were involved. The more he thought about it, as Zeb tried to convince him to play, the more it galled him that Zeb would even ask, even if Zeb wasn't aware of every single thing that white men had done to him in the past.

"We won't be gambling, it's just a game to pass the time. You play a few games. After each game, each person counts his points that he has, and after a few games, we see who the winner is. The only thing that can be won or lost is bragging rights. Come on, Sam! This is boring just sitting here with rain all around. I don't want to listen to Bill and those kids talking gibberish. It gives me a headache just thinking about it," Zeb pleaded.

Sam stopped trying to get away from Zeb. Zeb was right. It was boring, and he didn't want to listen to the gibberish either. "You better not be trying to get me in a gambling game!" Sam said as he turned and faced Zeb with his arms folded.

"I swear, Sam, it's just to pass the time. I play it with my kids all of the time," Zeb assured.

*****

Bennager and Rose woke up. The rain was falling. It wasn't a torrential downpour, but it was definitely coming down, and Rose and Bennager knew that it was going to be a long, wet day as they joined the rest of the party under the lean-to that protected the cooks.

"Long time no see, you two!" Zeb jibed as Rose and Bennager approached them, hand in hand. Both children ran to Rose and hugged her legs. They had been clinging to Bill's legs as he was fixing their biscuits, but they were happy to see Rose again. They were

439

afraid they wouldn't, and to them, she was their mother, but she didn't know it. Rose turned loose of Bennager's hand and knelt to give them hugs, and Bennager knew that they were back in the real world again where he couldn't have his sweet wife to himself any longer. The disappointment that washed over him caused him to smile and shake his head about how ironic reality always was.

"You two missed supper last night," Bill mumbled to Bennager.

"It was worth it," Bennager mumbled back to him.

"Do you reckon that missing supper just to tend to your own animalistic needs is the proper way to tend to my niece's well-being? It's likely that she's got a baby inside her by now, and she will need proper nourishment to keep herself healthy and safe from pneumonia," Bill quietly upbraided Bennager as the children attacked Bill's legs again.

Bennager was enraged with Bill for telling him how to take care of his wife and accusing him of being some sort of a monster. "Who are you, Mother Goose? My wife and I are perfectly capable of taking care of each other. You stick to tending to these youngsters and let me do the worrying about Rose." Then Bennager boldly helped himself to the biscuits and bacon that Bill had cooked and shared them with Rose.

"I don't know what those kids like more, Bill or those biscuits that he makes. I bet those rascals have eaten a hundred each this morning. They don't drop a crumb either. They shove 'em in whole and walk around a little until it goes down and then they run over and get another one," Zeb explained to Rose as they watched Bud and Blossom do the very thing that he was describing.

"Did you tend to the flea bites this morning, Uncle?" Rose asked loudly over the sound of the rain.

"I haven't had time yet," Bill replied.

Before the children could get another biscuit, Rose took their hands in hers and went to the tepee. Bud and Blossom were happy to have Rose rub the salve on their bites, and Rose could see a marked difference in their personalities already. They were happy, trusting, well-fed, and pleasures to be around. They gently hugged Rose and played with her hair and quietly chatted with each other and then with Rose, trying to tell her something that maybe was of great importance, but Rose didn't know, so she smiled and nodded her head.

When they went back outside, they found that the men were ready to get going. Sam and Stud were hitching up the team, Zeb and Bennager were taking down the tents, and Bill was putting the kitchen away. Rose handed the children over to Bill and started saddling the horses. Bud told Bill that he wanted to ride with Rose, but he said no. He explained to the little boy that the Roman was a mean horse and couldn't be trusted to be civil around little children. Bud pouted. He didn't like Bill's answer or explanation, and he was determined to ride with Rose. That was what he knew. He did not know how to argue, and he didn't think that Rose would ride a mean horse, but he also knew that he didn't want Bill to stop giving him biscuits either. Bud stood in one place thinking over what he should do as he watched his sister follow Bill around while he took the tepee down and the other adults bustle around like the little ants did around their mound.

Rose finished saddling the horses, and she went to help Bill with the tepee and collect things that had been in the tepee and put them in the wagon. Bud watched Zeb and Bennager go to Rose and Bill and the four of them stood in a group talking for a while with Blossom hanging on Bill's leg. Bud looked over at Sam and Stud who were busy arranging the wagon, and Bud decided that it was time to get mounted, on the Roman, of course.

Bud was far too little to get his foot in the stirrup, so he grabbed hold of it and jumped trying to pull himself up. The Roman looked back at Bud to see what was going on and out of curiosity, stood very still, and continued to watch the little guy's efforts. Bud lost his grip on the stirrup and fell back landing on his rear. He was frustrated but refused to give up. He got to his feet, walked under the horse's belly, and tried to pull himself up with the other stirrup. The Roman turned his head to the other side to watch. The boy tried and tried and finally walked up to the Roman's head and started jabbering at him, which caused Zeb to turn around and see what he thought was the Roman about to bite the baby's head off. Zeb gasped, and everybody turned to see what was going on. Bill started to run for the horse, but Bennager stopped him.

"God only knows what will happen if you spook that devil. Let's just ease over there," Bennager suggested.

Rose and Zeb watched the Roman, who had his head down so he could get a closer look at the boy while he jabbered at him and held their breaths, hoping that Bill could get the boy to come to him before the Roman bit his face off. Rose knew that if the Roman did anything to harm the boy, she would be a foot or riding in the wagon with Sam because Bill and Bennager would cook him and eat him. Sam and Stud were watching now and looked over at Rose. When Sam finally caught her attention, he smiled at her. Rose elbowed Zeb and pointed to Sam who was smiling at her. Rose looked quizzically at Zeb, and they observed the Roman closer. It seemed as though the Roman was listening attentively to Bud, who was very frustrated and about to cry.

Bill and Bennager saw Sam smiling at the same time, and both men wondered what the devil was the matter with him when suddenly, the Roman moved. The two men stopped dead in their tracks and held their breaths as they watched the dun fold his front legs, get down on his knees, and lie down. Bud smiled brightly, clapped his hands with delight, kissed the Roman on his nose, and scrambled into the saddle so he could ride with Rose for the day.

Tears welled up in Rose's eyes as she exhaled and looked at Zeb, whose eyes were as big as saucers. Sam knew a horseman when he saw one, and that is why he had been smiling, but now he was laughing heartily at Bill and Bennager as they stood in the middle of camp with their mouths gaping. Stud shook his head at the bizarre scene and later told Bill that Bud was better with horses than Stud was with a woman. A few moments passed before Bill could catch his breath. Then he told Rose that Bud really wanted to ride with her for the day.

Rose smiled. "Yes, I guess he does." Bud was smiling when Rose walked over to her horse and gave him a piece of hard candy. The Roman gently eased himself to his feet, making sure that his rider wouldn't topple off, and Rose spoke her praises to him as she hugged his neck and then prepared to mount.

The whole episode had added ten years to Bennager's life. He could feel his hair turning gray as he watched his wife sitting on that crazy damned horse. He was sure that he would have to kill the animal that Rose valued so highly, and he knew that if he did, Rose would never forgive him. Then the son of a bitch did the most remarkable thing that he had ever seen. Bennager was in awe until Zeb eased up beside him and said, pointing to the dun, "That is a witch horse who likes little Indian warlock boys like Bud. They speak the same language as witches. You should get a different horse for Rose as soon as you can and just give that one to the boy. Pablo will have many horses to choose from." Zeb was visibly rattled.

"Rose wouldn't give that horse up for anything, especially after what he just did. Don't worry, Zeb, I'm sure Rose speaks their language too," Bennager replied.

"You're a damned fool to let her keep that horse. He's a bad influence on her. He's bad luck. He can't be trusted. The next time the boy tries that little trick, that dun could very well bite him, and you know it!" Zeb argued.

Bennager squeezed his eyelids together, showing his irritation with Zeb. "I trust my wife to know whether or not she has a sound mount, and she believes that she does, and that's the end of it. When will we get to Pablo's?" Bennager attempted to change the subject.

Zeb didn't answer. He just marched to his horse, mounted up, and headed out.

THE WAIT

1

The Ramirez Rancho was picturesque and a sight for sore eyes after six hours of riding in the rain. Pablo walked out to intercept the party, hoping that there wouldn't be trouble. He told his family to stay in the house, and his son covered him with one of their old musket loaders.

Pablo resolved to be pleasant, but he was prepared to defend his home if he had too.

"You must be going blind, you old Mexican cock hound!" Zeb hollered at his old friend.

Pablo stopped at the remark and searched his memory for the man who always referred to him in that way and remembered Loco Zeb Jones. Pablo smiled. "Loco Zeb, what are you doing?" he shouted.

Zeb laughed and dismounted. The two men warmly grasped each other's hands and patted each other's shoulders. The rest of the party remained mounted, hoping that Pablo would ask them in.

"Loco Zeb, how is your family?" Pablo asked his friend. Pablo hadn't seen Zeb in over a year. Monterey was only a day and a half away, so that was the port where he did his business, and then he would stay with Zeb and his family for usually a day to rest up for his trip back home. Pablo was a distant cousin to Anna.

"My family is very well, Pablo. I've only been away for about three weeks, but when I left, they were well. I have too many daughters, and they are growing fast. They make me feel like an unwanted stranger in my own home, and I never know what to do or say to get them to be nice to me. I went to Sacramento City to look at the gold rush and to get away from the women for a while, and now I am missing my Anna so much that I have to go home and see her.

Pablo gave Zeb a queried expression for a moment and shook his head slightly. "You are taking these people to Anna's house? Are you bringing her a present in that wagon?" Pablo asked, surveying the strange-looking party.

Bill was translating the conversation to Stud Colt, and Stud was very interested in the fact that Zeb had daughters and then was disappointed in Zeb for wanting to get away from them.

Zeb chucked slightly. "No, Anna wouldn't be interested in anything that these people are doing. Pablo, these people want to start a cattle rancho way up north of here, up on the Yuba River, and they were wondering if you would be willing to sell some of your cattle to them. What do you think?"

"I think thieves, bandits, and miners will wipe them out before they get back to Sacramento City," Pablo said as he looked at the party with genuine concern. Pablo saw two old men, two babies and an Indian child, one man that looked like he could handle himself, and then his eyes lit on Rose and the ugliest horse that he had ever seen. Pablo took Zeb by the elbow, and they walked a short distance from the others, and he whispered, "Loco Zeb, what kind of idea is this? These people could not drive my milk cows. They do not know anything about wild cattle. My cattle are calving right now, and anyone of them would kill a man for even looking at their calves. These people will get themselves killed. You have found people who are more loco than you are."

"The woman on the warlock horse is determined, and she has money."

"If she is determined, then she should have left the old men and babies at home and hired vaqueros," Pablo argued and wondered at the ignorance of the people.

Zeb laughed heartily at the "old men" comment. Pablo was twenty years older than he was, and he was about the same age of Bill and Sam. It was funny to Zeb because he knew Pablo was dead serious. "You make me laugh, old friend. It is good to see you again. It has been too long. The old men are not that old. The ugly one on the tall roan is Horny Bill Ford. Do you remember the stories that I told you about him?"

"Yes, he is loco!"

"We can't help it about the babies Pablo. We just found them two nights ago. They lost their parents somehow, and they were starving. As for the woman, she is willing and able to hire vaqueros if she can."

The rain was starting again, and Pablo didn't have any intention of getting wet while he was trying to educate people about wild cattle during calving season. "Tell them to come." Pablo led them to his livery. He was a short, bowlegged man who looked like a fish out of water when he was afoot. He walked quickly to get out of the rain, and everyone sensed that he was irritated by the unexpected visitors who had no idea of what they were getting into.

Zeb figured that since his old friend hadn't sent them away, he might as well start in with the introductions. Even though the party was in out of the rain, they did not dismount until they were asked to. Pablo's rancho was self-reliant. His stables had forty stalls, more than any in the party had ever seen. He had his own forge. There was an orchard, big garden plot, and a vineyard started with vines that a priest had given him years ago in Monterey. His house was surrounded with short green grass and a flower garden that would rival anything that Rose had ever seen in Europe, and on the side of a hill behind the house, a flowered rock walkway led to a tiny chapel. There were various outbuildings to accommodate his vaqueros, and from the outside, each one looked very clean and tidy. There were not any flower gardens, but each house had short grass and rock walkways.

"Nobody, not even my vaqueros, can move my cattle when they are calving. These animals are wild beasts! They hide while they calve, and they defend their calves to the death. If you people are very serious about buying my cattle, then you will have to wait until they come out of hiding and start grazing again," Pablo explained.

"How long will that be?" Rose asked, wondering if she should have let Zeb purchase those extra beans and Bill the extra flour back in Stockton.

Pablo waved his hand in the wind and shook his head. "It will be two or three months."

Bud and Blossom were thrilled to have their feet back on the ground again. They were in the garden plot trying to catch one of a hundred of Pablo's chickens that were working the ground up for the next season and looking for morsels of corn that might have been left behind at harvest time. Bill was watching with a keen parental eye and waiting for when one of the children would finally get pecked.

Waiting in the rain was bad news for Bennager and Sam. Bennager had never waited for two months for anything with nothing to do. In the past, if he found that he was in a place where there wasn't anything to do, he would leave. But now, he couldn't leave his wife behind to go back to hauling freight. Angus had his team for one reason, but also, he would never leave his wife's side. Sam reckoned that he might just as well have stayed on the Cosumnes River, looking for rocks with Stud instead of traveling across the San Joaquin Valley, only to find out that they had to wait, camped out probably in the rain, tending to animals and people, instead of looking for gold.

Rose could sense the disappointment that Bennager and Sam were feeling when she turned to the Roman and scratched him under his chin. His big bottom lip drooped, and he closed his eyes at the pleasure that it gave him.

Finally, Zeb asked the question that everybody was waiting for. "Can these people hold up here with you, Pablo?"

"Sure, it is no problem."

"Will you teach them what they need to know about your breed of cattle?"

Pablo smiled broadly. "Sure, it is no problem." Pablo looked at Rose and her ugly horse. "How many of Pablo's cattle do you want buy?"

"How many do you have?" Rose asked with a smile.

"I have many cattle, too many cattle," Pablo said, smiling charmingly.

"I would like to buy two hundred pair and twenty bulls," Rose replied.

"And a pretty girl should have a handsome horse. I have many handsome horses." Pablo was being very pleasant as he insulted the Roman.

Rose smiled and stated. "Yes, and so do I."

Pablo smiled at the hardheaded woman. Loco Zeb was right when he defined her as determined, and Pablo quickly realized that the party wasn't as stupid as he thought.

The babies ran into the livery and hid behind Bill. Blossom was hiding her face with her hands, but she wasn't crying. Bill ignored them because he knew that they had finally tormented the hen into madness until she had to put her beak down. Blossom didn't like being reprimanded by the hen, and Bud sure wasn't going to take on the colorful creature by himself. Pablo observed the children and what they were wearing. He didn't usually have sympathy for Indians that roamed around on his land. They were ignorant. They would stay in one place until it was infested with filth and uninhabitable, and then they would move just far enough away so that they couldn't smell it anymore and start all over again. Pablo wanted to put the mystery to rest about the children's parents. "Renegade ex-soldiers leftover from the Mexican war make little campaigns once in a while. It makes them feel like big men again to ride out here to the middle of nowhere and pick off an Indian," Pablo said nonchalantly as he looked at the ground.

Bennager cringed when Pablo gave this information. Bennager had heard about this slow process of genocide over the last couple of years and knew that was probably the fate of the Indian parents, but he wasn't ever going to tell Bill about it. He figured Bill would go on a rampage that would alarm every human being from the Sierras to the Pacific and from Mexico City to the Cascades. But it was Rose that became unhinged at the news. Bill was already aware of the fact that Indians were being murdered.

"Do you know who these people are? Do you know their names? Which way were they headed?" Rose inquired of Pablo and his son who was wandering into the livery with his weapon. He laughed at the red-faced woman who was being loud with his father and the look of pain and aggravation that he had on his face because of her.

Bennager pulled Rose back by her shoulders and hugged her. "Forget about it now, Rose. I'm not going to let you ride off and track down a pack of crazy ex-soldiers. The children are safe and better off anyway."

"Sure, but what if they come for Stud?" Rose asked, still shaking with anger.

"Well, then, you can go get them," Bennager said to appease her holding her tight in his arms.

Zeb went over to talk to Pablo's son, and the young man laughed at seeing Loco Zeb again. "I guess you were in the house this whole time, fixin' to shoot us."

"No, I helped my mother make supper," he lied. "She says for all of you to come and eat."

Zeb smiled, but he knew better. On the way into the house, Zeb asked him if they had been having any trouble. "Yes, we have been having trouble with people who do not recognize our land grants from the Mexican government. They try to take our cattle and live on our land. We are afraid they will kill us one day."

"That is ridiculous. This land has been in your family for a hundred years!" Zeb exclaimed.

"Yes, but things are changing," Romero said sadly.

"You must not give in. You will have to fight to keep your home," Zeb encouraged the young man.

"Loco Zeb, you know we are not fighters. It's good that you have come to purchase cattle because I'm sure that the rest will be stolen eventually. Since the war, there is no law, there are no soldiers to keep us save from thieves, and the United States does not care what is happening to us and they do nothing to protect us either," Romero explained.

"When I go to Monterey to see my Anna, I will post some letters to people that I know in the government. In the meantime, you should teach your vaqueros how to use weapons," Zeb advised.

Zeb's statement shocked Romero, and then he laughed heartily at the idea. "Vaqueros know their lassos and how to ride, they know where every cow is and what calf they had five years ago, but they know nothing of weapons, and they don't want to know. We leave our fate in God's hands right now, but it's good that you have brought this strange group of people to buy cattle. Money will be good to have."

Zeb laughed at the comment and looked around at the people he had been traveling with and who had become his friends. Romero was right, it was a strange group.

Bill was having a hard time rounding up the children for supper. They had gone back to pestering the chickens, and he couldn't make them understand that they were going into the big house to eat. They had never seen a big house before, and they did not have any intention of going inside it for supper or anything else. Bill had taught them the words *biscuits* and *bacon,* and they pointed to the wagon and told Bill that was what they wanted.

Rose had ridden all day with Bud and had made friends with him, so she just grabbed him up and started for the house. Bill decided that it was best to do the same with Blossom since both children were being unreasonable, but the closer they got to the house, the more frightened they became. They didn't cry or scream, but they wriggled so violently that Rose lost her grip on Bud. As it turned out, Bud was as quick as a streak of lightning, and before Rose could capture him, he ran underneath the Roman back at the livery and hid in between the animal's two front legs, grasping one like he did to Bill all the time.

Bennager followed Rose back into the livery to help her, and when Bennager's girlfriend, the mule that he had named Caroline, saw Bennager next to Rose, surveying the situation that Bud was in, she cried and wailed for all she was worth. Rose held her head in her hands. She was powerless. Caroline would always hate her, and Bud knew that nobody would ever try to manhandle him as long as he had the Roman for his protector.

Bennager finally went over to console Caroline. He whispered things in her big ear, and Rose shook her head at the surreal scene that she was witnessing. Fortunately, the Roman was unaffected by Caroline's outburst and continued to stand perfectly still while Bud had a hold of his leg. Rose sat on an old barrel and took a deep breath. There wasn't anything that she could do except wait for the boy to come to her. She looked at him and smiled. Bud mumbled, "Biscuits and bacon!"

Rose smiled broader and crooked her finger at the big brown-eyed boy looking back at her, motioning him to come to her, but he wouldn't. In despair, she took out her plug tobacco and bit off a piece. This caused her greater despair when Toby went off like a Swedish clock. Rose was caught. Now Bennager would know that Rose had been feeding Toby's addiction all this time and that she was the cause of all his braying when there never seemed to be an apparent cause. Everyone had been keeping their eyes peeled for cougars, wolves, and bears.

"You have been sly about this since Sacramento City, my dear," Bennager teased.

"At least he's not in love with me like that crazy beast of yours," Rose teased back.

"You picked her out for me, dear."

"I know," Rose said, glaring at Caroline. The mule closed her eyes and shied away at Rose's insult. "This little boy is stubborn. He is a rascal. He is beginning to be a pain in my ass. Pablo's wife will call us all loco."

"Bud will fit in well with this family," Bennager remarked, and he wasn't joking. Bennager stood beside Rose, and he smiled at the boy.

Bud peeked around the Roman's leg again and mumbled, "Biscuits and bacon!"

Bennager smiled and repeated the boy's request and nodded his head. Bud came out and walked into Rose's opened arms. Rose said, "I'll wait with Bud at the wagon. Will you please go tell Uncle that his boy is demanding his attention?"

"Yes, if you will please keep him away from your horse," Bennager pleaded.

"Somebody will make him his biscuits and bacon, I hope. I don't want him to think that I'm a liar," Bennager said as he headed for the house.

Rose held Bud in her arms and let him scratch the Roman under his chin, and when she heard Bill coming, they quickly moved toward the wagon.

"I think Bud is afraid of houses, Uncle. He wants you to do his cooking. Where is Blossom?" Rose asked.

"Blossom was afraid of the house, too, but she likes it now. Pablo's girls took her right up and gave her a doll. The house and the ladies are very beautiful and very colorful. Go ahead and meet them and have your supper. I'll tend to Bud," Bill told her.

"Bennager promised him the biscuits and bacon."

"Why did he do that?"

"It was the only way that he would come out from under my horse. That boy is hardheaded like you, Uncle," Rose scolded.

"Like me, only a hardheaded woman would keep a man-eating horse with children around!" Bill exclaimed.

Rose ignored her uncle and headed for the house. She was greeted at the door by Señora Ramirez, and she never felt more out of place in her life. She wished that she had taken the time to put on her red dress. Señora Ramirez and her girls were wearing beautiful dresses, and their hair was done up with ribbons. Señora Ramirez had hers up in a bun with curly locks surrounding her face. As it turned out, the girls were actually her granddaughters, the daughters of Romero, but it wasn't easy to tell that by looking at Pablo's stunning wife who didn't look a day over forty. Even though Rose wasn't properly dressed, she was still treated like a queen as Señora Ramirez ushered her to the dining room table.

Rose was seated next to Bennager and across from Stud. Rose smiled at Stud as she observed that he was sitting up straight and doing his best with his table manners. Rose knew it was because there were so many gorgeous women in the room. Most young men would be intimidated by such femininity and shy, but Stud was charming in his own adolescent, masculine way. He smiled and looked each man and woman in the eye, trying to follow the conversation and the smiles of the young women at the same time.

Pablo was curious about Rose and her ambition to be a cattle ranchero and how the idea came to be, and now that she was at his table, it was his very purpose to ask, but he just couldn't take his attention away from the Indian boy that they called Stud Colt. Pablo asked Zeb, "Where is this Indian boy from?"

"He is a Miwok Indian from up on the Cosumnes River," Zeb replied.

"I do not think that this is an Indian name that you call him," Pablo responded.

"No, Bill Ford gave him that name," Zeb answered with a twinkle in his eye and making sure not to say "Horny Bill" or "Stud Colt." Zeb was about to laugh again at the San Joaquin ferry incident and was dying for Pablo to press this issue in front of the women.

Bennager elbowed Rose in the ribs. Bennager wanted her to make Zeb stop.

"That does not seem to be an appropriate name for such a nice young man. Tell Mr. Bill Ford to change this young man's name to something more appropriate," Pablo said as if his word was law.

"As a matter of fact, the boy has wanted Bill to change his name to—"

"Oh, Señor Ramirez!" Rose interrupted and scowled at Zeb who was bursting with pride at the mess he was about to make. "I was wondering if we could ride out tomorrow and have a look at some of your cattle. Everyone has been telling me that Mexican cattle don't have very much meat on their bones."

"Yes, this is true. For years, we only raised cattle for the tallow and hides, and for years, we did very well." Bill and Bud came in and joined the group at the table, and Pablo continued, "Zeb thought we should go to Texas and try out the longhorns. The longhorns are grand beasts compare to my little Mexican shorthorns, but we purchased fifty cows and brought them home. It was the biggest mistake I have ever made. The big longhorns are unreasonable beasts, and it has taken a long time to cull out the little shorthorns, and I had to hire these special men from the Mexican border country, my vaqueros, to handle this breed of animal. In the last four years, I have made two more trips back to Texas to look for bulls that would gentle these beasts down. All Loco Zeb did was cause me more work and more headaches, but I do have cattle with meat on them now. It took a lot of work for my poor little shorthorn bulls to breed those big beasts, and then we had to start selling off our little cows, and I was sorry to see them go. They were reasonable cattle."

"Were they sold for their hide and tallow?" Rose asked.

"No, I found a buyer for them in the Sandwich Islands. It made me happy to know that they were not going to be slaughtered. I like knowing I can buy that breed back someday when Loco Zeb decides to stay out of my business," Pablo said, glaring at Zeb.

Zeb only laughed at Pablo as if he had played a good joke on him six years ago by encouraging him to buy the crazy longhorns from Texas.

Supper was finished, and the Ramirez women were clearing the table. The men removed themselves to another large room. Rose helped the women, but Señora Ramirez told her to join the men. "You are buying cattle, not cleaning my dishes, Mrs. Rasmussen."

Rose smiled. "I can do both."

"You must sit with the men and learn. Besides, you are my guest."

"The meal was delicious, and I'll take all the advice from you that I can get. There is much to learn from all of you," Rose replied.

"It will be my pleasure, Mrs. Rasmussen." Señora Ramirez was very pleasant and gracious.

Sam and Bennager excused themselves to tend to the horses. Pablo had a large set of corrals, a pasture fenced off, and a large building on the side of it for their wagons, carriages, and tack. They decided to put the Roman in a stall so Bud couldn't use him for a hiding place anytime he took a mind to, and they left the cook wagon out so Bill could keep making his biscuits and tea whenever he wanted to. Everyone assumed that they would still be sleeping out, so they started to set up camp.

Zeb and Stud came out of the house. Zeb was laughing at the two men, and Stud just needed a rest from being charming. One of the girls was already in love with him, and he thought he should give her time to miss him. "You men won't be sleeping in tents in the rain as long as you are staying here. Don't you know you are among royalty now? The vaqueros went back to their own homes for calving season, so you will all being staying in their houses or in Pablo's house, and you will all be expected to show up to Pablo's table for supper daily. And if you have any other ideas about it, you will insult the poor man."

"I wouldn't want to sleep with a roof over my head. I haven't done that in thirty years," Sam explained.

Zeb put his arms out straight and said, "This is the life that Rose wants to make for herself. She isn't going to let you sleep outside any more than Pablo would. You should get used to this way of life, Sam. It's good, especially for old, arthritic men. It will be good for all of you to stay here for a couple of months. You and Rose have had too hard of a year, harder than anybody should have."

Sam remembered back to the hospitality that Grace Weatherford had shown him and what a comfort it had been to have a roof over his head and a bed to sleep in until the night that Doug had tied him to it. He wasn't going to argue with Zeb, but he wasn't ever going to sleep in a bed again either. Sam knew that this was Rose's dream, and until Zeb said it, Sam always thought that it was unattainable, but he also knew Rose wouldn't make him sleep in a bed or a house if he didn't want to.

"We are still going to leave the wagon here, if that's all right, Zeb. Bill is still going to have to make his biscuits and bacon for the kids or we will have a miniature Indian war on our hands. Bud stood underneath Rose's horse for fifteen minutes until I promised him that Bill would make him some," Bennager complained.

Zeb chuckled a little at the visual that he was having of the boy, and then in a very serious tone, he said, "That warlock horse is nothing but trouble. You should figure out a way to get rid of it."

"If it's a warlock, how can I get rid of it? Won't it come back to life if I shoot it?" Bennager asked gravely in a whisper.

Zeb looked stumped. "Well, I guess that's possible."

"What should I do then?"

"I have to go see my Anna tomorrow. While I'm gone, I'll think about it," Zeb said, heading back to the house.

Bennager turned to Sam and rolled his eyes. "That guy is a nut," Bennager said, shaking his head.

Stud was telling Sam about the young lady who was in the house and already in love with him because he had good table manners and didn't threaten war on the nice people. Sam understood that he was talking about one of the girls, but he didn't understand the rest of it. He hoped that he could ask Bill about it later.

While the others were outside, Pablo was getting to know this man that Zeb called Horny Bill Ford. He wanted to know if some of the stories Zeb had told him were true. Pablo found out that Zeb had embellished the truth, which Pablo had counted on, knowing Zeb the way he did. In return, Bill told a few stories about Zeb that delighted Pablo very much. After a little while, Pablo came to the subject of Stud Colt.

Rose quickly exited the room and begged Senora Ramirez to let her help. "They are not talking about business or anything that I haven't already heard. I have been traveling with these crazy men for three weeks. Please don't make me sit with them anymore." Señora Ramirez and her granddaughters were happy to show Rose around the house.

Pablo continued after Rose left the room, "I do not think that is an appropriate name for the young man."

Bill smiled. He knew that he was in the home of a very civilized, God-fearing man, and now he was going to find out if the old Mexican man had a sense of humor or if he was going to get them all kicked off Pablo's rancho and ruin Rose's chances of buying cattle. Either way, Bill was certain to have a good laugh about it. "It is precisely the appropriate name for that young man. That's why I gave it to him, Pablo. Didn't you see how he was with the ladies of the house?"

"Yes, I saw that he was a gentleman, and that is why he should have a gentleman's name. Zeb told me the boy asked you to change his name. What name would he like to have?"

"He wants me to change it to Stud Dick, and I was thinking about it until he let Little Rose beat him up."

Pablo gasped and clutched his chest at the shocking vulgarity he was hearing, but Bill sat before him as if nothing out of the ordinary was happening, refusing to participate in the drama. Then Bill looked at the fine china teacup and sipped his tea from it with his pinky finger pointing straight out. There was a long pause in the conversation while Pablo collected himself and observed Bill.

Finally, Pablo asked in a whisper, "Why would that boy want to be called such a thing?"

"Because his pecker is as big as a jack's," Bill said loudly, just as the men from outside reentered the room. Bill waved Stud over to him to have him show Pablo his pecker, and while Zeb laughed, Bennager cringed, but Stud was tired of these two old men always getting him into trouble every time he hauled out his big pecker that his older brother was jealous about, and he wasn't going to it anymore. Stud held on to his pants and shook his head no, and the pranksters had to give up. Bennager was proud of Stud Colt, but he was worried about Pablo. He was wide-eyed and still in shock and didn't know whether to believe Horny Bill's explanation, but he did understand now why Zeb was so loco. It was because of Horny Bill Ford. Just when Pablo concluded that Horny Bill probably needed a musket ball in his head, Bud and Blossom ran into the room and climbed on Bill's lap. They were tired and ready for sleep. Pablo studied how Bill was with these little children and decided that he must not be as bad as he seemed.

"Maybe we could call the boy Jack," Pablo offered.

"I'll talk it over with him," Bill assured the old man, now that the fun was over. "Did you boys set up camp out there?" Bill asked, looking at Bennager.

Pablo got out of his chair. "You are my guest, Bill Ford. We have a room prepared for you and your children." Pablo led the way through the vast house. Now it was Bill's turn to be shocked at the man's hospitality. Sam and Stud followed Bill because they intended to just sleep on the floor. After the warning they were given not to hurt Pablo's feelings, they didn't know what else to do, and Stud wanted to talk to Bill, and Sam wanted to talk to Stud Colt. Pablo wasn't sure what to make of it. He had enough rooms for everybody, and being proud of the fact, he wanted to make use of every one of them that he could.

Bill turned around to see what was worrying Pablo and laughed. "These are my children too." Then he said so as not to embarrass Sam, "Sam and I are working with these Indians to learn some of the English language. I tell stories, and Sam acts them out so they know what I'm telling. So far, we know more Yokut than they know English."

When Pablo wasn't looking, Bill gave Sam a confused look and shrugged his shoulders.

"Well, the room is very big, Bill Ford," Pablo said with pride.

"Thank you, Pablo," Bill said, sensing the self-esteem that abounded from the man. "Say, do you have a very small room to put the newlyweds in? They get so raunchy when they have room to roam at night that they keep everyone awake!" Bill complained.

Pablo stopped and clutched his chest again at Bill's perverted comment. Bill turned to look at him, and even though Bill was straight-faced, the twinkle in his eye gave him away, and Pablo knew that he was being teased. Pablo didn't know what he was going to do about this Horny Bill, but he was finding it hard to be a gracious host now that this man was under the same roof as all the lovely Ramirez women. Pablo glared and smiled at the same time. "I will be watching you, Bill Ford. Now I know why Zeb is loco and quit surveying to marry Anna."

"Zeb quit surveying and married Anna because he is a pussy!" Bill remarked wildly.

Pablo did not laugh in Bill's presence. He shook his head and walked back the way that he had come, shaking his head in disgust at Bill's vulgar words. Once he got away from Bill, he laughed robustly. Bill was full of spice and had come at a perfect time for Pablo. It was a boring time of year, and he lived with too many women. He would keep feigning shock and awe at Bill's outrageous behavior because he knew that Bill would keep it up, and he planned on coercing Bill into the chapel, but not with the women around, of course. Pablo knew that the mere mention of it would insight much profanity and give him much to laugh at when Bill wasn't looking. He only hoped that he could keep a straight face better that Horny Bill Ford could.

Bennager was sitting in the living room when Pablo returned. He looked lost. He didn't know where his wife had gone to, and Zeb was missing as well. Bennager had been admiring the family's bookshelf from afar but didn't dare to take a book from it.

"It is late. Let me show you to your room, Mr. Rasmussen," Pablo said, sweeping his arm in the direction that he wanted Bennager to go.

"I don't know what happened to my wife," Bennager chuckled.

"She is with the women. I am sure after such a long journey with those two crazy men, she was happy to be with ladies again." Pablo called his wife in a gentle voice but loud enough that she would hear. Pablo imagined that the women were in the sewing room. They spent all their free time there, making their fancy impractical dresses, although they did manage to find time to make the men's clothes as well.

Señora Ramirez came into the vast room that seemed to be Pablo's domain, and she had Rose with her. Pablo said, "Maria, it is late. Mrs. Rasmussen needs her rest if she wants to ride out and look at the cattle in the morning."

Maria smiled at Rose, and Pablo led the way as Bennager took his wife's hand in his and followed.

*****

It had been going on a week since the veterinarian had come to torment Douglas. Rufus Butler had cleaned Doug's wounds with soap and water and had done so as if he were scrubbing mud off an old pair of dungarees. Doug had lost a lot of blood, and the pain was too much to stand. When he passed out from the pain of it, Rufus would wait for him to wake up before he continued with his task. Rufus worked on Doug off and on for two days.

On the morning of the second day, Rufus set Doug's arm, and he wrapped his ribs very tightly. Rufus had asked for Dan's assistance in this, knowing that Doug would pass out again, but now he was in a hurry to get away from Weatherford. He was now lying in his own waste, and the man was the worst-smelling live human that either one of them had met before he started fouling himself. When it came time for them to set his leg, they realized that it was shattered, but they tried anyway just to hear Doug scream. Rufus and Dan often thought about what it was like for a young girl to be mounted by Douglas Weatherford, and they imagined that if the girls hadn't screamed, they had wanted to, and they both wanted to hear Doug scream out in pain so he would know what real pain was.

When the screaming was over and the iniquitous man had passed out again, Rufus and Dan cut off the shattered bone. Doug's leg was amputated, leaving only the thigh. Even though Rufus was a veterinarian and he hated Weatherford, he could not in good conscience leave the man to rot in his own filth. Rufus and Dan had left him on the floor with his bloody bandaged stump and left the shattered knee and shin on the bed of feces for Doug to smell when he woke up. Rufus and Dan took one last look before they left the room.

"Well, we've done all we can for the poor soul," Rufus Butler said to Dan.

"Yes, I can't think of anything else to do or anyone who would have done it better, Mr. Butler. Thank you for coming. What do I owe you?" Dan asked, flashing his perfect smile.

Rufus laughed and shook his head. "I wouldn't feel right about charging you, Dan, especially since I was trying to torture him to death. If it looks like he might survive, I would appreciate you telling me so I have a chance to defend myself."

"We will both be in his line of fire if that happens, but I don't see how it could," Dan replied.

As Doug slipped in and out of darkness and hell on earth, he heard the men talking about him, and he hated them. He heard what they said right before they slammed the door that night, and he vowed to himself he would survive their tortures and remembered thinking how stupid they were for letting him live because he was sure that the torture would be revisited upon them one hundred times over.

A Chinese man had been passing by the gambling hall when the sounds of torture intrigued him enough to sneak into the building. Wong cringed as he watched the two Americans laugh as they worked at setting the shattered leg and was relieved when they finally stopped hurting the man and cut it off. Wong hid when the two American men left the building, and then he tiptoed to the entrance to find out where they were going. When Wong was sure that he wouldn't be seen by them, he went home to the tent city and asked his brother to help him bring home a wounded man who needed medical care.

Doug felt pretty lucky that these strange little men had taken him in. They bathed him, kept his clothes and his bedding clean. They fed him food, the likes of which he had never even imagined, and it was the best-tasting food that he had ever had. Nobody had ever cared for him the way these two had, and the best part was they didn't speak his language, so they couldn't ask him questions, and they couldn't find out anything from anybody else either. For the first time in Doug's life, he was finally being treated with respect, almost as if he was a king, and he wondered if these men had any sisters.

Wong and his brother also possessed a most miraculous pain-killer called opium. Doug was sure he would live forever, and when he inhaled the opium, he would have visions about how he was going to get his revenge an all of the men who had done this to him, and then he would have visions about what it would be like to have a Chinese girl do unspeakable things to him.

As the week passed, he tried to convey to the wonderful, caring men who were seeing to his health that he needed a woman, but they only shook their heads. He didn't know if that meant that there were no women in the tent city or if the ignorant little bastards just didn't understand the international sign for woman. Doug would become annoyed, heated, and vocal when they wouldn't help him with his sexual needs, and the Chinamen would become revolted when Doug started touching himself. They gave him more opium to make him stop it.

Wong shook his head at his brother and said in his own language, "This was a mistake."

"When his leg scabs over, we can leave him and go to Marysville," his brother replied.

"I'm sorry, brother. I thought those two men were evil, but now I know that perhaps they had their reasons for torturing this man. I should have stayed out of the American's business," Wong said.

"Let's put him back where we got him. Without feeding him and giving him the opium, he might die after all."

"Yes, early in the morning, we will put him back and go to Marysville" Wong agreed.

2

Zeb left at first light the morning after he arrived at Pablo's rancho. Zeb knew Pablo would take care of Rose and the others. What he hadn't counted on was that Stud Colt was going with him. Bill left the children in the room with Sam, and Bill and Stud waited outside by a fire they had built so they could make breakfast.

"What are you two doing out here so early? Have you come to say goodbye to your dear old friend, you old buzzard?" Zeb teased.

"Sure, I have. I knew that you would want to take some biscuits along with you," Bill replied. Zeb laughed and reached down from his horse and graciously accepted the food.

"If a bear gets after me, I can stone him to death with your famous biscuits, Horny Bill," Zeb teased again.

Bill glared at the man and said, "You can use them as you see fit."

Stud was leading his horse from the corral to where the two men were carping at each other. "Where is Stud going?" Zeb asked.

Bill smiled sheepishly. "Stud has a lot of problems with being here. Apparently, we haven't gotten the smell off the children yet, he is afraid of the man killing cattle, Pablo wants him to change his name to Jack, which he will not stand for, and one of the girls is in love with him already. He wants to go to Monterey with you and see the ocean. What do you think, can he go with you?"

"I don't know. It would be strange to travel with someone you can't talk to." Zeb was apprehensive.

"He's picked up a few words. You can teach him some more," Bill suggested.

"I'm figuring on staying for at least a week, and I would appreciate it very much if he would not fall in love with my daughters. Anna has already decided who they will marry, and she would be very upset if Stud interfered with her plans. Tell him that for me," Zeb asked pleasantly.

Bill understood this was how things were done among the Mexican families, and he made Stud understand what Zeb was saying without hurting the boy's feelings.

Stud told Bill, "I can't help it if women fall in love with me. Zeb should talk to his daughters, not me."

"Your daughters haven't even seen him yet, and they're already in love with him. He said that you have to talk to them about it." Bill chuckled.

"By God, he's cocky, isn't he?" Zeb laughed and waved Stud to come along. Zeb couldn't help liking the boy. Only God knew what would happen when he took Stud home. His girls would probably think that he had brought them a gift to squabble over.

As Zeb and Stud headed west, Bill hollered after them. "Why didn't Anna have a prearranged marriage?"

Zeb stopped and turned his mount. "She did, but it was me she loved," Zeb said in a serious tone, and then he waited for Bill to say something outrageous or disgusting. Zeb would have waited all day. His favorite topic was love and he was willing to discuss it with Bill repeatedly. Bill tipped his hat to his friend and waved. He reckoned that there was a chance he might not see his friend again, and he didn't want to part with hard feelings. Zeb smiled and waved back, and he and Stud headed for the ocean.

*****

A week had passed at the Ramirez rancho, and Pablo had convinced the party that it was best to stay out of the rain. He didn't think that they would see much of the cattle through the rain and the fog, and if they did, they wouldn't have enough time to get away before the cow killed somebody. Rose didn't make a fuss. Her interests had changed from being a ranchero to learning how to cook, sew, and tend a household. She did take time out to let the Roman know that she was still alive. Every day, she would take Bud out to see the Roman. They fed him and cleaned out his stall. Rose thought that it was safer to set Bud on the Roman's back while she did the work, rather than let the boy wander around underneath him, and both Bud and the Roman seemed to appreciate her thoughtfulness. Maria handed Bud a carrot to feed to the Roman every day, and Bud learned how to laugh, an emotion that he had never known until he became Bill's son. Bud laughed, giggled, jumped up and down, and even did a little dancing jig while the Roman chomped on his daily carrot. Rose couldn't believe the transformation that Bud and Blossom had made in such a short time.

Blossom loved the Ramirez girls and followed them wherever they went with her new doll in hand. They had made her two new dresses and put ribbons in her hair, and then they handed the little girl a looking glass so she could see herself in it. Right away, Blossom became a Yokut princess, or so she thought. She had a newfound outlook on life, and her past was soon forgotten. The day that she saw herself in the mirror would be the last day that she would remember being clad in rotten deer hide. Blossom looked at herself for hours every day. The only time that Bill saw her was when she was tired or hungry.

One day, Blossom brought the mirror with her when she came to Bill for her nap. "What do you have here?" he asked her, smiling. He looked at himself and was shocked to see what he looked like. Like Blossom, he had never seen himself either, and he wanted to examine his reflection a little longer, but Blossom took the tool away from him.

"Mine!" she said.

"Who taught you how to say that?" Bill exclaimed as he took the child to their room. Since Blossom wasn't available for him to teach her English, he had to assume she was learning it from the women, which would explain her feminine attitude. He wasn't sure about the royal mentality she had acquired, and he thought that he liked her better when she was content to pester chickens.

After Bill tucked Blossom in for her nap, he headed for the kitchen. He barged into the women's domain and hollered. "What in the devil are you females teaching my girl?"

Maria's granddaughters were frightened and hid behind her. They had been leery of the hairy mountain man from the first meeting, but he had also kept his distance and said, "Please" and "Thank you" to them at suppertime. "You females are teaching my girl to be a spoiled, rotten brat!" Bill yelled and shook his finger at all of them.

Rose was embarrassed that her uncle was yelling at the Ramirez women. She looked at the two granddaughters and could tell that they were about to cry. After living with the family for a week now, Rose knew that these people didn't raise their voices or use harsh words to convey their thoughts. Rose quickly walked up to her uncle and kicked him in the shin. She didn't know what else to do to make it up to the girls for him yelling at them. "Don't you come in here and yell at these fine ladies! What is the matter with you, you crazy old buffalo hunter?"

Bill was holding his leg. "Stop spoiling that girl. She will turn out to be no good. She must learn things that will be of use to her someday. She doesn't need to worry about how she looks." Bill gently handed the mirror to Maria. He left the kitchen and ran into Pablo.

"I hear you making war on the women, Bill," Pablo said, smiling at the sight of Bill rubbing his leg. "Who won the battle?"

"Those women are spoiling my daughter. Pablo, I think it would be best for me and the children to get out on our own. They need to learn the ways of the people. Those women are going to convince Blossom she is someone other than an Indian girl, and she won't like it when she finds out she is, in fact, just an Indian girl," Bill explained as they sat down together at the dining room table.

"I understand what you are saying. You know this land is full of prejudiced people, and you want her to know her place. Times change, Bill. Her life does not have to be as limited as you think," Pablo said, trying to be helpful.

"Their parents were killed two weeks ago for no reason other than they were natives. Things are changing, all right, and for the Indians, the change is very bad. This place will soon be crawling with people who don't like Indians whether they have reason to dislike them or not. The Indians of California will die out, and Bud and Blossom will be lucky if they survive the wrath of the White man that will soon have them surrounded. It is important for them to know the ways of their people so they might have a chance to survive it."

Pablo nodded his head. Bill was wise in the way of the Indians, and he understood now why Bill had scolded the women. Bill Ford was right, and he was doing what he thought best to protect his children as any parent would. "Where will you go?" Pablo asked.

"I was just going to go where I could have the children to myself so that I could teach them something of value. I will come back when it's time to gather in the cattle that you'll sell to Little Rose," Bill said, hoping that his request wouldn't insult his host.

"Yes, I understand, but you must understand about the cattle. You must find a way to not let them kill you and the children. Stay as close to my home as you can and wait until tomorrow so Maria will have a chance to make something warm for Blossom to wear. Dresses of lace won't do for what you have in mind. Would you agree?" Pablo said. He was sorry that Bill had decided to leave, but he was correct in his reasons for doing it, and Pablo wanted his guest to be happy.

"Yes, I would agree, and thank you for your hospitality. Zeb said we were among royalty now, and he was right." Bill scratched his whiskered face and squinted. "Come to think of it, it's the only time that I've known Zeb to be right." Bill and Pablo laughed together, and the topic of Zeb lasted until it was time for supper.

*****

A couple of days after Bill and the children set up camp a mile from Pablo's headquarters, Sam and Bennager had finally found that they had absolutely nothing to do. They had fixed and greased every wagon wheel, patched every hole that they could find in the carriages, and replaced every rotten post that they could find in the corrals.

"How many weeks have we been here, Bennager?" Sam asked with a sigh.

Bennager rolled a smoke out of boredom. "We haven't even been here for two weeks, Sam, and I can't think of anything for us to do. I don't even get to see my wife until she comes to bed at night. Pablo says that we have to wait at least another six weeks before we can start gathering cattle."

"The horses will be fat and barn sour in six weeks. Maybe we should ride 'em out every day," Sam suggested.

"Maybe I should, You said that you didn't fit in saddles."

"I could handle it for a couple of hours a day, I reckon. I can't just lie around here, not doing anything. I wish I had just stayed on that river where we met Stud. I might be rich by now," Sam complained.

Bennager nodded his head. He only wished that he could see his wife more often, but he didn't complain about it to Sam. "Pablo has me feeling cautious about riding out without knowing where those cattle are hiding. I would hate to have to shoot one, especially if she had a calf on the ground."

Sam nodded his head and looked out at the rain from the shelter of the livery. "Maybe they hold up when it's like this."

"It's probably best if we do too. Maybe tomorrow, it will ease up, and we'll ride out and see Bill," Bennager said, taking his hat off and scratching his head. "Maybe Rose will ride out with us to see the kids, and maybe Bill will know something about those wild cattle."

"William is probably cooking one right now," Sam chuckled.

Bennager scratched his head again. "I could use a haircut."

Sam ignored the comment. He knew Bennager was looking for an excuse to be alone with Rose.

Bennager said, "Let's go in, maybe Pablo will let us borrow a book from his library."

"I'll be in after a bit. You go on ahead," Sam replied.

Bennager flicked his smoke into the mud and headed for the house. He decided that it was time to take some action. It was time for a bold move. He was happy that his wife was learning the things that wives should know about households, but he missed the days when she wanted to learn about him, and this particular rainy day reminded him of the day that they had spent together after they had found the children. He hadn't been able to get that day out of his mind all morning.

Bennager entered the mudroom of the house, took his boots, coat, and hat off, and headed for the kitchen. Rose was there, and she was wearing a dark blue silk dress trimmed with black lace that fit her perfectly, showing every splendid feminine curve that she possessed. Her hair was loosely pulled back with one braid streaming down her back, and she had curly locks of hair outlining her face in the same way Maria did her hair.

Rose was surprised to see her husband so early in the day, and all the ladies stopped what they were doing to see what the man wanted. The last man that came into their sanctuary yelled and pointed his finger at them.

Rose held her arms out flat to the side of her and twirled two times, just as she had done on the day that Bennager had been thinking of all morning. Instead of seeing his wife in her new dress, he was seeing her air-drying her naked body. His pulse quickened. "What do you think? I made this myself. Can you believe it?"

Bennager became oblivious to the fact that there were other ladies in the room. Pride abounded from Rose as she watched her husband come to her. He held her by her slender waist and slyly brushed his thumbs against her nipples. Rose knew what her husband wanted, and she knew that it wasn't because of the new dress. "Your dress is beautiful, and you did a wonderful job of making it. I told you to open a dress shop in San Francisco."

Rose's eyes twinkled as she admired her handsome husband. His black hair with bits of gray in it had become curly. She ran her fingers through it, admiring the way it fell and its length. "I don't think I would have had as much fun if I would have stayed in San Francisco," she whispered.

Bennager pulled her close to him and wrapped his arms around her, feeling her breasts against his chest. He kissed her passionately, and Maria's granddaughters giggled. Rose and Bennager pulled back, and Bennager could see that Rose was embarrassed to be kissing him in front of her peers, but he also knew that the longing between them was mutual. He didn't know what to say or how to behave in front of these females. He just wanted to spend the afternoon alone with his wife. He lovingly held her hands in his and gazed into her eyes. They were speaking now without words, and Bennager realized that Rose didn't know how to excuse herself from the kitchen either. Bennager scratched the back of his head. "Woman, I need a haircut." Maria quickly handed Rose a pair of scissors and directed them to the door with a sweeping motion of her hand.

Rose blushed and was grateful to Maria for treating her like a lady still, even though they both knew that Rose wasn't thinking of ladylike intentions toward her husband. Maria understood what it was like for a man when he needed a haircut.

*****

Angus and Trina spent three wet, rainy days exploring the foot-hill region of the Yuba River. Angus looked over the creeks that ran north into the river and the grass varieties and made rock monu-ments so others would know that he was in the process of claiming it. He didn't care for the land that paralleled the river because he thought that it was too rocky for cattle to graze on. He didn't think that sufficient feed would grow there, and he thought Rose would prefer to be hidden better in the rolling hills and oaks that he had found farther south of the river. The grass was much more abundant, and there were plenty of creeks that seemed to run year-round, one in particular that he was sure of.

Angus liked the rocks that he had seen on the shore of the Yuba River and measured out five acres for himself there. He thought of using the round blueish-gray rocks as building material, and he wanted to have access to it when spring hit and the miners went back to work.

Angus and Trina set up camp next to the flowing creek that he admired for Rose Mary to have, and he went to work with Trina and a riata that measured 137.5 feet. They used the rope to measure out one square league of land with the creek running through the center of it. They built rock monuments at every end of the rope. It took Angus and Trina five days to measure out the 4,428 acres. It was almost seven sections of land, and they had to walk a perimeter of ten and a half miles. That didn't count the five acres that Angus had walked at the river on the edge of the foothills.

Angus was thankful to find that creek where he did because his main objective was to be out of sight of the strange buttes that lay in the middle of the valley down below, and according to the map, he was that much closer to the lumber mill in Grass Valley anyway.

After all these days, he and Trina still hadn't run into another human and were beginning to feel they were on the edge of the earth. Angus was delighted and felt fortunate that his working companion was always willing to do whatever he needed her to do. She was always ready to go in the mornings. They did everything as a team from the cooking of breakfast to the cooking of supper and everything in between, and she never complained, even though she wasn't wearing proper shoes, and her clothes were so big for her that she was constantly adjusting them.

Trina had given up on her sullen demeanor when Angus discovered the creek. Trina thought that the Irishman would wander around for years looking for the land that would be perfect enough for the married woman who he was in love with. It was obvious to Trina how he felt about the young woman in the black chaps because after all these days, with just the two of them alone in the middle of nowhere, Angus still hadn't treated her like anything other than a coworker. Even at night, after supper around their campfire, he played with the puppies and talked of what they had to do the next day.

Trina's suspicions about Angus had changed dramatically. She knew now that he would never do anything to hurt her, but now she was afraid that she could never do anything to make him love her. Trina knew she should be careful and apprehensive about loving a man. Her heart had been tainted at the very least by what she had experienced in Sacramento City, and she knew that the only reason she was falling in love with Angus was because he was a decent man who didn't want her. She watched him on the sixth night since they had settled by the creek. She was waiting for a pot of water to warm up so she could have a sponge bath and wash her hair. He had all three puppies on his lap while he lay on a blanket with his back resting on a big oak branch that was on the ground. He was gentle with them all as he cuddled them and let them nuzzle his face and neck, but he paid special attention to the one he had named Me Lady. Trina noticed the care and gentleness that his big hands possessed, and she imagined those same hands on her body and how they might feel. Then she looked at herself in Angus' baggy clothes she was wearing and realized it wasn't much of mystery why he didn't see her as anything other than a coworker.

They had shared the same tent since she gave up sleeping in the wagon, and after the third night, she realized she could sleep easy because the big Irishman never paid her a bit of attention. In some ways, it was a relief to know he didn't want anything from her because she still wasn't ready to have another man touch her, but she imagined being loved by Angus Donovan someday. The more she imagined what it would be like, the more hopeless she felt about the whole thing. Sometimes she thought the big man was touched. He didn't always seem right in the head. Between his always being concerned with the dogs and the uncanny fear he had about the buttes in the valley, Trina really had to wonder if this man was for real. The only time he actually seemed normal was when he was working and planning the site that would one day be Rose Rasmussen's cattle rancho.

Trina's water was warm now, and her mind was drowning in thoughts about Angus. She shook her head in defeat and took her pot of water up from the fire. "I'm going to wash up. I'll need my privacy for a while. Is there anything that you need from the tent before I get started?" she asked.

Angus' blue eyes twinkled in the firelight as they looked into hers, and he simply shook his head.

Pleasantly, Trina said, "I'll see you in the morning then."

"Good night," Angus replied.

Angus had no idea that he was exasperating the redheaded beauty. He had spent six days and nights envisioning the rancho that he was going to build for his employers. He thought of what the house would look like and how big it should be for Bennager's family, if there should be guest rooms or guesthouses, where the out-buildings should be in relation to the house, and the best place for the corrals and barns. He thought that Rose should have chickens and a place for a garden. Angus hadn't had the time yet to examine all the property within the perimeter he and Trina had marked off, so he wasn't sure yet where the house would sit and what the view would be from it. Once the cattle came, the creek would strictly be for their use, so he would have to dig a well or hire someone to do it. He needed to get to Grass Valley and put a claim on the creek, but he also wanted to take a couple of days to explore the land that he was claiming as well. He couldn't figure out what to do first.

Angus was tired. He and Trina had worked hard the last few days. He didn't even know what day it was. He marveled at how Trina had walked the perimeter in her town shoes and never complained when she turned her ankles. Angus had cringed every time he saw her do it and waited for her to bellow as he imagined that Rose Mary would do, but she never said a word. Angus figured that she was happy with her new job, and he was happy she had agreed to come with him instead of continuing in her past profession.

He smiled when he thought of Trina trudging around all day in those dirty, baggy clothes. Since he had given her his only other set of clothes, he guessed that they would both look pretty shady when they arrived in Grass Valley. It didn't bother him to look like a working man, but it was starting to occur to him that Trina might be pretty embarrassed.

Angus put the pups away and walked out to gather more wood for the fire. The rain was a light drizzle, and it would be another wet and muddy day tomorrow. He brought the wood into the lean-to that they built so that it might be dry in the morning and gave up for the day.

An hour had passed since Trina had turned in, and he was sure that he wouldn't disturb her. Angus brought the puppies into the tent for Girl and shed his dirty clothes and crawled into his bedroll.

*****

Trina was already up and making breakfast when Angus awoke to the smell of coffee and bacon. He smiled at his luck at finding Trina when he did. He would hate to have to be doing all the work and the cooking by himself with no one to talk to. It wasn't daylight yet, so he couldn't see how dirty his clothes were, but he could feel how stiff and dirty they were with mud. He decided that it was time to go to town.

Angus walked out of the tent and greeted Trina by saying. "Look at us! We look like pigs!"

Trina raised her eyebrows. She knew Angus looked like a pig because he hadn't even attempted a sponge bath since she had known him. "Clothes don't make the man," Trina suggested quietly.

Angus looked at Trina's clean, red, curly hair flowing down her back and shoulders, and when she turned toward him to hand him a cup of coffee, he noticed her clean freckled face and bright blue shining eyes. She looked as if she was about to laugh.

"Ye don't look like a pig. I'm sorry I said that, but I look like a pig, and we're goin' to town to get some clean clothes and soap!"

Girl came out of the tent and looked at Angus to see what he was upset about. Angus looked back at her, and Trina watched the two of them, with one brow raised in bewilderment, have a bit of a staring contest. Girl became bored with it once Angus was quiet again, took a long stretch, and went back into the tent again.

"Will you be leavin' me once we get into town? I owe you some money. It's probably enough to get you started home."

"Are you firing me from my job?" Trina asked. It wasn't a surprise that Angus wanted to get rid of her, and Angus could see his question had made her down in the mouth suddenly.

"Nay, I want ye to stay, but if ye take it into your head to leave, then I would like to know ahead of time. I wouldn't want to be wastin' me time lookin' for ye," Angus explained.

"That's fair enough. I haven't thought much about going back home lately. I like this place and I like working for you." Trina spoke very calmly, trying not to show her feelings for Angus.

"Aye, ye're a good worker and tougher than me. Ye won't be turnin' ye're ankles one more day that ye work here. I can't bear to see it happen anymore. It's beyond me how ye keep goin'." Angus was serious.

Trina didn't reply. She only thought of how sore her ankles and knees were and the hard work that Angus had planned. Trina studied Angus as he finished his coffee, and it occurred to her that she couldn't imagine what would happen to her if she did go home on her own. She couldn't imagine not traipsing around in the foothills amongst the oak trees, in the rain doing this thing or that thing with the big Irishman and the Border collie dog. Angus always had something on his mind to do and someplace to go, and he always took her and the dog with him. He was honest and he thought about his job constantly until this day. Today was the first time he was more concerned about himself and his appearance since Trina had known him. He had not once treated her like the whore she had been just two weeks ago. He had always treated her as an equal and with the same respect he would have treated any man who he might have employed instead of her. It surprised her every night when she was bathing that he didn't find an innocent excuse to barge in on her, and it surprised her that he never found a reason to accidentally touch her or brush up against her.

Angus finally noticed that Trina was looking at him intensely. He looked back at her. The sun was just starting to peek over the eastern horizon and underneath the layer of clouds that would soon block it out for the day. They were having a short reprieve from the rain, and Angus hoped it would last all day. The morning light lit up Trina's face and fiery hair. Her pale blue eyes were sparkling, and there were only faint traces of scarred tissue where her cuts and bruises had been. He couldn't take his eyes away from her freckled face and beautiful eyes, and he couldn't believe how she was looking at him. Suddenly, he felt self-conscious again about his appearance. His pulse was racing, and he didn't know what to do or say to his partner about how she was looking at him because he wasn't sure why she was doing it.

"I look like a pig!" he blurted out as he quickly left to hitch up the team.

Trina smiled and raised her brows as she watched the crazy Irishman scuttle about. She shook her head and chuckled as she wondered what went through his mind sometimes. What was he thinking when he was searching her face and eyes just now? Trina thought that for a man, Angus was the most mysterious character she had ever known. She quickly picked up camp and put the boxes of food in the tent in hopes the gray squirrels would stay out of things. They hadn't been very welcoming of their new neighbors so far, and Trina was sure that they were bent on revenge. She put her quilt and Angus' bedroll over the things, but she knew it wouldn't do much good. The animals in the area were very curious about the goings on at the camp. Trina brought the pups out, and Girl followed.

"We are taking a day off from working, Girl. We are going for a ride." Trina was excited about seeing a new town and the country that lay ahead. She smiled as she told Angus, "I reckon the critters will destroy camp before we get back."

Angus was pleased Trina had brought the pups. She always gave him a hard time about playing with them so much. He smiled and nodded. "Aye, there's not much left of camp for 'em to do that. We need a shelter that has a door on it. It's not right for us to be sleepin' in the same tent anyway."

"Why not?" Trina asked with hurt feelings.

"Why not, ye say! Are ye serious, woman? Ye are a woman and ye should not be sleepin' and bathin' in a man's tent!" Angus exclaimed.

"Do you want me to sleep outside?"

"Nay, I don't want you to sleep outside, woman. I'm goin' to build a little cabin for ye to sleep in so ye don't have to sleep with pigs and dogs. I'm sorry ye've had to for this long," Angus said pleasantly.

Trina looked at the ground. He cared for her well-being, and again, he had surprised her. "I didn't mind," she stated softly. She didn't want to leave the tent. She felt safe when she heard Angus come in every night and settle in with his dogs, and it made her giggle to herself when he talked to Girl and her puppies as if they were people. But she didn't argue with Angus. Her mother had raised her to be a lady, maybe not a rich fancy lady, but she understood what Angus was driving at. Since she had fallen in with Weatherford, her only goal was to survive in any way she could. Compared to Weatherford's fancy whorehouse, the tent with Angus and the dogs in it was much better. Angus could go for years without a bath and never smell as rotten as Weatherford did on his best day.

Trina climbed onto the wagon after she helped Angus finish hitching up the team. Girl had become accustomed to riding in the wagon seat with Trina and Angus. The backs of the horses seemed to mesmerize her. Sometimes Angus would try to talk to her or pet her, but she would ignore him or duck his attempts. She didn't want to be bothered when she was watching the horses. Trina giggled at the dog's obsession as they headed east.

An hour or two of the morning passed as rolling grassland and oaks became thick with pines, brush, manzanita, and smaller oaks. They crossed creeks and tributaries and still never saw a house, tent, or person as they approached the bottom of a steep hill they would have to climb if they wanted to get to Grass Valley.

"Aye, that is a long, steep climb," Angus remarked as he stopped the team. "I better give them time to build up their strength." Angus surveyed the hill and wondered what it would be like to come off it with a full load. He turned to see where Trina was and realized she had taken a stroll. He knew she would always want to go to town with him when he went, but now he was thinking it might be too dangerous. He watched Trina and Girl come back to the wagon, and he was thankful they were making this first trip in the winter because Trina had her coat to cover up her pitiful garb. He shook his head as he thought of how she would look to the townsfolk if it was summertime.

Suddenly, Trina and Angus heard another freight wagon coming down the hill. Angus rushed to get a better look, and Trina followed. Angus was pleased to see that the wagon was coming without any trouble and with only a four-horse team. As the wagon approached him, he noticed that the horses were a lot smaller than Bennager's, and when the man stopped to introduce himself, Angus could see that the little critters were trembling.

"Whoa!" the man hollered, and the horses were happy to stop. "Ho, folks, I'm Jake. That's a fine team you've got there, sir."

"Aye, thank ye, but it's not mine, it's me boss'," Angus replied as he stepped up to Jake's wagon.

"Yeah, that's Rasmussen's outfit. What did he do, start a franchise?"

Angus smiled. "I'm Angus Donovan, and this is Trina."

Jake tipped his hat to the girl. "I guess that rich son of a bitch gave you two all of the rough ground to travel and he's got a brand-new team running up and down the valley," Jake surmised. He was visibly envious of Bennager Rasmussen.

"Aye, that's a devil of a grade," Angus said, waving his hand toward the hill that was now behind Jake.

"Stop at the top and check your tongue and traces and then ease off slowly and ride the brake just a little. You won't have any problems with that team. If that damned Rasmussen was going to have you take this route, he should have gone with you a couple of times," Jake carped.

"Aye, ye must be his competitor," Angus remarked.

"No, I ain't Rasmussen's competitor, I just have a little pig farm down by the river," Jake explained.

Trina giggled, and Angus wondered why the man didn't like Bennager.

Jake glared at Trina. "Is there something funny about a man who raises pigs, ma'am?"

"No, sir." Trina smiled.

Angus touched his dirty clothes and explained, "Aye, we've just been talkin' 'bout pigs this mornin'."

Trina approached Jake's wagon. "I've raised a fair number of pigs over on the Missouri River. My family made a fair living at it," Trina said, trying to be friendly.

"My pigs eat acorns," Jake stated. "I better get to 'em. Tell Rasmussen that he's a son of a bitch!" And abruptly, Jake was heading down the hill toward the Yuba River.

Angus looked at Trina incredulously. "Bennager seems to be well known in these parts," he grumbled as they climbed back on the wagon.

"And well liked too," Trina teased.

"I hope I won't have to get into a fight. I like bein' healed up," he grumbled again.

The hill was steep and arduous, but the incredible six-horse team pulled it easily, and Angus gave them a rest when he got to the top. Girl became friendly again when the horses were not in motion. She turned her head to see if her balls of fur were still there, and then she let Angus pet her. Trina figured she might as well take this time to stretch her legs again, and Girl followed her as she walked around the wagon and threw rocks into the draw that paralleled the trail. The rocks made noise in the brush at the bottom of the draw, and Girl rushed over to the side of the trail and cocked her head, waiting for an animal to appear.

They passed through a lovely mountain meadow, and Trina could imagine how green it would be this spring, and she wondered why the pig farmer hadn't settled there. *Not enough acorns,* she thought. The wagon trail continued through another mountain pass, and both Trina and Angus hoped that they wouldn't meet another freight wagon on some of the narrow curves. Trina and Angus pointed out elk and deer to each other as they traveled on. The sides of the trail were very thick in places with brush and trees, and they both watched for bears and mountain lions that might cause them trouble, although they didn't know what they would do if they saw one since neither one of them had a weapon, but on this day, they were lucky. They had arrived in Grass Valley without any such incident.

Grass Valley was a sweet, little, bustling town surrounded by tree-covered mountains. The people smiled at Angus and Trina as they arrived. The atmosphere was completely different from that of Sacramento City, and even though Angus knew that he looked filthy, he felt perfectly comfortable with his environment. Trina loved the place and vowed to live there if Angus didn't ever get around to falling in love with her.

Angus stopped at the mercantile, and two men tipped their hats to Trina as they passed by. Angus smiled and nodded to them and then scowled when they weren't looking. He held his hand out to Trina to help her from the wagon.

"What are you doing?" Trina asked.

"Do we have to do this every time, woman? I'm helpin' ye from the wagon!" Angus exclaimed.

"You didn't help me the other two times today," Trina argued.

"I didn't know ye were gettin' out those two times!"

Since they were in such a nice town, Trina stopped arguing and gracefully departed from the wagon with the assistance of her employer. The merchant was surprised to see it was someone other than Bennager walking through his entrance. He wondered what this man was doing with Bennager's outfit.

"Where is Rasmussen?" the man inquired.

Angus could tell he had better not beat around the bush with this man. This man would see to it that Angus was punished for stealing Bennager's team. Angus put his hand out. "I'm Angus Donovan, and this is Trina. Bennager gave me this note to show anyone I might run into who was curious as to his where 'bouts."

The man shook Angus' big hand and wondered what he would do about the giant if the note didn't satisfy him.

"This says that Angus Donovan has my permission to use my team and wagon for purposes that are nobody's business." The man was confused.

"Aye, I know what the note says," Angus said, smiling.

"Well, it's his signature. I've seen it a hundred times." The man shook his head, thinking it over and wanting to know where Rasmussen was and what he was doing. He looked at the hairy, muddy giant who stood before him and decided not to pursue the subject. Rasmussen could do whatever he wanted.

"How can I help you today, sir?" the merchant asked, handing Angus his note back and followed the redheaded woman around the room with his eyes.

Angus frowned at the man. "We'll be needin' some new clothes and food and directions to the nearest bathhouse."

"Will this be on tick?"

"Nay, sir, we have money."

"Very well, help yourself to whatever you need. The lady has already found the garment department." The man led Angus around the store, showing him food, kitchenware, hardware, tools, tents, lanterns, tack, shoes, candy, and liquor. "The barber and bathhouse are two doors down."

"Thank you, sir. We'll look around for a while, if ye don't mind." Angus helped Trina pick out a sensible pair of shoes, and then he tried to help her pick out her clothes.

"What are you doing?" Trina asked. "Why don't you pick out your own clothes and go have your bath instead of rushing me?"

"Fine!" Angus quickly grabbed a shirt and pair of pants. "Write these down for me, sir. I've been told to go take a bath. The woman will see to the grocery list."

The man nodded and was happy Angus was leaving. He wanted to look at the girl without having to worry about Angus catching him. Angus did catch him, though, when he came back to tell Trina something. Angus glared at the red-faced man. "I'm not goin' to have any trouble with ye on account of the woman, I hope."

"No, sir."

"Ye see that no harm comes to her while I'm gone then," Angus scowled.

"Yes, sir."

Angus went to Trina. "I thought ye might like to have the money ye earned, but I want ye to know ye won't be payin' for your boots and clothes. The Rasmussens would want to do that for ye. Also, I want ye to pick out some goin'-to-town clothes, a nice dress if ye want. We can never show up lookin' this way again if we're workin' for the Rasmussens."

Trina accepted $5 from Angus and smiled at his honesty and thoughtfulness. "Are you sure, Angus?" Her eyes were sparkling as he looked at her.

"Aye, I'll be back in a little while." Angus couldn't wait one more minute for his bath, and he left abruptly.

The merchant never looked at Trina again until she asked him if she could try on some clothes, and then he directed her to a small private room. It was easy to find her work clothes, but she wanted her going-to-town dress to be the prettiest one she could find, and with her $5, she bought a new coat that was much more stylish than her work coat. Trina didn't think that the Rasmussens would want to pay for an extra coat. She kept her new boots on under her pretty new dress and vowed that she would never wear anything on her feet except boots again. She asked the merchant to wrap up her clothes and throw her old shoes away for her, and he gladly took them from her hands. He intended to take them home and keep them and pretend that she was in them in his house and that he had the perfect little Irish girl all to himself. When he woke from his fantasy, Trina had an expression of puzzlement on her face.

"Yes, ma'am, will there be anything else?" he said, quickly coming back to his senses.

She slowly and suspiciously handed him a piece of paper. "Yes, can you help me round up the things on this list?"

"Of course, that's my job." The man chuckled nervously.

"Thank you," Trina said as she determined the man to be creepy and hoped that Angus would come back soon. Trina spent the rest of the time looking over the kitchenware, wishing that she had some money left to buy some sewing notions and scissors. The money she planned on taking with her when she left Sacramento City had been beaten out of her by Weatherford, and the thought of it sickened her. She shook her head, trying to shake the memory out of her mind and told herself the past was over. Maybe she could buy her sewing things next time. Suddenly she felt a hand on her back, and she knew by the size of it that it was Angus. She turned slowly, delighted that he was back finally.

"*Dia duit*," he said, smiling down at her. "Ye look lovely, woman," he said in a low voice.

She gasped at his transformation. He was an Irish gentleman and more handsome than she had ever imagined. He was a breathtaking titan, and there wasn't any question now about how she felt about her rescuer. She was in love and she wanted him. She had never seen him without hair on his face because he hadn't shaved since he left San Francisco. He had never smelled like anything other than campfire smoke, which Trina liked, and of course, there were the clean clothes. She wondered how she would ever convince such a man to love her. The thought of her past stopped her from trying to hold and kiss him, and she looked at the floor and tried to compose herself.

"Did I scare ye, woman?" Angus laughed. "Ye didn't know it was me, did ye?"

She looked into his eyes then and said, "I would know your hands anywhere." She paused and looked at the floor. "I could find you in the dark." She could feel Angus become tense with confusion, and she remembered his childlike qualities where she was concerned. She looked back at him and said, "You look lovely too, Angus." She said it in a way that a mother would talk to her son, and Angus relaxed.

"Did ye buy some soap?" Angus asked as he picked out another outfit, a lantern, and a bedroll.

"Yes, we have plenty of soap now," Trina answered as Angus purchased a shaving kit and a leather strop.

"Me brothers got the shaving kit when they went swimming in the bay. How do me cuts and bruises look now?" Angus asked as he handed the merchant the things and stopped in front of her so she could examine his face.

"You look pretty well healed up, except a couple of teeth are black. How do you feel?" she asked.

"I feel like a new man." Angus paid the merchant and eased out the door, opening it for Trina. They put the purchases in the wagon with the help of the merchant and then pulled ahead four doors to have a noon meal. Angus held his hand out to help Trina from the wagon, and this time, she didn't put up a fuss. Trina felt like a queen as they entered the restaurant. Angus had opened the door for her again and then put his hand on the small of her back as they proceeded through the dining room.

A very clean woman wearing a white blouse and black skirt came to the table and poured them coffee. Angus looked at her respectfully. For the first time since San Francisco, he felt confident again among strangers. "Me dog needs a steak!"

The woman looked at Trina and then back at Angus and put her hands on her hips.

Angus knew he had done something wrong, but he didn't know what, and then he remembered Zeb's story about the restaurant witch in Sacramento City.

Trina saved his reputation when she pointed at Girl who was visible through the window. The waitress thought that Angus was referring to Trina as being his dog.

"Oh, well, that's very nice of you to buy a steak for your dog, young man!" The lady laughed charmingly, and Angus was happy again.

Angus had a hankering for ham and eggs and told the lady as much, and then he handsomely pleaded for a glass of milk. Trina wanted steak and eggs, and she was glad to hear that she wasn't the only one who craved milk. She reckoned that they could have made a meal just out of milk alone. "Me dog needs some milk too!" Angus declared after he had drunk his first gallon.

Girl was very vocal when Angus and Trina rejoined her. Girl told them that it was the best day ever and that she loved Grass Valley.

The next stop was the lumberyard. Angus purchased as many two-by-sixes and one-by-twelves that he felt was safe to haul since Bennager's horses had been on vacation for a week, and he ordered the rest of what he thought that he needed to keep him busy and asked for it to be delivered.

"Delivered?" Matthew Harrison asked. "You're the teamster. You have the best team around. You have Rasmussen's team. You're the one who is supposed to deliver stuff! I'll deliver the lumber if you let me use Rasmussen's team to do it with." The man seemed irate.

Angus was taken aback by the man's outrage. Angus needed to get started on the construction rather than hauling materials for it, but he realized Matthew Harrison was right and Bennager might hate him if he let his horses go to seed. Angus simply said, "Fine" and turned to leave. He helped Trina onto the wagon seat, and she was surprised that he wasn't furious. Once they left town, she realized why.

Angus handed the reins over to Trina and said, "It's time for ye to learn how to drive this team."

"Like hell!" she said in protest.

3

Not only was Douglas Weatherford in debilitating pain because of his amputated leg, but he was also suffering from opium withdrawals. The Chinese brothers discarded the bloody filthy sheets and blankets from Weatherford's room the Americans had left the man to rot in.

After a couple of days, the room looked just as bad as it had before, and Weatherford screamed night and day until his voice gave out. It was hard for the citizens of Sacramento City to ignore the noise. Maggie told the newcomers from San Francisco, who stopped to eat, that the sound was coming from a lonely hound dog. Some folks were skeptical, and others were believers since they had never seen a hound dog.

Rufus Butler spent most of his time at the livery on the other end of town, and he had great success at ignoring Weatherford's cries of pain, but Dan Dunaway had a conscience, and he had women to deal with. The women couldn't bear to hear the man's screams. They knew with each scream that Weatherford was vowing revenge on every living thing he thought had anything to do with his pain, probably starting with the first person who he had known since birth.

Kate came down the stairs with her hands over her ears. "Do something, Dan!" she said as Dan smiled at her from the dining room table while he had his morning coffee.

"What would you have me do? Do you want me to make him better so he can come after us? Or do you want me to murder him?"

"It's like having the devil screaming at the back door, trying to get in! I can't take it anymore! You want this establishment and the people in it to be reputable, but you are proving this whole town and the people in it to be disreputable when you leave a man sick and dying in his own filth with no food and water or even whiskey to dull his pain, and the whole town is backing you up in your decision!" Kate complained.

Dan flashed his perfect smile. "Where did you learn to talk like that?"

"What do you mean?"

"You make a very compelling argument, Kate."

"My father is a lawyer," Kate explained.

Dan rolled his eyes and wondered how the daughter of a lawyer could wind up as one of Weatherford's whores. "Why in the world didn't you stay home and help your father in his law office?"

"I thought I could come here and open my own office. Weatherford said in California, the possibilities were endless," Kate answered. "The girls and I agree that something must be done, even though he doesn't deserve it. He needs something for the pain. He needs food and he probably needs to be cleaned up, and we are not going to do it, but we will pay for it to be done by someone else."

That was Kate's final say on the matter, and Dan knew it. Dan also knew eventually someone would get sick and tired of listening to the screaming and put Weatherford out of his misery. Someone might also go to a different town and tell folks what was going on in Sacramento City, and Kate would be right about folks in town being a notorious bunch.

Dan let out a long woeful sigh and said, "You gals can hang on to your money. I'll take care of Weatherford. You can take care of getting this hotel up and running."

"Please see that you do then. That creature's screaming gives us nightmares. Nancy is in such poor shape that she just cries and shakes all day and night. She hasn't slept in three days," Kate told Dan and then turned and left the room.

Dan went over to the livery and talked to Rufus and Jim.

"Let that bastard suffer!" Rufus said with rancor.

Dan had to explain what Kate had told him and how he felt that she was right about putting the townsfolk in bad light by letting the cruelty continue and that the girls were willing to pay for Weatherford's care.

"That's outrageous, it's absurd!" Rufus simply stated.

"The screaming gives them nightmares, and I can't say that I blame them," Dan explained.

"I don't have any painkillers to give him, Dan. We'll just have to rely on whiskey."

"Then you will come with me to tend him?" Dan asked.

"I guess I should." Rufus was reluctant. "I wish that big Irishman was around to see the trouble he caused."

Dan and Rufus went to the mercantile and bought whiskey, and then they asked Maggie for a plate of food. When they opened the doors to Weatherford's empty gambling house, they both began to gag. Dan set the plate of food down on a table and went back out for some buckets of water. By the smell of the place, he knew what he would find in Weatherford's tiny room.

Rufus followed Dan out to see what he was doing. Rufus wasn't going to get stuck dealing with Weatherford by himself. Rufus was relieved to see that he wasn't being abandoned, and he brought in two buckets of water as well.

The sight of Weatherford's room was more disgusting than the ugly, toothless, bald-headed, stinking, red-eyed man that occupied it. Besides the fact he had taken a sharp object and tried to cut off the end of his bloody stub for some reason, he had also thrown and smeared his fecal waste all over the walls and himself. Douglas screamed with what voice he had left when he saw the two men he hated most. They threw the buckets of water on him and went for more. Now Doug was bathing in his waste.

When the men were outside, they stopped, and Rufus suggested, "Let's burn the place down with him in it."

"The whole town would go up!" Dan exclaimed.

"Just this side of the street probably."

"My hotel is on this side of the street!"

"Oh, all right," Rufus said as if he had been scolded. When the men returned, they found Doug masturbating.

"Oh my god!" Rufus said. "Let's poison him with something. Let's just light him on fire and we'll put him out when he's dead."

Dan threw water on Doug again, and Rufus followed suit, and they went back outside.

Dan started rubbing his forehead. This was bad. He had never seen anything nor imagined anything this bad before, and he knew why Nancy wasn't sleeping because he didn't think he would ever be able to close his eyes again without the sight of Douglas Weatherford coming to his mind.

"If the people in this town could see what we just saw, they would tell us to put that worthless, crazy bastard out of his misery!" Rufus said after he tried to purge.

"That would be murder, Rufus. I'm not going back in there. Let's go," Dan said. They went to the tent city, and after being turned down by about fifty Chinamen, they finally found one that agreed to tend to Weatherford. Dan figured that it was going to take every bit of money that he had left to pay the ruthless Chinaman, and he hoped that the Chinaman would be the one to put Weatherford out of his misery. Lee followed the two Americans to the gambling hall and went to work immediately.

Dan and Rufus let out a sigh of relief and went back about their business. Dan went to the hotel. Kate was waiting for him with her hands on her hips. "Well, what happened?"

"You don't want to know."

"Well, nothing that animal could do would surprise me," Kate replied.

"I hired a Chinaman to care for him and keep him from screaming. I had to give the man half of my savings to get him to agree. That means I will have to leave for the diggings right now and pan for gold in freezing water so I won't go broke. Does that satisfy you?" Dan said, still rubbing his forehead.

"We'll hold down the fort," Kate said with indifference.

"Yeah, I bet you will. You best not be doing it with your legs in the air, though, or I'll kick you all out, and I mean it," Dan said, not looking at Kate as he passed by her to go get his trappings.

Kate wheeled Dan around and slapped him in the face as hard as she could. "How dare you speak to me like that! The girls and I have conducted ourselves as ladies since the day we agreed to work for you! Some of the townsfolk even smile and nod at us as a sign of respect! I ran into Maggie at the mercantile yesterday, and she told me she was proud of all of us girls for changing our ways! She was with us on that wagon train, and she knows we were taken in by that bastard! She knows it was never our intention to become whores!" Kate yelled with both lungs and tears in her eyes. She was furious.

Dan was holding his hand on his face. She might as well have held his face to the fire. It hurt so much. "Why did ya then? Why did you become his whore? You do have a say about what happens to you, you know! You just ripped my face off! Why didn't you do that to him? Oh, I know, because he would have beaten you for it! He beat you anyway, though, didn't he? And now you have the nerve to act just like him! I guess he must have sweet-talked you into screwing him, is that it? Well, you won't catch me ever sweet-talking the likes of a pack of stupid girls that would let something like that have at 'em, and if you ever hit me again, I'll hit you back!"

Dan got his trappings and left Kate standing in the kitchen, sobbing uncontrollably. Dan was right about everything he said except the sweet-talking part. Douglas had raped her and the others repeatedly, but they had never done one thing to prevent it from happening. They had been too scared to gang up on him and make him stop. They were afraid he would kill them. In most cases, Douglas had held a pistol to their heads to make them do what he wanted, and Kate knew where that pistol was.

*****

Kate clenched her jaw as she walked up behind Dan at the livery where he was saddling his horse. "Turn around and look at me, Dan."

Dan turned around and saw tears running down Kate's scorned face, but he couldn't bring himself to feel sorry for a woman who was holding him at gunpoint.

"Get down on your knees." Kate's words ground out of her clenched jaw, and Dan knew she was going to kill him. Weatherford had turned her into the same breed of monster he was. Dan got down on his knees silently and waited to be thwacked in the chest with a hot lead ball.

"Are you scared, Dan Dunaway?" Kate hissed. He looked at her in confusion. "Are you scared?" she screamed irately as her hand shook.

Dan wanted to beat the woman to death at this moment. He slowly nodded his head twice.

"That's why you let an animal like that mount you!" Kate tossed the empty pistol at Dan's knees and nonchalantly crossed the street to their hotel. Dan was in shock. He didn't take his eyes off her until she was inside and he couldn't see her anymore. He was ashamed of all the things that he had said to those young women. He got up from his knees and leaned on his horse and rubbed his forehead some more. He really had a headache this time.

He thought of Weatherford and what he had done to further disgrace the man, and he thought of all the mean things he had said to those poor girls. Dan had never felt the fear those young women must have felt, nor the pain, embarrassment, and humiliation. Then Dan thought of his grandfather, who Douglas had drowned in a stream in Kentucky. Daniel Evans' death had been the reason that Dan had followed Weatherford and waited for an opportunity to make him suffer, but he was going about his business in a detestable way.

Dan picked up the pistol and led his horse to the hotel. Kate was cooking something on the cast-iron woodstove when Dan walked in. She wouldn't look at him, and Dan was saddened by it. Until today, even after all the things Dan had said to the women, Kate had always been as pleasant as she could be to him, and Dan had taken her for a conniver every time. Dan set the pistol on the butcher block and said, "Keep it loaded and watch your back. I'll be out of your hair for a couple of days. Try not to shoot me when I return."

Kate watched from the front entrance as Dan headed north, out of town. She started to sob again. Weatherford had threatened to break her spirit, but Dunaway's words had broken her heart. He made her feel hopeless every time he looked at her. Quite a few times, she had woken in good spirits and high hopes that she might one day be able to work for a lawyer and get married and have children. Then she would walk downstairs and see the disdain that Dunaway had for her, and her hopes and dreams would be vanquished. So also would her spirit, and her heart sank as she settled into the job she was grateful for.

Dunaway certainly wasn't as bad as Weatherford. He had never offered to lay a hand on any of them in any way, shape, or form, and for that, Kate and the others were thankful. But Kate couldn't understand why Dan would offer them a way out and then treat them as if they were still in the business of whoring. Kate wiped the tears from her face and determined that all men must be sick in some way or another, except her father.

*****

Dan was at the Bear River by midday and decided that he would do a little panning there for a couple of days. He hoped he would be able to think of a more suitable revenge for Weatherford while looking for a few flakes of gold. He knew that he didn't deserve to find one meager speck after the way that he had been treating the women for that last couple of weeks.

He led his horse downriver. He wanted to be off the trail a good peace so travelers wouldn't bother him. He searched the area for rocks and gravel that the gold might be hiding under and studied the ripples of the water as they flowed passed by some boulders by the edge of the shore. He was hoping to find a gravel bar that he could pan without getting more than just his boots wet. It was good that he had left town. Being alone by the shallow river gave him a feeling of calm that he hadn't felt since he had started following Weatherford. He was sure that God was looking down on him with displeasure, but he was also pretty confident that Daniel Evans was smiling.

As he searched the water, looking for just the right spot, a piece of clothing caught his eye. He couldn't be sure at the first sight of it if it was a body or not. He ran into the water and plucked it out and recognized it to be the dress Trina was wearing the day she left town with the radical Irishman in the freight wagon. Dan knew he shouldn't be concerned, but he was, and if the women back at the hotel knew about this, they would assume that the Irishman had killed her. Dan sat down on a rock and rubbed his head. He looked at the dress for a long time and tried to think of different reasons why the dress was there and Trina wasn't. He picked it up and scrutinized it thoroughly; he determined it had not been ripped off her.

Just to make sure, he mounted up and rode a couple of miles on each side of the shore and didn't see any sign of where someone might have been killed. All he knew about Trina was that Weatherford seemed to favor her, and he also seemed to beat her more than the other girls. Other than that, he didn't know what kind of girl she was. Everyone in town agreed if she didn't fall in love with the Irishman, then she would be a fool, so maybe she threw her dress off and then threw herself at him. Dan could never believe the Irishman would do her harm after almost killing a man in her defense. Then again, the big Irishman might have as short a fuse and just go to killing people whenever he took a notion to.

Dan had wasted his daylight away by searching the riverbanks for Trina's body, so he started a fire and laid out his bedroll. The dress dried out after a couple of hours by the fire, and he rolled it up and put it in his saddlebag. Dan sat by the fire, trying to figure out what he should do. Should he go and find the Irishman and ask him about Trina? Or should he look for gold so he could keep paying the Chinaman? He figured on the latter since he told the girls he would be the one to keep them safe should Weatherford become able to come after them. Trina had figured a way out before he involved himself with Weatherford. If something had happened to her, it wasn't Dan's fault. He fell asleep by the fire, still wondering about the mystery of the dress.

*****

He was cold when he woke up some time in the middle of the night. He built the fire up and thought about the dreams that he had been having. He had seen Weatherford and Lee sitting peacefully on the boardwalk in front of the gambling hall, and then he saw Weatherford walk up to himself, pick him and his chair up, and set him down in the middle of the street. Then Weatherford got on his horse and rode south out of town, but the one-legged Weatherford was still sitting in the middle of the street. Dan thought that was a weird dream and couldn't make any sense out of it, but he didn't like the fact there was a mobile Weatherford who was capable of riding around and maybe doing harm to folks.

Dan was tired. The truth of the matter was he hadn't slept for three days either while Weatherford had been caterwauling. He fell asleep again, thinking about what he had said to Kate about her acting like Weatherford. Dan deserved the slap she had given him, and he deserved the lead ball that he was certain she was going to fire at him but didn't. It was he who was becoming as bad as Weatherford. It was he who had been a bastard to those poor women.

*****

Dan awoke to a frost covered morning and threw more wood on the fire. He hadn't brought any coffee. All he had was a little bacon, so he fried it up and went to work. He was determined to find a little gold before lunch and then head back to town. As the day passed, Dan had more success than he thought he would. By midday, he had panned out a dozen flakes that were the size of his thumbnail. He could hear people passing by throughout the day, especially the ones on foot. They were the ones that complained loudly when they crossed the river. Dan figured they were on their way to Marysville to get ready to head into the foothills at the first sign of spring. The men who passed by never noticed Dan. He was a little better than a quarter of a mile from the crossing, so he was never disturbed. He wondered why the men didn't stop at the Bear River and try to pan like he was doing, but he was glad they didn't. He wasn't in the mood to visit or to be robbed.

With only an hour of daylight left, it began to rain. Dan saddled up and went back home. All was quiet when he entered the mercantile that evening. He didn't bother to look in the direction of the gambling hall, and he was happy that Lee wasn't waiting outside to talk to him. Dan was washing his hands of his revenge. Weatherford could die or live or suffer and live and prosper, Dan didn't care anymore. He just didn't want the girls who worked for him to pay for his care. He gave some flakes of gold to the merchant, and he figured he and the girls could keep their heads afloat for a week or so.

He was downhearted about what he knew that he had to do. He led his horse to the livery and took his time unsaddling and currying him. He thought if things didn't go well with Kate, then he could come back and clean the horse's hooves. He took his bedroll and saddlebags and trudged to the hotel, hoping Kate wouldn't shoot him when he walked through the entrance.

His hotel sparkled, and he could smell something wonderful coming from the kitchen. He thought it was probably chicken. He could also smell apple pie. He stood in the entrance and remembered how the place looked and smelled on the first night, and he thought of all the hard work that the young women had done. If he could be sure Weatherford would never bother them again, he would sign the deed over to Kate right now.

Kate had heard someone come in, and she went out to greet who she thought might be a prospective customer, but she only found Dan standing there, looking stupid. Kate looked at the floor. "You'll be happy to know you have two guests this evening," she said softly and turned to go back into the kitchen. She didn't bother to invite him for supper. In the past, she would have been much more pleasant toward him.

"Kate, I'm sorry. I've been just as bad to you gals as Weatherford ever was, and I'll never act like that again. You gals have turned this place into a stunning hotel, and I didn't help by belittling you all the time. You made me understand what happened to you all, and I'm sorry for the way I've been treating you and for the rotten things that I've said," Dan said to Kate's back.

He would have said it over and over again, but he didn't have to. Kate turned and faced him, letting him off the hook.

"Imagine what the girls will be capable of when you start treating them like human beings," Kate said as she helped Dan with his things.

Dan followed Kate to his room. She opened the door and set his things inside and turned to leave. "Will you stay for a minute, Kate?"

Kate stopped and contemplated what the man might want and decided whatever it was wouldn't be bad. She entered the room, and Dan closed the door behind them.

"What I said to you yesterday after you slapped me was probably the worst thing I have ever done in my life. When you came out with the pistol, I knew I deserved to have you shoot me. You have never and will never be anything like that animal. I was the one who was turning into him. I followed him out here from Kentucky because he killed my grandfather a couple of years ago, and I wanted revenge. When I saw that big Irishman, who took Trina out of here, crush him into the boardwalk, I saw my opportunity. I don't really want to own a hotel. I just wanted to see him suffer, but I made you gals suffer too. If he dies, I plan on giving you gals this place to have for your own. You've earned it and you deserve to have it." Dan reached in his pocket and pulled out some gold flakes. "I want you to have these. You can use them for whatever you want, but I thought you could order some law books with them."

Kate smiled as if she had found the flakes herself. She scrutinized each one as if she was a jeweler. "You should save these for the business. There is still a lot of work to do. You don't owe us anything, Dan. You've been a bastard to us, but you have also given us jobs and a roof over our heads. Not many men out for revenge would have done that. As for the things that were said yesterday, I have heard worse."

"Not from me and not ever again."

"Well, I don't think we could manage the business without you, Dan. What if someone else comes to town and wants us to go back to being what we were? Who will protect us?"

"I will stay as long as you want me to, but you gals will have to learn how to protect each other one of these days," Dan told her.

Kate looked at the floor. "I might miss you," she said meekly, knowing that Dan would never want her. That fact made her cry.

Dan's heart ached at her sorrow that was caused by his past behavior, and his playful side came out in hopes that he could make her stop crying. "Oh, you wouldn't miss me for a minute," he said, taking her hand in his. She lunged into him, giving him a long, forceful hug. Dan was shocked and like a stone at first, but then he hugged her back, realizing that it was something that she needed. He knew that she hadn't been touched by a decent human being since she had left the comforts of home, and Dan was determined to be a decent man and more from now on.

Suddenly, Kate fell apart and began to wail. The small kindness that Dan had finally showed proved to her that there was hope. The hope was that she was capable of having a decent life. It also made her sad and homesick to have this man hold her the way he was. It was the same way that her father had hugged her when she left for California. Her sobs became uncontrollable when she thought of the nightmare that she had been living and the possibility that it might be over now.

Dan knew that Kate was having a breakdown and longed for the day that she would be strong and whole again. Dan had sisters and had seen them have fits of all kinds and run to his mother or father, and they would hold and rock the girls for hours if that was what it took. Dan knew that Kate needed that right now more than any girl that he had ever seen. Kate let the tears flow until her well went dry, and then she was worn out and just wanted to sleep. But she didn't want Dan to let her go.

He directed her to the bed. "You're tired. You've worked hard for a long time." He pulled the covers back and put her in bed. Kate took his hand and looked at him with her sad, wet, green eyes as if he was going to abandon her. The man eased into bed beside her, resting his back against the wall, and Kate curled up against his chest. Dan held her and rubbed her back until they both fell asleep.

During the night, Dan had made himself more comfortable, and when he woke, he saw Kate's blonde hair spread out across his chest. He hoped that she would wake in better spirits this morning and start the new day with strength in her heart. He gently pulled her hair away from her face as he watched the back of her head, waiting for her to wake up and wondering what she would do or say when she did. She seemed as content and safe as a little girl who had been saved by the monsters of the world.

Dan admired the simple prairie dress that Kate was wearing and imagined what she would wear if she ever opened a law office. Dan thought that she should study law that had to do with land, and then he laughed to himself at what he imagined her clients might think when they saw the sweet little blonde girl with big green eyes waiting to greet them. Dan could see every man for miles around going to see her, whether they needed legal advice or not. She would be wearing a smart businesslike dress and have her hair flowing down in big ringlets and would always stand up and greet every client with a big warm hug instead of a handshake. She would be the sweetest lawyer in all of California in a few years.

Kate continued to sleep for some time while Dan stroked her hair and daydreamed about knowing a lady lawyer in Sacramento City. He could brag to all the men at the diggings that he had been her first investor. They would be in awe because she would be the most well-known woman in Sacramento City. Other women would want to live up to her standards of fashion.

Finally, Kate began to stir, and Dan stopped stroking her hair. When she realized that she was in bed with Dan, she became embarrassed and didn't know what to do or say.

"Good morning," Dan said as softly as the voice of a dove. "Are you feeling better this morning?"

Kate slowly got out of bed, and Dan did the same. "I'm feeling stupid and embarrassed. You must think that I've gone insane. I'm sorry that I intruded on your privacy." Kate headed for the door.

"Kate, you didn't intrude on my privacy. You shouldn't feel stupid or embarrassed for needing a shoulder to cry on. Everyone needs to be comforted once in a while," Dan assured her.

"Thank you, but you should have kicked me out. This place will be like a hornet's nest now. The other girls will hate me and bother me all day about this," Kate complained.

"Why? Nothing happened that they should hate you for."

"They won't see it that way."

"Well, I don't understand." Dan shook his head in defeat. The woman was riddling him to death, and he was ready for a cup of coffee. Kate was not feeling better as far as he could tell, and somehow it was his fault, and he didn't understand why Kate was mad at him when he had only tried to help.

"They will be jealous, Dan. They will think that you made love to me, and it's all because I behaved like a little child. I was weak. I don't want them to think that I'm weak, so I will have to put up with them being jealous of me," Kate explained.

"Well, they should mind their own business. I'm sure that you are making a mountain out of a molehill anyway. You can tell them that I came home with a fever and you tended to me," Dan suggested with a smile.

"If I did that, then you would have to stay in bed all day," Kate said, beginning to blush at the way Dan was smiling at her.

"And if I did that, then I would have to have coffee and breakfast in bed." Dan smiled to make Kate feel better. He didn't want to stay in bed, but he didn't want an angry mob of women under his roof either.

"I'll be back in a minute," Kate said.

Minutes passed by as Dan wondered what he could do for the day, and Kate came back with his breakfast.

"Thank you, how did it go with the gals?" Dan asked.

"They believed me, but they still teased me." She turned to go.

"Wait, aren't you supposed to take care of me? If you leave, I won't have anything to do," Dan pleaded.

"What will you do if I stay?" Kate queried.

"I won't have anybody to talk to," Dan said. "Never mind, I'm sure that you have things to do."

"I was going to come back, but I was going to wash the sleep out of my eyes so I can see. I'm surprised the girls believed me. My eyes feel like they have sand in them," Kate replied. She thought about how quickly Dan had changed and wondered what he was up to. She hoped that she wasn't being taken in again, but she remembered what Dan said the first day she started working for him. What it had amounted to was that he would never be caught dead making love to any of his employees. He had been so kind and gentle with her last night that she had to wonder what it all meant. She didn't know this man yet. Was he a bastard or not? She wondered if she would ever really know who Dan Dunaway was.

She changed her clothes and scrubbed her face. She combed her hair, and she remembered how Dan had been tenderly playing with her hair as she was waking up this morning. She remembered smelling the campfire smoke on his clothes and how comfortable that single smell had made her feel, and she wondered why she felt that way. She thought of how she should still hate him for all the wicked things that he had said to her, but she couldn't bring herself to do it. She just wanted a nice life that was free from hate and pain. She had lived a happy life as a child, and she was determined to have that again. It would be nice if she knew that she would never have to see Weatherford again, but now that his leg was cut off, she didn't fear him as much. She knew that he would never touch her again if Dan kept his promise to stay and protect her. Dan acted like he was ready to move on, though, and Kate had to face the fact that he probably would and leave her and the other girls to fend for themselves. Dan had said many times now that they would have to learn how to defend themselves, but she couldn't imagine how he expected them to do that. They could never kill anyone.

Kate braided her long hair as she thought of all these things, and then she remembered the flakes of gold and the generosity with which they were given to her. She remembered the sincerity in Dan's voice when he was apologizing to her last night and the tenderness that he showed while he was comforting her. She smiled at the thought of what it would be like to capture such a man's heart and have it for her own one day. She knew that Dan would never want her, but maybe somebody else as tender as he was would come along.

Her spirits were high as she entered the kitchen. Nancy was there alone, cleaning up the breakfast mess. "How is Mr. Dunaway?" Nancy asked.

Kate wanted to say as little as possible about the subject since his illness was a fabrication. "I think he caught a chill when he was camped out. You know men, they can't take care of themselves," Kate said, not making eye contact when she told her lie.

Nancy dropped a plate, and Kate flinched. She looked at Nancy then and could see that she wasn't well. Nancy was worn out for many reasons. She took her job with Mr. Dunaway very seriously. She didn't want him to kick her out, and so she worked as hard as she could.

Besides fixing up the inside of the hotel, she had been working up a garden plot, trying to get it ready for starting a root crop. The screaming that had come from up the street for three days had made her a nervous wreck. "Nancy, I think you need to take a day off and get some rest," Kate suggested.

"Mr. Dunaway will call me a lazy, old whore," Nancy replied.

Kate cringed at the thought. He might have called the girl that a few days ago. "I will tell him you are not well. Go ahead and get some rest. We don't have to work as hard as we were anyway. Mr. Dunaway has told me that he is very pleased with the hotel. As a matter of fact, I was going to speak to him about making it to where we could all have some time off on different days, of course."

"I don't think he would like that, Kate. He thinks we owe him our lives. If he thinks we have spare time, he might want us to do the things that the other man always wanted us to do." Nancy was still trembling and began to cry at the thought of the past.

Kate hugged her and took her to her room. "You need to rest and quit worrying so much about Mr. Dunaway. I don't think he's as bad as he would have us believe." Kate went back to the kitchen for more coffee. She thought of how all the girls, including her, had been scarred for life, and now they were all waiting for the other shoe to drop with regards to Dan.

She knocked on Dan's door, and he told her to come in. "I gave Nancy the day off," she said, forcefully waiting for him to say something callous.

"She's the one that couldn't sleep," Dan remembered as Kate filled his coffee cup.

"That's right," Kate replied.

"Has she made herself sick?" Dan asked.

"Her nerves are shot," Kate said.

Dan nodded as he thumbed through an old book. "You ought to make out a schedule where each gal has two days off a week. You aren't slaves, you know? This place sparkles now, and you don't have to work on it night and day."

"Thank you, Dan, but some of the girls think that if they don't look busy, then you might want them to tend to you personally, if you understand my meaning, even though you have told us many times that you would never want anything to do with us in that way." Kate hoped that this comment would not conjure up his mean-spirited behavior but expected that it would.

"That does it!" Dan jumped up from the chair he was sitting in and went to his saddlebags. Kate had to step out of his way. "Go get yourself a cup and join me while we transact some business."

"What do you mean?" Kate was shocked at his swift movements.

"You are a lawyer's daughter, I'm sure that you've heard that term used before. Go do what I asked, please," Dan said amiably.

Kate had heard the term, but she didn't know what a cup had to do with it. She did as Dan asked and came back.

"Sit down at the table Kate." Dan filled her cup with coffee and then sat on the bed. "I know I have given the girls cause to hate me, and I deserve it, but I have never given them cause to distrust me. Given the circumstances, though, I don't blame them. I don't want to be their boss anymore. From now on, I would like to be a silent partner, and when this place starts doing really well, then I will just be a patron once in a while. I just wanted to see you gals get away from what was going on before, and you know my other reasons beyond that. I don't really want to be a hotel owner." Dan got up

and put a piece of paper in front of Kate. "This is the deed. Put your name on it."

Kate did as he said.

"Now we are partners. That makes you the boss of the girls. My job will be to watch over you for a while until I go to the diggings," Dan started to ramble. "I grew up with sisters, big ones and little ones. I come from a big family. I would never do anything to hurt a girl and I wouldn't like anybody that could hurt a girl. I have been terrible, I know, but I said those things because I thought it would toughen you up. I thought it would put you in a fighting spirit. It finally worked on you yesterday, although I would admit that I might have taken it a little too far. One of my sisters was beaten to death by her own husband, and now I'm surrounded by girls who think that I would harm them."

"Did you know that I was in the same wagon train that you were in? I kept my distance, but I saw what that man was doing and there wasn't anything that I could do. I was afraid of him too. He had killed my grandfather and made it look like an accident. He even managed to kill his own wife before he left Kentucky, and I was afraid of him too. I wish that I had been the one to crush him instead of that Irishman. I wish that I had killed him out on the trail, but only he can kill someone and get away with it. Those people would have had a trial, hung me, and maybe you gals would have been stuck in the middle of nowhere. I'm sorry that I didn't do something sooner, but I honestly thought you knew what his intentions were."

"When you get over your fever, you should tell the girls what you told me," Kate said, knowing now what kind of man Dan was.

"I'll tell them that I'm sorry for hurting their feelings. They don't need me to tell them the rest of it. I doubt they would give a rat about me having a passel of sitters and all the rest of it," Dan said, looking at the wall remorsefully.

Kate looked out the window at the garden that Nancy had been working on. "Certainly, you don't think of us as sisters?"

"Why not? Surely you are all somebody's sisters."

Kate looked at Dan. "Well, I would prefer to think of you as anything other than a brother."

"Why, did you have a mean brother?"

"No, Dan, I didn't." Kate waited for Dan to look at her, and he could feel her eyes burning a hole through him. Finally, he looked into her smiling face, and she said, "I don't have a brother." She could feel him become nervous, and she didn't want to hear him say he would never make love to her. She got up from the table and handed him the deed. "Thank you, Dan, maybe this will put the ladies at ease, but you didn't have to do it. They would have figured you out eventually." She poured him another cup of coffee.

"As long as it happens sooner rather than later. They shouldn't have to spend one minute, worrying about me doing them harm. They need to make dresses and go to church and find husbands."

"This town doesn't have a church, Dan, and they would probably shoot the first person who tried to build one."

Dan chuckled. Kate said. "I'll get to work on that schedule." And then she reached for the door.

Dan took her free hand. "You can do it, you know? You can be a lawyer if you want to be."

Kate looked at his hand that was holding hers and said, "I would prefer to be a wife and mother. That is what I want more than anything. I suppose I could have some law books lying around, though."

Dan had hoped to inspire her, but it didn't work. The girl was still downhearted. "You can do whatever you put your mind to. Don't ever let anyone tell you that you can't," Dan said optimistically.

"I'll consider that, Dan, but I'm sure my possibilities are limited," Kate whispered.

"Why would you say that?" Dan asked.

Kate smiled modestly, but she didn't answer. Her answer would have embarrassed Dan or caused him to leave, and she didn't want either one of those things to happen. She wanted him to stay close. She wanted to know him better. She wanted to be with him in any way that he would allow her to be. She wanted to see his handsome face and his flawless smile. She wanted to be in the company of a man, a real man; it was something that she had sorely missed.

Dan began to rub her shoulder as he waited for her to answer, just as a brother might do.

"I should check on Nancy," Kate whispered.

"Are you about to cry again?" Dan asked.

"No, but I should go," Kate answered.

"All right then," Dan said and patted her on the shoulder as she left.

Once Kate entered the kitchen, she began to catch her breath. She was sure that her heart had stopped beating, but for how long, she could not guess. It seemed like many minutes had passed while Dan was holding her hand, and she smelled his masculine scent. "Oh, Brother Dan!" she said to herself, knowing that she would never have him.

4

"Hey, you old witch doctor! What in the devil are you doing living out here?" Zeb yelled as he and Stud approached Bill's camp. Bud and Blossom were chasing each other around Bill's tepee, but when they saw riders coming, they ran inside and hid. Bill was putting his rifle away.

Zeb wondered at the children and Bill's uneasiness. "What's going on around here?" Zeb asked.

"I'm huntin'!" Bill shouted. "Look over yonder at what I've bagged so far." Bill used his thumb to point behind him toward a thicket of low brush.

Zeb rode toward it, but his horse smelled the death and reared up. Zeb stayed in the saddle and was able to get close enough to see two dead horses. He rode back to Bill. "Why are you killing horses, Bill Ford? Are they Pablo's? Are you and the children making war on my old friend?" Zeb was scared and confused. He was afraid that crazy Horny Bill had finally lost his mind. Stud dismounted. Regardless of the stinky children, Stud was going to stay with Bill. He had things to speak to him about.

"No, you batty bastard, I'm not killing Pablo's horses. Those dead men over there with their dead horses were on an Indian killing spree. They really thought they had something when they saw this tepee," Bill said, smiling with pride.

"Christ, Bill, you're not in the Rockies anymore!" Zeb exclaimed as he dismounted. "I guess that's why the kids ran and hid. But why are you out here anyway? Why didn't you stay at Pablo's?"

"Those women were spoiling Blossom!" Bill stated.

"Oh, what a crime! So you brought her out here to be attacked by Indian killers. That is brilliant, Bill!"

"She's an Indian! She needs to learn how to survive as an Indian!" Bill shouted at Zeb's sarcastic remarks.

"Why should she? She's just a little girl who will be raised by a White man! If you would only act like a White man and raise her right, she wouldn't have to worry about how she is going to survive!" Zeb explained by shouting back at Bill.

"That's what I'm doing!"

"Not hardly, you ignorant bastard!" Zeb mounted and continued on to Pablo's rancho. He had been away from Bill for three weeks, and it had been glorious. Now he was back, and he found Bill to be crazier than ever and killing people to boot.

Stud walked over to the dead bodies of the men and horses and came back. In his native tongue, he and Bill talked. "Were they bad men, Bill?"

"Yes, they kill people like you. It did not bother me to kill them and the horses because when they don't make it back home, people will wonder what happened to them and think that the Indians are hard to kill," Bill explained.

"Those people will try harder to kill us," Stud stated.

"I think that what I did will make those people stop trying. I think the ones over there killed Bud's mother and father."

"My mother and father say we will all die of disease," Stud said.

Bill nodded sadly. "They are probably right." The children came back out of the tepee and started running again. Stud wrinkled his nose and scowled at them for a moment and then shook his head at Bill.

Bill laughed and changed the subject. "How did you like the ocean?"

"Zeb's wife is dead. She died two years ago. His daughters are handsome and good for me. They are all in love with other men. They were too young for me anyway. I have decided that I like older women. The ocean is big, but it is boring, and the air makes my nose burn. I would rather smell that than your kids though. Zeb's trees are very big. Are you going to sit here and wait for the vultures to come so you can watch them eat your kill?" Stud asked. Stud wanted to stay with Bill, but he didn't like the fact that the dead men were lying fifty feet away.

Bill didn't hear anything after "Zeb's wife is dead." He couldn't believe his ears. "What do you mean Zeb's wife is dead?"

Stud looked at him like maybe he didn't understand the Miwok word for *dead*. "She does not live anymore." Stud shrugged his shoulders.

"How do you know?"

"He took me to the place where she sleeps in the ground."

"Why?"

Stud shrugged his shoulders. "I think he told the ground who I was, and then he kept talking until dark. I had to stay there with him because I did not know where else to go."

"Didn't you go to his house first?" Bill queried.

Stud shook his head no. "We went to a place where there were many people in the ground. I had to wait for many hours before I could see his daughters."

"How do you know that it was his wife who was in the ground?"

"There was no mother at home. He was not with a woman while he was at home. He talked to his daughters, and their lovers came over to visit him, and we ate well and went to the ocean. We stopped at some places in town, and he visited with the men who worked there. There was no woman for Zeb," Stud explained. Stud looked Bill in the eye as if he was daring him to call him a liar.

Bill shook his head. He still couldn't believe Anna was dead. He went and got a stick and came back and sat next to Stud and wrote Anna's name in the mud. "Did you see this at the place where she is buried?"

Stud pointed to it and said, "Yes, that is who he talked to for hours."

Bill scratched his hairy face and thought of all the ways he had tormented Zeb about Anna, and then he wondered if Zeb was completely mad. "Did he go to see Anna every day?"

Stud nodded his head. "Yes, but he didn't make me go. He let me clean his ditches in his pastures."

Bill raised one brow. "He made you work?"

"He did not make me. I told him that the ditches were overgrown with weeds, and it needed to be done," Stud explained.

Bill wanted to chuckle, but he was still shocked about Anna. "You are a good man, Stud Colt. I might change your name yet."

"How long are you going to live with these dead men?" Stud asked.

Bill looked around nonchalantly at the Indian-killing bastards and thought about what Stud had said about the vultures. "Rose will be getting ready to look at the cattle soon. We could probably head back to Pablo's. I'm sure those women have learned not to cross me."

Stud furrowed his brow at the old mountain man. Stud knew men were small harmless prey for women. Women loved to torment them the way a fat cat does to a mouse. Stud knew the only thing a man could do to make a woman happy was to love them. Bill was ignorant with woman. Stud shook his head in disappointment. He wondered how such an old man could live so long and not understand women. Bennager knew about women, and Zeb knew about women, but why didn't his best friend know about women? He would not waste his breath to ask this thing. Stud would always have something to laugh at as long as Bill didn't change, and Stud would be superior to Bill in this area as well.

Stud didn't want to travel alone to Pablo's house with the threat of Indian killers in the area, so he helped Bill take down the tepee, and then Bill gathered up the children. Bud wanted to ride with Stud. Stud disliked the idea, but he couldn't be mean to the smelly little boy. Stud knew he would have to bathe before he presented himself to Juanita, but he needed to do that anyway after such a long journey. He already smelled like a horse, so he might as well be nice to Bud. Bill was surprised Stud allowed this and reiterated the fact that Stud was a good man.

"Zeb is a good man too, Bill. Zeb knows how to love a woman," Stud said later as they were riding.

Bill looked at Stud and realized he was wise for his age and never missed anything that had to do with women. He didn't comment on Stud's statement, but he knew Stud was right. Zeb knew how to love a woman better than he knew how to do anything else. He had loved Anna from the first time that he saw her, and he still did. So much so that he rode for two days in the rain just to be able to talk to her at her grave. Bill started to think of Grace Weatherford. He hadn't even stayed long enough to know where she was buried, and Rose must not know either because she knew nothing of her grandmother. Bill was suddenly overwhelmed with sorrow. He could actually feel physical pain in his heart. These thoughts activated his compulsion to get drunk and try to forget that he didn't know where his own mother was buried.

The clouds were starting to sprinkle rain down on Bill and the kids when they arrived back at headquarters. They hadn't been able to see the sun set behind the clouds, but they knew that it had. Bud and Blossom wanted to get down and find Rose right away, but Bill had taught them some manners and discipline while they were alone together, and the children behaved and waited while Bill and Stud put the horses and tent away. They walked quietly with Bill to Pablo's house when it was time to go in.

Bill's haunting thoughts of his mother had passed. With Bud and Blossom in tow, he didn't have time to let his regrets bog him down. He couldn't go back to the bottle either; he had to be a responsible parent now. As he went to the house, he wondered what he would say to Zeb about Anna, and if he should tell the others what Stud had told him. He also wondered if Pablo would scold him for defending himself and the children against the vermin he had killed.

Pablo greeted Bill at the entrance to his home. "Bill, my old friend, how are the children?"

Bill shook Pablo's hand. "See for yourself. They are filthy but well behaved." Bill chortled.

"I was worried. Zeb said you had to kill two men."

"Zeb is a tattletale. Yes, I believe they were the ones who killed their parents," Bill said, nodding toward his children.

"Yes, you are probably right. I believe they have taken cattle from me as well. Zeb is upset about it. He thinks you are loco, but I am glad I have two less people to have to kill myself," Pablo said, smiling. "We will go to the chapel and say a prayer for those men," Pablo commanded.

"Like hell I will, señor! They are filthy murderers and thieves. Why would I say a prayer for the likes of them?" Bill was appalled.

"Come with me, Bill, and say one for yourself then."

Pablo seemed determined, and Bill couldn't understand why the man wanted him to go to the chapel. "I'll say a prayer for the buzzards that are eating them if I go to that chapel with you, Pablo," Bill told him, thinking that Pablo would let him off the hook.

"I'm sure that the buzzards will appreciate it," Pablo said.

Bill scowled at the curious man and followed him. Pablo had been very hospitable to him and the others. He was also a delightful person to be around. He was kind, gentle, and had a very good sense of humor. Bill had tried to rile the man by being loud, vulgar, and overbearing, and Pablo had only smiled or laughed and extended his hospitality further. Bill liked the gentleman very much. He was honest. He protected his family as a good man should, and he was kind to his neighbors, but Bill thought that he ought to keep his chapel to himself.

Bill shook his head as he reluctantly followed Pablo into the tiny building. Pablo crossed himself and then knelt in front of the tiny altar. Bill rolled his eyes as Pablo prayed. Bill could feel his mother looking down at him and laughing. Grace was the only thing that Bill was willing to think about in such a place; she was the worthiest person he had ever known who he would pray for if he was a praying man. He thought long and hard about her while Pablo prayed on and on about only God knows what.

Finally, Pablo stood up and smiled, and they walked out together. Bill wanted Pablo to think he was grateful for the gesture. "Thank you for bringing me to your chapel, Pablo."

"It is nothing. I only insisted because Zeb and I made a bet. Zeb said my chapel would catch on fire if you went in it," Pablo told him.

Bill was wide-eyed and furious. Pablo laughed heartily and slapped Bill on the back. "Come, my friend, let's have supper," Pablo said after he stopped laughing at Bill.

Bill shook his head and smiled at the prankster. He looked back at the chapel and then to the heavens where he knew his mother was laughing, too, and figured that he had that joke coming.

Before Bill and Pablo got back to the house, Bill stopped to talk to Pablo. He couldn't keep his concern about Zeb quiet anymore. "Pablo, my friend Stud Colt went with Zeb to his home. Stud tells me that Anna is passed away."

"Yes, it was almost two years ago," Pablo said sadly.

"Zeb talks about her as if she is still alive."

Pablo nodded his head. "Yes, to Zeb, she might as well still be alive. To Zeb, she watches everything that he does and hears everything that he says. She can see him now from heaven, so you see, he has to be a better man now than he was before."

"Then he does know she is dead, but he is just paranoid he will do something she wouldn't approve of," Bill said, trying to puzzle out how Loco Zeb's mind worked.

"Yes, he is very devoted to Anna and her memory."

Bill smiled mischievously. "I will have to remedy that."

"Oh no, Bill Ford, you should not interfere with Loco Zeb's devotion to his Anna. He might become dangerous or violent. You should leave him alone when it comes to this, Bill," Pablo advised.

"I can't make any promises, Pablo, but I'll consider it," Bill said, but Pablo could see the wheels turning in Bill's head. Pablo wondered what Bill meant when he said that he had a remedy for Zeb's devotion.

Pablo and Bill entered the house, and the smell of the wonderful meal drew them into the dining room. Everyone was there, except for Stud, and Rose asked about him. Bill simply said, "Oh, he'll be along, I reckon."

Rose looked at Bennager and smiled. Stud hadn't been boasting when he had told Bill that Juanita was in love with him. Stud was all Juanita had talked about and thought about since he had gone away to Monterey with Zeb, and now she was very excited to see him again. Rose had told Bennager all about Juanita's inquisition. Juanita now knew almost everything that Rose knew about Stud. Rose didn't dare to mention how he got his name.

Rose and Bennager never told anyone about Juanita's feelings for Stud. They knew there would probably be trouble about the whole thing. In some ways, Rose and Bennager thought that it was funny, but in other ways, they worried about it together. They didn't think Pablo would welcome Stud into the family as easily as Juanita thought he should. And Juanita's father, Romero, probably wouldn't like it much either.

Juanita had made sure to set an extra place at the table for Stud, and she also made sure that the place was next to her. When Isabel, her sister, came out of the kitchen, she saw that the only other extra place at the table was next to the wooly old mountain man that had yelled at her that day in the kitchen, so she took the seat next to Juanita. Juanita had an emotional, adolescent fit about it and eventually pushed Isabel out of the chair and onto the floor in front of their guests. The girls embarrassed Pablo, and he was beside himself. He couldn't understand what the matter with the girls was, so he sent them to the chapel.

The guests knew such a display would humiliate Pablo, so they tried to ignore what was going on, except for Bill. He looked on, amused by the comical scene and remarked while laughing, "I saw two Crow Indian girls scrap like that one time over a tin of blue beads." Since Bill knew nothing about girls, he assumed that they were really fighting about the chair, just as he figured the Indian girls were really fighting over beads. Bill never would have considered that a boy was the underlying cause of either dispute.

Zeb observed that Rose and Bennager had taken particular care not to notice the royal row, and because of that, Zeb knew exactly what was going on. He also knew women and girls. Rose could feel Zeb's eyes burning a hole through her, and she held out as long as she could without looking up from her plate. Finally, she shot daggers back at him, daring him to speak up about what was on his mind, but he didn't. For Pablo's sake, he brought up the subject of cattle.

"Pablo, when will your vaqueros come back? Mrs. Rasmussen had a deadline to keep with all the miners between here and Sacramento City."

"The vaqueros will start drifting back in about a month."

"Maybe we should go see the cattle tomorrow. Maybe Mrs. Rasmussen will get to see a calf be born," Zeb suggested.

"Yes, tomorrow will be a good day to look for cattle, but you know you shouldn't intrude when those devil cattle are calving Zeb. It is much too dangerous. Would you like to go tomorrow, Mrs. Rasmussen?" Pablo asked her.

"Yes, Señor Ramirez, Zeb is right. I need to get as much business finished as I can so I can see how my rancho is coming along. I don't even know if I have a rancho. I worry all the time I don't even have a place on the Yuba to put these cattle. I can't wait to see these devil cows of yours, as you put it. It figures their breeding is inspired by Zeb," Rose said, smiling at her little joke.

Pablo shook his head. "Yes, they are Loco Zeb's inspiration. Well said, Mrs. Rasmussen. Oh how I miss my sweet little Mexican cows."

Bill said, "It's going to be an interesting trip, all right. Loco this, devil that, witches and warlocks, Indians and man-eating horses, and one pregnant boss woman!"

The women at the table gasped. They knew where the mountain man was headed with this line of conversation, so they cleared the table and scurried into the kitchen.

"If Little Rose isn't pregnant by now, she surely will be in a month. How are you going to keep her and the baby safe on this trip, Rasmussen?" Bill asked boldly.

Bennager looked directly at Bill, who was sitting across the table from him, and said, "I've told you before you shouldn't concern yourself with my ability to take care of my wife."

"You can tell me that all you like, but it won't keep me from being concerned." Bill's cold, old, blue eyes glared back at Bennager.

Sam felt bad for Bennager, and it looked like there was about to be a fight. Sam knew Bill should stop trying to test Bennager. He was a good man and loved Rose very much. Sam also knew Bill's concern had merit because of the way Grace had passed. The confrontation made Sam uncomfortable, but he stayed in case he had to break up a fight.

Bennager ground out the words, "We are not ready for children yet, Bill, and we have been careful."

"Care is the very thing that I see in your face when you look at her! You bet!" Bill was sarcastic.

That was it. Bennager lunged across the table and grabbed Bill by the throat, and Sam and Zeb pulled the two men apart. The women came out of the kitchen to see what was going on and then quickly scampered back to where they had come from. Rose stayed. There was a problem, and she felt that she should stand up for her husband. Besides, she couldn't let him kill her uncle.

"Why don't you tell Bennager why you are so concerned about Rose instead of pretending to be a nosy, know-it-all, old mountain man?" Sam suggested.

Bill shook free from Sam's hold and went outside. Bud and Blossom never moved from their seats. Rose saw them both look at the doorway where they had last seen Bill. She was impressed with their behavior, but she was saddened by it too. Rose took them by their little hands. They hadn't had a bath since Bill had taken them out to live in the brush, and Rose figured it was high time.

Pablo wanted to retire from the dining room, as he did every night, and the men followed. Bennager was still mad. His jaw muscles rippled as he sat down in one of Pablo's luxurious cowhide-covered chairs. Pablo poured them all a drink. He had been made aware of the fact that Sam preferred brandy for his arthritis, and that is what they all had.

"Bill thinks he is a doctor with all of his teas and plants and salves," Zeb finally said after there had been a long silence. He wanted Bennager to stay mad at Bill. Bennager didn't pay any attention to Zeb, though. He knew Zeb could be a troublemaker where Bill was concerned, and he didn't want to encourage him. Bennager did wonder what made Bill act like such an ass when it came to the subject of Rose and babies. If Rose was to become pregnant, it would be wonderful. Bennager wouldn't let her ride that crazy horse, and that would escalate into a devil of a battle, but she was young, and she would be fine and well cared for. She would have to ride in the wagon and she would have to lay off the booze, and Bennager would have to make sure that the wild cattle didn't get near her. He could do that.

He could win the battle about the horse with one lead ball and could keep her safe. Why did Bill think that he couldn't?

After the brandy drink was sipped away, Bennager loosened up. "Sam, you told Bill to tell me something. What was it?"

"I'm sorry, Bennager. Bill should be the one to tell it," Sam replied.

Bennager left abruptly to go have Bill tell him. Zeb's eyes widened as he looked at Sam. "Do you think that was a good idea, Sam?"

"Yeah, they're goin' to have at it one way or the other, and I believe Bennager is plenty able to defend himself. No two men will love Rose more than they do. They need to get straight with each other, and the sooner, the better," Sam answered.

"I agree!" Pablo said, just to be contrary to Zeb.

"Well, I want to see this!" Zeb jumped up from his chair.

Sam quickly grasped his arm as he passed by. "It's private, Zeb. Old wounds will open, and it's not our business," Sam said with a persuasive look.

Bennager had cooled off, and now he was curious about Sam's comment. He rolled a smoke, lit it, and waited for his eyes to adjust to the dark so he could spot Bill. He half expected Bill to sneak up on him, and that would have been fine. Bennager wouldn't have to go look for him then. When Bill didn't come around, Bennager decided to go find him, and he did find him behind the house. Bill had been on his way to the chapel, but he saw something there that made him change his mind. Bill smelled Bennager's tobacco smoke and whispered to him, "Hey, come here, look what I found."

Bennager peered through the darkness and saw it too. "Oh my Lord!" he whispered.

Bill held his hand to his mouth and giggled as Bennager flicked his cigarette away. "Romero isn't going to like this, Bill," Bennager whispered as they spied on Stud Colt and Juanita kissing by the chapel.

"Let me sneak up on them. Maybe it will embarrass the girl and she'll stay away from Stud. Maybe she'll think I'll tell her old man if I catch her in the act," Bill plotted, finding it very hard to stop giggling. Even Bennager had his hand to his mouth, trying to stifle a snicker. Bill started out, and Bennager hid behind the house, watching the two youngsters. It was obvious to Bennager that Stud had no intention of letting Juanita go, and that seemed to be all right with her, so Bill had plenty of time to get there. The boy held Juanita with his arms and his heart, and she held him back with all the love that she could muster. Rose had been telling Bennager for three weeks now about Juanita's affinity for Stud, but Bennager never thought that it would come to this so soon.

Bennager looked for Bill to see where he was, but he couldn't see him, so he watched the kids and waited. Pretty soon, Juanita jumped out of her skin, and then she kicked Bill in the leg for scaring her, but she didn't run away. She grabbed Stud's hand and held her ground while Bill rubbed his bony old shin. Bill grimaced as he looked at Stud. He wanted to tell Stud to stay away from the little witch girl, which she was because she had kicked him, but he knew Stud wouldn't stand for that kind of talk about his woman. Bill limped down the hill to where he had left Bennager.

"My plan didn't work," Bill said.

"I can see that." Bennager chuckled. "We better get out of here. I don't want to be around when one of the Ramirez's catch Stud Colt," Bennager said as he walked, and Bill limped out to the corrals.

Bennager rolled another smoke and looked at the stars that were visible between the clouds as he smoked it. "Sam said you might have something to say to me other than accusing me of being a poor husband."

"I don't think that about you, Rasmussen. I know that you love my niece, and she loves and trusts you. You are a good husband to her," Bill confessed.

"What's with the hard time then, Bill? Why all the concern?"

"I'm worried about what will happen if you get her pregnant," Bill said, looking at the ground.

"She is young and strong, and she will be cared for, Bill. I won't let her ride that horse if that's what you're worried about," Bennager said, shaking his head. This man drove him crazy, but he still wanted his friendship and his approval.

Bill let out a long sigh. "Babies kill women, Bennager. My mother had our friend Lucy and a doctor by her side, and she died. My wife had women of her tribe by her side, and she died. There ain't no doctors around here, Bennager. There ain't no women around to help out either, and there ain't one damned thing that you can do to keep a woman from dying during childbirth. No matter how much you want to or how hard you pray or how much you cry, you can't stop it from happening. It makes you feel like the lowest, most worthless, inept son of a bitch in the world, and of course, you know that it's your fault. It's you that did the thing that made the baby that killed your wife. That's how you feel, and you never stop thinking about how you couldn't protect or save her. Sam knew about my mother, but he doesn't know about my wife. Nobody does, and I don't want them to. It was a lucky thing I was able to help Rose with her arm back there on the river. It was just pure luck that I came by when I did, but I can't help a woman have a baby. Do you understand that?"

Bennager nodded his head. Bill had driven his point home and had put the fear of God into him. Bennager realized Bill was absolutely right. He couldn't imagine losing Rose at all but especially in that way. He also understood Bill's ways with the Yokut children and why he was so different from anyone that he had ever met. He covered his sorrows with jokes and pranks and self-righteousness. He could make you laugh one minute and want to kill him the next. "I understand you, Bill, and I'm sorry for your losses."

"I speak from experience when I say things to you about Rose. You should have seen my wife. She was so beautiful. She was tall and slim, and she had the most beautiful green eyes in the world. Her father had been with the Hudson Bay Company in the early twenties. She was beautiful, but the men of her tribe wouldn't have her because she was half Scottish. Boy, I felt like the luckiest son of a bitch in the Absaroka Range when I ran across her and her people. I knew the men had to be jealous. They weren't blind, they knew she was pretty, but they just couldn't take her for a bride. She felt lucky that I came along too. Boy, she was ripe for the pickin' and pleasant to be around. Lord, how I miss her." Bill sighed. "Stud told me that

I don't know anything about women," Bill said, turning around to look at the chapel. "The truth is I've been trying to forget everything that I ever knew about 'em."

"Stud seems to know about women, all right," Bennager chuckled. He was hoping that Bill would keep talking about his life. He knew there was much to learn from Bill if he listened. It was a rarity to see the serious, sincere side of Horny Bill Ford.

"I buried my woman and my baby, and I never looked back. It's the same thing that I did with my mother, only I didn't even stick around for the burial. I might have if Sam hadn't been hurt, but I doubt it. Zeb, on the other hand, makes folks think that his wife is still alive when she ain't. He rode through the rain for two days to talk to her at her grave. Why would a man revisit that pain?"

This was news to Bennager, and he didn't have the answer. "I don't know," he said.

"Pablo says now that she is in heaven, she can see and hear everything that he does. He allows her to haunt him! I don't think that's love. I think he should let the poor woman rest in peace. She deserves it after having to live with him."

"How did she die?" Bennager asked.

"I didn't ask because I didn't think Stud would know," Bill replied.

"You didn't know Anna was dead then?"

"No, and I was shocked to hear it," Bill answered. "I've been giving him such a hard time about her, you know?"

"Yeah, I heard something about a wandering vaquero," Bennager said. "What do you say to him now that you know?"

"Well, I'll have to think on it, but I think I'll leave it as it is. If he wants to make out that she can see him and hear him, then I will try to get him to do things that she would disapprove of," Bill said with a wide grin on his face. "It will give me something to think about."

*****

There was an argument the next morning between Pablo and Rose. Pablo wanted her to ride with him in the carriage to go find the cattle, but she wouldn't have it. She thought it all had something to do with the men deciding that she was pregnant. She wasn't pregnant and she wanted to ride the Roman. She felt safer with him under her than she did being trapped in a carriage if one of those cows came after it. Pablo just wanted her to be dry in case it started to rain while they were out. Neither one of them stopped smiling nor did they stop being pleasant during the dispute, and Pablo finally gave up on the hardheaded woman. Sam didn't mind taking her place. He knew Rose was likely to stay out all day, and he didn't think that he wanted to ride that long.

Stud Colt never had any intention of riding out to find cows, and he told Bill as much when Bill told him to get up and get going. "You are not going to stay here all day, sneaking around with what's her name and kissing her and God knows what else. Your actions are bound to get us killed. You can't be fooling around with that girl anyway. She already has a husband picked out for her somewhere, so just stay away from that," Bill whispered in Stud's language.

"She loves only me, Bill. I'm staying here to be with her when you go away with the cattle," Stud argued.

Bill eyeballed the boy, and then he said, "They will turn you into a vaquero."

Stud shrugged his shoulders. "Then I will be a vaquero, and I will be her lover."

Bill turned away from Stud so he wouldn't see him laughing at the boy. Stud was a romantic dreamer, and his big ideas tickled Bill right down to the bone. After a while, when he knew that he could hold a straight face, he turned back to Stud and told him, "You will have to prove yourself to be a vaquero before you will be allowed to be her lover. This is how these things work."

Stud shrugged again. "Then I will do it."

"Do you even know what a vaquero is, you adolescent cock hound?" Bill whispered with force.

Stud shook his head no.

"A vaquero rides for cows and commands them, you idiot. Now go get your horse and mount up and stay the devil away from what's her name," Bill said, shaking his head.

"Her name is Juanita," Stud said, pouting.

"I don't care," Bill stated.

Stud and Bill were running late. As they approached the livery, they saw that everyone else was just about ready. Zeb and Bennager were talking and almost ready, and Rose was mounted and visiting with Sam and Pablo in the carriage.

"There are a couple of early risers!" Zeb shouted, referring to Bill and Stud.

Bill didn't give Zeb the satisfaction of a reply. Bill knew that he would have to spend the whole day looking after his sullen Miwok friend who wouldn't pay a lick of attention to the business at hand because he was going to be thinking about a girl all day.

"Where have you two been? We've been waitin' for you for half the day. It's pert near suppertime," Zeb continued on.

Bill rolled his eyes and shook his head. It was still dark, for heaven's sake. Bill pulled his cinch strap tight and ignored Zeb. He decided that he would pretend to be mad at Zeb today. It would drive him nuts.

"I suppose Bennager kicked the devil out of you last night, and now you won't talk to anybody, is that it?" Zeb finally asked after several moments of putting up with Bill's cold shoulder. Bill and Stud were mounted now, and they rode out and waited for Rose and Pablo to lead the way.

"Hey, don't put me in the middle of you trying to rile Bill. There was not a fight last night, we just talked," Bennager warned Zeb.

"Oh, he knows I'm just giving him a hard time." Zeb chuckled.

Pablo and Sam rolled out of the yard and headed southwest, driving on a trail that took them over little rolling hills with oak trees scattered about and brush too thick to ride through. Pablo warned that the thick brush was where the cows liked to hide. They crossed a few shallow creeks and went by a big pond. After a couple of hours, Pablo finally came to a place at the top of a hill and told the others to look around at the other low hills that surrounded them.

Sam couldn't see anything, and Stud didn't care to see anything, but Bill's keen eyes spotted movement in the brush everywhere he looked. The others finally saw some movement as well. The cattle that hadn't calved yet were running hard and fast in the opposite direction of the people. They had already been three quarters of a mile away when Pablo stopped.

Bennager and Rose were leaning over their saddles, watching the cattle run away. Rose looked at her husband in despair, and he displayed a wide grin. His wife looked beat, and she hadn't even started yet.

"Those cattle of yours are as skittish as elk, Pablo," Bill remarked.

"I know," Pablo said, shaking his head.

"Look at 'em go!" Zeb hollered. "At least they're headed south. Your vaqueros can bring 'em back home in a month."

Pablo gave Bill a look that showed his frustration with Loco Zeb. Pablo wished he would have gone to the Sandwich Islands with his reasonable little Mexican cattle or he should have left Zeb in Texas and never listened to him. "What do you think, Mrs. Rasmussen?" Pablo finally asked after the hillsides stopped moving.

"They look meaty, Señor, but they're not very tame critters, are they? How in the world would we ever get them to the Yuba River?" Rose asked in bewilderment.

"The vaqueros make them cooperate. I do not know how, but they do," Pablo assured.

"Vaqueros are cattle warlocks," Zeb offered as further explanation. Everyone ignored his remark, and Pablo sighed.

Rose didn't know what to think about the cattle, but she couldn't wait to see a vaquero in action. She wanted to see how any man could make such an animal cooperate. She looked at her husband again and tried to imagine what he was thinking with that great big smile on his face. She felt defeated, and if she spent all her money on these cattle, only to have them scattered in the wind between here and the Yuba River, then she would be defeated. How would they live? What would they do? He had been doing just fine before she came along, and now he had stopped what he was doing to traipse around with her on a misadventure at best and fatal mistake at the worst. The realities of being a cattle baron were starting to soak in, and she was beginning to think that she might be in over her head if she decided to be one.

As they all eased back to headquarters, Rose was deep in thought about how Angus was coming along or if he was even there, building her rancho. She had no doubt he had gone to do as she had asked, but she had no way of knowing if he had made it. She figured she needed to know for sure before she shelled out all her money to Pablo. She would talk to her husband about all of this when they were alone.

The loud bellow of a cow sounded after they had traveled the better part of an hour, and everyone stopped and waited for a cow to come barreling out of the brush. Stud figured if he wanted to be a vaquero, then he shouldn't show fear like the others were doing. He nonchalantly rode in the direction of the sound.

"Bill, tell Jack to come back! Now is no time to be brave! I warned you all what can happen," Pablo pleaded.

Bill knew what Stud was up to and laughed when Pablo called him Jack. Bill wanted to see what the romantic was made of, so he didn't tell Stud anything. Sure enough, a big cow with a bloody rump came running out of the brush, aiming to kill Stud's horse with her big, pointed horns. Stud's horse moved out of the way so quickly that Stud tumbled off his mount, onto the ground, and dislocated his shoulder. Fortunately, the big cow was more concerned with the horse than she was with Stud, and it gave Bill, Zeb, and Bennager time to rescue Stud and get out of there.

Zeb couldn't stand just to help the boy out, though. He favored tormenting the cow to get it away from Stud's horse. The cow had no intention of running very far away from her calf; she only wanted to chase the horse a little bit. Bill watched Zeb as the others widened the gap. Zeb chased the wicked cow down on horseback, grabbed her bloody tail with his right hand, and then he took a hard left, throwing the poor, devoted mother down onto her side. Rose had ridden back to witness Zeb's efforts and was amazed. The old cow was stunned and didn't know up from down. Bill was pretty impressed with Zeb's skills, and he thought he might like to try that maneuver sometime, but he wouldn't tell Zeb that. He was being mad at Zeb today, so he rode off and joined the others.

"Well, that's a terrible thing to do to something that has just had a baby!" Rose scolded.

"It's better than shooting her, which is what you would have done!" Zeb said in a charming way. "Come here and look at her calf before she gets to her feet and comes after us."

Rose's eyes twinkled with excitement as she followed Zeb into the brush. In a few moments, Zeb held his hand up for Rose to stop and then pointed to a little secluded patch of dry grass. Rose pulled a branch down that was obstructing her view and saw it. It was a little heifer all cleaned off and trying to stand up. Her little legs were long and spindly. She was light brown with dark brown legs, and her little nose was the prettiest pink Rose had ever seen. The heifer bawled for her mother. "We better get out of here, let's go," Zeb whispered.

Bennager was waiting for Rose to come out of the brush, but the others had gone on. They were going to find a safe place where Bill and Sam could put Stud's arm back in its socket.

"Go on ahead, you two, I'll get Stud's horse and be along in a minute," Zeb suggested.

"Will the cow come back for her baby?" Rose asked.

"She sure will, and you better be long gone when she does," Zeb hollered over his shoulder as he rode fast to find the quick horse.

Rose wasn't worried or depressed anymore. Seeing that little calf made her want to have many calves of her own running around in the foothills of the Sierras. The determined, excited look on her face told Bennager everything he needed to know. His wife was not going to earn her living being a dressmaker, even if she was quite good at it. As they rode on to join the others, he thought of how much fun he was having. He looked to the future and imagined all the crazy things his wife was going to get him into. She was always trying to figure out how to make her money grow, and she had added so much spice and excitement to his dull, lonely life that he just couldn't stop smiling. How were they going to be able to tend these crazy critters by themselves once they got them to their rancho? Bennager knew that it would be something he would be able to tell his children and grandchildren about, and all he had to do was hang on tight and try to keep up.

Rose gently slapped her husband on the leg while he was in deep thought. "Are you laughing at me or what? You've had that silly grin on your face all day."

"I'm happy, Rose Mary Rasmussen. Is there a law against having a silly grin on my face now?" Bennager glared at her in a playful way.

"What are you so happy about? Did you see those critters hightail it for Mexico?" Rose asked excitedly.

"Yes, those critters seem to suit you. They should fit in perfectly with your dreams of being a ranchero," Bennager teased.

Rose smiled. "You should have seen that little baby back there in the brush."

"I know. For a minute there, you were thinking of being a dressmaker, and then Zeb had to be the hero and show you that calf. Now we will all be damned," Bennager joshed.

"I don't think I was ever going to be a dressmaker, dear, not for a living anyway. If you think we will be damned, then why are you smiling?" Rose inquired as she reached out for his hand.

"You just tickle me, that's all," Bennager said honestly and shook his head a little, trying not to blush. She didn't need to know his every thought.

They saw the others up ahead and trotted to join them. Not only was Stud not much of a vaquero, he also wasn't very tolerant to pain. He had mud all over his backside from squirming around on the ground while Sam had been holding him down so Bill could set his arm. Stud was visibly furious with the two men but mostly Bill. Bill had been badgering him the whole time about how he would never get his name changed to Stud Dick and how Pablo was calling him Jack whether he liked it or not. He was also fuming because he had just bathed the night before for Juanita, and now he was filthy again, and a week hadn't even passed.

Stud and Bill argued constantly in Stud's language until Zeb arrived with Stud's horse.

Rose didn't know that Stud was capable of such fierceness. Even when he wanted to make war over the pie, he hadn't been infuriated about it. Rose thought she could calm him down, so she dismounted and asked if he would be all right.

He was livid when he heard the question. "I am a man!" he hollered at her, and then he mounted.

Rose jumped back at the loud Miwok words and got out of his way. Bill couldn't help but laugh at his radical, hormonal, Indian friend, and this made Stud even angrier. He rode hard and fast back to the rancho to be with Juanita and away from Bill.

"Jack is really mad at you, Bill Ford," Pablo stated as he headed toward his home.

Bill looked at Bennager, who was the only other one who knew what Stud was up to, and Bennager raised his brow and grinned. Rose happened to catch the exchange and knew there was a secret between her two favorite men. This was quite a switch from the dining room table incident that happened the night before, and Rose was curious about the details.

Zeb rode beside Bennager the rest of the way to the rancho and talked of cattle, breeding, and the techniques that the vaqueros used when tending the cattle.

Rose rode with her uncle and listened to Zeb intensely. Finally, when Bill was tired of being ignored, he whispered to his niece, "You're not listening to that rotten old buzzard, are you?"

Rose was caught; she had been listening because he was being so serious. He hadn't used the W words since they had seen the cattle heading south. She smiled at her uncle. Rose bit off a piece of tobacco. "How long would it take me to get to the Yuba River from here on horseback?" she asked Bill.

"Why?"

"I want to go check on Angus. I need to know if he found a place for me to put these cattle. I can't buy them if I don't have a place to put them."

"Stud and I will go check it out. I should be able to find Angus easily, and I think Stud is getting too domesticated by staying with the Ramirez's," Bill said.

Rose looked at her uncle in a confused way. "He has only been here for two days," she reminded him.

"Well, that seems to be all the time it takes for a boneheaded Miwok," Bill stated.

"What about the children?" Rose asked.

"Bennager and Sam will be in charge of them. I don't want any women spoiling them again," Bill said loudly and defiantly.

Bennager and Sam turned and scowled at Bill. They weren't babysitters and they didn't want the job. Sam glanced up at Bennager from the carriage and shook his head in disgust.

"Why can't I be in charge of the rascals?" Zeb asked, but Bill wouldn't answer him. Bill was mad at him today.

"You should go with Bill Ford and Jack," Pablo suggested, wanting Loco Zeb out of his hair.

"Let me be in charge of the kids. Those guys don't know anything about little kids," Zeb pleaded with Bill, but Bill ignored him. When Zeb turned around to pout, Bill winked and smiled at Rose, and she caught on to his game.

Rose said, "He doesn't want them to be spoiled or turned into witches, Zeb."

"You should go with Bill Ford and Jack," Pablo reiterated.

"Who in the hell is Jack?" Zeb hollered at Pablo. Bill held his hand to his mouth to hold back a laugh.

"Jack is the Indian boy who has been kissing Juanita!" Pablo yelled back.

Bill, Bennager, and Rose all rolled their eyes and grabbed their hats at the same time. "His name isn't Jack, you old Mexican fart, it's Stud Colt!"

"I like Jack better, you damned Loco Gringo!" Pablo yelled to Zeb.

Bill and Rose were having a hard time controlling their laughter during Zeb and Pablo's bickering, and when Zeb quickly turned in his saddle, he caught them trying not to laugh. Zeb was whole again when he realized that Bill had just been messing with his head all day. "Let me tend the children, Bill," Zeb begged again.

"You can't make biscuits. Sam can!" Bill said defiantly. "And Bennager needs the experience," he added.

"Not yet he doesn't, Uncle," Rose whispered playfully.

"He will," Bill stated.

5

Bill woke up to a crisp, clear February morning and kicked Stud in the foot. "Get up, it's time to go," Bill said in Miwok. Stud was down in the mouth. Apparently, Juanita's grandmother had a talk with her about Stud while he was out hurting his arm for her love, and the girl had been cold toward him when he came back to be comforted by her. He was sad and didn't understand why she hadn't come to his aid when he needed her love and her sweet kisses. The other women in the family had shown Stud aid and kindness when he returned, but Juanita had stayed hidden. Stud thought that Juanita would meet him at the chapel again, so once it got dark, he went there and waited, but the only one that showed up was Bill. Now Bill was making him leave again, and he would never know where he stood with his woman.

Bill and Stud had argued about his leaving the night before when they were at the chapel. Stud knew there was no use in arguing with him now about it, so he got up and quietly went to the corrals with Bill and caught his horse.

Rose brought the children to say goodbye to Bill. He had made them understand the night before that he was going to leave, but he would be back, and to be good for Sam and Bennager. The children weren't frightened or worried. They knew that Rose would keep them safe. They didn't care what Bill had conveyed to them about Sam and Bennager because Rose was their mother and their rock.

Pablo came out to see Bill off. "Thank you for understanding my thoughts about Jack kissing my granddaughter behind my chapel, Bill Ford. They are too young to be in love. Maria tells me that Juanita has been crying all night. Please take Loco Zeb with you, my friend."

Bill laughed at the dear man. "Pablo, I doubt that I can keep Stud Colt away from here. You might just as well consider putting him to work for you when we get back. He agreed to take this trip with me because he wants to check on his mother on the way through and tell her about the ocean and the girl, but he tells me that nothing will keep him away from your granddaughter, and I believe him. He's a good worker, Pablo. He knows nothing of cattle, of course, but he's been working on and off for Jared Sheldon for the last three years, and he seems to be sitting on quite a nice gold claim that's in my name, so his family won't lose it."

Pablo looked at the ground and shook his head. "They are too young to be in love."

"What about two years from now if he learns how to be a vaquero?" Bill negotiated.

"I don't think Jack wants to be a vaquero. He just wants to make babies. Will you please take Loco Zeb with you?"

"I asked Zeb to stay here and watch in case more murdering thieves show up, Pablo. I know he'll help watch over Rose when she takes it in to her head to go off and do something she shouldn't," Bill said so Rose could hear. "Rose can help keep Zeb out of your hair too. She knows how to talk to him."

Pablo shook his head in disappointment, but he understood Bill's concern, and he knew Bill was determined to leave Zeb with him whether he liked it or not. He couldn't blame the man for his wise decision.

"Besides, I might be bound to find Zeb a new wife if he went with me," Bill jibed, grinning widely at Pablo.

"Oh no, I told you about that, Bill Ford. You must not interfere!" Pablo said, holding his hands up and waving them in front of his face.

"Well, I'm going to be scouting for one on this trip, so watch out." Bill laughed. He loved to worry the sweet man and make him sweat.

Rose, Pablo, and the children headed back for the house. "Señor Ramirez, what did Uncle mean about finding Zeb a new wife?"

"Zeb never told any of you? Anna has been dead for almost two years. He acts like she is still alive because she can see him from heaven. Bill Ford does not understand this kind of devotion, and he wants to corrupt Zeb," Pablo explained. He could see that Rose was shocked to hear this information, and he was surprised that Bill hadn't told her.

"How long has Uncle known about Anna?" Rose inquired.

"Just a couple of days. Jack told him when they came back from Monterey," Pablo said.

"I'll be damned!" Rose whispered.

Pablo smiled at Rose's language but didn't say anything about it. His wife would never use such language, but he thought that it was funny that this beautiful little American girl did. She was a good girl, but she had a poor upbringing, Pablo concluded, and let it go at that. Rose's upbringing made Pablo think of something.

"Where did you and Mr. Rasmussen have your wedding?" Pablo asked.

Rose snickered. "We were married on the Sacramento River by a steamboat captain."

Pablo scowled at the image. Rose continued, "I was sick with my infected arm and a bashed head, and Bennager went and got Charlie, and he married us up while we were both lying down in the tent."

Pablo gasped. "That is not a real wedding!"

"According to Charlie, it was a real wedding," Rose argued with a smile.

"It might be legal but not a real wedding. You will have a real wedding in my chapel when Bill and Jack come back. I will send for a priest from Monterey and Maria will help you make a dress. I will speak to Zeb," Pablo said.

"Señor, my marriage is wonderful just the way it is. I don't need a wedding with a priest in your chapel," Rose argued.

"You must! You must have the ring and the dress and the priest!" Pablo was unwavering. "I will speak to Zeb."

"Señor, is this just an excuse to send Zeb away?" Rose asked, glaring at her host.

"Yes, please let me do this. It will be good for the girls to see a wedding, and it will give us something to do while we wait for the calves and the vaqueros. It will please Zeb to go to Monterey again before your drive to your Yuba River."

Rose thought that Pablo made a compelling argument. It would be something to do and it would be fun for the girls. "Maybe it would cheer up Juanita."

"Yes, think of poor Juanita. Think of how lovely you will look in a wedding gown. Someday, I will be forced to let Juanita marry Jack, and you will come and help her with her wedding, and you will have to tell Jack that chapels are not just a place for kissing," Pablo said pleadingly.

Pablo made Rose giggle. The sweet man was wise and hated to be bored. He didn't miss anything that had to do with his family, and he made Rose feel like she was part of that family. His attitude toward Zeb was very comical. "Oh, señor, say what you want, but this is all about Zeb."

"Yes, Loco Zeb needs something to do."

Rose laughed. "You are right about that. I will ask my husband."

"He will say yes," Pablo assured her.

*****

Five weeks had passed since Angus had last seen his boss. As he looked around the property that was becoming a rancho, he was satisfied with his progress and pleased with all the hard work that Trina had helped him to accomplish. He was getting ready to make his fifth trip to Grass Valley for lumber, and Angus was noticing how well the grass was coming up. It was as green and lush as anything that he had seen in Ireland, and he hoped that the Rasmussens would be happy with his choice of land. In the last three weeks, he had fallen in love with the area, and today he would be putting in a claim for some property north of Rose's land. He didn't need as much as Rose did; he only wanted a little home in the oak trees to call his own.

During his trips to Grass Valley, he had met some people who had led him to some men who would dig a well for the rancho house. The only problem was that they said they should wait until summertime for the water table to drop, and autumn would be even better. Angus intended to talk to the men again today because it was his opinion that they just didn't want to leave the saloon. Angus knew about water tables, but he also knew Mrs. Rasmussen would want some water, and it was his job to see that she had it.

Angus had also become acquainted with men who knew Bennager quite well. The pig farmer, as it turned out, was a good friend of Bennager's, and he only cussed him because he was jealous of his team and his good fortune. Bennager and Jake Gates had come out from Illinois together in '42. Bennager tripped over a rock in Grass Valley that turned out to be a big gold nugget. Since he figured it was a once in a lifetime occurrence, he bought a little mule with part of his last $50 and rode to Marysville, crossed the Feather River and traveled onto the Sacramento River to Hugh Glenn's wheat rancho, and started acquiring his six-horse team. Glenn took the gold nugget and sent Bennager to pick up four more horses and a freight wagon from Bidwell's rancho farther up the Sacramento Valley, and Glenn paid Bidwell in script and gave Bennager quite a lot of change back.

Jake told Trina and Angus that he dug around the same spot, where Bennager had tripped, for a week until one day when Bennager showed up with his matched team and a slightly used freight wagon. Jake had been cussing his friend ever since. The news about him marrying a beautiful woman with her own money made Jake Gates and Matthew Harrison and all his other friends cuss him even more.

"First, he falls on his face 'cause a gold nugget tripped him up, and the ignorant bastard doesn't even bother to look for any more, then he makes a fortune hauling freight all over the damned countryside when everyone else can't rub two cents together, and now you mean to tell me that he actually met a woman? That alone is a blessing in these parts, you know. But then she actually married the son of a bitch?"

"Aye, and she loves him very much," Angus explained to the exasperated Jake Gates.

"What a rotten son of a bitch! You know that rotten bastard still has the first dollar he ever made. He invested some of his money in Harrison's lumber mill, I think he owns 20 percent of it, and he doesn't do a damned thing but haul freight out of there once in a while. Doc Glenn invests money for him too, but I don't know what he does with it. Leave it to that damned Rasmussen to trip over another gold nugget, that sorry bastard."

Angus and Trina heard the same complaints about Bennager wherever they went, and they concluded from the jealous rhetoric that Bennager was fairly well off and well known. Angus was happy to find out that Bennager had a reputable name and past. He didn't know what he would have done if he had found out that the man was a cad and the father of countless little children running around the state of Illinois, but according to Gates, Bennager hadn't even been in love before. Gates claimed that he felt sorry for Bennager's new wife because Bennager wouldn't know what to do with a woman if he had one.

Jake Gates had come to visit Bennager's new rancho site the day before, and when Jake made the claim about Bennager, Trina had found the remark and the humorous way that he said it to be quite amusing. When she laughed heartily at it, Jake was surprised. Angus saw him blush and then smile at Trina. Angus got it into his head that the two pig farmers were about ready to unite, and he had been awake half the night thinking that he might lose his partner. He had to drink a quarter of a jug of whiskey to get to sleep.

Now while he was waiting for Trina to come out of her tiny cabin and petting Girl by the warmth of the fire, he thought of the blush and the smile again. He thought of Gates' statement and reckoned he might not know what to do with a woman, but a woman with Trina's past would be able to train him just fine. Angus shivered at Jake's misfortune should he decide to fall in love with an Irish woman. He shook his head at the idea. Angus knew Irish women, and he knew how mean and unreasonable they could be. His life as a free and simple pig farmer would come to an end the first time she went to telling him his business about this thing and that thing. Trina didn't seem to be as bad as his sisters were, but he figured if she had a husband to pick on, she would change overnight into a typical Irish woman.

Angus looked over at Trina's cabin and could see there still wasn't any movement. This was out of the ordinary for Trina. The sun was up over the horizon now, and she still hadn't come out for breakfast. Girl was growing impatient as well. She hadn't had her piece of bacon yet, and her pups were getting on her nerves. They were starting to walk and roll around now, and they followed her wherever she went. She couldn't go to town with Angus anymore because he was afraid they would fall out of the wagon and be killed, so she had to wait all day in the tent or by the cabin for Angus and Trina to get back. She was grateful to the titan, though; he never forgot to bring her a good piece of meat.

Angus and Girl walked over to Trina's cabin, finally. He knocked on the door. "Come in!" Trina said.

Angus didn't open the door. He was fearful that he would intrude on her privacy. "Are ye goin' to town with me, lassie?" Angus shouted through the door.

Trina rolled her eyes. Why wouldn't he just come in? "I'm sick, Angus," Trina replied.

"What's the matter with ye?"

"I don't know. I can't keep my food down and I have a fever."

"I'm comin' in," Angus said. He opened the door to find Trina in her bedroll and red in the face. He put the back of his hand to her forehead. "Aye, you have a fever all right. Ye must be gettin' a chill at night. Ye can't stay warm in this place."

"I think I ate something bad, Angus. I'll be all right after a while," Trina assured him.

Angus didn't listen. He picked her up and carried her to the fire. The day was dry, so he didn't have to worry about her getting wet. "I've been makin' ye work too hard, lass." He took a bucket to the creek and filled it with clear, cold water. He sat it beside her and went to his tent for a clean cloth. He soaked it in the water and laid it across Trina's forehead and then went for more blankets. He figured that he could sweat the fever out of her.

Trina looked at the freshly shaven face of the man whom she had come to care for so much. "What are you doing? I told you that I'd be all right in a while. You don't have to fuss like this."

"I'll make sure ye're all right," Angus said as he boiled water to make some tea.

"You need to go to town and roust those well diggers out of the saloon. You don't need to stay here and worry about me," Trina told him.

"No, I can't leave ye here with a fever. Ye work for the Rasmussens, and they would want me to take care of ye," Angus replied. "If they were here, they wouldn't be worried about a well, they would be worried 'bout ye."

Trina closed her eyes and wondered why Angus just couldn't worry about her because he cared for her. Her heart broke at his indifference toward her. He was talking about her as if she was a piece of property that needed to be tended to as if she was one of the horses that had a fever. "If you were sick, I'd take care of you because I care for you Angus, not because you work for the Rasmussens." Trina sighed in disappointment.

Angus raised his brows. He didn't know what she was trying to say, but she seemed vexed with him, and he didn't know why. He figured that between being a redheaded Irish girl and having a fever, she was probably just talking nonsense. He dismissed her confusing remark and kept trying to cool her down with the wet cloth.

"Angus, put me in my cabin. I don't want to be out here on the ground like this. I can take care of myself," Trina pleaded.

"No, I want ye here by the fire, ye have to sweat the fever out of ye."

Trina sighed again. The man was stubborn and exhausting. There was no use in arguing with him. She had been awake half the night, purging, so she decided to try to sleep.

After Trina fell asleep, Angus gathered more wood and stood watch over her as he made coffee and breakfast. Trina's nap was cut short when she smelled the bacon frying. The smell woke her up and made her stomach turn, and she rolled over and purged again. She had been doing this for the last six hours. At first, it came on about every ten minutes, but now it had slowed to about every hour. She didn't have anything left in her stomach except acid, but apparently, her body wanted that out too. Trina moaned when she was finished. She wondered when it would end. Angus took the mess away with a shovel and rushed back to her. He cleaned her mouth and kept cooling her forehead. "Ye need to drink a little water."

"No, it will just come up again. Please put me back in my cabin. I don't want you to see me like this."

"Nay, ye have to be by the fire."

"I can't stand the smell of the food!" Trina moaned and began to cry.

Angus quickly finished cooking the meal and put the food in the tent and cleaned up the mess so Trina couldn't smell it. While he was cleaning, Girl ate all of Angus's bacon and then quickly left the vicinity of her crime with her babies in tow. When Angus returned to find his bacon gone, he wasn't really disappointed. He had only made it so Girl could have some, but he figured she wasn't in the sharing mood today. He settled for cheese and dried fruit and went back to Trina's side. She had fallen asleep again.

The day passed by slowly for Angus. Trina finally started to sweat, and she had only purged two more times and slept the rest of the day away. Toward the end of the day, Angus could hear riders coming. Girl barked from somewhere out in the distance, and Angus stood up to greet whoever was coming. He hoped that it was the well-diggers, but he was very surprised to see it was Bill Ford. Bill eased up when he saw the camp, but he knew that he had the right place when he saw Zeb's dog and three little balls of fur following her.

"Hello at the camp! It's ol' Bill Ford, and I'm coming in!"

Angus was happy to see him. He took off his hat and waved Bill and Stud in. Bill hopped off his horse with ease and put his hand out and Angus took it. "It's good to see ye, Bill!" Angus laughed cheerfully.

"Yeah, I'm glad to find you here Angus. You've picked a fine spot for the rancho." Bill noticed Angus was looking at the Indian, who was not in a pleasant mood, with curiosity. "Oh, this here is Stud Colt. He's a Miwok Indian brave from the Cosumnes River country. He's been riding with us because his mother is having a baby, and he doesn't like the smell of babies."

Angus offered him his hand, and Stud took it and patted Angus hard on the shoulder, but he never smiled. As a matter of fact, he was downright gloomy. Angus figured this was probably the way with Indians and didn't think much about it.

"I can see you've started on a good bit of work here, Angus. Is that going to be the barn or the house?" Bill asked as he looked at the building that Angus was framing on top of a little knob.

"That is the house I've been workin' on," Angus replied.

"How many acres do you have on the books?"

"One league, almost forty-five hundred acres."

"That's a fair amount, I reckon."

"I would like to take ye out and show ye the perimeter, but I have a sick woman on me hands," Angus told him.

"Oh, is that right? Maybe I better have a look," Bill said with concern. Stud followed, leading the horses. "What has she been doing?"

"She threw up all night and part of the mornin' and she has a fever."

Bill knelt beside Trina, and Stud did the same on the other side of her. Stud touched her red hair and looked into her face. This made Angus a little nervous, but he noticed it didn't bother Bill, so he stayed calm.

"She said that she probably ate somethin' bad. We were supposed to go the Grass Valley today for more supplies and to pick up the well-diggers, but I thought it best to tend to her," Angus explained.

"His woman is striking," Stud commented to Bill.

"What did he say, Bill?"

"Stud said that your woman is pretty. Where did you find such a beauty, you ol' dog?" Bill teased.

"Do ye think she'll get better, Bill?" Angus asked.

"Yeah, I think she's all right, did she stop throwing up?"

"Aye, she quit that 'bout noon."

"I bet she'll be back on her feet tomorrow. Who is she?"

"Her name is Trina. She needed a job, so I hired her, she is a good worker."

Bill wondered about the tiny scars on Trina's face, but he could tell that Angus wasn't being forthcoming about the girl, so he didn't bother to ask. "Are you really expecting me to believe that she just works for you, Angus? There's no crime against having a woman, you know." Bill chuckled at the shy Irishman.

Trina was waking up to the sound of the men's voices.

"Aye, but not this woman. Irish woman are mean, Bill. I know 'cause I grew up with them being mean to me every day."

Bill laughed robustly. "Is this one mean to you?"

"Nay, she is a good worker. She does everythin' that I ask her to do, and I pay her $5 a week."

Bill couldn't contain his laughter. Angus was a dandy. Bill told Stud what Angus had said, and Stud shook his head at the Irishman's ignorance.

"How can he live with this woman and not make love to her?" Stud asked Bill as he looked into Trina's face and gently touched her scars. "What happened to her face, Bill?" Stud asked with a tinge of anger in his voice.

Trina opened her eyes and saw Stud's smiling face and his concern. Bill asked, "How are you feeling, Miss Trina?"

"I'm soaked! Where's Angus?"

"He's here. I think your fever is gone," Bill whispered and smiled.

Trina smiled graciously at the men. "Angus, will you please take me back to the cabin? I am embarrassed to be seen like this."

Angus picked her up off the ground and did as she asked. He came back to the fire. The sun was going down, and there wasn't enough time to show Bill the boundary lines. Angus started to get supper prepared before it got dark.

"It's good to see you, Bill. Did Rose send ye two to help me get the rancho ready?" Angus asked as he bustled around camp.

"No, we just needed to make sure that you had a place picked out and where it was, although we could stay for a couple of weeks. She's fixing to buy about two hundred pair, and for that, she's going to need more land, so we'll start work on that tomorrow. Also, I think we ought to lay off on the house building and start on a sturdy set of corrals. These cattle are pretty wild. We'll have to hold 'em for a while so they will know where their new home is. Are there anymore good creeks like this one around?"

"There are a couple, but not as good as this. Maybe we should get some land on the river," Angus suggested.

"That's where the miners will be, and they will just take what they want."

"Aye, that's what I thought. The grass isn't as good next to the river either. East of here, we will find more creeks, I think, but I don't think they run year-round," Angus explained.

"We'll have to move the cattle around throughout the year then. Somebody will, that is." Bill chuckled.

"What happened to that woman's face?" Stud posed his question to Angus this time. Angus raised his brows. The boy was clearly irritated, and Bill translated.

Angus nodded his head and explained, "She was with a bad man when I met her, and she came here with me."

"Where is the bad man?" Stud asked.

Angus was shy about what had happened, and he didn't want to speak about it. "He's probably dead. I doubt he survived what I did to him," he said as he looked sadly at the ground.

Stud smiled broadly when Bill translated for him. Stud liked Angus now, even if he was ignorant about loving the woman. He wanted to talk to Angus some more, so Bill translated for the better part of an hour. Stud told Angus about his Juanita and Bill's scheme to keep them apart. He told stories about the man-eating horse that Rose loved and the poor mule that was in love with Bennager. He spoke of the ocean and how Zeb had talked to the ground for hours, and he told Angus his opinion of Bill's smelly children and the mean cattle that Rose wanted.

His last topic of conversation was of love. The love between Bennager and Rose and the love between Zeb and his dead wife. He told Angus that he was a fool for not loving the beautiful woman and that he was ignorant like Bill. Angus had laughed, been shocked, and then offended. Bill rolled his eyes and shook his head a lot while he translated Stud's stories. Finally, Stud picked up one of the puppies and left.

"Mr. Colt had a lot to say," Angus remarked.

"Well, he should. He quit talking to me when we left the Ramirez Ranchero. He's mad at me for making him leave that little shin-kicking girl, but we had to split them up. His pecker is so big he would have split her in half if he had poked her with it," Bill said, seriously shaking his head.

Angus fell over backward off the old log that he was sitting on. That was the funniest thing that he had ever heard. Now he understood why Bill called the boy Stud Colt, and he laughed even harder when he pictured in his mind the young boy convincing some girl to make love to him. After some time had passed, Angus was able to speak again. "I don't remember ever laughin' like that in me life! I would have laughed at ye and Zeb that night by the river, but I didn't have the energy. That boy is too young for that kind of love," Angus said.

"That's what Pablo and I thought too," Bill said.

Stud rushed back to the fire and screamed, "I am a man!" in his own language.

Angus jerked a little and Bill squinted with pain and waved at Stud to go away. He knew that he would hear that one Miwok phrase long after he was dead in the ground. Those were the only words that Stud had spoken on the whole trip. Stud petted the little puppy and gently set her down with her mother and went to make his own camp under a big oak tree that they had passed when they came in. He knew Bill had said something about him that had made the big man laugh.

Trina never came back out of her cabin, so Angus checked on her. She told him that she preferred to wait until morning before she met the men, so Angus and Bill made ready to bed down for the night.

Trina fell asleep, thinking that the fever had made her crazy. The hairy mountain man she saw when she woke up by the fire had the same eyes as her former employer. She knew who the man was, though. She remembered seeing him that fateful morning in Sacramento City on the day that Angus had hauled her out of town. She remembered seeing the mountain man with the others at the corrals. She never dreamed the man would be a dead ringer for Weatherford, and she hoped her eyes were playing tricks on her.

*****

Trina was up early the next morning, but she didn't beat Bill to the fire. He was already awake and brewing his tea. He had picked up a book to read in Stockton because Stud wouldn't talk to him. He decided he would bother Stud on the trip by reading the book out loud in English. It worked pretty well. Stud had become accustomed to sleeping out of earshot of Bill and making his own fire and eating alone. Bill thought that Stud was a piss-poor traveling companion.

"Good morning, Miss Trina," Bill said lowly as he stood up and took off his wide-brimmed hat. He held out his hand and Trina graciously shook it. "My name is Bill Ford," he said, smiling.

"I'm Trina Harper. I'm pleased to meet you," she said, scrutinizing Bill's eyes and concluding she had been right about his resemblance to Weatherford. She started coffee and breakfast and then sat on the old log and looked at Bill. "I expect that you shortened your name up some, sir," she said bluntly. "You look a lot like my last boss. If I had known I would be working for a member of his family, I wouldn't be here right now."

Bill was shocked by her honesty. She was free, and it would be easy to assume that she had never been a whore. She looked like a hardworking farm girl getting ready for another hard day of work. Bill could have gone the rest of his life without knowing about the relationship they shared with Doug. Bill hated the fact this girl thought of him to be the same caliber as Doug based on looks alone.

"I doubt you'll believe me, but the rest of us ain't anything like that bastard, and we damned sure don't call him family, and we haven't since he was ten years old." Bill got up to get Stud. It was too early to go to work, but he didn't want to be alone with Trina, and waking him up would make him mad, so he did it to be contrary. Trina never took her eyes off the man until he was out of sight, then she scurried into Angus' tent and woke him up.

"That man out there is Weatherford's brother! Wake up and get out here! I don't want to be alone with that man!"

Angus got up, but he was confused about what Trina was saying. Trina stayed close to the tent and watched breakfast from afar while Angus got dressed.

"What are ye frightened about, lassie?" he said as he waited for the coffee to boil.

"Bill Ford is the brother of the man who beat me!" Trina whispered hysterically. "I quit, I want you to take me to Grass Valley today and leave me there. I'll get a job in town."

"Easy now, lass, calm down. Ye are mistaken about Bill. He'll do ye no harm." Angus couldn't understand why Trina was so confused. Trina slapped Angus on the arm out of frustration.

"I quit, I tell you!" she whispered.

Angus flinched when she hit him. She had never been violent before. "Ye just want to run off with the pig farmer? Go ahead then, but I already warned him 'bout livin' with an Irish woman." Angus laughed. He felt indestructible now that he wasn't alone with Trina.

Trina's heart broke when Angus' remark hit her ears, and she saw red. Why didn't he understand that she loved him and not Jake Gates? When he laughed at her, that was it. She attacked him, toppling him over off the old log and onto the ground. She slapped him, punched him, kicked him, and kneed him, and he never did anything but close his eyes, hold his hands up to cover his face, and try to squirm away from her.

Bill and Stud were watching, and when Trina came to her senses, which was when she was all worn out, Bill helped her to her feet. Bill laughed at Angus when he helped him up. "What the devil did you do to deserve that?" Bill asked.

"I quit!" Trina screamed.

Stud had to move quickly to keep from being trampled by the beautiful woman. He looked at Angus and shook his head in disgust. He told Bill to tell Angus his words.

Bill said, "Stud says that she wants to be loved by you and that you are a big dumb idiot."

"She just beat me up!" Angus exclaimed.

Stud went to Trina's cabin, where she had gone to hide, and when she opened the door, he gave her a long warm hug. She started to cry and hugged the boy back. He said things in his own language that she didn't understand, but the way he said it soothed her. He pulled away from her after quite a few minutes had gone by and rubbed the tears away from her face. He took her hand and led her back out to the fire where Bill was ignoring him, and Angus was puzzled by what the boy had done. Stud asked Bill to translate.

Bill told Stud that he was lazy and needed to learn English and that he never would even try, no matter how much time Bill had spent teaching him, and he wasn't translating anymore.

This made Stud very angry, and he shouted, "I am a better man than you, Bill Ford!"

"If you are so much better than me, then you don't need me to tell folks things for you," Bill said defiantly.

"Tell this woman that the big man is a fool," Stud demanded.

"No!" Bill said boldly. "This isn't any of your business!"

Stud was madder than a hornet. He wanted to beat Bill the way Trina had beaten Angus. Trina saw how angry he was and patted him on the back. She directed him to eat with her, and he did.

Bill and Angus got the team harnessed, and Trina went to go get ready to go to town. She put everything that she owned in the wagon.

"Ye don't have to go to town today, lassie. I want you to show Bill the property that we marked off, and tomorrow, Bill wants to mark off some more," Angus said as if it was a typical day.

"I told you, I quit, Angus. I'm not working for anybody that is related to that man!" Trina shouted for everybody to hear.

Angus looked at her sadly. "Don't leave me, lassie, I need ye."

"You need me for what?"

"I just need ye."

"You just need me to help you work. I can work someplace else!" Trina was disgusted and turned away in anger as she climbed onto the wagon seat.

Angus looked at Bill in frustration and walked over to him where he was saddling his horse. Stud was playing with the pups.

"She wants to leave me, Bill. She claims that ye are related to the man that beat her, and she wants to leave this place." Angus sighed with disappointment. "I guess we'll look at the boundary tomorrow. I'll have to hire someone to take her place." Angus looked at the sad girl. "I'll probably have to hire two men to take her place. She is a good worker, and she is usually very pleasant."

Bill looked at the girl. He thought about how hard it was to find good help and how the girl probably did love Angus, but he was an idiot, just as Stud had said. He thought that it would be better for her to stay, and maybe he and Stud could convince Angus that she wasn't as mean as the other Irish women he had known, even if she had just tussled with him a little. "Do you want me to talk to her?" Bill finally asked.

Angus was relieved. "Do ye think ye can talk her into stayin' with me?"

"Come with me," Bill said boldly. "Miss Harper, what is the problem here? Why are you so hell-bent on quitting this outfit?"

"He knows why!" she said, pointing at Angus.

Bill knew that he would really have to lay on the charm to convince Trina that he and Rose were nothing like Doug. When Bill held his hand out and asked Trina to come down from the wagon, Stud came over to observe what Bill was doing. He had never seen Bill act this way with a woman before, and he wanted to stick around and help the girl, if need be. Stud scowled at Bill's obvious trickery.

"I think that it's time to have a nice talk. You need to come, too, Angus. That is a lovely dress, by the way, did you make it yourself?" Bill asked Trina.

Trina walked with Bill back to the campfire. "No, I haven't had time to make a dress. Angus bought it for me. He said we represent the Rasmussens, and we should look nice when we go to town."

"Angus is right about that." Bill was laying it on thick now. He wasn't aware of any dress code, and he would have been the last one to adhere to it if there had been one. Stud sat across from Bill so he could watch his eyes and his facial expressions as he tricked Trina. Bill was getting sad and serious. Bill continued, "I am Doug's brother, but I wish that I wasn't, Miss Harper, and Mrs. Rasmussen feels the same as me about it. She is his daughter. I wish the man had died at birth, but he didn't. Rose ran away from home to get away from him, and we found out in Stockton about him and you gals being in Sacramento City. My friend, Sam, knew that Doug was in Sacramento City because he could feel Doug's eyes on him. That is how badly we hate him, Miss Harper. Doug branded Sam when we were young. Me and Sam left home that night, and I've been known as Bill Ford ever since. Sam and I figured that Doug would follow us out of town, and then we would kill him, but the coward never came around. Now I don't blame you for wanting to leave out of here, but if you stay, you will be safe. No one of us will do you harm, and if Doug comes around lookin' for you, we'll kill him."

Trina looked at Angus. She wondered if Angus would tell Bill the truth and what Bill would say or do about it. Stud followed her eyes and looked at Angus too.

"Bill, it could be that your brother is dead." Angus seemed to feel bad about it. "He was the one beatin' Trina when I first saw her."

Bill was shocked but not angry. "Was he dead or not?" Bill asked elatedly.

"He still had a pulse," Trina answered.

"Well, that bastard is probably still alive then," Bill said with discouragement. "That must be the reason why he didn't follow us, though."

"He killed his own wife!" Trina blurted out.

Bill wasn't surprised, but he felt bad for Rose. "How do you know that?" Bill asked softly.

"He threatened us with that all the time. He would say that he had killed his wife, and it wouldn't bother him to kill us. He held a gun on us when he…when he wanted to be alone with us." Trina began to cry. It felt like yesterday that he had beaten her. Her life was good now, but she couldn't forget the past. Bill motioned to Angus to comfort her. Angus scowled, and Bill scowled back at him, so Angus did it. Bill and Stud walked away from camp to give the two of them a chance to be alone. Bill thought that Angus would come around to Trina's way of thinking if the two of them weren't watching.

"Bill, you are tricky like a fox. You told Angus to be a man," Stud commented.

"I did not, you silly Miwok. If you would learn English, then you would know what was said. My brother was bad to her, and she thinks that Rose and I will be bad to her too."

Stud nodded. "She wants to leave."

"Yes, and Angus wants her to stay."

"That is because he loves her." Stud smiled.

"I don't know if he loves her, but he wants her to stay," Bill said in a tired tone.

A half an hour later, Stud said, "I think he loves her, Bill, look at them." Bill looked and saw that Angus was comforting her with kisses. Bill looked at Stud and snickered. "I was right, Bill. You are tricky like a fox. Take me back to Juanita now."

"We are going to stay and help out for a couple of weeks, and then you can go see that girl," Bill explained. "You'll have to see her in your dreams until then."

"Let's work then," Stud said hastily.

Bill sighed. "Can't you enjoy anything?"

"Like what?"

"Like how things will work out for the beautiful lady."

Stud smiled. "I will enjoy it when things work out for me."

"You have to learn English or Spanish to be a good man for your girl," Bill told Stud.

"My woman and I don't need words," Stud said, smiling.

Bill rolled his eyes. "Let's go get started on the corrals."

6

Two and a half weeks had passed since Pablo had declared Rose and Bennager would be married in his family chapel. Bennager thought the idea was ludicrous, but at the same time, he knew it was something to do and think about while they were waiting for the vaqueros to turn up. The delight he saw in his wife's eyes was all he needed as encouragement, and he never mentioned to her that he thought the whole thing was silly.

Maria Ramirez had sent Zeb and Juanita to Monterey for the fabric and lace for the wedding dress that Rose was going to make. Rose was embarrassed to learn that Maria had done this. Of all the things that Rose would be comfortable having Zeb do for her, picking out fabric for her wedding dress was not one of them. Rose also figured that Zeb would not want to do it. Rose told Maria the story of Zeb and Bill arguing over beans and biscuit makings back in Stockton, but Maria only shook her head and smiled.

Bennager figured on going to Monterey too. After he and Rose had been married by Charlie, he figured on buying her a wedding ring in Sacramento City. He searched quite a bit but never found one that he liked so he bought her the dresses and other things instead. Bennager didn't want to go to Monterey with Zeb and Juanita. He knew Zeb would drive him crazy. Zeb would make an issue out of picking out the fabric for Rose, even though Bennager knew that Zeb was only escorting Juanita so she could do it. He also didn't want to witness Zeb talking to his dead wife at her grave.

Sam and Bennager kept their promise to Bill about taking care of the children. Keeping them clean, fed, and out of trouble was a full-time job for the two grown men, and Bennager wondered how his mother had managed it when he was a boy. Sam went right to work teaching them English. He spent hours with them every day at the stables, scratching letters and numbers into the dirt, and he taught them all the names of the different animals. Bud and Blossom liked it when they could walk around and learn the plants and animals, but they hated the letter and number sessions.

Sam was really starting to think that his teachings were a lost cause until one day when he was making their biscuits and bacon, he saw Blossom showing Bennager some letters. She had even gotten them right, and since Bennager was so impressed by her newfound knowledge, Bud started paying more attention.

As the second week passed, Sam realized that Bud liked the numbers better because there were fewer of them than there were letters. Sam reckoned that if the twins stuck together, then they would probably do all right.

Sam and Bennager were happy to have their jobs of watching the children. Pablo's house had become mad with women who thought of nothing else, except wedding preparations. There was no chance the children would have been spoiled by that bunch on account of them being so busy. Even Pablo was crazed with the excitement of it all. He and Romero had butchered two pigs and had been smoking them. They made a trip to Monterey to invite friends and to purchase hard liquor, and when Bennager heard about it, he wanted to grab Rose and head out.

"Sam, don't you think these people are just looking for an excuse to party and get drunk?" Bennager asked. He was beginning to become anxious over being the center of attention.

"Probably," was Sam's only reply.

"Well, don't you think they could just have a party without making me and Rose get all dressed up?"

"I reckon Pablo thought that it would make Rose happy," Sam said.

"I think Rose has fallen in with a bad bunch," Bennager stated. His remark made Sam laugh. "Don't laugh, Sam, it's true! Pablo's wife told Rose that she couldn't sleep with me until after the wedding!"

"Well, we wouldn't have to break out the shotguns," Sam teased. "What did you tell Rose about that?"

"Fortunately, I didn't have to tell her anything. She spoke for both of us when she told Maria there was no way in tarnation that she was kicking me out of her bed." Bennager blushed and shook his head.

"She didn't say it exactly like that, did she?" Sam asked incredulously.

"I reckon she did Sam. She was still furious about it that night when she was telling me the story."

"What did Señora Ramirez do?" Sam inquired.

"Rose said she turned on her heel and left the room." Bennager and Sam continued to speculate on whether the relationship between the two women had been severed. They still hadn't figured out that Señora Ramirez was a little joker in her own right. She had a very cutting sense of humor and knew the precise thing about people to get their backs up. Maria had turned on her heel and left the room so she could have a fit of uncontrollable laughter without Rose catching her. Pablo reprimanded her that night when they were alone for being such a wicked old woman, and then they laughed together.

After Zeb and Juanita returned from Monterey, Bennager quickly tired of what he knew Zeb, the great savant of love, would do. The boasting never ended. Although he couldn't say anything at all about the fabric, he still found ways to talk about the role that he played in purchasing it.

Bennager and Sam both knew all Zeb did was to give Juanita a ride to the mercantile, and then he went around town, shooting the breeze with his friends until she was finished. Bennager simply tried to look busy when he saw Zeb coming toward the stables every day, but finally, at the beginning of the third week, Bennager decided to sneak off to Monterey. He got up early and saddled his mount. When Sam and the children came out for biscuits and bacon, Bennager told Sam, "Tell Rose I'll be back in three days."

"That's news you had better tell her yourself," Sam said in a demanding way.

Bennager smiled mischievously and headed west.

Sam shook his head. He didn't think that he would ever forgive Bennager for leaving him with such a task. Rose would want details, and he didn't have any and wouldn't like it. She would get it into her head to follow her husband, and Sam knew that he didn't want to be followed. Hopefully, she would be too busy to ask him anything until it was too late for her to follow him because Sam wasn't going to tell that woman anything unless she made him.

Everyone was starting to consider where Bill and Stud were. Rose had expected them to be back by now, and she was getting worried that something had happened to them. The wedding was planned with the idea that the two of them would be there for it, but Rose was sure that they were missing because she didn't think Bill would leave the children for that long, even though he had left them in good hands. Bennager and Sam hadn't ever caught her, but she had been sneaking out to the stables every day to see how the men were doing with the children.

Rose had grown bored with sewing and cooking. She couldn't wait to get started for the Yuba River and get to work on her own rancho. She missed the excitement of meeting new people and seeing a new country, and she was starting to feel confined in the Ramirez house. The food and conversation were wonderful, but she was beginning to feel trapped, almost like the way she had felt on the ship that had brought her to California. She wished she had gone with Bill to check on Angus, but she had been busy learning how to sew, and now she really regretted making that choice. If Pablo hadn't have talked her into having a real wedding, she would have gone stir crazy by now. For the last week, the only real pleasure she had was spying on her husband and Sam.

Her melancholy was now turning into anxiety about where her uncle was. She worried that her father had something to do with his delay, and she reckoned that Sam might have some sense about it. On the same morning that Bennager left, Rose went to the stables to question Sam. She had gotten so good at sneaking up on him that he hadn't even seen her coming.

"Hey, Sam," Rose greeted him. Sam nearly jumped out of his skin. She had not come out of the house in two weeks, to Sam's knowledge, and now here she was on the very day that Sam didn't want to see her.

"Hello, Rose," Sam replied. The children were happily surprised to see her in their school. Bud and Blossom grabbed her hands and made her sit with them to learn their letters. Rose snickered at their enthusiasm.

"Sam, I'm worried about Bill. I'm worried that he ran across my father, and something happened to him," Rose said uneasily.

Sam contemplated what Rose said for a few moments. "I think William is all right, and I reckon he'll be back in due time. He wouldn't leave these little ones. If it wasn't for them, I'd say that there's no tellin' where he is or if he would even come back. As for your father, William wouldn't be bothered by him."

"Maybe he hired someone to do harm to Bill."

"From what folks were saying about your father, I doubt he could hire a pig to clean his supper plate," Sam replied wittily.

Rose shook her head. "I hope you're right, Sam. We're holding off on the wedding until he gets here, but Maria said people will start rolling in tomorrow. I don't want the Ramirez's to have to feed a bunch of people until Bill gets back. He probably wouldn't care to attend it anyway, I reckon." Rose seemed disappointed by the thought as she watched the children draw in the dirt.

Zeb was following his usual course for the day. He always lingered in the house long after breakfast was finished to bother Pablo. His new scheme involved him, Pablo, and Romero going to Oregon to purchase Durham Shorthorn bulls to bring back and breed with the Mexican and Longhorn crossed cattle that Pablo now had and wished that he didn't. "With the money that you are going to get from Mrs. Rasmussen, you could buy bulls and some cows too," Zeb urged.

Pablo waved his hands at the man as if he was swatting a fly away from his face. "You have me in enough trouble, Loco Zeb. I will never buy cattle with you again."

"Well, you old ungrateful Mexican yellow belly! What's the matter with you? Do you even know what a Durham is? It would settle those longhorns down to a trot, I tell you!" Zeb exclaimed.

"You have made a mess out of me and my ranchero, Loco Zeb. I'm going to the Sandwich Islands and find my lovely little Mexican cattle, and I'm going to stay there with them so you can't bother me every time you take it into your head to do so!"

"Romero will listen to me, you old fart bag!"

Pablo shook his head and went to the chapel. It was the only place where Zeb wouldn't follow him. He had a jug of tequila hidden behind the altar, and every morning he had to deal with Zeb was a morning he had to calm his nerves at the chapel.

*****

Bennager had ridden hard and got little sleep. He managed to get to Monterey by midmorning of the next day. He had only been to Monterey just one time before, and it had been four years ago. He was surprised to see how the town had grown, but he didn't take the time to make note of every new business. It was enough just to see all the new rooftops. He was in a hurry to pick out Rose's wedding ring and get back to her. The weather was mild and pleasant that day, even though he was close to the ocean. The shopkeepers had their doors propped open so the fresh air would clean away the stagnation that had developed in their buildings during the rainy month that had just passed.

"Can I help you, young man?" a portly older gentleman asked as Bennager carefully looked around in his store.

"Yes, I'm in the market for a wedding ring."

The man smiled. "Spring is on its way when I see young men buying wedding rings. You are a little early. I just sent away for wedding ring sets last month, but I did anticipate that young fellers would want to get a jump on the nuptials this year due to the gold rush." The portly man looked Bennager in the eye and smiled, wondering if Bennager had picked up on the pun. "I have a fair selection right over here."

Bennager followed the man to the back of the store. Bennager started looking at each ring while the man went back to dusting his merchandise and a few impractical knickknacks that the established

Mexican wives liked to purchase for decorating their homes. "Just give me a holler if you see one that you like, young man."

As Bennager peered at and scrutinized each ring, trying to imagine what it would look like on Rose's hand and keeping in mind that she was intending to be a ranchero woman who would have her hands where most other women wouldn't, he could hear men talking outside the store. He was so engrossed with his own business that he wasn't listening to them until one man got excited, and the conversation became heated. At this point, Bennager raised his head up from the jewelry counter and listened with curiosity. He became even more intrigued when the storekeeper stopped dusting and watched the men outside, standing with his hands on his hips and hoping that the glass on the store front wouldn't be shattered.

Bennager listened and realized that the men were arguing about their two missing comrades. Apparently, they had ridden east about three weeks ago and hadn't returned. A couple of men in front of the store were sure Indians had killed their friends, and they wanted to ride out and seek revenge. The young man that had gotten excited was against heading east because he was afraid that the Indians would kill them all. Another man suddenly appeared and told the others that if they wanted to head east and kill Indians, then they should have gone with Joe and Bob this morning. The fourth man told the others that Joe and Bob would find the missing men one way or the other, and they'd kill every Indian they saw along the way.

Bennager knew that they had to be talking about the two men that good old Uncle Bill had killed. This was one time he was going to mind his own business. He only wasted one more minute in Monterey. He picked out the ring that he admired most, went to the livery, and traded his horse for a fresh one and eased out of town. He hoped he could pick up Bob and Joe's trail, and he also hoped he could get back to Rose before the carcasses of the dead men's horses were found. Sam and Bennager had buried the men for lack of anything better to do but had left the horses for the birds.

*****

Stud Colt and Bill had made it across the San Joaquin River with the dimwitted ferryman still on the job. The man was so slow in the head that he didn't even remember Stud Colt or the fact that the boy had showed him his pecker a couple of months ago. Bill didn't like wasting his jokes and charm on idiots, so he and Stud just ignored the man as they made the crossing and paid him when they were finished.

Stud was becoming happier and more excited as they neared Pablo's rancho. Bill had worked him to death, pert near, digging postholes for the set of corrals that Angus and Trina were left to finish, and he wanted to get back to Juanita and have her feel sorry for him and his pain. Pablo would surely let him have Juanita when he showed him his callused hands.

Bill was happy to be getting back to see the children. He chortled to himself now and then at the torment that they might be causing Sam and Bennager. Bill thought back to Angus and Trina and wondered if the big man would ever figure out what to do with the pretty redheaded woman that was so in love with him.

The kiss between the two Irish people, which Bill and Stud had giggled about, was never repeated. Stud was always trying to convey advice to Angus about how he should love Trina back, but Bill wouldn't translate for the boy. Bill told him to mind his own business. Bill was suspicious that Angus might be in love with someone else. He couldn't imagine any other reason than that for Angus to keep rejecting Trina. Bill and Stud were both sure that Trina was going to have her way after they saw the two of them kiss that day, but Angus made it a point to leave the three of them behind every day while he went to Grass Valley to purchase lumber.

Bill thought Trina was a good girl and a good worker. Trina took Bill and Stud out and showed them the property boundary, and Bill told her that they would stake out another league of land to the east. She worked all day every day digging postholes with Bill and Stud and was very hospitable at every meal. Bill always took pity on the poor girl at mealtime and helped her with the cooking and cleaning. When the drunken well-diggers finally showed up to work, she had to stop what she was doing and check their progress every hour because Angus told her to.

Bill chuckled to himself as he remembered the second day that the well-diggers had been on the job. Trina was the most beautiful woman that they had seen in years, and not just because they generally had blurred vision. The first half of the first day, they thought that she was coming to the well site just to be friendly, and they delighted in it. They assumed Angus was her man, but since Angus wasn't there, she was taking the opportunity to become better acquainted with them. By the end of the day, the men figured that their theory was wrong because she only inspected the depth of the hole but never stayed to chat.

On the second day, the men thought they should investigate and find out if their first theory was right. Trina knew men well enough to know that something was bound to happen if she kept checking on the men every hour, but when one of them looked into her eyes pleadingly and then caressed the calf muscle of her leg, she had a knee-jerk reaction and kicked the well-digger in the face. He fell to the bottom of the fifteen-foot hole, landing partially on his partner. The other man had a bad temper and scrambled out of the hole as fast as he could to beat Trina for what she had done, but wisely, she had taken her shovel with her to the hourly inspection. The sight of the woman about to use her long-handled implement as a weapon slowed the man down, but he still proceeded to call Trina every foul name he could think of, and he knew a lot of them.

The man became more enraged and tried to take the shovel away from her. Bill and Stud had been on their way to help her when the physical engagement broke out. The man had miscalculated the strength Trina possessed. Trina kicked the man in the knee, took her shovel away from him, thrust the tip of the handle into his stomach, shoved him over onto his back, and stood over him, threatening to cut his head off. Needless to say, the man crawled back into his hole from where he had come.

Bill and Stud had stopped in their tracks and snickered when the row was over. Bill asked Trina if she wanted him to have a talk with the men, but she only smiled and went back to digging postholes. Stud yammered for the rest of the day about how if Angus had been there to see that, he would take her in his arms and never let her go. Bill wished that Trina wasn't in love with Angus so he could have her for himself. For the next week and a half, Bill was the sweetest man on earth in hopes that Trina would begin to favor him. He kept forgetting that he looked too much like his brother for Trina to ever love him and reckoned that people could never forget their past. He knew because he had never been successful at doing it either.

Bill didn't dwell on such things the way that young men like Stud did. He could feel Stud's joy and anxious anticipation as they camped for the night in almost the same place where they had given the babies their first bath. Bill reckoned he was lucky to be loved by a woman once and lucky that he had even gotten to meet an all-round, good, hardworking woman like Trina, even if she did favor an ignorant Irishman to him.

*****

Rose hadn't bothered to ask where Bennager was on the day he left for Monterey until suppertime. Her husband had made sweet passionate love to her that morning, and it never occurred to her that he intended to leave her. When she finally asked Sam that afternoon, and he sheepishly answered her, she was furious. "Three days? Why didn't he tell me? Why didn't he ask me to go with him? Who does he know in Monterey that he doesn't want me to know?"

Sam didn't have any answers for her, which made her even more livid because she was sure Sam did have her answers and wasn't telling her what they were. "What are you protecting my husband from?" To make matters worse, Zeb's feelings were hurt too. He asked all the same questions that Rose asked. Zeb was sure that Bennager would have a much better time in Monterey if he had gone along to show him the sights. Zeb was also suspicious that Bennager had gone to see a woman. Why else would he keep it a secret and just cut out on his wife? That wasn't what galled Zeb, though. What galled him was that he wanted to know which woman it was. He knew everybody in Monterey.

558

Sam knew this would happen. He took a break from teaching the children numbers and letters and just spent most of his time playing with them in the stables, staying away from Rose and Zeb and thinking up ways to pay Bennager back for leaving him alone with all these people.

On the second night of being in trouble with Zeb and Rose, he decided that he would take the children to the pond the next morning to play and maybe catch a fish. That was something he hadn't attempted since he and William were boys. Sam asked Pablo if he had any objections, and Pablo warned him again about the crazy cattle and then told him to take a carriage. Sam was delighted. He was going to spend a warm springlike day away from the glares, hurt feelings, and suspicions Rose and Zeb had been dishing out to him for two days and watch the children do something other than scratch in the dirt at the stables.

*****

Sam and the children were up the next morning before the chickens. The children were excited to go for a ride in the carriage. Once they were on their way, the children stood on each side of Sam on the seat and jumped up and down for the first mile. Sam rolled his eyes as they banged and bumped into him and waited for the time to come when they would wear themselves out and sit still. Sam could feel, in his arthritic bones, that this day was going to be just as pleasant as the day before. There wasn't a cloud in the sky, nor was there much of a breeze this time of day to indicate otherwise. He was able to see in the distance about fifty head of cattle with their calves as he made his way to the pond and reckoned that as flighty as they were, he shouldn't have much trouble with them. He also knew that the pond was always a drinking hole for them and to heed Pablo's warnings. He was sure that he would lose the battle if he was up against it with a protective longhorn mother.

The day eased by slowly. Sam was always on the lookout as he watched the children play. They splashed rocks into the water, marveled at the pollywogs and tiny fish that were swimming just under the water's surface, and examined various bugs that were clinging to the weeds and the willows. They were particularly impressed with the dragonflies and were pleased when they were able to catch them. Sam laughed at their intrigue with everything that was new to them, and he told them what they were seeing to improve upon their understanding of the English language. By midmorning, they needed a snack, and Sam was quick to comply.

Bud tried to share his sandwich with the horse, and Sam chuckled at the boy as he led the twins to a willow tree. He thought that it was a nice little spot for a picnic. As he admired the beauty of the day, he smiled at the children talking to each other. Their language was now about half Yokut and half English. With the English thrown in, Sam could almost make out what they were talking about. He quickly surveyed the surroundings for cattle again. Pablo had him so worried about longhorn mothers that he had completely forgotten about the tendencies of Indian killers.

There was no time to get to the carriage. He and the children had already been spotted by the two strange men who were only one hundred yards from them. Sam knew that this would be the end of him. If these men were here to kill Indians, they sure as hell wouldn't spare a Black man. He stood up and told the children to go to the pond and catch pollywogs, and they ran and jumped away playfully. Sam hoped that these men would spare babies. All he could think to do was to say a little prayer to Grace Weatherford to watch over them.

"Would you look at what we have here, Joe!" Bob said as they approached Sam who was waiting.

"Yeah, look at this; This here must be a runaway," Joe replied.

"I work for Señor Ramirez. These are his grandchildren," Sam lied.

"I never heard of a Black runaway nursemaid like you before. I reckon you're a kidnapper," Joe told Sam.

Sam chuckled, trying to remain calm. "Pablo Ramirez will tell you. I'll load up the kids and we'll go back and ask him."

"We ain't askin' anybody nothin', you Black son of a bitch! We just found two fresh graves and two dead horses on your boss' property about a mile or so back," Bob said, leaning ahead in his saddle and resting his arm on the pommel in a menacing way. "We don't give a damn who you are or who you work for."

Sam smiled broadly, and his last thought was, *You will.*

The children jumped in the water and hid in the cattails when they saw the two strange men shoot Sam down. Each man put a bullet into him, one after the other to prolong his pain for an extra few minutes. Joe rode over to the pond to look for the children, and Bob rode over to the carriage and stuck a knife into the horse's lung.

"Did you get those kids?" Bob hollered to Joe.

"You go in after 'em, I don't fancy being wet all day," Joe said defiantly.

"You damned whelp!" Bob replied angrily. They rode around the pond and concluded that the kids had to be in the cattails.

"How many bullets do you reckon we ought to waste on those cattails?" Bob asked.

"I don't know, how many do we have?" Joe questioned.

"We have about twenty-five a piece, stupid!" Bob always got rankled with Joe's ignorance.

"Let's use 'em all," Joe said.

Bob rolled his eyes. "Maybe we oughta just use five a piece. We came out here to get revenge. We can't do that unless we have a lot of ammunition, you damned idiot," Bob said, gritting his teeth until they hurt.

Joe shrugged his shoulders.

Bud and Blossom knew that the strange men wanted to hurt them the way that they had hurt Sam. They quietly edged into the cattails until they were up against the bank of the pond. While the men were arguing, Bud and Blossom were holding their breaths. A volley of lead and the loud sound of gunfire made the children start to shake and cry, but they were still silent as they hugged the bank even harder.

*****

Bennager rode into Pablo's rancho about five minutes ahead of Bill and Stud. Bennager rushed into the house to find Rose. Her safety was Bennager's first concern. He found her all right, and the first thing she did was to light into him about leaving without telling her. He simply hugged and kissed her and said, "Where is Pablo?"

"You don't need to talk to Pablo. You need to tell me what you think you've been doing for three days!" Rose said in frustration.

Bennager put his hands on Rose's shoulders and shook her gently. "Tell me where Pablo is!"

The expression on her husband's face scared her. "Try the chapel."

Bennager ran through the house and out the back door. He waded through a sea of people that he failed to notice upon his arrival, who were waiting for the matrimonial ceremony to start.

Rose had stood in the house for a moment thinking that her husband had a change of heart about her but soon realized that his eyes had told her that there was serious trouble about her. She ran out to catch up with him.

Bennager barged through the chapel doors with a crash. Pablo and Zeb were chatting with the priest and Maria and the girls were decorating. "The groom has finally arrived!" Zeb shouted rattling the stained glass.

"I followed two men from Monterey who are looking for their two dead friends. Have you seen them?" Bennager asked, a little short of breath.

"No," Pablo and Zeb answered in unison.

"I know that they found the graves. I saw their tracks," Bennager said as Rose entered the chapel. Bennager reached out and took her hand in his. "Are you sure that you haven't seen any strangers?"

Pablo and Zeb rushed to the doors to survey the crowd that was accumulating for the wedding. Pablo knew every person in attendance. Bennager let out a sigh of relief and hugged his wife. "Now you can go back to giving me heck. I just had to make sure that everyone was safe. I still have a bad feeling, though."

Rose could feel his tense body against hers and began to have the same bad feeling that something was wrong. She had worried all week about Bill and Stud, and then she had to pile on jealousy when Bennager left her, and then to make matters worse, she was stuck with Zeb all week. Zeb had finally told her that Anna was dead, and that was why she wouldn't be attending the wedding. Rose had spent the last three days consoling Zeb and listening to his apologies. "Where have you been?" she finally asked her husband as Bill and Stud entered the chapel.

Stud rushed across the room into Juanita's opened arms, and Rose hurried over to hug her uncle. "I've been worried about you. You are long overdue."

Bill laughed. "There's no need to worry about Bill Ford. What's with the crowd? Are you about to have a cockfight, Pablo?"

Pablo was aghast at all the blasphemy that was happening in his precious little chapel. "No, there is to be a wedding, Bill Ford."

"So you have decided to let Stud Colt marry the girl," Bill commented, knowing that couldn't be the case.

Pablo put his hand on his chest. "No, it is a real ceremony for Rose Rasmussen!"

"That's nonsense! That will only make her twice as raunchy!" Bill said waving away such a silly waste of time. Rose slapped him and he laughed. "Where are my children?"

Pablo turned pale and looked at Bennager. In all the excitement over the wedding, the men finally getting back, and the guests that he was entertaining, he had forgotten that Sam had taken the children to the pond.

Bennager's heart sank when he saw Pablo's expression. "Where are they?"

"Sam took them fishing at the pond early this morning," Pablo replied.

Bennager said to Bill as he rushed past him. "I hope you didn't put your horse up."

Rose ran as fast as she could, unbuttoning her dress as she plowed through the crowd. She quickly changed her clothes and got her weapons and ammunition together and screamed for Maria to tell Romero to do the same. She saw Bill and Bennager already heading south, away from the headquarters, as she raced to the stables to saddle the Roman. She had to dodge Zeb as he hurried to catch up.

Romero made it to the stables just as Rose was mounting up. "You must not go, Mrs. Rasmussen. This is not for a woman. You might be killed." The Roman let out an evil, ear-popping whinny that frightened Romero enough to step back, and Rose passed by the man, taking no heed to his advice.

*****

"Oh, my Lord," Bennager said quietly when they saw the dead horse in the distance still in its traces.

Bill was in a profound state of grief as they eased by the carriage and saw Sam's body under the willow tree. He knelt beside his childhood friend and looked into his old, battered face. Sam had a strange grin on his face that made the hairs on Bill's neck stand up. *Why would this man grin into the face of death?* Bill wondered. He had seen more dead men than he would willingly admit to, but he had never seen one with a grin on his face. Bill had been about ready to fall apart until he saw that. He thought of Sam and how he was in life and felt that, even though Sam's body was cold, his presence was still near. "All right Sam, what does it all mean?" Bill said out loud as he stood up.

Bennager looked at Bill strangely. Bennager wouldn't admit it, but the grin had given him pause too. Bill and Bennager started tracking the killers' every movement and came to know what they did and how they did it as Zeb arrived at the scene.

Bill was sure the killers had taken the children. There were so many of their little footprints near the water's edge that it was hard to say that they had gotten away.

"Why would they ride around the pond and then stop in front of these cattails?" Zeb asked. He walked over to where Sam was and could see that the killers had interrupted a late breakfast. *What would Sam do, knowing that he was caught like that?* Zeb wondered. He took the shortest distance back to the pond looking for the little footprints that would indicate that Sam had told the babies to hide.

Bennager saw Rose coming in the distance. "Oh my Lord." He was sick to his stomach at the thought of how this would affect his wife.

"Damn it! I told Romero to keep her out of this!" Zeb exclaimed.

Bennager quickly mounted to catch her before she could see Sam's dead body. It was no use, though. The Roman was more in charge of the situation than anybody else. The horse ignored his dead stable comrade, the dead Black man that he had come to trust, Rose's attempts at reining him and Bennager. Zeb and Bill ran to get out of the way as he skidded to a stop at the edge of the cattails with such force that Rose was put into flight, landing about ten feet from the bank of the pond and into the middle of the muddy clump of cattails.

Bud and Blossom were freezing and too afraid to come out when they heard the men's voices, but when they saw Rose flying into the pond, they knew they were safe.

The Roman carefully stepped off the bank with his two front feet, put his head down, and snorted at Bud. Bud was shaking so much from fright and from being cold that he couldn't move, but he was glad to see his old friend come for him. The horse snorted again as Rose tried to get her balance in the waist deep muddy water and navigate through the forest of water weeds that was between her and the shortest distance to her horse.

Bennager started to wade in to help his wife, but she angrily held her hand up and shook her head. Bill was in shock at the loss of his friend and couldn't wrap his mind around what was going on with the crazy horse. Zeb looked on in awe at the scene and was too afraid of the warlock horse to get involved in its business. All he could think of was why that horse would choose today of all days to be so wicked.

The Roman snorted three more times at Bud and Blossom before Rose discovered them hiding. The Roman whinnied as Rose scooped them up one by one and set them on the shore. She went into a fit of uncontrollable sobbing as she looked past the shivering, traumatized children and saw her friend's dead body under the willow tree.

Bennager saw Rose haul the twins out of the water, and he waved to Bill and Zeb to come get them. Rose stood in the waist-deep water and leaned over the bank; she rested her head on her arms and cried into the grass. Bennager came to her side and tried to comfort her. "I'm sorry, Rose."

She nodded her head but didn't look up. Bennager took her elbow. "Come on, let's get you out of that water." The Roman put his head up, and Rose grasped the reins, and with Bennager's help, she was removed from the deep muck on the bottom of Pablo's pond.

Bill and Zeb were tending to the twins. They were stripping them of their wet clothes and getting ready to build a fire as Rose dropped the reins and let her feet slowly drag her to where Sam was lying. The Roman followed her to give Sam one last sniff. Rose knelt beside her grinning friend and put her face on his chest and wailed.

Bennager began to cry at his wife's grief, and as he watched her, he became overwhelmed with sorrow. All Sam ever wanted was to be free and look for gold on the Cosumnes River with Stud again. Bennager took off his hat and knelt at the edge of the pond and waited for the sorrow to pass so he could help his wife find her peace.

Romero arrived at the pond. He was astonished at what had taken place. He hadn't rushed the way the others had because it never occurred to him that anyone would dare to murder a guest of Pablo Ramirez. This was the worst scene he had ever witnessed, grown men and the woman crying over Sam's death, the wicked horse pawing at the earth as if it was digging a grave for the man, and Zeb, of all people, being the only one who was trying to hold them all together.

"Take over here with these little ones, Romero. I want to see which way those bastards went," Zeb told him.

Bill came out of his shocked, bewildered trance for a moment. "I'll come with you."

"Rest up a bit, Bill, I'll be right back," Zeb said.

Romero was warming up the twins and looking at the grief-stricken woman. He asked Bill if Rose would be taking the children back while the rest of them went after Sam's killers.

Bill couldn't answer; he didn't know what would happen next. He couldn't get Sam's grin out from in front of his eyes. He tried to imagine what it was like for his babies to be so badly frightened again in their short little lives. He didn't know if it would be right to leave them again to go after the killers.

Bennager pulled himself together and went to Rose. When he got to her, she lifted her head up from Sam's chest and was saying something to her horse. Bennager thought that it was a shock-induced reaction and that she needed to go back to Pablo's and rest. Bennager put his coat over Sam's face, and Rose stood up.

Bennager and Rose went to where Bill was, and Rose knelt and held the children. Time passed as they sat by the fire, and Rose finally asked Romero, "I think Sam would like to be buried by that willow tree. Would your father mind that?"

"My father would like the priest to speak over him and for him to be buried in our family cemetery," Romero replied.

"No, Sam had happy moments at this place with the children. This is where he would like to be buried. Pablo can have the priest speak over him if he wishes," Rose said.

"Yes, Mrs. Rasmussen." Romero knew not to argue.

*****

More time passed by, and Bud warmed up enough to get up and thank the Roman for finding him. The adults looked on in awe at the way the dun was with the boy. Rose got up and went to the boy to pick him up and held him in her arms so he could pet her horse. Blossom curled up in Bill's lap and told him about Sam and the bad men in her new language, half Yokut and half English, and Bill was impressed with her knowledge.

The tracks of the murderers had led southeast, and Zeb knew the scum would be easy to follow. He even knew the men who he was tracking, and Bennager had been right about them being from Monterey. Zeb wished that the vermin had gone back to Monterey so that they and their friends could all face justice at the same time. He ran his mount hard back to the rancho. He saddled two fresh horses, outfitted two pack horses, tore Stud away from Juanita, and headed back for the pond.

Zeb arrived in the middle of an argument that Bennager and Rose were having, which was a very rare thing to witness. All that he heard was Rose screaming, "Like hell I will!"

When Rose saw Zeb come back with the pack horses, she knew he was prepared to track down the odious men who had killed the man she was supposed to be protecting from such a crime. Rose mounted up and said, "Let's go, William."

Bennager shook his head in despair and prepared to follow his wife to the end of the earth.

Bill called out to Stud Colt. He told Stud what needed to be done, and then he repeated his instructions to Romero. "I want Stud and Pablo to take care of the children. I want Sam to be buried by that willow tree just as Rose requested. I want both of you to take the children home first, and I don't want Stud to be alone for one second while I am gone. Come back with more people and more weapons and bury Sam as soon as you can. Apologize to your father for me for the trouble we have caused him." Bill hugged each child and pushed them toward Stud Colt, commanding them to stay just as he had done the last time that he had left.

7

Lee liked to think of himself as a scientist, but he wasn't. He liked to experiment on how much pain certain people could endure. Doug was his fourth experimental subject, and he determined that Doug was his weakest subject so far. Lee's only purpose for keeping Doug alive was to torture him, but in his mind, it was for scientific purposes.

Douglas had always considered himself lucky for never being caught and punished for the things he had done in his life, but he knew now that his luck had run out and perhaps he had never been lucky at all. Someone or something had simply saved him for Lee.

The first thing that Lee did for Doug after he cleaned his room was to tie his hands up to the bed. He didn't feel that Doug should be able to pleasure himself when Lee was trying so hard to gauge the man's pain. The only thing that Doug was grateful for was the cleanliness of his room and himself. Lee couldn't observe the man and be surrounded by filth. Now that the days were warming up, Doug could even get a whiff of fresh air during his hallucinations.

Lee kept Doug on the brink of pain, hunger, and thirst always. He gave him just enough opium to keep him from screaming and just enough white rice and water to keep him alive. Gangrene had gotten into the amputated leg, and Lee took great pleasure in scraping it off every day. The more he scraped, the more it spread, so every day, the task took longer and longer.

After two weeks, Doug was unrecognizable to anyone who might have known him. What was left of his hair and teeth had fallen out from stress, and his body had eaten away most of his fat to keep itself alive, but it was a losing battle.

Doug was in a nightmare whether he was awake or not. His state of hallucination brought the faces of the people he hated to his mind constantly. Lucy was most persistent. She did everything. She glared, laughed, cooked biscuits, did laundry, but mostly, she glared, and her face would turn into the faces of her daughters and then to bone. His mother walked up to him and slapped his face every other second, it seemed, while William and his father stood in the background, glaring at him. The woman who had died in his bed, who he had trampled, liked to sit up in his bed and talk to him in a friendly way, but he couldn't understand her language, and he desperately wanted to because she was the only one who was nice to him in his dreams. He saw the faces of Evans, his wife, and the girls that he had picked up on the Missouri River. He saw Sam's face, and his chest was on fire where he had branded him. They all hated him. They hated him worse than he knew a person could hate, which was a lot considering he had spent his whole life hating them.

Lee heard someone holler at the door. He left Doug and went to see that it was the man who had given him the gold. The man gave him some more little pieces of gold and left. This was the first time Lee had ever been paid for doing his scientific experiments, and he was sure he would have a prosperous future in America. He returned to his subject and continued with his scraping of the gangrene that had spread into Doug's hip. Lee wondered if the scraping would get easier or harder when the man was down to just skin and bones.

*****

Dan Dunaway never entered the gambling hall when he paid Lee. If he had known what was going on in Weatherford's room, he would have put Weatherford out of his misery and killed the sick, iniquitous Chinaman. Dan had no idea of what was happening and assumed that Lee was doing his best. The folks hadn't heard any screaming coming from the north end of town, the girls had almost forgotten to fear the man, and Sacramento City was becoming more reputable every day.

Kate and Dan's hotel was full of patrons every night, and a new gambling hall was being built on the west side of town by the river. Spring was coming, and so were more miners. Kate had customers from back east, the southern states, and Europe. As she served her customers, she picked up on information from Washington DC, world affairs, and general news, none of which was more exciting than the California gold rush that she was right in the middle of already. She was soon to realize that her hotel would be the hub of activity for years to come. She hadn't realized the position that Dan had given her and the other girls in the community of Sacramento City.

Kate's position as half owner put her in association with the other business owners in town, and they met once a week to discuss supply and demand topics, combining forces to get supplies to town expediently, the direction that the town would take, if it was time to build schools and churches, where new saloons and gambling halls would be built with respect to more reputable businesses, and the tent cities. They all agreed that the tent cities were a scar on the face of a bright new town and that come summertime, it would stink to high heavens. Those were Maggie's words. Kate brought up the fact that a passing doctor had told her, a day prior to the meeting, about the diseases that would surely manifest due to the filth and measures needed to be taken throughout the whole town to deal with the human waste.

Rufus Butler was at the meeting, and visions of Douglas Weatherford came to his mind. He shook his head in disgust and said, "I'll round up some men and take on those measures."

Kate ran into Dan on her way out of the meeting, but Rufus started talking to him about sewage issues before she could say hello. The look and the smile between them were enough for Kate to know that Dan would stop in for supper and check on the business. Dan was irritated with Rufus for dragging him away from Kate, especially when he heard the topic of discussion.

"You aren't going to find men to dig trenches this time of year. They're all going to the diggings, and so am I. That's winter work. Draw up your plans between now and winter, raise money to pay the men, and start the work when we all come back. It's simple. I'll help you, but not right now," Dan said.

"How's that Chinaman doing?" Rufus asked.

"I just gave him a little gold, and he seemed pleased. I didn't go in to see what was going on, and I'm not going to."

Rufus nodded his head. He didn't blame Dan. He wasn't ever going into that building again either. "I haven't seen you for a few days, where have you been?" Rufus inquired.

"I've been in the foothills, scouting out claims and checking on how the rivers are running. I like the looks of a creek that runs into the Yuba. It's only a couple of days away so I can come to town once in a while."

"A lot of folks are heading south," Rufus remarked.

Dan nodded his head. He had always hoped to run into Trina and the big Irishman. Since the day that he had found her dress in the Bear River, he had never stopped wondering what had become of them. He never inquired about them in his travels, but he always hoped to see them sometime. He was sure that eventually, someone would mention an attractive redheaded woman being in the area. He stopped at every saloon that he came across, sipped coffee, and listened but hadn't heard of her yet. He was beginning to think that she might be on the Feather River, but he liked the looks of the creek that he had spotted on the Yuba. Trina's whereabouts weren't all that important to him so that he needed to travel every river in California.

Rufus was in the mood for gossip. "That young Kate sure did turn into something, didn't she?"

Dan raised one brow. "I believe she probably always was something, Rufus."

"Yeah, probably. If she keeps going the way she is, she'll be married before summertime. She'll run off, and you'll be frying eggs every morning for your patrons," Rufus predicted.

"She would like that. Who's going to marry her? You?" Dan queried.

"I'm fairly sweet on Ginger. My heart melts when I watch her hang the bedding on the clothesline," Rufus whispered.

"I doubt you have a heart, Rufus, and I bet you've never said two words to Ginger," Dan teased.

"I've tipped my hat to her!" Rufus exclaimed.

"You can't conjure up children by tipping your hat. Do I need to explain to you how babies are made?"

"I know as much about babies as you do, Dan!" Rufus was good and riled now, so Dan was welcome to leave and check on Kate. Dan chuckled to himself about the veterinarian who probably hadn't touched a woman in his life.

Dan entered his hotel, and Kate rushed out from the kitchen to greet him. "Well, I'll be, Dan," Kate said pleasantly. "I didn't expect to see you until suppertime." Dan didn't say anything for a couple of moments. He was admiring Kate's delightful demeanor and smile. It was pure, free from fear, humiliation, and sorrow. Kate thought that she might melt because of the way Dan was looking at her, especially when he finally smiled. Kate continued so he wouldn't see the effect he was having on her. "Let's you and I have a cup of coffee, and I'll show you the books. I think you will be pleased. You've been gone for a while. Will you be staying long?"

Dan still couldn't answer as he watched her bustle around the kitchen, preparing their coffee, and then she went to her room to get the accounting books. Dan took a deep breath. He wondered what was the matter with him. Why couldn't he talk to Kate? She came back to the kitchen and sat down beside him so she could show him how many customers they had had while he had been gone. She smelled lovely. The numbers were a blur to him, and her talking about them sounded like jibber-jabber. Dan took in another deep breath. He could tell by the excitement in her voice that business was good. "Yes, that looks fine," he said.

Kate could tell he hadn't heard a word she had said. It disappointed her, but she continued, "Let me get your share of the profits." She stood up from the table, and Dan caught her hand.

"Sit here with me. Don't you know how to rest for a minute? Tell me how you and the gals have been. Tell me about your meeting," Dan pleaded.

Kate sat back down and pushed the accounting books aside. She took in a breath and let out a long sigh. "You're right, it feels good to rest for a minute with a friend."

Dan smiled with satisfaction and let her hand go. "Are the other gals doing as well as you are? Did Nancy ever get caught up on her sleep?"

Kate smiled. "Yes, she did, it's nice of you to ask. She stopped shaking and just loves to work in the garden. She'll probably be able to supply the whole town with fresh vegetables this summer. She is very excited about being able to do it. Ginger told me that Mr. Butler tipped his hat to her the other day."

At this, Dan covered his mouth with his hand because he had just taken a sip of coffee and wanted to swallow it before he laughed. Kate thought that he had burned his mouth or perhaps he was choking. "Are you all right? Oh dear!" She got up to do something for him, and her reaction made him want to laugh even more. He finally got his coffee down and let out a hearty laugh. Kate smiled and began to laugh as well at his amusement. She had never seen him laugh before. "What is so funny?"

"Mr. Butler told me that he tipped his hat to Ginger too." Dan laughed hilariously.

Kate shook her head and smiled. She didn't understand why Dan found the occurrence so amusing. She put her hands on her hips.

"Have you two men been making fun of Ginger?"

Dan laughed wildly and shook his head innocently. "No, ma'am!" he said.

"Well, what is it that you find so funny? Ginger was thrilled to have a nice man tip his hat to her," Kate said with hurt feelings for her friend. She sat back down when Dan began to gain control over his laughter.

"I'm sorry, Kate. I'm not laughing at Ginger, I'm laughing at Rufus. Rufus will go on just tipping his hat to her for the next twenty or thirty years if she doesn't convince him to do otherwise. I doubt Rufus knows very much about women," Dan explained.

Kate smiled and let out a sigh. "Yes, well, most men don't, I guess." Kate was thinking of the man who was sitting beside her.

"Tell me about the meeting now," Dan said.

"You should be at those meetings too, Dan," Kate scolded.

Dan smiled at her reprimanding tone. "No thank you, I see what happens at those meetings. Folks end up being recruited to dig ditches! The hell with that! Rufus already talked to me about that!"

Kate nodded her head and smiled. "I suppose that project will have to wait until winter."

"That's just what I think too. I told Rufus to draw up the plans, start raising funds, and put men to work this winter."

Kate nodded. "That sounds like a solid plan. We also think that the tent city is a disgrace."

"Yes, but folks have to live somewhere." Dan had empathy for the folks living in the tent city.

"They can live out of town and walk a little farther for their supplies," Kate said sternly.

Dan smiled thoughtfully. He could see that Kate wouldn't put up with any argument about the subject.

"So how long will you be staying this time, Dan?" Kate asked, looking into the bottom of her empty cup. She had a good many things to do, but sitting beside the man that she favored most was hard to walk away from. She poured more coffee.

"Not long. As a matter of fact, it might be best if I sleep at the livery and let you rent my room out. You'd make some extra money to put toward your municipal project," he replied, still taking in whiffs of her perfume.

"Why would you do that, Dan? This place is your home," Kate argued.

Dan shook his head. "This was never my home. This is your place now. You and the girls are respected citizens of the community, and everyone here will look after you and make sure that you're not harmed. You should be able to run this business—and the whole town, for that matter—without my advice or interference."

Kate was downhearted. She was afraid that Dan was washing his hands of the business and her as well and that he wouldn't ever want to see her again. She got up from the table. She felt she might be delaying him from pressing business someplace else. "I see," she said softly.

Dan scowled at her curiously and got up too. "Kate, what is the matter now? I thought you would be happy to have sole ownership of this place. You have plenty of hands to help you. You don't need me coming and going as I please. You will be one of the most eligible women in town if I stay out of your hair."

Kate gasped back a cry and quickly left the room. Dan could hear her running up the stairs and wondered if she was still afraid of Weatherford. He stayed in the kitchen, hoping she would come back. He sipped his coffee and walked around looking at how the rooms sparkled. He watched Nancy working on her hands and knees in the garden, thinning her carrots, onions, and parsnips. He strolled to the back of the building and saw Ginger hanging the bedding on the clothesline. He tried to figure out where Rufus would have to stand to be able to see Ginger without Ginger seeing him spying on her.

Dan walked over to a window in the parlor that faced north and saw Rufus leaning on a post across the street, pretending to be in deep thought about something so he wouldn't be bothered by passersby. He wanted to go pester Rufus, but he had to make sure that Kate would be all right. He went upstairs and tapped on her door.

"Come in," Kate said.

Dan entered and found Kate cleaning the room that she shared with two other girls. Most men would have been intimidated to walk into a room that was filled with so many feminine things, but Dan's upbringing had made him immune to the ways of girls. "Kate, are you all right? I think I have upset you." He could tell she had been crying.

"I just suspect that I won't be seeing you anymore. I'll miss you."

Dan watched the lovely woman who was trying her best not to look at him, and his heart swelled with the fondness he had come to feel for her. He smiled and said brusquely, "By God, woman, I'll be expecting a home-cooked meal and a cup of coffee every time I'm in town, and it better be free too!"

Kate turned around to glare at him for a moment. His tone had startled her, but his smile put her at ease.

Dan added, "And I will expect to be seated next to you while I am enjoying my free meal whether you are married or not."

Kate wanted to cry again. She feared that she would never marry unless it was to Dan, and it didn't seem as though he would ever go back on his words about the subject. She looked away from him and tried to control her emotions.

Dan crossed the room and stood behind her, looking at how pretty her golden hair was and remembering the morning he had been able to touch it. He held his breath and said, "Well, what about it? Do I get free food or not?"

Kate wheeled around and hugged him as though she would never get to again. "Anytime, Dan," she whispered into his ear.

"Good, I reckon I'll be starving every time I show up!" Dan said jovially and hugged her back. "Quit now with this cleaning nonsense and come with me. I'm going to have a little fun with Ginger and Mr. Butler." Dan took Kate's hand, and they went downstairs. He showed her what Rufus was up to across the street, and Kate snickered at the sight of the man. He had a serious expression on his face, his clothes were dirty from hanging around horses all day, and his hat was ridiculously lopsided. Kate shook her head.

"That's what you're going to look like if you live at the livery," Kate teased.

"Well, I actually take a bath once a week year-round." Dan chuckled. "Now stay right here and look worried."

Kate nodded her head to acknowledge his command. She didn't know how she could look worried about Rufus Butler, but she would give it a try.

Moments later, Dan and Ginger came into the room. Dan pointed at Rufus. "That's the man, Ginger. Do you see him?"

"Yes," Ginger said meekly.

"He's been spying on you all afternoon!" Dan said protectively.

"He has!" Ginger said with delight.

Dan pretended to be angry. "Yes, he has. I'm going over there and set him straight!" He turned to leave.

Ginger grabbed Dan's forearm with both hands. "Oh don't!"

Dan stopped and looked at her curiously.

"Don't go over there, Mr. Dunaway. I don't want any trouble." Ginger blushed and looked at the floor.

"He'll just go on spying on you if I don't say something to him. He's a friend of mine. I know him too well. He's pitiful," Dan explained like a brother would.

"He is?" Ginger asked, wide-eyed.

"Is what?"

"He's pitiful?" Ginger asked again.

Kate kept a straight face. "Perhaps pitiful Mr. Butler would enjoy a home-cooked meal. Perhaps you could bring him along with you sometime, Dan."

Dan had a distasteful look on his face. "Oh, I couldn't do that. The poor man smells like the wrong end of a horse."

The disappointment was visible on Ginger's face. Kate suggested, "Perhaps you could convince Mr. Butler to clean up a bit."

Dan shook his head. "Well, I could try," he said doubtfully and trudged out of the hotel.

He headed toward the mercantile, and Rufus met him on the boardwalk and joined him. "Is that place making you rich yet, Dan?" Rufus jibed.

"No, I'll never be rich enough to dig ditches for you and Kate for free, Rufus, especially in the summertime. Hopefully, I'll figure out how to get out of it completely," Dan said.

"Oh no you won't, you're a business owner in this town."

"No, I'm not. I just turned the place over to Kate."

"Do you mean to tell me that you gave the place away so you wouldn't have to help me with the trenches?" Rufus was incredulous.

"No, but that's a better reason than why I did it."

"What did you do it for?"

"Kate should have it. The ladies made the place what it is. I don't want a business. I don't want to have to go to a bunch of damned silly meetings and have to go run off the people in the tent city," Dan declared.

"Oh yeah, the women in this town hate the tent city."

"I have no intention of telling people what to do. Pretty soon, you'll be wanting the law hanging around and churches and schools. This place is getting too busy to suit me as it is," Dan complained. "It's getting organized by God!"

"Kate told you about the schools and churches, did she?"

"What?"

"Never mind," Rufus said.

The men were sitting on a bench in front of the mercantile, watching the people coming and going. Dan was trying to figure a way to convince Rufus to take a bath and buy a clean shirt. Dan sniffed the air. "I'm surprised they let you into those government meetings. It's no wonder why you got the job of tending to the sewage problems."

"I volunteered!" Rufus said loudly.

Dan rolled his eyes and turned away. "That figures."

"Somebody's got to do the work around here. What will become of Weatherford's building over there, you reckon?"

"I reckon you ought to give it to the Chinese. Get some of them out of the tents."

"Hey now, that's not a bad idea," Rufus whispered. Moments passed as the two men watched the hustle and bustle on the street.

"Well, I'm going to buy a new shirt and get cleaned up for supper," Dan said, standing up and stretching his back. "I believe I'll get a shave while I'm at it." He looked at Rufus. "Do you want to come with me and see how such things are accomplished?"

"I know how to clean up for supper!"

"Why don't you then?"

"Why would I get cleaned up just to eat beans with Jim at the livery?"

"Why not come and have supper with me over at Kate's?"

Rufus jumped up and stayed hot on Dan's heels for the rest of the afternoon.

*****

Bill was filled with remorse. He knew the men who he had killed a few weeks back were the reason why Sam was dead now. He wished that he could turn back time, but those men might have ended up killing Sam anyway if he had let them go. He couldn't make sense of it, but he knew justice was going to be served for Sam's death.

Rose was in her own world of revenge. She imagined a dozen different ways that she wanted to kill the men they were tracking. She hated herself for not protecting Sam as she had promised to do. She hated her selfishness in wanting to have a rancho and not letting Sam see his dream through by being a rich gold miner. She wouldn't look at anybody. She only stared tenaciously ahead. Bennager reached out to hold her hand to comfort her, and she took it, but only for a brief moment. She only had one thought on her mind right now, and it wasn't her husband or being comforted by him. Only one thing would give her comfort right now, and it was more death.

Bennager remembered the day in Stockton when Sam had laughed at him for getting mixed up with Rose and Bill, and he wondered what he was getting into now. He didn't want to be a party to a killing spree led by Bill Ford. He was a simple man from Illinois who had led a fortunate, simple life in California, hauling freight for the last seven years. He had good friends in the foothills and the Sacramento Valley who had helped him get his business started. He knew all the influential families from Red Bluff to Sacramento City, and he knew that they would think he had become a vigilante.

Bennager looked at his wife's grim face, and his stomach knotted at the thought of how this would change her. *What if she was involved in killing a man? Wouldn't that change a woman for the rest of her life? What if seeing a man be killed by someone else could change a woman for life?* He knew that she had to kill once before, but he hadn't been around that time. In his heart, he knew he was going to have to do something to keep her from participating in an act that men shouldn't even have to see.

The days were growing longer now, and Bennager couldn't wait for the night to fall into darkness. He prayed that Zeb and Bill wouldn't find the culprits before then, but he had his doubts that his prayers would be answered on account of how easy the men were to track. The party had followed Zeb at a lope all afternoon.

"These are the stupidest sons of bitches that I have ever tracked. Don't you agree, Bill?" Zeb said as they forged ahead.

Bill nodded, and the expression on his face told Zeb to be quiet. Zeb didn't know why, but he figured that it had something to do with Rose, so he stopped talking and just smiled at Bill. They were getting close to the vermin that they were hunting, and they knew that the issue would be resolved before the next morning.

It finally became too dark to actually see the tracks, even though Zeb reckoned that if he was afoot, he would surely trip over them. Bill could almost smell the murderous bastards. Bill pulled back on his reins. "We better stop for the night." Zeb turned and gave him a look of astonishment, and Bill looked back at him with a definitive nod and a vengeful look in his eyes.

"Yeah, we'll rest up here and catch those bastards first thing in the morning," Zeb stated.

"That's my thought too. We'll get up real early and catch 'em when they're still sleeping." Bill gave Bennager a serious look. "That means we'll have to turn in early."

Bennager peered at Bill and nodded to the man. Rose wasn't paying any attention to the men. She thought of Sam, and she missed seeing him. He wouldn't have liked being on a mission like this, and he wouldn't have wanted to kill a White man for any reason. She couldn't help wondering what had made him grin like that in the end. Bennager startled her from her unpleasant thought when he warmly put his hands on her shoulders as he came up to her from behind.

Bennager didn't think that his wife wanted to be hugged or kissed. She only had retribution on her mind. "Rose, did you hear Bill? He wants to turn in so we can get up early and catch those men," he said softly.

Rose turned around and leaned on her husband for comfort. She was tired. She had woken early that morning to prepare for her wedding, spent a couple of hours sobbing like she had never done before, and had spent the last five hours on the back of the Roman, chasing murderous bastards and wasting her brain away with the thoughts of what she wanted to do with them, and on top of that, her undergarments had never dried out after being dumped in the pond by her trusty steed. She held her husband tight around his waist, buried her face in his chest, and cried. Bennager graciously comforted her, and when he heard her sniffles from crying, he held her closer and rubbed her back.

Bill shrank away from the sight of his niece being so sick with grief. He strolled away from the couple, pretending to look for firewood, and Zeb stealthily followed. They knew that they were close enough to find their prey in the dark, but Bill wanted to get a look at them. "Stay here and get a little fire started so Rose won't smell their smoke. I want to run over and get a peek at just how stupid these sons of bitches are."

"What if they smell our smoke?" Zeb whispered.

"I doubt they're very smart or even worried about being followed, but if they smell us, we'll meet 'em in the middle," Bill replied.

Zeb nodded and returned to camp. Rose was unsaddling her horse, and Bennager was unloading the pack saddles. "There's a little brandy in there for Rose," Zeb said suggestively.

Bennager smiled at the old renegade. "She could probably use some tonight. Thank you for thinking of her, Zeb. What did you do with Bill?"

"Oh, I think he's out in the brush doing the only thing that he's any good at, taking a big sh—"

"Never mind," Bennager interrupted. "I get the point."

Zeb chuckled at his grotesque answer and Bennager's reaction to it. Zeb quickly got the fire going and helped Bennager with the pack saddles. "I doubt we'll need all this stuff, but if I hadn't brought it, Bill would have had a fit. He thinks that he is a better outfitter than I am because I've been out of the game for fifteen years."

Bennager nodded. He was as tired as anyone there. He hadn't had more than six hours of sleep in the last three days, and he hoped that he was right about what Bill and Zeb had planned. "I've been going through these packs looking for Rose's tent, but I can't seem to find it," Bennager said mostly to himself.

Zeb threw his hand to the top of his head smashing his hat as he did it. He grimaced at Bennager. "I forgot the tent. Damn, Bennager, I'm sorry."

"That's all right, I could sleep anywhere, Zeb."

When Rose was finished unsaddling the horses, she eased up to the fire, hoping to dry her clothes out better. Zeb had brought along tamales that had already been prepared for the wedding guests, so all that needed to be cooked was some water for the tea. Bennager was still going through the packs, looking for coffee. He desperately wanted a cup because he wanted to make sure that Rose was asleep before he was.

"Zeb, do you remember where you put the coffee?" Bennager asked.

Zeb slapped one hand into the other. "Damn it, I forgot that too," he lied. The smell of coffee traveled far in the open air, and he didn't want the hunted men to smell their camp.

Bennager grabbed the bedrolls and the brandy, joined his despondent wife by the fire and handed her the jug.

A half hour passed as Zeb added wood to the coals but kept the fire small. Bennager got up to get the saddles for he and Rose to use as back rests, and he gently convinced Rose to settle in so she would be warmer. She stopped staring blankly into the fire for a moment and did as she was asked. Zeb had offered her food and tea, but she had declined, taking small sips from the brandy jug as her only sustenance.

Bennager hadn't eaten since he left Monterey, trailing after Bob and Joe. He gladly ate Rose's share and would have eaten Bill's, too, if he hadn't finally showed up. Zeb heard him coming and turned to see what information he could glean from the expression on Bill's face.

"How did it all come out?" Zeb asked.

Bill knew what Zeb had told the others about his whereabouts. "I think I only got out half of it, maybe a little more," Bill replied.

Bennager scowled at the two men curiously and realized what they were up to. Bob and Joe were about a half a mile ahead, and Bill had already seen them. Zeb didn't ask any more questions which meant that they already had a plan, and Bennager was still hoping he wouldn't have to be a part of it.

"Why don't you have your wife warm inside a tent?" Bill asked Bennager.

"We don't need a tent on this trip," Bennager said. "It's been too nice out to neglect the stars like we've been doing all this time."

"Zeb forgot the tent, I take it," Bill said, shaking his head.

Zeb and Bill sat by the fire until they figured it was about midnight. Rose was fast asleep for sure; it was always easy to tell with her. On this night, even Bennager was snoring slightly because he was so tired. Bill put more wood on the fire and turned to warm his back. "I think Rose is rubbing off on her husband," Bill whispered.

Zeb smiled and nodded. "That is always apt to happen when people stay together long enough."

"Are you ready to go?" Bill asked.

"Yep, I'm just waitin' on you," Zeb replied.

The two men walked for what Zeb thought was closer to a mile rather than a half mile, and Bill stopped to rest. He could hear Zeb starting to breathe hard, and he wanted him to be quiet when they walked into the vermin's camp. Zeb could smell their fire and hear their loud snores. He shook his head as he caught his breath. He gave Bill a glaring look, and he reciprocated it with one of his own. Bill let another minute pass, pulled his skinning knife out, and looked at Zeb. No words were needed between them; they knew what needed to be done and how to do it. Bill nodded to Zeb, and he nodded back.

They softly walked into camp, and Bill went to the smallest man, knelt, and slit his throat from ear to ear. Bill got up and looked at Zeb. Zeb kicked the bigger man to wake him up.

"What? What do ya want? Get the hell away from me, you little whelp!" Bob groaned.

Zeb kicked the man in the face, and Bill stood behind the man's head, waiting for him to get to his feet. "Get up, Bob!" Zeb said.

When Bob realized that it wasn't Joe, he got up as quickly as he could. "Zeb, what in the hell are you doing way out here? What are ya kicking me in the face for?" he asked innocently.

"I woke you up so you could tell Joe who killed him when you get to hell, Bob. Oh, by the way, you can also tell him that the man you killed today was a friend of mine and Horny Bill Ford's."

Bob looked on in confusion at Zeb words. It seemed like a big riddle to him that Zeb had known the Black man, known they had killed the Black man, and was now standing before him, talking about hell. Zeb reckoned that expression on his face would stay with him into his fiery eternity because Bill slit his throat before he could unravel the knot in his small brain.

"What now?" Zeb asked, looking at the dead men.

"I believe I'll dump them in the San Joaquin River and give the horses to the little toe-headed children that belong to that dimwitted ferryman. The kids will have a better chance of running off that way or maybe Mama will just hack the horses up and eat 'em. That's what I'm hoping for, and the sooner the better."

After Bill and Zeb got back to camp, Zeb said, "I'll see you at the wedding then." He said it with a feeling of numbness. He didn't like seeing dead men, but he wasn't sorry, remorseful, nor sickened by what had happened. He still cringed at the thought of Joe and Bob shooting into the water, trying to kill the twins. Now he hoped that he could clear things up with Rose. Bill had taken her chance to inflict vengeance away, and Zeb reckoned that she would be beside herself with madness about it.

*****

The morning sun was well above the horizon when Rose opened her eyes. She panicked and quickly jumped up. Sam's murderers were getting away, and everyone was still asleep. She looked a second time and realized that Bill was gone. Bennager and Zeb began to stir, and they both saw Rose standing in camp, holding her face in her hands and crying out of frustration.

Both men got up to talk to her. Zeb went first. "Bill wouldn't want you to be a part of what happened last night. A human being shouldn't ever have to do such a thing, and Bill made sure that you didn't have to. It's done now. There isn't anything more that can be done to those men for what they did to Sam. It's time to head back to the rancho now." Zeb looked to Bennager, and they both wondered what Rose's reaction would be when she stopped crying. Zeb warily went back and retrieved his bedroll and started packing things up.

Rose sought comfort in her husband's arms. He received her and hoped that she would take Zeb's explanation reasonably. Several long moments passed as Rose commanded herself to let go and accept that Sam was gone and couldn't be brought back. His killers were gone, and she hadn't been the one to make it so. She willed herself to move forward. She willed herself to remember the good times she and the others had shared with Sam and to let him go in peace. Finally, her red, wet eyes looked into Bennager's, and she asked. "Do you think that they have buried Sam yet?"

"I don't know, honey, let's go find out," Bennager said.

Rose solemnly started saddling the horses while Bennager helped Zeb finish with the packs. The Roman followed her like a pet as she saddled Bennager's horse, and then Zeb's. He wanted to console her too. He rested his chin on her shoulder at one point, and she turned and hugged his neck. The Roman was as disappointed as Rose was about being left out of the retribution that was served up in the middle of the night.

Zeb led Bennager and Rose back to the pond at a slower pace than what they had traveled the day before. They arrived back at midafternoon to find that Sam had indeed been buried. Pablo, Romero, and Stud were still at the gravesite. They were building a sturdy miniature corral enclosure around the grave to keep the cattle from trampling it. Tears welled up in Rose's eyes at the thoughtfulness and care that Pablo was giving to her deceased friend, especially since she knew this was not the place where Pablo would have buried him.

They dismounted, and Rose went to the grave. Bennager started to follow, but Zeb drew his attention to all the carriage and wagon tracks and the footprints of all the people who had attended Sam's funeral.

"I'll be damned. I bet Sam didn't expect that," Bennager said.

Zeb smiled and shook his head. "He probably didn't expect a lot of things. His death is a great loss, but I reckon Pablo gave him a proper send-off."

Bennager and Zeb joined Rose at the grave for a moment, and then they spent the rest of the afternoon finishing the fence.

VAQUEROS AND ROSES

1

The wedding guests had departed after Sam's funeral. Pablo had no way of knowing how many days the bride and groom would be chasing after Sam's murderers. Bennager was relieved the big wedding was off. He had never liked the idea of being watched by a passel of strangers, and he gave up churching when he left home several years back.

Rose was still in a state of depression when she awoke the next morning. Bennager had gotten up early, and he was waiting for her to wake so he could bring her breakfast in bed and take care of her for the day.

"Good morning, beautiful," Bennager said to her when her eyes finally opened and locked with his. He was sitting in a leather chair across the room reading a book. Bennager was planning on spending the day with Rose alone in their room together to console and rest after the arduous experience of loss.

The fact that Bennager was sitting in a chair rather than being in bed with her reinforced the previous notion that Bennager had gone to Monterey to be with another woman, that he was becoming bored with her, and the marriage was not real after all. This notion complicated with her grief had her in a mood Bennager had not witnessed before. He attributed it all to grief, not considering the other factor Rose had on her mind. She did not answer her greeting. She just glared.

"Do you feel like having breakfast? If so, I will go get it."

Rose continued to glare.

"What is the matter, my love? Have I done something wrong?"

"You left me."

"Because I wanted to surprise you," Bennager said in defense.

"It was a surprise to realize you had another woman in Monterey."

Bennager was dumbfounded, and then he started to laugh.

Rose threw a boot at him and began to cry. "It's not funny, you son of a bitch."

Bennager's expression quickly changed. Grief or no grief, Rose had earned a corrective response from him. He leaped from his chair to the bed like a cougar and quickly rolled Rose onto his lap and gave her a stern spanking. He would never tolerate that sort of name-calling from anyone, let alone the love of his life.

"I hate you!" Rose shouted as she tried to leave the room.

Again, Bennager's cat like action surprised her as he beat her to the door. "What on earth has gotten into you? I do not understand this behavior. Did you have a bad dream or something?"

"You wanted to see another woman before you had to swear your fidelity to me in a real chapel."

"That sounds like something Zeb or Bill put into your head," Bennager said as he dug into his shirt pocket and then produced a small box. He handed it to Rose with a handsome grin on his face.

*****

Bill had come back to the rancho in the night and was at breakfast when Bennager and Rose returned from their hiatus. Pablo, Zeb, and Bill stood up at the sight of Rose, and Bill gave her a hug. She returned it, and Bill knew that what had happened a few nights before was an issue that wouldn't be spoken of at Pablo's dining room table and hopefully never.

The children were excited to see Rose. They knew nothing of grief. They hugged her because they had missed her the day before, and then they ran back to Bill.

Zeb and Pablo assumed that she had spent the day before grieving for her friend and were pleased to see that she could manage to smile for the children. Zeb nodded his head to Bennager. He admired him for taking care of his wife so well during her time of sorrow.

The priest hadn't left yet. It was a rare thing for him to be at Pablo's rancho, and Pablo had insisted that he stay and perform services at his chapel on Sunday. The priest was only too happy to stay. The bed was softer than his, the food was better than his, and the wine was abundant. Bill was seated across from the man, who appeared to be in his thirties, that morning at breakfast. The priest had been there all week, and it had slipped Pablo's mind to introduce Bill to Father Chavez. Bill was gentlemanly enough to wait until he had his children seated and behaving, including Stud Colt. Bill reached his hand across the table, and Father Chavez noticed blood on his deer skin fringes hanging from his sleeve. "I'm who they call Horny Bill Ford, this is my friend Stud Colt, and these are my children, Bud and Blossom."

Father Chavez kindly took Bill's hand.

"Oh, Horny Bill, I'm sorry I have forgotten my manners. I forgot that you haven't been introduced to Father Chavez," Pablo apologized.

Bill was pleased that Pablo fell in with him about his name and smiled at him. "That's quite all right, my friend."

Zeb rolled his eyes at the idiotic mountain man, and the Ramirez women tried very hard not to giggle in Father Chavez's company.

Father Chavez said, "I have already met the young man. I was told that his name is Jack."

"Jack is his Mexican name, Father. His Miwok name is Stud Colt. That's what I call him, and he likes it," Bill explained.

"So he is a man with two names, I understand."

Bill smiled and nodded. He could see that he would have to work at making Father Chavez disgusted with him. "Do you want to know why I call him that?"

"No," Father Chavez replied. Rose and Bennager snickered.

"It will help you to understand why his Mexican name is Jack," Bill said to enlighten the man.

"No explanation is needed, my son. I am well-versed in the knowledge of names and many other things as well," Father Chavez said amiably with a devilish smile. "I do hear confessions and would be more than happy to hear yours."

As Bill stared the man down, Rose had an emotional fit of laughter and everyone at the table joined in her amusement. Father Chavez was too angelic to be fazed by Bill's antics, and Bill promptly behaved and helped the children with their food.

Father Chavez pressed on, "Where is your wife, Mr. Ford?"

Bill glared at the man for asking this question and then realized that he assumed the children were really his. For a moment, Bill was confused. "I don't have a wife, Father. These children were orphaned. They think of Little Rose as their mother now."

"I'm sorry to hear about their parents. It's a wonderful thing you are doing by taking them on as your own," Father Chavez said.

Bill nodded, but he didn't agree. "Anybody with half a brain would have done the same thing."

Rose was seated next to Pablo, and he noticed her wedding ring. He took her hand in his. "My, my, my, look at this, Mama," he exclaimed as he held Rose's hand in the air for his wife to see at the other end of the table.

Rose smiled with pride and got up to show the ladies. It hadn't occurred to her that anyone other than herself would take interest in such a thing, but the women went crazy, especially the young ones. Rose caught Juanita giving Stud a special smile after she examined the ring closely, and Stud reached out to Rose so he could have a look. He had never seen such a stone on the Cosumnes River. He would have to look harder now. He knew that quartz wouldn't pass in Juanita's eyes. Rose was taken aback when the men wanted to see it, too, and the approval in Bill and Zeb's eyes made her even prouder. She lightly kissed Bennager when she returned to her seat.

"Pablo, my husband has agreed to marry me today in your chapel," Rose told him with the happiest grin on her face that Pablo hadn't seen on a woman since Maria had agreed to marry him. Almost all Spanish weddings were set up years in advance between families, but it was a very special thing to have the bride wholeheartedly look the groom in the eye and agree to it. He had always thought of the day between him and Maria as the day when his life truly began.

"What time will the happy event take place, my lovely lady?"

"Just as soon as I can get my dress on," Rose replied.

The people scattered, like Pablo's wild cattle, to all corners of the house. They had to hurry to get ready. The dishes were left on the table for the egg yolks to dry on, and Rose and Bennager were sitting alone together. They looked down the table and saw Bill taking bacon off Father Chavez's plate, and then he cleaned off Juanita and Isabel's too. Rose and Bennager shook their heads at Bill's fortune and unconcern for what everyone else seemed to be in a panic about. Moments passed as Bill and the children crunched on their extra bacon, and Juanita and Isabel scampered out of the sewing room and snatched the children away without saying one word about it to Bill.

Bill was shocked at the kidnapping and looked at Rose in disbelief. Rose smiled at the old goat. "Will you be coming to our wedding, William?"

He puffed up his chest as he stood up from the table. "Do you want me to?"

"Yes, I want you to give me away. I saw it happen that way once when Mother dragged me to a wedding back home," Rose explained.

"How am I to give you away? Can I throw you? Can I kick you in the ass?" Bill teased loudly in hopes that Maria and Father Chavez could hear him. He could see that Rose was as ignorant about wedding procedures as Stud Colt was.

"No, you'd probably tear my dress," Rose replied.

"Well, go get it on, I don't have all day," Bill grumbled.

Rose was delighted that her uncle wasn't opposed to being a participant. She kissed her husband and scurried to her room.

Bill stared at Bennager for a few minutes, and then he said, "I heard that you are a wealthy, well-known man, Rasmussen, but I didn't think that you were fool enough to squander your fortune away on a crazy little squirrel like that!"

Bennager turned and glared at the man for his comment. Bill laughed, slapped him on the back, and dragged him to the chapel. "Come on, you can't see the bride in her dress," he teased.

*****

It was the last week in March on the Rasmussen rancho, and the new oak leaves were peeking out of their buds to greet a new season. The bushy-tailed gray squirrels were just about out of acorns and digger pine nuts. They were cranky with worry this time of year and complained profusely about the dogs snooping around in their business. Girl didn't bother with them very much because she was a cow dog, but her pups were becoming premier squirrel dogs, and the squirrels lamented constantly and threw pinecones from the treetops at the pups whenever they could.

Angus gave the squirrels at headquarters a reprieve when he made the pups follow him and Trina out to mark off the second league of land that Bill had pointed out. He and Trina were able to finish the corrals in three long days since the posts were already set. The well-diggers had come and gone, and Angus figured that the money they earned was drunk away after two days.

Angus and Trina were able to mark out the perimeter in less than three days' time. They only had to mark out three sides, and Trina wasn't having any trouble staying on her feet. As a matter of fact, Trina could make her 137 feet in half the time that it took Angus. Every time he turned around, he saw her making the rock monuments bigger as she waited for the end of the rope to get to her. He started using fewer rocks after that, and the job went quickly. His partner surprised him every day. She picked up on every job they did, and he never had to tell her something twice. It was usually Trina who could come up with an easier way to do something.

"Tomorrow, we will go back to building the house. I want it framed and roofed at least when the Rasmussens get here," Angus stated when they got back to camp and started an early supper.

"Tomorrow, you will take me to town. I need a window for my cabin since you won't let me sleep in the tent. The air is stagnating in there, and if I leave the door open, the squirrels vandalize the place. It will be too hot in there this summer. Besides that, Girl and I haven't been to town for a steak in a month. We haven't had a day off in all that time either. Girl perked her ears up when her name was mentioned and eased over by Trina to stand firm with her about going to town for a steak and to get a pet, of course.

"People will be able to see ye in your cabin if ye have a window," Angus said.

"What people? You? I doubt you'd bother to look through my window, Angus Donovan," Trina grumbled.

"Yes, I had better take ye to town. Ye are beginnin' to sound like those squirrels. And I will buy ye three windows so people can look at ye from all directions."

"Again, I ask, what people?"

"Bill and his children, the Rasmussens, Zeb, and the vaqueros that Bill told us 'bout, woman, those people will be here soon."

"Angus Donovan, they have an invention here in America called curtains, so you shouldn't have to worry about folks seeing my naked body on the hot summer nights that are sure to come," Trina jibed with a sly, devilish, suggestive tone in her voice. She hoped to make Angus blush, but it didn't work. She saw something else altogether different in his eyes. She was sure that she saw what she had been waiting for: interest.

"Oh, ye are a clever one with the words, Miss Trina." Angus remained his same old self for the rest of the evening, so Trina didn't know what to make out of his failure to blush.

*****

They woke early as usual the next morning, and Trina had the team hitched and grained before Angus had the fire hot enough to make coffee and fried biscuits. "Don't ye want breakfast this mornin', lassie?" he hollered at her.

"Yes, but I still have to change my clothes, and I didn't want to get my dress dirty while helping you hitch up the team," she said as she joined him by the campfire.

"I can hitch the team up meself," Angus mumbled.

"You couldn't live without me helping you hitch the team up," Trina sniped.

Angus gave her a smiling scowl but didn't answer her comment. Trina was becoming surlier every day, and Angus realized that there was still much to learn about his partner. Since he had known her, she had been beaten down, suicidal, mean toward and afraid of him, quiet, diligent, tough, and now she was friendly. Every week, she seemed to develop a new personality, and every week that passed, she became stronger in every way, and she was beginning to remind Angus of his sisters more and more. He already knew that he couldn't live without her, but he wasn't sure that he could live with her either. He figured to give it more time and find out who the real Trina Harper was.

Angus had been awake half the night, thinking about Trina and her windows. He imagined that she wouldn't make her curtains until the Rasmussen party showed up, and he wondered if he would be able to keep his distance that long. Each day that passed was a day that his brain became weaker over the battle it was having with his heart, and his will was fading fast. He watched her go to her cabin when breakfast was finished, and it weakened him to know for a fact that she was in there, taking clothes off and putting clothes on. He could picture in his mind her firm, pale, muscular body as she pulled on her going-to-town dress, and his heart felt like it would explode.

Trina came out of her cabin, dressed and ready to go, and Angus hadn't noticed. He was still sitting next to the campfire, daydreaming. "What are you doing?" she asked.

Angus remained stoic as he looked up at her. "I'm finishin' me coffee, lassie."

"Your cup is empty, you big ox! Are we going to town or not?"

"Yes, woman, get the dogs!" Angus said, mocking insanity. The fiery redhead was sure to make him squirrel crazy, just like those pups.

*****

Dan Dunaway was sitting in the cafe in Grass Valley, thinking. He thought of how he was finally free from the hate and vengeance he had been harboring toward Douglas Weatherford. Weatherford was dead now and had been for three weeks. He had stopped by to pay Lee for his services one day, but Lee was nowhere to be found. Dan was afraid that Weatherford had recovered and sent Lee away, but the smell of death in the gambling hall gave him the courage to investigate. The corpse that Dan found was beyond recognition, except for the amputated leg that was nothing more than black, rotting flesh and bone. Dan lost his stomach and eased over to the livery to get Rufus to help him get rid of what he had found. As Dan sat in the café, thinking of how they had disposed of the carcass, he started to gag. He closed his eyes and shook his head and willed himself to think of something else.

Thinking of something more pleasant led Dan to think of Kate. She hadn't reacted to Weatherford's demise in the way Dan had thought she would. He figured she would want to have a party, but the news made her melancholy. Dan had asked her why she was feeling that way instead of rejoicing, and Kate said that she didn't know. She knew it was a strange reaction, and Dan figured that Kate had never expected Weatherford to die. She wouldn't talk about it, and Dan reckoned she would get over whatever she was feeling. Dan didn't bother telling her what Lee had done to Weatherford. Dan and Rufus made a pact they would never tell anyone on earth what Lee had done to Weatherford. When Dan left Sacramento City three weeks ago, he did so knowing that Kate would be fine. She had shirked off the short phase of depression that she had felt and went back to work at trying to disband the tent city. Dan thought that she was becoming obsessed with those folks who were just waiting for the rivers to recede so they could go to the diggings. Dan told her they would leave soon enough, but that wasn't soon enough for Kate.

Thinking of the diggings led Dan to think about when he could get started at working his claim. He hoped that there weren't any fussy ladies on his creek that wouldn't let him live in a tent. He laughed to himself about lovely Kate and her town meetings and imagined her poring over her law books, looking for a law that prohibited people from living in tents.

The lady of the cafe came and filled Dan's coffee cup. "It sure is a beautiful day out there. If I was rich, I'd close up for the day and go out and enjoy the smell of spring."

"Yes, it is a pretty day. Maybe you should close up anyway," Dan said with his gorgeous smile. "It isn't every day you can enjoy the smell of spring."

Helen looked deeply into Dan's face, and he could tell that she was considering the idea.

Dan could tell that the woman, who was about the age of forty, had worked most of her life serving people, and one day off, after all those years, wouldn't hurt anybody.

They looked out the front windows as they heard the six-horse team and freight wagon pull up and stop. "Oh, oh, if this place was closed up when Angus Donovan came to town to eat, he'd turn the whole town upside down," Helen remarked.

Dan smiled at her comment and watched her rush off to the kitchen. Dan was quick to match up the Irish name with the six-horse team, and he quietly waited for the chance to get a close look at the man who almost killed Weatherford and took Trina out of Sacramento City.

Angus was having a difficult time traveling with Trina today. Between her beauty and the pretty day they were having in the foot-hills, he was intoxicated with the kind of bliss he knew was dangerous. The fresh smells of grass growing, flowers blooming, and trees leafing out was all the more incentive for Angus' inhibitions to weaken toward the woman who was seated beside him, who acted like and smelled like spring every day. *What if loving her and living with her was like living this lovely day over and over again?*

As they approached the cafe, Angus wiped the silly thought from his mind. It was time to focus on the list of lumber he had pictured in his mind, and he didn't want to forget the items he had come to town for. Angus hopped out of the wagon and headed for the cafe entrance.

"Angus, what are you doing?" Trina asked from the wagon seat.

Angus turned and scowled at Trina as if to say, "What does it look like I'm doing?"

"Will you help me down from the wagon so I won't rip my dress?" Trina asked in a whisper.

Jake Gates happened to be coming out of the mercantile when he witnessed the little scene between Trina and Angus. He beat Angus to the task by a head. "I'd be happy to help you out of there, Miss Harper," Jake said, holding his hand out to her.

"Oh, hello, Jake," Trina said with delight. "Thank you, I'd be much obliged to you."

Angus watched Trina lean forward and let Jake Gates take her by her waist and lift her to the ground as she secured her dress from catching and ripping on some piece of hardware on the freight wagon.

"Thank you, Jake," Trina said as she straightened out her dress so she would look her best. "It's a lovely day to come to town, isn't it?"

"Yes, and the place sparkles now that you're here, Miss Harper," Jake complimented.

Trina was too wise to blush, but she flashed a dazzling smile at Jake, and Angus rolled his eyes.

Angus used his arm as a barrier between Jake and Trina and gently eased Trina toward him. They walked into the cafe together, and Jake followed. "Do you mind if I join you? I have a hankerin' for a piece of pie," Jake said.

Angus let out a sigh as Trina invited Jake to come along. She would take great pleasure in ruffling Angus' feathers today. She knew how quickly he tired of the topic of pig farming. "How are the pigs doing, Jake?" Trina asked once they were seated. It delighted Trina to watch Jake blush whenever she asked him this question. Her interest in his pigs pleased him. Angus glared at their annoying courtship ritual as Helen greeted them with coffee in hand.

"I should have known that I would see you on such a beautiful day like today, Angus. Are you still hard at it?" Helen asked.

"Aye, it's a beautiful day, Helen, I should be workin' today," Angus grumbled. Angus had noticed the black-haired young man in the dining room eyeballing Trina, and he could tell that the young man was visibly pleased to see her. Angus watched the man sip his coffee and pretend to stare out the window, but Angus knew that the man was listening to the ridiculous pig palaver that Trina and Jake were engaged in because every so often, the black-haired man would snicker to himself.

Finally, Angus elbowed Trina in the ribs. "Ouch, Angus what are you doing?"

"Shhh, do ye know that young fella?" Angus whispered.

Trina rubbed her ribs and vowed to hurt Angus later when he least expected it. Trina peered at the young man for a moment and said, "No, I don't know who he is."

"Are ye sure, woman? He acts like he knows ye."

"Why would you say that? He's just sittin' there, mindin' his own business, Angus," Trina said in frustration. She reckoned that Angus was just looking for an excuse to interrupt her conversation with Jake. Angus ate his meal hastily and was finished before Trina was halfway through. She was talking to Jake too much.

Angus saw Dan get up and leave. "I'll be right back, Trina. I have to check on somethin' at the mercantile." He shot Jake Gates with a departing glare and left.

Angus caught up with Dan outside. Dan had stopped to roll a smoke and was letting the warmth of the sun hit his face. "*Dia duit*, I'm Angus Donovan," Angus said with his hand out.

"I'm pleased to meet you, I'm Dan Dunaway." Angus observed the man to be genuinely pleasant.

"I think ye know that woman," Angus said bluntly.

Dan flashed his perfect smile. "I don't know her personally. I know her as well as I know you and that team, though."

Angus nodded and knew what the young man was driving at. He became sick to his stomach and embarrassed that Dan remembered them from Sacramento City. Dan saw the robust man wilt in front of him and felt he should elaborate.

"I was in Sacramento City the day that you crushed that man and took Trina out of town because I had followed that man all the way from Kentucky. It was my intention to get him back for killing my grandfather. Later, after you left town, I was over on the Bear River, and I came across the dress that Trina was wearing that day. Since then, I've always wondered what became of her. It's good to see that she is well."

"What happened to that man?"

"He's dead now, and I can assure you it wasn't all because of you," Dan smiled.

"How is it ye know the woman's name?"

Dan looked at the ground and then back into Angus' eyes. "There were others in Trina's situation. I got to know the ladies pretty well and am happy to report that they are doing as well as Trina is now. They have their very own hotel and are prospering."

Angus was stunned.

"I figured if Trina was alive that the two of you would be married. It surprises me to see that she is so smitten with the pig farmer when it was you who saved her from such a deplorable life." Dan smiled at Angus' confused expression. "You should know that what you did that day saved the lives of six women and the reputation of Sacramento City."

Dan Dunaway had given Angus many things to think about. Dan Dunaway was as pleasant as the spring day that they were enjoying, but he was also a reminder of the cold, foggy past. Angus had played a part in yet another man's death, and Dan knew it. Dan knew of Trina's past, and Angus didn't like it. Even though Dan said all the right words, Angus still had an overwhelming feeling of regret for having followed Dan out of the cafe. Angus could have gone the rest of his life without knowing that he had killed Rose's father.

Dan wondered at the big Irishman's reaction to the news. For the second time now, a person had the audacity to be saddened by Weatherford's death when they should be celebrating it. Dan shook his head slightly and put his hand out. Angus took it reluctantly. "It's good to find you and Trina well, Mr. Donovan. I hope to be seeing you again sometime."

"Aye, same to ye, Mr. Dunaway," Angus lied. He took a deep breath and tried to forget the day that he left Sacramento City. He focused on the fact that he was surrounded by the beauty of the foothills of the Sierras and went back inside the cafe to join Trina.

As Angus entered the cafe, he had to wonder if Jake Gates would follow them around all day and what he could do to get rid of the man. Jake was a good man, but Angus found him to be intrusive. Trina looked into Angus' eyes as he approached the table. He could tell that she was happy to see him; her smile was broad, and her eyes twinkled. The sight of her broke his will. Even though she enjoyed talking about pig farming with Mr. Gates, and even though she could make Mr. Gates blush, and even though it was obvious that Mr. Gates would take her home in a heartbeat, Angus had never seen her smile that way at anyone, except him.

Trina's heart skipped a beat when Angus smiled back at her in a pleasing way that she had never seen before. He came to the table and said, "If ye're finished stuffin' your face and flappin' your jowls, then we better be gettin' your windows." He held his hand out to her.

Angus' offensive words were so ridiculous that it made Trina giggle. Angus never stopped smiling as she put her hand in his. He gently took it as she lifted herself out of her seat. He didn't move as she rose. She was forced to brush up against him. Some uncontrollable urge overcame Angus as he looked into Trina's dazzling eyes, and he brought her hand to his lips and kissed it. Trina would have made love to the Irishman right there in the dining room of the cafe in front of God and everyone, and Angus knew it. Angus knew that Dan Dunaway was wrong about Trina being smitten with the pig farmer, and Angus knew that he wanted this woman, and he wouldn't wait another day to have her.

Trina could feel and see every thought Angus was having. It was as clear to her as if she was reading a book. She put her calloused hand to Angus' face and pleaded with her eyes for him to kiss her as she held her breath.

"Will you marry me, Miss Trina Harper?"

Trina reached her lips to his and whispered, "Yes" into his mouth and kissed him with all the passion she had reserved for him during the months they had been together, forgetting they were not alone.

"What a rotten son of a bitch!" Jake grumbled. He threw down his napkin, planted his hat on his head, and left the cafe without one word of congratulations.

Angus smiled at the insult and reckoned that Jake Gates wouldn't be attending the wedding.

Helen clapped her hands with excitement. "Now I'll have a reason to close the cafe and take a day off. I wouldn't miss seeing the two of you get hitched for anything. I hope you don't mind me inviting myself."

Trina smiled, but her eyes never left Angus' face. "Of course, you'll come, Helen. You'll be my witness, that this was his idea." She wrapped her arms around Angus' neck and hugged him. "When should Helen have her day off?" Trina whispered as Angus hugged her back and smelled her hair.

"This day, lassie, we're goin' to wed right now."

Dan watched the dejected Jake Gates plod out of town. He leaned on a post and rolled another smoke. His instincts compelled him to hang around and wait to see Trina one more time.

Minutes passed as he nonchalantly let the sights and sounds of the town invigorate him. Men were getting ready to go to the diggings, and soon, he would be going as well. Finally, Angus and Trina came out of the cafe, hand in hand. Helen and her husband were following. Dan watched Helen lock the front door, and he saw Angus feed the black-and-white dog a big piece of meat.

Dan could only assume that Angus had won out over the pig farmer, and Helen was closing the cafe to witness a matrimonial ceremony. Dan smiled with delight and wished that he knew Angus Donovan better. He hoped that he would treat Trina as well as he treated the black-and-white dog. Even from where he stood, he could feel Trina's happiness radiate from her. He could see her smile and rosy cheeks, and he could tell by the bounce in her step and the lack of effort that Angus used to help her into the wagon that she was walking on a cloud.

Dan flicked his cigarette into the street. He decided to make one more trip to Sacramento City before he started to work on his claim.

2

Once Bill had given Rose away to Bennager, he sat down with Zeb and started making animal noises. Zeb turned four shades of red. He was embarrassed that Bill would do such a thing in front of Pablo's family and Father Chavez. Stud and the twins thought that it was part of the ceremony and joined in with Bill. Zeb leaned over and held his head in his hands and looked at the floor. Stud was an expert at mimicking doves and songbirds, and after a few minutes, Bill gave him the floor. Rose wept at the lovely sounds that Stud was making for her wedding music, and when the vows were said and the bride and groom had kissed, Stud was given a standing ovation. Bill scrambled to get out of the chapel before Rose could catch him, but Juanita met him at the exit and kicked him in the leg again.

Zeb and Bennager got quite a chuckle out of watching Bill limp around for the rest of the day, but Stud couldn't understand why Juanita had kicked him this time.

Later, Stud asked, "Why did my woman kick you, Bill?"

"Because she is evil. Soon she will be kicking you for no reason. She does not do it now because she has me to kick. Someday, when the two of you are alone, she will kick you," Bill explained.

Stud watched Juanita for the rest of the day. She was busy with the women's business and didn't make time to do anything more than smile at him once in a while.

Toward suppertime, Stud told Bill, "She kicks you because you keep taking me away from her. She wants me, Bill."

"Who are you talking about?"

"I am talking about my woman, Juanita!"

"Which one is that?" Bill said, peering at the small crowd of women.

Zeb had been sitting with Bill. "What did he say?"

"He's confused about why what's-her-name kicked me," Bill explained with a childish snicker.

"It was a good thing she did. If she hadn't, Ol' Bennager might have throttled you."

Bill looked up into the branches of the tree they were sitting under and sighed. "He's apt to throttle me anyway if I don't get out of here pretty soon. This place is making me nuts."

"You're already nuts, Bill."

"How in the devil are we going to get Rose, Stud, and my babies up to that rancho without getting them killed, Zeb?"

"Maybe we ought to send them up there before the drive starts. Do you think Stud remembers how to get there?" Zeb asked.

"I can't send the Indians by themselves, and Rose wouldn't leave the turmoil that she's caused or her husband. She's going to be right in the middle of those vaqueros. You know it, and so do I."

Zeb scratched his head and thought out loud, "You and I will have to be on horseback. The vaqueros will find a use for us. Bennager will have to be on horseback to keep up with Rose and keep her safe. That leaves Stud Colt and the kids in the wagon."

Bill sighed and rolled his eyes. "Stud Colt can barely ride, let alone control four hardheaded burros if they take it into their heads not to follow along. I doubt that he'd have much patience with my children day in and day out either. Bennager's the only one that could do that, but I think that it will take both of us to keep Rose out of trouble."

There was a pause in the conversation as both men tried to solve the dilemma, and finally, Zeb had a thought and smiled. "If I could get Pablo to help us out, maybe I could convince him to go with me to Oregon and get those Durham shorthorn bulls. I could tell him that we might as well go since we're halfway there already."

"That's a long trip for Ol' Pablo. If he agrees, then we better have the girls make some pillows for that wagon seat," Bill suggested.

"Yes, we might have to spell him once in a while, but the trip would do him good, and I think that he would like to know how to find Rose and Bennager someday."

"Well, if he won't go, then I reckon that we will just have to hogtie Rose. She's bound to get us all killed if we don't."

*****

Six days later, Rose was in the kitchen, helping with breakfast when a group of twenty-five men showed up in the yard. Alarm showed on her face as she rushed out of the kitchen to get her weapons, but Maria caught her and smiled. "Those men are the vaqueros."

Delight came into Rose's eyes. She went back to the window and watched as Pablo made his way from the chapel to greet them. Soon, Zeb came from the stables followed by Bennager, Bill, and Stud. Rose had never imagined what a vaquero looked like, but if she had, she would have gotten it entirely wrong. They all looked like princes from another land. Their clothes fit them perfectly and were clad with silver buttons. Every button was buttoned on their coats, and their boots were polished. Each man was straight, lean, and tall in their saddles, which were all decorated with silver as well. Even the bridles were decorated with silver. "How much do you pay these men?" Rose asked.

Maria laughed. "They are a special breed of men. Just wait until you see them work."

Rose observed their wide-brimmed hats and the beauty and power of their horses. She noticed how their saddles differed from hers. The stirrups were covered with leather, protecting their feet; each saddle was equipped with a lariat hanging from a horn perched above the pommel. The lariat was the only thing that wasn't decorated with silver. "They look more competent than any army that I have ever seen. Do they know about these men back in Washington DC?" Rose said as she turned to Maria with wonder in her eyes.

"Your Washington knows nothing of this place," Maria reported proudly.

Rose heard one of them greet Loco Zeb with a laugh, and she reckoned that they knew each other pretty well. Rose could not believe her eyes. *Why would these handsome men bother with cattle? They look like they should be running the Mexican government.*

"You should go out there. This is your business," Maria said to Rose. Rose gave Maria a hug and went outside to stand beside her husband.

The conversation was spoken in Spanish. Zeb understood every word, and Bill knew about half of them.

Pablo told the men to find two hundred cows with the oldest calves and twenty bulls to sell to the Rasmussens. He told them that ten of them would be going to the Yuba River to take the cattle to the Rasmussen Rancho. The vaqueros didn't bat an eye at what they were told.

One of them told Pablo that they would be ready to go in three days.

Bill understood the words "three days" and became excited instantly. He couldn't wait until Rose was settled. Summer was coming, and he figured on being in the Rockies when it got there.

Rose was in awe as she watched the men march out of the yard. She looked on in curiosity when one vaquero kicked his horse into a fast gallop and reached all the way down to the ground from his saddle to catch a chicken.

"Oh that was my little Rosa!" Pablo gasped as he put his hands to his face. They watched the vaquero slow down to a trot, and he let the hen flutter away. Pablo let out a sigh of relief. "He was showing off for you, Mrs. Rasmussen. I thought that he was going to eat my little Rosa!" Pablo fearfully exclaimed as he teetered back toward the chapel.

Bill took Zeb by the elbow away from the newlyweds. Stud followed. "Did you talk to Pablo about going with us?"

"Not yet. I'm beginning to think that Pablo does more than just pray up there in that chapel of his."

"What do you mean?" Bill inquired.

"I think we would have to fill Sam's wagon full of tequila just to get him to Stockton!" Zeb declared.

"Oh Lord Almighty, are you serious?" Bill said with disappointment.

"I'm afraid so, Bill. I've been watching him. He goes out there right after breakfast, comes in for an afternoon nap, back out there until suppertime, and then he has his evening brandy, and off to bed he goes."

"Do you reckon he's just bored?" Bill asked hopefully.

"That could be it. I'll go ask him about going with us right now before he prays himself silly."

"I'll go with you. He seems to oppose anything that you suggest," Bill said as they headed for the chapel. Stud followed. The two old men were up to more tricks, and he wanted to see who they were deceiving now.

Bill burst through the chapel doors, and he cringed when he saw Pablo slyly hiding something behind his back. It looked like Zeb was right about the tequila. "Pablo, my friend," Bill said as the troop surrounded the man who was praying to be alone with his tequila bottle.

"Horny Bill Ford, you have something on your mind?" Pablo stated.

"Yes, I was wondering if you would go with us to the Yuba River."

Pablo's eyes were glistening as he smiled. Bill couldn't tell if it was because of the spirits or if he was pleased. "Yes, I will go with you to the Yuba River, Horny Bill Ford."

"It's not a pleasure trip, Pablo. We lost Sam, and now we need a driver for the cook wagon, and you would have to put up with the twins because I can't have them riding with us while those spooky cattle are trying to kill us all day," Bill told the smiling, intoxicated man.

Pablo nodded his head. "Yes, I will drive the wagon and watch the children."

"Won't you miss Maria too much?" Zeb asked out of sincere concern.

"Yes, but what is better than that is Maria will miss me." Pablo smiled.

Stud was trying hard to follow along with the conversation. He had been learning English for the last two months, but he refused to speak it mainly because he knew that it bothered Bill if he didn't. It appeared to him that the two old mountain men were making Pablo happy, which was a switch from their usual behavior, and Pablo was going to the Yuba River. This would be Stud's chance to get in good with Juanita's grandfather, and maybe the old man would let him come back to be Juanita's lover. Stud kept his wits about him and thought of all the ways that he could impress Pablo on their journey.

Bill said, "Well, thank you, Pablo. It will be good to have you come along with us. We better go get ready. Three days, right?"

"Right!" Pablo exclaimed.

The troop left Pablo to his chapel and headed for the corrals. Bennager and Rose were in the stables, playing with each other, and Caroline was having a fit. Bennager had no sympathy for the love-stricken mule, and Rose had become immune to her loud complaints. Stud thought the newlyweds were mean, and he took poor Caroline out of the stable and let her go out in the corral to eat some fresh green grass and forget about her affection for Bennager. Shortly thereafter, Stud watched Rose and Bennager leave on their mounts.

Stud was bursting with want for Juanita. His thoughts led him back to impressing Pablo. He went to Bill. "I want to show Pablo my home and the gold on the Cosumnes River and my creek."

"You can't buy what's-her-name, Stud Colt," Bill wisecracked.

"I want him to see that I'm a man!" Stud shouted.

Bill closed his eyes at the old annoying Miwok phrase and shook his head. "A good man does his work, and every day, he gets better at it. Learn from the vaqueros the way that you learned from Sheldon's men, show Pablo the work that you've done on your own place, but don't try to buy the girl."

"Juanita!" Stud shouted, and then he turned and stomped away.

"Good God, that rotten little shin-kicking girl is becoming the bane of my existence," Bill grumbled. "I'll be glad to get going out of here."

"Yeah, I'm excited about it too, Bill. I can't wait to see what Angus has done on Rose's rancho," Zeb commented.

Bill thought of Trina and her refusal to love any other man except Angus Donovan. "Yeah, it will be good to see Ol' Angus again." Bill laughed.

Rose and Bennager decided to get their fat barn sour horses back in shape for the drive. They were fully armed and alert to cattle and cattle thieves. They weren't going to find themselves in the same situation that had killed Sam. Rose hoped to see the vaqueros in action, but they had disappeared in the brush like ghosts, or so it seemed. Bennager couldn't believe that the time to go home was finally so near. He thought of his friends in the foothills and the hard time they would give him for getting married. They would really raise a fuss when they found out that he had done it twice. He wondered how long it would take to get there and what the rivers would be like to cross this time of year with the snow melt coming out of the Sierras. He was excited to see what Angus had done on the rancho and couldn't wait to have a home. He hadn't had a home since he had left Illinois. He had camped every night, no matter what the weather was, until just recently when Pablo invited him in. He had taken a room, maybe once a year, just to indulge himself, but from now on, he would have a home. Hopefully, he would fill it with a family. Bill had scared the devil out of him about Rose having children, but women had children every day, and Bennager wanted a son.

Bennager's silence throughout the day was starting to make Rose uneasy. It wasn't like him keeping his thoughts to himself, and Rose had to wonder if he was mad or worried about something. The Roman was starting to sweat. "I think we had better head back. The Roman will be pretty lathered up by the time we make it back to headquarters."

"Yeah, I bet I'll be a little sore tomorrow too," Bennager remarked as they wheeled their horses around.

"Well, don't tell me that you're starting to fall apart on me, old man," Rose teased.

"I've been eating too well lately."

Rose laughed. "Yeah, me too."

"You are more beautiful today than ever before," Bennager complimented.

"Oh, nonsense, it will do me good to get back on the trail. I bet I won't even be able to walk tomorrow."

Bennager chuckled and went back into his silence. Rose reckoned that he was enjoying the warm day. Rose wondered where her father was, if he was still in Sacramento City or if he had been run out of town, who he had killed recently, if he would find a way to scatter her cattle to the four corners of the world, or if he had just gone back home. She thought of Sam and how she missed him. She would always remember their ocean voyage and the fact that he had stayed with her to purchase cattle instead of striking out on his own to find gold. She would miss him on the trip back home. It would be hard to travel the same country without him. She wondered why horrible things like that had to happen. Why did there have to be men in the world like her father who would hurt and kill good men like Sam?

Despite the gorgeous day, Rose's thoughts were dark. She wouldn't stand for her father living in California. She wouldn't stand for him to be a constant threat to the wonderful life that she wanted to have with Bennager or a disgusting monster to those girls in Sacramento City or anyone else, for that matter. She set her jaw and decided that she wouldn't stand for him to live or breathe at all if he was still in Sacramento City. She wondered what the others would think of her pressing on ahead of the herd to finally put an end to the threat that she had been pushing away for the last couple of months.

The Roman spooked slightly at the sound of animals coming out of the brush, and Rose squeezed her legs into him, hoping that he wouldn't rock her out of the saddle, but he stayed calm and alert, waiting to see what was coming. Rose and Bennager readied themselves for the appearance of a longhorn mother but were glad to see that it was just a small herd of deer.

"We had better skedaddle, Rose. Those deer are probably trying to get away from a herd of cattle being driven this way," Bennager said as they loped up the trail. They didn't waste time getting back to the stables. They were both aware of the fact that a passel of longhorns and an army of vaqueros could overtake them at any time.

While they were currying the horses, Rose said, "You were quiet today, is something bothering you?"

"No, ma'am," Bennager replied. He liked it that Rose was concerned about him, and he wondered if she would continue her questioning or let it go, so he didn't elaborate.

Rose tried to leave him be but found it impossible. She couldn't stand not knowing what her husband had been thinking about all day. Since their rift from the week before, she had learned not to push her husband; he had taught her that it was a battle she couldn't win. She concentrated on how to pry him open without pushing.

Bennager knew that he was driving her mad and laughed to himself. He wondered how long she would be able to stay calm when he knew that she was scheming.

Finally, after the horses were turned out in the corral with Caroline, Rose decided to use her feminine wiles to get him to tell her what was on his mind. Since they were alone behind the stables, she figured that she could test him a little without getting into trouble.

Bennager was delighted to have Rose seduce him and was glad that she had picked this way out of all the other schemes to find out why he had been so quiet all day. He soaked up her touch and her kisses like a sponge and responded to her in kind until it became evident that she had forgotten the purpose of her assault. When it seemed that they might lose control, Bennager took a step back. "What are you trying to do to me, woman?" he teased.

Rose became embarrassed. She looked at her handsome husband and wondered why he would have anything to do with her. "I don't know!" she stated after thinking about it for a couple of moments.

Bennager finally showed mercy to his confused, passionate wife. "I can't wait to settle down with you in a real home, in our home. It's all that I could think about today. I hope it's a tiny little cabin, so I won't have to spend a second looking for you when I need you. I'm going to put you in there and take all of your clothes outside and burn them so you can never leave, and you will always be there when I need you," Bennager explained as he came to her and hugged her around the waist. He squeezed her into him and held her tight, moving his hands from her back to her bottom.

Rose playfully scowled at him with a wrinkled nose. He was demonic when he teased her about locking her up. She only shook her head and kissed him sweetly on the cheek. "I can see where that line of thought could keep you entertained for an entire five hours."

"Yes," he whispered, feigning remorse.

"I believe you to be a bit of a heathen."

"Yes, can you help me?"

"You are so perverse I don't know if I can," Rose remarked with a smile.

"Will you try?"

"Yes, I guess I had better."

Zeb and Bill had spied on the couple for a few minutes, and Zeb was giggling at the faces that Bill was making while he was mocking them. When it looked like the newlyweds weren't going to wait for nightfall to show their love for one another, Bill grabbed Stud, and they all left the stables. Halfway to the house, Bill stopped, put his hands on his hips, and said, "Now what are we going to do?"

"We should have been making more noise while rearranging the wagon instead of spying on them. Now we'll have to wait around for them to come out of there," Zeb complained.

Stud heard someone hanging out fresh laundry on the other side of the house and hoped that it was Juanita. He could hear her lovely voice humming a tune. Stud burned with desire for his woman as he sneaked around the corner of the house. A light afternoon breeze was drifting in from the ocean. Stud stopped and admired the sight of Juanita's dress flowing in unison with the sheets and dresses that she had already hung on the line. The sheets made a wall of privacy between her and the west side of the house. Stud looked around for Pablo and Romero but didn't see anyone that would reprimand him for kissing his girl.

While Stud was closing in softly on Juanita, Bill and Zeb were hiding on the south side of the house watching as Stud Colt took a chance in broad daylight. He was becoming bolder. It was one thing for Juanita to come to him in the dark, behind the chapel, but Stud was really looking for trouble now.

Bill and Zeb weren't laughing this time. Bill had hoped that Stud would forget about the girl once they headed for home. Now he was concerned that Stud's actions were going to ruin the deal that Rose had made with the family, and the party would continue to roam the south, looking for cattle to buy. Bill wasn't up for that prospect. The weather was already too hot for his liking, and he was in a hurry to get back to the Rocky Mountain Range.

"Go stop him," Bill told Zeb.

Zeb watched as Stud and Juanita held each other and kissed. "I don't want to get kicked. That looks like it really hurts."

Bill nodded. "It makes you want to piss your pants."

"Just tell him to come on, we have work to do," Zeb suggested.

"You tell him, he doesn't listen to me anymore."

Just as Zeb was about to keep Stud out of trouble, Maria came running out of the house with a broom and beat Stud as if he was a rattlesnake. Bill and Zeb hid behind the house so Maria wouldn't beat them just for being there, and after a moment had passed, Stud came running around the corner, headed for the corrals, with a big smile on his face. Juanita came to the corner of the house to wave to her sweet Miwok Stud, but she didn't see Bill and Zeb until they couldn't contain their laughter anymore. She scowled and came toward them, but they quickly followed the path of their young friend so they wouldn't get kicked, and Juanita happily went back to work.

Bill looked over at the stables and reckoned that his niece wasn't finished romping with her husband yet, so he and Zeb sat under a tree in the backyard. "I didn't notice Juanita getting whacked with a broom, did you?" Bill asked.

"I didn't notice anything. I was hiding," Zeb answered.

"Well, you're a coward. Do you reckon that Stud is the first boy that Juanita has ever seen or what?" Bill inquired.

"No, Pablo has big gatherings here two or three times a year. I'm sure that Juanita and Isabel know plenty of young men."

"Well, why does she have such a hankerin' for that silly Miwok? Why in the world would she consider him to be a good choice?"

"Stud has a gift with women and sufficient equipment, I guess. I don't know what goes through Juanita's head," Zeb replied.

Bill shook his head. "I can see that this is a matter to take up with a woman. Maybe Maria can talk some sense into that girl." Bill got up and headed for the house.

"Hey, don't talk to Maria about this. Pablo is the head of the family. You should talk to him about this matter," Zeb implored.

Bill waved Zeb away and said, "Women know how other women think. I'm sure Pablo's too busy to be bothered by such palaver anyway."

Zeb hurried to catch up with Bill, who didn't take his advice. He wanted to hear how Bill intended to have an adult conversation with the woman of the house.

Bill burst through the kitchen door. Maria turned and smiled graciously at her two guests. Bill took his hat off, and his hair stuck out in every direction. The sight of the man was comical to Maria, but she tried not to show it. "Hello, Mr. Ford, are you hungry?" she asked.

Bill shook his head and looked at the floor. "No, ma'am, I ain't hungry. I want to talk to you. What in the devil does that girl want with a silly Miwok Indian boy anyway?" Bill asked, waving his dirty old hairy hat robustly around in Maria's immaculately clean kitchen. "Doesn't she have a more suitable beau out in the brush or in some town somewhere? Why does she have to pick on Stud Colt? He's ignorant, you know. He won't learn English or Spanish. All he's good for is digging ditches and postholes. He's not even any fun to travel with. You should tell the girl to forget about the big-peckered, baby-hating little whelp and find a rich man with cattle somewhere else."

It was hard for Maria to concentrate on what Bill was saying because the more he waved his dirty hat over the food that she was preparing for supper, the more disgusted she became about the dried flakes of scalp and hair that was coming out of it. Maria would have preferred Bill to show his respect by keeping his hat on his head in her company.

Zeb's eyes twinkled as he watched Maria's eyes grow wider, following the path of the hat. When Bill was finished making his point, he solidified it by smacking his hat with his hand, and oily dirt really flew then. Zeb closed his eyes tightly and shook his head. Bill proved again that he wasn't fit for society. He couldn't believe that Bill would bring up the subject of peckers in front of a lady such as Maria. He heard Maria let out a long sigh, and he opened his eyes to see what would happen next.

Maria decided that she would have to converse with Horny Bill Ford in a language that he could understand. Years later, Zeb would make her little speech famous when he repeated it at her funeral, and everyone who had known her would gasp. "What right do you have to say bad things about that boy or to accuse Juanita of having men out in the brush?" she asked as she approached Bill, backing him up a step or two. "What woman wouldn't want a sweet, big-peckered boy like Stud Colt?" she argued loudly. "Juanita takes after me. Those were the exact qualities that I wanted Pablo for, and I got him by doing just what Juanita is doing to Stud Colt."

Bill was the one who was wide-eyed now as he backed up three more steps toward the door.

"Now if you ever step foot in my kitchen with that damned dirty hat again, I will take it and your filthy deerskins and burn them!" Maria shouted. "You have just spread hair and filth all over my kitchen, Horny Bill Ford! You are not to enter this house again until you have bathed, shaved, and cut your ridiculous hair!" Maria screamed.

Bill was pressed up against the door now. Zeb was being as still as a statue, not knowing if he should run out with Bill or stay and apologize to Maria for Bill's behavior. Bill stuffed his hat onto his head and eyeballed Maria for a moment. "I can see that my niece has had a bad influence on you, ma'am. I'm sorry that you have been corrupted by her foul mouth and raunchy behavior," Bill finally said.

"Get out!" Maria bellowed.

Bill held his head high as he slowly opened the door. He walked through it as if nothing out of the ordinary had happened and left the house, leaving Zeb on his own.

Maria turned on Zeb, surprised to see that he was still in the room. Zeb's mouth opened to say something, but Maria held her hand up, and he closed it back up again. She glared at him and pointed to the door. Zeb hung his head and quietly left feeling ashamed and embarrassed.

When Bill entered the stables, he yelled, "I hope you fornicators are finished! I've been kicked off the rancho!" Bill went to work collecting the burros. Zeb came along after a minute, and once Bennager and Rose had dusted themselves off, they came out of hiding too.

Zeb knew that Bill was too hardheaded to do something about meeting Maria's requirements for gaining entrance into the house. Zeb knew it was best to help Bill get the wagon ready and hitch up the team. Bill had probably just caused Maria to do and say the most horrific things in the history of Spanish hospitality, and Zeb was still in shock over having to witness it. He couldn't even speak, and his thoughts were of Anna and how she had probably seen the event from heaven and what she must be thinking of her husband for running around with such a man as Bill Ford.

"What in the devil are you doing, William?" Rose said with her hands on her hips.

Bennager was standing behind her, trying to be sly about picking bits of stable out of his wife's hair.

"I'm taking the wagon and the kids out to the place where we found Bud and Blossom. I'll be waitin' for you there," Bill said, smiling. "Señora Ramirez doesn't favor me or my hat."

"What in the devil is that supposed to mean?" Rose asked as Bennager was helping Bill along with his departure plans.

"That wicked woman told me that I was filthy!" Bill said loudly, remembering the shimmer in Maria's eyes when he had maddened her. It reminded him of when he used to get his mother riled.

"Well, you are filthy. I'm surprised that it bothers you to hear that," Rose said with a puzzled expression.

"She said that I can't come into her house anymore!" Bill explained.

"She said that you can't come back unless you bathe," Zeb corrected, even though he knew that it was a waste of his breath.

"What did you do to that woman?" Rose suspiciously questioned.

Zeb knew that Bill wouldn't tell the truth, so he answered for him. "He went into Maria's kitchen and waved that old bug-infested hat around as if he was killing flies with it."

"Oh Lord, no wonder why she kicked you out. It wouldn't hurt you to clean up and get a haircut, you know," Rose said firmly as she tried to hide the fact that she thought her uncle was funny.

"It ain't summertime yet!" Bill said incredulously.

"Oh, forgive my ignorance." Rose rolled her eyes and headed for the house to smooth things over with Maria.

Pablo came to the stable yard when the burros were hitched, and Bill was collecting the children and his saddle horse. "Hello, Horny Bill Ford, where are you going with my job?" he asked jovially.

"Your wife is making me leave," Bill explained.

Pablo smiled proudly. "I heard my Maria yelling at you, Bill Ford. It was very funny, no?"

"Yes, I thought it was funny. Your wife is stunning when she gets mad, Pablo," Bill said with a smile.

"Yes, I know," Pablo remarked mischievously. "Are you going to take Jack with you?"

"Nope, Stud Colt is Maria's problem now. She seems to think that the kids make a fine match. Don't tell Stud that, though, or else he won't go on with the cattle. He intends to impress you while we're out on the trail."

"Maybe I should go with you now, Bill Ford," Pablo suggested.

"You can if you want to. It will give your wife another reason to hate me." Bill laughed.

Zeb and Bennager had gone to clean up for supper. Pablo looked around the barn to see if Zeb was in hearing distance but didn't see anyone. "Do you think Loco Zeb will follow us?"

Bill shrugged his shoulders. "He probably will."

"I will sneak out tonight and catch up with you. Maria can tell him that I'm sleeping, and maybe he won't look for me," Pablo whispered and patted Bill on the back. Bill smiled as he watched Pablo wobble to the house for supper.

The children were excited to go for a ride in the wagon. They hadn't gone anywhere since the day that Sam was killed. Bill didn't make it more than a couple of miles with the slow burros before he had to stop and make supper. The days were growing longer, but he reckoned if Pablo was going to catch up with him in the dark, then it would be best if he didn't have to ride far.

Several hours later, Pablo rode into Bill's camp. The children were asleep in the tent, and Bill was waiting up by the fire, drinking tea. "Well, was Maria happy to get shed of you?" Bill hollered.

Pablo smiled sheepishly. "I had to wait around for her to give me a kiss goodbye. She said that I cannot let Horny Bill Ford corrupt me while I am away." He sat down by the fire.

"Did she mean with women or with dirt?" Bill teased.

Pablo laughed and nodded his head. "She meant with those things and many others that I will not bother to mention."

Bill laughed heartily. "I'm a clean-livin' man, Pablo I'm just not clean enough for your missus."

Pablo fell asleep easily that night. His belly was full, his wife had made sweet love to him before he left, and he was sure that he wouldn't have to see Zeb in the morning. Pablo knew that Zeb was back at the rancho, waiting to get him alone so he could apologize to him for Bill's remarks to Maria. Pablo had convinced Maria to bring supper to him in his bedroom and to tell Zeb that he was too distraught to see anyone on account of Bill upsetting his wife. Pablo imagined Zeb waiting and wringing his hands with worry, and it made Pablo grin as he drifted off that night.

*****

There wasn't any hurry to get moving the next morning. Bill made breakfast at a leisurely pace and let the children run and play. Pablo watched Bill and learned where everything was in the wagon, and then he watched the children play. Pablo had been perfectly content to sip Bill's tea that morning. He ate and drank whatever Bill gave him, and he was glad to get it. Bill noticed that his eyes were clearing up from all the tequila that he had been drinking since Zeb's arrival. He already looked brighter, even though he had slept on the ground the night before. Bill could tell that Pablo was going to be a splendid traveling companion.

Pablo took the wagon, wanting to get used to his new job before the days got long and rough, and Bill led the way on horseback. They were sure to get farther along today now that the burros had a horse to follow. Bill got to see the vaqueros in action a couple of miles down the trail. Bill and Pablo stopped and watched them until they were out of sight.

The vaqueros were a half mile away, galloping their horses on the side of a ridge that was thick with brush. Four vaqueros had about thirty cow-calf pairs surrounded and were pushing them toward Pablo's rancho. Bill waited to see if one of the cows would try to hook a horse with its long horns, but he never saw it happen. The cattle just wanted to get away and hide, but the vaqueros wouldn't let them. Bill admired the men's horsemanship as they raced to keep up with the skittish cows, all the while ducking low oak branches and weaving through the gigantic bushes, some of which were very thorny.

"I'll be damned," Bill remarked. "I could watch that all day."

"They are very talented men," Pablo said proudly.

"You bet they are. I've been on buffalo hunts out on the plains, but we never had all that brush to contend with. Those buffalo hunts would be a piece of cake to your vaqueros if they could shoot arrows," Bill commented.

"The vaqueros only need corrals to put buffalo in. Then you could just kill the fattest ones. They do it during slaughter time with a long knife that they keep in their boot. They stick each steer just one time, and it dies before it knows what has happened," Pablo explained.

Toward the end of the day, the children became very frightened. They recognized the terrain where they had lived before, and they were certain that Bill was taking them back to leave them. They became sullen and wouldn't get out of the wagon when Bill stopped for the day. Pablo thought that they were sick and probably got into something in the wagon when he wasn't watching. He confessed to Bill that he had been more interested in the countryside that he hadn't seen in many years rather than keeping a close eye on what the children were doing.

Bill put his arms out loving to the twins, and, timidly, they came to him. They clung to him, and he could feel them both trembling. He checked for fever but found nothing and hugged them tightly. "This is about where we found them, Pablo. They think that I'm going to leave them here," Bill said with sadness. "Can you imagine feeling that way for even one minute, let alone the last couple of hours?"

Pablo simply shook his head and began to gather wood so Bill could stay close to the twins. Bill was able to convince them to let him go so he could make camp for the night, but he had to be careful not to step on them or knock them down because they were never more than a couple of feet from him. They understood Bill's words now, but it broke his heart to know that they didn't trust what he said. Pablo had to stake out the burros because Bill was afraid that the children were so overwhelmed with fear that they wouldn't get out of the way. Their spirits had reverted to the night that Bill had first seen them.

In Pablo's eyes, Bill had taken on a different character. He had known Bill to be more like a child himself, rather than a caring compassionate man, and Pablo respected him for it. He wanted to go to the Yuba River because he knew that it would be a fantastic adventure and the last adventure that he would ever have. He wanted to see the gold rush and the men running into the hills to work in cold, knee-deep water all day in their pursuit to become rich. He could not imagine the poverty that would drive men to do such a thing.

Most people had been content to live off the land for centuries and now, suddenly, they were determined to be rich. Pablo knew that greed was a sin, and up until now, he thought that everyone else knew it too. He watched the way Bill was with his children. He was kind, loving, and patient, and that was all that people should need from one another. "Will you look for gold when the cattle are settled on the Yuba River, Bill Ford?" Pablo asked as Bill, and the children sat down with him by the fire.

"I reckon Rose will get us all killed before we get to the Yuba River, but if I make it that far, I figure on heading for the Rockies this summer. I want the children to see where I have spent most of my life, and they will be safe there," Bill replied.

"You are not hungry to be rich?" Pablo asked.

"I wouldn't stand in a creek all day if you paid me!" Bill laughed.

"Oh, that is right, my friend. You are opposed to submerging yourself into water." Pablo laughed loudly.

"You're damned right!" Bill said defiantly.

"Hello in the camp!" a voice came from the darkness, and it sounded like the voice of a female.

Pablo's hearing wasn't as acute as Bill's, but even Bill thought that he was imagining it until he looked at the faces of his children. He popped Pablo in the leg. "Did you hear that?"

"I thought I heard a coyote. Are you afraid of coyotes, Horny Bill Ford? Zeb told me that you made love to one once."

Bill wrinkled his nose and scowled at Pablo. "You have a filthy mind, for Christ's sake!" he scolded.

"Hello in the camp!"

The children jerked and huddled into Bill. He patted them on their backs and got up. The children quickly scurried to huddle with Pablo. They knew that it was a woman's voice, and it wasn't Rose, and they also sensed that there was something very wrong about it.

"Come on in!" Bill bellowed. He waited for several minutes and was astonished to see who he had invited in. A very pregnant woman on a horse plodded into camp with a blonde child in front and behind her, and she was accompanied by three other blonde children on the back of another horse being led by yet another blonde child about the age of twelve.

"Oh my Lord, it's Mrs. Harding!" Bill exclaimed.

3

Dan had decided to trail after Angus and Trina after their wedding. He wanted to know where they lived and what they did, but he didn't intrude on them. He got the feeling Angus was uneasy around him and feared what would happen to him if he was to anger the man. When he saw the freight wagon come to rest at what was obviously a building site, he stopped and looked on at what appeared to be a house under construction and was impressed with the size of the corrals. The site was pretty this time of year, and Dan surmised that Angus must be a wealthy man to be able to afford so much lumber. He figured that Angus was going to raise horses and was glad to know that Trina was going to be well off with the man. He watched the big man grab Trina up in his giant arms and lovingly kiss her. He petted the dog as he and Trina entered the tent hand in hand.

Dan felt compelled to stay within earshot of the newlyweds. The thought of his sister being beaten to death by her own husband is what convinced him to stick around, even though he didn't want to. He was certain that Trina knew what she was doing in agreeing to marry the Irishman, but he also reckoned that she was able to put up with more abuse than most women would, even if it was half as much as she had survived before.

Dan's horse grazed quietly as he whittled on one stick after another until it was too dark to see what he was doing. Finally, as the night wore on and on, he heard the newlyweds talking while they started the evening fire and supper. Everything had seemed to go amiably; now all Dan had to do was to wait for the moon to come up so he could get out of there before the dogs noticed him.

As Dan heard Trina and Angus chatting and laughing, his thoughts turned to Kate. He couldn't get the pretty blonde girl out of his head. The conversations they had plagued his mind. Her desire to be a wife and a mother was what he thought about most of all. It was becoming very difficult to think of her as just a friend, even though he continued to push away the feelings that were becoming romantic. The moon finally came up, and Dan mounted, heading southwest for Sacramento City. He blamed Angus and Rufus for giving him the idea that it was a good thing to get romantically attached to a troubled woman.

Being a good friend to Kate would be the wisest approach for him. Besides, he knew that he had already burned that bridge by being so hard on her and the other girls when they worked for him. He rode a couple of miles away from Angus' camp and then made one of his own. Sleep didn't come easy to him that night, but when it finally did, he dreamt of Kate.

*****

Dan woke the next morning with conflict in his heart and mind. He didn't bother to make coffee or breakfast. He drank from his canteen and rolled a smoke. When he mounted, his only thought was of Kate and how much he needed one of her home-cooked meals.

By midmorning, the west wind was blowing hard, and by noon, Dan was surrounded by clouds of every kind. The wind would gust at times that forced him and his horse to nearly topple over. Dan got tired of hanging on to his hat, so he tied it down with the sleeves of an extra shirt. He hoped that he wouldn't run into anybody that he knew because he looked ridiculous. Once he got to the valley floor, he and his horse found themselves having to endure one hailstorm after another. During these storms, the temperature would drop twenty degrees. The hail was painful when it hit him, and even though he had made the time to put on his coat, it wasn't much protection against the force of Mother Nature.

In between storms, Dan was able to take a look at his surroundings to see if he would be granted a reprieve. He was amazed, at one point, to see a tornado to the west of him, twisting and turning its way up the valley. After witnessing the tornado, he made sure to kick his mount up into a gallop between hailstorms, and the horse was very obliging. The gelding wanted to get back to Jim's livery just as badly as Dan did.

Dan was a sight when he finally got to Sacramento City. The wind had made him cranky and tired, and there were still hailstones all over him and his horse. The brim of his hat held hundreds of them, his saddle was white all over, except for where he had been sitting, and the horse had hail sticking to him as well.

Jim had been undercover all day. "You look like you just left Donner's Pass!" Jim joked as he finally realized that it was his friend, Dan, coming in.

"Yeah, that was a devil of a thing to ride through. Did you see any twisters?"

"I didn't see a damned thing. Do I look like the kind of idiot that would stand out in that weather?" Jim smiled broadly. "Only a fool in love would ride through weather like that."

"A hungry fool would ride through it too," Dan mumbled.

"Yeah, you're hungry all right," Jim jibed.

Dan ignored the comment. "Where is Rufus?"

"Rufus Butler is doing what he does every day at this time. He is bathing, shaving, and probably buying a new shirt. He spends a half hour every day cleaning the dung out of his boots and shining them up, then he heads off for his afternoon ritual of getting ready to go see Ginger. That woman has made a dandy out of him. He used to be content to eat beans and play cards with me, but not anymore," Jim complained.

"Haven't they gotten married yet?" Dan asked incredulously.

"I don't think the boy has even laid a hand on her yet," Jim said with a laugh.

"Well, that figures. Rufus is timid, I reckon. I'm going to have a drink. I need to get the chill out of my bones. Do you want to come with me?"

"Yeah, it's a good day for a drink."

The men finished tending to Dan's horse, and the animal was very appreciative for the grain and to be out of the weather. Dan talked to him and rubbed his neck before they went next door to the saloon. They saw Rufus up the street, leaning against the bathhouse, eyeballing the hotel and waiting for the weather to break. Dan elbowed Jim and pointed. Jim shook his head and smiled. "Let's get Rufus drunk before he goes to see Ginger," Dan suggested.

"Yeah, maybe she'll pity him more than she does already," Jim said.

"Hey, Rufus, come have a drink with us!" Dan hollered up the boardwalk.

Rufus was happy to comply. He wanted to know what Dan had been up to anyway. He comically ambled down the walk to join his friends. "By God, Rufus, you are handsome. Jim had to tell me it was you. I didn't even recognize you," Dan commented. Jim held back a chuckle.

"Thank you, Dan. I took your advice about cleaning up for Ginger. She has asked me to supper every night since you've been gone," Rufus said, still looking as silly as ever under his bent-up old hat.

"Yeah, I reckon she must be getting tired of you by now," Dan joked as he ordered a jug of whiskey.

"My Lord, Dan, are you planning on getting drunk tonight?" Rufus was wide-eyed.

"I plan on warming up. I was pert near hailed to death today right after being almost blown to pieces by the wind," Dan replied. All three men swallowed down their first drink. Dan poured another round.

"Oh, so you were out in the weather today, huh? You should have gotten undercover," Rufus said with wisdom. The men downed a second glass, and Dan poured another.

"That would have been a good idea, except there wasn't any cover to be had. You should see what's left of the tent city. I saw one tent blow thirty feet in the air and head east." Dan watched Rufus down his third glass, and he knew that if he kept his glass full, Rufus wouldn't stop drinking until someone told him to. Jim had no objections to having a few more either. He didn't expect to have much more business for the day.

Dan continued on, "I even got to see a twister today. It was heading north. That was quite a sight." Dan began to smile as he noticed that the spirits were starting to cloud Rufus's mind. "So how are Ginger and the other girls doing?"

"They are busy all the time now. It takes every one of 'em to keep that place tidy," Rufus said, waving his hands and slurring his words. "Miss Kate has been spending a lot of time with a surveyor. Ginger told me that she is investing a lot of money in the city building lots that he's been marking out."

Dan raised an inquisitive brow at this information. Young, beautiful Kate was a bright woman, and Dan imagined that she would own most of Sacramento City before she was finished, but he felt his heart sink at the news that she was entertaining a surveyor. The feeling seemed inexplicable, but it was definitely real. Dan stifled it with another drink, and Rufus and Jim joined him.

"What have you been up to all these weeks?" Rufus slurred. "You must have a woman up in those hills."

"I don't have one, but I saw a couple of 'em. They were already taken, of course. It looks like that will be the story of my life." Dan grudgingly chuckled.

A couple of hours quickly passed in the saloon, and Jim felt that he had had enough to drink and decided to splurge on supper. "I'm going to go see if Maggie will let me through the door. If she will, then I'm going to eat a piece of meat tonight."

Dan barely understood Jim's words as he ran them all together, but as he watched Jim stand up, he got the point that the man was finished drinking for the evening. Dan nodded his head to his friend, and Jim wobbled out the door. Rufus had completely forgotten about supper, but when Jim brought up the subject, Ginger entered his mind as well.

"Damn you, Dan, you went and got me drunk! I can't go see Ginger now!" Rufus complained as he drank another glass of whiskey.

"Why not?"

"I don't want her to see me falling and tripping over my lips!" Rufus explained.

"Oh, that's nonsense. Ginger will like seeing you no matter how much you fall over. Women like to take care of men when they're drunk," Dan lied.

"They do? And here I've been being careful not to get drunk before I see her."

Dan shook his head in disbelief. "I can't believe you didn't know that, Rufus! Come on, I'll walk over there with you."

Rufus couldn't walk by himself, as it turned out, so Dan helped him along. Once they got to the hotel, they had five steps to ascend, and Rufus tripped and fell on every one of them while Dan only fell twice. Dan was surprised to see that the wind had stopped blowing and the sky was clear. The evening star was winking at him, and when he tried to focus on it, it became one of many, so he gave up. Rufus decided to sit down and take a break at the top of the stairs. The exertion of climbing them had caused his stomach to start flip-flopping, and he wasn't confident that Ginger would want to take care of him if he threw up on her clean floors. Dan was swaying in every direction but was still coherent enough to find Rufus' plight amusing. He smiled as he watched Rufus suck up the clean night air. "You better get in there before your supper gets cold, Rufus," Dan advised clumsily.

Rufus got up, and Dan opened the door for him, pretending that he would be right behind him. The heat from inside the hotel hit Rufus like a rock. He turned to say something to Dan, but before he could, he passed out on the floor. Dan chortled and closed the door. He thought of joining Jim at the restaurant, but he knew it would be too hot in there as well, so he headed for the livery. Perhaps Jim would have some leftover beans that he could dip into to sustain him until morning.

Kate came out of the hotel and stood on the top step, watching Dan Dunaway navigate the quiet street. He seemed to be trying to follow an invisible line between the hotel and the livery. He swayed from side to side of it but was determined to stay on course. She knew because the only time he advanced forward was when he was on it. Kate walked out.

"Hello, Dan, it's good to see you again. Why don't you come in and have some supper?"

Dan looked at the blurry woman for a moment, and then he closed one eye. He balanced himself by putting his hands on her shoulders, and Kate obliged him. She smelled lovely. She smelled like the fragrant soap that she used and fried chicken. He took in a deep breath through his nose and was able to identify the smell of apple pie as well. "I can't come in for supper, Kate. You're busy enough without worrying about me. It's too hot and crowded in there," Dan mumbled, and then looked at the ground to find the line that he had been on. He eyeballed the space between him and the livery and continued on his path.

Kate helped him along his way. "There isn't anyone at the supper table, Dan, and I don't think I would ever be too busy to fix you a plate of food," she said sweetly.

"Ha, a plate of food. Okay, tomorrow I will come for a plate of food, Kate!" Dan said maliciously.

Dan gave Kate a feeling of uneasiness, so she left him on his own. She remembered how he used to be when he was mean and hateful, and she wasn't going to purposely involve herself in whatever his problem was now. She watched to make sure that Dan didn't pass out on the public street, and then she went back to help Ginger drag Rufus up from the floor.

*****

"Mrs. Harding, what in God's name are you doing out here in the dark with all your children? Where is that idiotic husband of yours?" Bill asked as he helped her children from the horse and then her. Bill would have been surprised if the poor, malnourished woman weighed an ounce over one hundred pounds. The children gathered around the fire. Pablo took the oldest one with him to gather more wood in the moonlight.

"I lost my man. These warm days got the river up and knocked over some trees and brush somewhere. They tipped the ferry over and took my man downriver with 'em," Mrs. Harding explained.

"Well, that's bad news, Mrs. Harding. I'm sorry for your loss," Bill said. Mrs. Harding nodded her head with indifference. "Where are you headed then?"

"This is the road to Monterey, ain't it?"

"Yes, ma'am, it is," Bill answered.

"Well, that's where I'm goin', I reckon."

Bill shook his head at the despairing sight that was sprawled out before him. "Well, Mrs. Harding, I don't know if it's safe for you to travel alone with all of these children. Besides that, you can't ride those horses into Monterey. I thought I told you to cut 'em up and eat 'em."

"I never got around to it. I thought I'd wait until after the baby was born. It's a lot of hard work to hack up horses," Mrs. Harding said calmly.

Bill observed the woman and her children. It didn't seem to bother them much that the head of the household was lost, nor did they seem too concerned with the fact that they were poor as poor could be and probably starving. Bill was nervous about being around a pregnant woman. He cringed at the thought of his bad luck in prior experiences and wished that he had left the San Joaquin Valley last week. "When do you reckon your baby will come, Mrs. Harding?" Bill finally asked as he got supper working for the big, toe-headed family.

"How should I know? I reckon babies come when they have a mind to," the woman replied.

Bill rolled his eyes. "Is that what your husband told you, ma'am?" Bill could feel the woman scowling at his back but didn't say more that would encourage her to talk. The woman was as ignorant as her husband had been, and Bill had heard enough.

Pablo and the Harding child came back with the wood, and Pablo advised, "Mrs. Harding, when you get to Monterey, you need to look for Father Chavez. He will help you get settled." Pablo joined Bill to help him with the late supper.

"That's a funny name for a man. He must have as many kids as I do," the woman said as she sipped a cup of tea that Bill had given her.

Bill looked at Pablo, shook his head, and rolled his eyes. Pablo smiled. "Yes, señora, he has many children."

"He is a man of religion, ma'am. His children are not blood relations like yours are," Bill said loudly, thinking that she would understand him better that way.

Bill turned to see that the woman had a confused expression imprinted on her face, so he didn't say anymore. It was obvious the woman was having a deep thought. Minutes passed by as Bill and Pablo cooked, and Bill was amazed by the fact that not one child was concerned about their empty stomachs. Bill figured that they would be swarming him by now on account of ham and fresh eggs frying over the fire. Pablo had another frying pan going with biscuits frying in lard. When they were finished, Pablo sprinkled them with sugar and passed them around. Bill handed Mrs. Harding a plate, but she held onto her stomach and shook her head no to the food.

"Ma'am, there's plenty of food, go on and take it. You won't shortchange the kids," Bill pleaded.

She shook her head rapidly. "No, I can't, I'm busy right now!"

Bill was puzzled at the sight of her just sitting there. "What are you busy doing, ma'am?" he inquired.

"I reckon this baby is workin' its way out!" the woman shouted.

"Oh, for Christ's sake, I knew it!" Bill shouted back at her as he grabbed the brim of his hat with both hands.

Pablo found Bill to be quite amusing in this situation. Within a moment, the man was in a perfect panic. Pablo let out a laugh as he watched Bill pace back and forth in front of the woman, never taking his eyes off her face. "Bill, take my horse. My rancho is only three hours away if you ride hard. Get Maria and bring her here in a wagon. Maria will take care of Mrs. Harding."

Bill saddled up and mounted as quickly as could be done. "Bill, bring Juanita, too, so she knows what it is like to have a baby!" Pablo shouted after him. Bill was swallowed up by the darkness before Pablo was finished speaking his request.

Bill and Pablo hadn't gone as far as they thought, and Pablo's horse made it back to the rancho in two hours instead of three.

*****

Bill burst into the quiet, dark Ramirez home. "Maria, Pablo needs you! It's Bill Ford! Come quickly and don't shoot me!" Bill bellowed, almost shaking the house.

Maria was frightened for her husband's life. "What has happened to Pablo?" she asked, glaring at Bill.

"Nothing, he needs you to come help a woman have a baby. He said to bring Juanita and a wagon." Bill dashed out the door, hopped on the horse, and raced to the livery. He hitched up the wagon for Maria with a two-horse team, and by the time he was finished, Maria, Zeb, and Juanita were there, talking to Bill.

Zeb started asking questions about what was going on, and Bill explained while he saddled up a fresh mount. He never noticed that Maria was saddling a horse as well. "Well, what did Mrs. Harding say about the condition of the ferry?" Zeb hollered as Bill raced out of the yard with Maria following.

About a mile down the trail, Bill actually fell from the galloping horse at the scare that Maria gave him. She had ridden up beside him, and Bill's first thought was that he was being attacked by a thieving bandit that had been trailing him all night.

"You can't lead the way from down there, Horny Bill Ford!" Maria said smiling widely. Her teeth sparkled in the moonlight, and she began to laugh at the bewildered expression on the silly man's face.

"By God, you old witch woman, you damned near got your ass blown off!" Bill yelled as he collected his hat and leaped in the saddle. Maria shook her head and giggled. The man was so ludicrous that there wasn't anything else that she could do.

Later, they eased their horses down to a walk so they could catch their breaths. Maria began to scold Bill. "I knew you would corrupt my Pablo if he went with you to the Yuba River."

Bill glared at the woman, and then he smiled. "Woman, when I'm finished corrupting Pablo, you won't recognize him, let alone sleep with him. He won't be fit to be around humans, let alone women. I met a big female brown bear up on the Yuba River last fall, and I asked if I could live with her, but she told me that she favored an old Mexican gentleman with a big pecker to an old hairy mountain man with a dirty hat. I reckon when Pablo meets that nice young sow, he'll forget all about you and you'll never see him again!" Bill said boisterously.

Maria grabbed Bill's deer skin sleeve and stopped her horse. "Bill, I'm afraid I might not see my Pablo again if he goes to the Yuba River. I'm afraid I'll lose him." Maria's eyes were worried.

Bill put his hand on Maria's. "We'll make sure he comes back home to you Maria. The vaqueros will watch the cattle, and the rest of us will watch Pablo. That's all we're good for anyway." Bill smiled. "I won't let him marry up with that young sow no matter what he says. I'll whack him on the head if I have to."

"You are a good boy, Horny Bill Ford, but you just need to take a bath," Maria said with pity in her voice.

"My beloved mother used to say the same thing. Clean men scare the game away. That's what I say!" Bill said loudly as he slapped his horse into a gallop, and Maria followed with love in her heart for the misguided young mountain man.

An hour later, Bill and Maria arrived at the camp. All the children except for the oldest girl, who had led the horse on foot, were asleep. Some of them were in the tent with Bud and Blossom, and the rest were spread out by the fire, sharing blankets that Pablo had given them since they hadn't brought their own. Pablo had hot water going on the fire and had managed to maneuver a canvas underneath Mrs. Harding so the poor baby would have something clean to land on when it came out. He had also covered her with a blanket so he wouldn't have to see it when it did. The oldest girl oversaw that end while Pablo took the head and spoke words of encouragement to the woman.

Pablo was very happy to see his Maria, and he wanted to shout for joy, but he stayed calm for Mrs. Harding until Maria took over.

"That was a fast trip, Bill. I bet that you did not know my Maria could ride like the wind," Pablo said when the men were alone.

"I sure as hell didn't! She scared me plumb out of my saddle when I noticed her riding beside me. I thought a bandit was after me!"

Pablo laughed and slapped Bill on the shoulder. "I would have given my left nut to see that, Horny Bill Ford!"

"You might as well. You ain't got no use for it anyhow," Bill teased. "Yeah, the old woman got quite a kick out of it."

Both men laughed loudly, and Maria could only wonder what they thought was so funny about the present situation. There was no time to ask because lucky number seven was working his way into the world, and Maria couldn't be distracted. The Harding girl was a great help to Maria. She considered the possibility that she didn't even need to be there. Mrs. Harding had plenty of practice giving birth, and she knew just how to conduct herself.

Zeb and Juanita arrived in the wagon just minutes before number seven came into the world, and Juanita was able to witness the miracle of birth. It didn't have the effect on her that Pablo had hoped for on account of the fact that Mrs. Harding made it look so easy.

Dawn wasn't far off, so Bill got busy in his kitchen. Poor little Mrs. Harding had missed out on supper the night before, and he knew the kids could use another good meal. Pablo and Zeb helped with the wood for the fire and started the coffee. Maria came to the back of the wagon with the new baby boy and observed Bill mixing up his biscuit dough. Bill said in a low voice, "What are you doing with that thing in my kitchen, you old witch woman?"

"Mrs. Harding thought you might like to hold the baby. She wants to name him after you," Maria said, ignoring Bill's teasing.

"You didn't tell her my name, did you?" Bill whispered. "I don't want some ignorant brat in the world with the name of Horny Bill Ford."

"I agree that one is enough," Maria said in a scolding tone.

"Tell her my name is Bennager. That's a good name for a dim-witted, toe-headed boy child." Bill looked at the baby's face. "Yeah, he looks like a Bennager," Bill snickered mischievously. "Rose will think Bennager's the father when she hears that. Now get out of my kitchen woman!" Bill bellowed to embarrass Maria.

Maria rolled her eyes and took the baby to Pablo. He took the little child and examined him like Maria, being a woman, would expect him to do, and then he gave the baby back to her. Maria turned to leave, and Pablo looked at Bill and shrugged his shoulders.

Zeb was talking to Mrs. Harding about the condition of the ferry when Maria gave her back her baby. The woman flapped her long, disfigured, well-used tit out of her blouse, and the baby who was already a master of survival went right to sucking. Zeb wasn't embarrassed at all by the sight and waited for his answer about the ferry.

"The ferry is still there, it just tipped over, and my man fell off. There ain't nobody there to pull it across now," Mrs. Harding said. Zeb noticed that she hadn't looked down to admire her new addition to the family like most women did. She handled him more like a piece of split oak than a human being. She mothered him, all right, like any animal would, but there didn't seem to be much love in her demeanor. Zeb reckoned she was pretty tired.

Zeb went to go talk to Bill and met him as he was bringing a plate of food to Mrs. Harding. Zeb waited, and when Bill saw the mother feeding her baby, he started gagging. Juanita glared at him and took the plate so he wouldn't spill it on the woman. Zeb shook his head and laughed. "Why didn't you warn me about that, you damned idiot?" Bill said scolding Zeb.

Zeb ignored the remark. "We better go check on that ferry. It's probably swaying in the middle of the river, and if it does that then the ropes are bound to stretch out and break."

"Yeah, you're right, I know, but I hate like hell to leave these people here alone, Zeb," Bill said grudgingly.

"Pablo's here, he can take care of things," Zeb assured.

"Yeah, and old Maria's a woman to stand aside of too, but that's a day's ride from here, and the only horse that ain't played out is mine. I say we wait until the vaqueros get here. Pablo and I will get to the crossing first, and if we can't haul the ferry in, then we will. If it's gone, then we'll get to work at building a new one. I promised Maria that I wouldn't let anything happen to her old man, and I don't feel right about leaving him alone with this mess for two or three days. It's bad enough that we have to trade horses with Mrs. Harding. It wouldn't do for Pablo to get caught with dead men's horses. I'm also running out of food having to feed that mob, and I can't expect Pablo to stay here and do all of the cooking while he's waiting for us to get back," Bill explained.

Zeb nodded and scratched his head. "This is a bit of a mess, isn't it?"

"Yeah, Mrs. Harding wants to go to Monterey, and Pablo told her that priest would help her out, but she can't show up in town with those horses, so take her and the kids back to Pablo's in the wagon. Maria can tend to her until she's ready to travel again. Have Rose buy two more horses from Romero and meet us at the ferry as quick as you all can. We'll wait for the cattle there. As soon as we get the other horses and the ferry in working order, I'll take these others to the other side of the river and turn 'em loose."

Zeb nodded. "That's about all we can do, I guess."

"Pablo and I will get going as soon as the children have been fed." Bill was irritated that the Harding children weren't awake yet. He reckoned they were getting a good night of sleep because their bellies were full.

"We better wake them up, Bill. You need to get to that ferry and get those horses out of here. They are closer to the rancho now than they were when we found them."

"You're right about that." Bill started for the burros. "We have to get going, Pablo."

Zeb woke up the children, and they ate as much as they could while Bill hitched up the team, and then he and Pablo broke camp down. Zeb helped put the kitchen away. They had to give up the blankets and canvas to Mrs. Harding to make her ride more comfortable. Pablo got to kiss his wife goodbye again, and Bud and Blossom were glad that they weren't being left behind.

*****

It was going to be a long day getting to the ferry crossing. Bill led the extra horse in hopes that the burros would follow along a little faster. If Bill got out too far ahead, the burros would slow down. It drove Bill crazy all day, but Pablo kept the poor little critters moving at a steady pace, and they made it to the crossing about an hour before dark.

"I'll be damned, Pablo. We haven't lost the ferry yet. It's not that far away from the shore either." Bill stood at the edge of the shore and tried to determine how deep the water was. "Well, I reckon I'll have to ride in and capture the damned thing."

"You need a boat, Horny Bill Ford," Pablo said as a log rushed past them in the water. "There you go, make a boat out of that log," Pablo said cleverly.

"If you can catch it, I'll carve it out," Bill said with confidence.

Pablo laughed and shook his head. "No, Horny Bill Ford, that log will be in the bay in a few minutes." Pablo walked over to the wagon and took out a sixty-foot-long, braided, rawhide lariat. "Watch this, Horny Bill Ford." Pablo smiled. In his left hand, he held the coiled rope, and in his right hand, he made a big loop by turning the first loop backward twice and letting out slack from his left hand. He lined up with a snubbing post that had been built on the ferry for securing the horses that made the crossing. He began twirling the lariat over his head. The big loop grew even larger, and Pablo let it go. The loop fell right over the post, and Pablo pulled the slack. Bill looked on in awe; he had never seen such accuracy with a rope. Pablo handed the rope to Bill. "Pull it in, Horny Bill Ford."

Bill put all his weight against the rope, and Pablo laughed as he went to get his horse that had his saddle on it. He was mounted and rode up next to Bill. "Do you think you will get it to shore before dark, Bill Ford?" Pablo looked on with concern.

"It hasn't budged yet. I reckon it's hung up on something!" Bill grunted as he kept pulling. Pablo let Bill slip and slide and fall three times and laughed each time it happened, but Bill was tenacious and wouldn't stop trying. Pablo smiled as Bill began to curse at his dilemma as if the cursing would miraculously bring the ferry to shore.

"Horny Bill Ford, watch this." Pablo reached over and grabbed the lariat away from Bill. He wrapped it around his saddle horn, turned his horse, and headed away from the shore. Bill ran over to secure the ferry and then detached Pablo's lariat for him. Pablo coiled it up and looped it around his saddle horn and dismounted.

"Well done, old man. Did that little trick just occur to you?"

"No, but you won't forget it, Bill Ford." Pablo laughed, slapping Bill on the back.

"You are ripsniptious, old friend. I wish Sam could have been here to see you throw that rope. That would have impressed him," Bill said, smiling.

Pablo thought Bill would have been riled at him for not helping sooner, but Bill took the lesson and the joke well.

The children had been sitting on the wagon seat, watching all the activity. Bill put his arms out, and they both leaped into them. He hugged them and told them they could play now and to stay away from the river. Another night of camping would soon commence.

*****

Rose and Bennager got up to join the family for breakfast, but nobody was there. They knew that Romero had taken Stud Colt out to learn about the cattle and the vaqueros, but it was strange and eerie that there wasn't any movement in the house. Rose checked the kitchen, and it was empty. They both looked outside and could see no evidence of what could be going on. Bennager went to Zeb's room, and Rose went to find the women. When they met back in the dining room, Rose had Isabel with her and no one else.

"What in tarnation is going on around here?" Rose bellowed.

Bennager was very concerned. He couldn't imagine what was going on but something out of the ordinary had happened. He quickly surveyed the house and determined that there hadn't been a struggle, and then he went outside. His instinct led him to the stables and the livery, and he saw that one saddle horse was missing along with the two-horse team and the wagon. As he walked out of the stables, he noticed that the horse Pablo had taken was back.

Bennager pulled the gelding out of the stall to examine him. He had been ridden pretty hard and hadn't been tended to before he was put up. Bennager checked his feet and found that his frogs were in good shape which meant that whatever had happened hadn't been an awful emergency. Bennager quickly groomed the horse and grained him and went back to the house.

Rose and Isabel were in the kitchen. Isabel was crying. She knew that something terrible had happened to her family. Rose was trying to comfort and reassure the girl when her husband came into the room. Rose looked at him with curiosity.

"It looks like they all went somewhere in the wagon, Isabel. I'm sure they are fine. One horse was missing, but it wasn't Zeb's. That's the only thing that doesn't make sense to me. I'm sure they are just fine. Let's have a quick breakfast, and then we'll ride out and see what they're up to." Bennager didn't speak of Pablo's horse being back in front of Isabel.

Rose could tell by the especially pleasant tone of Bennager's voice that something was still out of sorts. If he knew for a fact that the family was fine, then he would have said so, but he hadn't, and he was anxious to find them. Bennager continued on with a reassuring smile. "How about this? I'll go get the horses saddled while you gals fry us some eggs, and then we'll head out."

Rose set her jaw. She knew it was important to keep Isabel calm, and that meant she had to feign calmness too, but her instincts told her to forget about the eggs and go find out what was going on. She smiled at Isabel through her gritted teeth and said, "Well, I guess he's the only boss we have at the moment. It looks like it will be a nice day for a ride." Isabel stood toe to toe with Rose and didn't believe her pretending for a second. Isabel heard the worry in Rose's voice, and tears welled up in her eyes again. "No, don't do that, Isabel. Go get dressed, and then we'll have some damned eggs and go."

Isabel nodded her head rapidly. She heard truth in Rose's voice with the last remark and knew to hurry because Rose suspected trouble.

"Nobody has time for a bunch of damned eggs, for Christ's sake." Rose mumbled once Isabel had left the room. Rose hurried to her room to collect their weapons. She gathered up their coats and bedrolls in case they had to sleep out, and Bennager met her at the door. "Isabel will be ready in a minute," she told him, and then she rushed out to tie down their trappings to their saddles. When she came back, she bellowed, "Isabel, let's go!"

Bennager grabbed his wife. "Settle down, Rose, you'll scare the poor child. I thought we were going to have breakfast."

"Isabel was scared when she got up, and she's going to stay that way until we find the others, and I don't blame her. There's a sack of food over there on the counter. Grab it and let's go," Rose demanded as Isabel rushed by them and got mounted. "See, she doesn't need any damned eggs!" Rose caught up with Isabel, and Bennager had to hurry so he could lead the hasty girls in the right direction.

When Bennager headed east, Rose was sure Bennager knew more than he had told them at first. "Why are you sure they went this way?" Rose asked.

Bennager pointed to the ground. "I'm following these wagon tracks."

"Why don't you tell us what you didn't tell us in the kitchen?" Rose implored as they galloped down the trail. "You have some idea of what happened or else we would still be in the kitchen."

"Since you insist, and you must want to frighten Isabel, then I guess I will tell you." Bennager scowled at his demanding wife.

"Isabel wants to know the truth, Bennager."

"Fine, the truth is either Pablo or Bill came back last night and left again. I reckon maybe something happened to one of them."

Rose turned to Isabel, and the girl nodded her thanks to Rose. At least now she knew what to expect. Everyone was quiet until they slowed their horses to a walk. They had ridden for about an hour. Rose wondered if the Roman would ever get back into shape. He had enjoyed his feed too much over the wait while Rose had become domesticated.

"You are a handsome rider, Isabel," Bennager remarked to try to take her mind off the task at hand.

"Papa says that ridding well is more important than reading," Isabel replied. "I've ridden for as long as I can remember. Do you think my Papa is hurt, Bennager?"

"No, I don't think anybody is hurt. Your Papa's horse was in too good of shape. Whatever is going on, I'm sure it's not a dire situation. I think it's more curious than dire," Bennager explained. Isabel looked to Rose to see if the man was telling the truth, and Rose nodded and smiled. Bennager started off again at a trot a few moments later, and the ladies followed. Isabel felt safe with these two people. She noticed how their eyes never stopped scanning the horizon all around them, always vigilant for danger.

Less than an hour later, they found what they were looking for, and they couldn't believe their eyes. Rose said, "Would you look at Maria? That woman is lovely no matter where she is."

Bennager's eyes squinted at all the blonde heads that were apparent in the back of the wagon, and he couldn't fathom where they had all came from. It was also confusing that Bill and Pablo weren't with them.

Zeb was pleased to recall the story of the midnight rescue of the Harding family and how Bill was still his charming self. The wagon eased along at a snail's pace as he quietly retold the events of their journey. Rose looked in the wagon and saw that Mrs. Harding was sleeping. She eased over alongside Maria and said, "That woman's bleeding a good bit."

"I've been watching her. So far, she is doing as is expected."

"You mean that's normal?" Rose inquired with disbelief.

"Yes, she will bleed like that for a few days," Maria said with a smile. "That's why you should avoid having babies while you are traveling. She should have stayed in her home, but I do not think she cared if the baby survived or not," Maria whispered.

Rose nodded. "Well, I think this family has had a hard time. There's no tellin' what goes through that poor woman's mind."

"Guess what she named the baby?" Zeb asked Bennager.

"What?"

"She named him Bennager after the man that fed her family and rode all night to get her help. Bennager Ford Harding is his full name," Zeb said with a childish grin on his face.

Bennager shook his head once. "I wonder whose idea that was," he said sarcastically.

Zeb laughed and then proceeded to give Rose and Bennager the orders that Bill had told him to. "Go on ahead. When I get back to the rancho, I'll get Stud, and we'll come too."

"You won't get there until midnight at the rate you're going!" Rose declared.

"This is true, Mrs. Rasmussen. We're not going this slowly for my health," Zeb pleasantly reprimanded.

Rose scowled and looked at Bennager. He nodded his head to the weakened Mrs. Harding, and Rose understood then. "Well, I guess we'll get the horses and the rest of our things and see you on the way back, unless you want us to ride along with you," Rose reasoned.

"No, we'll be fine. Go on ahead," Zeb replied.

"Are you armed, Zeb?" Bennager asked.

"This bunch and me are ready for anything!" Zeb joked.

4

"Are you prepared to ride the whole night through?" Bennager asked as they packed Caroline down with their trappings and collected two more horses.

Rose shrugged her shoulders. "Well, I reckon we've rested enough lately. If the moon isn't covered with clouds, then I don't see why we can't."

"Good! Are you ready to go then?"

Rose looked around at the rancho that they had spent the last couple of months at. She remembered Sam and the children in their makeshift school. And she recalled the many atrocities that her uncle had performed during their stay. She fondly remembered the playful, magic day that she and Bennager had made love in the stables. She missed Sam. "I wish I had time to say goodbye to Sam," Rose said sadly.

"We can go if you want to," Bennager said. He knew Rose would feel bad about it for days if they didn't go, and Sam deserved one last visit.

"There isn't time. Bill and Pablo probably need help with that ferry."

"We can worry about that ferry when we get there. Come on, I want to say goodbye to Sam too."

Rose didn't argue, and she was pleased that her husband understood her. Bennager pulled the string of animals, and they headed south to Sam's Pond. That was its name now. Pablo had called it that one day when he was describing it to Zeb during an argument they were having about the villainous cattle. Rose liked the fact that Sam had a place in the world named after him at least.

On their way to Sam's Pond, they happened across Romero and Stud Colt. They were a couple of miles ahead of the cattle that the vaqueros had picked out for Rose. "Will we have time to visit Sam's grave?" Rose asked.

Romero shook his head. "They will probably come while you are there. I will go with you, and we will wait on a hill until they pass. You will get to see the cattle that you have purchased."

The news was exciting to Rose. They rode with Romero and Bennager told him all that had been happening. Then he told Stud to be ready to go when Zeb got back to the rancho. Stud Colt understood his words and nodded his head.

Romero saw the dust up ahead and led the others off the trail and to the west. They rode over one rolling hill after another until they could look down and see the cattle. This is what Rose had dreamed of when she had been on Charlie's steamboat last winter, engulfed by the fog. Ten vaqueros, riding magnificently and calmly, had the longhorn cattle surrounded. They didn't act like wild elk anymore. They were almost as docile as Zeb's Border collie dog.

Rose was amazed at the sight she was beholding. This was going to be her life. She thought of how much her life had changed since she had hit the shore of California. She was hardly the same person anymore, and then her father's face came to mind. There would be one more matter to tend to before her new life could really get started.

When the cattle were out of sight, Romero said his goodbyes. "I have to get up ahead and open the gates in the corrals. You will see the cattle at the San Joaquin River about four days from now, maybe five. They travel about ten miles a day unless they get frightened and stampede. If this happens, then you had better get far away from them and let the vaqueros stop them. They will kill you if you are in their way," Romero warned. Bennager and Rose shook hands with the quiet, friendly man, and they parted ways. Rose wondered if she would ever see him again as they headed for Sam's grave.

Bennager and Rose stood together outside of Sam's fenced place of rest. Later, Bennager took the stock to the pond for water while Rose finished what she was saying or thinking to her dear friend and business associate. Bennager waited patiently, and soon it was time to go.

"We'll just cut across until we hit the east trail. How does that suit you?" Bennager suggested.

"That's all right with me. I guess if we see dust, we had better get out of the way, though," Rose reminded him.

"Yeah, you didn't leave anything behind at the rancho, did you?"

"I can't think of anything. If I do, I'll tell Zeb to pick it up."

Bennager smiled. He was glad that Rose seemed as ready to head home as he was. He thought of what Romero had said about the cattle traveling ten miles a day and quickly figured how many days it would take to get to his new home. With any luck, they would be there in about twenty-two days, and part of that luck would depend on the San Joaquin River crossing being in working order. He quickly mounted up and led the way.

The couple trotted at a steady pace in silence for about an hour until they hit the eastern trail. Bennager stopped and determined that the others hadn't got there yet. He told Rose, and they pushed on. Shortly thereafter, they ran into Zeb's party. Mrs. Harding was awake now and faring the trip well. Rose and Bennager got to see the baby boy and meet the mother who seemed to be in better spirits than what Maria had previously described. The Ramirez women hugged Rose and Bennager goodbye. Rose promised to come back and visit when she could, and the couple was off again.

When they got down the trail a fair piece, Bennager asked, "What, no tears?"

Rose smiled. "It's hard to explain, but I'm being pulled to a home that I have never seen and know nothing about. It tugs at my heart as if they were attached by an invisible lariat. Besides, we'll see Maria again."

The couple continued on until it was almost dark, passing by the second place where Bill had camped. "Let's stop for supper. It's going to be a long night. I bet we don't make it until morning," Bennager remarked.

Rose could barely walk as she hobbled around to Caroline for the food they had packed. Bennager drank from the canteen and then rolled a smoke. "It looks like it will be a clear night anyway," he said. Caroline began to have a verbal fit, so Rose hurried to get away from her.

"No more tamales for us, I reckon," Rose commented as she handed Bennager the old diet of dried fruit, cheese, hardtack, and bread.

"You can make us some when we get home," Bennager said as they watched the horses graze.

Rose liked the way her husband said the words. She walked around as she ate to get the stiffness out of her legs. The soreness was a good feeling. It made her feel alive with purpose again. "It's going to get cold tonight," she said.

"Yeah, I can feel it already," Bennager replied. "The sky is going to be as clear as a bell."

Rose got their coats. Bennager took his and put it on. They stuffed their pockets with fruit and hardtack, and Rose went to get mounted. Bennager attacked her from behind. Rose laughed and turned to receive his kisses. He held her tight. "It feels good to be back to work, doesn't it?" he said.

"Yes, it does." Moments passed as Rose buried her face in his chest. "Will you go back to hauling freight when we get home?"

"I haven't thought about anything except for being with you. Will you haul freight with me?"

"I think I'm supposed to watch over the cattle," Rose replied.

Bennager laughed. "I should probably help you with that then. We better get going."

"Well, I'm ready just as soon as you unhand me," Rose joked.

Bennager slapped her bottom as she mounted, and Rose let out a yipe that made the Roman crow hop one time, but Rose managed to stay on and get in the saddle. Rose laughed heartily at the look on Bennager's face. He knew that he had made a mistake that had almost caused Rose to be bucked off again. He shook his head at her laughter, gathered up the stock, and they continued onward to the San Joaquin River.

It was a long night as Bennager had predicted that it would be. They traveled slowly for three hours before the moon finally came up to light their way. The sky had put on a spectacular light show, full of shooting stars during that time. Rose was as delighted as a small child would be at such a sight. Her amazement tickled Bennager, and he found yet another thing to love about her. He enjoyed the ride immensely. He especially enjoyed the fact that Bill and Zeb weren't around to spoil it with tricks, bickering, and bad jokes.

An hour after the moon had been up, Rose started to complain about needing a rest. "I think my knees are broken," she said.

Bennager chuckled. "Let's stop and make some coffee."

"That sounds good." Rose was grateful for the suggestion.

"I think we're making pretty good time. Are you getting tired? We can stop and sleep for a while if you want to," Bennager said.

"I'm not sleepy, I'm just out of shape."

"Well, we've been at since yesterday morning. My butt hurts too, you know," Bennager said with a laugh.

"Let's see how we feel after we have our coffee," Rose advised.

Rose paced while they waited for the coffee to boil. Bennager asked, "Are you going to make it?"

"I'll live, I reckon." Rose bit off a piece of tobacco and continued on with her moving about and stretching. The coyotes started in with their tribute to the moon, and Rose discovered that there was something in the world that Caroline hated worse than her. "Sam told me that mules hated dogs and coyotes with a passion. He told me that mules would protect other livestock from coyotes. Did you know that?" Rose shouted at Bennager over Caroline's braying.

"No, it never occurred to me to ask anybody about all the things that a mule could hate," Bennager shouted sarcastically.

"Well, Caroline, is particularly hateful, that's for sure."

The coyotes decided to cut their song short for the night since they knew that Caroline might be looking for them so she could stomp them. The mule settled down in time for the couple to enjoy their second cup of coffee in peace.

"So what do you think? Should we stay here for the rest of the night?" Bennager asked.

"I can keep going. This is fun. I've never stayed up all night before," Rose replied.

"Not even when you were on the ocean?" Bennager asked.

"No, I was sick most of the time and willed myself to sleep so I wouldn't have to face the reality of where I was. Now that was a long night compared to this."

"What did you dream about when you were doing all of that sleeping?"

"I dreamt about pie, steak, and getting pig drunk!" Rose replied.

Bennager laughed at his wife and thought back to that afternoon when he had picked her up off the ground after having passed out from drunkenness and what he had thought of her at the time. He stood up and kicked the small fire out. "Let's go, then, before you change your mind, woman."

The coffee was a good idea. Rose's body was getting used to the abuse now, and they were able to push on without any more breaks. Rose heard Little Toby in the distance about an hour before sunrise, and they suspected that they were nearly to the river. Caroline brayed to her comrade, and Bennager and Rose picked up the pace so they could finally stop and rest.

Bill and Pablo were standing by the fire, waiting to make sure that they had, in fact, heard Caroline and not some other silly mule.

"Hello at the camp!" Bennager hollered.

"Come on in!" Bill hollered back at him. Bill waited for them to get closer. "Hell's bells, what did you do, ride all night?"

"Yes, Rose insisted that you would need help with the ferry," Bennager said when he dismounted. He shook hands with both men. "I hope you have some biscuits and bacon fried up. We're in need of a hot meal." Bennager looked up at his wife who was still mounted. He smiled. "Do you need help, dear?"

Bill ignored Rose's preference to stay mounted and said, "I do need some help with the ferry. I had to ferry two different outfits across last night. Folks are starting to head for the Sierras already.

Pablo and I made $100 last night, but now we can't lift our arms." Pablo smiled and showed Bennager his ten-dollar eagles.

Rose finally got up the courage to dismount, but her legs wouldn't work, and she fell. The Roman turned his head and looked at her curiously.

Pablo and Bennager each grabbed an arm and pulled her up. "You exerted yourself, Mrs. Rasmussen. You better get some rest," Pablo stated. Bennager held her up while she tried to get her hip socket to move again.

"Oh, she's probably drunk!" Bill said, waving away Pablo's concern.

"You old bastard, I am not drunk!" Rose said defensively.

"Well, what's your problem then!" Bill joked as he handed her a cup of tea. "The coffee will be ready shortly," he said.

Rose finally started to loosen up, and Bennager let her go and began to tend to the stock. She walked toward the river and looked at the ferry.

"Watch yourself, Little Rose, that water is swift," Bill warned.

"So the ferry is still in good shape, huh? I thought that it would have been swaying out in the middle of the river if that guy fell off of it," Rose commented.

Bill nodded his head. "It was out there about fifty feet, but Pablo lassoed it and dragged it back in with his horse. It's a lot of fun dodging trees on that thing. Two big trees, roots and all, went by last night just on one trip. I had my customers pissing their pants." He laughed.

"So you didn't need us after all," Rose remarked.

"Well, we had no way of knowing what we needed when we sent Zeb back, except we knew we needed new horses."

"Zeb never told us why you needed the extra horses. What's wrong with the ones you have?" Rose asked.

"Those horses used to belong to those bastards from Monterey, and Mrs. Harding was going to Monterey. I never told you what I did that night, but I thought that if I gave the horses to her, she would feed them to her family, and no one would ever see them again. When it gets light, I'm going to take 'em across the river and turn 'em loose."

"Are they both geldings?" Rose asked.

"Pablo's been riding a mare."

"We'll take the mare with us then. Piss on anybody from Monterey that doesn't like it." Rose went to help Bennager unsaddle the stock.

Bill smiled at his niece's idea and started cooking breakfast. "Are the cattle coming yet?" he asked.

"Yeah, we saw Romero and Stud before we left. They're starting out this morning," Bennager answered.

"That will give me time to ride into Stockton for more supplies. The Harding family ran my supplies thin. It will be tricky making it to Stockton if I don't go," Bill suggested. "Bennager can give rides on the ferry all day and finally start earning a decent living."

"The first thing I'm going to do is get some rest." Bennager chuckled. He began to set up their tent. He felt like he was about to drop and wondered how he would be able to sleep once the sun came up. He could kick himself now for not convincing Rose to stop for the night back at their little fire. Bennager and Rose stayed up long enough to eat breakfast, and then they turned in for a nap.

Bill and Pablo sat by the fire and watched the sun come up over the Sierras. It looked as if it was going to be another warm day. "We should ride downriver today and see if we can find that poor fella's body," Bill said softly. "When the newlyweds wake up, I'll ask them to watch the children, and we'll take a ride."

"Yes, that would be a decent thing to do, Bill Ford. I don't think Mrs. Harding looked for her husband before she ran away from home."

"Well, I met the man a few times, and I don't blame her a bit," Bill remarked, shaking his head.

*****

Dan Dunaway woke the next morning to a pain in his head that made him certain that his eyes were bleeding. He surveyed his surroundings, and after a few minutes, he realized that he had used some sacks of grain as a bed, and he was in the livery. Jim had been waiting for Dan to wake up so he would have someone to blame for his own headache, but Dan hadn't woken up soon enough to suit Jim, so he had been tickling his face with a long piece of straw. When Dan woke, he saw Jim leaning on a pole, sipping coffee.

"Hey, tin pan, you look worse than I feel, you son of a bitch," Jim said.

"Yeah, we were just supposed to get Rufus drunk. What happened?" Dan asked.

"We accomplished that task. I saw the two of you falling up the steps of the hotel. I also saw you talking to Kate in the middle of the street. I think you were a jackass toward her," Jim said with a warning tone.

"I thought that was a dream. She smelled like lilacs and fried chicken."

"I noticed that you really started pouring down the sauce when Rufus mentioned that she was spending time with another man," Jim accused.

"No, that's nonsense. I just couldn't get warmed up after riding in the hail all day. Kate should have a man. She wants to be a wife and a mother, and she ought to hurry up about it before she becomes an old maid," Dan said, feigning happiness that he didn't feel.

"Maybe so, but it looks like you probably owe her an apology. I don't know what you did or said, but the girl had hurt feelings when you parted company last night."

"She was probably mad about Rufus showing up drunk. I told Rufus that women like to take care of drunken men," Dan said as he rolled a smoke and went to the barn door to get some fresh air and a look at the hotel. Nancy was already working like a demon in her garden. Dan chuckled and shook his head at the woman. She had actually purchased a hoe while he was gone, and he found it humorous that she had waited so long to do it. "Do you have any more coffee?"

"Sure, coffee is the one thing that I have a lot of," Jim replied.

"I'll have some then and get my head straight." Dan thought of how Jim acted more like a matchmaker every time he saw him these days, and he had to wonder why the man cared about him being rude to Kate or her having her feelings hurt. Dan thought about telling Jim how he had seen Trina and the big Irishman in the foothills and then decided against it. Dan was beginning to think that he was going to live in the foothills permanently. If Kate was going to take up with a surveyor, then there really wasn't any reason to keep checking on her. "It looks like it's going to be another blustery day," Dan commented.

"It could be. I suppose you'll be traveling in it again today."

"No, I reckon I'll stick around for a couple of days. I'll see you later, Jim."

Dan thought a bath, haircut, and shave would do more to straighten out his head than hanging around Jim and drinking bad coffee would. After he finished cleaning up, he went to Maggie's for breakfast.

"Now here comes a handsome young man!" Maggie bellowed as Dan walked through the door. Dan hoped that it would be the end of her shouting, but he knew that it wouldn't be. Maggie gave everyone she knew a hoot and a holler when she greeted them.

"Good morning, Maggie. Could I have some of your good coffee and breakfast, please?" Dan spoke softly.

Maggie peered into Dan's bloodshot eyes. "You also need some hair of the dog that bit ya."

"Oh Lord, not yet, Maggie, maybe later."

Maggie poured Dan's coffee. "I'm surprised that you're not having breakfast with Kate," she said assumingly.

"I reckon Kate has her hands full. I hear tell that she's a busy woman."

"Yep, we're all busy these days," Maggie replied cheerfully and then left for the kitchen.

Dan watched the door while he waited for breakfast. He observed the people coming in and going out. Maggie and her husband had to hire a young couple to help them out in the restaurant. The young man was a dishwasher, and the young girl was a waitress. The mostly male population that passed through Maggie's place enjoyed seeing the young lady bustle around the tables to serve them. They knew they probably wouldn't see another woman until next winter, so they were very generous about leaving the girl a little something extra for waiting on them. A prominent-looking older gentleman, about the age of thirty-five years old, came in and sat down, and Maggie greeted him in the usual way. Dan held his hands over his ears.

Maggie brought Dan his breakfast. "That's the man that's surveying the city lots for us. Mr. Gowans is his name."

"Is that right?" Dan said, feigning interest. Maggie moved along to tend to her business, and Dan wondered why Mr. Gowans wasn't having breakfast with Kate. Shortly after he had that thought, Rufus Butler entered the establishment. Dan smiled mischievously at his drinking partner. He wasn't about to tell Rufus how silly he looked because Rufus didn't own a mirror. One side of his shirt was hanging out of his pants, one pant leg was in his boot, his lopsided hat was on sideways, and his face was almost jaundiced.

"You got me in a peck of trouble, Dan," Rufus complained. "And just so you know, women do not like to take care of drunks. Ginger left me sleeping on the floor right in the middle of the parlor, and then she chased me out with a broom this morning, right in front of a dozen people having their coffee and reading the *California Star* from a week ago." Rufus held up his aching head with his hand and braced his arm up with the table. "I fear she hates me now."

"I reckon she just wants to embarrass you for showing up drunk to supper," Dan said. "I really thought you would wake up in a softer place other than the floor, though."

Mr. Gowans came to their table. "Good morning, Rufus. May I join you, men?"

"Sure, Josh Gowans, this is Dan Dunaway. Dan, Josh is the surveyor that I was telling you about," Rufus explained.

"Yeah, that's what Maggie was telling me. I'm pleased to meet you," Dan said as the men shook hands. The two men commenced in eyeballing each other, sizing each other up, and making small talk about everything except young Miss Kate.

"I heard that you used to own the hotel but you gave it up," Josh queried.

"Yeah, I didn't favor town life that much, especially once it started to get organized," Dan replied.

"And I'm doing the organizing," Josh said.

"Well, it suits you, I reckon, you look like an organized fellow."

"I understand that you have the deed to the abandoned gambling hall on the north end of town," Josh said.

"I don't have it. Who told you that?" Dan asked.

"I did, Dan, I thought you had it," Rufus said.

"Miss Kate also told me you might have it." Josh had finally said her name to Dan's great satisfaction.

"Well, I don't have it." Dan smiled, showing his perfect teeth. "Why are you asking about it?"

"I need some office space, and it appears to be large enough to live in as well," Josh explained.

Dan's smile grew broader. He knew Kate would never walk into that building as long as she was alive. "I reckon if that deed is still in the building, then you can just have the place. It's better than letting it fall down. Rufus and I were just going to give it to the Chinese anyway. You could probably ask about it at one of the government meetings." Rufus smiled and nodded his head, thinking that Dan had a very generous idea. Dan finished his coffee and got up. "It was nice to meet you, Josh."

"Yeah, the pleasure was mine. I think I'll walk over and take a closer look at that place."

Dan and Rufus nodded to him, and they left. As they walked back to Jim's livery, Dan said, "Sometimes town life can be fun, I reckon."

"How's that?" Rufus asked.

"There are just a lot of things to watch," Dan said vaguely.

"I guess that's true. I wouldn't know. I spend all of my time watching Ginger."

Dan watched the hotel and waited for the folks to start leaving. He thought about Maggie's suggestion of having a drink to clear the cobwebs out of his head. He gave his breakfast another hour to settle and then went to the saloon, got one drink, and then came back.

"Well, I guess I'll go over and see how much trouble you're in, Rufus," Dan finally said while Rufus was trimming the hoof of a burro for an old gentleman who had come into town from the south.

"Put in a good word for me, Dan," Rufus implored.

Kate watched from the window as Dan crossed the street, wiped his feet, and took off his hat. She was apprehensive about seeing him. It seemed to her that he had gone back to his menacing ways and if that was the case, then she didn't want to talk to him. She busied herself in the parlor and pretended like she didn't hear him come in.

"Hello, Kate," Dan said softly.

Kate turned to face the man who looked ill. *As well he should,* she thought. "Hello, Dan, how have you been?" she asked kindly.

"Jim tells me that I've been a jackass. I'm sorry for getting Rufus drunk and throwing him on your floor. I played a bad joke on him last night."

"So that was all your doing, was it? Well, my patrons found it amusing this morning when Ginger chased him away," Kate said with half of a smile.

"Jim said that I was rude to you in the street. I'm sorry for that too," Dan apologized.

"You only seemed opposed to having a late supper. I should have known better than to try to reason with a man who has been drinking," Kate replied.

Dan turned his hat in his hand, looked at the floor, and nodded. "Yes, you're right about that. Will you tell Ginger that it was my fault and that Rufus won't be coming in that state of drunkenness anymore?"

"Yes, I will tell her for you, Dan."

Dan heard indifference in Kate's tone and decided that it was best to be on his way. Kate would have asked him about his trip and how long he was staying in town by now, but since she hadn't, he reckoned that she wasn't interested in his life anymore. He reckoned that she was sweet on Gowans, the organizer, and she would probably be better off.

Downheartedly, he skulked toward the door and left. He stood on the top step, put his hat back on, took in a deep breath, and resolved to spend another day in the saloon.

Kate saw the path he was taking once he got to the street, and she cringed. She hadn't known Dan to be a drinker and wondered why he had chosen to take it up now. She wanted to rush into the street and stop him, but everyone in town would see her and start talking. She didn't suppose that Dan would want people to think that an ex-whore of Weatherford's was concerned about him or that she might be in love with him, so she let Dan go to his business of drinking, and she went back to work.

*****

Zeb decided that he and Stud Colt might as well ride along with the vaqueros instead of rushing off to help the others with the San Joaquin ferry crossing. He knew the vaqueros were not going to use the ferry to transport two hundred pair of cattle across the river anyway. The wild beasts would have to swim across, and more than likely, they would have to wait a month for the river to recede so the calves wouldn't drown. He knew there would be plenty of time to work on the ferry later. For right now, he was more interested in staying with the cattle. He loved driving cattle with the vaqueros. It was almost as good as when he was able to spend a day with Anna. He was a vaquero at heart, and he tried his best to be useful on the drive and to learn everything he could from the superior horsemen.

Zeb talked to the vaqueros about what to do with Stud Colt, and it was decided that Stud would be safe with the remuda. Stud didn't understand the word, but Zeb conveyed to him that it was a very important job consisting of bringing along the vaqueros' extra horses. No man rode the same horse two days in a row. The cattle might only move ten miles a day, but a man on horseback might travel four times that amount to keep the cattle together and under control.

The cattle always had a bad habit of doing just the opposite of what the vaqueros wanted them to do, and that was why driving cattle was real work and not just a pleasure trip. Stud understood that it was his job to keep the saddle band together and under control, and if it was lost, then the drive to the Yuba River would be over. He smiled and nodded his comprehension to Zeb. He was pleased to be awarded such a high-profile job. This would certainly impress Juanita's grandfather.

It was the morning of April first, 1849, when the vaqueros started pushing the cattle east. Zeb had said his goodbyes and gratitude to the Ramirez family, and Maria had implored him to keep her Pablo safe and to bring him back home. Juanita and Stud did not hide their love in front of the vaqueros or Maria. The kisses they gave one another were many, passionate, and long. The vaqueros took their hats off and hooted at the young couple, and Stud was satisfied to see Juanita crying for him as he led the remuda out of the corrals, following along after the herd of cattle.

Tomas drove the supply wagon. He was the oldest vaquero in the group and was retired from traveling on horseback. His wagon seat was adorned with a long, soft, lavish pillow. It was purple, the color of royalty, with gold-colored fringes. Tomas carried a flintlock pistol with him for the sole purpose of scaring people away who might try to take his pillow.

Thunder clouds began to move into the area by the noon break when the men stopped for water and a bite to eat. Zeb had been eyeballing Tomas' pillow all afternoon. He imagined how Bill would talk about it when they finally joined up with Bill's group. He also imagined Tomas having to shoot Bill for fooling around with it. Zeb laughed at the scene that he had pictured in his head. "Tomas, which whorehouse did you steal that pillow from?" Zeb asked.

"Do not touch my pillow, Loco Zeb. I will poison your tamales," Tomas warned.

"I'm not touching it."

"Do not look at my pillow, Loco Zeb."

"It's impossible to keep my eyes off of it, Tomas. It is very pretty. My friend, Horny Bill Ford, will want to take it when he sees it."

"I will kill your friend!" Tomas explained simply.

Zeb figured he could get Tomas to shoot Bill whether Bill noticed the pillow or not. Zeb kept company with Stud Colt for the rest of the break. He looked at the sky and noticed the clouds coming in from the south, but the wind was coming out of the north. Stud noticed it, too, and Zeb told him that the cattle would go wild during the storm and to stay away from them. "I will help you with the remuda for the rest of the day. The horses are apt to scatter too."

Stud was becoming more familiar with the English language and understood Zeb very well.

"We have to look after Tomas too," Zeb said, pointing to the man and the supply wagon. "If you see his pretty pillow on the ground, you better pick it up for him. He will tell Pablo that you are the best vaquero who ever lived."

Stud nodded and smiled at the suggestion.

"Do not talk about my pillow, Loco Zeb!" Tomas hollered.

Zeb made a face at Stud that indicated he was in trouble with Tomas, and Stud was grateful for the smidgen of comedy because he was bored already. He didn't have Juanita to look at anymore; he didn't have time to explore rocks, plants, animal tracks, and songbirds, and the cattle were dirty, and they smelled bad. His love for Juanita was great, but he missed his freedom to roam. He hoped to show Pablo his home on the Cosumnes River and the gold he had found there. He hoped Pablo would let Juanita come live with him so he wouldn't have to learn how to be a vaquero. He imagined Juanita walking with him on the Cosumnes, looking for gold and quartz. It was a better-smelling life than the life of a vaquero.

The splendid horsemen were ready to go again. Each one gave Stud Colt a pat on the back before he mounted, jarring Stud from his daydream. Each man smiled genuinely at Stud, and he smiled back. Stud felt better about his occupation now. He figured he must be doing a good job. He was energized and filled with purpose when he mounted. These men were better to travel with than Bill was.

Zeb was pleased with the men for remembering to encourage Stud Colt along. Driving the remuda wasn't much of a job, but it was a dirty one, and Stud was in a safe position. The horses would have trailed along with the cattle just fine without Stud being there.

Zeb had fibbed to him to keep him from being killed by one of the longhorns. Zeb hoped that the young man would forgive him one day when he found out about the charade.

The respect the men showed to Stud was sincere. They were very impressed with the tenacity he showed with regard to Juanita Ramirez. They were amazed by his temerity in the way that he had kissed her goodbye in front of her father and everyone else and had feared nothing in the process. He showed no sign of embarrassment, threw out all inhibitions, if he had any to start with, and took the young girl in his arms as a man would. Now he was proving himself as a man would, and the vaqueros were in awe of him. They couldn't believe that Romero Ramirez would stand for such a thing to happen to his daughter, and yet the man stood dumbfounded this morning by Stud's performance.

An hour after the drive had started up again, the strange spring storm that everyone had predicted did indeed come. The cattle did as Zeb said they would. They sought shelter from the pelting hailstones that might just as well have been rocks coming out of the sky. Everyone wanted to seek shelter, especially Stud Colt. He was the only one that didn't have a sombrero on his head for protection.

The vaqueros worked hard to keep the cattle in line and out of the brush, but when the cattle couldn't have their way, they resolved to make a run for it. Now the horsemen had something to think about besides how miserable it was to be hit by hailstones repeatedly. The race was on to keep the running cattle headed in the right direction and altogether at the same time, but they had to be stopped or else the calves would suffer. The men on the left flank dropped back once they saw two men on the right flank get up ahead of the herd. The two men in the lead were able to turn the cattle until they were circling back into the middle of the herd. The rest of the men continued on with the circling process until the cattle slowed down and finally stopped. No calves were lost this time, and the vaqueros were certain that it was a miracle. The cattle had traveled two miles in a matter of minutes, and the first hailstorm of the day had passed.

The day wore on in such a way with one hailstorm after another. When it wasn't hailing, it was raining. The vaqueros worked so hard at keeping the cattle under control that they didn't even have time to put on their ponchos. Eventually, two calves were trampled to death during the next stampedes, but they traveled about fifteen miles that day instead of ten.

The entire crew was miserable, wet, cold, and hungry at the end of the day. The night was going to be frigid, and at least three men would have to stay with the herd to keep it from running back into the brush at Pablo's rancho in the middle of the night. The violent winds had blown the tempestuous clouds away and to the east. The night sky was clear, but all was calm in the San Joaquin Valley by the time the sun hid itself behind the coastal range.

The first hour of night watch was a game of one vaquero riding in and out of camp to change into dry clothes and have one hot cup of coffee. They repeated this process again until everyone had their bellies full of tamales and beans. Finally, they were able to settle into a routine of taking two-hour shifts at watch. Zeb and Stud took a shift halfway through the night, even though they weren't needed. Zeb wanted to show Stud Colt how the vaqueros slowly eased around the resting herd, softly singing to the cattle so as to calm the cattle's always nervous, restless habits. Zeb didn't think it was right for Stud and him to be the only ones on the crew with a full night's rest, and Stud was eager to learn how these men continued to command such wild beasts.

When their night watch shift was up, Zeb and Stud quietly eased back into camp. It was important to do everything softly and slowly when the cattle were bedded down for the night. Loud noises, loud voices, and pans clanking were a sure way to spook the cattle. Nobody could know which way the cattle would run when they were frightened, so the nights were very dangerous. There were only three men standing in between the herd of wild longhorns and a camp full of men and supplies. In camp, everything was said in a whisper.

Stud whispered in English, "Do you think the men will let me sing to the cattle?"

Zeb gasped and then quickly covered his mouth as if he had accidentally made a loud noise. "Stud, you can talk to me now!" he whispered with delight.

"Sam and Juanita teached me, but do not tell Bill. I like it when he tells people I am ignorant. Juanita told me he said that to Old Mama." Stud smiled.

Zeb closed his eyes and giggled at Stud's name for Maria Ramirez.

Stud went on, "I do not want Bill to think that I understand him. It makes him mad with me when I won't learn English."

"I will be happy to keep your secret, Stud Colt." Zeb smiled and slapped him on the back. "You are a smart man. Tomorrow, I will watch the remuda for you while you sing for Tomas. He will say if you can sing for the cattle."

Zeb went to sleep thinking of how far Stud Colt had come. The best part was his desire to bother Bill. This led him to think about how he was going to convince Bill and Rose to be quiet when the cattle were bedded down for the nights in the future. He hoped to sway them into going on ahead to their new rancho and putting Stud Colt out in front of the herd to lead the way, but he was certain that Rose wouldn't go for it.

Tomas was up while the stars were still bright in the sky. Eggs, cheese, corn cakes, apple cakes, peppered beef, and coffee was the vaqueros' breakfast of the day and would continue to be until the eggs were gone or broken to pieces or until they could get more. Zeb hadn't had such an elaborate breakfast since his Anna had passed away. He couldn't wait to see Tomas outdo Bill's trail breakfast of salty biscuits and bacon. He was sure even Bud and Blossom would leave him to dine with Tomas. "Did your pillow dry out, Tomas?" Zeb asked.

"My pillow is frozen. Do not think about my pillow, Loco Zeb."

Tomas had a pair of pillows, and to Zeb's amazement, later on in the morning, Tomas was sitting on the dry one, but Zeb thought that it was the same pillow.

"You will get the piles from sitting on a wet pillow, Tomas," Zeb warned.

Tomas had enough and simply pointed his unloaded pistol at the man without speaking. Zeb quickly galloped away to get out of his range.

Zeb scanned the cold, clear sky and the majestic Sierras. He hoped the unseasonable cold weather would continue so the muddy rivers could clear up and recede. He didn't like the idea of swimming with trees.

The calves were tired and sore from the stampeding of the day before. The cattle plodded along slowly, grazed, and waited for their babies to catch up. The day wasn't as dusty or hectic as the day before. The vaqueros practiced lariat tricks as they eased along with the cattle. It was important to let the cattle eat to make up for the weight they lost the day before and to heal their muscles and spirits for the long drive that was ahead of them. The vaqueros had no intention of racing to the Yuba River. They enjoyed being on horseback and seeing new country. They had never been north of Stockton and were excited to see what was ahead of them, although the superior horsemen would never admit it or show it.

Stud tried to see what the vaqueros were doing with their lariats as they threw wide loops under a cow's belly and waited for her to step into it with her hind foot. The vaquero would then pull the slack in the lariat and capture the hind foot and let it go again. Stud realized that it was a trap and wanted to learn more about it.

Zeb spelled Stud so he could sing for Tomas. Tomas liked the smiling Miwok boy, and he liked his singing, but he wanted the boy to observe the vaqueros for two more nights and to sing in camp after suppertime for the next two nights as well. It was too hard to tell if Stud's voice was soft enough because the wagon and harnesses were making too much noise. Stud told Tomas that he wanted to trap cattle.

Tomas stopped the wagon, got off, and went to the back. He handed Stud a brand-new sixty-foot raw hide lariat and explained to the boy that he would have to train it. It was very stiff and wouldn't work as easily as the older ones that were being used until Stud had practiced with it for many, many days.

Zeb rode with Stud for the rest of the day, showing him how to manipulate the loop. Stud kept getting it caught in his stirrup, but Zeb told him that was perfectly normal for a beginner, and Stud smiled and kept on trying.

"That's a handsome gift from Tomas. He must like you, Stud Colt. A man would normally have to pay a month's wages for such a thing or make it himself," Zeb said.

"I did not look at his pillow."

5

The cattle arrived at the San Joaquin River crossing on April fifth. Zeb's prayers had been answered about the river clearing up. Pablo had convinced Bill, and the others to set up camp on the east side of the river after they had found Harding and buried his remains by his abandoned house. Bennager, Rose, and Pablo had spent their spare time ferrying travelers across the river, and Bennager was tickled to have his own eagles to show off to Rose. It certainly wasn't his job of choice, but it was a living.

Bill rode into Stockton with Caroline before the herd arrived and packed her down with supplies. Rose had put in a request for cocoa and brandy, and Pablo seconded that request, so Bill didn't give his niece a hard time about it. He brought back some hard candy for the kids, but they didn't like it any more than Stud had, so he let Bud feed a couple of pieces to the Roman.

While Bill was in Stockton, he told Peter Harlan of their progress with the cattle, and he asked if Peter's competitor on the north end of town was still in business. A mischievous grin appeared on Bill's face when Peter told him that the man was there and doing well now that so many people were passing through town on their way to the diggings.

"Put in a good order of merchandise, Pete, I intend to have some fun with that bastard when those longhorns come to town."

Peter was shocked at the ghastly plan that Bill Ford had conjured up and tried to talk Bill out of it. "You can't do that, Mr. Ford," Peter implored.

"Well, you better close up shop and watch me, Pete. That son of a bitch won't ever forget me or my dead friend when I'm through with him!" Bill laughed as he pictured the vengeful scene in his head. "Come over to the Howells with me. I'll buy you a piece of pie and a cup of coffee," Bill said.

The store still had nine other customers waiting and shopping. "I can't come for at least another hour, Mr. Ford. I wish I could, I'm hankerin' for a piece of pie. I've been smellin' 'em all day."

"Yeah, me too, that's why I mentioned it. I'll wait for you," Bill said generously. "I made a fair amount of money working that ferry for two days. I can't think of a better way to spend it right now. I don't know who will work the son of a bitch once we're gone, but I reckon they'd make a right livin' at it." Bill nodded to Peter. "I'll see you after a while, Pete."

"I'll be lookin' for you, Mr. Ford," Peter replied.

Bill had it in mind to ride around town and get a better look at the bigot's mercantile building from all sides, but he was followed out of Peter's store by a burly looking young man about the age of seventeen. He didn't have as many whiskers as Bill did, but he was working on it. He had a new haircut, but the glint in his eyes told Bill that he wasn't the sort of young man who worried about how he looked. He was young and full of piss and vinegar, just as Bill had been at that age. He wore the garb of a farmer and looked like he was ready for a change of clothes and of occupation. Bill could see it in his eyes before the boy said. "Let me see them ten-dollar eagles again, mister."

"What in the devil do you reckon on doing, boy? Robbing little 'Ol me?" Bill asked in a daring way.

"No, I heard what you told Pete about that ferry. I reckon on riding out with you and taking the job over," the young man said.

"Is that right? Well, do you have a horse?"

"No, does it look like have a horse?"

Bill glared at the boy curiously. He was taken aback by the boy's brusque behavior toward him, but he liked the particular quality as well. "Well, how in the devil do you reckon on riding out there with me if you don't have a damned horse, boy?" Bill asked, trying to keep a straight face.

"I reckon since you're so kind of rich, you might loan me the capital that I need to get started in my new business," the young man said boldly.

Bill shook his head, looked at the ground, and laughed. "You sure are in a hurry to quit your old man, ain't ya, boy?"

"You're damned sure right about that, mister!"

"What's your name, boy?"

"My name is Henry Cooper. What is yours, old man?" Henry asked with a bucktoothed smile.

"I'm Horny Bill Ford from the Great Rocky Mountain Range," Bill said, puffing out his chest. "I have a gelding over there that I brought to town to trade for a mare. I was going to turn him loose in the valley since I killed his owner and don't currently have a use for a gelding, but I reckon you might as well have him. As far as capital goes, Hank, that's all the capital that you're going to get out of this old man. You'll have to get the rest of it from your own blood relation."

"I'll take it!" Henry thought for a moment and added, "Besides, I ain't got any blood relation."

"Well, that fine by me, Hank, I didn't mean to pry," Bill said indifferently.

"Let's get going then," Henry demanded.

"Well, Hank, when you had your big ears flappin' at my conversation with Pete, you should have heard that we're having pie and coffee later. What's wrong, are you afraid that your pa's coming to town to whip your backside or what?" Bill harassed in a knowing way. "Ain't you big enough to whip your pa yet?"

Bill could see the hate in Henry's eyes as he thought about how to answer Bill's questions. The wait was so long that Bill gave him a slap on the back. "Come on, give your horse a try while we wait for Pete." Both men mounted up, and Bill went on about his business of surveying the bigot's building.

Henry Cooper sat proud on the bare back of his new mount. Bill could tell that he had never had his own horse before. "How did you get to town today, Hank?"

"I walked."

"How far?"

"I walked about eight miles. I was told to go to town and get a haircut." Henry thought about the row he had with his stepfather that morning. "I haven't whipped him yet, but I sure as devil don't let him cut my hair anymore. I'm plumb tired of him hackin' up my ears and callin' me a pussy when I complain about it."

Bill thought about Maria giving him heck about his dirty hat. "I only bathe but once a year myself," Bill remarked.

"Yeah, and it looks like it too, old-timer," Henry replied.

Bill sneered at Henry. He thought maybe Henry might need his ass kicked, but he wasn't sure he was the man for the job, and he didn't think it would do any good anyway. He thought the boy might want to watch his mouth around Bennager, though, and he wondered if he could get Henry to make some sort of crude remark about Rose once they got back to the river.

Bill and Henry were wandering around the outskirts of the north end of town. "Do you do much business in that mercantile, Hank?"

"No, I don't do business anywhere. I like to go into Mr. Harlan's and look, but I can't buy anything."

Bill nodded. "Well, that will change when you become a rich ferryman."

Henry had settled into his new job the day before the cattle arrived. Bennager was pleased to have the young man take over for him. Rose and Pablo had quit him in favor of playing with Bud and Blossom while Bill was gone off to Stockton. Bill observed how Henry Cooper was cordial and polite to everyone except for him. He had to scratch his head and wonder why people always seemed to treat him with disdain. It was only a fleeting thought, though, as he started to concentrate on the scene he had planned in Stockton.

Henry was surprised to see the cattle operation coming his way on his second evening on the job. He was even more surprised when the vaqueros stopped at the water's edge and got bare-assed naked. Generally, the men would keep their long handles on, but Zeb had talked them into taking it all off so Bennager would haul Rose away from the activity. He was still certain she and Bill would cause a midnight stampede, and Zeb didn't want them to botch up a perfectly smooth undertaking.

Rose peered across the river at the men and surmised that they intended to take a bath before they crossed the river. That made sense to her, so she found something to do out of their line of sight so as to give them their privacy.

Henry was waiting on the west side of the river, and he observed the horsemen putting their boots and clothes inside Tomas' wagon. Zeb and Stud were the only ones who kept their undergarments on. Zeb joked with Tomas about how the size of their peckers would frighten the cattle into another stampede. Tomas glared at Zeb as if he was sickened by the sight of him and eased his wagon over to the ferry.

Henry pulled Tomas across while the vaqueros did indeed have their baths. Tomas would have time now to start supper while the men swam the cattle across the river. All that Bill could see once Tomas was on land again was his big Mexican whorehouse pillow. Tomas could see the man's scheming mind behind his eyes and made a big show out of loading his flintlock pistol. He made a point of glowering at the mountain man who seemed to be nothing but trouble. Loco Zeb was right about one thing, and it was that this man needed to be away from his operation.

Bill wondered what he had done to make the man hate him. After giving it some thought, he decided to glare back at the man. Bill figured he was probably an old bandit anyway and wondered if he could hit the broadside of a barn with his old dirty pistol that had never once been cleaned. Rose and Bennager introduced themselves to Tomas again as the first introduction at the rancho had quickly turned into a celebration. Tomas wouldn't look at them or shake their hands. Pablo was embarrassed by Tomas' rudeness and apologized to the Rasmussens, explaining the man was old, grouchy, and lacking in humor once he was on a drive. Rose and Bennager shrugged and nodded. They left Pablo and Tomas while they went to go play with the children. Bennager wasn't going to leave his wife's side for one second. He was sure that she would find a way to sneak a peek at the vaqueros.

"Tomas, what is wrong with you? There is no reason for you to be rude to those people," Pablo scolded when the young couple had gone.

"Women and dirty mountain men are not welcome on my drive! Make them go away from these cattle!" Tomas demanded.

"I cannot make them go away. The woman owns these cattle, and she is paying your wage!" Pablo was outraged with the man.

"Make the dirty one go away then. He wants my pillow!" Tomas shouted.

Bill was listening to the conversation. It hurt him to be called "the dirty one" by an old Mexican bandit. He waved his children over and told them that Tomas wanted to give them some bacon. Bud was the first one to attack Tomas' legs in his race with his sister. Bennager and Rose ambled over toward Tomas' supply wagon to bear witness to what would happen next.

Tomas screeched at the sight of the little Indian children as if he was being attacked by a violent tribe. He was afraid they were trying to bite his legs. The children smiled at the face of Tomas and held on for all they were worth as Tomas danced around the camp, trying to shake and push them off. Bud and Blossom laughed and giggled and held on tighter. While Tomas had been fending off his savage foe, Bill had taken the purple pillow, put it on top of his dirty hat, and was turning his head from side to side rapidly so the gold fringes would swing out and jiggle. When Tomas saw Bill had his pillow, he became vicious toward the children. He didn't know whose children they were, and he didn't care. For all he knew, they had just appeared from under the ground. Tomas grabbed each child by their hair, and before Bill and Rose could get to him to make him stop, the Roman was at Tomas' side, biting him on the shoulder. The man dropped to his knees in pain.

Pablo and Bennager could see tears well up in his eyes from where they stood together at the supply wagon, each one of them horrified at what was taking place. The Roman reached down to bite the man again, but Rose got there in time to kick her horse in the jaw while Bill picked his children up. The Roman let out a bloodcurdling whinny, reared up, and struck Rose with his front hoof just as Bill got the children away from the horse's wrath. Rose had turned to protect Tomas and was struck on the back, damaging her ribs.

Tomas was so enraged by Rose falling on him that he elbowed her in the mouth to make her get off. Bill told Bud and Blossom to run, and when they did, the Roman followed Bud. When Bill tried to help the man to his feet, while Bennager was tending to Rose, Tomas hit Bill in the mouth and went to the wagon to get his pistol. Bill was stunned, but Tomas hadn't knocked him down. Suddenly, Pablo was screaming. "No, Tomas! Put it away!"

Bill knew that the crazy man was going to try to shoot him. He began to laugh in a mocking way that made it very difficult for Pablo to stop the man.

Bennager became deranged with anger when he saw the blood spilling out of Rose's mouth and left her on the ground to suffer while he went after Tomas.

Tomas had been so focused on Bill for dropping his pillow on the ground that he never saw Bennager coming. Bennager rammed his head into the man's stomach as he grabbed him around the waist and ran the man into the ground with the fierceness of a fallen tree. Tomas' pistol flew from his hand with such force that it landed in the river forty feet away. Bennager was able to hit Tomas in the face two times before Bill and Pablo could get him pulled from the man. Tomas had never been so abused in his whole life. Not by man, woman, nor beast had he been so ill-treated in such a short matter of moments, and today, he had been harmed by all three and two Indian children as well.

Bennager was in a killing mood for the first time in his life, but he didn't know who he wanted to kill more—Tomas, Bill, or the Roman. He figured that he could kill all three of them and never shed a tear. His face was red, his jaw was rippling, and his fists were still clenched as he approached his wife.

Rose's smile revealed her crimson teeth, and she spat out another mouth full of blood. Bennager shook his head as she held her hand out to him. "For Christ's sake, woman, what in the devil are you laughing about?"

"You have a temper, Mr. Rasmussen." Rose cringed as she got to her feet. "I think my ribs are broken," she added with a chuckle.

"Well, I bet they are. You were just stomped by your own horse. You better say goodbye to him because I'm going to kill the son of a bitch and then I'm going to kill your idiotic uncle," Bennager replied.

Rose laughed. "Did you see the face he was making when he had that big purple pillow on his head?"

Bennager stopped in his tracks. "I don't think it's very damned funny, Rose Mary! People were fixin' to die a few minutes ago, and it's all because of Bill's stupid sense of humor. I'm tired of finishing what he always starts!"

Big Henry Cooper had been leaning on the rail of the ferry, watching the entire commotion. Bill happened to glance his way, and the young man stood there and shook his head at Bill in a disappointed way and then turned his back to him.

Bill looked at the ground and saw Tomas' pillow. He picked it up and dusted it off and went to where the man was still lying on the ground with Pablo at his side. "I'm sorry, Tomas. I'm a pitiful joker. I didn't know your Mexican whorehouse pillow meant so much to you. She must have been a very special woman," Bill said with as much sincerity as he could muster.

Bennager and Rose overheard the apology, and Rose laughed again at what Pablo called Tomas' lack of humor as she watched Tomas snatch the pillow out of Bill's hand.

Bennager waited for the man to get up. When Tomas glared at the young couple, Bennager stood toe to toe with him. "Don't expect an apology out of me, you stupid son of a bitch. If you ever touch my wife or those children again for any reason, I will kill you! Do you understand that? Or do you need a translator?"

Rose's eyes grew wide at Bennager's threat. The smile had been wiped from her face, and she looked at the ground in shame. Her husband lacked humor as well. What had started out as a harmless joke had suddenly turned her husband into a lunatic, in her opinion. Rose wanted to pull Bennager away from Tomas, but her instincts told her not to interfere with his rage. She thought about feigning a fainting spell, but she knew he would kill her horse while she was pretending to need his full attention. Not knowing what else to do, she took out her plug tobacco and bit off a small piece.

Caroline could see the tension in Bennager now and started up with her woeful braying. Toby joined her because he could smell Rose's tobacco.

Tomas shook his head slightly at Bennager. "My point has been proven. Dirty mountain men and women don't belong on the trail with longhorn cattle. You people are noisy and unruly, and so are your animals. You will cause the cattle to stampede because you are full of jokes. When cattle stampede, people die in a most unpleasant way. People don't die when Tomas is the boss. If you want to be the boss, then you can be the gravedigger too. You lost two calves on the day of the hailstorms. The cattle stampeded four times that day. We have been blessed that the wild dogs, wildcats, and bears have not caused other stampedes during the nights, and we have been blessed that no one was killed on the day of the storms. God is with Tomas and his vaqueros. Is God with you?" Tomas' wisdom poured from him as he asked Bennager this question.

Bennager blinked his eyes at Tomas in exasperation as he took in all that Tomas had said. "Does it look like God is with me?" he finally said softly.

"No, señor, it does not!" Tomas answered.

Rose turned away from Bennager and Tomas and caught her uncle watching her. They exchanged broad bloody smiles with one another, and Bill waved his niece over to the wagon so he could bandage her ribs. Tomas was happy that the camp was finally quiet, and he waved at the vaqueros to start the cattle across the river. It was a slow process, and Tomas started supper for his men right away. Bud and Blossom were under the Rasmussen wagon, watching the man who had played with them and then pulled their hair. Tomas didn't know if the loco people would stay with the herd and be quiet or if they would ride on ahead. He feared that the woman wouldn't be going anywhere with her damaged ribs. He thought that it was fortunate she hadn't been killed by the ugliest horse he had ever seen.

When the cattle arrived to their unknown destination, Tomas would apologize for this day and drink tequila with these people, but for now, he had to stand his ground against their antics. All their lives depended on it. It was bad enough that he had to put up with Loco Zeb, but at least he understood the stupidity of cattle and how to act around them.

Bill stood by quietly and watched in amazement at how the expert horsemen managed to move the cattle into the water and keep them from turning back without scaring them or abusing them in any way. The cattle slowly plodded up the bank of the eastern shore upriver from where the camp was. It became loud with the sound of cows bellowing for their calves that were still in the water, trying to catch up with their mothers. The cows crowded the bank, waiting for their offspring. Once the calf made it to shore, it was then his job to dodge mothers who didn't love him until he found the one that did. This was a dangerous prospect because if he suckled on the wrong udder for even an instant, he was apt to be kicked or swatted at by the longhorn of the wrong mother. Bill observed that some calves appeared to be brighter than others in that they were able to find their mothers promptly.

As the cows and calves paired up, the naked vaqueros would ease them away from the water's edge until they were in a long line. The vaqueros stopped almost a half of a mile from camp and let the cattle graze. This was where they would bed down for the night. As more cattle came out of the water, so too did the vaqueros. One by one, as the cattle settled down into their grazing, the men came to camp and dressed for supper. Each man made it a point to locate Rose Rasmussen after they had dressed, tip their hats, and smile in a most noble way and then go back to work. Rose didn't know whether they were being silly or if they really were that magnanimous.

There were two naked vaqueros left in the river when Zeb and Stud Colt started the remuda across. Pablo stood with Bill so he could observe the young man who wanted to make babies with his granddaughter. Pablo folded his arms and glared at Stud, hoping to make the boy nervous, but it was an impossible task. Zeb and the two other men were astride their mounts downriver from the crossing. As the last of the calves approached the eastside, Stud led the remuda into the water. Zeb and the others promised Stud that they wouldn't help him in front of Pablo unless it was a matter of life or death, and because the saddle band had no reason not to follow Stud or the rest of the troop that they had been following, it didn't come to that. When Stud came to the deepest part of the water, he gracefully slid off the back of his mount and held onto its tail until the horse hit bottom again. Then, just as elegantly, he pulled himself back into the saddle, led the mob to the shore, and then to where the cattle were, never once giving Pablo the slightest indication that he knew that the man had been watching him.

Stud Colt hadn't completed a remarkable task in crossing the San Joaquin River with the assistance of his horse, but it was remarkable to Bill because that wasn't something that the boy would have done a couple of months ago. One of the reasons why Indian families in California didn't move around much was because they didn't like to swim, and he knew this to be the case where Stud Colt was concerned. Bill was proud of the boy, and it showed on his face when Pablo looked at him and said, "Jack will have to do more than that before he can be in my family!"

Later, with impeccable manners, the twins waited for their turn to be served supper with the vaqueros. They smelled Tomas' tamales, and their mouths watered for them. The young, tall vaqueros thought the children were sweet and adorable. They smiled and patted the children on their heads as they settled down to eat. Tomas glared at the big-eyed little beggars as they approached him with their plates in their hands. "You are not my vaqueros!" Tomas told them brusquely.

Tomas was then ridiculed by the younger men who were his vaqueros, and Bennager, who was still in a killing mood, was grateful to the men for reprimanding Tomas. Tomas gave the children a mocked smile and plates full of beans and tamales. The children said, "Thank you." They were earnest as they looked kindly at the man, and then they went to be with Bill.

Bill was sitting with Zeb and Stud Colt. He told them of his visit to Stockton and what he had planned for the cattle once they got there.

Zeb shook his head. "Tomas will not allow such a thing to happen Bill. This is his business, and he is a professional."

"Don't you remember how that bastard treated Stud Colt and Sam?" Bill said loudly. Zeb and Stud shushed Bill in unison. Zeb shook his head at the intemperate man.

"Yes, but Tomas won't allow it," Zeb whispered.

Stud nodded his head and smiled. He pointed to himself, and Zeb understood what the boy was trying to convey. Zeb shrugged his shoulders and shook his head. "You can try, but I don't think he will allow it."

"What's he going to try?" Bill asked.

"He's going to try to talk Tomas into it," Zeb replied.

"Does Tomas speak Miwok?" Bill asked in disbelief.

"Yes," Zeb lied.

"I'll be damned!" Bill exclaimed.

Bennager observed all that was before him and thought about what Tomas had told him earlier. He thought of all the reasons why he should get Rose away from the cattle and the men, and then he thought about the fight the two of them would surely have about it. Bennager looked at his wife who was by his side. "Will you be able to ride tomorrow in the shape you're in?"

"Bill said they are just cracked. If they were broken, I'd probably have a punctured lung," Rose said as she sipped her cocoa and brandy.

Bennager couldn't wait for the darkness of the night to come. Every time he saw Rose's swollen mouth, he wanted to kill Tomas all over again. "I think we ought to ride on ahead to Stockton in the morning and see if they have a doctor who could check you out. We can wait for the cattle there and you can sleep in a soft bed."

"Well, I don't intend to walk, and as soon as you get the Roman away from these cattle, you'll shoot him," Rose replied wisely.

"I won't shoot him if you promise to give him to Bud and you get a new mount in Stockton," Bennager negotiated.

Rose set her jaw. "I'll give him to Bud when I get home," she countered.

"Fine, but you'll quit riding him when we get to Stockton."

"No, I'll quit riding him when I get home. When I get home, I intend to have a baby with you, and I'm not going to want to ride anyway."

"You probably won't be able to have babies if that beast kills you first, Rose Mary. I have had enough of seeing you in pain because of that animal," Bennager said, becoming angry.

"He didn't mean to strike me. He was after Tomas," Rose argued.

"You shouldn't have an animal that would bite or strike anybody!"

"He can't help it if he loves the boy, Bennager!"

Bennager became furious when Rose called him by his name. She hadn't done that since they had wed. He gritted his teeth, clenched his fists, and walked away. Rose was saddened by the argument, and she wanted to follow him, but she thought it might be better to let him simmer down. She had hoped he would be pleased at the mention of starting a family, but it didn't seem as though he had even heard her. She finished her drink and went to the tepee to settle in for the night.

Bill saw that Henry Cooper was minding his own business by his own campfire, and he couldn't stand the fact that the young man was being so unsocial. Bill asked Zeb and Stud to come with him to meet Hank. Bill took some food with him to give to the young man.

"Well, Hank, I reckon we'll be leavin' you tomorrow," Bill said as he approached his fire. "These are my friends. This here is Zeb Jones, and this is Stud Colt."

Henry got to his feet and shook hands with the men. "I'm pleased to meet you both."

"So does this job beat farmin' for your pa?" Bill asked.

"It doesn't look as interesting as what you folks do," Henry confessed. "I reckon I had better stick with it, though." Henry flashed his bucktoothed grin. "I see somebody finally hit you in the mouth, old man."

Zeb and Stud both smiled at Henry. They liked the young man already. Bill replied to the comment, "That man doesn't have a sense of humor like we do, you pecker head."

"Yeah, neither does that other mean son of a bitch. I can't believe he hasn't killed you yet."

"Who are you guys talking about?" Zeb asked.

"We're talking about Bennager. He pert near killed that whore-house bandit earlier," Bill explained.

"He did? What for?" Zeb was incredulous.

"Tomas hit Rose in the mouth after her horse bit him."

Zeb held his hand to his mouth and snickered. "Well, I can see how that would bother Ol' Bennager, all right." Stud just shook his head at the information.

"Yeah, and this silly son of a bitch was trying to get me to make eyes at her because she didn't have a man and was ripe for the pickin'," Henry told the men as he pointed to Bill.

Zeb squinted at Bill. "Why in the devil would you say that?"

"I wanted Bennager to hit him because he's too damned mouthy."

Henry smiled broadly at Zeb and Stud. "I didn't fall for the old fart's trick, though. As soon as I saw that big son of a bitch, I knew that I had better stay on his good side. That little gal of his is a looker, though. It's too bad I didn't see her first."

All three men laughed heartily at Henry's confidence. They couldn't imagine Rose with anyone except Bennager, and Henry's comment seemed absurd to them.

Bill noticed that even Stud Colt was quick to laugh at Henry's remark. When Stud noticed Bill eyeballing him, he motioned to Zeb that he had to go sing for the cattle.

The wheels were turning in Bill's head as watched Stud Colt leave. He decided he would try out a little of the Miwok language on his new friend, Tomas. He continued on with Henry. "With a big head like that, you had better stay right here on this river, Hank. You're apt to get into trouble with the wrong gal."

"No, I wouldn't, I'm not as stupid as you look, old man," Henry replied.

Bill shook his head and sneered at the mouthy youth while Zeb slapped his knees and laughed. "Do you see why he needs his ass kicked?" Bill asked Zeb.

"Get after it, old man!" Henry challenged.

"Piss on you, you little whelp!" Bill waved the challenge away, and Henry flashed his bucktoothed smile at the man and laughed.

"You'll miss me after tomorrow. You won't have me to kick around anymore, and you can go back to loping your mule when nobody's watching," Bill jibed.

"My Lord, you're a sick old bastard!" Henry pretended to be appalled.

Zeb couldn't stop laughing as he said, "I don't know why you'd leave Hank here. He seems to be the perfect traveling companion for you."

"The next traveling companion I get will be of the female variety. I don't think young Hank wants anything to do with what I have in mind for my next companion."

"You're damned straight about that!" Henry exclaimed. After a moment of thought, he added. "Good luck finding a woman who would have anything to do with you anyway. I'll bet you a hundred dollars that I'm married before you are. Hell's bells, man, you smell like a dead animal, for Christ's sake. You're too old for a woman anyway."

"Like hell I am, boy! You've got a bet, and when I bring her around to show you, she'll be smilin'."

Henry put his lips together and blew, making an offensive sound. He shook his head at Bill's ludicrous idea and then laughed with Zeb who was holding his stomach at the pain he was in from laughing so hard.

Tomas approached the three men. "If you want to get your singing friend killed, you are doing a good job of it," he said as a warning. "You are being noisy and reckless."

Bill repeated Tomas' words back to him in the Miwok language after all three men stood up from the fire and quieted down. Zeb rolled his eyes at Bill. He knew that Bill was aware of Stud Colt's secret.

Tomas gritted his teeth. "You people owe me a new pistol!"

"What happened to your old one, Tomas?" Zeb asked smiling.

"It is in the river now, Loco Zeb, but I can still find a way to kill you," Tomas said glaring at the man.

"Well, a pistol is owed to you, Tomas, but it will take me a couple of weeks of dragging one around in the mud before it's as dirty as your last one," Bill teased.

Tomas looked wearily into Bill's face and ground out the words, "You will give me a new pistol before you leave my operation in the morning."

Bill folded his arms and smiled. "Maybe I will and maybe I won't. Has Stud talked to you about Stockton yet?"

"Yes, he has," Tomas replied.

"Well, will you let me do it?"

"Will you take these people away from these cattle and give me a new pistol if I agree to your evilness?"

"Yes."

"Then I won't see you until I get to Stockton," Tomas said, pleased that he was getting his way.

Bill put his hand out to shake on the agreement, but Tomas ignored him and left.

Bill and Zeb turned to Henry. "Well, Hank, I reckon I had better turn in for the night. If things don't work out for you here, you can look Zeb up in Monterey or you can look Bennager up on the Yuba River. I'll be seeing you again with my new bride sometime soon," Bill promised.

"Yeah, well don't forget to bring that hundred dollars with you, you crusty old bastard. I'll be kickin' my kids out of the house before you find a woman stupid enough to marry you," Henry replied.

Zeb and Bill shook hands with Henry and went back to camp. Zeb mounted up to join Stud Colt and asked Pablo to come along to hear the boy sing.

"I heard Jack's voice in my chapel at Rose's wedding." Pablo waved Zeb away as Tomas had done earlier, and Zeb left. Pablo was amazed.

Bill spent an hour going through his supplies, weapons, and ammunition. He figured that if they were traveling without the herd and straight through to Stockton, then he could spare some supplies to leave with Henry. He boxed up tea, flour, coffee, sugar, salt, dried fruit, beans, and some salt pork. He figured that Henry could round up some cooking utensils from the Harding house, but he would have to hunt or fish for his meat. He went through his saddlebags and found the pistols and ammunition he had taken off the vermin who had killed Sam. He cleaned the pistols and tried to recall which pistol went with which horse to make sure that they didn't match so Henry wouldn't get into trouble, but he couldn't remember, so he gave up and decided to switch horses with Henry in the morning.

When Bill was finished, he brewed a cup of tea and waited for Tomas to sneak up on him, but the man never came. When his cup was empty, he took the pistol and headed out for where the cattle were bedded down. He wanted to hear Stud's crooning. Tomas met him halfway out.

"You are frightening the cattle," Tomas whispered.

"I was quiet," Bill argued.

"Things that are too quiet will frighten the cattle as well," Tomas explained. "You are quiet like a wild cat. Do you understand?"

Bill nodded his head and gave the pistol to Tomas. "I had to kill a man to get this for you." Bill smiled.

Tomas took the pistol, ignoring Bill's comment, and eased back to camp.

Bill stayed and listened to his singing friend for a few minutes and then headed back to turn in for the night.

Tomas disregarded Bennager's glaring eyes as he passed by their tepee where Bennager was having a smoke and grinding his teeth. Bennager was afraid for his wife's safety, but he hadn't realized it yet. He was still angry at Tomas, Bill, and the Roman over what had happened earlier in the evening. He hadn't stopped to consider what the root of his anger was. The mere sight of Tomas made him want to finish what he had started with the man when Bill and Pablo pulled him off, especially when the man continued to overlook his presence as if he was an object of lesser value than one of his cows.

Bill approached Bennager as he rolled another smoke. "Where is Little Rose?"

"She's asleep." Bennager scowled.

Bill put his ear to the tepee. "No, she's not," he argued.

"Well, I suppose she is resting then."

Bennager could tell Bill had it in his mind to make some sort of nasty comment. Bennager's eyes dared him to do it, but he didn't. He said instead, "I had to make a deal with that whorehouse fiend to pull out and get to Stockton. I promised him that he wouldn't see us until he got there."

"That suits me right down to the ground, Bill. I was going to do that anyway. I want to find a doctor for Rose."

"Oh, she'll have a bad bruise, but I think she'll be all right," Bill said, waving away Bennager's concern.

Bennager reached out and grabbed a fist full of Bill's coat, shirt, and chest hairs with such speed that Bill's jaw opened to yipe, but he didn't because he would spook the cattle. "Rose Mary wouldn't be in any pain if it wasn't for you acting like a damned fool!"

"You're the one that cowed down to her when she bought that rotten horse!" Bill said in self-defense.

"When you see that horse lying dead on the ground, you better start hightailing it for your precious Rockies because you'll be next, Bill, and I mean it!"

Bill pushed Bennager's hand away from him. He considered how Bennager felt about his niece, but he still didn't like Bennager's threats. "Careful of what you say, boy. You're on your way to being the next thing to cause your wife pain." Bill eyeballed him for a moment and then walked away.

Bennager went back to grinding his teeth. Pablo came up behind him with a cup of brandy. "Take a drink of this, my friend," Pablo offered and smiled angelically at the younger man.

Bennager was startled but soon relaxed in Pablo's company. He took the brandy and swallowed it down. Pablo was surprised. He had never seen Bennager imbibe in such a way. Pablo put his hand on Bennager's shoulder. "Do not be angry with me for saying this. I have been watching, and you and Tomas are similar men. He has no humor because he worries that the longhorn beasts will bolt and kill his men, and you worry that they will kill your wife. Your worries are the same. This is not Tomas' first time on the trail with these wild animals. Tomas lost his humor many years ago. Tomorrow, we will be in front of the herd, and you will get your humor back, my friend."

"Perhaps when my wife's bruises go away, then I will get my humor back," Bennager replied. "She is so stubborn and as childish as Bill at times that I become very frustrated. She called what happened to her today an accident. Did that look like an accident to you?"

Pablo nodded in agreement with Bennager. "She was very fortunate today, my friend." Pablo shook his head as he remembered and poured Bennager another cup of brandy. "Everyone was very fortunate today. I liked what Bill Ford said, though. Do not be the next thing that hurts Rose." Pablo patted Bennager on the shoulder and turned in for the night.

Bennager looked into the cup and nodded his head. He flicked the cigarette away and drank down the brandy. He said a silent prayer to his maker that they would all see the sun again and then turned in for the night.

The tepee was filled with the scent of Rose, and his anger started to dissipate. A small fire in the middle of the tent would keep them warm until morning, and in its light, he could see her lying on her back. As Bill had argued before, it was obvious that she wasn't asleep yet, but for some reason, she wanted him to think that she was. Bennager contemplated what he should do in such a situation. Maybe she wanted to surprise him or maybe she wanted to be left alone to rest. Maybe she was upset about his threats toward her horse. The more he wondered about it, the more he wanted to know the answer.

Bennager undressed and laid down beside his wife. He gently took her hand in his silently as if he was trying not to disturb her. She squeezed it to let him know that she was awake but didn't say anything.

"How do you feel?" Bennager whispered.

"I'll be sore in the morning."

"Do you want me to get anything for you?"

"You are all I need," Rose whispered. "What will you do with me after you've killed my horse and my uncle?"

Bennager was silent. He wasn't sure how he should answer her question, and then he realized how ridiculous he had been all evening. He felt like an idiot. He tried to let go of Rose's hand, but she held on tight. She brought his hand to her lips and kissed it.

"You people, as Tomas says, are making me insane," Bennager whispered. "You are incorrigible!"

"Yes, and stubborn and childish. Is there anything about me that you like besides your obsessive need to protect me?"

Bennager was ashamed that he had caused her to ask such a thing. "I love everything about you." It seemed like a silly answer after everything that had been said that evening, but when he thought about it, he remembered what his life would be like without her and her damned uncle in it. "I am obsessed with you, not the need to protect you," he added.

"Come to me then," Rose demanded.

6

The Roman was on his best behavior on the morning of April sixth when Rose gingerly mounted. Bennager was ready to shoot the animal on the spot, the cattle be damned, if the horse did one demonic thing. The morning was chilly, but there wasn't a cloud in the sky. The party was certain that it would be a warm, glorious day. Bill left the extra food for Henry Cooper, and the men said their last round of goodbyes.

"If you see a raggedy, little man looking for his lost farmhand, don't tell him where I am, you crusty old bachelor!" Henry yelled after Bill.

"I won't be a bachelor for long, you pup," Bill retorted as he waved at the young man.

Bennager and Rose pushed on ahead of Bill and Pablo. Bennager was in a hurry to find a doctor for Rose and find a comfortable place for her to recover from her injuries. Rose was still positive her husband wanted to kill the Roman once they were out of sight of the others.

She didn't know what she would do to stop him if he decided to do such a thing. She started to think that the Roman belonged with Bud, and if she could find a nice mare to purchase in Stockton, then she would do it to make her husband happy. It wasn't right that he should have to worry about her safety all the time. The more she thought about how her spirited mount had abused her in the past, the more she realized that her husband was right. The Roman loved Bud more than her anyway.

After Bennager and Rose were a few miles up the trail ahead of Bill and Pablo, Rose said, "If I can find a nice mare in Stockton, then I think I will give the Roman to Bud."

"That's what I told you to do yesterday!" Bennager exclaimed.

"I need mares anyway, and the Roman really does love Bud," Rose said, ignoring Bennager's comment.

Bennager rolled his eyes. "Did you just think of this? Or have you been considering it for a while?"

"The Roman just tolerates me, but he really does love Bud. Bud would be proud to have his very own horse, you know."

Bennager was beginning to think Rose wasn't even talking to him. She seemed as though she was trying to convince herself of her decision.

Rose continued, "Of course, it depends on if I can find a nice mare to ride."

Bennager nodded his head in full support of her brainstorming and said nothing more about the subject. As the miles passed, Rose's pain increased, but she wouldn't complain nor ask to stop. She reckoned that she had saved the Roman's life for the last time. Finally, she asked for a nature break, and Bennager was quick to agree. He needed one as well. The pain was so bad that Rose cried while she was hidden behind a big oak. She didn't know how she would get to Stockton in one day, feeling the way she did, but the mere thought of a real bed and Howell's pies gave her strength. She bit off a big piece of her plug tobacco as she walked up to her mount. She looked in all directions and couldn't see her husband. She took out the jug of brandy and guzzled as much as she could before she had to pull it away to breathe.

Bennager shook his head as he watched her put the brandy jug away and wipe the tears from her eyes. He thought of how he had been a fool to threaten her about her evil horse and wondered in awe about her strength and stubbornness. He watched her rest her forehead on her saddle and figured that she was still crying. The Roman turned his head and looked at the woman who he had struck the day before. As he had done for Bud on occasion, the Roman knelt, first his front legs and then his back legs so Rose wouldn't have to strain herself getting mounted.

Bennager's jaw muscles rippled at the sight of the horse helping his wife. Surely, she would change her mind now about giving the wicked animal to Bud. Bennager waited for the horse to get back on its feet, and then he came out of the brush. He pretended to be unaware of Rose's pain. "Are you ready to push on?" he asked.

"Yep," Rose answered.

Bennager mounted with ease, and Rose envied his health. Bennager knew that within the next half hour, his wife would probably pass out. What a sight she would make when they finally arrived in Stockton, Bennager thought. Bennager watched the love of his life like a hawk for the next hour. Finally, she did as he predicted. He was surprised that the Roman hadn't taken advantage of her sloppy state and thrown her to the ground again. Obviously, the horse knew that it would be the last thing he ever did.

Bennager stopped and tied Rose to her saddle. He wanted to put her on his mount and just hang on to her, but he was afraid that if he handled her, he would injure her further. He took the Roman's reins and led them the rest of the way to town.

As Bennager got closer to town, he saw that the population of the trail was growing. He could see by the look in the miners' eyes that they were curious about the woman who wasn't well. Some of them minded their own business while others asked if they could help.

"Do you know if there is a doctor in Stockton?" Bennager would ask of them.

Finally, one miner answered his question. "Yes, there is a doctor. When you get to town, ask for Dr. Beanblossom. He arrived a month ago from Rhode Island. What's troubling your wife, mister?" the miner asked.

"Her horse struck her in the ribs yesterday. The ride into town was bothering her so bad that she drank a half gallon of brandy when she should have been having lunch."

The miner's eyes widened at the story, and then he peered at Rose's face. "What's the brown stuff dripping from the corner of her mouth?"

Bennager shook his head. "That would be her plug tobacco."

"My Lord!" the miner said.

"Where are you headed for, mister?" Bennager asked.

"I'm heading for the Tuolumne River. I aim to stake a claim."

"There's a herd of longhorn cattle coming up the trail. It would be a good idea to avoid them if you can. You might want to pass the word along to the others," Bennager warned.

"Cattle, huh? Where are they headed for?" the man asked.

"They're headed for the Yuba River."

"Whose are they?"

"You can think of this woman right here someday when you sit down in Marysville or Grass Valley to eat a steak dinner." Bennager smiled as he observed the look on the man's face. The miner took a closer look at Rose Mary Rasmussen, and then he squinted in disbelief.

"Don't take this the wrong way, mister, but I doubt I would ever stop thinking of this woman whether I eat steak or not." The miner turned and headed down the trail.

"Good luck to you!" Bennager hollered after the man. Bennager saw the mining pan and pick among the other utensils and trappings in the man's pack.

"And to you, mister," the miner replied with a wave.

After another hour of listening to various comments by men that Bennager didn't know ranging from how he was a wife-beater to gossip about malaria, he finally made it to the Howell's restaurant. He dismounted, and Mr. Howell met him outside.

"What has happened, Mr. Rasmussen?"

"Well, she is dead drunk at the moment, but she also has some broken ribs. The trip was too painful for her, so she drank a lot of brandy while I was in the brush, tending to nature. Where is the best hotel in town?"

"The Stockton Hotel is the nicest one in town, Mr. Rasmussen. Did you folks find some cattle to purchase?"

"We did, and they will be passing by in three or four days."

"Well, now, that is what I call excitement!" Mr. Howell exclaimed.

"I was told that there is a Dr. Beanblossom in town."

"Yes, there is, I'll send someone to bring him over to you. Can I make you folks some supper and perhaps a pie?" Mr. Howell asked.

"I would be much obliged to you. I'll come around and pick it up in about a half hour."

"No need for that, Mr. Rasmussen. I'll send it over to you."

"Oh, well, thank you so much, Mr. Howell." Bennager paid Mr. Howell for the supper and led the horses to the hotel. Even toward dusk, the town was still bustling with men who were planning on striking it rich. Rose was starting to wake from her drunken nap. She was surprised to see that they were already in town and that she was tied to her saddle. Bennager stopped in front of the Stockton Hotel and turned to untie his wife who was still in a daze. She stoically watched him at his task and then saw him smile at her.

"How are you feeling, dear?" Bennager asked.

"I'm just fine," Rose mumbled.

"Can you dismount by yourself?"

"Of course, I can," Rose slurred. "Where are we?"

Bennager shook his head as he watched Rose try to read the large sign on the front of the hotel and then start to roll backward from her horse. He quickly caught her and asked her to dismount. "Come on, now, it's time for you to hit that soft bed we were talking about."

Rose started off the Roman, and as she did, the excruciating pain made her pass out again, and Bennager had to catch her. He cringed at the possibility that she might have been further damaged. He put her good arm around his shoulder and guided her by wrapping his arm low on her waist.

"I need the nicest room that you have available," Bennager said to the man at the desk. "This woman is in a lot of pain. When Dr. Beanblossom gets here, I need you to send him to our room."

"Yes, sir!" the man said as he hastily retrieved a key to room number seven and led the way. "Is there anything that I can to do to help, sir?"

"You're already doing it, sir," Bennager replied kindly.

.

Mr. Collins opened the door, and Bennager was pleased to see that the room was very nice indeed. He gently laid Rose on the bed and turned to pay the man. "How much do I owe you, sir?"

"How long will you be staying, Mr.—"

"Rasmussen. I guess that will depend on what the doctor says." Bennager looked at his wife and back at the man. "I reckon we ought to stay for at least five days."

Mr. Collins could see the worry in the younger man's eyes, but he wasn't going to waver on his price. "I charge $6 a day, Mr. Rasmussen."

"That's fine. May I ask your name?"

"Yes, my name is Collins. Can I help you bring in your trappings?"

"Yes, I'll be down in just a few minutes. Thank you, Mr. Collins," Bennager said as he handed the man three ten-dollar eagles. Mr. Collins looked at Rose one more time before he left.

"Is your wife fevered up?"

"No, she's drunk. She got her ribs broke yesterday, and then she downed a jug of brandy on the way into town today."

"Oh, the poor thing, I'll send for a doctor."

"No need, Mr. Collins, I've already asked Mr. Howell to do it. He'll also be sending someone over with our supper."

"Very well, Mr. Rasmussen, I'll tell the doctor where to find you," Mr. Collins said as he quickly left the room.

Bennager let out a long, exhausted sigh. He hoped that the doctor and the food would arrive soon. He was eager to join his wife in the soft bed and be alone with her. He had longed for months now to have her to himself and enjoy some peace and quiet for a change. He sighed again and went downstairs to retrieve his belongings, and Mr. Collins told his young son to lead the horses to the livery.

"No, sir, I better do it myself. That dun has a wicked streak. I'll do it after the doctor gets here. Thank you anyway," Bennager said.

"Dr. Beanblossom is tending to a broken leg right now," the boy said.

"Thank you for the information. I guess I'll have time to go to the livery now then," Bennager told the boy.

"Can I go with you?"

Bennager smiled at the boy. "It's a free country. What's your name?"

"My name is Curtis, what's yours?"

"It's Bennager."

"Huh, that's funny name," Curtis said.

"You are the first person who has ever noticed that." Bennager laughed.

"I saw you bring that woman in. Is she your wife or your sister?" Curtis inquired.

"She is my wife. Her name is Rose Mary Rasmussen."

"I saw that she had a fat lip. Did you have to cuff her for runnin' her mouth?"

Bennager shook his head and chuckled. "No, Curt, I didn't cuff her. A vaquero cuffed her yesterday after this wicked horse bit him on the shoulder and kicked her in the back."

"You mean to tell me that some other man hit your wife? What did you do to him?" Curtis asked.

"I didn't do enough to him, I can tell you that. The son of a bitch is still breathing. My wife told me that it was just an accident," Bennager explained.

"What's a vaquero doing in these parts anyway? Was he fightin' you for a mining claim?"

"No, he and nine other vaqueros are trailing a herd of cattle up to the Yuba River for my wife. They work for her," Bennager replied.

"I'll be damned! Curtis exclaimed. "No wonder why he hit her, I never heard of men working for a woman," Curtis said, shaking his head at what the male gender and the world had come to.

"How old are you, Curt?" Bennager asked as he looked curiously at the boy.

"I'm ten years old," Curtis answered.

"Well, look out, by the time you're fifteen, all of us men will be working for women," Bennager teased.

"I'll be damned if I will!" Curtis declared. He promptly left Bennager's sight just in case Rose came out of her room and tried to put him to work. In Curtis' eyes, Bennager was a foolish man to live with such a woman.

Bennager paid the man at the livery and warned him about the Roman's evil disposition. "How many horses do you have for sale?" Bennager asked.

"You must be a crazy man. If those miners could ride goats and pigs, there wouldn't be anything left in town to eat. I'm plumb sold out, mister. I bet I could get you a fair price for this dun if you don't want him. I bet I could get $200 for him," the man said, trying to be helpful.

Bennager reluctantly shook his head. The offer was tempting. "No, he's not for sale, I'm afraid. You just tend to him and make damned sure he's still here along with the other one when I'm ready to leave town."

"Sure enough. I'll see to it, mister."

"Thank you, sir," Bennager said as he hastily walked back to the hotel. He was thinking that Rose might be awake again and wondering where he was. As he opened the door to room number seven, he was pleased to see that she was just waking up. Bennager lit the lamps in the room and waited to see what Rose's condition would be this time. He stood by the window and watched the street, hoping that somebody would show up soon with their supper. He knew that food would cheer his wife up.

"Where am I?" Rose groused.

"We are in a hotel room in Stockton, waiting for a doctor and our supper. I ordered a pie for you, dear. How are you feeling?"

"I think I'm drunk!" Rose grumbled.

"Well, however did that happen, darlin'?" Bennager teased.

"I don't recall," Rose retorted.

Bennager shook his head at his silly wife. "How are your ribs feeling?"

"Oh, they're just fine. What are you doing way over there by that window? Why don't you come to bed with me?" Rose implored.

Bennager smiled and sat on the bed, giving his wife a kiss and a gentle hug. Rose asked, "Did you shoot my horse?"

"No, and you'll be pleased to know that there are no other horses to be had in this town." Bennager whispered as they continued their embrace.

Rose inhaled and let a long, pungent sigh that made Bennager's eyes water. There was a knock on the door. Bennager opened the door to see an older man with white hair, small in stature and no hat, holding a black bag, two supper plates, and a pie, all stacked up on one another. The man smiled and said, "I'm Dr. Beanblossom."

Bennager quickly relieved him of his burden and asked him in. "Dr. Beanblossom, this is my wife, Rose Mary Rasmussen. She is in poor shape," Bennager explained as he set the food down on the table.

"Yes, Mr. Rasmussen, I've already heard all about it. Between the Howells and young Cursing Curtis, I think everybody who's left in town has heard of your wife's trouble and yours, too, for that matter." The doctor chuckled.

"What in tarnation did you say your name was?" Rose slurred.

"It's Beanblossom, ma'am!" the slight man repeated loudly.

"That can't be right, I must be drunk. We've been arguing about beans and calling a little Indian girl Blossom," Rose said with a look of confusion.

"It's just a coincidence, ma'am. Take your shirt off and roll over onto your stomach."

Rose looked at Bennager as his mouth watered for supper, and he nodded to Rose to do as the doctor asked. The doctor cut off the binding that Bill had put on the day before. "Well, what a lovely bruise you have, Mrs. Rasmussen. One rib is broken, and that is why riding into town today gave you such pain. You shouldn't leave this bed for four to six weeks, and if you do, you will have to do it lying down," Dr. Beanblossom said.

"My uncle said they were just cracked!" Rose moaned.

"I'm sorry, Mrs. Rasmussen. They might have been before you rode into town or your uncle could have been wrong. What is this heinous scar on your arm?"

"That's where my husband tried to cut my arm off," Rose replied.

Dr. Beanblossom looked at Bennager who was discreetly nibbling at the pie. "I wasn't married to her when that happened, Doc," Bennager said, smiling.

"What about the scar on the back of her neck sir?" Beanblossom questioned in an accusing way.

"That one is from a shovel two men used to rob her," Bennager answered.

"This girl appears to have bad luck," Beanblossom said, still eyeballing Rose's husband.

"You haven't seen anything yet, Doc. Just wait until her herd of longhorns comes to town. You might just as well follow along with us, I'm sure that you could make your fortune if you did," Bennager said sarcastically.

Dr. Beanblossom got up from Rose's bed, took her fork, and helped himself to a piece of pie. "The news is all over town that she is bringing in a herd of longhorns. What is a longhorn, Mr. Rasmussen?"

"A longhorn is a skittish beast of a cow with long horns that seem to come out of Texas, Doc."

"It is a cow then. I was afraid to ask Cursing Curtis for fear that he would curse at me. This appears to be a momentous feat of daring according to the town gossip."

"It figures that people in these parts would say that," Bennager said as Rose began to snore. Beanblossom was either ignoring her or he was hard of hearing. "I think that folks in these parts think that the miners will eventually steal the cattle," Bennager continued.

"And will they?"

"Not without a fight, Doc."

"This is very interesting, Mr. Rasmussen. I'm glad I ventured to this land. Nothing interesting ever happens in Rhode Island, you know. The people here in California are colorful. They are always doing and saying things that I would not have imagined. I should have left Rhode Island a long time ago, but my Emma wouldn't have it. She would have fainted hourly in a place like this. Just hearing of your wife trailing cows to some unknown place would have made her faint."

Bennager chuckled as it occurred to him to cover his wife. Dr. Beanblossom could see that the young man was weary, so he prepared to leave.

"What do I owe you, Doc?" Bennager asked, pleased to see that the man would be leaving him alone.

"I would like to come back when Mrs. Rasmussen has recovered from her exertions of today. It will be better for me to bandage her when she is in full control of her movements." Bennager smiled and nodded. He thought that it was nice of the man not to use the words "drunken stupor." Dr. Beanblossom headed for the door. "Oh, by the way, Peter Harlan sends his regards and intends to pay you a visit tomorrow night after he finishes at his mercantile."

"Oh, well, that's very nice of him. I'll probably pay him a visit. I'm sure my lovely wife will send me out for something tomorrow."

"Yes, Cursing Curtis made sure to tell him of your arrival. He said something inflammatory about men working for women. I hope that boy never gets married. He will be in for a rude awakening."

Bennager kindly laughed as Dr. Beanblossom finally crossed the threshold of room number seven. Bennager let out a sigh of relief as he closed the door.

*****

"Dan, you're becoming plumb worthless! You'd be better off going to the diggings rather than sitting in this saloon day in and day out. What's gotten into you, for God's sake?" Rufus said as he worried and watched his friend turn into someone that he didn't want to know.

Dan ignored Rufus and continued sipping his whiskey.

"Dan, come on with me to the hotel. You haven't had anything to eat in two days. Ginger will make us a nice supper," Rufus implored as he grabbed Dan's elbow. Dan quickly pulled away from him and Rufus put his hands up in defeat. "You ought to take your own advice and clean up, you stinking son of a bitch. You smell much worse than I ever have." Dan ignored Rufus and was grateful to see him leave.

Kate was waiting on the porch of her hotel, confident that Rufus would succeed in bringing Dan out of the saloon. Her hopes were replaced with disappointment when she saw that Rufus was alone. She watched the man approach her, and he could see the sadness and worry in her eyes.

"I'm sorry, Kate, but you're on your own. He just almost hit me! If I was you, I think I would let him rot," Rufus said matter-of-factly.

Kate looked at her feet and considered what her life would be like if she didn't try to convince Dan to love her. She couldn't imagine loving another man and didn't want to give up on her dream of being a wife and a mother. Kate began to cry.

"Oh, don't cry, Kate. Dan has turned into someone that isn't any good. You're too good for a rotten, stinking son of a bitch like that."

Kate jerked her head up, and her big tearful eyes looked into Rufus' face. "What do you mean I'm too good? I was a whore! That's why Dan won't love me. He's not all those things you said. He's kind, and he's smart when he wants to be."

Rufus laughed. "He is many things when he wants to be, and right now, he wants to be a rotten, stinking son of a bitch. And don't be calling yourself a whore. Nobody thinks that of you. You are a fine lady, and you'll stay that way as long as you stay away from Dan Dunaway. He's a bastard."

Kate looked down again and wailed. "Dan thinks of me as a whore."

"Dan thinks you're in love with Gowans, and he's too stupid to come out and ask you about it. Jim told me that Dan has been in love with you for months, but he won't admit it."

"He won't admit that he is in love with a whore," Kate cried.

Rufus felt pain and anger as he watched the lovely woman continue to demean herself. He couldn't believe that she had such little confidence. He had watched her conduct her business and herself as a lady for months. She was well respected, and when she spoke at the town meetings, everyone listened. Finally, something occurred to Rufus. He put his hands on Kate's shoulders. "Kate, did Dan actually call you a whore?"

"Yes, but then we became friends, and I thought there could be a chance for us," Kate said.

Rufus didn't hear what Kate said after the word *yes*. He was enraged. *How dare that man say such a thing to any of those poor girls*, he thought. As he marched back to the saloon, it occurred to him that Dan might have called Ginger a whore as well.

Dan didn't bother to turn his head when Rufus burst through the saloon doors. If he had, he still wouldn't have had the time to defend himself. Rufus grabbed him by his shoulders and shoved him out into the street. Dan fell from drunkenness, and Rufus was aware that Kate was watching. Rufus didn't want her to see what he was going to do, so he picked Dan up, forcefully grabbed him by the elbow, and took him to the livery. Rufus decided that Dan needed to clean up before he beat the devil out of him, so he shoved him out to the corral and threw him in the horse trough. Dan sat there in defeat. He didn't care about what Rufus had in mind to do to him. He didn't care if Rufus killed him. He didn't care about anything anymore.

Rufus was glad that Dan didn't want to put up a fight. Rufus put both hands on Dan's head and said, "This is for calling Kate a whore!" And then he pushed Dan's head under the water. Jim watched as he leaned on the rail of the corral. Dan didn't struggle, and bubbles came to the surface immediately.

After a few moments, Jim said indifferently, "Ah, ya better let him up, Rufus."

Rufus had to pull Dan's head out of the water because he wouldn't do it for himself. Rufus patiently waited for Dan to catch his breath and cough out the water that he had swallowed. Then he said, "This is for calling Ginger a whore." Rufus dunked Dan again with the same result.

Jim asked, "Are you going to do this on behalf of all the ladies? Because I was fixin' to have supper at Maggie's place and I'm gettin' hungry."

"No, I'm finished with it for now. He's so pathetic he won't even defend himself," Rufus answered in disgust.

"Let's get him out of there then. Don't lay him on the grain sacks, though. Just prop him up against the wall over there," Jim said, pointing to the outside of the building.

"I'll prop him up, all right," Rufus said as they took Dan out of the trough and threw him on the ground next to the building.

Dan heard Rufus tell Jim, "I hope Kate has enough sense to give up on that stupid son of a bitch."

*****

Rose awoke the next morning well after dawn. Bennager felt fortunate he had been able to sleep comfortably for six hours before Rose woke him with her snoring and painful moaning. The Howells finally opened their restaurant at six o'clock, and Bennager went for coffee and to take their supper plates back to them. Rose had never woken the night before, and Bennager didn't have any trouble cleaning up all the food that had been sent over.

Bennager visited the Howells momentarily and then excused himself to be with Rose. He was afraid that she would get up without his help.

As Rose finally awoke, she saw her husband enjoying pie and coffee while reading a newspaper. Her body felt like it was shaking, and she held her hand out in front of her to check. She was shaking indeed, and she felt like she had been poisoned. She moaned in despair at what she had done to herself and started to get up.

"Lay still!" Bennager ordered.

"I have to go to the outhouse," Rose whispered.

"You can't do it by yourself, dear," Bennager said as he got up to help her. "The doctor said that one of your ribs is broken. You'll have to be in bed for four to six weeks."

"What doctor told you that? I didn't see a doctor." Rose thought her husband was teasing her again about locking her up in a room.

Bennager shook his head as he helped her down the stairs and out the back door. "Dr. Beanblossom was here last night. Don't you remember talking to him?"

"No, I think that I've been poisoned."

"I think you drank a jug of brandy yesterday. Don't strain yourself in there, you're apt to break the other two ribs clean through too," Bennager warned as Rose closed the outhouse door. "I'll have to see about getting you a chamber pot."

"That is disgusting!" Rose commented through the door.

"Well, I would do anything for you, dear," Bennager said as he caught Cursing Curtis spying on them from the back door. "Come over here, Curtis," Bennager ordered. Curtis was embarrassed to be caught spying but still walked over to Bennager. "Go scare me up a chamber pot, and tell your father that my wife is ready to have a bath."

"The bathhouse is up the street," Curtis informed.

"Your father assured me this morning, while you were still sawing logs, that you would haul water to our room so that my wife could have a bath in private. Women don't belong in bathhouses, Curt, you know that."

Cursing Curtis rolled his eyes and did what he was told. He was big and surly for his age, but Bennager got a chuckle out of his attitude toward general labor. Bennager rolled a smoke as he waited for Rose. "Are you still alive?" he jested with his wife.

"Yes," Rose said exhaustedly. "Who were you talking to?"

"That was Cursing Curtis Collins. He's ten and has a foul mouth just like you. He is opposed to men working for women, and his father owns the hotel. You would know that if you hadn't been drunk when you got to town."

"Oh my Lord, why don't you just shoot me?" Rose grumbled. "Hey, you didn't shoot my horse, did you?"

Bennager sighed and rolled his eyes. "No, I sold him for $200. The doctor said that you can't ride anymore anyway. You'll have to travel on a cart pulled by a Billy goat." Bennager smiled as he imagined the scene. "The gold miners have taken every horse, mule, and burro out of this valley."

Rose came out of the outhouse after a few moments. She put her hands on her hips. "You…did…not…sell…my…horse," she said, glaring at her husband.

"No, but I should have!" Bennager said, scowling back at her, and then he smiled. "Come on, this is the last of you walking around for a while."

Bennager put Rose in bed and waited for the hot water to start arriving. Mr. Collins had already put a bathtub in their room. "Do you want some pie and coffee while you're waiting for your bath?" Bennager asked.

"I'll just have some coffee."

"What, you don't have an appetite this morning?"

"Not right now I don't." Rose was irritated.

There was a knock on the door. It was Curtis and his father bringing in buckets of scalding hot water. Curtis scowled at Rose as Mr. Collins bid her a good morning and then quickly left for more water. Curtis stayed behind for a moment to tell Rose, "You still look drunk to me!"

"I was poisoned by a wicked vaquero!" Rose said in self-defense.

Curtis raised his eyebrows and pitied the woman's denial. He turned to Bennager and shook his head.

"Get along now, Curt, and get that water," Bennager threatened the boy by pretending to kick him in the backside.

"I don't know why you're having them go to all that trouble. I don't even want to take a bath," Rose said, folding her arms.

"It's high time for you to take a bath and fix yourself up. Dr. Beanblossom is coming back to bandage you. Pete Harlan is coming for a visit, and I expect Bill and Pablo to get here shortly. People are talking about you all over town, dear. They will want to see the woman who intends to have a rancho on the Yuba River."

"That's ridiculous, who would want to see me?"

"I just told you," Bennager said as he squinted at his wife's lack of understanding.

Cursing Curtis was right. Rose was still drunk. Bennager spiced her cup of coffee with a touch of brandy, and Rose didn't even comment about it as she drank it down and asked for another.

"Would you go to the mercantile and buy me some of that smelly soap I like so much?" Rose asked.

Bennager smiled as he remembered the scent. "Will you promise to stay in bed while I'm gone?"

"Yes."

"Do you want me to bring this pie over to you?"

"No, I'm not hungry right now."

"I'll be right back then."

Bennager met the Collins men on the staircase. "Go right in. She's still decent," Bennager told them. Bennager scanned the southern horizon as he walked to the mercantile, looking for Bill and Pablo, but didn't see anything resembling the little wagon that Sam had put together. Bennager shook his head slightly as he remembered Sam working on his kitchen unit in front of this very mercantile, and then he entered the building.

"Ah, Mr. Rasmussen, I heard that you were back in town," Peter greeted him as Bennager closed the door. "How is your wife feeling? I heard she had an accident. Dr. Beanblossom told me that she has a broken rib," Peter continued.

"Yes, she'll be laid up for a while and easy to catch for a change," Bennager said as he looked around the store for reading and sewing material that would give Rose something to do while she rested.

"You're not planning on resting here in Stockton all that time, are you?"

"Well, yes, she's not supposed to move around. Why do you ask?" Bennager queried.

Peter was thinking of Bill's plans for his competitor on the north end of town, but he got the feeling the Rasmussens were not privy to it, which Peter knew would be Bill's way to keep it a surprise. Finally, Peter said, "Well, it's just a shame that you have to hole up here. It gets really hot here. I hear there is a lovely hotel in Sacramento City, and the owner is a pioneering young woman just like your wife. I hope you folks get the chance to stop in there. I hear the place is the talk of the Sacramento Valley."

Bennager nodded as he brought the items to the counter. "I'm sure we will be in Sacramento City for a day or two. We'll try the place out."

Peter leaned across the counter and whispered, "I hear that it is ten times nicer than the Stockton Hotel, and you wouldn't have to put up with Cursing Curtis."

Bennager chuckled. "Curt isn't near as bad as the lunatics that I've been with lately, my wife included."

"Yes, Bill Ford is a handful, isn't he?" Peter said as he laughed nervously.

Bennager eyeballed Peter for a moment as the man tallied up his purchases. "Mr. Harlan, did Bill cause some trouble when he was here the other day?"

"Oh no, not at all," Peter said, looking up at Bennager.

Bennager believed him and sighed with relief.

"I wonder, though, if Mr. Ford had a young man with him by the name of Henry? His pa has been looking for him since last week."

Bennager nodded. "Bill brought a young man by the name of Hank Cooper to operate the ferry down on the San Joaquin River. Bill said Hank didn't want to be a farmer anymore and took the ferry over."

Peter looked at Bennager and smiled. "Oh, yes, I recall Bill telling me that he had been making his fortune operating the ferry. Hank followed Bill out of the store that day, and I was afraid that the boy had gotten on his nerves." Peter laughed.

"Bill deserves to have somebody get on his nerves, but Hank is safe and sound, at least he was yesterday morning when we left."

"That's good to know. Give your wife my regards."

"I will. Come around after you close up and have some pie with us. I expect Bill and Pablo to arrive sometime today. The lead vaquero won't allow Bill to be anywhere around the cattle herd because he is too noisy."

"I recall Mr. Ford being noisy, as you put it, in front of my competitor's mercantile." Peter snickered.

"Yeah, he does things like that all of the time. His antics with Tomas are the reason why Rose has a broken rib right now. I had better get back to her, Mr. Harlan. She is having a hard time understanding that she has to stay in bed," Bennager explained.

"Good day to you. Perhaps I will see you later." Peter watched the younger man hastily rush back to the hotel. He was relieved to find out that Bill Ford wasn't traveling with the longhorn cattle. His bigoted competitor was getting a reprieve, at least from Bill's original plan, and Peter had to wonder what Bill would think up next as retribution for the man up the street. Peter knew that Bill wouldn't give up. Peter was also glad that he hadn't revealed Bill's plan to Mr. Rasmussen now that he knew it wasn't going to actually happen. He could tell that Mr. Ford was a thorn for the young man who obviously liked for his wife to smell like lilacs and roses.

*****

Bill and Pablo finally arrived in Stockton near suppertime. They had taken their time getting to town because they were visiting with miners who would stop long enough to give them the time of day. Most of the men were in a hurry and didn't see anything curious about Bill and Pablo so they continued on their quest to get rich. Pablo was amazed at how many men passed by them and on foot no less. Pablo couldn't believe their determination. Bill warned the men of the herd of cattle they might encounter if they kept heading south. The men that actually stopped to chat were pleasant and grateful for the warning.

Bill and Pablo stopped at the Howell restaurant first. Bill figured the Howells would know where Rose and Bennager were, and he also figured that Pablo would be ready to feast on a decent meal. Bill was shocked to learn from Mr. Howell that Rose had a broken rib and that the doctor told her to stay in bed for a few weeks. Bill scratched his hairy chin with his dirty, long fingernails and said, "That won't do, and I don't think she'll stand for it. She can't stay here after the cattle pass through, that's for sure. Pablo, we'll have to build her a travois. That stupid horse of hers will probably go to the moon. Bennager will have to pull her along, and Bud can ride the dun."

Pablo nodded in agreement. Pablo was confused about the urgency in Bill's voice. He thought Bill expected him to build the travois right away, even though the cattle wouldn't be there for three or four more days. Pablo followed Bill to the Harlan mercantile after they finished supper.

"Hello, Pete, how in the devil are you doing?" Bill asked loudly, causing one potential miner to drop a tin pan that he was looking at. "I want you to meet Señor Pablo Ramirez. He has about three other names mixed up in that, but I haven't memorized them yet."

Peter held his hand out to Pablo; he smiled and took it in friendship. "Señor, I think you should know that you're traveling with a troublemaker."

"Yes, Pete, I know this. I had to travel with him because he made my wife kick me out of my own house," Pablo joked.

Peter nodded his head. "I believe you, señor."

"She was an old witch woman anyway," Bill said in a serious tone. He was aware that he was making a spectacle, and he liked the fact that Peter's customers had stopped shopping just to look at him.

"Pete, I need some canvas. I have to build a travois to haul Rose out of town on."

"What is a travois, Bill?" Peter inquired.

Pablo was glad that he asked because he had been wondering about the same thing since Bill first mentioned it.

"It's a bed pulled behind a horse. I'm going to make a square frame out of some poles, if I can find some, and stretch a piece of canvas across it and rig up a harness with some rope to pull it behind Bennager's horse," Bill explained.

"Does it have wheels?" Peter asked as everyone listened to their conversation.

"No, it's a drag. The Indians make them to tote the sick or wounded people around after a fight, and sometimes they use them just to tote their belongings from one place to another." Now Peter's customers were really intrigued.

"What will you do when you have to cross water?" Peter queried.

"Oh, hell, it won't hurt her to get a little wet! She's got a broken rib, not pneumonia!" Bill shouted.

Peter looked at Pablo who was smiling at Bill's insanity. Peter looked back at Bill. "Why don't you just let Rose rest here in Stockton?

I'm sure that's what her husband intends for her to do. He was in here earlier today, and I'm sure that is what he told me."

Bill's eyes twinkled as he held an unblinking stare with Peter. "No, Pete, I think Ol' Bennager will want to move on up the trail once those cattle hit town."

"Oh, Bill, for Christ's sake, you're not still thinking—"

Bill interrupted, "You're damned straight I am, Pete."

"I think Rose's husband will kill you, if you do what you're thinking," Peter warned.

"Maybe so, maybe so, but I bet Rose will enjoy the show," Bill retorted with a laugh.

"Yes, and then she will have to be dragged through two rivers and countless creeks, just so Mr. Morris won't look her up with his hand out," Peter reasoned.

Bill giggled. "Yeah, I know her. She'll get a kick out of it."

Peter shook his head in disbelief. He knew that he had better warn Bennager of Bill's plans and find a different way to get Rose out of town. He smiled at Bill and Pablo. "Where are the two of you staying while you wait for the herd then?" he asked.

"Pablo and me ain't babies like Bennager and Rose are. We're going to camp here on the south end of town."

Peter nodded his head. "Maybe I'll come around in the morning for a cup of coffee."

"We'll be there. You can meet my children," Bill said in a lower tone and quickly left with his canvas and cotton rope.

Peter was puzzled by Bill's last comment, but he was more worried about Bill's life expectancy if Bennager Rasmussen found out what Bill was up to. He was sure Bill would pay his niece a visit before he made camp for the night. He would have to wait until the couple was alone before he implored them to hurry on to Sacramento City. He didn't want to ruin Bill's plans, but he didn't want Bennager to kill the man either. Peter Harlan closed his store a half hour early that evening, just so he could figure out a way to convince Bennager Rasmussen to take his wife and get out of town.

7

It took Peter all night to figure out what to do. He thought of fifty different schemes and two dozen different lies, and he finally decided to tell the truth, but not to Bennager. Bill's fate would lie in the hands of his niece. He wrote a long, detailed letter of Bill's plans and what he perceived the consequences to be. He outlined a plan for Rose and Bennager to leave town in his own wagon with his own bed in it. He pleaded with Rose, in his letter, to use her wisdom, common sense, and feminine intuition when deciding if she should stay in Stockton or push on to Sacramento City, and then he explained to her what a travois was. He folded the four-page letter twice and stuffed it in his coat pocket.

Peter joined Bill and Pablo for coffee that morning, just as he said he would, and was delighted to meet Bud and Blossom. It didn't surprise Peter in the least to learn that Bill had taken two little Indian children into his life and intended to raise them as his own. Peter sipped his coffee, and the three men talked and laughed. Bill and Pablo told stories about each other, and Peter learned from Bill what had become of Henry Coleman and how he didn't want his pa to know where he was.

"Well, I wish I could stay longer, gentlemen, but I guess I had better get to work. Bring the children by later. I got in a new shipment of hard candy, maybe they will find one they like this time," Peter said as he left camp. As soon as he had a building in between him and Bill, he hurried to the Stockton Hotel, ran up the stairs, and tapped on door number seven. He was glad to see that the Rasmussens were awake and ready to receive visitors. "Good morning."

"Good morning to you, Mr. Harlan. Come in," Bennager said as he shook hands with the man. "We were expecting you last evening."

"Oh, I'm sorry about that. I'm afraid that something came up. I should have sent over a note with Cursing Curtis."

Bennager and Rose chortled. "Oh no, no, Mr. Harlan, I wouldn't ever want you to go to that kind of trouble," Bennager replied sarcastically.

Peter made his way to the side of the bed and took Rose's hand. There was a chair beside the bed, and Bennager told him to make himself comfortable. "I'm sorry for your troubles, Mrs. Rasmussen. Are you feeling any better since Dr. Beanblossom's visit?" Peter asked as he watched Bennager out the corner of his eye. Peter had seen a book on the table and hoped that Bennager would go back to reading it. A light conversation ensued between the three of them, and then Peter decided to talk to Rose about his mother and his sisters when he was growing up as a boy.

Rose generously listened with compassion, and Bennager finally took up the book. Peter slyly handed Rose the note as he continued on with his stories from his childhood and then, abruptly, rose to leave. "I have to open my mercantile now. I see that I have customers waiting already. It's been very nice chatting with you folks, and I hope to see you again before you leave." His eyes pleaded with Rose as he departed, and then his expression quickly changed when he nodded to Bennager.

"Thank you for coming by, Mr. Harlan," Bennager said as the man walked out of the room. Bennager turned and smiled at his wife. "That was an interesting visit. It sure seems like he misses talking to the females."

Rose chuckled. "It was a long visit. I wonder if the Howells have opened up their restaurant yet?"

"Oh, I bet they have. I'll go get us some breakfast." Bennager kissed his wife and headed out.

Rose read the letter Mr. Harlan had given to her ever so slightly and laughed. The poor man was obviously worried sick about Bennager killing Bill, but he was also right about them getting out of town. She knew Bennager would explode if Bill followed through with his plan. Rose wished that she could stay and watch and laughed at the scene that she had pictured in her mind. Now she just had to figure out a way to convince her husband to let her travel.

Bennager came back with their breakfast and Bill, Pablo, and the children. Bud and Blossom ran in and got right into bed with Rose. "What kind of trouble do you two have planned until the cattle get here?" Bennager asked.

"Pablo seems content to take in the sights, so I reckon that's what we'll do for a couple of days," Bill replied.

Rose and the children chatted while the men talked at ease for about an hour. Bill decided that the town was starting to wake up and that they had better get back to camp and keep an eye on things. Bill never let on about his plans for Mr. Morris and Bennager was thankful for the short visit.

"Darlin, I want to finish my bed resting in Sacramento City," Rose said, moments after Bill left.

"I thought you were worried about your father being there."

"If my father is still there, then that's all the more reason to go. That situation needs to be resolved once and for all."

"How do you expect to get there? You can't ride and there aren't any wagons for sale," Bennager reasoned.

"We can borrow one. I bet Mr. Harlan would let you borrow his wagon."

"What's the hurry all of a sudden?"

"I liked it better when we were alone and people weren't barging in on us all of the time. Sacramento City is a special place for us. Don't you remember?"

"Oh, yes, I remember it well, dear."

"Let's go there then. I'll be that much closer to home when I'm ready to ride again," Rose pleaded. "It will also give me more time to figure out what my father is up to and what to do about it."

Bennager liked the idea of being alone with Rose and getting away from Bill. He was growing weary of life in Stockton, and the memories of his honeymoon night in Sacramento City were happy ones. He knew more people in Sacramento City and was sure that he could find something to do there while Rose was recovering. He might even take some time to go check on his investments. He got into bed with Rose. "How do you intend to deal with your father?"

"He is as bad as they come, dear. I'll have to do whatever it takes, especially if he is abusing those girls that we saw there. I'll take him away in the night and kill him if I have to," Rose said with sadness and reluctance as she held Bennager's hand.

He gently hugged and kissed her. "I don't think it will come to that. I won't let it. If your father is still there, we will deal with him together."

"You shouldn't have to get involved. I don't even want you to see the man that made me. You'll throw me back when you see that grotesque bastard. I have to see him, though. I have to know what happened to my mother."

"I'll go and ask Pete about the wagon. I'll be back after a while," Bennager said as he kissed his wife goodbye.

*****

Dan woke himself by slapping flies off his face the morning after Rufus left him outside by the corrals. The flies were buzzing excitedly around in the warm morning sun and were pleased to have something new to taste other than horses and horse droppings. Dan was still too drunk to do much more than swat them away with a casual late reaction. Finally, he mustered up enough energy to sit up with his back leaned up on the barn wall. The morning sun was beating down on him, blinding him to his surroundings. He looked for his tobacco so he could roll a smoke, but when he found it, it was ruined from being in the horse trough with him.

He curled his knees up and hung his head down to keep the sun out of his eyes and fell back to sleep. He dreamt of Kate. He dreamt that Kate was laughing at him, and Gowans and Rufus and twenty other people that he knew were standing behind her and laughing. He woke again, abruptly, when he saw Weatherford standing amongst the people. He was smiling at Dan the same way Dan had smiled at him the night that Angus had crushed him, and then Weatherford took Kate by the elbow, and she gladly walked away with him.

Dan jumped to his feet. He was wet with sweat and short of breath. He focused his eyes, trying to figure out where he was and how he got there. He looked at his clothes and smelled the front of his shirt. He stunk to the high heavens. He emptied his pockets looking for money but couldn't find any. He figured that he must have been robbed.

Jim was sitting in the shade of the livery playing solitaire when Dan hobbled in hastily. "Hey, Jim, did you see who robbed me?"

"I don't think anybody robbed you, Dan. I think you drank your money away," Jim said without looking up from his game.

Dan wanted to ask for a loan so he could clean himself up, but he was too embarrassed. He knew that he had probably drunk his money away, and he also knew that he had to see Kate, but he couldn't see her looking and smelling the way he did. "Jim, can I borrow a bar of soap?"

Jim looked up at the man then and smiled. "Take it and keep it, Dan," Jim said as he tossed the soap to him.

Dan struggled to saddle his horse. He smelled so bad that his mount didn't want to cooperate. Dan's balance was still off, and when the horse quickly turned, Dan fell over. Jim snickered to himself but didn't offer to give Dan a hand. Dan couldn't stop seeing Weatherford in his mind and was becoming aggravated with his horse and himself as well. "Jim, have you seen Kate today?"

"Yes, I think I saw her headed for Gowans office this morning," Jim replied.

"Dan's heart fell, and he would have, too, but he leaned on his horse instead, and then after thinking about it for a few moments, he purged. Jim shook his head at the sight of his lovesick friend but didn't offer any words of encouragement.

Dan mounted and headed for the Sacramento River. As he was wiping the tears from his eyes, he saw something peculiar. A man was driving a wagon that contained a bed with a woman in it. At first, Dan could only assume the man was advertising. As the wagon got closer, Dan could see that it probably wasn't the case. The man driving the wagon looked like he had been hearing vulgar proposals all morning and wasn't amused by it. Dan stopped his horse and watched the wagon pass. He was astonished to see who the young woman was in the bed.

*****

In the two more days Bill and Pablo had stayed in Stockton, Bill became acquainted with Cursing Curtis. Mr. Collins never saw his son in those two days because Curtis had become Bill's shadow. Bill told the boy wild stories day in and day out, and some of them were true.

Pablo was amused as well and enjoyed having supper at Howell's restaurant but was growing restless. At camp, both Bill and Pablo sat facing south, waiting for the herd.

Cursing Curtis was very startled when he saw Stud Colt ride into camp. He thought he was about to be attacked by one of the Indian warriors Bill had described to him from the Rockies. He was also surprised to hear the boy speak English, as were Bill and Pablo, for that matter.

"The herd will be here in an hour, Bill," Stud Colt shouted and then raced back to his job.

"Did you hear that, Pablo? I told you that your granddaughter's lover could speak English now. I bet she taught him that. I bet she taught him a few other things too," Bill teased as he started packing up camp.

"Where in the devil are you going, Bill?" Curtis asked.

"It's time to get the hell out of here, kid. I want you to go to that mercantile where that son of a bitch Morris is and tell the people to get the hell out of there. Let the rest of the store owners know to close their damned doors and come watch the cattle drive. Tell them they might consider watching from their rooftops, though." Bill laughed as he gave Curtis a friendly shove.

Bill and Pablo hitched the burros to the wagon and loaded the children. Pablo eased the wagon through town, and as he did, he saw that Cursing Curtis was doing as Bill had told him to. Pablo kindly tipped his hat to miners and shopkeepers who took notice of him and continued on his way. He wanted to stay ahead of the herd by a considerable distance, and he wished that Stud Colt had given him more notice. He made it out of town and another half mile before he heard Bill's war cries. Pablo decided to get off the trail. He headed west for another quarter of a mile and then turned the wagon so that it faced south. He took out his eyeglass and watched Stockton.

Bill watched and waited to see the Longhorn cattle and the vaqueros make their way toward town. He smiled when he finally saw them all plodding along in a nonthreatening way. The cattle looked good. The vaqueros had given the mothers plenty of time to eat the fresh green grass that had been growing throughout the spring. The calves were fat and healthy as well. Bill watched for a moment and saw the calves were nibbling the grass, mimicking their mothers as they eased along.

Tomas gave the order to cut out the twenty bulls from the herd. He figured that would be enough cattle to fulfill Bill's plan, and he didn't see any sense in unsettling the cows and calves. Tomas sent four vaqueros with the bulls, and the rest of the men stayed with the herd and started taking them around the town instead of through it.

Bill leaped on his horse and remembered what Morris had said on that foggy afternoon back in February about his friend, Samuel Washington. He let out his Arikara war cry and raced through the main street of Stockton. Back and forth he went on his horse at a quick pace, just as he had done that day.

Cursing Curtis stepped out on the road to watch his new friend, and Bill counted coup on him by knocking off his hat. When the bulls approached the south end of town, he hurried to the front of Morris' mercantile and started in on his intimidating war chant. Mr. Morris walked out of the store and stood on the boardwalk with his hands on his hips, looking at the spectacle before him. He remembered this crazy man from before, but he had completely forgotten what was said or done that had provoked him or even when it had happened. While he stood there, trying to puzzle it out, the vaqueros started up with their own particular brand of war cry, screaming and waving their coats in the wind until the bulls became frightened by their actions. The bulls looked around and saw they had lost their cows somewhere, and they started to turn around. It quickly became a battle of wills between man and beast, and as the engagement wore on, the beasts became frustrated, and just like clockwork, they bolted. The vaqueros funneled the bulls right toward the storefront and Mr. Morris.

Morris continued to stand on the boardwalk looking at Bill and then at the cattle with wonder and bewilderment. Peter Harlan and the Howells were watching from the rooftop of the Howells' restaurant while Cursing Curtis Collins and his dad had crossed the street to watch from the balcony of the miners' flop hotel where they charged a dollar a night, but the men slept fifty to a room.

Morris refused to immediately accept what was about to happen to him. His eyes widened as the angry bulls got closer and closer to him until finally, he realized that it was time to run for cover.

The bulls crashed through the windows and door of the storefront and continued on through, wreaking havoc as they thrashed their long horns from side to side, flinging a surprising amount of snot around in the process. The fact that they were inside a building for the first time in their lives made them nervous, causing them to release the weight in their bowels. The longer they were in the building, the angrier they got.

Their bellowing made the cows on the outskirts of town very nervous as well, and the cows called back to their male counterparts. The bulls desperately wanted to be out of the building and back with their herd. Being in the building was a harrowing event for them, and they didn't like it. When they finally made their break, the vaqueros recalled later, eight bulls took out the west wall, and twelve bulls took out the north wall. When the bulls made it back out to the light of day and saw their herd, they ran and kicked and tossed their heads from side to side, trying to fling away the merchandise that was still stuck to their horns and bodies. They were covered with flour, sugar, and coffee. Some of them had men's shirts and pants wrapped around their horns, and one bull had impaled a can of smoking tobacco with one of his horns. The bull was fearful of the thing that wouldn't leave his sight, and as the south and east walls collapsed, the bulls bolted again, taking the herd with them.

Pablo saw the wreck and laughed robustly as he threw the eye-glass down and prayed that he could get the burros out of the way in time to be missed by the stampede. Bill saw Pablo was in the line of destruction and cringed. He knew that he couldn't get to Pablo before the cattle did. He would have to get in front of the herd, which would only cause them to run right into the man and his children. Bill was on the wrong side of the herd to be of any use, but the young superb horsemen had the situation under control.

The vaqueros lined out on the west side of the herd and raced to keep themselves in between the cattle and Pablo, turning the herd eastward all the while. Once the cattle passed by Bill, he hurried out to where Pablo was. Of course, by that time, the cattle were long gone and headed for the Calaveras River.

Stud Colt was still leading the saddle band and was mildly amused by the sight of the man who had once been rude to him over a pair of boots. Morris was now red-faced and pulling what was left of the hair that was on top of his head. Stud wanted to say something glib to the man now that he could speak English but thought better of it. He feared the man might kill him instead of Bill, and Stud didn't think Bill was worth dying for. Besides, Pablo might look down on him for causing the man anymore misfortune than he already had. Morris was oblivious to the fact that Stud Colt was passing by, and Stud thought that was all right as he galloped out toward Bill and Pablo.

Peter Harlan shook his head in silence as the angelic Howells snickered quietly. In Peter's greatest imagination, he never thought that Mr. Morris' building would actually collapse. He was glad that he had taken Bill's advice and ordered extra merchandise. The town's economy would surely suffer if the only mercantile in town failed to carry sufficient inventory to sustain the needs of the miners, especially this time of year.

Cursing Curtis knew that he had just witnessed the grandest display of destruction that he would probably ever see. "Father, I've decided I'm leaving town now, and I'm going with Bill."

"You aren't going anywhere until I tell you that you can. You're not old enough to go traipsing around with that crowd of people," Mr. Collins told his son.

"The hell I'm not! I'm just as big as that Indian kid that's riding with them!" Curtis argued.

"Watch your mouth, Curtis," Mr. Collins said as he pulled his son's ear. "The commotion is over now. Go get back to doing your chores."

Curtis mumbled words of discontent as he shuffled out of the flop hotel to do as his father had told him.

*****

"Holy smokes, Pablo, I thought you were a goner! I'm sorry about that. I had no idea those bulls were going to bring half the store out with 'em. Did you see that bull with the can of tobacco hooked on his horn?" Bill started to laugh. He and Pablo laughed so hard that tears began to stream down their faces. Pablo wanted to stay and laugh all day, but he thought that eventually, the store owner would recover from the shock of the catastrophe and come after them. Pablo wheeled the wagon around and headed north behind Stud Colt and the remuda.

Later, Zeb came riding back to inform the party that the stampede was over. Tomas wasn't very happy about the stampede having to happen, but he knew that if Bill was involved, then he should be ready for just such an occurrence, and he was, and so were the men. They just hadn't expected Pablo to be right in the way.

Zeb laughed and asked, "Do you think Sam saw that from heaven, Bill?"

"I sure hope so, Zeb." Bill laughed. "I did it for him. Now I have to settle the score with my brother. I haven't decided what to do with him yet, but I'm thinking of staking him out in the street and running those bulls right over the top of him."

"I thought you said that Angus pert near killed him," Zeb recalled.

"It would be nice if he was already dead, but I won't believe it until I see it. Of course, it won't be as funny as demolishing a bigot's mercantile, but at least it will finally be finished," Bill replied with a grim, serious expression.

*****

"Rose Mary Weatherford, is that you?" Dan Dunaway asked as he tried his blurry vision.

Bennager stopped the team and turned to look at the man who appeared to know his wife. Bennager had feared that Richard Hawthorne would be in Sacramento City, and he squinted at the wreck of a man who was approaching the wagon.

Rose sat up slightly and used her elbows to hold herself up. The couple could smell the rancid whisky oozing out of Dan's filthy pores, and both wondered who in the world this man could be. Bennager assumed by the confused look on his wife's face that it was not Richard.

When Dan smiled showing his perfect teeth, Rose recognized him. "Dan Dunaway, what in tarnation has happened to you?" Rose shouted with delight, happy to see the boy she used to visit at Mr. Evans' plantation every summer as a child.

"I fell in love with a woman, Rose Mary. What happened to you?" Dan said with a smile as the two of them shook hands.

Rose motioned to the Roman who was tied to the back of the wagon. "The Roman kicked me in the back and broke me up some," she answered.

Dan nodded his head drunkenly and peered at the dun. He shook his head in disgust. "My Lord, I think that is the ugliest horse I have ever seen, Rose Mary. How in the devil did you get all the way out here from Europe?"

"I never went to Europe. I got on a ship bound for San Francisco. I've been out here since January." Rose's eyes began to water at the smell of Dan. She put the back of her hand over her nose to try to cover up the stench, but it didn't help. Bennager dismounted from the wagon to join in on the conversation. He was very curious about how Dan and his wife were acquainted. Bennager could see that the reek of Dan was causing Rose discomfort, and he smiled and laughed.

"Rose Mary, is this one of your old beaus?" Bennager asked as Dan clumsily sat astride his mount trying to be personable.

Rose looked at her husband with a mischievous smile and made the introduction. She ended by saying. "Dan wasn't my beau, dear, he is my friend."

Dan nearly fell from his horse when he reached down to shake hands with Bennager and Rose asked. "Christ, Dan, how many days have you been drunk? I can't believe your woman lets you drink so much. Bennager always makes me sober up and bathe!"

"Now you can see why I do that, can't you?" Bennager chuckled.

"Yes," Rose agreed as she scrutinized her old friend.

"I don't usually drink at all, Rose Mary," Dan said shamefully looking down at the ground. "You sure are a sight being hauled around in the back of that wagon." Dan turned his horse to go bathe and to wash his clothes.

"Hey, Dan, where in tarnation are you going? I want to talk to you some more," Rose hollered.

"I'll be back in town after a while. I suppose you'll stay and rest up for a while, won't ya?" Dan replied.

"Yeah, we'll be here for a couple of weeks probably," Rose answered.

"I'm sorry you had to see me looking like this, Rose Mary. I'll see you later after I've cleaned up."

"Make sure you do, Dan. There's something important I want to ask you," Rose yelled after him. She looked at Bennager strangely. He could see the wheels turning in her head.

"What is it, dear? Do you reckon he followed you here?" Bennager asked.

"No, he was surprised to see me, but I reckon he followed my father out here, and I bet my father has something to do with whatever is eating at him right now. My father killed his grandfather by drowning him in a creek. Everyone around figured that Mr. Evans had a heart attack and fell in the water, but I didn't, and I bet Dan didn't figure it that way either." Rose loaded her weapons mercilessly, and Bennager did the same for moral support.

Bennager was ready for the cloud that hung over his future to be blown away. On this subject, he was behind his wife entirely, but he prayed that there wouldn't be a killing.

Rose looked at her husband. "Let's go to town and get settled in. I would like to wait for Dan so I can ask him about my father, but I had better be ready in case I see the bastard before Dan gets back."

"What will you do, shoot him down in the street?"

"Yeah, I'll make it look like my derringer went off accidentally and pretend like I never saw him before in my life."

*****

Dan knew what his old childhood friend wanted to ask him. As he bathed and washed his clothes, he wondered how Rose would take the news of her father's long overdue demise and the events that took place leading up to his death. Douglas Weatherford was fresh on his mind after dreaming that he took Kate away by her elbow. He couldn't get the image out of his head. As he sobered up in the cold water of the Sacramento River, it occurred to him that Rose Mary probably had no idea her father had ever been in Sacramento City, and her questions probably had to do with news from back home. Dan's first priority was to check on Kate.

*****

Rufus came to the livery and was shocked at the news that Jim gave him about Dan Dunaway's decision to actually use a bar of soap instead of a jug of whiskey to cure his ailments. "I think I'll ride out and see how he's gettin' along. I intend to cure him of calling those girls bad names." Rufus saddled his horse, and as he rode out of town, he noticed Bennager and Rose approaching. Being a member of the town council, he took it upon himself to find out what their business was. If the man was fixing on opening a whore house, he was starting out with a short supply of merchandise, and Rufus didn't think the town needed a whorehouse anyway. "Hello, folks, my name is Rufus Butler, are you folks prospecting?"

Bennager shook his head. "No, and if your next comment has anything to do with why I'm hauling my wife around in this fashion, I believe I'll blow you out of your saddle. It's been a long trip from Stockton, and if I hear one more wisecrack about my wife and that bed, I'll see red, and I mean it."

"Well, that's all right with me, mister. What's your business then?"

Bennager leaped from the wagon, wrapped Rufus up with his arms in midair, and they both fell to the ground. Bennager didn't see any sense in hitting Rufus just yet, so he jumped to his feet and stood over him. "I'm Bennager Rasmussen. I've been hauling freight in this part of the world for eight years now. I've been driving a wagon of one sort or another up and down this trail long before this place was ever called Sacramento City. I've been in this valley, hauling freight for John Sutter, Doc Glenn, John Bidwell, and countless others. Where were you when I was hauling freight for the army back in '46? My business is my own, and I'd thank you to keep your nose out of it!" Bennager took in a deep breath, put his hands on his hips, and waited for a response.

Rufus didn't say anything as he got up and dusted himself off. He put on his lopsided hat and looked sheepishly at Bennager.

"Who in the devil are you to be asking me my business anyway?" Bennager added.

"I'm a member of the town council, sir. We had a problem in the past with a corrupt man, and I just didn't want to see it happen again," Rufus said in an apologetic tone. "I wasn't aware that you're a native of this valley, sir."

"Well, this place is growing, and from what I can see, it's growing up a lot of smart-asses. I don't put up with smart-asses," Bennager replied.

"Yes, sir, neither do I. I was just on my way to confront one when I ran into you."

"Well, get to it then and quit bothering me!"

Rufus was mildly confused when Rose waved and winked at him provocatively as he mounted, tipped his hat, and rode away to fulfill his mission. Of course, Bennager hadn't seen her tease the poor man as he was wearily climbing back onto the wagon.

Rose giggled at the episode as she told her husband, "I want to go to the restaurant and see Maggie. She is a wealth of information. She'll tell me what my father has been up to."

"Yes, my dear, as you wish."

"I used to think that you were a sweet, mild-tempered man," Rose remarked.

"And what do you think now?"

"I think you are my hot-headed angel."

"Well, you must be rubbing off on me," Bennager replied gruffly.

Rose became anxious when she started to smell the holding pens of the livery. This was where Sam had felt her father looking at him, and she felt vulnerable. She wasn't in any position to do anything but shoot if she happened to see the man, so she held her weapon in a readied position. She was surprised to see the lovely garden that was growing in the lot next to the building that her father was surely in. As Rose passed by, Nancy cut the first rose that ever bloomed in Sacramento City and took it in to show the other ladies and also to tell them what she had just seen.

Rose saw Ginger for a moment in the back of the hotel, hanging out laundry. The ladies she saw didn't seem to be the sort of ladies she had seen before, and that story that Pete Harlan had told her in Stockton didn't seem to add up now. The ladies didn't look abused, they didn't look like whores, and the hotel looked beautiful. Her father couldn't possibly have anything to do with this place.

As Bennager stopped in front of Maggie's restaurant, Rose noticed another lovely, young blonde lady walking down the board-walk on the opposite side of the street. Kate didn't notice the arrival of Rose and Bennager. Her mind was full of thoughts about business, money, investments, the law, and Dan Dunaway. Rose distinctly remembered her passing by the men on their first day in Sacramento City. The blonde hair was a dead giveaway, but the young lady looked different now. Her garb was appropriate attire for a businesswoman, and her gait was full of purpose instead of devilish mischief.

Bennager helped Rose down from the wagon, and the two of them quickly took in the sights. Bennager looked over at the hotel that he had spent his honeymoon night in, and Rose looked at where the gambling hall had been on the north end of town. Rose peered at the sign that was on the front of the building now that said "Josh Gowans—Surveyor."

Bennager caressed Rose's back and kissed her. "Well, did you see him?"

"No, and I don't believe he's here anymore. That's too bad because now I will have to go look for him. I hope he doesn't know about Angus or where he is," Rose said as they walked through Maggie's door.

*****

"Hey, you no good son of a bitch, you called my woman a whore, didn't you?" Rufus yelled, after finally finding Dan hidden behind some brush downriver from the ferry.

Dan could hardly hear Rufus hollering at him over the noise of the river rushing by over the rocks. He slowly looked up, and then around, and saw Rufus sitting on his horse, glaring at him. He ignored the man and went back to work scrubbing his clothes.

Rufus was perturbed that the naked man would have the audacity to ignore him when he was in the process of picking a fight with him. Rufus dismounted and stood on a rock on the edge of the shore. "Hey, you rotten son of a bitch, Kate told me that you told those poor girls that they were whores."

Dan shook his head at his ignorant friend but didn't say anything as he beat his trousers on a rock. His feet felt like they might break off on account of the water being so cold, and he wanted to quickly finish his task before he had to deal with Rufus.

"Do you deny saying such a thing?" Rufus asked.

Dan shook his head.

"Well, come out of that water then. I'm going to beat you to death!" Rufus bellowed.

"Oh, in that case, I'll be right out, Rufus," Dan lied as he rinsed the soap out of his pants.

Dan laid his clean clothes on the big rocks that surrounded the pool of water that he was standing in and then sat on one, waiting for Rufus to come in after him.

"Are you comin' out of there or not?" Rufus yelled wildly.

"No, I'm not coming out of here, you silly son of a bitch." All Dan could think about was getting to Kate, but he couldn't leave until his clothes were dry. He was starting to get his appetite back, but Rufus was standing in between him and his chances of finding some old, dried-up hardtack in his saddlebags. He also wished that he could have a smoke while he waited, but that appeared to be out of the question at the moment as well. "Hey, are you the one that tried to drown me in the horse trough?"

"You're damned right I did!" Rufus declared.

"What the devil for?" Dan asked.

"For calling Ginger a whore, damn it!"

"Well, we're even then. Besides, they were whores when I called them that, and you know it. They know it too!" Dan said in self-defense.

"Well, you smart son of a bitch, it hurt Kate. It hurt her right down to the bone. She's got it in her head that you still think that of her."

"What does she care what I think of her? She's with Gowans now," Dan replied, being careful not to reveal his feelings for Kate.

Rufus didn't think that Dan deserved to know how much Kate loved him. Kate was better off without a mean drunk in her life, in his opinion, and he also thought that it would be better for Dan to go be a mean drunk up at his mine so Kate could get started on having a normal life. "I guess it's hard for her to have anybody think that of her. You should apologize for saying it and move on out of town."

"Who in the devil do you think you are to tell me my business? I'll go when I'm damned good and ready to go and, if you must know, I have apologized to Kate for calling her that and for the poor behavior I exhibited when I first took the hotel away from Weatherford."

Rufus cringed at the name being spoken out loud. It made him recall what everyone had gone through in the past, and he thought of how many things had changed since that time.

Time passed as Dan waited for Rufus to either leave or come in after him, but as was usually the case with Rufus Butler, he decided to sit down on the rocks and contemplate. Dan figured that Rufus was over his desire to beat him to death, so he sloshed out of the water, slipped his boots on, and made for his saddlebags. He didn't have any hardtack and remembered eating it all on the day of the hailstorms. He figured it was probably for the best anyway. "What day is it, Rufus?"

"It's the twelfth of April. You would know that if you would keep your head out of the jug." Rufus got to his feet nonchalantly.

Dan continued to rifle through his trappings and found another set of dirty clothes. They didn't smell as bad as the last set, but they weren't clean enough to wear for Kate either. He went through the pockets and was surprised to find some money. There was quite a lot of money, actually, and he couldn't recall how he came by it. He figured maybe he won at a card game and wisely rat holed it for another day. He was disappointed in not finding any tobacco in his dirty pockets and continued to dig in both saddlebags until he finally found some makings in the bottom of one bag. As he stood there in the sun with nothing on except his boots, he realized that he was a rich man—still hungry but rich. He smiled at his fortune of having tobacco and then turned to join Rufus.

*****

The next thing he remembered was waking up again to the familiar sound of flies and bees buzzing around him. He had been laid out, flat on his back, in the sun, on the rocky shore of the Sacramento River. By the look of his red flesh, he had been there for about three hours. Rufus had gotten his way finally and knocked him out.

Dan raised his hand and was pleased that he hadn't dropped his tobacco, but his emotions quickly changed to debilitating fear when he heard the warning tail rattle of the diamondback rattlesnake that had quickly coiled when Dan raised his arm. The snake had sought extra warmth on the breezy spring day by lying in the sun next to Dan, using the man as a wind break. The warm man was warmer than the rocks as the rocks hadn't completely warmed up after the cold winter.

Dan was too afraid to move, and the rattlesnake was confused as to why its shelter had suddenly shifted for the first time. Dan couldn't understand why the snake continued to linger but didn't offer to eat him. Minutes passed by, but it seemed like hours to Dan. He began to sweat as he realized that he was going to bake to death while he waited for the snake to either leave or kill him. The arm that had been suspended in space was beginning to hurt as every muscle in his body began to cramp due to dehydration and being in a state of rigid fear.

The snake began to relax and stop rattling its tail. As Dan continued to sweat, the snake could smell the foul odor of rotgut whisky coming out of the pores of its windbreak. As the snake repeatedly and rapidly stuck out its forked tongue to examine what it was smelling, it was all Dan could do to keep from pissing all over himself. As he watched the snake move its tongue closer and closer to his torso, he knew that if he let his bladder go, he would be a goner. He closed his eyes and waited for the snake to take its fatal bite out of him. If the snake would just hurry up and bite him, then he could piss.

Dan thought of what he would do to Rufus Butler if he managed to get out of this predicament alive. He thought that he would have been better off to stay a drunken, filthy mess than to clean up for Kate. He was beginning to think that being in love with Kate was more trouble than it was worth, especially if he was going to keep denying it. He could feel his skin burning in the hot midafternoon sun. He opened one eye at the sound of an old leaf rustling and saw the rattlesnake making its way toward the brushy embankment.

Dan slowly got up, put his tobacco back in his saddlebags, and waded back into the river for another bath. Even he could smell what the snake had sensed with its forked tongue and made use of every bit of the soap that he had left. When he figured that he had done all he could, he stood on the rocks in the shade of his horse and rolled a smoke. Rose Mary Weatherford came to mind, and he wondered if his dream had been more about her than her father. He thought that the spirits were still clouding his mind. He couldn't seem to puzzle anything out. Why would he want to bother Kate when she was in love with Gowans? Why would Rufus want to hit him? Why didn't the snake bite him? How was he able to not piss himself when he thought that the snake was going to bite him? Why did Rose Mary Weatherford have to show up? After having two cigarettes, he decided to get dressed and go find the answers to his questions.

8

Bill and Pablo rode with the herd and camped with Tomas at the Calaveras River. "Was your wish for the evil man who said bad things about Stud Colt fulfilled?" Tomas asked Bill after supper had been cleaned up.

"Yes, Tomas, thank you for making my dream come true. I didn't imagine that the building would collapse, though. I reckon if you would have given me the whole herd, then there wouldn't be anything left of the town," Bill replied in a whisper.

"That man will be lucky to sell a pair of boots to anybody now." Tomas still didn't see any humor in it, not in Bill's laughter, not in the building falling or the look on Morris' face that Bill kept recalling and mimicking every ten minutes. He was satisfied that justice had been served, and that was all. Pablo noticed Tomas stop in front of Zeb and glare at him. Zeb hadn't said or done anything to deserve it, but as long as Tomas remembered to glare at him once in a while, he wouldn't. Even though Tomas demanded that Zeb didn't talk or cause trouble, Zeb was still having the time of his life. Zeb was certain that Tomas would raise a glass with him once the cattle were safe and sound in their new home.

Zeb loved working with the vaqueros. He loved escaping death daily as he experimented with new ways of commanding the cattle. Often, the vaqueros would dare him to lasso a particular cow that they knew would try to hook Zeb's horse. Today, his dare was to get the tobacco can off the bull's horn. Zeb rode beside the bull time after time and just tried to grab it and pull it off, but even though the bull was worn out from the stampede, he was still angry about that can, and Zeb didn't help his temperament by continuing to fuss with it.

Tomas had scrutinized Zeb's line of thought in the matter and shook his head in disgust. Tomas knew there was only one way to get the can short of killing the bull, and he wondered why Zeb was being so idiotic. Why wouldn't he just do it and be finished with it? Sooner or later, the bull would hook his horse, burst a lung, and then Zeb would be afoot because Tomas would have to make him walk for being so stupid in the first place.

Finally, Zeb slipped a loop over the bull's horn, let out some slack, dallied, and galloped his horse out ahead of the bull, slipping the can right off along with the lariat. It was then that Tomas realized that Zeb just enjoyed tormenting things. Zeb just didn't realize that he had been tormenting Tomas in the process. The young vaqueros laughed and praised Zeb for his efforts and ingenuity while Tomas coughed up a piece of lung and spat it out.

At camp, the twins followed Tomas' every movement. If he moved out of their sight, they would crawl under his wagon to see where he went. Tomas liked Bud and Blossom. They never looked at his pillow and they were very quiet. He was always aware of when he was being watched. He had been very good at intimidating people, so they wouldn't watch him and wouldn't do anything to cause him to have to watch them, but the twins were impossible. Every time he scowled at them, their smiles and big brown eyes melted him. He wished that he had found them before the filthy mountain man had. When no one was watching, he had pity on the little beggars and gave them some soft candy that he learned how to make when he went to Mexico with his crew. It was the same place where he had acquired the two purple pillows. Tomas didn't smile at the children as he gave his gift, but they knew that he was a good man.

Tomas told Bill, "Now that justice had been served, you and Pablo will ride onto Sacramento City and wait."

"We'll wait for you at the Cosumnes River. Stud's family lives there, and he wants Pablo to meet his mother," Bill kindly informed. He didn't like men telling him what to do the way Tomas did, but he had a deep respect for Tomas, even though he would never admit it.

Tomas glared at Stud Colt for confirmation, and Stud gave it with a nod of his head. "We will stay for one day by this Cosumnes River," Tomas declared without hesitation or mirth.

Bill and Pablo obeyed Tomas' command the next morning and rode away from the herd.

They spent the day warning the miners to beware of the cattle that were coming up the trail. They made the Mokelumne Ferry crossing just before dark and stopped on the north shore to make camp.

The ferryman recognized Bill and asked if the little lady's cattle herd was coming. "Yeah, they'll probably be here tomorrow sometime," Bill answered.

"I saw Miss Rose about three days ago. It's too bad about her accident. I guess I'll have a lot of ferrying to do once those cattle show up."

Bill smiled knowing that the cattle would swim the river. "Yep, I reckon you'll be at it for a day and a half, and you'll have folks waitin' in line for you to finish. You should have built a bigger ferry while we were gone. I heard you had a bet with that girl. It was something like if she made it back by June, then you would ferry the outfit over for free."

The man nodded his head in despair. "Yes, sir, I did. I would have built a bigger ferry, but I didn't believe she would make it back. It didn't surprise me a bit to see her being carried out of the San Joaquin Valley either."

"Oh, that's just a minor setback. I'm sure you'll see her again on some other such endeavor once she's all healed up," Bill teased.

"Well, I won't be making any more bets with her, I can tell you that. I lost my ass on this one," the friendly ferryman said with a smile.

Bill wanted to camp by the river and wait for Tomas so he could see the look on the ferryman's face when the cattle and the naked vaqueros made the crossing, but he was afraid that it would cause Tomas to recant his offer to give the vaqueros a day off at the Cosumnes River. He reckoned he would have to rely on one of the vaqueros to recount the story for him.

The Mokelumne Riverbanks were full that night with miners who wanted to cross the next morning and others who were planning on going upriver to make their fortunes. Bill and Pablo took turns on watch, although it wasn't necessary. The miners slept the whole night through, weary from walking day in and day out in pursuit of their golden quest. Bill and Pablo marveled at how diverse the men were from one another and how they all sought the same outcome. Each man that stopped to visit throughout the evening had a different story and background. Some were married, their families still being back home, and poor. Some were married and had closed their businesses to become millionaires. Some were already wealthy but just wanted more and the younger crowd mostly wanted adventure. Some were tired of home life; others were sick of their jobs. Some had been encouraged to go by their parents, and others had willingly run off from their parents. Some were avoiding the war that they knew was sure to come between the Northern and Southern states, and others were dodging the law for being drunk and disorderly a time or two in their short lives.

Bill and Pablo listened and chuckled at the stories that the men told, and out of all the men, they never met a mountain man or a Mexican cattle baron in the bunch, and the miners had never met anyone like the two of them. Pablo had made the trip to meet men who would leave their families on a lark, and now he had. Their faces would be remembered by him for the rest of his life, short though it might be.

It had been a long while since Bill had seen so many men gathered in one area. He hadn't seen such an event since the Rocky Mountain Rendezvous days. He missed seeing the women. The Rendezvous events were always spiced up with women, and lately, the love of a good woman filled his mind with carnal thoughts. He didn't speak about the seriousness of the matter. He only joked and boasted about his desire to be with a woman, knowing full well that there weren't any women to be had within the newly discovered land that was filling up more and more every day with male competition.

Bill told Pablo, "You know, if a man wanted to get his pecker wet, I reckon he would head east, don't you think?"

Pablo snickered and shook his head. "That is good thinking, Horny Bill Ford."

"Let's leave the children with Rose, get some fast horses, and go check it out. Do you want to?" Bill said encouragingly.

"Maria told you not to corrupt me, Bill Ford." Pablo laughed at Bill's plan and thought that if he was twenty years younger, he would gladly go with Bill and take on all the lonely ladies in the east. "Maybe you should ask Zeb to go with you," Pablo added.

"Yeah, I should, it's about time for him to give up on this notion that Anna is watching him. I'm sure Sam has already given her an earful about Zeb anyway."

"Yes, maybe you are right. Perhaps it is time for Zeb to have a fresh start."

"I know damned well it's time for me to have one!"

*****

The next morning, Bill and Pablo started out for the Cosumnes River. Pablo was surprised by Bill's insistence that he should meet Jack's mother. Pablo had seen many Indian camps in his life and had never been impressed by them. The more he thought about having to meet some silly Indian woman, the more the idea aggravated him. He would die soon, probably before Juanita was of the age to wed, and she would do what she wanted to anyway. He didn't see the need in meeting Jack's mother.

"It will be another story for you to tell Maria," Bill said when Pablo grumbled and complained about having to do it. "Besides, you might as well since it seems that Tomas is going. I think that's why he's taking one day off. If you stay behind, you'll have to listen to Zeb because Tomas won't be around to keep him quiet."

"Yes, Maria will like to hear a story of Jack's mother," Pablo acquiesced.

*****

Maggie's restaurant was filled to the brim on the day Rose and Bennager walked through the door. Maggie's help was gone, the gold fever had taken its hold on the young couple, and they lit out one early morning to make their fortune. Maggie figured that the young man wanted to keep his wife sheltered from the eyes of so many men, many of whom were better prospects than he was.

Maggie remembered Rose and Bennager, greeted them with a holler, and rushed into the kitchen. When she came out, she asked Rose what she was crippled up about this time as she delivered plates and coffee to her other customers. Maggie and everyone else in the room heard the answer that Rose bellowed out to her. Maggie continued to stay on the move and required her customers to just shout out what they wanted from the kitchen so she wouldn't have to stop. Rose reckoned that if she hadn't been banged up, she would have taken pity on the poor woman and gave her a hand.

Rose and Bennager settled for pie and coffee, but the pie had just run out. Rose quickly realized this wasn't the time to pick Maggie's brain. "I think we had better get our room so I can lie down. Either that or you can pull me up and down the street in the wagon some more," Rose told Bennager with a mischievous smile.

"I suppose you were amused by all of the crass comments hurled at you by those men over the last four days," Bennager scowled.

"Oh yes, my dear, I reveled in them. I particularly enjoyed the city council member with his old horse and floppy hat." Rose giggled.

"What would it take to keep you from getting into trouble, Mrs. Rasmussen?" Bennager asked passionately.

"You look like you have an idea brewing, Mr. Rasmussen."

"Let's go back to that room that we had to leave so prematurely."

The couple got up, hollered thanks to Maggie, and walked out into the hustle and bustle that was Sacramento City. The place resembled a wild frenzy. Wagons and carts of all shapes and sizes rolled up and down the street. The street was so packed with them that they ran into each other. There was no order, except for whoever was bigger got to go first. In some cases, a big man driving a little cart being pulled by a little burro would win the engagement because everyone's haste and desire to head out seemed to be worth fighting for as three fights broke out along the street before Rose and Bennager were able to cross it to get to the Sacramento Hotel.

Bennager's heart sank with disappointment when they learned that there wasn't a room to be had in his sentimental, all-time favorite place in the world.

"The hotel on the south side of town is lovely, Mr. Rasmussen. It's more expensive, but I hear that it's worth every penny. I know that you want the best for your wife and young Miss Kate's hotel is the finest," the desk clerk and owner explained.

Bennager looked at his wife. He was sure that she would balk at the idea. Rose asked the gentleman bluntly. "Didn't that place used to be a whorehouse?"

Bennager and the man behind the desk turned four shades of red to hear the accusation come out of the young woman's mouth.

"Oh no, ma'am, it was always a hotel, but it's under different management now."

"What happened to the old management?" Rose queried.

"Well, I couldn't say for sure, ma'am."

"Is the son of a bitch still around here or not?" Rose said with malice.

Bennager put his hand on Rose's back, thinking that it might calm her. Her quest for information was hardly subtle and terribly embarrassing.

The gentleman behind the desk sensed Rose's anger and became curious about her association with the man she was asking about. Obviously, there was one or else she wouldn't have known that he was a son of a bitch. "I really couldn't say what became of the old management, ma'am." Every business owner who knew Kate and had witnessed her blossom into what she was now was not inclined to speak of the past. Kate and the ladies were well-respected citizens in the community, and not one member of the city council would ever speak Weatherford's name again, not even to someone who seemed to hate him as much as they all had. To speak of him would conjure up the memories of the foggy nights when the man in question would wail the whole night through. The townsfolk wondered if they would hear the wailing again once the wintery fog arrived next season. California was a place for new beginnings. Douglas Weatherford's new beginnings weren't fit for hell, though, and no one cared to retell his story.

Rose could see that the man knew more than he was telling. She knew that something out of the ordinary had become of her father. She desperately wanted to hear what it was. She smiled at the secretive man but didn't push him any further. Dan Dunaway would tell her what she wanted to know without having to admit to this man before her that she had a right to know where her father was. She knew that she had already caused her husband some embarrassment. He was close to home now. His business revolved around what people did in this town. The man held eye contact with Rose while she thought of her husband's livelihood. "I'm sorry to have troubled you, sir," Rose finally said.

"It's no trouble at all, ma'am. Enjoy your stay in Sacramento City, Mr. and Mrs. Rasmussen."

"I'm sure we will," Bennager assured as he escorted his wife out the door.

Once outside, Rose asked, "What do you make of that?"

"I figure he knows more than he's saying," Bennager replied as he rolled a smoke.

"That's what I think. Something strange happened in this town while we were gone just as Sam said it did. He should have followed us because he saw Sam, but he didn't because something happened." Rose looked at her husband and smiled. "What a mystery. Dan Dunaway knows, and if he won't tell me, I'm going to turn this damned town upside down."

Bennager wasn't shocked or alarmed by his wife's statement. He would do anything to help her put an end to her obsession. "Maybe we better get you healed up first. This town looks pretty heavy," Bennager said as he took in the sights.

"It will be easier if I walk than if I climb back up in that bed. It's not very far," Rose suggested.

Bennager walked slowly with his wife. He put himself between her and the street and kept his hand on the small of her back. She was wearing one of those dresses that she had made, and Bennager was sure that the mere sight of her would create havoc and chaos amongst the men who were already primed to fight at the drop of a hat.

They both noticed Rufus Butler riding back into town. He tipped his hat to them as he passed by and quickly went to work straightening out the mess in the street. Everyone that was heading south was to line out on the right, and everyone that was heading north was to do the same. Bennager and Rose stopped at the shade of a tree and watched as more fights broke out over the suggestion. Rufus' city street plan was brilliant, but the miners enjoyed the constant state of pandemonium. For most of them, this would be their last day in town until next winter.

Bennager and Rose laughed heartily when Rufus unwillingly became part of the fray and was wrestled down to the ground by three young men.

"No wonder why his hat is lopsided," Rose remarked with a laugh.

"Yeah, I feel bad about lighting into him now, the poor devil," Bennager replied as they continued. They passed Ginger, who was keeping a close eye on the fracas. They noticed how she was biting on her knuckle and cringing with worry.

"That must be Lopsided's, sweetheart," Rose suggested under her breath. Bennager nodded in agreement as they entered the yard of Kate's Hotel.

As they entered the grand lobby, Kate rushed out to greet them. Rose noticed a tiny scar over her right eye.

"Hello, folks, and welcome," Kate said with a lovely, sincere smile. "I'm surprised that you're not taking in the spectacle in the street. It seems to be our city's only amusement these days."

"It looks like somebody has taken quite an interest," Rose said, referring to Ginger.

"Yes, that is Ginger. Her beau insists on trying to make those crazy men cooperate with each other. Ginger just has fits about it because he gets roughed up for his efforts." Kate looked at the second most handsome man that she had ever seen. "How did you make it through town with this lovely lady without falling victim to the disruption, sir?"

"I've been lucky so far. Once my wife is settled, I'll have to go back for my wagon. I'm sure that is when my luck will wear out," Bennager said, feigning fret.

"Well, you had better hurry, sir, unattended wagons, horses, mules, burros, and oxen usually wind up missing eventually," Kate warned.

"Yes, miss, that I could believe," Bennager said.

"Go on ahead. I'll wait for you in the lobby," Rose said as she kissed Bennager, and he headed for the door. "Dear, keep your eyes peeled for Dan and bring him to me when you see him, will you, please?" Rose added.

"I'll do it, dear."

Both women watched Bennager until he was out of sight. Rose smiled at Kate's interest while Kate was curious as to whether his first stop would be the saloon.

"May I lie down?" Rose asked quietly.

"Yes, of course, let me show you to your room," Kate replied.

"I'd rather wait for my husband, but I can pay you for my room right now."

"That won't be necessary. Is there anything that I could get for you while you wait?" Kate asked as she eased along with Rose to the large sofa. "May I ask what happened to you, Mrs.—"

"Oh, I'm Rose Rasmussen," Rose said with her hand out.

"I'm Kate McGuire," Kate said as they shook hands.

"My horse kicked me in the rib cage, and Doc Beanblossom told us that I was supposed to be in bed for four weeks," Rose said as she gingerly positioned herself on the sofa. "It's a damned nuisance, and I still have three weeks to go. Can you have us for that long?"

"Of course we can," Kate said without hesitation. She was relieved to know that Rose wasn't an abused woman but confused about who Doc Beanblossom was. Sacramento City didn't have a doctor to her knowledge, and she would know. "Where is this Dr. Beanblossom?" Kate inquired.

"He's the doctor in Stockton."

"Why didn't you stay in Stockton to recover?"

"I was encouraged to leave by Peter Harlan, who recommended this hotel, incidentally, due to certain events that were about to happen that my husband wasn't supposed to see."

Kate didn't want to pry, but she just had to know. She had heard of a mercantile in Stockton being demolished by a herd of cattle. "Such as?" she asked.

Rose smiled. "Such as my wild uncle had a score to settle with a merchant who offended two of our friends."

"Your uncle would be the one I heard about, and you're the same Rose Rasmussen who's bringing a herd of longhorn cattle up from the south."

Nancy ran into the lobby and put her hands on her hips. "Those cattle better stay out of my garden!" She turned and scurried back to where she had come from.

Kate smiled at Nancy's outrage. "I believe she's serious, Mrs. Rasmussen."

"I can see that. Her garden is lovely." Rose chuckled and yelled, "If my uncle ruins your garden, I'll shoot him dead!" Rose looked back at Kate, and they talked of Rose's adventure for a spell. "Can you see if my husband has made it back to the livery yet?" Rose asked.

Kate looked out the window. "I don't see him or a wagon."

I reckon I'll take you up on a cup of coffee then, Kate. I guess he couldn't avoid the fight." Rose laughed. "It will do him good, he's been in a fighting mood lately anyway."

*****

Bennager had managed to avoid a row until he got back to the wagon, but that's when his trouble began. He was accosted by six men.

"Hey, where are you going with my wagon?"

"Where are you going with my bed?"

"Where do you think you're going with my horse?"

"Hey, that's my horse!"

Then they argued with each other.

"What's your bed doing in my wagon?"

"Why are those horses tied to my wagon?"

"Why did you put your bed in my wagon?"

The Roman pinned his ears back and snorted. Bennager figured they were just joshing him and ignored their jeers until one of them grabbed his arm. He became ready to fight instantly.

Maggie poked her head out the restaurant door. "Leave this man alone, you rascals. He's a friend of mine!" Maggie was too busy to see her request through as she went back to work.

"Hey, you're the guy that brought that whore to town!"

"Yeah, where did she go?"

"What did you do with her?"

Jim was leaning on the wall of one of the storefronts, watching and waiting to see how Bennager, a man who he knew well, was going to tend to the wayward miscreants.

The Roman let out his ear shattering whinny, and the fight was on. Bennager quickly broke the arm of the man who had dared to grab him while the Roman bit the arm of a man who was leaning on the wagon. Bennager grabbed another man by the back of his neck, the one who had called Rose a whore, and began to beat his head repeatedly against the bed of the wagon. Jim cringed while another man, who had claimed that the wagon belonged to him, ran around the end of the wagon to come to his friend's aid. The Roman kicked the man squarely in the side of the knee, knocking him to the ground in excruciating pain, and then he kicked him again, this time in the side of the head. Jim shook his head at the brutality of it all.

The last two men were in awe of the madman and his horse and knew that they didn't stand a chance against the man who had obviously been sent to them from hell. Their eyes were as big as saucers when Bennager leaped, flat-footed, from the boardwalk into the middle of the bed and proclaimed at the top of his lungs that the wagon, bed, horses, and whole damned town was his. The fracas in the street came to an abrupt halt. Men returned to their business at hand, and everyone kept to the right, just as Rufus Butler had suggested they do.

"Hello, Jim, how have you been?" Bennager said as they both looked at the man that the Roman had probably killed.

Both men sat down on a bench in front of the mercantile. "I've been all right, Rasmussen. What have you been up to lately?"

"Oh, I've been traveling some. I went to Monterey here a few weeks ago."

Jim nodded, and there was a pause in the conversation as Jim studied the Roman. "Say, didn't I sell that horse to your bride?"

"You sure did, Jim, way back in January as I recall."

"I'll be damned," Jim simply stated as he watched Rufus finally get up off the street and look for his hat. "Where is that crazy girl of yours?"

"She's over at the hotel on the end of town. That damned horse roughed her up some about a week ago."

"Was she trying to beat you up?" Jim asked sarcastically.

"No, that son of a bitch just goes crazy when he takes a mind to," Bennager explained.

Jim noticed that Rufus found his hat, finally. He looked back at the young man on the ground that was starting to open his eyes. All he could see was the Roman's backside, so he slowly dragged himself away from the horse's reach. The Roman snorted nonchalantly as if he had done nothing unusual. "Have you ever seen a leg look like that, Rasmussen?"

"It serves the stupid son of a bitch right," Bennager said with disdain.

Jim stood up and hollered, "Hey, Rufus, come over here. You have a customer." Jim sat back down and waited. They watched Rufus amble up the middle of the street. He stopped when he saw the poor man dragging himself along.

"What in the world happened to you?" Rufus asked him with compassion.

"We were just having some fun, and that damned horse kicked me," the man whined.

"Like hell! You called my wife a whore! You're lucky you're still breathing!" Bennager yelled. Jim chuckled and jabbed Bennager in his side with his elbow.

"There's another one over here, Rufus," Jim told him, pointing to the side of Bennager's borrowed wagon.

Rufus rounded the wagon and saw the man with the bloody head. Upon further examination, he said, "Holy cats! You pert near scalped him!" Rufus let out a long sigh and sat down on the bench. "Hey now, I remember that horse!" he exclaimed. "I wondered whatever happened to that devil."

"I think you're getting sidetracked, Rufus," Jim said. "Are you going to patch these fellas up or what?"

"Aw, piss on 'em. They called your wife a whore, didn't they?" he asked Bennager, and he nodded. "Well, piss on 'em then. They ought not be sayin' things like that." Rufus gave the matter some more thought. "I'm all worn out anyway. Let's go have a beer."

"I think I had better get this wagon down to the livery, Jim." Bennager said. "I'd hate to have to kill a man today."

"There's a saloon next to the livery," Rufus informed Bennager.

"Yeah, I see there's about thirty of 'em now," Bennager remarked.

"This place is really turning into something," Jim said.

"Yep, it looks like I need to quit fooling around and get back to work." Bennager sighed.

"Oh yeah, there's plenty of freight to haul, that's for sure."

The men took a few minutes to contemplate the future and then reluctantly got up. Jim and Rufus walked to the livery and waited for Bennager. It took him longer to circle around the outskirts of town, away from the congestion, than it took the men to walk through it.

Three hours later, as the men enjoyed their beer in the coolness of the saloon, Dan walked in. He wanted to kill Rufus, but he was afraid that his skin would rip from his body if he moved too hastily, especially the skin around his groin. Dan ordered a beer.

"I owe you, Rufus, you son of a bitch!" Dan muttered with Bennager standing between them.

"How do you figure that, Dan? It seems to me like we're even," Rufus replied.

"Bullshit! I laid on the rocks in the sun for three hours. I was accompanied by a rattlesnake during those three hours, and he didn't like it much when I came alive, you stupid son of a bitch."

With a few beers under his belt, Rufus was feeling feisty again. "Well, Dan, I'll tell you again, it's about time for you to leave town and go be a rotten bastard someplace else."

Bennager raised his brows and set his beer down. He was supposed to take Dan to the hotel, but he reckoned he'd wait for the argument to finish up or escalate, whichever came first.

"I reckon I'll leave for the diggings when I'm finished with you, Rufus."

"Why wait? Let's finish it now!" Rufus said loudly.

Dan finished his beer and slammed his mug on the bar. "Now how in the devil am I supposed to do that with a burnt pecker and nut sack?" Dan yelled and then gingerly headed for the door. Bennager followed him out while the rest of the patrons laughed heartily at Dan, including Jim and Rufus.

Once outside, Dan shook his head and rolled a smoke. Bennager joined him. "Dan, I was told by my lovely wife to bring you to her."

Dan was shocked by the man's statement. He didn't recognize Bennager from before, and his expression reflected it.

"My name is Bennager Rasmussen, and my wife is Rose Mary Weatherford. She's Rose Mary Rasmussen now, of course," Bennager explained.

"Oh yeah, all right, I'm going to see her, but I have to check on a friend of mine first."

"Well, Rose is chomping at the bit to see you. Can your friend wait?"

Dan smiled. "I'm afraid she can't, Ben. Where are you staying?"

"Right across the street there," Bennager said, pointing to Kate's hotel.

Dan nodded and chuckled. "Imagine that." Dan thought of the irony. "That's where my friend should be. I don't think it's a government meeting day."

Bennager squinted at the man. They both flicked their cigarettes away and crossed the street.

*****

"Your husband is finally coming, Rose," Kate said with excitement in her voice on account of Dan being with him. "Was it Dan Dunaway that you wanted to speak to?"

"Yes, it's about damned time, for Christ's sake!" Rose grumbled.

"Oh." Kate said with disappointment as she left the room wishing that Dan was coming to see her.

The two men tromped through the entrance. Bennager sat down in the lobby and sighed. "I finally found him, dear."

Rose peered at her husband. She had heard blow by blow accounts of his deeds and whereabouts all day, and they didn't include him combing the town looking for Dan Dunaway. She smiled as she found humor in her silly husband and said, "Thank you for your efforts, dear. Hello again, Dan. You look in better shape than you did this morning."

"Hello, Rose Mary."

"Dan, I need some information," Rose stated.

"All right, but it will have to wait, Rose Mary. I have some pressing business to tend to just now." And then Dan left the room.

Rose was agape as she looked at Bennager. He slapped his hands down on his knees and smiled. "It's a woman, my dear. Maybe we should get you settled while we wait. What in the world are you doing in the lobby anyway?"

"I was waiting for you. I didn't know it would take you so long to find Dan, my love." Rose smiled at her husband's fibs. "Did you bring our trappings over?"

"No, ma'am, I plumb forgot," he said as he leaned over to help her up.

Rose took in his smell. "Were the beers refreshing?"

"Yes, they were, my dear." Bennager was unabashed.

"Well, I'll take a whole bucket when you come back then," Rose demanded.

"Yes, my love."

*****

"Kate, I have a lot that I want to say to you!" Dan said as he burst into the kitchen. He hadn't counted on his voice to crack or his body to tremble, and he was surprised by it. Kate looked up at him briefly and then went back to chopping up vegetables. Dan sighed. "I know it's probably too late to say this, Kate, but I'm sorry. I'm sorry for all the things that I said to you and to the other girls back on that first morning. It was cruel, crude, and crass, and it makes me sick to think about it. I'm sorry for every cruelty that I did to you and the other girls after that. I should have never used the cruel word in reference to you, and I'm sorry. I wish that I could take it back, but I can't, Kate."

Dan waited for a reaction, but it was as if Kate had gone deaf as she continued to chop the vegetables. "Kate, you're all I think about." He paused to wipe his brow. "I love you, Kate McGuire. I know you're in love with Gowans, and that's good because the truth is, Kate"—he paused to take a breath—"I'm not good enough to clean the bottoms of your shoes, let alone make love to you. I wish you all the good things in life, Kate, because you deserve them and so much more." He looked at her one last time. She was crying, but Dan saw that she was also cutting up an onion. He wished that Rose Mary had stayed somewhere else. He wanted to leave this building and never come back to it again. He decided to see Rose Mary when Kate was at a government meeting, and he headed for the door.

"I don't know what makes you think I'm in love with Josh Gowans," Kate said softly.

Dan stopped in his tracks. "They tell me you've been taking carriage rides with him, having him to supper, and Jim told me you went to his office this morning." Dan turned around to face her. "Now I know you wouldn't walk into that old gambling hall unless you were in love with the man in it."

"Yes, that was unpleasant."

"Why did you go there then?"

"Why did you spend the last two weeks in the saloon?"

"Thinking of you constantly was driving me mad, Kate. Seeing you with Gowans made me irate, but I didn't have any right to ask you to stop."

"Why didn't you just come and talk to me?" Kate asked. "Was it because you still thought of me as a who—"

"Don't say it, Kate," Dan interrupted. "I thought of you every minute that I was away, dreamt of you when I slept. I dreamt of you when I was passed out from drunkenness, but it took me until this morning to know that I was in love with you. It took me all day to sober up and bathe and clean my clothes and gather up the courage to come and tell you that I'm in love with you, Kate. But as I said before, I'm nowhere near being good enough for you."

"I believe you to be, Dan, when you're not being mean," Kate said in her quiet, gentle tone.

Dan went to her and took her hand. "What about Gowans?"

Kate smiled. "Dan, I noticed a while back that you had a tendency to wander more than you worked." Dan furrowed his brow and looked at the floor guiltily. Kate put her hand on his face. "I've been investing your share of the hotel profits in land speculation. I've been buying and selling city lots. Josh surveys them, and I buy and sell them. Have you noticed the new buildings going up that you could have been working on, by the way, while you were in your drunken stupor?"

"Hey, don't knock me too hard, Kate, I won some money in a card game."

"No, you didn't, Dan. I put some money in your saddlebags when Rufus happened to mention that you were broke and owed the saloon $78."

"Oh my Lord, Kate." Dan couldn't believe his ears as he sat down at the table and put his head in his hands. Kate wasn't sure what she should say now that the man she loved appeared to be on his last leg. She set down a plate of ham, cheese, bread, and dried fruit in front of him.

"Have something to eat. You'll feel better after a while. "Kate went back to fixing supper. "I don't want you to apologize to me and the girls anymore, Dan. We all want to forget the past. We all know who we are now, and the unfortunate time was just a mere short chapter in our long lives. It's only good things from now on that we want to talk about and think about."

"Rufus was right. I am a worthless son of a bitch."

"No, you're not, Dan. I think the past was worrisome to you. You were put through an ordeal too. It's just that women adapt quicker than men do. No matter how you look at it, we owe what we have now to you."

"Not really. Angus Donovan was the real hero."

"Who is Angus Donovan?" Kate inquired.

Dan took Kate's hand again and looked deeply into her warm, beautiful eyes. "Kate." He swallowed hard. "The woman who arrived today is Weatherford's daughter."

Kate gasped and clutched her heart with worry and fear.

"Don't fret, Kate. She hated her father. She came here to get away from him. She wants to talk to me, and I owe her the truth. We were good friends growing up together in Virginia. I'm sorry that it's not over yet. I thought she was in Europe or I probably would have never followed her father, and if I had known that she was here, I would have asked her to help me get rid of him. Will you come with me to tell her the story?"

"She'll want the hotel, it's hers by law," Kate said with disappointment.

"No, she won't, Kate. You hold the deed. Will you come with me?"

Kate thought of how she had talked to Rose all afternoon without knowing who she was, and she thought of how she liked the unruly woman very much. "She's a strange woman, Dan."

"Yes, she's always been a little strange, but she's nothing like her father."

"I know that," Kate said as she got up with Dan to go see Rose.

*****

"Come in!" Rose hollered when she heard the knock on the door. She smiled when she saw that it was Dan and Kate, hand in hand. "So you're the one Dan's in love with!" she said to Kate. "Good for you, Dan, Kate's sure to be a wealthy woman. Kate, this room is lovely. Pete Harlan was right about this place. I especially love the balcony. Can I offer you some beer?" Rose asked, holding up the gallon pail. "I made my husband feel bad for drinking without me."

They all looked at Bennager who was napping in a chair.

"Don't mind him. He's all tuckered out. I reckon the townsfolk wore him down to a frazzle."

"No, thank you, Rose," Kate replied with a smile.

Rose poured her a glass anyway along with one for Dan. "Drink up, there's more where this came from, I'm sure."

Dan chuckled, remembering now how he missed his crazy Rose Mary.

"Dan, I can see that you are a busy man, so I'll get right to the point. Where is my father?"

"He's dead, Rose."

"Good, who killed him?"

Dan's stomach began to knot up, and Rose could sense his discomfort.

"Dan, I know he had it coming. I know he had some girls he was abusing. I know what he was and what he probably did to them. I reckon he killed your grandfather in that creek, and I'm glad he's dead, but I still want to know what happened. I want to know how he got here, where my mother is, and whatever became of Lily, and I'm certain that you know. I came here to start a new life, and I want to get shed of the past and never look back."

Dan nodded as Kate looked into her glass of beer and then drank it down. Rose held up the pail to pour another, and Kate accepted it.

"You are one of the girls, aren't you, Kate?" Rose surmised.

"Yes." Kate nodded. "All of us here now were brought here by your father."

Rose shook her head and clenched her jaw. "I'm sorry for what happened to you, Kate." Rose looked at Dan then.

"Your mother died right after Lily's wedding. She married that Richard Hawthorne that you liked so well. Your mother died from the bite of a rabid raccoon that had made its way into her henhouse. The doctor investigated around that henhouse and made your father nervous. When he realized that he had spent all your mother's money and owed every merchant in town, he traded the farm to Hawthorne for Lily's dowry, which was more than the farm was worth, of course. That's where he got the money to come out here."

Rose's heart ached for her mother, and she wished that her father was still alive so she could kill him herself.

"How much do you really hate him, Rose? Isn't it enough to know that he's dead?" Dan asked after he let the story of her mother sink in.

Rose handed the pail of beer to Kate and broke out the brandy jug that Bennager had stuffed under the bed for her. Rose peered at Dan gravely. "I think you know better than that, Dan. Let's have a drink to my mother before you continue on." The three of them drank, and Dan took Bennager's since he was incapacitated.

Dan burped. "Well, Rose, one foggy day here a couple of months back, the wrong man—or the right man, depending on how you look at it—was driving his freight wagon through town when he saw your father beating on a woman named Trina."

"Trina Harper," Kate interjected with a nod.

Dan looked at his love and smiled. "She's Trina Donovan now."

Rose's ears pricked up, and Kate was mildly confused as to how Dan would have such knowledge. He put his hand on her leg. "This big Irishman with his six-horse team lunged from the wagon, crushed Doug's right side entirely, and then beat the devil out of him."

Rose laughed. "You're describing Angus Donovan."

"Do you know him?" Dan asked.

"Yes, he's building my rancho in the foothills."

"Oh my Lord, is that your place?"

"Yes, have you seen it?" Rose asked with delight.

"Yes, it's going to be beautiful, Rose Mary."

"Well, go on. What happened next? Did Angus kill him?"

"No, but his injuries finally did him in a couple of weeks later, Rose Mary. There really wasn't much left of him when we hauled him away with the gangrene that had set in. He died a long and miserable death, I assure you."

"Did you bury him somewhere, Dan?"

"He's under a rock pile east of here, Rose Mary. I'm afraid I didn't put much effort into his burial. I only wanted to hide him from prying eyes."

Rose laughed at the guilt that Dan displayed. "Well, you did better than I would have, that's for sure!"

Dan laughed with Rose and was glad the story was finished and that he was right about Rose's attitude toward her father's demise. She was the only one that he had told who possessed the proper frame of mind about the whole thing. He wasn't sure what she would think of Lee the scientist. She might have enjoyed hearing about that, too, but he and Rufus had sworn to never tell anyone about him.

When they had finished having their laugh, which was morbid in Kate's view, Rose asked, "Dan, will you take me there?"

"You bet. Just say the word, and we'll go." Dan filled his glass with beer and offered to fill Kate's, but she shook her head.

Kate looked at Rose and said, "There's more that you should know, Rose. Your father owned this hotel and the gambling hall up the street."

"Yeah, I heard about that from Maggie, but she didn't give me a name, and then when I got to Stockton, Pete Harlan could have mopped the floor with me when he told me who owned this place," Rose explained.

"To make a long story short, we took the place over and made it what it is now, but by law, it's rightfully yours."

Rose looked at Kate with wonder as she took a sip of brandy and offered the jug to Dan. He declined, vowing to stay sober from now on and make something of himself. Rose respected Kate's honesty but thought her to be a fool. "You're too damned honest, Kate McGuire! By law, I reckon the rightful owner would be my slaveholding sister. She's the one he stole the money from," Rose corrected.

"Yes, I suppose you're right."

Rose eyeballed Kate as she looked at her empty glass. "I asked a citizen of your fair city some questions regarding this matter earlier today, and he refused to answer. I know that he was hiding the truth from me. Isn't that the usual case regarding my father?"

They waited for Kate to answer, but she only looked blankly at Rose.

"I believe that it is, Rose Mary. Kate and the other ladies are loved and well respected by the townsfolk. Kate is a city council member," Dan said proudly.

"Well, then, I say let sleeping dogs lie. If Lily or Richard ever make it out this far, which I doubt will ever happen, just don't say anything. Have you written home, Dan?"

"Nope, I've been busy being an ass," Dan replied with Kate in mind.

"Good, we only have one more problem then."

9

Bill blasted through the hotel entrance with Pablo right on his heels, followed by Bud and Blossom. His intention was to kill Doug and take the place over. It would be a coup. Everyone had been warned about Bill, and Dan and Bennager had been waiting for him at the livery for five days. Just when they had given up on him and figured that Tomas had let him ride with the herd, he showed up. The ladies were cleaning up breakfast, and the lobby was packed with patrons sipping coffee and reading their papers.

Bill bellowed, "Where are all the women? I hear this place is full of 'em! Let me at 'em!"

Kate came into the lobby and extended her hand graciously with a smile and kindly said, "Hello, Horny Bill Ford, and welcome."

Bill immediately became aware of what an idiot he was when he looked at the lovely young woman that stood before him. She wasn't any Maria Ramirez, but her loveliness made him wish that he had taken Maria's advice about bathing. He didn't know who the girl was that was taking his hand, but he was in awe of her and knew that he wasn't fit to be in the same town with her, let alone the same room.

"My word," he whispered.

A tall, thin, gorgeous girl with long, straight, brown hair and big, brown, inviting eyes walked up behind Kate and tapped her on the shoulder. Kate moved aside, and Bill took in the full, voluptuous form that was approaching him. His every sense became electrified with desire. Her name was Della.

"Your bath awaits you, Mr. Ford," Della said, leading him away by the hand.

Pablo smiled at how easily Horny Bill Ford could be sidetracked, and then he saw Bennager and Dan snickering at the kitchen door. The children stayed quiet and kept their eyes peeled for Rose. Kate knew what to do and took them upstairs to see her.

"Hola, my friend. Where is a bathtub for Pablo?" Pablo said with a laugh to Bennager as they shook hands.

"You better stick with us, Pablo. We've made other arrangements to keep Bill quiet for a while," Bennager explained.

"Yes, I see. Bill Ford came here to kill his brother, but now he has forgotten about it. I think you are corrupting my amigo," Pablo said jovially.

"Well, not in the way you think, my Catholic friend. We're just trying to persuade him into a bathtub. Rose doesn't have anything better to do these days other than hatch plans," Bennager said as Dan handed the man a cup of coffee. "Señor Pablo Ramirez, this is Dan Dunaway."

"I'm pleased to meet you, Señor Ramirez," Dan said.

"Yes, and the same to you, but where is the brother. If Bill is too busy, then I should kill this man," Pablo said with indifference.

"Oh, he's long gone now, Pablo. We only have Della and the longhorns to fear now," Bennager joked.

"They are nothing to fear, my friend, they are only women."

Pablo's comment made Bennager think of Stud Colt. "Did you meet Stud's family?"

"Oh, yes, Jack's mother is wealthy in every way, much like Miss Della, if you will understand." Pablo raised his brows and chortled. "They are wealthy in other ways as well. When we arrived, we became involved in a war over her creek. We had to run off some miners that didn't belong there. Jack was irate and nearly beat a man to death for being too close to his lovely mother, and Bill shot the man's friend in the foot. Tomas lassoed another and dragged him down the creek bed and then down the river for a while, and the fourth man ran for his life.

"Jack is a very tender, loving young man. He and his mother love each other very much. Jack has a very nice family, but they didn't understand the piece of paper Bill gave them, giving them ownership of the creek. Indians can be ignorant creatures. Fortunately, Jack was finally able to make them understand. They do not believe in owning anything, you know," Pablo stated.

"I know, that's why it's so easy to take advantage of them," Bennager said.

"They have a wonderful orchard and quite a few chickens. I must say I was impressed by their little log home and the cleanliness of their place. It is not an average Indian camp like I am used to seeing, and Jack's mother is quite a woman." Pablo raised his brows and chortled again.

Bennager looked at Dan who was smiling at the pleasant old Mexican ranchero. "Are you starting to miss Maria yet?"

"Oh yes, very much. She made love to me before I left, you know."

"Yeah, I recall you saying that a time or two before." Bennager chuckled.

The town was starting to fill up as it did every day at about that time. Bennager and Dan had been helping Rufus keep a semblance of peace in the streets. It didn't pay anything at all, but it made Ginger feel better at the end of the day, and Bennager and Dan took turns buying the beer every afternoon.

"Well, I guess we had better get out there, Dan. Do you want to come with us and watch our attempts to contain the town, Pablo?" Bennager asked.

"My friend, I am still jealous that Bill Ford is getting a bath and I am not, and not just because of the young señorita. I'm filthy, and so are my clothes," Pablo said.

"Come with us, we'll get you fixed up," Bennager said as he left the kitchen. "Just a minute, Pablo, I better say goodbye to my bride."

Pablo nodded as both young men dashed away in opposite directions.

Dan found Kate outside helping Ginger to fold the sheets. "Kate, I'm off to do my civic duty."

Kate was still leery of Dan. She had listened to his words that day and she had been kind and civil to him. She wanted him more than ever, but she hesitated to give him her heart because she knew he would grow weary of town life and leave for the diggings again. Every time he left, he left her not knowing where she stood with him. He seemed to be changing. He came for breakfast and supper, and he was taking interest in the town, but she didn't think that would last for very long. Dan was apt to pick up and go at the drop of a hat. He might even be apt to go back home for all she knew. She was determined to build her life in Sacramento City, but she didn't believe that Dan should have to follow suit if he didn't want to. She smiled at Dan as he approached her and made ready to receive one of his long, warm hugs.

Dan did as she expected, but then he embraced her and kissed her passionately in a moment that seemed to Ginger, as she looked on with envy, to last forever. He held her and said, "I love you, Kate, and I'm not going anywhere unless you tell me to." It was as if he could read her mind. Kate was flabbergasted as she watched Dan leave for the day.

"You're blushing, Kate," Ginger teased. "I can't believe this. Rufus has been snooping around me for weeks and has never done more than kiss my hand. What do you suppose that silly man is thinking?" Ginger complained.

"Maybe it's time for you to take charge of the situation. Do to him what Dan just did to me," Kate suggested.

"Oh, I don't think so, Kate," Ginger said downheartedly.

"Forget the past, Ginger. The man is just shy and uncertain of himself, not you."

Della came out to the clothesline with a smile on her face that stretched from ear to ear. The other ladies had never seen her smile one time since they had known her. She was quiet and kept to herself. She worked hard and tried to stay away from people, even the other girls. If she had to be near another human being, she mostly listened, never contributing much to the conversation. Ginger and Kate observed her smile but didn't comment on it. They had always been frightened of the young woman. Rose's plan had consisted of Kate luring Bill into a bath, with Dan's consent, of course. Kate had been very surprised and grateful when Della suddenly took the chore upon herself.

Della had Bill's buckskins and hat in her hands along with a few of his undergarments. She hung the buckskins and hat on the clothesline and threw the underwear on the fire. Still smiling, she took up the rug beater and went to work. Ginger and Kate hurried away with their clean sheets but stopped before they entered the back door to watch as the cloud of filth enveloped Della.

Kate held her hand to her mouth and shook her head. "Do you think she was smiling because she hoped to ruin the sheets with the dirt that she is beating out of those clothes?"

"I don't think so," Ginger said with certainty. "If you ruined sheets that she had washed, she would kill you."

"Go ask her what she's smiling about," Kate said.

"I'm not going to ask that girl anything, Kate, but it's nice to see her smile. She almost looks human," Ginger retorted.

Kate and Ginger both jerked out of their skin when they heard Bill. His room was next to Rose's and was also equipped with a balcony. He was standing on it, hollering at Della. His naked body was as white as snow, except for his chest and groin that was covered with hair. "Well, woman, here I am without any clothes! Now what are you going to do with me?"

Kate and Ginger giggled. Della scowled at the silly man, dropped the rug beater, and pointed at him with a worn finger. "You get your silly, hairy ass in that tub, Mr. Ford!"

"It ain't summertime yet!" Bill hollered in defiance.

"It damned sure is close enough!" Della argued. The two of them had a staring contest for a few minutes. This suited Bill right down to the ground. He smiled at the young woman, and her eyes softened. He finally returned to the privacy of his room, reluctantly climbed into the tub of tepid water, and started scrubbing.

Della went back to her chore, and her smile returned.

"I guess we have our answer to the big mystery," Kate whispered.

Ginger's eyes grew wide. "Oh, mercy, you must be joking."

"Don't take my word for it, go ask her."

"Never mind, it's easier to take your word for it."

Della quickly turned to look at the two girls who were talking about her, and they scurried away into the hotel.

*****

It was all that Rose could do to keep Bud and Blossom entertained and away from her balcony door while Bill was out there, showing off for Della. She didn't really have anything for them to do, so while Bill was outside, they sang a song. They kept this up until the children knew the song by heart.

Finally, Della passed by on her way to Bill's room, and Rose stopped her. "Pardon me, I'm sorry to be such a bother, but would you please go out and purchase some writing slates for the children? They will draw on the walls if we don't find something for them to do. I should have thought about this before my husband left this morning."

Della boldly stepped into Rose's room and scrutinized the twins. The kids stopped what they were doing immediately and quietly looked back at her, wondering what they had done to deserve her unnerving attention. "Do these children belong to you?" Della was confused. Rose had been there for some time now, and Della hadn't seen the children before.

"No, they belong to Mr. Ford. We found them after they had been orphaned," Rose explained.

"Then Mr. Ford doesn't have a wife?" Della said gleefully.

"No, he doesn't have a wife." Rose smiled, knowing why Della was inquiring.

Della looked at the children again and left the room, continuing on with what she was doing and never agreeing to anything about the writing slates. Rose figured she was too busy and hoped that Kate or Bennager would check on her soon.

Bill was mildly surprised to have Della burst through his door. He had hoped she would but never expected it to happen. "I burned your old, worn-out underwear, Mr. Ford. I'm on my way to the mercantile to replace them. Is there anything else that I could get for you while I'm there?" Della said as she laid the buckskins on the bed and then turned to face him.

Bill felt like a little boy for the first time since he had been one. He was in a vulnerable situation, and the most beautiful woman left on earth was staring him in the eye. The only thing that he wanted was to be out of the tub of water and into the bed with her.

"Cat got your tongue, Mr. Ford?" Della said, knowing full well that her intimidation tactic seemed to be working.

Bill stood up in the tub, exposing himself to her. "Here, let me give you some money for my new underwear. It's about time that I had a new pair before I head for the Rockies," Bill said softly as he walked across the room to his saddlebags, reached over, and picked them up. He stepped up toe to toe with Della and handed the money to her. "Will that be enough?"

Della had admired his lean, muscular body, but her eyes held with his. "Mrs. Rasmussen asked for writing slates for your children. This will be enough for those too." Della put her hand on Bill's neck. His body throbbed, but he wouldn't show it. "You had better get back in the tub, Mr. Ford. You've missed a spot."

Bill could feel her breath. It was alarming to him as to how badly he wanted this woman. He wanted to take her, but her youth made him think twice. "I'll cut your hair and beard when I get back, Mr. Ford. I won't be gone for more than a few minutes." Somehow, to Bill's ears, she made her words sound seductive. Bill was stunned. She intended to come back. There was hope yet.

*****

The Sierras had finally been blessed with warm weather, even though the valley temperatures had been mild. The rivers had started to swell and become dangerous for the ferrymen and any man who dared to cross the smaller rivers on foot. Tomas sent Zeb into Sacramento City to tell his boss that they would be delayed at the American River. Zeb didn't argue. Even though Tomas had never seen the American River before, they could tell when they left the Cosumnes that Tomas was right. Stud Colt confirmed what the rivers were like this time of year. They had all hoped for the snow melt to wait for them to cross the river, but Mother Nature waited for nothing. There would be plenty of grass for the cattle to graze until the river receded, but the men needed supplies.

Zeb arrived in Sacramento City only an hour after Bill and Pablo. Henry had caught up with Zeb just before he got to town.

"Well, well! How do, Hank? Did your arms give out?" Zeb teased.

"Nope, but that ferry was still too close to my stepfather. He found me, whipped me, and tried to haul me back home. I think I'll venture out a little farther than his old mule can travel this time."

"That explains your banged up face," Zeb said with a smile.

"Where in tarnation is that crazy Ol' Bill?" Henry asked.

"I'm hoping he is still in town here. I need his help getting supplies to Tomas. They're going to have to hold the cattle on the south bank until the river recedes," Zeb said. "Where are you headed?"

"Nowhere in particular."

"Good, you can help me gather up what we need and find Bill," Zeb suggested.

"That shouldn't be too hard," Henry chuckled.

Zeb and Henry saw Pablo's wagon at the livery but continued on toward the closest mercantile that they could find. Henry finally had some money in his pocket for the first time in his life and rushed into the building. As he jovially looked back at Zeb for being slow, he ran into Della. She scowled at him as he gasped for air at the sight of her ample, curvaceous body. She wanted to slap him senseless for the way he was looking at her, never once making eye contact. Grudgingly, she only pushed him aside and walked away. This was why Della hated people and kept to herself. Men had been looking at her like that since she was twelve years old, and jealous girls had been talking about her for just as long.

Henry watched her with delight until she closed the hotel door behind her. "Did you see that?" he asked Zeb excitedly.

"First of all, she wasn't 'a that.' And second, that was a pure, 100 percent witch woman. You'd be smart to stay away from her, Hank. She made the hairs on my neck stand up."

Henry followed Zeb into the store and looked around while Zeb inquired about the Rasmussens. The storekeeper told him what he knew, and Henry was jumping for joy when he heard they were going to the hotel where he had last seen the girl of his dreams. Zeb gave the man an order to fill, and they headed across the street.

Kate met them in the lobby. "Hello, gentlemen, and welcome."

Zeb held his hat in his hand and elbowed Henry to do the same. Henry didn't take his eyes from Kate's breasts as Zeb said, "Howdy, miss, I'm looking for Mrs. Rasmussen."

"Of course, right this way, sir."

Zeb was embarrassed by Henry and told him to wait on the porch and behave. "Mrs. Rasmussen doesn't need a room full of visitors."

Kate smiled at the young man's disappointment, and led Zeb up the stairs.

"Zeb, you're here already," Rose said in a bittersweet tone. The cattle were already in Sacramento, and she was missing out on all the fun. Zeb sat down in a chair next to the bed, and the children climbed on his lap.

"How are you feeling, Rose?"

"I'm bored to death and mad as hell about missing all the fun. Tell me what happened in Stockton," Rose demanded.

"I don't recall anything happening in Stockton, Rose," Zeb lied.

"Oh, bullshit, Pete Harlan gave me a letter telling me what was going to happen and for me to get Bennager out of town. Bill's life depended on it he said, now tell me!" Rose laughed again over Pete's concern.

"Oh, Lord, Rose, you should have been there! You would have loved it!"

*****

Della walked in on Bill again. He admired her boldness. She looked down at him. "Did you wash your hair, Mr. Ford?"

"I did my best, Miss Della."

"Would you like me to cut your hair while you're in the tub?"

"As you wish, Miss Della."

Della pulled a chair around to the foot of the tub. "Let me see your feet," she said as she pulled up one side of her dress, revealing her leg.

Bill wondered why she did that and what she was up to, and then she began to cut his toenails. "Miss Della," Bill said in a whisper. "While you were gone, I remembered why I came here." Bill paused, not wanting to tell her.

"You came here for women. I'm not deaf, Mr. Ford."

"I came here to kill my brother, Miss Della. Where is he? Where is Douglas?"

Della didn't look up from her work. "Douglas Weatherford is dead."

"Are you sure? Are you sure that he didn't just crawl off somewhere?"

"I'm sure, Mr. Ford," Della said, looking into his eyes. "He died from the injuries that were given to him by a big Irishman." There was a long pause as Bill admired Della's lovely hands and the way she used them to touch him.

Bill smiled. "What do you do besides cut toenails?"

"These are the first toenails that I have ever cut other than my own, Mr. Ford. It's important for you to know that. Kate ended up with the hotel, and we all work here." Della looked at Bill again. "I repeat, we work here. We aren't whores anymore, Mr. Ford. We keep the rooms, cook, do the laundry, keep the yard, and scrub the floors, walls, and ceiling." There was a long pause as Della concentrated on her work. "By the way, Mr. Ford," Della said as she slid the chair to the middle of the tub and took his hand to work on his fingernails, "we heard what happened in Stockton, and Nancy is very worried about the cattle destroying her garden when they pass through here."

"Are Nancy's eyes as gorgeous as yours are?" Bill asked in a whisper.

"I wouldn't know, Mr. Ford, but I can assure you that they will be red with anger if the cattle trample that garden of hers," Della said with a smile. "Give me your other hand."

Bill sighed as he watched the witching woman at her task. "There's no need to bring the cattle through town. I've been taking a perfectly good trail to the rancho that is east of here."

"Oh, you've been by here before then?"

"Yes, a couple of times now."

"We could have met sooner," Della said as she coaxed Bill to lean forward so she could wash his back.

"Miss Della." Bill chuckled and stood up. "I appreciate your attention, but I've bathed long enough for one day. I'm sure that I have things to do."

"Yes, Mr. Ford, you have to get your haircut now," Della said as she stood up from her chair to meet Bill's eyes.

"Girl, you don't understand, if you're still in this room a minute from now, I'm going to make love to you!" Bill was exasperated with want. "Now you better get going before I find a way to embarrass you!"

Della turned her back while Bill put on his long underwear. She smiled to herself and said, "I'll give you your haircut outside on the balcony then, Mr. Ford."

She heard Bill growl and knew that she might be pushing the man beyond his limit but refused to leave. She had to know how a man who called himself Horny Bill Ford would conduct himself when faced with a temptress. She never considered herself to be such a thing until this morning when she saw the man that everyone had talked about all week. Della had quietly listened to stories of Bill's bold, amusing recklessness and thought of how nice it would be to meet someone interesting for a change. She had already decided before Bill arrived that if he was at all decent, then he would be hers. She hesitated to be too bold, though, since her last bold action had landed her with a scoundrel, but Weatherford had never gotten around to using her, and neither had anyone else. Weatherford had tried once out on the overland trail, but for some reason, he changed his mind and never bothered her again. In his employment, she had taken care of the gambling hall, and that was all until Dan put her to work at the hotel.

"Are you still here?" Bill growled.

Della smiled and waved her scissors. "Please let me give you a haircut, Mr. Ford."

Bill came to her and grabbed her around the waist. "You're a brave girl to stay here after I warned you of what would happen." He looked into her smiling eyes as moments passed between them. "I know I must be a frightful sight, but I reckon my haircut will have to wait. If you keep touching me, I'll burst and make an old fool out of myself."

"The hair goes, Mr. Ford." Della couldn't stop smiling.

*****

Henry recognized Bennager walking on the side of the street with two other men and rushed over to talk to him. The daily street fight hadn't commenced yet, and the men were visiting, getting to know the new faces. Bennager had led Pablo to the bathhouse, and the men were staying in the vicinity, waiting for him to finish and join them.

"Howdy, Mr. Rasmussen, do you remember me?" Henry asked.

Bennager gave him a long look. "Well, hello Hank, did your pa catch up with you down on the ferry?"

"Yes, sir, he did, and I'm looking for work."

"All right, Hank, but why didn't you stay with the herd?"

"I figured if that old vaquero could run Bill off then he would probably run me off too. I thought I should ask you first anyway. I was hoping that I could go to the rancho to work. Do you think that fella would let me help him?"

"I have a better idea, Hank. How would you feel about hauling freight?"

"All right, I reckon, as long as I didn't have to haul it on my back."

"Since Bill is here now, I think I'll have him look after Rose while I go up north and put a couple of teams together." The men found some shade and sat down. Henry was thinking of how he could get inside the hotel while Bennager tried convincing him and Dan into driving freight wagons with him. Dan was reluctant to agree until he talked to Kate about it. He had his claim and now a good job offer, but he was afraid that Kate wouldn't want him to leave.

"I'll tell you what," Henry proposed. "If you'll get me into that hotel, I'll do whatever you say, Mr. Rasmussen. I saw a damned fine-looking woman go in there this morning, and I want to see her again!"

Dan and Rufus stood up, but Henry didn't notice. Bennager smiled and prepared to witness the first fight of the day. "So you're already sweet on a girl, huh, Hank?"

"Oh, you got that right. Zeb called her a fearful witch or something, but I want her to be the mother of my children."

"Did you ever have a mother, Hank?" Dan smiled broadly.

"Yeah, for a little while."

"What did this woman look like?" Rufus asked.

"She had big tits, wide hips, and long hair!" Henry said excitedly.

The three men raised their brows at Henry's description. "Was she short?" Rufus asked.

"Was she blonde?" Dan asked.

Henry's mind was hard at work to recall the details. Finally, he said, "I think she had long dark hair."

"Oh." Rufus and Dan sat back down. Dan shook his head. "I think you're talking about Della. Forget it, kid, Zeb's right, you're in over your head. That girl won't talk to anybody. She might be mute. I've never heard her say a word."

"Yeah, I've seen her. No man in his right mind would approach her. You say you seen her today?" Rufus asked.

"Yeah, I bumped into her coming out of the mercantile," Henry said.

Dan and Rufus looked at each other quizzically. Rufus said, "She never shops!" Dan nodded in agreement. "We can take you over to meet Nancy and Belle, if you want, but you'd be wasting your time looking for Della. She's like a ghost!" Rufus assured.

Henry was ready to meet anybody. He wasn't picky. "Well, let's go then!"

"We'll go over for a minute, but then you'll have to help us for the rest of the day," Bennager said.

"Zeb told me I have to help him," Henry said.

"Where is Zeb?" Bennager asked.

"He's with Mrs. Rasmussen."

"Let's go see what he has for you to do that's so important."

When Bennager walked into Rose's room, he was surprised to see that she was visibly irritated and embarrassed. Bennager had never seen his wife embarrassed before. The French doors to the balcony were open, and he caught a glimpse of a man's leg. Something wild was happening on the other side of the wall. Rose looked up at her husband, rolled her eyes, shook her head, and then hid her face with her hand. The children were huddled together against the opposite wall because the noises that were coming from the room next door were strange and out of the ordinary. Bennager thought so too, but his first priority was to find out who was on the balcony.

He rushed out to see that it was Zeb. Zeb was trying to look through the French doors of the other room to spy on the couple next door. This was why his wife was embarrassed.

"Zeb, come away from there, for Christ's sake!" Bennager whispered as he noticed Ginger looking up at them from the clothesline.

"Shhh." Zeb put his finger to his lips and spat. "That's Bill in there!" Zeb giggled. "The old horny goat has been at it for half an hour."

"What?" Bennager elbowed Zeb over so he could look too but the curtains were too dark. They couldn't see anybody. "Who is he with?"

"Devil if I know!" Zeb whispered.

"I bet it's that girl we were just talking about who took his hand this morning," Bennager surmised.

"Is it the witch woman?" Zeb asked giggling.

"Yes," Bennager answered in a worried tone. "Come on." Bennager dragged Zeb into Rose's room where she was still holding her face.

"Would you please help me and the children downstairs?" Rose asked without making eye contact.

Bennager and Zeb went right to work. Zeb took the children and their slates and went to the lobby.

As Bennager helped Rose down the stairs, she said, "Zeb was telling me about how Tomas was holding the cattle at the American, and all hell broke loose in there! I can't tell you how awkward it was for Zeb and me to be sitting there, trying to have a civil conversation with all of that raunchy racket going on next door. You should have seen Zeb's face when I told him who it was." Rose held her back as she laughed, recalling how fast Zeb rushed out the French doors. "I guess the children have never heard the likes before either."

Bennager was impressed with ol' Bill. He found himself a woman and was living up to his reputation. Dan, Rufus, and Henry were in the kitchen. They were introducing Henry to Nancy and Belle. Nancy was too high strung to be introduced to anyone, and Belle didn't want to be bothered while she was polishing the wood. Dan cut Henry a big piece of pie. "I guess that's the best I can do for you, kid. Rufus and I have our hearts set on the other two," Dan said with a smile.

Henry ate his pie in four bites. "Pie will do for any reason. Thanks anyway."

"How was it?" Dan asked.

"Damned good!" Henry praised.

"How could you tell?" Rufus asked. The three headed for the lobby, and Henry shook hands with Rose.

"How are you feeling, Mrs. Rasmussen? I hear you have a broken rib after all."

"I'm doing all right, Hank, how about yourself?" Rose asked kindly. She could see by the marks on Hank's face why he had followed them.

"I'm looking for a woman and a job, Mrs. Rasmussen."

Rose nodded her head. "I heard that you had a hundred-dollar bet with my uncle that you'd be married before he was."

Dan and Rufus were looking at the ceiling and wondering why it was shaking. Rose sneaked a wink at Zeb as Henry answered her. "Oh yeah, I had a bet with that crazy old son of a bitch, but I won't hold him to it."

Rose couldn't help but smile as Bennager looked at the floor. "Hank, I reckon you missed gettin' here by one pitiful hour," Rose teased.

Kate came in from her Independence Day meeting. The town was already making plans for the celebration. "What in the world is going on here? From outside, it sounds like the walls are falling in. Did that crazy uncle of yours bring a bull in with him, Rose?"

Everyone laughed heartily, especially Rose. When she caught her breath, she said, "In a manner of speaking, Kate." And everyone laughed again, except Henry. He didn't get the joke.

Kate blushed and didn't know how to react. She pretended to have important business to do in her office. She knew she could get away with it since her arms were full of papers. She sat in her chair and looked at the ceiling. She smiled as she thought of how Della had finally met her match and would probably be following Horny Bill Ford out of town. When Ginger could convince Rufus to be less shy, she would lose another lady. She wondered how she would ever find someone to replace them.

She heard a gentle tap at the door. "Come in."

Dan had a look in his eye that made her smile. She could see that he was being inspired by the commotion coming from the second floor. She could also see that he was going to kiss her again whether she was busy or not. Kate stood up from her chair, and they embraced each other.

"I love you, Kate." Dan couldn't stop saying it now that he knew for sure how he felt, and he wanted Kate to believe it. He continued to hold her. "It sounds like Della won't be around for much longer."

"Who told you that?" Kate whispered.

"The walls told me, Kate."

Kate blushed, and Dan chuckled. "They're just doing what we should have been doing a long time ago, if I hadn't been so stupid." Dan moved a lock of hair out of Kate's face and admired her beauty. "Do you doubt my love for you, Kate?"

"No, but I doubt that you will stay in this town with me day after day."

"What would be the harm in leaving for a few days at a time as long as you knew that I loved only you and I would come back?"

"I want to have a family, Dan. I think a father should be at the supper table every night. I cannot raise children by myself," Kate whispered.

Dan looked into her eyes, filling with disappointment. "I can see your point, Kate. You are right, but the question is, do you want me to be their father?"

"If living in this town is going to cause you to drink hard, then the answer is no, Dan." Kate was a negotiator and a great business-woman, and she didn't hesitate to employ her tactics.

"Will you ever trust me to never drink again?" Dan asked, feeling like Kate might not give him a chance.

"We would have to see how you do, Dan."

"How long will we have to watch, Kate?" Dan's anger was starting to show.

Kate pushed away, and Dan let her go. Dan thought about the situation for a moment and said, "Perhaps you don't love me, Kate. Just because I'm in love with you doesn't mean that you feel the same way."

Kate didn't answer. Dan waited, and his heart sank with every second that passed by. The times he had shared with Kate flashed in front of his eyes. He had hurt her, probably more times than he knew, and he could never make those times up to her. He didn't love her soon enough. They had agreed to be friends with no chance of anything more. Dan had been thankful for the friendship, knowing that it was his fault they couldn't have more. His rueful words had ruined his life. He had already pictured in his mind what their children would look like and act like and grow up to be like, and their mother didn't love or trust him. Maybe she thought she could do better. Maybe Gowans had found out about Dan's confessed love and had made her a better offer.

"Well, I love you, Kate. I want you to be the mother of my children. I want us to raise a family full of lawyers or doctors or whatever they want to be. I'll be home for supper every night like a good pa should be." Dan paused and swallowed hard. "I guess you can send word to me at my claim if I'm the man for the job, Kate. I can't sit around this town, watching you traipse up and down the boardwalk planning your celebrations and government meetings, not knowing how you feel about me. At least if I'm at the claim, I can pretend that you think of me once or twice a day." Dan's impatience was his downfall in life. He knew it as he slammed every door between him and the livery.

Pablo thought Dan to be a curious sight as he marched by him. Pablo was also curious about the noise coming from inside and wondered if the two were connected. Pablo walked in the hotel and looked up at the ceiling in a confused way and then noticed the people who had taken up residence in the lobby. He noticed that Bill was not among them, and then he smiled when he saw Rose. "Hola, Mrs. Rasmussen, you look rested," he said as he took her hand and kissed her cheek.

"Thank you, señor, how has your adventure been so far?" Rose asked.

"It has been interesting. I would have never believed that all these men had come here unless I saw it for myself." Pablo looked at the ceiling, pointed to it, and smiled. "Is that my friend, Bill Ford?"

Zeb answered, "Yes, Bill is with one of the witch women in this town."

"Is he with my witch woman?" Henry was incredulous.

Zeb and Bennager both nodded their heads.

"Well, that dirty, old, rotten son of a bitch! I saw her first!" Henry declared.

"Come on, Hank, we have to get those supplies over to Tomas' camp," Zeb said, getting up. Henry complained about Bill taking his woman all the way out the door and across the street.

*****

Rufus watched the livery as the others chatted about Bill, the condition of the river and the cattle. He had a feeling that Dan was leaving town, and fifteen minutes later, his suspicions were confirmed.

"You just lost a freight hauler, Ben. Dan just lit out, heading for his claim, I reckon," Rufus said as he sat back down.

"Huh, I was hoping that he would take Pete's wagon back to Stockton for me," Bennager said.

"Oh, the rivers are too full," Pablo said. "The ferryman at the Cosumnes said that your cook wagon was the last one that he would take for a while."

"Are you going back to hauling freight, dear?" Rose asked her husband.

"I was hoping to. I could be making a fortune right now if I had a couple more teams. I was going to ride up north while you were resting, get my teams, and put Dan and Hank to work."

"You were going to leave me here by myself?"

"No, not a chance, you'd figure a way onto the back of that biting horse and head for home where there aren't any doctors."

"I heard the Roman helps you to keep the peace in this town," Rose smiled proudly.

"You have big ears, don't you?" Bennager smiled sheepishly. "I thought I could have Bill look after you. It was a risky thought, though, even before he met Miss Della. I guess there will still be freight to haul in a couple of weeks," Bennager said cheerfully without regret.

"It seems like a shame to miss out on making money," Rose said, thinking of profit. The wheels were turning in her mind. "We still have Pete's wagon. Why don't you just take me home in it?"

"There wouldn't be room for the cattle for all the miners that would follow us home! I'm sure it would please them to see you move your operation to the foothills, my love," Bennager said, backed by mischief in his eyes. Rufus blushed at the reference to Rose operating a whorehouse while Pablo continued to watch the ceiling.

"What could that man be doing to that poor girl?" Pablo asked in bewilderment.

No one was willing to answer the question that he posed. The men didn't want to speak of the witch woman, and Rose didn't want to think about it. If Bennager wasn't so hell bent on her lying around, she would have been long gone by now.

Rose sighed. "Miners or not, if you take me home, then I will promise to rest until I'm healed. You can tell Angus and Trina to shoot me dead if I don't. Bill's apt to be here with Della forever, and I'm not going to lie in my room and listen to that racket for the next two weeks. Take me home and go make some money," Rose demanded.

"Do you want to go right now?" Bennager asked as a loud feminine screech came from overhead.

Rose couldn't hold a straight face. She smiled with partial amusement and fractional embarrassment and said loudly, "Yes, get me the hell out of here! If I leave now, I won't have any reason to climb those stairs again, and I'm already at the front door."

Bennager looked at Pablo. "I guess I'll get the wagon and pack it up. Do you think there is any way that you could talk Bill into coming downstairs so we can tell him our plans? We need to make sure that Tomas is covered for his delay, and we need to make sure that Bill is not too occupied to take care of the children. The witch woman might have taken his brain out when he wasn't watching."

"It sounds like he is starting to wear down. I will see if he can be available," Pablo said with a smile, hoping to catch a peek at Della.

"Thank you, Pablo." Bennager kissed his wife and left to prepare for the trip.

*****

Kate came out of hiding when the hotel stopped moving. "Is there anything that I can get for you, Rose?"

"No, thank you, Kate." Rose could see that she had been crying. "Bennager has decided to take me home. We're going to leave shortly. I think Bill will follow, but I can't make it a promise, I'm afraid. I'm sorry if he has embarrassed the reputation of your hotel."

"I don't think too many people noticed," Kate said as she sat down. "Della sure did surprise me," Kate whispered. "I never thought she would let a man touch her. Weatherford never even attempted to cross her."

Rose looked away at the mention of her father. "Well, Della must like crazy, old, hairy mountain men, I guess."

"I doubt we will ever know, Rose. She's not the kind of girl I would want to question." Kate looked at her hands as she wrung them together. "Will Mr. Ford take Della away with him or leave her behind?"

Rose looked at Kate then. "I was wondering the same thing, Kate. What would Della do if he left without her?"

"I don't know." Kate couldn't think of Della anymore. She thought of what she should do about Dan leaving her behind and if he would come back if she asked him to. She feared that she had demanded too much from Dan Dunaway. She feared that she had hurt him, maybe as much as he had hurt her in the past. She watched the Yokut Indian children play quietly and draw, and her heart was torn between the life that she thought she wanted and the exciting, rewarding life that she thought she had now.

Bill and Della came downstairs, hand in hand, and Kate disappeared again. Pablo followed behind, and Rose noticed that her uncle hadn't gotten around to having his haircut yet. She had to bite her tongue not to mention it.

"Hello, Uncle," Rose said with a personable smile.

"Hello, Little Rose. Pablo tells me that you're going on ahead to the rancho."

"Yes, I promised that I would rest there. Bennager wants to get back to hauling freight. He's going to put your friend Hank to work. Tomas is going to graze the cattle along the side of the river until it recedes, and I was hoping that you could see to him being well provisioned and take care of the expenses before the outfit leaves out of here."

Bill squinted at Della and then at Rose. "How long have I been here?"

Rose squinted back. "Just a couple of hours. Why do you ask?"

"Is Tomas at the American already?"

"No, he sent Zeb up ahead."

"Where did Hank come from?"

"His pa ran him off again. He got here this morning," Rose explained.

Bill scratched his head. "I was planning on heading for the Rockies." He looked admiringly at Della. "I guess it can wait a little longer," he said softly and kissed her young hand.

"Uncle, I want you to personally guarantee me that nothing will happen to Nancy's garden or to anything else in this town resembling what happened in Stockton," Rose said, trying not to smile.

"I have no more scores to settle, Little Rose."

Rose thought of the daily fights in the street and looked to Della. "You better keep him off the streets, Della. He'll have the town leveled within the week if you don't. Kate's already worried that she'll have to rebuild the second floor," Rose said boisterously.

Della only smiled from ear to ear, not commenting. Rose waited and watched at how Bill never let her hand go. She waited for him to say something even more outrageous and was surprised to see him quieted by the gorgeous young woman who was probably the same age as herself.

"Will you be able to tend the children, Williams?" Rose asked.

"You bet. I have plenty of help now. They will have the chance to get to know their new mother better if you're not around to spoil them."

Rose smiled at Della. "It looks like you're going to have your hands full," she said as Bennager walked in to start packing their things. "Is my wagon out there, Uncle?"

"Yep, your bed awaits you."

"Help me out there then. I'm ready to see my new home." Rose looked at Della and shook hands with her once she was on her feet. "I'll be seeing you again, I reckon. I'm trusting you to keep my uncle out of trouble, but don't take it too hard if you fail. It's an impossible task."

"Thank you, Mrs. Rasmussen. Take care of yourself," Della said with sincerity.

"I'll be right back, girl," Bill said as he lightly kissed the young woman.

Pablo didn't want to be alone with Della, so he followed Bill and Rose outside. Kate wasn't far behind as she wanted to say goodbye to someone she thought of as a friend.

Bill asked Rose, "How are you going to live without Bennager if he's off hauling freight?"

"I've held him up long enough with my dreams. He is a freight hauler. That's how he makes his living, and he likes it. I wouldn't have met him if he wasn't a freight hauler. I don't want him to feel that he needs to be on the rancho everyday if he doesn't want to be. Besides, while he's gone, he will miss me. Isn't that right, Pablo?"

"You'll need more help. You'll need more men if Bennager isn't there all of the time," Bill said with worry.

"I reckon I'll steal some of Pablo's men. If they won't stay, then I'll find others. The foothills are crawling with men, Uncle."

Bennager made his first trip out with their trappings and then went back for the rest of it as Bill helped Rose into the wagon.

Rose gave Bill some money to see the vaqueros through. "By God, Uncle, don't let any of the calves drown in that river because that's the last of it."

"No wonder why you want your husband to go back to work," Bill said sarcastically. "Don't worry, Little Rose, you married a wealthy man."

"I did?" Rose acted surprised by Bill's statement.

"I can see that he failed to mention that he was rich." Bill laughed.

"He is?"

Bennager crawled up on the wagon seat. "I guess we'll be seeing you up on the Yuba, gentlemen. I'm glad to have met you, Kate."

"Goodbye, Mr. Rasmussen. Goodbye, Rose." Kate waved as Bennager rolled up the street. She thought of what Rose had said to her uncle about her husband being away from home. She thought of Dan and wondered if she would ever see him again.

10

————

Angus and Trina were on the roof of the two-story house, nailing shingles on it, when Bennager and Rose rolled into the yard with Dan leading the way. Dan had stopped at the Bear River to poke around when the couple caught up with him. Angus and Trina hadn't even noticed them arrive. They were on opposite sides of the roof, and each time they checked each other's work, an argument would commence over the way each one of them was doing their job.

"You should stagger the light-colored ones with the dark-colored ones so it looks like a basket weave," Trina hollered.

"Shut up, woman! Don't tell me 'bout me shingles. They will be the same color within a month of the sun beatin' down on 'em. Ye have to stop puttin' the thin side down ye silly red head."

"I'm not, you blind Irishman!" Trina shouted.

"Ye are. Ye are so worried 'bout the weavin' that ye aren't payin' attention to what side goes up!" Angus bellowed.

"Like hell I'm not!" Trina screamed and stood up with a handful of shingles and started throwing them at Angus' head.

Girl had been out with her pups and heard the argument escalate. She ran back to the house to referee and was startled by the newcomers. She began to bark viciously, and Trina stopped to see what was going on. Angus stood up to see the curious sight of the Rasmussens and the man from Sacramento City who he had met in Grass Valley.

"Dia duit!" Angus waved. Everyone smiled and waved back as they dismounted. Girl was still upset and ran onto the porch of the house to protect it from the intruders.

Trina looked at Angus in amazement as they headed for the ladder. "Did your Mrs. Rasmussen turn into a queen while she was gone? I pictured her having her nose in the air, but I never imagined her being carted around on a bed, for heaven's sake."

"Quiet, woman! She's not a queen, she's probably hurt. Mind your tongue."

"Oh, yes, sir." Trina felt her jealousy return. She had always wondered if Angus would change once Rose Rasmussen got there.

Bennager was in awe of the sight before him. He hadn't imagined anything more than a tiny log cabin and a six-horse stalled stable. Nothing was finished yet, not even close, but the buildings were framed, and the boards were up on the outside walls of the house. Bennager's freight wagon was loaded with shingles, and his team was grazing in the newly built corrals. The location of the place was beautiful, and there was already a small rose garden started on the southwest side of the house. Angus had sent away for the bushes the first day that he had gone to Grass Valley. They arrived a week after the well was finished.

Rose cried with joy as they approached the new house. She laughed and cried at Angus and Trina's spat and at seeing Girl again. Angus' face had been pale and battered badly the last time she had seen him, and now he looked healthy, well, and happy, just like the first day she had met him on Charlie's steamboat.

"Angus, it's so wonderful to see you again!" Rose cried with happiness and exhaustion. Rose was so overwhelmed with emotion that she couldn't stop crying.

Dan and Bennager had helped Rose down from the wagon while Angus and Trina were getting down from the roof. Angus could see that Rose was stiff and sore. He hesitated to hug her and only took her hand after he shook hands with Bennager.

"What has happened to ye, Mrs. Rasmussen?"

"Oh, for heaven's sake, don't call me that, you big Irish angel!" Rose kissed Angus on the cheek with tears streaming down her face. Rose saw the worry in his eyes and laughed. "Do you see that dun?" Rose said, pointing at her horse. "I call him the Roman. He's an evil, wicked critter. He bites and kicks, and he kicked me in the back a couple of weeks ago and broke one of my ribs. The only person in whole world that he likes is Bill's little boy. Bud talks to him in his native tongue, and the Roman does whatever the little boy asks."

"I thought it was somethin' like that or else I would have hugged ye and threw ye up in the air a time or two." Angus looked at Dan then and took in a deep breath. He held his hand out to the man, and he took it.

"Dan Dunaway," Dan said.

"I remember, Dan. How have ye been?" Angus asked.

"I'm down in the mouth at the moment. My Kate won't have me," Dan said bluntly since Kate was all that he thought about.

"Angus, I've known Dan since I was a small child. Did he tell you that?"

"Nay, I didn't know he knew ye, Rose Mary."

Rose looked at Trina and put her hand out.

Angus said proudly, "Rose Mary, I would like ye to meet me lovely wife, Trina Donovan." The ladies shook hands. "Trina has helped me with everythin' that has been done here."

Rose began to cry again as Bennager shook hands with the gorgeous, freckled, redheaded woman.

"You two have done a lot of work. Everything is wonderful. It's so much more than we could have imagined, Angus, I just can't believe it," Bennager remarked graciously.

Angus proudly put his arm around his wife and nodded. "We argued some 'bout how large the house should be. It's four times bigger than the house that I grew up in, but Trina said that ye would like it."

Bennager stroked Rose's hair as she continued to bawl. "I think that it's safe to say that we love it, Angus. The two of you do excellent work."

The five of them walked into the house. It was completely empty, and the inside walls weren't up yet. Only the studs separated the rooms. "Trina designed the inside, Rose Mary," Angus said as they stood in the foyer. Rose took Trina's hand. Trina smiled proudly as she showed Rose the kitchen and dining room. Angus was particularly proud of the blue rock fireplace that they had built. He told of hauling rocks up from his claim on the Yuba River and showed the men the gold nuggets that he had found while gathering the rocks. Remorsefully, he thought of his brothers but didn't speak of them.

After seeing the double fireplace that was on a wall in between the kitchen and living area, Trina took Rose to the bedroom that she and Bennager would occupy. Like the hotel in Sacramento City, it was to be equipped with French doors leading onto the wraparound porch that wasn't finished yet. The room was very spacious, and the morning sun would wake them and then be cool in the evenings. The windows faced east and north. Trina had thought of Rose raising her babies in this room and wanted her to have plenty of space. The upstairs consisted of three more modest-sized bedrooms, but Rose was too tired to explore them. The banister wasn't on the stairs yet, and she didn't want to risk falling on the way down.

"Well, we might as well move Pete's bed in here for you to lie on since we can't take it back to him," Bennager said to his wife. "I'll go to town tomorrow and order the furniture," he said as he made for the door.

"I've already ordered a bed and two chairs Mr. Rasmussen. They should be coming by the first part of next week," Trina said timidly. Angus had made her pick out and order an item that she felt was a personal thing to be picked out by the couple who would be using it. "If you don't like the bed, Rose, Angus and I will buy it from you," Trina said softly.

Rose smiled mischievously. "As long as it's sturdy, it will do, Mrs. Donovan."

Trina squinted at Rose's vulgar innuendo, and then she laughed heartily as the men blushed and went to get the bed.

"Dan, did you decide about hauling freight for me?" Bennager asked.

"Yeah, Ben." Dan smiled. "I'm sorry, but I've decided to stay at the claim in case Kate sends for me. She thinks I won't make a good pa because I wander around too much. If I'm not at the claim when she sends for me, her point will be proven, and I'll miss my chance."

"She seems like a hard woman to please, Dan," Bennager commented.

"It might be taking her some time to forget the past or it could be that she doesn't love me. I don't know. I can only hope for her to come around."

As Dan and Bennager hauled the bed in, Angus brought in the feather mattress. Angus commanded, "Quit flappin' your lips and get supper workin' for us, woman!"

Rose raised a brow at Angus' behavior but noticed the evil smiling eyes of Trina as she glared at her husband. Trina left to do as she was told but only because she was hungry, and it was well past suppertime.

Over supper, Angus and Trina talked of Rose's father for the last time. Rose assured him that he had done nothing wrong. Rose and Dan told of all the heinous things that the man had done in his life and how his long and painful death had been deserved.

They told of Bill and Della getting together, and Trina told them of her jealousy toward Della and how Doug had been too frightened to harm her.

Angus told of how Rose's money had run out, but every business that he had dealt with had extended credit to him in Bennager's name. He told of the friends they had made who were also friends with Bennager. Rose was delighted to hear about Jake Gate's complaints of Bennager's good fortune, and she was dying to see the town of Grass Valley.

A half hour before dark, Dan said his goodbyes and left for his claim. When he opened the door of the big empty house, Girl rushed past him, jumped on Rose's bed, and rested her chin on Rose's leg.

"Oh, so you remember me now!" Rose exclaimed.

Angus and Trina stayed and told of how the pups chase the squirrels and how Girl is waiting for the cattle to come. That led to stories of Pablo's rancho and the magnificent vaqueros. Bennager and Rose grudgingly told of Sam's murder and how Anna had been dead for two years.

Trina had spent the last two months reluctantly anticipating the arrival of Rose Mary Weatherford Rasmussen. She didn't realize it until today how much it had eaten on her nerves. She knew that Rose would look like her father, act like him, talk like him, eat like him, and it had driven her mad thinking of how she was working for someone like that and how she would leave the instant the woman arrived, no matter what Angus and Bill had assured her. Trina waited all evening and long past dark for Rose to show her resemblance, but Trina never saw it. Rose didn't favor her father in one single mannerism or expression, and she quickly determined that Rose wasn't the daughter of Weatherford. She just couldn't be as far as Trina was concerned, even though there was no way to prove it, and she would never say it out loud.

Everyone was tired, and the Donovans said their goodbyes and turned in for the night. Girl stayed in bed with Rose, and Bennager threw his bedroll on the floor. "I'm sorry my dreams have cut into your finances, Mr. Rasmussen. How long will you have to haul freight to pay for this house? The windows aren't even in yet." Rose was trying to get Bennager to confess that he was wealthy.

"You'll be able to pay for it yourself when you sell the calves." Bennager stripped down in front of his wife in the moonlight so she could see what she was missing. She had missed out on everything that was fun, and Bennager liked to rub it in. "We'll make out all right with the payments until then," he said.

Rose had taken Kate's advice and gave her $2,000 to invest in city lots in Sacramento City. Rose figured that she would make more monetary gain from that than she would with the cattle.

Bennager smiled as he lay down on top of his bedroll and thought of his investment with Matthew Harrison and how much lumber Angus had purchased. The price of lumber had climbed considerably in the last year from four cents a board foot to a dollar. Bennager hoped that Angus wasn't Matt's only client. He couldn't wait to check on Jake Gates and Matt. He couldn't wait for them to meet his wife who would soon be known as the cattle baron of the foothills.

There was much to do over the next week. He had to help Angus with the roof, get a look at the property, and go to Grass Valley and drink beer with his old friends. He heard Rose start to snore as he wondered what the price of wheat was up to now, and he couldn't wait to see Hugh Glenn and have Hank help him round up two more teams and wagons. It was good to be home. Tomorrow would be the beginning of a long, good life with the woman that he loved.

*****

Angus and Trina were up and moving the next morning at the usual time, even though they had stayed up later than usual the night before. Bennager was awakened by Girl when she jumped out of bed and onto him in her quest to help Angus fry bacon. It had become their morning ritual. No matter what, Angus fried bacon every morning. Bennager slipped his pants on and let the whining dog out.

Bennager finished dressing and went out to sit with Angus. Rose was still sleeping, and she needed her rest. He nodded to Trina who was tending the coffee and who looked as fresh as morning dew and dressed for another day of work.

"Angus, you said that you ran out of Rose's money. How much do I owe you folks for what you've done for us?"

Angus chuckled. "I've been payin' Trina her $5 a week that I promised. She said she'd leave me if I didn't. We only ran out a couple of weeks ago."

Bennager looked around at all the couple had accomplished, and he looked back at Trina who was unconcerned about the conversation until she noticed the man staring at her. She looked him in the eye and smiled. "Five dollars a week, huh?" Bennager laughed heartily as Trina scowled at him and then at her husband. "Angus, do you remember me telling you that you would one day be a rich man, erecting brick buildings?"

Angus laughed as he recalled their conversation on the steamboat. He hadn't thought of it since he left Sacramento City. He had only dreamed of the place he would create for his friends to grow old together in. "Aye, that was a long time ago."

"Well, you won't get rich charging $5 a week, old man." Bennager laughed. "Let's throw these shingles up on the roof and go to town. I need to see some men in Grass Valley, and then I want to go over to Jake's."

"All right, woman, you tend to breakfast," Angus said as the men stood up.

Trina glared at the men as she hadn't had her coffee yet.

"Mrs. Donovan, will you see to it that my wife stays in bed? She promised me that she would rest if I brought her home, but I didn't believe her for a minute. She'll be up trying to get her strength back so she can go up on the roof or some such nonsense. I'd be obliged to you if you would do this for me," Bennager requested.

"Surely, Mr. Rasmussen, I could use a day off anyway, although I doubt it's Sunday."

"Thank you, Mrs. Donovan."

Angus and Bennager grabbed a handful of fried biscuits and bacon and left with the wagon just as the sun broke over the horizon.

Trina fixed plates for her and Rose that were filled with cheese, dried fruit, fried potatoes, eggs, and bacon. She set them down on the sawhorse table that she and Angus had set up the night before and went back for coffee. By the time she got back, Rose was awake and sitting up.

"Our men went to town already, Rose."

"My husband is glad to be back home. I reckon he'll spend the day drinking beer with Angus and his other friends."

Trina laughed at the idea of Angus being in a saloon. "The only time my husband was ever in a saloon in Grass Valley was when he pried the well-diggers out to go to work for us here."

Rose raised her brow and chuckled. "Well, maybe we'll luck out then."

"Your husband asked me to make sure that you stay in bed and rest," Trina confessed.

Rose nodded her head. "I'm sure he did. He doesn't believe my promises, but I'm determined to heal up and be back on my feet when the cattle arrive." Rose shook her head. "It's been damned exasperating having to lie on my back like this. Since I've hit land, I've had one accident after another, most of them due to that crazy horse out there," Rose whispered when she said it, thinking that the Roman or Bennager might hear her.

The ladies talked for the better part of an hour and then they heard a rider coming at a fast pace. Rose checked her pistol, which surprised Trina, and then nodded her head. Trina opened the front door to see that it was Jake.

"Hello, Jake, how are the pigs doing?" Trina smiled. "I haven't seen you since the day Angus and I got married."

Jake walked up on the porch. "Well, I was pretty sore about that, Mrs. Donovan. It took some time to get over it." Jake chuckled. He seemed to be in good spirits for a change. "Where's Angus? It's time to cut the pigs, and I was wondering if he would help me out."

"He's already gone off to town, Jake. Come in and have a cup of coffee with Mrs. Rasmussen," Trina said leading the way.

"I'll be damned! Bennager finally made it back!" Jake exclaimed. "Where did he go, Grass Valley?"

"Yes, he's gone visiting with Angus. They were going to visit you tonight," Trina explained.

Jake saw Rose lying on the bed and quickly took off his hat. "Ah, that rotten son of a bitch!" he whispered, but the ladies still heard him and smiled. Jake rushed over and shook hands with Rose. "Your husband is the luckiest son of a bitch I know, ma'am."

"Thank you, Mr. Gates."

"He's a good man, ma'am, you've married well. I can't stay for coffee. I've got to catch up with those two. It's a pleasure meeting you." Jake stuffed his hat back on his head and raced away.

"I bet the pigs don't get cut today," Trina said, shaking her head.

Rose's eyes sparkled. "I bet your husband comes home drunk too."

Trina sighed and nodded her head. "I bet you're right."

*****

Jake caught up with his friends while they were climbing the long and arduous Pet Hill. They all arrived in Grass Valley before noon and went straight to the lumber mill. Bennager had to wait for Matt to see him and turn off the saw.

"Hello, Matt!" Bennager hollered.

"How do, stranger? You son of a bitch. I suppose you want your wife's money back!" Matt said with a hearty handshake.

Angus and Jake left to load more lumber in the freight wagon while Bennager, and Matt went to the office.

"How's business, Matt?" Bennager asked.

"You're a wealthy man, Benny. Have you heard what the lumber prices are these days?"

"Yep, I have. That's good because I'm just about tapped out. I want to go over to Glenn's and Bidwell's and pick up a couple more teams and wagons. The valley is booming with freight to be hauled. Can you give me some money?"

Matt laughed robustly. "I can't give you any money. It's all at the bank. Why do you want to haul freight anyway? You're a rich man, Benny. Why don't you stay home and look at your wife?"

"My feet are itching, Matt. I miss the life. Did you say there's a bank here now?"

"Yeah, old Dixon finally built a bank."

"Did he buy the lumber from you?"

"Yeah, but not as much as your wife did. His bank is about as big as this office." The men laughed about the banker being frugal.

"How much do I have in the bank, Matt?"

"Let me show you the books, Benny." Bennager was pleasantly surprised to see the figures, and the men talked of the recent population growth as Matt had his midday snack. Bennager could see through the office window that his friends were finished loading the wagon with one-by-twelves, and he prepared to go.

"Benny, I want to buy you out."

Bennager smiled at his friend. "I bet you do. Let me think about it for a while, all right?"

"All right, Benny, it's good to have you back," Matt said as he went back to work.

The next stop was the new bank. Bennager went in and opened an account for Angus and Trina and put $2,000 in it. He added Rose's name to his account and took out $1,000 for himself.

"Take good care of this, Angus," Bennager said when he handed Angus the bank book.

Angus almost wept. He wished that Trina had been with him at that very moment. "What do you boys say to having a drink?" Bennager asked.

"It sounds all right to me," Angus replied.

"I should be cutting pigs," Jake complained.

"We'll help you with the pigs tomorrow if you help us for a day on the house."

"I ain't much of a carpenter," Jake said, trying to get out of the deal.

"I know, I've seen that shack you live in," Bennager joked.

"If it wasn't for your rich wife, you'd never have a roof over your head," Jake reminded his lucky friend.

The men spent the better part of the afternoon drinking beer and catching Bennager up on the local events, and then they went to the mercantile. Bennager put in a large order of furniture and house wares to fill his home with Rose, and then they headed down the hill.

*****

Six days later, Bill, Della, and Hank showed up. Bill was ready to take his family to the Rockies, and Henry was eager to learn how to haul freight. Tomas wouldn't have him, and Sacramento City was too busy for his liking.

Trina busied herself outside when she saw Della coming. The roof had been completed three days earlier, and Bennager and Angus were working on the wraparound porch. Della and Trina simply glared at each other when their eyes met but said nothing.

Rose was feeling much better by this time and tried to convince her husband that she was completely healed, but he still wouldn't let her get out of bed.

"Did you take care of everything in Sacramento City?" Rose asked Bill.

"Yep, you're debt-free, the river is starting to recede, and Tomas is stocked with enough provisions to get him back to Pablo's, probably."

"What did you do with Pablo?"

"He's going to come along with the cattle. He's been camping with Tomas. I'm taking my family to the Rockies, Little Rose. This climate is too hot, humid, and populated to suit me."

Rose started to cry. "Will I ever see you again, Uncle?"

"You bet, I'll come back next fall. We'll camp out with the cattle over on the north side."

Rose laughed through her tears at how ridiculous her uncle was to expect Della to camp out for the rest of her life, regardless of what season it was.

"We plan on leaving in the morning, if that is all right with you Rose. Della is going to kill Hank if she has to look at him for another day."

"I thought you might lead the herd, Uncle."

"Stud Colt remembers the way."

"I can always do that," Bennager said, thinking of what a relief it was to hear that Bill was leaving them for a while, even though he had become more civilized now that he had Della by his side.

*****

Bill and his family left early the next morning. Rose bawled when her uncle kissed her on the cheek and then the children. Della smiled at Rose's sadness and shook her hand goodbye. Rose told Bill to take the Roman with him for Bud. Rose cried as she watched them all leave.

The men and Trina went to work that day, boarding up the walls on the inside of the house with the one-by-twelves. For the next two days, Rose felt like she was being assaulted in the ears by a flock of woodpeckers.

Bennager went to town on the second day for the windows and replacement glass that he would surely need before the place was finished. He didn't get all the windows on that trip, but he got enough for one side of the bottom floor.

Rose cried two or three times a day. She was overwhelmed with gratitude for the work that everyone was doing. She was filled with excitement about the cattle coming soon and everything finally coming to fruition so quickly. She was mad at herself for not being allowed to help, and she missed her uncle and the twins. She was consumed with worry about if she would really ever see him again, and she desperately wanted to see her property and meet her neighbors and see the towns.

"Hey, Bennager?" Angus said when they were putting in a window.

"Yeah?" Bennager queried.

"Why are those mountains sittin' in the middle of that valley down there? Anyone can see that they don't belong there. I think they are evil," Angus remarked.

"Oh my Lord, not this again!" Trina exclaimed as Bennager chuckled.

"Ye shut up, woman!" Angus told Trina.

"You big, silly, damned Irishman, how many times do I have to tell you that mountains aren't evil? They're just mountains!" Trina hollered, exhausted by her husband's obsession.

"I am not talkin' to ye, woman, shut your trap so Bennager can answer me!" Angus bellowed.

Rose painfully began to laugh hysterically at the conversation.

"They tell me the Sutter Buttes used to sit on top of the Tabletop Mountains over by the Feather River," Bennager said.

"What did they do? Grow wings and fly away?" Angus asked incredulously.

"They say a big slab of ice sheared them off, and they lit out there by the Sacramento River."

Angus' eyes widened.

"That would have been a hell of a thing to see, wouldn't it?" Bennager said.

"Aye, but I don't believe that. Ye are tellin' me stories."

"It's damn sure more believable than what you said about mountains growing wings, you big ox," Trina jeered.

"I've 'bout had it with ye, woman!"

Trina giggled as Rose continued to laugh at the noisy, boisterous couple.

"I'm going to be traveling all around those buttes when I go to see Glenn and Bidwell. Why don't you come with me and Hank and get a closer look at them?"

"Oh no, I don't want to be anywhere around those mountains," Angus said.

"Oh no, you want to be up here where they can't see you. That's why he picked this place, you know. He didn't want the evil mountains to be able to see you, Rose. Have you ever heard of such a thing?" Trina said mockingly.

Rose laughed and said, "Thank you for your consideration, Angus."

"That does it!" Angus bellowed as they finished the window. He rushed across the room where Trina and Hank were nailing up the one-by-twelves, picked his wife up, and threw her over his shoulder. Trina kicked, screamed, and laughed as the big man hauled her away and out of sight.

"I expect we won't see them for a while, Hank." They all laughed at the jovial Irish couple. "Come help me with the rest of these windows."

*****

A few days later, Rose convinced her husband that she was well enough to get out of bed. She took the dogs and walked as far as she could while looking for the property markers, having to rest from time to time on the way back.

The next night, while Bennager and Rose were in bed, Bennager told her that Hank and he were leaving the next morning for the valley. The love they shared that night was heartfelt, passionate, and long overdue. Rose bawled the next morning to see her husband mount up. "When I get back, we'll throw a party and get you acquainted with some people, darling. I love you. You be good now," Bennager said as he rode away.

"See you later, Mrs. Rasmussen," Hank hollered as he followed Bennager out of the yard.

"Hurry home!" Rose finally bellowed through her tears. Trina and Angus waved goodbye. Angus and Girl started frying their bacon, and Trina invited Rose to have coffee with them.

Angus went to town that day for more windows while Trina and Rose worked on the porch.

"You know, Rose, Angus told me quite a lot about you. I admit, I didn't like to listen because I figured he was in love with you and also because of who you were in my imagination." The women looked up from their work to face each other. Trina smiled. "I never imagined you to be such a bawl baby. Angus told me you were pretty tough. He told me he heard that you even killed a man. I figured you to be some sort of a giant. He said you cursed, drank, and chewed tobacco like there was no tomorrow. All I see is a woman who cries at the drop of a hat."

Rose began to cry again. "I know, I don't know what's the matter with me. The Roman must have kicked my head or else I rotted my brain that day I drank a half gallon of brandy."

"I don't think it is as bad as all that, Rose. You might want to consider the possibility that you're pregnant, though. Mood swings are one of the symptoms."

Rose thought about it for a minute. "I haven't had my cycle since before we left Pablo's rancho. I thought it was because of the injury, though."

"I guess you'll know in another month. Have you been sick in the mornings?"

"No, but my tobacco hasn't agreed with me since I was in Sacramento City."

"Well," Trina said, smiling and shrugging her shoulders.

"Well." Rose smiled and cried. "I bet you're right. I bet I'm going to have a baby!" she exclaimed, hugging Trina. The two of them laughed with joy and went in to have a cup of tea. "I'll be damned. It must have been the day we were playing around in Pablo's stables!" Rose said, shaking her head.

*****

Bennager and Hank crossed the Sacramento River that afternoon. They waited in the shade of Dr. Glenn's yard for him to return from his fields with his foreman. Dr. Glenn's wife was in Paris for the spring, but the maid treated them to lemonade while they waited. Bennager thought of riding out to look for him, but his fields were so vast, and the maid didn't know which direction he had even headed for. Glenn had so many people working for him that he had a mercantile built and well stocked with anything that his men could possibly need. He had the latest farm implements on the market in a big barn and dozens of different wagons and tons of leather, metal, and chain for making harnesses and any other contraption that he could think of to make farming easier and faster.

Dr. Glenn was delightedly surprised to see Bennager again and to meet Hank. Hank was impressed to meet him. Hank thought that he had been farming all his life until he saw Dr. Glenn's operation.

"Bennager, my boy, it's good to see you. I heard you got married," Glenn said as they sat down to supper.

"News travels fast in this valley, doesn't it, Doc?" Bennager chuckled.

"Not for long. This country is filling up with strangers."

"It sure is. That's what I've come about. I need to get my hands on two more teams and freight wagons. Hank and I have itchy feet. A man could get rich hauling freight these days."

Dr. Glenn chuckled at Bennager curiously. "Where is your other outfit?"

"My friend Angus Donovan is using it in the foothills. He's building the house and rancho for my wife."

"For your wife? You mean to tell me the rancho is your wife's?"

"Yes, sir, I hope you will come and see the place when it is finished. Angus built her a fine two-story house surrounded by oak trees."

"Well done, young man. You've married a woman who wants to make money instead of spending it. I heard you went south to buy cattle. I didn't know they were for your wife."

"I didn't buy anything. That was all her doing."

"Didn't you ever tell her of your own wealth and that she didn't have to kill herself raising beef?"

Bennager laughed. "She's a spitfire, Dr. Glenn. She wanted something of her own. She wants to raise cattle, breed horses and mules, and have a family."

"Well done, well done, Bennager. You have married a woman who is quite the opposite of my wife."

When supper was finished, Dr. Glenn's Indian foreman took Hank out to show him around. Dr. Glenn had a pasture full of fine yearling colts, and the Indian thought it would be a good place to visit and have a smoke. Glenn and Bennager went into the office.

"I didn't want to speak of it in front of the young man, but why do you want to haul freight? Do you realize how much money you're going to make on wheat this year? We won't even ship half of it. We finished building the flouring mill this last winter, and we're going to grind it up and sell it right here in California. Didn't you buy any flour on your adventure?"

"No, my wife bought it." Bennager chuckled. "I'm aware of the price of flour, sir, but I enjoy my work, and it's a necessity in this country, more than ever now."

"Don't you think your wife will want your help and her rancho?"

"The hills are crawling with men who will need work soon. It will be good to provide a few jobs for the men who can't make it as gold miners."

"I only have four horses that I can afford to give up. I'll need the rest for my own farming. I heard Bidwell has quite a few if he hasn't already sold them. Come back here for the wagons, though. I have plenty of those and a man who will build more."

"That sounds good, Dr. Glenn, and thank you," Bennager said shaking the man's hand.

"You never told your wife how rich you are, huh?"

Bennager laughed. "I told her we would manage making the payments until the calves were sold."

"You are a devil." Dr. Glenn laughed.

"She deserves it. Her uncle Bill demolished a man's mercantile in Stockton, and she kept it from me, knowing full well that I'd kill him for it."

Dr. Glenn laughed. "Do you mean to tell me that madman is your wife's uncle?" Dr. Glenn sat down again. "I never put it together. Those bulls belonged to you!"

"Not me, Doc, those bulls belong to her. I didn't hear about it until I was sitting in Sacramento City, having a beer. By then, it was too late to kill Horny Bill Ford, so I just sat and drank some more beer. The merchant was a despicable man, but I sent a rider down to Stockton with a banknote to cover his loss. I won't be doing in hauling in that town, you can believe that."

Glenn couldn't stop laughing. Bennager sat back down, and Glenn poured them some cognac. Glenn caught his breath. "You can tell your wife to expect me after harvest. I can't wait to meet this woman."

*****

The next morning, Bennager and Hank headed north along the east side of the Sacramento River. They passed by the mysterious buttes consisting mostly of volcanic rock.

"You'll want to watch for rattlesnakes around here, Hank. These little mountains grow the biggest rattlesnakes that I have ever seen," Bennager said. "That's the only thing evil about these mountains. Remind me to tell Angus that when we get back."

Henry chuckled. "All right, boss."

The day was hot and humid. Bennager reckoned they would have a storm by midafternoon, but a cool west wind came in from the coast to relieve them, and they continued on, eating only once before finally arriving at Bidwell's late that evening.

"Rasmussen, I heard you got married." The remark was wearing thin with Bennager as he had heard it probably twenty times between the foothills and the Sacramento River, but he smiled and told John a little bit about his wife. After a long visiting spell, Bennager finally asked if he had horses to sell.

"I'm glad you came along, Rasmussen. I'm horse poor. Take as many as you want," John said.

"If you're horse poor, you should sell them in Marysville. There isn't an animal with legs to be had in the mining towns."

"Those miners should have brought their own horses." Bidwell laughed.

"Do you have eight of them to sell me?" Bennager asked.

"Of course, I do. You two should go find an empty room and get some sleep. I'll show you what I have in the morning."

Before the two men fell asleep that night, Henry confessed, "Hey, Bennager, that crazy Bill Ford tried to tell me that Rose was single and ripe for the pickin'. I'm sure glad that I didn't believe him. It sure is fun riding with you and meetin' all these rich people. I never knew such people were here abouts."

Bennager chuckled as he thought back to when he found that big gold nugget and thought the same thing years ago. "Get some rest, Hank. We have to make that trip all over again tomorrow." Bennager thought of how much he missed Rose. He had only been gone for two days, and he'd probably be three of four days getting back. He thought that he was ready to return to his old life now that he was home. He hadn't counted on it being so difficult to spend a few days away from his bride. He imagined that she was there beside him as he drifted off to sleep.

The next morning was a long one. John took them out to look at the horses, and Bennager made his picks. One team was a perfectly matched set of bays and the other two were sorrels. They weren't matched as well as the six bays, but he had to pick and choose because he didn't want any with white feet.

Bidwell took the men and showed them his orchard and vineyard. "Do you think you could get these to grow in the foothills, Rasmussen?" John asked of the peaches, apricots, grapes, and nut trees.

"It's mighty rocky in places. I don't know if they'll grow or not." Bennager desperately wanted to be on his way back, but he knew that he had to be personable.

"Come on, let's get you on your way," John said suddenly after glancing up at the sky.

Bennager was afraid that he had let his anxiety show, and he started to have a guilty feeling about it. Once they were back at the house, Bidwell said, "I have a wedding gift for you, Rasmussen. The wagon is for you, and the trees and vines are for your wife. Tell her to take good care of them and of you too. I'll be over to meet her after the harvest is finished."

"Thank you, John, thank you very much. She'll love your gifts and probably tend to them more than me."

"Don't let her get away with that Rasmussen," John said, slapping Bennager on the arm as they shook hands.

John's men had the team hitched up and the wagon loaded. Bennager and Hank left directly and headed south back to Dr. Glenn's. They had to travel well past dark to get there. Glenn was still awake going over his books. One lantern was still glowing when the weary men arrived.

"Come in, come in," Glenn said, opening the door. "You men look beat. Could you stand a drink? Are you hungry?"

Henry said yes to both, and the men had a midnight supper.

"I take it John still had horses. It sounded like quite a herd coming in."

"Yes, I have another matched team and two others. He gave me a wagonful of fruit trees for my wife," Bennager stated.

"I've never known Bidwell to be so generous." Glenn chuckled. "Did you boys get wet today? It looked like it was pouring a fair amount of rain up north."

"We got into one squall of hail, but the rain missed us. The river looked like it was rolling pretty well when we came across it on the ferry."

"Yeah, I bet it is. I hope that rain makes its way here. The wheat could sure use it."

Henry thought that no matter how rich a farmer was, they always worried about the rain. He had heard his stepfather say the exact same thing a thousand times.

Glenn didn't sleep all night while Bennager and Henry rested. He racked his brain trying to figure out what a woman like Rose Rasmussen could use for a wedding gift without having to steal something from his own wife. He finally decided on a one-horse carriage. That was as good as what Bidwell had given, and perhaps the woman would be apt to stay out of harm's way.

Glenn went to Miguel's house early that morning. Miguel Skinner was one of the older men who worked for him. Glenn asked Miguel to drive the carriage to Mrs. Rasmussen when Bennager and his man left. They went to the big implement barn and spent the next two hours cleaning the little carriage and greasing its wheels.

Glenn hurried back to the house at breakfast time while Miguel picked out a pretty little bay mare to pull the carriage, and then he crossed the river and started making his way slowly toward Marysville. Glenn didn't want Bennager to know about the gift until he was on his way home.

Bennager knew he was getting a late start when he woke to a lighted room. Glenn was chomping at the bit to start his day, but he wanted to see Bennager off. They had breakfast so young Henry wouldn't have a screaming fit, and then they prepared to go. Bennager made Henry drive the mismatched team, and the rain finally came to Glenn's wheat as the men said their goodbyes.

The river was muddy and rolling fast. He thought it would be wise to wait a day or two, but he didn't want to spend another night away from Rose. He had Henry cross first, and while he waited for the ferry to get back, the rain poured out of the sky. He thought of how he wouldn't dry out for days. The matched team plodded onto the ferry without incident, and the ferryman started to pull them across the rapid river. Bennager looked over at Henry who was waiting on the other side and imagined Rose's reaction when she saw the fruit trees that were in Henry's wagon. He smiled as he thought of her face and how she would laugh and love him when he got home. He was certain that she missed him as much as he missed her.

Suddenly, the wagon was rolling. The horses were panicking and diving sideways into the water. Bennager leaped for all he was worth into the water, trying to grasp anything that he could get his hands on. The horses were swimming with all their might trying to get their footing and get to shore. The wagon pulled them downriver, but they were young and worked as a team to get to shore.

Henry lunged to the ground from his wagon and ran downriver as the trees that caught the ferry broke loose and continued their journey southward. Henry ran until he collapsed, and he never saw Bennager. He figured he ran seven miles. His boss was lost, and it was his job now to tell his wife. On his way back, it occurred to him that Bennager must have been able to latch on to the ferry when he went over. Henry jogged all the way back, knowing that was what happened and thought of the teasing Bennager would give him when he got back.

Henry's hopes were dashed when he didn't see Bennager back at the wagons. The ferryman was shaken and had gone to shore to sit down. He knew that he should have closed the ferry that morning. He had watched it rain the whole day before in the north and knew that it had rained all night. He knew that the snowmelt in the Siskiyou Mountains would put him out of business for the rest of the week, and he knew that the two young men would pester to him to no end with wanting him to take them across the river for that whole week. His poor decision to go ahead and take them across had cost the life of a young man that he knew and respected and almost his own as well.

"Are you sure that he didn't grab the ferry when he went over?" Henry asked.

The man shook his head remorsefully. "No, kid, he'd be standing here with us if that had happened." The man held his head in his hands. "I saw him in the water, and when the trees broke loose, I saw him downriver trying to stay afloat. He's gone, kid. No man can survive swimming with trees, and right now, the river is full of them. I watched four more pass by while you were gone. The water is ice cold. It's full of mud. He's gone, kid. All you can do now is take your wagons and go tell his wife. A man named Miguel is up ahead in a carriage, waiting for you fellas. The carriage is a wedding gift from Dr. Glenn, so you had better see that she gets it."

He helped Henry tie the traces of Bennager's wagon to the wagon with the trees in it and rearranged the horses. He shook his head. "Wedding gifts," he said softly to himself.

Henry climbed on the wagon sadly.

"You better watch yourself crossing at Eliza, kid. If there's any debris in the Feather River, then you had better wait to cross. That water is so cold that you'd die in a few minutes." The water was cold, but the man lied, hoping the young man wouldn't take any chances.

Henry met up with Miguel, and they reluctantly continued on eastward. It was the longest journey that Henry would ever make in his life. He was exhausted with fret about how Mrs. Rasmussen would take the news. He didn't know if he wanted to cross the Feather River or not, although Miguel said it was safe to do so. If he crossed, there was no place to go except for the Rasmussen rancho. If he crossed, then he would have to tell Rose she was a widow before the end of the day.

Miguel told the young man that it was his duty and part of growing up into a man to do unpleasant things and to realize when things had to be done, no matter how unpleasant they were.

"Yes, sir," Henry said and shook his head all the way. He thought of dozens of different ways to tell Rose the news, but each way came to the same reaction in his mind. It was shear hysteria ending with her killing him for bringing the news. Henry voiced his concern to Miguel, and Miguel assured him that he wouldn't let the lady shoot him.

Henry's heart throbbed with fear and sadness as they stopped in front of Rose's grand house. Henry noticed that they had finished the porch and had most of the windows in now, even on the second story. It was a couple of hours past suppertime and Rose, and the Irish newlyweds were sitting on the porch, enjoying the night air. They all stood up when the wagons stopped.

Rose stood on the porch, waiting for Bennager to appear, run to her, and give her a hug and a kiss. She had been waiting for days to tell him that they were going to have a baby. Henry climbed down from the wagon, and Miguel got out of the carriage, but Bennager didn't appear. The men took their hats off and looked at the ground as they approached her. Rose brought her hands to her mouth, and Trina grabbed her around her shoulders. They all knew what the men had to say.

"I'm sorry, Mrs. Rasmussen." Henry couldn't look the woman in the eye. "I'm sorry, but your husband was lost early this morning crossing the Sacramento River. A couple of trees caught hold of the ferry and flipped it sideways. The horses swam out, miraculously, but we couldn't find Mr. Rasmussen. I looked for him for about five or six miles, but the ferryman told me to go home. He said there was no use."

Rose wailed and went down on her knees. She held the life that was inside her and tried to scream, but her voice was paralyzed. Trina cried for her friend's anguish and rocked Rose Mary Rasmussen as if she was a small child. Henry thought that he'd rather be shot than to see someone in so much pain and misery. He looked at Miguel and shook his head. The men left to take care of the stock and put the wagons away, and Angus helped them.

They walked away from the house, but the sound of Rose's wails echoed against the rolling hills and oak trees. The dogs followed. Even Girl knew that there was nothing that could be done for Rose now. Miguel sat on a rock a mile from the house and rolled a smoke. The men talked of all the men that they had known who had died and how they died. Henry recalled his mother's death.

"We'll have to go find his body. I wouldn't want him to be buried by somebody who didn't know him," Angus suggested. "I'll ride over and get Jake and we'll go look for him. This is no place for a man to be right now anyway."

Hours passed as Rose finally cried herself to sleep in a state of grief. Moments later, she woke, scaring Trina. The woman seemed to be touched and almost ghostly. Rose looked at her redheaded friend and said, "Why would that river give me that man and then take him away from me? I don't believe it! I won't believe it!" Rose ran outside and saddled a horse.

Trina knew she was in shock and out of her mind with heartache. She tried to stop her. Trina hollered for Angus and the others to help her while Rose fought her off.

Finally, Rose grabbed the woman. "Look at me! Look at me, Trina! I'm not crazy! My husband is not dead! I know it! I feel it! I'm going to find him!"

"You are crazy if you go alone! Wait for one of the men to go with you."

"I'll give you just one minute to round one up!" Rose said with gritted teeth.

"Rose, think of your baby. You shouldn't ride full out right now." Trina grabbed Rose's hand. "Right now, that baby is all you have left of him, Rose," she whispered with tears in her eyes.

Miguel had heard Trina's shouting and ran with Henry back to the house. They saw the women in the moonlight, and Rose was mounted. He heard what Trina said about the baby.

"Mrs. Rasmussen, what are you doing?" Miguel asked.

"I'm going to find my husband."

"The big man left to get another man. We will leave in the morning to find your husband."

"I'm leaving right now!" Rose said with contempt.

"I will drive you in the carriage. That is the only way you can go."

"I'll go any damned way I please!" Rose raged.

Miguel smiled. "You must listen to Miguel. Hank has hobbled your horse, so you must listen to Miguel," he said.

Rose cried with frustration, and the ladies waited while Miguel and Henry hitched up the carriage.

*****

Charlie was docked in Sacramento City. The water was full of debris, and he spent the day cursing beavers and raking bushes away from his steamboat. He looked up when he heard a man yelling in the distance. He saw the trees and realized that he was about to be slammed. He cursed and ran into the wheelhouse to take hold of something sturdy. Six tree roots were coming toward him all at once. "Them damned, stupid beavers!" he hollered, knowing that the trees had met up on a beaver dam and broke through at the same time. The trees made a tremendous crash when they hit his boat and pushed it sideways, threatening to separate it from the dock. He heard a man yell again, but it sounded closer this time.

He ran back out to see the damage and was surprised at who he saw. "Well, well, howdy, Benny! It looks like you've been swimmin'!"

ABOUT THE AUTHOR

Noel Hill was inspired to tell this story for those who lived and worked in the foothills of the Sierras during the Gold Rush of the mid-1800s. She feels it is important to share their history and the challenges the growing nation faced during this time. She wants others to really feel what it might have been like to live in those times and hopes to spark interest in others to explore the realities of our nation's history further.

Printed in the USA
CPSIA information can be obtained
at www.ICGtesting.com
CBHW030748050824
12635CB00001B/1